Mary Moore

THE GREEN YEARS
and
SHANNON'S WAY
(two complete novels)

A. J. CRONIN

The Green Years
and
Shannon's Way
(TWO COMPLETE NOVELS)

BOSTON

LITTLE, BROWN AND COMPANY

THE GREEN YEARS
COPYRIGHT 1944, BY A. J. CRONIN

SHANNON'S WAY
COPYRIGHT 1948, BY A. J. CRONIN

LIBRARY OF CONGRESS CATALOG CARD NUMBER 60–9353

PRINTED IN THE UNITED STATES OF AMERICA

THE
GREEN
YEARS

BOOK ONE

CHAPTER ONE

HOLDING Mama's hand tightly, I came out of the dark arches of the railway station and into the bright streets of the strange town. I was inclined to trust Mama, whom, until today, I had never seen before and whose worn, troubled face with faded blue eyes bore no resemblance to my mother's face. But in spite of the bar of cream chocolate which she had got me from the automatic machine, she had so far failed to inspire me with affection. During the slow journey from Winton, seated opposite me in the third-class compartment, wearing a shabby grey dress pinned with a large cairngorm brooch, a thin necklet of fur, and a black-winged hat which drooped over her ear, she had gazed out of the window, her head to one side, her lips moving as she maintained a silent yet emotional conversation with herself, from time to time touching the corner of her eye with her handkerchief as though removing a fly.

But now that we were out of the train she made an effort to put away her mood; she smiled at me and pressed my hand.

"You're a good man not to cry any more. Do you think you can walk to the house? It's not too far."

Anxious to please, I replied that I could walk, so we did not take the solitary cab which stood outside the arches, but set off down the High Street, Mama attempting to interest me in the points of importance which we passed.

The pavement kept lifting and falling; the rough seas of the Irish Channel were still pounding in my head; I felt a little deaf from the thrumming of the *Viper*'s propellers. But opposite a handsome building, with polished granite pillars, set back from the street behind two iron cannon and a flagstaff, I heard her say, with gentle pride:—

"These are the Levenford Municipal Offices, Robert. Mr. Leckie . . . Papa . . . works there, in charge of the Health Department."

"Papa," I thought, giddily. "That is Mama's husband . . . my mother's father."

My footsteps were already flagging and Mama was looking at me with solicitude.

"It's too bad the trams are off today," she said.

I was much more tired than I had thought; and rather frightened. The town, harshly lit by the grey September afternoon, was full of cobblestones and sounds far less reassuring than the familiar, steady hum of traffic flowing past the open window of my home in Phoenix Terrace. A great ra-ta-tap of hammers came from the Shipyard, and from the Boilerworks, which Mama pointed out with a cracked gloved finger, there arose terrifying spurts of flame and steam. They were re-laying tramway lines in the street. At the corners little gusts of wind eddied up the dust into my swollen eyes, started off my cough.

Presently, however, we left the noise and confusion behind, crossed an open common with a pond and a circular bandstand, entered a quiet suburb which seemed part of a small country village very pleasantly situated beneath a wooded hill. Here were trees and green fields, a few old-fashioned little shops and cottages, a smithy with a horses' drinking trough outside, and prim new villas with painted cast-iron railings, neat flower beds, and proud titles like HELENSVILLE and GLENELG lettered in gilt on the coloured glass fanlights above the front doors.

We stopped at last, halfway along Drumbuck Road, before a tall semi-detached house of grey sandstone with yellow lace window-curtains and the name LOMOND VIEW. It was the least imposing of the houses in the quiet street—only the facings of the doors and windows were of masoned stone, the rest had been left rough, an appearance vaguely unprosperous, yet redeemed by a front garden surprisingly aglow with yellow chrysanthemums.

"Here we are, then, Robert." Mrs. Leckie addressed me in that same tone of anxious welcome, heightened by a sense of arrival. "A beautiful view of the Ben we get on a clear day. We're nice and near Drumbuck village too. Levenford's a smoky old town but there's lovely country round about. Wipe your eyes, there's a dear, and come away in."

I had lost my handkerchief throwing biscuits to the gulls, but I followed obediently round the side of the house, my heart throbbing anew with the dread of things unknown. The matronly yet misguided words of our Dublin neighbour, Mrs. Chapman, as she kissed me good-bye that morning at the Winton docks, before surrendering me to Mama, rang in my ears: "What'll happen to you next, poor boy?"

At the back door Mama paused: a young man of about nineteen, working on his knees in a newly turned flower plot, had risen at our approach, still holding a trowel. He had a ponderous and stolid air, heightened by a pale complexion, a bush of black hair, and large thick spectacles which condensed his nearsighted eyes.

"You're at it again, Murdoch." Mama could not restrain an exclamation of gentle reproach. Then, bringing me forward: "This is Robert."

Murdoch continued to gaze at me heavily, framed by the trim back-green with iron clothespoles at the corners—a bed of rhubarb at one side; on the other, a rockery of honeycombed grey lava, spread with soot to kill the slugs. At last, with great solemnity, he expressed his thought.

"Well, well! So this is him, at last."

Mama nodded, nervous sadness again touching her eyes; and a moment later Murdoch held out to me, almost dramatically, a large hand, encrusted and stiff with good earth.

"I'm glad to meet you, Robert. You can depend on me." He turned his big lenses earnestly upon Mama. "It's just these asters I got given me from the Nursery, Mama. They didn't cost a thing."

"Well anyway, dear," Mama said, turning, "see you're washed up before Papa comes in. You know how it riles him to catch you out here."

"I'm just finishing. I'll be with you in a minute." Preparing to kneel again, Murdoch further reassured his mother as she led me through the doorway. "I set the potatoes to boil for you, Mama."

We passed through the scullery to the kitchen—arranged as a living-room with uncomfortable carved mahogany furniture, and diced varnished wallpaper which reflected the furious echoes of a "waggity" clock. Having told me to sit down and rest, Mama removed the long pins from her hat and held them in her mouth while she folded her veil. She then pinned hat and veil together, hung them with her coat in the curtained recess and, putting on a blue wrapper that hung behind the door, began with greater confidence to move to and fro over the worn brown linoleum, giving me soft encouraging looks while I sat, stiff and scarcely breathing in this alien house, on the edge of a horsehair-covered chair beside the range.

"We're having our dinner in the evening, dear, seeing I was away. When Papa comes in, try and not let him see you crying. It's been a great grief for him as well. And he has a lot to worry him—such a responsible position in the town. Kate, my other daughter, will be in any minute, too. She's a pupil teacher. . . . Maybe your mother told you." As my lip drooped she went on hurriedly: "Oh, I know it's confusing, even for a big man like yourself, to be meeting all his mother's folks for the first time. And there's more to come." She was trying, amidst her preoccupations, to coax a smile from me. "There's Adam, my oldest son, who is doing wonderfully in the insurance business in Winton—he doesn't stay with us, but runs down when he can manage. Then there's Papa's mother. . . . She's away visiting some friends just now . . . but she spends about half of her time with us. And lastly, there's my father who lives here always—he's your great-grandpa Gow." While my head reeled with this jumble of unknown relatives her faint smile ventured forth again. "It isn't every boy who has a great-grandpa, I can tell you. It's quite an honour. You can just call him 'Grandpa,' though, for short. When I have his tray ready you can take it upstairs to him. Say how do you do, and help me at the same time."

Beside laying the table for five, she had, with a practised hand, prepared a battered black japanned tray, oval-shaped and with a rose painted in the centre, setting upon it a moustache cup of ribbed white china filled with tea, a plate of jam, cheese, and three slices of bread.

Watching her, I wondered, aloud, rather huskily: "Does Grandpa not eat his food downstairs?"

Mama seemed slightly embarrassed. "No, dear, he has it in his room." She lifted the tray and held it out to me. "Can you manage? Right up to the top floor. Be careful and not fall."

Bearing the tray, I climbed the unfamiliar stairs shakily, confused by the steep treads and the shiny, waxcloth "runner." Only a fragment of the dwindling afternoon was admitted by the high skylight. On the second landing opposite a boxed-in cistern, I tried the first of the two doors. It was locked. The other, however, yielded to my uncertain touch.

I entered a strange, interesting, dreadfully untidy room. The high brass bed in the corner, with its patchwork quilt and lopsided knobs, was still unmade; the bearskin hearthrug was rumpled; the towel on the splashed mahogany washstand hung awry. My eye was caught by a black marble time-piece of the "presentation" variety lying upon its side on the littered mantel-piece with its inside in pieces beside it. I felt a queer smell of tobacco smoke and past meals, a blending of complex and intricate smells, forming, as it were, the bouquet of a room much lived-in.

Wearing burst green carpet slippers and dilapidated homespun, my great-grandpa was sunk deeply in the massive ruin of a horsehair armchair by the rusty fireplace, steadily driving a pen over a long thick sheet of paper which lay, with the original document he was copying, on the yellow-green cover of the low table before him. On one hand stood a formidable collection of walking sticks, on the other a box of newssheet spills and a long rack of clay pipes, with metal caps, filled and ready.

He was a large-framed man, of more than average height, perhaps about seventy, with a pink complexion and a mane of still faintly ruddy hair flying gallantly behind his collar. It was, in fact, red hair which had lost a little of its ardour without yet turning white, and the result was a remarkable shade, golden in some lights. His beard and moustache, which curled belligerently, were of the same tinge. Though the whites of his eyes were peculiarly specked with yellow the pupils remained clear, penetrating and blue, not the faded blue of Mama's eyes, but a virile and electric blue, a forget-me-not blue, conspicuous and altogether charming. But his most remarkable feature was his nose. It was a large nose, large, red and bulbous; as I gazed, awe-struck, I could think of no more apt simile than to liken it to a ripe, enormous strawberry, for it was of the identical colour, and was even peppered with tiny holes like the seed pits of that luscious fruit. The organ dominated his entire visage; I had never seen such a curious nose, never.

By this time he had ceased to write and, bestowing his pen behind his ear, he turned slowly to regard me. The broken springs of the seat, despite the brown paper stuffed around them, twanged musically at the shifting of his weight, as though ushering in the drama of our acquaintance. We stared at each other in silence and, forgetting the momentary fascination of his nose, I flushed to think of the wretched picture I must make for him standing there in my ready-made black suit, one stocking falling down, shoelaces loose, my face pale and tear-stained, my hair inescapably red.

Still silent, he pushed aside his papers, made a gesture, nervous but force-ful, towards the cleared space on the table. I put the tray down on it. Barely taking his eyes off me, he began to eat, rapidly, and with a sort of grand indifference, partaking of cheese and jam indiscriminately, folding over his bread, soaking his crusts in his tea, washing everything down with a final draught. Then, wiping his whiskers with a downward sweep, he reached out instinctively—as though the business of eating was a mere preamble to tobacco, or even better things—and lit a pipe.

"So you are Robert Shannon?" His voice was reserved, yet companionable.

"Yes, Grandpa." Though my answer came strained and apologetic, I had remembered the instruction to omit his "great."

"Did you have a good journey?"

"I think so, Grandpa."

"Ay, ay, they're nice boats, the *Adder* and the *Viper*. I used to see them berth when I was in the excise. The *Adder* has a white line on her under-strake, that's how you tell the difference between them. Can you play draughts?"

"No, Grandpa."

He nodded encouragingly, yet with a trace of condescension.

"You will in due course, boy, if you stay here. I understand you *are* going to stay."

"Yes, Grandpa. Mrs. Chapman said there was no place else for me to go." A forlorn wave, warm with self-pity, gushed over me.

Suddenly I had a wild craving for his sympathy, an unbearable longing to unbosom myself of my terrible predicament. Did he know that my father had died of consumption, the spectral family malady which had carried off his two sisters before him—which had infected and, with terrible rapidity, destroyed my mother—which, it was whispered, had even laid a little finger, beguilingly, on me . . . ?

But Grandpa, taking a few musing puffs, looking me through and through with an ironic twist to his lips, had already turned the subject.

"You're eight, aren't you?"

"Almost, Grandpa."

I wished to make myself as young as possible but Grandpa was implacable. "It's an age when a boy should stand up for himself. . . . Though I will say there might be more of ye. Do you like to walk?"

"I've never tried it much, Grandpa. I walked to the Giant's Causeway when we went on our holidays to Portrush. But we took the miniature railway back."

"Just so. Well, we'll take a few turns, you and me, and see what good Scottish air does to us." He paused, for the first time communing with himself. "I'm glad you have my hair. The Gow ginger. Your mother had it too, poor lass."

I could no longer hold back that warm tide—almost from habit I burst into tears. Ever since my mother's funeral the week before the mere mention of her name produced this reflex, fostered by the sympathy it always brought me. Yet on this occasion I received neither the broad-bosomed petting of Mrs. Chapman nor the snuff-scented condolences which Father Shanley of St. Dominic's had lavished upon me. And soon the consciousness of my great-grandpa's disapproval made me painfully confused; I tried to stop, choked, and began to cough. I coughed and coughed, until I had to hold my side. It was one of the most impressive bouts I had ever had, rivaling even the severest of my father's coughs. I was, to be truthful, rather proud of it and when it ceased I gazed at him expectantly.

But he gave me no solace, uttered not a word. Instead he took a tin box from his waistcoat pocket, pressed open the lid, selected a large flat peppermint, known as an "oddfellow," from the number within. I thought he was about to offer it to me but to my surprise and chagrin he did not, placing it calmly in his own mouth. Then he declared severely:—

"If there is one thing I cannot abide, it is a greeting bairn. Robert, your tear-bag seems precious near your eye. You must pull yourself together, boy." He removed the pen from his ear and threw out his chest. "In my life I've had to contend with a wheen of difficulties. Do you think I'd have won through if I'd laid down under them?"

Grandpa seemed about to launch forth on a profound and rather pompous dissertation; but at that moment a hand-bell tinkled on the ground floor. He broke off—disappointed, I thought—and with the stem of his pipe made a wave of dismissal, indicating that I should go below. As he resumed his writing, I took up the empty tray and crept, abashed, towards the door.

CHAPTER TWO

DOWNSTAIRS, Mr. Leckie, Kate, and Murdoch had come in and, with Mama, were awaiting me in the kitchen, their sudden silence, which immobilized the room, indicating that I had been the subject of their conversation. Like most solitary children I had a painful shyness, exaggerated in my present state, and, with a confused understanding of the deep estrangement which had existed between my mother and Papa, I shrank into a kind of daze when, after a pause, he limped forward, took my hand, held it, then after a moment bent down and kissed me on the brow.

"I'm pleased to make your acquaintance, Robert. No one regrets more than I that we haven't met before."

His voice was not angry, as I had vaguely feared, but subdued and depressed. I told myself I must not cry, yet it was hard not to, when Kate also bent down and kissed me, awkwardly, but with generous intention.

"Let's sit in then." Mama, showing me to my place, again put on her veneer of brightness. "Nearly half-past six. You must be famished, son."

When we were seated, Papa, at the head of the table, lowered his eyes and said grace: a long, strange grace which I had never heard before, and he did not bless himself either. He began to slice the steaming corned beef in the oval ashet before him, while Mama served the potatoes and cabbage, at the other end.

"There!" Papa said, with the air of giving me a nice piece, his movements precise and correct. He was a small, rather insignificant man of forty-seven, with a narrow face, pale features and small eyes. His dark moustache was waxed out straight and his hair streaked over his scalp to conceal his bald-ness. His expression was marked by that faint touch of resignation seen on the faces of people who know they are conscientious and industrious yet have not been recognized or, in their own opinion, adequately rewarded by life. He wore a low starched collar, a made black tie, and an interesting, if unexpected, double-breasted suit of blue serge with brass buttons. A uniform cap, with a glazed peak, not unlike a naval officer's, lay on the chest of drawers behind him.

"Eat your cabbage with the meat, Robert." He leant forward and pat-ted me on the shoulder. "It's very nourishing."

Under all these eyes I was finding it difficult to manage the strange bone-handled knife and fork, much longer than my own, and very slippery. Also, I did not like cabbage; and my small slice of beef was terribly salt and stringy. My father, in his gay style, had insisted that "nothing but the best" should appear on our table at Phoenix Crescent and he often came home from the office with some extra delicacy like guava jelly or Whitstable oysters —indeed, I was a thoroughly spoiled child, my appetite so pampered and capricious that often in the past six months my mother had bribed me with sixpence and a kiss to eat a slice of chicken. Yet I felt I could not displease Papa; I choked down some of the watery vegetable.

With my attention apparently diverted, Papa looked down the table at Mama, reverting, guardedly, yet in a worried fashion, to their interrupted conversation.

"Mrs. Chapman didn't ask anything?"

"No, indeed." Mama answered in a lowered tone. "Though she must have been out of pocket over the fares and what not. She seemed a good, sensible woman."

Papa exhaled a little breath. "It's a relief to find some decency left in the world. Did you have to take a cab?"

"No . . . there was nothing much to bring. He has grown out of most of his things. And it seems *the men* took everything."

An inward spasm seemed to grip Papa, he stared at a painful vision in the air, murmuring: "One extravagance after another. Small wonder there was nothing left."

"Oh, Papa, there was such a lot of illness."

"But not much common sense. Why didn't they insure? A good sound policy would have taken care of everything." His hollow eye fell upon me as, with growing languor, I tried hard to clear my plate. "That's a good boy, Robert. We waste nothing in this house."

Kate, who sat across the table moodily viewing the twilight through the window as though the conversation were devoid of interest, gave me an odd sustaining kind of smile. Though she was twenty-one, only three years younger than my mother, I was surprised how little she resembled her. Where my mother had been pretty she was plain, with pale eyes, high cheekbones, and a dry, chapped, florid skin. Her hair was colourless, as if caught in a neutral state between the Gow red and the Leckie black.

"You've been to school, I suppose?"

"Yes." I flushed, simply from being spoken to; speaking was a great effort. "To Miss Barty's in the Crescent."

Kate nodded understandingly. "Was it nice?"

"Oh, very nice. If you made a good answer, at Catechism or General Intelligence, Miss Barty gave you a sugar dragee out of the bottle in the cupboard."

"We have a fine school in Levenford. I think you'll like it."

Papa cleared his throat. "I thought the John Street Elementary . . . with you, Kate . . . would be very suitable."

Kate removed her eyes from the window and gazed directly at Papa—resistant, almost sullen. "You know John Street is a wretched little school. He must go to the Academy, where we all went. In your position you can't do otherwise."

"Well . . ." Papa's eyes fell. "Maybe . . . but not till the half term. . . . That's October fourteenth, isn't it? Give him some questions and see what standard he's fit for."

Kate shook her head shortly.

"At this moment he's dead with tiredness and ought to be in bed. Who is he sleeping with?"

Startled out of my growing drowsiness, I blinked at Mama while she meditated, as though her perplexities had prevented her from considering the matter before.

"He's too big a boy for you, Kate . . . and your bed is very narrow, Murdoch . . . besides you're so often up late, studying. Why don't we put him in Grandma's room, Papa? While she's away, I mean."

Papa dismissed the suggestion with a shake of his head. "She pays good money for her room. We can't disturb it without consulting her. And she'll be coming back soon."

So far Murdoch had been silent, eating stolidly, scrutinizing his food closely, inspecting each slice of bread like a detective, and from time to time picking up a textbook that lay beside his plate, holding it so close to his face he almost seemed to smell it. Now, he glanced up with a practical air.

"He must go in with Grandpa. It's the obvious solution."

Papa made a sign of agreement, though his face clouded at the mention of Grandpa's name.

It was settled. Half asleep though I was, my heart sank at the awfulness of this new prospect, this fresh link in the chain of my miseries, binding me to that strange and intimidating personality upstairs. But I was afraid to protest, too weary even to hold up my lids as Kate pushed back her chair.

"Come then, dear. Is the water hot, Mama?"

"I think so. But there's the dishes. Don't run off too much."

In the cramped bathroom Kate helped me to take off my clothes, her face flushing queerly as I reached a state of nakedness. There were only six inches of tepid water in the boxed-in bath which was yellowish at the waste and rough from re-enamelling. She stooped to wash me with the cloth and the block of gritty yellow soap. My head was nodding, my eyes were too heavy to exude further tears. I submitted as she dried me and again put on my day shirt. The bolt on the bathroom door clicked. We were going upstairs. And there, on the landing, looming out of the haze, the waves, the ship's vibration, the roar of tunnels, holding out his hand, to take me, was Grandpa.

CHAPTER THREE

GRANDPA was a difficult sleeper, snoring loudly, tossing on the lumpy flock mattress, squeezing me flat against the wall. In spite of this, I slept heavily, but as dawn came I had a bad dream. I saw my father in a long white night-shirt, breathing in and out of his green tea inhaler, that little brass tank with red rubber tubes which one of his business friends had recommended to him when the other medicines did no good. From time to time he paused, his brown eyes full of fun, to laugh and joke with my mother, who stood watching him with her hands clasped feverishly together. Then the doctor entered, an elderly man with a grey unsmiling face. A moment later there came a clap of thunder, a great black horse with nodding black plumes charged into the room, and I hid my face in grief and terror as my mother and father mounted upon its back and galloped off.

I opened my eyes, perspiring, my heart quivering in my throat, to find the morning sun streaming into the room. Standing at the window, almost dressed, Grandpa was rolling up the creaky blind.

"Did I wake you?" He turned. "It's a grand day, and high time you were up."

As I rose and began to pull on my clothes he explained that Kate had already set off for her teaching and Murdoch was on his way to get his train for Skerry's College in Winton—where he was preparing for a position in the post office branch of the Civil Service. Whenever Papa departed for his work the coast would be clear for us to go down. It came to me as a mild shock when Grandpa told me that Papa, despite his fine uniform, was only the district Sanitary Inspector. Papa's great ambition was to be Superintendent of the Waterworks, but his present duties—Grandpa smiled indescribably—were to see that everybody kept their garbage cans and water closets in good order.

Almost immediately, we heard the slam of the front door; Mama came to the foot of the stairs and called us.

"How did you two get on?" She greeted us with a faint confederate's smile on her troubled face, as though we were schoolboys, up to all sorts of tricks.

"Nicely, Hannah, thank you." Grandpa answered courteously, seating himself in Papa's chair, with the wooden arms, at the head of the table. This morning meal, I soon learned, was the only one he took outside the confines of his room and he set much store by it. The kitchen was cozy from the range fire; there were crumbs and stains at Murdoch's place; a sense of intimacy bound the three of us as Mama spooned out cocoa into three cups from the Van Houten's tin and poured in boiling water from the big black-leaded kettle.

"I was wondering, Father," she said, "if you'd take Robert with you this morning?"

"Certainly, Hannah." Grandpa answered politely, but with reserve.

"I know you'll help all you can." She seemed to speak for his ear alone. "Things may be a little difficult at first."

"Tuts!" Grandpa raised his cup with both hands. "There's no need to meet trouble halfway, my lass."

Mama continued to gaze at him with that sad, half-hidden smile, a particular expression which, equally with that half-shake of her head, I saw to be the mark of her fondness for him. As we finished our breakfast she went out for a moment, returning with his stick and hard square hat, and the documents which I had seen him copying the day before. She carefully brushed the hat, which was old and faded, then retied more securely the thin red tape which bound the papers.

"A man of your parts shouldn't be doing this, Father. But you know it helps."

Grandpa smiled inscrutably, got up from the table and put on his hat with an air. Mama then saw us to the door. Here she came very close to Grandpa and gazed deeply, meaningly, with all her anxious heart, into his blue eyes. In a low voice she said:—

"Now you promise me, Father."

"*Tch*, Hannah! What a woman you are to fash!" He smiled at her indulgently and, taking my hand in his, set off down the road.

Soon we reached the tramway terminus, where a red tram stood waiting, the conductor swinging the trolley-pole, making contact with the overhead wire amidst a crackle of blue sparks—still quite a novelty in that year. Grandpa led me to the front seat on the open upper deck. I held his hand more tightly and he gave me a side glance of communicative ardour as we slid off with gathering momentum down the slight incline from the Toll, making swift and bounding progress through the morning air towards Levenford.

"Tickets please. All tickets please." I heard the *ping* of the conductor's punch approaching, the rattling of the coins in his bag, but Grandpa, staring ahead, with his chin on his stick and his hair flying in the wind, had fallen into a kind of trance from which my appealing look, and the official's demand, entirely failed to rouse him. Such was his absorption, so statuesque his attitude, that the conductor paused doubtfully beside us, whereupon Grandpa, without a movement of his position, infused into his immobile countenance such a protestation of good-fellowship and secret understanding, topped off by a wink so full of complicity and promise, that the man broke into a kind of sheepish grin.

"It's *you*, Dandie," he said, and, after a moment's hesitation, brushed past us.

I was overcome by this example of my grandpa's prestige, but presently I recognized that we were in the High Street, opposite the Municipal Offices. Here Grandpa descended, with dignity, and led the way towards a low building with a short outside flight of steps and a big brass plate, the name almost polished away: DUNCAN McKELLAR, SOLICITOR. The windows on either side of the door were half screened by a kind of gauze, the one bearing, in faded gilt letters, the title LEVENFORD BUILDING SOCIETY, the other ROCK ASSURANCE COMPANY. As Grandpa entered this office much of his swagger was replaced by a sort of limpid humility, which, however, did not prevent him from throwing me a comical grimace when an unprepossessing woman with glossy cuffs put her head through a hatch and told us severely that Mr. McKellar was engaged with Provost Blair and that we must wait. I was soon to learn that sour women always disagreed with Grandpa and made him pull this face.

After about five minutes the inner door opened and a prosperous, dark-bearded man came through the waiting room, putting on his hat. His attentive glance confused me; and suddenly, with a disapproving frown at Grandpa, he drew up before us.

"So this is the boy?"

"It is, Provost," Grandpa answered.

Provost Blair stared me through and through, like a man who knew my history better than I did myself, so manifestly reviewing in his mind events connected with me, incidents of such a terrible and discreditable nature, that I felt my legs shaking beneath me from shame.

"You won't have had time to make friends with boys of your own age?" He spoke with reassuring mildness.

"No, sir."

"My boy, Gavin, would play with you. He's not much older than you. Come over to the house one day soon. It's quite near, in Drumbuck Road."

I hung my head. I could not tell him I had no desire to play with this unknown Gavin. He stood for a moment rather indecisively stroking his chin, then, with another nod, he went out.

Mr. McKellar was now free to give us his attention. His inner office, although old-fashioned, was very handsome indeed with a mahogany desk, a red-patterned carpet into which my feet sank, several silver cups on the mantelpiece and, on the dull green walls, framed photographs of important-looking men. Seated in his swivel chair Mr. McKellar spoke without looking up.

"They've kept you cooling your heels, Dandie. Have you the work done? Or is some poor lass suing you . . ." Raising his head he noticed me and broke off as if I had spoiled his joke. He was a solid red-faced man of about fifty, clean-shaven, close-cropped, and sober in his dress. His eyes, beneath sandy tufted brows, were dry and penetrating but there was the hint of good nature behind them. His red underlip, naturally full, protruded judicially as he took the papers which Grandpa handed him and cast a glance over them.

"God help us, Dandie, but you're a bonny writer. Fair copperplate. I wish ye'd made as good a job of yourself as ye have of this deed of transfer."

Grandpa's laugh sounded a trifle forced. "Man proposes and God disposes, lawyer. I'm grateful for the work you give me."

"Then keep away from the demon." Mr. McKellar made a note on the book before him. "I'll credit this with the rest. Our friend Leckie," his tongue went into his cheek, "will get the cheque the end of the month. I see you have the new arrival."

He sat back, his eyes resting on me perhaps more shrewdly than the Provost's. Then, as though admitting a fact against his better judgment, as if implying, indeed, that he had expected some fearful and distressing freak to stand before him as the result of that horrible chain of circumstances which had passed before his vision, he murmured: "It's a nice enough boy. He'll not have his troubles to seek, or I'm much mistaken."

With due deliberation he selected a shilling from the loose change in his pocket and handed it across the desk to Grandpa.

"Buy the little son of Belial a lemonade, Dandie. And away with you. Miss Glennie will give you another deed. I'm rushed to death."

Grandpa left the office in excellent humour, inflating his chest as though savouring the breeze. As we came down the steps, he directed my attention to the other side of the street. Two tinker-women were making the rounds with baskets and wickerwork. One, the younger, stalwart and brown-faced, with that flaming orange hair so often seen amongst the roving Scottish gypsies, was carrying her burden on her head, swaying a little as she walked, her upstretched arms making firmer her strong bosom.

"There, boy," Grandpa exclaimed, almost with reverence. "Is that not a pleasant sight on a fine fresh autumn day?"

I could not follow his meaning—indeed, the two beshawled gypsies seemed to me quite beneath our notice. But I was very much cast down by certain obscure implications of the scene in the lawyer's office and, feeling myself more of a mystery than ever, I did not press the matter, but wrinkled my forehead in thought as we began our leisurely return. Why was I such a curiosity to all these people? What made them shake their heads over me?

The truth, though I could not guess it, was simple. In this small, prejudiced Scots town it was accepted history that my mother, a pretty and popular girl "who might have set her cap at anyone," had thoroughly disgraced herself by marrying my father, Owen Shannon, a stranger whom she had met while on vacation, a Dubliner, in fact, who had no family connections, held only an unimportant post in a firm of tea importers and had nothing to recommend him but his high spirits and good looks—if indeed such attributes could be considered a recommendation. No account was taken of the years of happiness which ensued. His death, followed so sensationally by hers, was regarded as a just retribution; and my appearance on the Leckie doorstep, without means of support, as certain evidence of the judgment of Providence.

Grandpa took the "Common way," which afforded us a view of the pond, and at the end of half an hour brought us, by an unexpected twist, to Drumbuck village—which Mama and I had skirted the day before—just as the noon hooter sounded musically from the now distant Works.

It was a pretty place, set beneath a slow rise of woods and traversed by a brook which ran beneath two stone bridges. We passed a little sweetshop filled with "lucky bags" and "bouncers" and licorice straps, with the sign TIBBIE MINNS, LICENSED TO SELL TOBACCO above; then the open door of a cottage where a weaver sat working his loom. Across the road I could see the blacksmith shoeing a white horse, bent, with the hoof in his leather apron, a glow of red in the dark forge behind, a delicious smell of singeing horn wafting over.

Grandpa seemed to know everyone, even the hawker selling finnan haddies from a barrow and the woman who cried: "Rhubarb, jeelie rhubarb! Twa bawbees the quairter stane!" In his passage of the village street he gave and received most cordial salutations—I felt him to be a really great person.

"How do, Saddler!"

"How's yourself, Dandie?"

The stout red-faced man standing in his shirt sleeves on the step of the Drumbuck Arms was so especially friendly in his greeting that Grandpa stopped, pushed back his hat and wiped his brow with an air of pleasurable anticipation.

"We mustn't forget your lemonade, boy."

While he entered the Arms I sat on the warm stone step of the open side door, watching some white chickens pecking at spilled corn in the dusty yard with the greedy haste of intruders, conscious of the drowsy noontime peace of the village, and of Miss Minns, guardian of the sweetshop, peering across at me from behind her sea-green window, her dark shape dim and a little distorted by the blown glass so that she looked like a small marine monster swimming in a tank.

Presently Grandpa brought me a tumbler of lemonade which fizzed over my tongue, thickening my saliva deliciously. I watched him as he returned to his place amongst the midday gathering in the cool dim interior, first emptying a small thick glass with a single expert tilt, then, while he talked very prosily and importantly with the others, drinking from a big foamy tankard, in slow draughts, washing in and consolidating that first superior golden liquid.

At this point I was distracted by the cries and evolutions of two little girls who were bowling their hoops upon the village green across from the inn. As I was lonely, as Grandpa looked settled for a very long time, I rose, and in a gradual and indirect manner approached the edge of the green. I might not care much for strange boys but most of Miss Barty's pupils had been girls and I was almost at ease with them.

While her companion continued to strike her hoop furiously in the distance, the younger of the little girls had paused in her exertions and seated herself on a bench. She was about my own age, wore a tartan skirt with shoulder straps and was singing, singing to herself. While she sang I placed myself, unobtrusively, upon the extreme edge of the bench, and began to examine a scratch on my knee. When she had finished, there was a silence; then, as I had hoped, she turned to me in a friendly and inquiring fashion.

"Can you sing any songs?"

I shook my head sadly. I could not sing a note, indeed the only song I knew was one my father had tried to teach me about a beautiful lady who had died in disgrace. Still, I liked this little girl with brown eyes and curly dark hair pressed back from her white forehead by a semicircular comb. I was anxious not to let the conversation die.

"Is your hoop made of iron?"

"Oh, of course. But why do you say 'hoop'? We call it a 'gird.' And this stick we guide it with is a 'cleek.'"

Ashamed of my ignorance, which had revealed me so quickly as a stranger, I glanced at her companion, now attacking her gird to drive it towards us.

"Is that your sister?"

She smiled, but quietly, and with kindness. "Louisa is my cousin, visiting me from Ardfillan. My name is Alison Keith. I live with my mother over there." She indicated an imposing roof, embowered by trees, on the far side of the village.

Humbled by my fresh mistake and the sense of her superior dwelling, I greeted the bouncing arrival of Louisa with a defensive smile.

"Hullo!" Arresting her gird with great skill, Louisa, rather short of breath, looked at me askance. "Where did you spring from?"

She was about twelve, with long flaxen hair, which she tossed about with a bossy importance, which made me long to shine before her, for my own and Alison's sake.

"I came from Dublin yesterday."

"Dublin. Good gracious!" She interpolated in a singsong voice: "Dublin is the capital of Ireland." Then paused. "Were you born there?"

I nodded my head, warmly aware of the interest in her gaze.

"Then you must be Irish?"

"I'm Irish and Scottish," I answered rather boastfully.

Far from impressed, Louisa considered me with a patronizing air.

"You can't be two things, that's quite impossible. It all sounds most peculiar." A sudden thought seemed to strike her, she grew rigid, gazing at me with the sharp suspicion of an inquisitor.

"What church do you go to?"

I smiled loftily—as if I did not know. "To St. Dominic's," I was about to answer, when suddenly the gleam, the burning, in her eye awoke in me primeval instincts of defence.

"Just an ordinary church. It has a big steeple. Quite near us in Phoenix Crescent too." Flustered, I tried to dismiss the topic by jumping up and beginning to "burl the wilkies"—my sole physical accomplishment, which consisted in turning head over heels three times.

When I got up, red-faced, Louisa's disconcerting stare remained upon me and her tone held an artlessness more cruel than any accusation.

"I was beginning to be afraid you were a Catholic." She smiled.

Redder than ever, I faltered: "What ever put that idea in your head?"

"Oh, I don't know. It's lucky you're not."

Overcome, I gazed at my shoes, more painfully embarrassed by the fact that Alison's eyes were reflecting something of my own distress. Still smiling, Louisa tossed her long hair back.

"Are you going to stay here?"

"Yes, I am." I spoke from between stiff, unwilling lips. "I'm going to the Academy in three weeks if you want to know."

"The Academy! That's *your* school, Alison. Oh, my goodness, it's lucky you're not what I thought. Why, I shouldn't think there's a single *one* in the whole Academy. Is there, Alison?"

Alison shook her head, with her eyes on the ground. I felt my eyelids smart; then, with a plunging movement, Louisa laughed gaily, finally.

"We must go for lunch now." She took up her gird primly, crushing me with her bright compassion. "Don't look so miserable. You'll be quite all right if what you've said is *true*. Come along, Alison."

As they departed, Alison winked to me, over her shoulder, a look filled with sorrowful sympathy. But it did little to lift me, so overwhelmed was I by this terrible and unforeseen catastrophe. Frozen with mortification, I stood watching their dwindling figures in a kind of daze until I became aware of Grandpa calling me from the other side of the street.

He was smiling broadly when I went over, his eyes bright, his hat cocked at a jaunty angle. As we started off in the direction of Lomond View he clapped me approvingly upon the back.

"You seem very successful with the ladies, Robie. That was the little Keith girl was it not?"

"Yes, Grandpa," I mumbled.

"Nice people." Grandpa spoke complacently, with unsuspected snobbishness. "Her father was captain of the P. and O. *Rawalpindi* . . . before he died. The mother is a fine woman, though not overstrong. She plays the piano something beautiful . . . and the little girl sings like a lintie. What's the matter with you?"

"Nothing, Grandpa. Nothing at all."

He shook his head over me, and to my acute embarrassment started to whistle. He was a beautiful whistler, clear and melodious, but quite careless of his own loudness. Approaching the house, he fell into a sort of hum:—

> "Oh, my luve is like a red, red rose,
> That's newly sprung in June . . ."

He put a clove in his mouth, murmuring to me, with a confidential air:—
"You needn't mention our little refreshment to Mama. She's an awful one to fash."

CHAPTER FOUR

I THINK it was Mama's strategy, at this early stage, to keep me out of the way of the other members of the household. Often I did not see Papa until the evening, for, when he had a "smoke test" or a "milk prosecution" on hand, he did not return for lunch. His devotion to his work was exemplary; even at night he seldom relaxed, seating himself in his corner chair with an official report on plumbing or adulterated foods. He went out only on Thursday evenings to attend the weekly business meeting of the Levenford Building Society.

Murdoch was away most of the day at college. When he came in he lingered as long as possible over his supper; then, although he often seemed to want to talk to me, he spread his books all over the table and placed himself, with an air of heavy resignation, before them.

Kate reappeared from her teaching for the midday meal, but she was oddly uncommunicative and in the evenings she rarely joined the family circle. If she did not go out to visit her friend Bessie Ewing, she retired to her room to correct exercise books or to read, banging the door behind her, those queer bumps on her forehead standing out plainly as evidence of her inward turmoil.

It was not surprising that, while awaiting my beginning at the Academy, I fell more and more into Grandpa's hands. Apart from his copying he had little to do, and although he pretended to regard me as a nuisance he did not altogether disdain my awed companionship. Most afternoons when it was fine he took me to Drumbuck Green to watch him win at "the marleys," a game of china bowls which he played majestically with two friends: Saddler Boag, a stout short-tempered gentleman who had kept the village harness shop for thirty years, and Peter Dickie, a small and sparrowy ex-postman who told me that in his time he had walked a distance equal to halfway round the world, and who was now deeply interested in Halley's Comet—which, he feared, might strike the earth at any moment. Grandpa's bowls were pale pink checked with brown. How wonderful to see him raise his last bowl to his eye with a calm ironic smile and "scatter the white" when Mr. Boag, who hated to lose, was "lying three"!

On other days Grandpa took me to inspect the Public Reading Room, to view a practice of the Levenford Fire Brigade—of which he was severely critical—and once, when Mr. Parkin, who hired out the boats, was away, for a lovely free row on the Common pond.

Sunday, which in any case gave me a peculiar hollow feeling in my stomach, brought a different programme. On that day Mama always rose earlier than usual, and when she had brought Papa a cup of tea in bed, she put the roast in the oven, and laid out his striped trousers and tail coat. Then began the general scurry and confusion of getting dressed, Kate running up and down stairs in her slipbody, Mama trying to get her fingers into gloves which had washed too tight, Murdoch at the last minute, in shirt and braces, putting his tousled head over the bannisters and calling, "Mama, where did you put my clean socks?"—while Papa, his stiff collar hurting his neck, champed, watch in hand, in the lobby, repeating: "The bells will start any minute now."

More than ever conscious of myself as an acute embarrassment to these good people, I kept out of the way in Grandpa's room, until the distant bells began caressing the still morning air, those sweet importunate bells which always increased my loneliness. Grandpa never went to church. He seemed to have no desire to go; besides his clothes were not good enough. When the others had set out for the Established Church on Knoxhill, where the Provost and the baillies of the town attended service, he gave me a kind of privileged sign with his eyelid that permitted me to accompany him while he "slipped across" to pay a forenoon visit to his friend Mrs. Bosomley, the lady who owned the house next door.

Mrs. Bosomley was the widow of a pork-butcher and had once been a leading member of a touring dramatic company, her most notable performance being that of Josephine in "The Emperor's Bride." She was about fifty, quite stout, her brown hair frizzed by tongs, with a broad face, small good-natured eyes which vanished when she laughed and tiny red veins on her cheeks. Often, peering through the privet hedge, I would see her pacing up and down her little garden, followed by her yellow cat, Mikado, and stopping to strike an attitude and recite something out loud. Once I distinctly heard her say: "Strike for the green graves of your sires! Strike for your native soil!"

Levenford was not her native soil; her origin and early life were obscure, and later on boys at school hinted to me that she had not really been on the stage but had travelled with a circus and was tattooed upon her stomach. I shall speak of Mrs. Bosomley again; now it is enough to say that her hospitality made a sharp contrast to the Spartan economy next door. In her front room she gave me milk and sandwiches while Grandpa and she drank coffee; and she startled me so dreadfully by smoking a cigarette—the first time I had seen a lady do such a thing—that to this day the name of the brand upon the flat green packet remains printed on my memory. It was "Wild Geranium."

On Sunday afternoon while Papa, with his collar and tie unloosed, took a nap on the sofa in the cool depths of the parlour and Murdoch departed

with Kate to teach in Sunday school, Grandpa again gave me his sign and
sauntered off with me in the direction of the village, now steeped in
digestive torpor. Turning up the lane beyond the Green he paused, with
a detached and purposeful air, outside the hawthorn hedge of Dalrymple's
market garden.

This was a beautiful garden, with the sun-blistered sign A. DALRYMPLE.
NURSERYMAN spanning the gate, kale and cabbages and carrots sprouting in
rows, the orchard still heavy with pears and apples. Grandpa, having first
surveyed the deserted lane, peered carefully over the hedge; then, with his
tongue, made a clicking sound of regret.

"What a pity! The dear man's not here." He turned, took off his hat
and handed it to me with an urbane smile. "Just nip through the hedge,
Robert; it'll save you a walk to the gate. Take the honey pears, they're the
best. And keep your head down."

Following his whispered instructions I crept through and filled the hat
with ripe yellow pears, while he stood in the middle of the lane, carefully
scrutinizing the landscape and humming.

When I rejoined him and we began to eat, the juice running down our
chins, he remarked gravely:—

"Dalrymple would give me his last gooseberry. He's just devoted to me,
the dear man."

Although I was a melancholy child I will not deny that I found great, if
temporary, comfort in Grandpa's society. There was, unhappily, one odd
detraction from the pleasure of our expeditions which shocked and baffled
me. Grandpa, cordially saluted, everywhere acclaimed, was greeted by a certain juvenile section of the community with shouts of unbelievable derision.

Our tormentors were not the Academy boys, like Gavin Blair, whom
Grandpa had pointed out to me across the street, causing me to redden
furiously, but the small village boys who gathered at the bridge to catch
minnows with their caps in the stream. As we went by, these boys stared
at us rudely and jeered:—

> "Cadger Gow! There he goes!
> Where did he get that terrible nose?"

I turned pale with shame, while Grandpa stalked on, his head in the air,
pursued by the awful chant. In the beginning I pretended not to hear. But
at last, my curiosity conquered my dismay. I besought him with wide eyes:—

"Where *did* you get that nose, Grandpa?"

A silence. He glanced at me sideways, aloof and very dignified.

"Boy, I got it in the Zulu War."

"Oh, Grandpa!" My shame melted in a quick flood of pride, of anger
against these ignorant little boys. "Tell me about it, Grandpa, please."

He gave me a guarded look. Although reluctant, he seemed flattered by
my interest.

"Well, boy," he said, "I am not one to brag . . ."

While I trotted spellbound beside him, a great troopship glided out amidst the weeping of beautiful women, and made stealthy landfall of an arid shore bearing a gentleman coronet in that exclusive brigade, Colonel Dougal Macdougall's Scottish White Horse. Swiftly promoted, through a daring sortie against the Matabele, Grandpa soon had risen to be the Colonel's righthand man and was picked to carry dispatches from the beleaguered garrison, when the White Horse were cut off. I scarcely breathed as, in the darkness of night, a revolver in each hand, a knife between his teeth, he crawled over the rocky veldt. He was almost through the enemy lines when the moon—oh, perfidious moon!—sailed out of the clouds. Instantly the savage horde was upon him. *Pim! Pam! Pim!* His smoking revolvers were empty. Planted on a boulder, he slashed away with his knife. Bloody black writhing forms lay all around him, he whistled musically, and out of the night bounded his favourite white charger. Oh, the stark suspense of that midnight ride. After him came the fleet-footed Zulus. Flights of assagais darken the air. *Whish! Whish!* But at last, faint and bleeding, clinging to his horse's neck, he reached the cantonment. The flag was saved.

I drew a long breath. Excitement and admiration gave me starry eyes. "Were you badly wounded, Grandpa?"

"Yes, boy, I'm afraid I was."

"Was it then that you got . . . your nose, Grandpa?"

He nodded solemnly, caressing the organ with reminiscent tenderness. "It was, boy . . . an assagai . . . poisoned . . . direct hit." Tilting his hat over his eyes against the sun, he concluded reminiscently: "The Queen herself expressed regret when she decorated me at Balmoral."

I contemplated him with a new awe, a new tenderness. Wonderful heroic Grandpa! I held his hand tightly as we returned from the Drumbuck Arms to Lomond View.

When we entered the house Mama was in the lobby, studying a postcard which had just come in, that first day of October, by the afternoon delivery.

"Grandma is coming back tomorrow." She turned to me. "She's looking forward to seeing you, Robert."

The news affected Grandpa strangely. He did not speak but gave Mama his particular grimace, as though he had swallowed something sour, and began to climb the stairs.

With her face upturned Mama seemed to offer consolation. "Would you like an egg to your tea, Father?"

"No, Hannah, no." The intrepid fighter of Zulus spoke despondently. "After that, I couldn't eat a thing."

He went upstairs. I could hear the melancholy twang of the springs as he flung himself into his chair.

* * *

Whatever Grandpa's reaction, mine was one of expectation. On the following day, which was Saturday, the dramatic sound of a cab drew me, running, to the window.

Excitedly, I watched Grandma lower her head and, treasuring her purse against her black-beaded cape with one hand, pulling her skirt from her elastic-sided boots with the other, climb carefully from the cab. The driver seemed out of humour. When Grandma paid him he flung up his arms; but at last, as though acknowledging defeat, consented to carry in the carpetbags. Grandpa had departed for a walk, silently, at an unusual hour, but Kate and Murdoch came out deferentially to welcome her. In the lobby Mama was calling: "Robie! Where are you? Come and help your great-grandma with her things."

I ran out and, in the general confusion, began to carry the lighter packages to the top landing, glancing hurriedly yet with shy interest at Grandma. She was a big flat-footed woman, bigger than my grandpa, with a long, firm, yellowish, deeply wrinkled face, nicely set off by the immaculate white frill which lined her black mutch. Her hair, still dark, was parted in the middle, and at the corner of her long, seamed upper lip was a brown mole stain from which sprouted a tuft of crinkling whiskers. As she talked to Mama, relating the events of her journey, she displayed strong, discoloured teeth which, however, were somewhat unmanageable and made little clicking noises.

Upstairs the secret door was open and while Grandma refreshed herself with a cup of tea downstairs, I sat on a bag in the doorway, satisfying the curiosity which I had so long experienced. It was a neat and well-ordered room, smelling of camphor and beeswax, two hooked rugs making oval islands upon the stained boards, and between them a heavy mahogany bed with turned legs and thick magenta eiderdown, a gleaming chamber pot discreetly tucked beneath. In one corner was the sewing machine; a plush-backed rocking chair draped with an antimacassar waited expectantly at the window. Three coloured lithographs, magnificent and terrifying, hung upon the walls: "Samson Destroying the Temple," "Israelites Crossing the Red Sea," "The Last Judgment." In a lugubrious ebony frame shaped like a tombstone, and near the door, where I could read it, hung a black-bordered poem, entitled "Auspicious Day," praising Abraham for having taken Samuel Leckie to his bosom and inflicting such heavy sorrow on Samuel's bereaved and beloved spouse.

Grandma came up slowly, but steadily, pressing each stair firmly into its place, while I hung about against my will, magnetized, rather in the manner of those small fish which, by instinct rather than desire, gravitate submissively to escort the leviathans of the deep. She was inspecting her room to see if anything had been disturbed, moving the chairs a fraction of an inch, testing the treadle of the sewing machine with her foot, and all the time observing me with a serene yet penetrating eye.

At last, not wholly satisfied, she shook her head and, opening her Gladstone carrying-bag, took out her spectacle case, a Bible, and a number of bottles of physic which she arranged, with the utmost precision, on the little table, covered with a lace doily, beside her bed. Then she turned and addressed me in her broad "country" accent.

"Have you been a good boy while I was away?"

"Yes, Grandma."

"I'm glad to hear it, dear." Her soberness yielded to a warmer note. "You may as well help me to get things straight. I cannot leave this place a day without someone tampering and tinkering with it."

I helped her to unpack while she put away all her folded and laundered garments in a deep cupboard. Then handing me a flannel, and remarking that cleanliness was next to godliness, she set me to rub the fire brasses while, with a feather duster, which she took from the same cupboard, she began to flick the china dogs upon the mantelpiece.

Pleased with my activity, Grandma further relaxed her strictness and bestowed on me a look of deep and meaningful solicitude. "You *are* a good boy, in spite of all. Your grandma has something nice for you."

From the top lefthand drawer of her chest she brought out a handful of the hard peppermint sweets known as "imperials," took one herself, and pressed the rest on me.

"Suck, don't crunch," she advised. "They last longer that way." She stroked my brow protectively: "You're going to be your grandma's boy. You bide with me, my lamb. I'm taking you out for your tea."

True to her promise, Grandma kept me with her most of the day, conversing with me from time to time, even telling me something of herself. She came of a good country stock: the nephew with whom she had been staying was an Ayrshire potato farmer. Her husband had been the head timekeeper at the Levenford Boilerworks, a "saint" who had helped her to find grace. One never-to-be-forgotten day, as he crossed the yard, a ton of steel had dropped from a travelling crane on to his head. Poor Samuel! But he had gone to the Lord, and Marshall Brothers had behaved most handsomely: she drew a pension from the Works every quarter-day in life. She was independent, thank God, and could pay decently for her board and lodging.

At four o'clock in the afternoon, she told me to wash my face and hands. Half an hour later we set out for the village of Drumbuck.

By this time Grandma's austere and Christian spirit was having its effect on me, and in my desire to win her approbation I became serious, old-fashioned, even began primly to imitate her way of nodding her head. I was filled with a godly sense of importance as I walked beside her in all her "braws," for, although the day was warm, she had resumed the full state robes of her arrival, carrying, like a sceptre, her long tightly rolled umbrella with a gold and mother-of-pearl handle. No one dare shout after *her*.

"Remember, dear," she warned me as we drew near the little sweetshop between the horse trough and the smithy. "You are to behave nicely. Miss Minns is my bosom friend—we go to the same Meeting. Don't make a noise when you drink your tea, and speak up when you are spoken to."

Little had I dreamed, when I pressed my face longingly against Miss Minns's low greenish windowpanes, that I would so soon have the honour to be her guest. The door went *ping* as Grandma pushed and I followed in her wake, stepping down to the delightful dim interior of the little cave which smelled of peppermints, aniseed balls, scented soap, and tallow candles. Miss Minns, a small bent woman in black bombazine with steel spectacles on her forehead, was seated behind the counter at her knitting; but, as we entered, taken unawares, she gave out a startled exclamation of affection and surprise.

"Good sakes, woman, you're not back!"

"Aye, aye, Tibbie, it's me and no other."

Delighted to have caught her friend unprepared, Grandma, with unsuspected playfulness, submitted to, and returned, an affectionate greeting, interspersed with many effusive cries from Miss Minns.

Then, hobbling from her rheumatism, Miss Minns led the way into the back shop where, very quickly, she laid out cups and saucers on the round table and set the kettle upon the fire, all the time giving her close attention to the account Grandma had launched into of her visit to Kilmarnock, which pertained largely to the "Meetings" she had attended.

"Yes, woman." Miss Minns sighed at the conclusion in resigned and subtle flattery. "You have had a profitable time. I wish I had heard Mr. Dalgetty. But better you nor me."

Pouring the tea, she began to relate to Grandma everything which had taken place in her absence: the births and the burials and, though I did not then suspect it, the various pregnancies which had occurred. But presently, when these secular trivialities had been disposed of, there came a veiled silence, they glanced at me with the expression of two gourmands who, having exhausted the light dishes, now turn, with whetted appetites, to the main item of the repast.

"He's a fine boy," Miss Minns said, openly. "Take another piece cake, my big man. It's very wholesome."

I could not but feel complimented by this extra attention. Miss Minns had already given me, all to myself, a plate of Abernethy biscuits and an extra cushion for my chair, to raise me to the table. Then, finding that I did not drink my tea, she had fetched from the shop a bottle of delicious yellow aerated water named Iron Brew, with a label showing a strong man in a leopardskin lifting dumbbells of tremendous weight.

"Now, dear," she said kindly. "Tell your grandma and me how you've been getting on. You've been with your grandpa a good deal?"

"Oh, yes, indeed. I was with him nearly all the time."

A meaning, mournful glance between the two ladies; then, in a tone which seemed to veil the forebodings of her spirit, Grandma asked:—

"And what did you do nearly all the time?"

"Oh, lots of things," I said rather grandly, reaching of my own accord for another Abernethy. "Played bowls with Mr. Boag. Hunted the Zulus. Gathered fruit in Mr. Dalrymple's Nursery. . . . Grandpa had permission, of course, to send me through the hedge." Flattered by their attention, I paid full homage to my grandpa, not forgetting our visits to the Drumbuck Arms, even mentioning the two tinkers whom Grandpa had liked in the High Street.

In the pause which followed Grandma continued to regard me with un-affected commiseration. Then, with great discretion but firmly, as though resolved to know the worst, she began to probe into my more distant history, drawing from me an account of my life in Dublin. So tempered was her approach, I soon found myself giving forth, without a qualm, the full record of my upbringing.

When I concluded the two women looked at each other, charged with a strange silence.

"Well," Miss Minns said at last, in a suppressed voice. "You know where you are, woman."

Grandma gravely inclined her head and glanced towards me. "Robert dear, run out and play a minute by the door. Miss Minns and I have something to discuss."

I said good-bye to Miss Minns, then stood by the horse trough in gathering uneasiness, until Grandma rejoined me. She did not speak during our return; although she held my arm with a kind of sober pity. Leading me immediately to her room, she closed the door and removed her cape.

"Robert," she said. "Will you say a prayer with me?"

"Oh, yes, Grandma," I assured her with nervous fervour.

As though her heart bled she took my hand, guided me to my knees, then got down heavily beside me, amidst the growing darkness of the room. Her supplication, full of confidence and devotion, was for my welfare. Agitated, my face drawn by anxiety, I was nevertheless moved by the stead-fast and personal quality of the prayer, and my eyes filled with tears when Grandma, having begged forgiveness for a sinner, and unceasing patience for herself, commended me tenderly to Heaven. When she concluded she got up, smiling cheerfully, drew the blinds and lit the gas.

"That suit you're wearing, Robert . . . it's a pure disgrace. What they would think of you at the Academy I do not know." Summoning me, she deprecated the frayed shoddiness of the material between her finger and thumb. "Tomorrow I'll begin to run you up something on my machine. Fetch me the inch tape from my drawer."

While I stood very still she measured me from every angle, jotting down figures with a moistened stub of pencil on a brown paper pattern which she took from a copy of *Weldon's Home Dressmaker*. Then she opened her cup-board, reflecting aloud: "I have a good serge petticoat somewhere. Just the thing!"

While she rummaged there came a tap on the door.

"Robie." It was my grandpa's voice outside. "Time for bed."

Grandma turned from the cupboard.

"I will put Robert to bed."

"But he sleeps with me."

"No, he is sleeping with me."

There was a pause. Grandpa's voice came through the door.

"His nightshirt is in my room."

"I will provide him with a nightshirt."

Again silence, the silence of defeat, and in a moment I heard the sound of Grandpa's slippers in retreat. I was now thoroughly alarmed, and must have shown it in my pallid face, for Grandma's manner became calmer and more protective still. She undressed me, poured water from her ewer and made me wash, then, wrapping me in a flannel bodice, she helped me into the high bed. She sat down beside me, stroking my brow, as though facing a disagreeable task.

"My poor boy." She sighed with genuine compunction. "I want you to prepare yourself. Your grandpa never fought in any war. He has never been fifty miles beyond the county of Winton in all his life."

What was she saying? My pupils dilated in shocked incredulity.

"It's not my nature to speak ill of anyone," she continued. "But this is a solemn duty which affects your future." As her voice went on, my whole being revolted, I tried not to hear what she was saying, yet the words, from time to time, broke through relentlessly. ". . . A failure in all he did . . . thrown out of every situation . . . exciseman in the bonded warehouse . . . hand-to-mouth for years. . . . It was the end of his poor wife. . . . And then the drink . . . see it in his face . . . his nose. Even the company he keeps . . . Boag, three times a bankrupt, and Dickie, one foot in the poorhouse. . . . Now not a penny to his name . . . dependent on the charity of my son . . ."

"No, no," I cried, covering my ears with my hands and thrusting my head into the pillow.

"You had to know, Robert." She straightened the bedclothes. "He's not the right influence for a growing boy. Don't cry, my lamb. I'll take care of you."

She waited patiently till I was composed, then rose, and declaring that she, too, was tired, she quoted: "Early to bed, early to rise, makes us all healthy, wealthy, and wise," then proceeded to take her clothes off.

Fascinated, despite my desolation, I could not help but watch her. She began by removing her black mutch: the little black bonnet which sat on her bun of still brown hair. Then from her bosom she unpinned her thin gold watch, which she wound, carefully, and hung on a hook above the mantelpiece. Next to come off was the white shawl which kept warm her shoulders. A pause for unbuttoning the front of her tight long-sleeved black bodice, then this, too, lay folded on the rocking chair. The slipbodies followed, white strips of cambric, perhaps four of them, the ends tied with tapes, until Grandma was seen to be encased in dark stays, which encircled her and rose high to the dark hollows of her armpits.

At this point she paused to remove her teeth, with one swift, almost magical pass of her left hand, a feat of legerdemain which caused her face to collapse in staggering fashion. Her austere features sank into an agreeable softness. However, once the teeth had been placed in a tumbler of water by the bed, Grandma put on a white bed-cap, the ribbons of which, tied tight under her chin, seemed to restore, partly, the rigidity of her facial structure.

Now she dropped and stepped out of her skirt, a process repeated with all her petticoats. The number of petticoats that Grandma wore became one of the great perplexities of my early life: first, a black alpaca, then three of white cotton, two of creamy flannel . . . but I never solved the ultimate and elusive mystery for at this point Grandma looked at me, sternly yet coyly.

"Robert! Turn to the wall."

When I obeyed, I heard more stepping out, the snapping of whalebone; other sounds; then the gas went out and Grandma was in beside me. She was a quiet and peaceful sleeper, but her feet, which she immediately placed against me, were very cold. Lying on my side in the darkness I fearfully studied her teeth as they grinned luminously at me from the bedside table: a heavy double set, of greenish colour, old-fashioned but immensely strong, with a powerful connecting spring. Grandpa had no such teeth; but I longed —oh, despite his wickedness I longed suddenly with all my heart to be back beside him.

CHAPTER FIVE

THE old greystone Academy, with its high square clock tower, worn stone steps, long damp corridors, and hot classrooms filled with the smell of chalk dust, children, and illuminating gas, had for more than a hundred years exposed to the High Street its deep, dark archway, an entrance comparable, by my nervous fancy, to the opening in the mountain of Hamelin.

On the very morning that I must pass through that opening, when I woke up filled with anxiety and excitement, Grandma informed me that my suit was ready. She led me, complacently, to the window where it was laid out, complete, on tissue paper, to surprise me.

The first sight of my new suit, to which I had looked forward, so took me aback that I scarcely knew what to say. It was green, not a dark subdued green, but a gay and lively olive. True, as she treadled, I had seen this material piled on Grandma's machine, but, in my innocence, I had assumed it to be the lining.

"Slip it on," she said, with pride.

It was large, the jacket engulfed me, the wide breeches fell in straight lines like a pair of long trousers amputated below the knee.

"Fine, fine." Grandma was patting and pulling me here and there. "It covers you well. I made it for your growth."

"But the colour, Grandma?" I protested feebly.

"Colour!" She removed a white basting thread, speaking from lips which compressed a pin. "What ails the colour? It's wonderful stuff, stands by itself. It'll never wear out."

I blenched. Looking closely at my sleeve I now perceived in the material a faint stripe, composed of little raised whirls: oh, heavens, a pattern of roses, beautiful for Grandma's petticoat, but scarcely the thing for me.

"Let me put on my old suit for this morning, Grandma."

"A pack of nonsense! I cut it up for dusters last night."

Grandma's praise of her creation sent me from the room partly convinced, but immediately Murdoch dashed me to the ground. Meeting me on the stairs he stopped in mock terror, shielding his eyes, then lay back against the bannisters with a wild guffaw. "It's come! It's come at last!"

In the kitchen Mama's odd silence, her air of extra kindness as she handed me my porridge, did not reassure me.

I went out into the cold grey morning, unnerved, conscious that on the whole of that drab, wintry Scottish landscape there was one strange vernal note: myself. People turned round to gaze after me. In my timid shame, I shunned the main street and took the "Common way," a quieter but longer road, which made me late for school.

After some difficulty, having lost myself in the corridors, I found the second standard—to which, on Kate's recommendation, I had been assigned. The partition was thrown back, the double class assembled, as I entered; and Mr. Dalgleish, at his desk, had already given out the first lesson. I tried to edge, unobserved, to a vacant desk, but the master stopped me in the middle of the floor. He was not, as I discovered, a habitual tyrant, for he had days of splendid affability when he dowered us with a wealth of interesting knowledge; but there were other spells, dark and bitter, when a glowering devil seemed to rage within him. And I now saw, with dismay, from the manner in which he chewed the corner of his moustache, that his mood was unfavourable. I expected a reprimand for my lateness. But he did not shout at me. Instead he climbed down from his desk and walked round me in a leisurely fashion, with his head slightly to one side. The class sat up, startled and excited.

"So!" he said at last. "We are the new boy. And it appears we have a new suit. The age of miracles is not over."

A titter of expectancy went round. I was silent.

"Come, sir, don't sulk at us. Where did ye buy it? Miller's in the High Street or the Co-operative Stores?"

Pale to the lips, I whispered: "My great-grandma made it, sir."

A roar of laughter from the class. Mr. Dalgleish, his blood-threaded eye unsmiling, continued to walk round me.

"A remarkable colour. But appropriate. We understand you are of Hibernian extraction?"

Great laughter from the class. In all that amphitheatre of grinning faces, magnified by my shrinking sensibilities to the vastness of a colosseum, yet seen minutely, vividly, there were only two that did not smile. Gavin Blair, in the front row, was gazing at the master with a kind of cold contempt; Alison Keith, across her lesson book, kept her brown, troubled eyes steadily upon me.

"Answer my question, sir? Are you or are you not a disciple of Saint Patrick?"

"I don't know."

"He does not know." The sneering tone took on amazement, a more leisured deliberation; the class rolled about the benches with merriment. "He bursts upon us, garlanded, as it were, with shamrocks, the walking apotheosis of that heart-moving ballad 'The Wearing of the Green,' yet he blushes to admit that the holy water still bedews his brow . . ."

This continued until, suddenly, he turned and, with a cold stare, stilled the class. Then he spoke to me in his natural voice.

"It may interest you to know that I taught your mother. It looks now as if I wasted my time. Sit over there."

Trembling and humiliated, I stumbled to my place.

I hoped that this might end my suffering. Alas, it was only the beginning. At playtime I was surrounded by a crowing, jeering mob. Already I had been marked as someone different from the others, now I was confirmed as a freak amongst the herd.

Bertie Jamieson and Hamish Boag were my worst tormentors.

"Green's the colour! Blue's its mother." The wit was cruder than Mr. Dalgleish's, but it followed the same pattern. The unhappy petticoat of an old woman had stirred racial and religious hatreds to their dregs. At the lunch hour I locked myself in one of the cubicles of the lavatory, my piece of bread, spread with rhubarb jam and wrapped in paper, resting untouched on my knees. But I was discovered and forced out to the light of day.

That afternoon we had drill, which was conducted in the school hall by the janitor, an ex-sergeant of the Volunteers. Here, as I removed my jacket with the others, Bertie Jamieson and Hamish Boag approached me with a threatening air. Bertie was a loutish boy with a bulging forehead who was always running and scrambling with the girls. He said: "We're going to give it to you after."

"But what for?" I faltered.

"For being a dirty little Papist."

During the next hour, I executed my "arms raise" and "knees bend" in shivering foreboding. Whenever the exercises were over and the janitor had gone I was crowded back into the hall cloakroom. Most of the bigger boys were there, and when I had been pushed and kicked into a corner, Jamieson, catching hold of my arm, began to twist it painfully behind my back. In trying to escape I slipped and fell. Immediately, while Hamish Boag collared my legs, Jamieson sat on my chest and began to bang my head on the floor.

"Give it to him, Bertie," cried several voices. "Knock the stuffing out of him."

This gave Jamieson an idea. He released my hair and exchanged a glance with the others. "Who's got a knife? We'll see if he's green inside as well as out."

"No, Bertie, no," I cried. I could scarcely speak for the frightened beating of my heart. Suddenly the bell rang and they were obliged to let me up. As I reached the corridor, from which we were to march to the classroom, Mr. Dalgleish, waiting, with his hand on the tongue of the bell, gazed at my dusty dishevelled form.

"What's all this?"

The others answered for me—a sycophantic chorus: "Nothing sir." Then little Howie, pert as a squirrel, cried out from behind: "We were just admiring Shannon's new green suit, sir."

Mr. Dalgleish smiled sourly.

All that week I felt the full misery of life. There was no end to the violations committed upon me. After school, opposite the Church of the Holy Angels, which stood quite near the Academy, there was usually collected a predatory band. Though I had never put foot within the edifice I was ribaldly urged to nip in and have my sins forgiven, to rifle the poor box, to kiss the priest's toe—and other portions of his anatomy. My tormentors were merciless and when, in desperation, I struck out at them I was always overwhelmed by the mob.

To avoid them, constantly on the lookout and ready to run, I took circuitous and unfrequented paths—especially the "Common way," which led past the Boilerworks; yet even here I was not immune—that dreadful suit was on my back and the young engineers and fitters from the works would shout: "Hey! Green Breeks! Does your mother know you're out?" Their remarks were good-natured, yet, by now, I was too cowed to know the difference between humour and abuse. I sank deeper into despair, I made a bungle of my homework, blotted all my copybooks in class, I was behaving like a halfwit. Once when Mr. Dalgleish asked me to stand and recite a poem we had learned I hesitated so long he shouted: "What are you waiting for?" I answered absently, vacantly: "Please, sir, for my green suit." Stupefied silence. Then a great howl of laughter.

I could endure it no longer. That evening I burst into Grandpa's room. The first whiff of the familiar fusty yet beloved smell—tears gushed from my eyes. Since Grandma had adopted me our estrangement had been complete, and though I had been prepared to offer him my forgiveness, he had passed me with his head in the air, wearing his chilly, aloof, disdainful smile, meeting my stammered explanation with the indifferent remark: "Sleep with who you like, my boy." Now, he was seated, philosophically, yet with a certain air of apathy, doing nothing.

"Grandpa," I wept.

He turned slowly. Was I mistaken? Or did his eye brighten at the sight of me? A pause.

"I thought ye'd come back," he said, simply; then, unable to resist his dreadful sententiousness, he added: "Old friends are better than new."

CHAPTER SIX

CALMED at last and seated on Grandpa's knee—joyful proof of our reconciliation—I poured out my heart. He listened to me in silence. Then, with a firm hand, he took a charged pipe from his rack.

"There's only one thing to do," he said, in his most reasonable voice—and oh, how, after days of bedlam, I blessed its tranquil logic. "The question is, will ye do it?"

"I'll do it," I cried fervently. "I will, I will, I will."

He lit his pipe and took a few calm puffs.

"Who is the strongest . . . sturdiest . . . stubbornest boy in your class?"

I need reflect only an instant: there was but one answer to that question. Unhesitatingly I declared: "Gavin Blair."

"The Provost's son?"

I nodded.

"Then—" He took his pipe from his lips. "You must fight Gavin Blair."

I stared at him, appalled. Gavin was not really one of my tormentors. He had kept himself contemptuously aloof from the whole miserable disturbance. Indeed, at the Academy, he had only spoken to me twice. He was a superior boy: bright yet self-contained, the top boy of the class, a favourite even with Dalgleish. In all the games he was the best; it was acknowledged that he could beat Bertie Jamieson with one hand behind his back. I tried to explain this to Grandpa.

"Are you feared?" he asked.

I hung my head, thinking of Gavin's wiry figure, small yet determined chin, his clear grey eye. Unlike the heroic boys of the fiction which had come my way, I was painfully afraid.

"I don't know how to fight."

"I'll learn you. I'll take a week and learn you. It's not size that counts but spirit." He shrugged his shoulders. "We'll write a letter to Dalgleish if you like, asking him to speak to the boys. But they'll scorn ye all the more for it. It's a matter of principle, to go in and whip the best of them. Will ye do it?"

I shivered; yet, strangely, in my extremity I found a certain resolution: perhaps the sort which makes suicides jump off high buildings. I gulped an incoherent: "Yes."

My training began that same evening after I had dried the dishes for Mama. It was agreed that Grandma should be kept in complete ignorance of our design. Grandpa placed me in a series of stiff and uncomfortable attitudes with my knuckles advanced and my chin so drawn in I could see nothing but my own boots. Facing me in a corresponding pose, he then commanded me to "let go with my left," which I did with such precipitancy I caught him full in the midriff, doubling him up, gasping, in his chair.

"Oh, Grandpa," I cried, shocked. "I did not mean to hurt you."

He was very cross. I had not in the least hurt him, it was merely that I had taken a most ungentlemanly advantage in striking him in a region known as "below the belt." When he had got his wind back he lectured me severely on foul blows, then sent me out to run to the road end and back to improve my legs.

In the days which followed he strove hard to advance me in the noble art of self-defence. He told me bloody and inspiring stories of Jem Mace, Gentleman Jim, and Billy the Butcher, who had fought eighty-two rounds with a broken jaw and one ear hanging off. He bade me drink no water, or as little as I could, to toughen my skin. He even sacrificed his dinnertime cheese, the one food he cared about, making me eat it slowly as I stood before him while a bead of saliva ran down his whiskers.

"There's nothing like Dunlop cheese, boy, to put real pith in you." I did not doubt him, but I suffered dreadfully from heartburn.

On Saturday afternoon he took me along with him to the cemetery and demonstrated me to his friends. As I struck my pugilistic postures before them he explained, darkly, the reason of the coming conflict. I heard the Saddler laugh offensively.

"What about your grand ideas now, Gow? You're aye talking about live and let live, and yet you start a fight."

"Saddler," Grandpa answered stiffly, "sometimes it is necessary to fight so that we *can* live."

This silenced Mr. Boag but I could see he held a poor view of my prospects of success.

The fateful day dawned. Grandpa called me to his room as I crossed the landing and solemnly shook me by the hand.

"Remember," he said, looking me in the eyes: "Anything . . . but don't be feared."

I felt like bursting into tears—despite Grandpa's cheese the soft and tender years at my poor mother's apron strings were not entirely undone. What made it worse was that, although my persecution had not abated, Gavin had lately shown signs of taking my part: he had cuffed Bertie Jamieson for shouldering too roughly in a game of Hopping Charlie, and once, in class, seeing me in need of a rubber, had silently pushed his own across to me. But I had given my word to Grandpa, and nothing, nothing must hold me back. The hour selected for me by my mentor was four o'clock, immediately following the dismissal of school. All day long, in a continuous tremor, I sat watching Gavin's calm, intent, intelligent face across the classroom. He was handsome, with deep-set dark-lashed eyes, a short proud upperlip: it was a Highland face, for his father was from Perth and his dead mother had been a Campbell from Inveraray. Today, perhaps because he was going out with his grown-up sister that evening, he wore his kilt, the dark Blair tartan, austere leather sporran, black brogues. Once or twice his eyes touched mine, which must have seemed strangely pleading. My heart lay heavy in my side. I felt almost that I loved him. Yet I must fight him.

Four strokes from the old clock in the tall grey tower of the Academy . . . My last hope that Mr. Dalgleish would keep me in had vanished. I was dismissed with the others, I was even crossing the playground, Gavin striding ahead of me, his satchel slung carelessly across his back. The need for urgency —if I were not to return to Grandpa a pitiful failure—goaded me beyond my senses. Suddenly, I ran forward and pushed Gavin hard. He spun round to find me confronting him with my fists arranged one on top of the other, rather as though I were holding a candle in a procession.

"Knock down the blocks." I croaked out the phrase, which, in case it is not fully recognized, is the traditional invitation to combat in Levenford. Immediately a shout, between wonder and expectation, went up from the other boys. "A fight! Gavin and Shannon. A fight! A fight!"

Gavin flushed—his fair skin coloured easily—and he glanced in annoyance at the ring of boys who already swarmed round us. He must accept the challenge, feeble though it was. With the palm of his hand he slapped my fists apart. Immediately I set them up again, holding them sideways from my body.

"Spit over the blocks."

Gavin spat expertly over the blocks.

I proceeded with the ritual. With boots that seemed dissevered from my fluid legs I traced a wavering line on the gravel surface of the playground.

"I dare ye to step over it."

Gavin, I perceived with dread, was growing angry. He promptly stepped over it.

I trembled in all my bones. Only the final act remained. Dead silence from the surrounding boys. With dry lips I whispered: "Give the coward's blow."

He rapped me, without hesitation, on the chest. How hollow my breastbone sounded—as though made of cardboard! How pale I felt myself to be! But there was no retreat. I clenched my chattering teeth and rushed at the beloved Gavin.

I forgot everything Grandpa had taught me, everything. My thin arms flailed the air in wild circular sweeps. I hit Gavin often, but always in the hardest and most resistant areas, like his elbows, his cheekbones, and especially the square metal buttons of his kilt. The unfairness of these dreadful buttons moved me to a surging bitterness. Always when I struck him I seemed to hurt him much less than I hurt myself. While his blows, on the contrary, sank painfully into my softest places.

He knocked me down twice, to the accompaniment of cheers. I had never before recognized in myself the capacity for rage. These base cheers helped me to discover it. Yes, surely the basest of all human beings were those who, while standing by, drew enjoyment from the strife and anguish of their fellow creatures. Fury against my real enemies welled out from my very marrow;

their blurred yet grinning faces incited me to show them what I was made of. Rising from the gravel I rushed again at Gavin.

He went down before me. Deathly stillness. Then, as Gavin got up, the voice of little Howie, the squirrel: "You only slipped, Gavin. Give it to him! Give it to him!"

Gavin was more cautious now. He circled a good deal and did not appear to enjoy my rushes. We were both the worse for wear, and breathing like steam engines. I was flushed and warm, the clammy coldness had left my skin. I observed with strange wonder that one of his eyes was of a purplish hue and closing fast. Had I really inflicted such a mischief, on such a hero? Then, through the haze, the tumult, the confusion, a voice fell deliriously on my ear. One of the "big" boys, from the upper forms . . . A group had stopped on their way to the gymnasium.

"By God! Green Breeks is making a fight of it!"

Joy and ecstasy! I was not disgracing my grandpa. I was not such a coward as I had feared. I rushed again at my dear Gavin, as though ready to embrace him. Suddenly, but without intention, as we wrestled about, he raised his head.

I received the stunning impact of his skull upon my nose.

It began to bleed. I could taste the warm saltiness in my mouth, feel the river running down my nostrils, splashing all over my front. Heavens! I never knew there was so much blood in my puny body. I was not in the least inconvenienced. My brain, indeed, was more and more clear, though my legs, once again, had ceased to belong to me. Dizzily, I landed my knuckles once again on Gavin's buttons. Dazzling lights, shouts, rockets in the sky . . . Halley's Comet, perhaps! I was still swinging my arms when I discovered that someone was holding me back. Another of the big boys had Gavin by the collar in like fashion.

"That's all, youngsters, for the time being. Shake hands. It was a dam' good scrap. Now run in for the hall-door key, somebody. This little brat is bleeding like a pig."

I lay flat on my back on the playground with the huge cold key pressed in at the back of my neck while Gavin knelt beside me with a smeared, concerned face. My clothes were sopping, the big boys were worried that the bleeding did not stop. At last, by plugging my nostrils with shreds of a torn-up handkerchief soaked in salt and water, they were successful.

"Lie still for twenty minutes, young 'un, and you'll be right as the mail."

They went away. All my classmates had gradually drifted off, all except Gavin. We were alone in the strangely empty playground, a battleground, stained, scarred and kicked up by our feet. Dreamily, I tried to smile up at him, but my plugged nose and the stiff film on my face prevented me.

"Don't move," he said, softly. "I didn't mean to hit you with my head. It was a foul."

I shook my head in disagreement, almost starting the bleeding again. Somehow, I managed to smile. "I'm sorry your eye got closed." He explored the shut optic tenderly, then smiled, his warm beautiful smile, which radiated through me like sunshine.

Carefully, when the little tails of handkerchief hanging from my nose ceased to drip, he pulled them out. Then he helped me to my feet. Together in silence we began our pilgrimage to Drumbuck Road.

Halley's Comet still flashed about the sky. Opposite his house he paused. "You can't go home like that. Come in and have a wash."

I accompanied him diffidently between the twin entrance lamp-posts, insignia of the Provost's residence, each with the town coat of arms painted on the glass, then up the carefully raked drive, with shrubs on either side. The garden was large and splendidly maintained: a handyman was working beside a wheelbarrow in the distance. At the back of the villa we approached a large coach-house with an outside water tap. As we started to get the worst off, a maid in a neat black-and-white uniform viewed us nervously from the window and, presently, a lady in a brown dress came hurrying out.

"My dear boys. Have you had an accident?" She was Julia Blair, Gavin's grown-up sister, who had kept house for his father since his mother died. After her first inquiring glance she stopped asking questions. She took me up to Gavin's room—a beautiful room of his own full of photographs, rods and fishing tackle, and fretwork pieces he had made himself. There she bade me strip off my clammy garments and, while the maid took these away, not without disgust, to wrap them in a brown paper parcel, she made me put on a good grey tweed suit of Gavin's.

"I knew your mother very well, Robert," she said in her kind, matronly voice. "Why don't you come round to see Gavin when . . ." She glanced round, but he had been detained in the kitchen to have treatment for his eye. "When you're both better." Downstairs, as she handed me my parcel at the front door, a flush came over her mature, earnest face. "We certainly don't want Gavin's suit back, Robert. He has quite grown out of it." She stood alone on the steps for a considerable time watching me vanish into the dusk.

I came up the road slowly towards Lomond View. Now I felt my full weariness. I ached all over, my head was whirling, I could scarcely move my dragging limbs. And with this growing lassitude, my spirits also drooped. Gavin's grand house had depressed me. That peculiar despondency which, in my later life, was to follow swiftly, and thus spoil, even my most apparent successes now began to gnaw at me. From the standards of perfection I viewed my recent performance with increasing dissatisfaction. After all—if the big boys had not stopped the fight . . .

I reached the gate and there, alone, waiting for me, was Grandpa.

A long pause. His look encompassed my pale strained features. His voice was gentle.

"Did ye win?"

"No, Grandpa." I faltered. "I think I lost."

Without a word he took me to his room, and seated me in his own arm-chair. I broke out:—

"I wasn't feared . . . not after we had started . . ."

He drew from me, haltingly, the story of the fight. I could not under-stand his excitement. When I had finished, he shook me, in a kind of exalta-tion, by the hand. Then he rose and, taking the brown paper parcel which contained the cause of my misery, cast it square upon the fire. My green suit took an awful time to burn and made a bad smoke in the room. But at last it was gone.

"You see now," said Grandpa.

CHAPTER SEVEN

IN THE wintry weeks which followed, with hard frost and long dark evenings, the feud between my two great-grandparents, which had its origin in dif-ferent viewpoints and unequal privileges, continued to manifest itself in a silent struggle for possession of me.

Grandma was very cross indeed about the change of suits; she gave me a good slap and, at night, as we lay in bed together, lectured me soundly on the baseness of ingratitude, telling me I must do much better if I wished to remain "her boy." Her fears for my health, always grave, seemed to deepen, and I could not sneeze without her endowing me with an inflammation of the lungs against which she dosed me freely with a dark horehound-and-senna physic of her own compounding. In spite of this I was happier than I had been before.

At the Academy, my fight had helped me greatly; perhaps less my fight than my Homeric loss of blood. This threatened to become historic, for al-ready boys spoke of events in relation to it: as before, or after, "the day Shannon had his nosebleed." At all events, decently clad in grey, for which I blessed Miss Julia Blair, I was no longer derided. Indeed, Bertie Jamieson and his allies went out of their way to offer me signs of their regard. It was recognized that Gavin was my friend.

Gavin, as I have implied, stood apart from the other boys, not in a snob-bish sense because he was better off than they—his father had an old-established corn-chandler's business—but in his character and disposition—really, in his interior life. He played all the ordinary games skilfully, yet sparingly, for he had other tastes and recreations far beyond the common lot. In the bookcase of his cozy room were volumes of natural history crammed with glossy coloured pictures of birds, insects and wild flowers, the names printed underneath. He had a superb collection of birds' eggs. On one wall was a framed photograph of himself, in knickerbockers, holding a great fish —his father, a noted angler, frequently took him to Loch Lomond, and the previous autumn, Gavin, not yet nine, had brought to the gaff a twelve-pound grilse.

Yet these magnificent accomplishments were as nothing beside that inner fibre, that spiritual substance for which no words suitable can be found. He was a silent boy, silent and Spartan. The firm line of his mouth, the small resolute chin, seemed to say to life, quietly: "I will never give in."

On the Friday following our encounter he had waited for me after class and, without words, with only a shy smile, fell into step beside me, along the High Street. After weeks of fleeing down the back ways, how I thrilled to this distinction! We stopped for half an hour at his father's warehouse, where, in the stables at the back, we watched Tom Drin, the head vanman, dose a sick horse, recovering from the hives. Provost Blair beckoned us, on our way out through the big storerooms full of forage and cornbins, piled sacks of meal, beans, and oats, with white-aproned handymen bustling about.

"You two came together the right way." He gave us his dark smile, an Olympian, godlike smile—and a double handful of the sweet carob pods which we called "locusts."

As we ate our "locusts" together, on our way home in the dusk I tried to tell Gavin how wonderful, how lucky, it was to have a father like his, which made him flush with pride—the best thing I could have said. Then, as we stood at the gate of Lomond View, he gazed towards his boots, gently kicking the pavement edge.

"When it's spring I'm going nesting . . . in the Winton Hills . . . for a golden plover's egg, if you'd like to come . . ."

Oh, the joy of being chosen, the picked companion of Gavin for these promised rambles amongst the Winton Hills! And a golden plover's egg! That night I could scarcely sleep for thinking of it. A prospect of tremulous wonder was opening out before me. . . .

But wait. . . . Before I pass to these delights I must record, dutifully, a visit which introduced me to the last member of the Leckie family.

At the beginning of January, Mama, on her evening pilgrimage to the letterbox, gave a cry of joy, as if she had received a message from the archangels.

"From Adam." She bore the letter into the kitchen, where we sat at high tea. "He's coming Saturday at one o'clock. A flying visit. On business."

Reluctantly, she surrendered the letter as Papa jealously reached out. It went round the house. Only Grandpa, who seemed to set little store by the news, and Kate, whose forehead was again sulkily gathering, remained unmoved.

I found myself growing excited as Mama related what a boy Adam had been for winning marbles; how his "head was screwed on the right way," how he bought and sold a bicycle at a profit of ten shillings before he was thirteen; how a year later he went into Mr. McKellar's office with no advantages whatsoever; how, after hours, he did evening collecting work for the Rock Assurance Company, how he saved all his money; how, not yet twenty-seven, he was himself established in the insurance business, representing both the Caledonia Company and the Rock, with an office in the Fidelity Building in

Winton, and earning at least four hundred pounds a year, even more—Mama held her breath—than Papa, himself.

Mama also showed me, proudly, his gift: her very yellow gold brooch which—Adam himself had told her—was worth a great deal of money.

At a few minutes before one o'clock on Saturday a motor car drove up to the door. Let me create no false impressions, no false hopes—it was not Adam's. *Still—a motor car!* An early Argyll model, bright red in colour, having a small brass-bound radiator stamped with the Argyll blue lion, a high wide body with handsome side seats and a door at the back . . .

Adam entered, confident and smiling, wearing a coat with a brown fur collar. He embraced the waiting Mama, who had been up since dawn preparing for him, shook hands vigorously with Papa, suitably acknowledged the rest of us. He was dark-haired, of medium height, and already beginning to be burly, with a fine blood in his clean-shaven cheeks from his wintry drive. As he sat down to the steak, cauliflower, and potatoes which Mama, with fervent prodigality, whipped out of the oven and put before him, he explained that Mr. Kay, a partner in the new Argyll works, had given him a lift from Winton on his way to Alexandria. They had done the fifty miles in under two hours.

While we all sat round and watched his solo banquet—we had eaten our dinner of shepherd's pie an hour ago—he told us that he had already spent half an hour in the town, and transacted some insurance business with Mr. McKellar. His eye, small like Papa's, but of a clear brown colour, caught mine, almost jocularly. I blushed with pleasure.

Mama, having stolen out to the hall to examine her son's beautiful new fur-collared coat, was back, serving him adoringly.

"One thing we must discuss." Adam interrupted his talk to smile up at her. "The old man's policy."

"Yes, Adam." Papa, who was taking time off from his work, drew his chair into the table close to Adam's. His voice was confidential, respectful.

"It's about due now." Adam spoke thoughtfully. "February seventeenth . . . Four hundred and fifty pounds net, payable, as agreed, to Mama."

"A nice sum," Papa breathed.

"Very tidy." Adam concurred. "But we could do even better."

Smiling a little at Papa's earnest perplexity, he went on to explain. "If we continued the existing policy—which I could easily arrange—the amount, payable at the age of seventy-five or death if earlier, would run, with profits, to something like six hundred."

"Six hundred!" Papa echoed. "But that means we wouldn't touch the cash now."

Adam shrugged. "It's there. The Rock Assurance is safe as the Bank. It's a gilt-edged opportunity. What do you say, Mama?"

Mama was looking very unhappy, her hands fluttering about. "I've said before . . . I don't like making money out of my father . . . not that way . . ."

"Oh, come now, Mama." Adam's smile was indulgent. "We straightened that out long ago. He owes you it for board and lodging. Besides, look at the history of the policy. When Grandpa started it years ago, it was only a miserable five-shillings-a-month collection affair with the old Castle Company. And you know it had lapsed and was lying buried with the Castle Company when I went in with the Rock. It would still be there if I hadn't dug it up, and persuaded McKellar, as a personal favour, to make it the basis of a new endowment on Grandpa's life."

Mama sighed but did not speak.

"Would you want your commission on the extension?" Papa asked guardedly.

"Well, naturally." Adam laughed, not in the least offended. "Business is business all the world over."

There was a reflective pause; then Papa spoke with cautious decision. "Yes. . . . Yes, Adam. I think we should extend."

Adam nodded approval. "You're wise." He opened the bag at his feet and brought out a folded document. "Here's the policy all drawn. I'll leave it with you, Mama. Get Grandpa to sign before the seventeenth."

"Yes, Adam." There was still a shade of reproach in Mama's voice.

Although it conveyed to me a deep impression of Adam's business acumen, I had not in the least understood this conversation. Afterwards, when Papa had returned to the office, Adam found time to have a word with me, alone, before leaving for the two-thirty express.

"I hope you'll see me to the station, Robert." He stood up, using a quill toothpick, his small eyes genial with friendship. "I'd like to make you a little present. Commemorate our first meeting. See this." From the coin case at the end of his watch chain he pressed out a half-sovereign and held it up between his finger and thumb. "Money . . . fresh from the Mint . . . a fairly useful commodity in spite of the disparaging remarks of those who haven't got it. Not a bad idea to get a notion of the value of money while you're young, Robert. Don't mistake me. I'm not one of your stingy ones. I like to get the good of my money . . . eat the best, wear the best, stop at the best hotels, have everybody running after me. That's my side of the picture. For the other . . . Well, look at Grandpa . . . not a farthing to bless himself with, bread and cheese in the attic, dependent even for his half-ounce of shag . . ." He broke off, glancing at his watch, smiling so infectiously I could not help smiling in return.

Waiting for him in the lobby, I found myself in warm agreement with his views on the gravities of life and the importance of money. I longed for that moment when, with jingling pockets, I, too, should walk into a restaurant and, in lordly style, order myself beefsteak, while the waiters scurried at my behest. I trembled, in joyful anticipation of the present he would buy me with that lovely half-sovereign.

"You won't mind carrying my bag?" Adam lightly asked me, as Mama helped him into his coat.

I fervently expressed my desire to serve him and picked up the Gladstone bag, which, showing lumps that could be neither books nor papers, was more burdensome than I had expected. Mama kissed Adam again. We departed for the station, Adam walking with a springy step, while I, half running, continually changing the bag from hand to hand, managed to keep pace with him.

"Now what sort of present would you like?"

"Anything, Adam," I gasped, politely.

"No, no." Adam insisted. "It's to be something you'd like, young fellow my lad."

What generosity! What understanding! Thus encouraged, I dared to express my preference. The Common pond was safely "bearing," covered with four inches of good ice and, on my way to and from the Academy, I had paused to watch the skaters with the regard of one who could not attain such happiness.

"I would be very glad of a pair of skates, Adam. They have them in Langland's window in the High Street."

"Ah! Skates! Well, I don't know. You can't skate in the summer, can you?"

Disappointed, I still had to admit the logic of his argument.

"A football might be better." He went on. "Only trouble is you've got to share it with the other boys. They boot the life out of it, burst it, lose it. The thing isn't really your own. How about a pocket knife?" Adam suggested next, acknowledging a greeting from across the street. "No, you might cut yourself. Dangerous. Think of something else."

The heavy bag was killing me, as I sweated after him, in lopsided fashion, one shoulder weighted to the ground.

"I . . . I can't think, Adam."

"I tell you what!" he exclaimed, reflectively. "It would please Mama if I gave you something useful. In fact—" His tone quickened with enthusiasm. "Now I think of it, I have the very thing!"

"Oh, thank you, Adam." I hoped that with this burden I should reach the station alive.

He looked at his watch. "Just two minutes off the half hour. Quick, youngster. And don't bump the bag."

He pressed ahead while I toiled up the station steps behind him. The train was already at the platform. Adam leaped into a first-class smoking compartment, took the bag, which I surrendered with a sob of relief, and burrowed in its depths. Then he leaned from the window and placed in my small damp palms a solid brass calendar, rough-hewn like a nugget, shiny as Mama's brooch, with knobs for turning the days of the week and handsomely engraved:—

ROCK ASSURANCE COMPANY
Semper Fidelis

"There," said Adam, as though handing me the crown jewels. "Isn't that handsome?"

"Oh, yes, thank you, Adam!" I answered in a startled voice.

The guard blew his whistle; he was off.

I came away from the station grateful to Adam, yet vaguely disconsolate, a trifle bewildered by this new possession, and the rapid strangeness of the day. When I got home I went upstairs and displayed my trophy to Grandpa, who viewed it in silence, with oddly elevated brows.

"It's not gold, is it, Grandpa?"

"No," he said. "If it's connected with Adam you may be sure it's brass."

A short pause, while I reread the inscription.

"Grandpa, has it anything to do with your policy?"

He turned dark red, his expression wounded, outraged, suffused with anger. In a loud fierce voice he answered:—

"Never mention that swindle to me again or I'll wring your neck."

There was a silence. Grandpa rose and began to pace up and down, much upset. Majestic with indignation he declared:—

"The worst crime in the calendar . . . the unforgivable iniquity . . . IS MEANNESS!"

With an expression at first bitter, then ironic, then soothed, he repeated this maxim several times. At last, as though regretting his outburst, he turned and studied my cowed form.

"Do you want to go skating?"

My heart sank deeper. "I have no skates, Grandpa."

"Tut! Tut! Don't be so easy beat. We'll see what we can do."

Choosing a moment when the coast was clear, he went down to the cellar, behind the scullery, and brought up a wooden box filled with old nails, bolts, doorknobs and rusty skates which—since nothing, I repeat, nothing, was ever thrown out at Lomond View—had accumulated during many years. Seated in his chair, pipe in mouth, while I sat on the floor in my stocking feet, he fiddled about with a key, trying to adjust the smallest pair of Acme skates to fit my boots. My disappointment was great when I saw he could not succeed. But, when everything seemed lost, he found at the bottom of the box a pair of wooden skates which had been Kate's when she was a child. What joy! Screwed into my boot-heels they fitted exactly. We had no straps, it is true, but Grandpa had plenty of strong string which would serve equally. He unscrewed the skates, I put on my boots, and we set out, with animation, for the pond.

What a pleasant and exciting scene: a sheet of ice perhaps half a mile long and a quarter broad, covered with darting, swooping and wobbling figures, moving gaily, tracing intricate patterns, colliding, falling, rising again, all under a clear blue sky to which ascended the high incessant ring of the ice and the shouts of the skaters.

Grandpa fastened on my skates and began to teach me, patiently, with many scientific explanations, how to keep my balance. He lumbered along beside me, guiding and supporting me until I was able to strike out for myself. Then he retired, joined Mr. Boag and Peter Dickie on the bank, lit his pipe and watched me.

Enchanted by this new form of motion, I floundered over the ice. In a quiet corner of the pond some good skaters had put down an orange, which made a brilliant speck of colour on the grey surface, and were doing figures round it. Miss Julia Blair was amongst them and, to my surprise, Alison Keith and her mother, both of whom skated very neatly indeed. Presently Alison came over and, crossing her arms, took both my hands. By imitation, picking up the rhythm of her strokes as she steered me round the pond, I began to make real progress. At my gratitude she smiled, shook her head slightly, and darted back to her mother and the orange. During our circuit she had not said a word.

Later Grandpa summoned me to the bank, with his enigmatic smile. "Enjoying yourself?"

"Oh, Grandpa, wonderful, simply wonderful."

Later that evening: an opinion drowsily revised . . . I don't think I want those scurrying waiters after all. What fun it was with these old skates and Grandpa's pieces of string! It was just a pity I did not see Gavin on the pond. Yes, Grandma, I will be a good boy tomorrow. I'm sorry I was ungrateful, I promise faithfully to count my blessings in the future. But now . . . now, I am asleep.

CHAPTER EIGHT

SPRING came quickly that year and the three chestnut trees in front of the house nodded their white plumes before a boy dazzled by freedom, intoxicated with strange and undreamed-of joys.

On the fifteenth of April Grandma left, according to her custom, to spend a few months with her Ayrshire relatives—as I have indicated, she divided the year pretty equally: autumn and winter in Levenford, spring and summer, "the growing months," at Kilmarnock.

We had progressed, she and I, in our grave private devotions. No one, I must here insist, could have been more restrained than Grandma in her handling of my delicate situation. A fervent member of the small but intense sect into which her husband had led her, her convictions were absolute, yet not once did she attempt to impose these upon me. Her attitude never transgressed the correct limits of patient hopefulness. Her strongest action came after dinner on Sundays, when she drew me to her room, and kept me at her knee reading aloud selections from the Scriptures. Approving my account of the war between Saul and David, she rocked gently in her chair by the window, on which the flies buzzed drowsily, viewing the regular Sunday promenade to the Drumbuck cemetery on the road outside and sucking, not the flat soft oddfellow recklessly preferred by Grandpa, but a hard round imperial which rattled lastingly against her teeth. (It seemed to me that the opposite characteristics of their favourite sweets exactly symbolized the difference between my two great-grandparents.) From time to time she interrupted my reading to give me little homilies on good living and the dangers of constipation, and to exhort me, above all, to stand firm against Satan.

Satan, the Evil One, Lucifer, or, as she also named him, the Beast, was for Grandma a Personal Enemy, perpetually gnashing his teeth at the elbows of the Just; and indeed, as her stern theology imperceptibly reinforced my earlier instruction, the Devil began to assume for me a terrifying reality.

On those winter evenings when Grandma was out upon some Gospel activity it was my duty to take up to our bed a stone hot-water jar, which she named her "jorrie," and if she had not returned by eight o'clock, to undress and retire in solitude. There was never much light upon the upper landing and frequently Grandpa was out also, though not of course at church. As I lay in the dark whispering bedroom, menaced on all sides by the shadowy walls and creaking wainscoting, I knew, with every shrinking nerve, that I was not alone. The Evil One was there, hiding in Grandma's "press," ready to pounce upon me the instant I relaxed.

Long moments of stiff and scarcely breathing anguish passed until at last I could bear it no longer. With that thin courage which streaked my natural timidity I jumped up and faced the awful cupboard. There, with shaking knees, a white small figure barely illuminated by the feeble glimmer which ascended from the street lamp outside, I raised my trembling voice in exorcism.

"Come out, Satan. I have the number of the Beast."

Then, blessing myself three times for good measure, I threw open the door. For a second my heart stood still. . . . But no, there was nothing there, nothing but the dim outlines of Grandma's dresses. With a sob of relief I would turn and fling myself beneath the sheets.

Grandma never knew of these nocturnal conflicts, yet I think she was satisfied with her tactful shaping of my tender and unconscious spirit. As she departed for Kilmarnock, in a new bonnet, she pressed a sixpence into my hand and, having exacted from me a promise to take my physic, after many admonitions and exhortations towards "perseverance" she murmured: "When I come back, my lamb, we'll see what's to be done for you."

My heart had come to brim, like a fountain, for my grandma. Yet, strangely, her absence gave me a queer feeling of relief which was intensified when Mama transferred me to a makeshift cot behind a curtain in the kitchen alcove. Oh, the sweet privacy of this little screened recess: almost a room of my own!

Grandpa seemed liberated too. His first act was to take the big bottle of medicine Grandma had left me and decant it, with an impenetrable smile, out of his window. Almost at once the ferns in the plot beneath yellowed and died, causing Murdoch to gloom and mutter, quite mistakenly, against Grandpa's intimate habits.

But never mind, never mind; the household at Lomond View was finding a momentary tranquillity in the miracle of the grey earth's rebirth. Soothed by the peace on the upper landing, Grandpa went placidly every day to the green to beat Saddler Boag at the marleys. Papa put a smart white cover on his uniform cap and actually took me on a Sunday afternoon to the Waterworks, to admire, over the red spiked railings, the big reservoir and the trim official dwelling which he hoped to inhabit when Mr. Cleghorn, the Superintendent, retired. Mama, less worried, ceased those interminable little calculations dealing, in pence and farthings, with her problem of making ends meet. In the morning, while he whittled his downy chin, Murdoch could be heard intoning sonorously: "I love a lassie, a bonnie Highland lassie." Only Kate seemed disturbed, angered even by the swiftly flowing sap, the swooping of the robins bearing straws to the eaves, the distant enchanting whinny of a stallion at Snoddie's Farm.

Before I reveal my own happiness I must probe, with careful tenderness, into this enigma which is Kate.

With the window open and the fragrance of the lilac bush in the back garden drifting in to us, we are seated at the dessert of our midday dinner in perfect amity. Mama, who hates to see anything left, picks up with the serving spoon the last three stewed prunes remaining forlornly in the dish. "Who will have these?" she inquires. "Very good for the blood in the springtime." She makes a tentative offer to the brooding Kate, then, receiving no response, drops them into Murdoch's plate. Immediately, Kate jumps to her feet, the bumps on her brow, like patches of headache, turning fiery red. She cries hysterically: "I am *nothing* in this house. And I am earning too . . . bringing in good money . . . teaching these smelly little beasts of infants all day long. I will never, never speak to any of you again." She rushes from the room, followed in consternation by Mama, who returns, a minute later, repulsed, shaking her head, and sighing: "Kate is a strange girl."

Murdoch wishes magnanimously to surrender the prunes; but Mama prepares her universal panacea, a cup of tea, which she bids me take up to Kate in her room. I am chosen because I, surely, cannot have offended her. I find Kate in tears upon her bed, her mood soft and self-commiserating.

"They all hate me, every one of them." She sits up unexpectedly on the bed and turns towards me a tear-ravaged face. "Tell me, dear, do you think I'm terribly plain?"

"No, Kate, no . . . far from it." I am startled into the lie.

"Your mother was much prettier than me. Simply lovely." She shakes her head dolefully. "And I have such a horrible name. Think of it . . . Kate. Who would take *Kate* on a Moonlight Cruise . . . or out to the Minstrels at the Point? If you ever do find me in the company of a strange young man, call me Irene. Promise now."

I promise, dutiful but amazed. Kate, in other ways, is so eminently sen-

sible, a conscientious teacher with a creditable record at the Normal Training College, a good hockey player, a beautiful knitter, a member of the
Women's Institute. She exhibits to perfection that wonderful Scots quality
—"dourness." In her struggle to keep "nits" from the heads of her poor pupils
she, who is violently clean, often picks up vermin on her own person and
must stand and shake her clothing in the bath whenever she comes in, pale
with disgust, yet grimly uncomplaining. Outsiders remark approvingly of
Kate: "Such a *worthy* girl." It is to Kate that I owe my sound teeth, for she
took me, without a word, to Mr. Strang the Levenford dentist, when they
started to decay the month before. She it is who gives me, from her small
library, solid books like *Ivanhoe* and *Hereward the Wake*. Yet I know there
exists in the same case, for I have perused them breathlessly, volumes
wherein the dark handsome hero kneels, in the last chapter, murmuring
brokenly before the sweet, womanly figure in white satin he has hitherto
ignored. . . .

"Oh, well, Robie," Kate concludes our present interview with a sigh, "I
suppose we may as well rot here as anywhere."

When I descend I tell Mama that she is much better. But she is not. She
confines her family conversation for a fortnight to scribbled messages on
torn-off scraps of paper. She quarrels tempestuously with her best friend,
Bessie Ewing, so that Bessie, faithful bespectacled Bessie, comes in late in
the evening for long perturbed confidences with Mama in the privacy of the
scullery. Bessie, who has supported Kate's temperament since they were
schoolgirls together, is the intelligent daughter of a refined Knoxhill family.
She works in the local telephone exchange all week and every Saturday night
dons the blue-and-scarlet uniform of the Salvation Army. Short and anaemic,
but with nice fluffy hair, she has an angelic disposition and a way of looking
at Murdoch when they meet in the kitchen.

Now I hear her say, earnestly, to Mama: "Really, Mrs. Leckie, I'm
worried. It's lack of an interest. Now if only we could get her to take up, say,
the mandolin . . . or even the banjo . . ."

Little talebearer that I am, I run to Grandpa with the news: "Grandpa!
Grandpa! I think Kate is going to learn the banjo."

He gazes at me, a faint ironic twist to his golden moustache. "I fear that
instrument will do her little good, my boy."

I gaze at him blankly; perhaps he means that Kate must learn the piano
in the parlour: McKillop Brothers Upright Iron-framed Grand. But no matter, I toss my head, and dart away, merely for the sake of running. I run
errands for everyone: for Mrs. Bosomley, who on my return rewards me with
her ripe smile and Bovril-spread toast, a sandwich which makes water run
from the very substance of my teeth. Forgetful of my precarious position, a
little outcast, barely acknowledged, poised on the edge of the unknown, I am
happy . . . happy that I love, and am loved by, Gavin.

We had begun, Gavin and I, to comb the uplands together: brave expeditions which made my previous voyagings with Grandpa seem babyish in-

deed. Gavin sought, ceaselessly, and passionately, the sole specimen lacking to his collection, this egg of the golden plover, rarest of all the Winton birds. Yet, as we traversed the lower woods, bent on this quest, he had the patience to instruct me: finding for me in unseen and impossible places all the commoner nests, parting the branches of a hawthorn bush and calmly murmuring: "Missel thrush with five," while with bright eyes I peered at the neat cup of straw and mud, wherein lay, warmly fragile, the speckled blue eggs. He initiated me in the delicate art of "blowing." He swore me to the oath of the woodsman: never to take more than one egg from a nest, his small face turning white with anger as he spoke of boys who "harried" the nest of all its eggs, causing the mother bird to "desert."

Then we climbed Drumbuck Hill. It was a new country we gained, with a breeze that came cool and sweet as spring water on my cheek. Distantly, beneath us, lay a free and sweeping panorama of the world laced with white roads and split by the estuary of the Clyde, a wide bar of shimmering silver, with tiny ships upon it. The town of Levenford was lost in a merciful haze, out of which reached the rounded hump back of the Castle Rock. The toy houses of Drumbuck village crouched far, far down, at our feet. Swathes of green rolled away to the west, and as my gaze followed this meadowland I started, almost in fear, to see a great high shape towering sharp and blue above the flying white clouds.

"Look, Gavin, look!" I cried shrilly, keeping close to him and pointing to the mountain.

He nodded solemnly. "It's the Ben!"

I could have gazed for ever, but again he drew me on, past a whitewashed farmhouse in the fold of the moor with its byre and steadings grouped in a square around it. There was a smell of cows and straw in the yard; a bush of broom, already flaming yellow, shaded the back porch. The curlews were wheeling overhead and the bees droned amongst the blazing gorse as we crossed the farm lands where the cows lay in the shade, all facing in the same direction, barely troubling to chew their cud, only their ears twitching the flies away as they stared at us sideways with their big liquid eyes.

At the end of the fields we began toiling upwards towards the higher peaks. The moorland Gavin took me to was almost in the sky, a singing wilderness, swampy in parts and split by limestone peaks. As we advanced, bent forward, our eyes seeking amongst the purple orchis and the spongy bog myrtle of the heath, we seemed to be dodging the woolly clouds which scudded across the blue just above our heads. Now and then Gavin would stop to point out silently some rarity: the sundew plant which stickily entangled and consumed insects, the pure white bee-orchid, scented beyond belief. Once an adder streaked across our path and before I could cry out, Gavin crashed his boot heel upon its skull. We ate our picnic lunch on a flat rock, Windy Crag, attained by the dizziest of climbs.

For a month Gavin sought the egg with all his skill and resolution—but fruitlessly. One afternoon as we came back, discouraged, from the farthest horizon we had yet attained, I lagged behind at a rushy swamp. Strangely, my interest had turned to these upland marshes and the teeming life which abounded in their waters. I bent down to cup some tadpoles in my hands. Then, as in a dream, my eyes fell upon a careless litter of coarse straw, dropped upon some adjacent moss. Three eggs lay on the straw, large eggs, golden green with purplish splashes.

The cry which broke from me arrested Gavin's small dark figure against the skyline. He was tired. But my wildly waving arms brought him plodding back. Speechless now, I pointed to the moss. I could not see his face, but I sensed by his sudden immobility that we had found the nest at last.

"That's it." He waded in over his boot-tops and brought back one of the eggs. We sat down on the edge of the marsh while, gently, with the utmost care, having first floated it to see if it were addled, he blew the egg, and placed it in my hand. "There. It's a beauty, isn't it?"

"A perfect beauty." I gloated. "I'm so glad we got it at last." When I had admired my fill I held it out. "Here you are, Gavin."

"No." He gazed straight ahead at the remaining eggs which I knew he would die rather than touch. "It's yours, not mine."

"Don't, Gavin! It's yours."

"No, it's yours." He persisted stoically: "You found it and finding's keeping."

"I wouldn't have found it except for you," I pleaded. "It's yours, absolutely yours."

"Yours." He insisted palely.

"Yours," I cried.

"Yours," he mumbled.

"Yours," I almost wept.

We bandied the word desperately until at last, in a frenzy of surrender, I blurted out the naked truth. "Gavin! Will you believe me? It's a lovely egg. But I don't want it. I've hardly any collection and you have. The things I'm really smitten on are frogs and tadpoles and dragonflies and that! If you don't take the egg I swear I'll . . . I'll . . . I'll throw it away."

Convinced at last by this awful threat, he turned and faced me, delight flooding his grey eyes. His voice quivered. "I'll take it then, Robie. Not for nothing, that wouldn't be fair. I'll trade you something in exchange for it . . . something I have that I know you like." He wrapped the precious egg in cotton wool in his collecting tin and smiled at me, that shy and somewhat sombre smile which came from beneath his half-lowered lashes and filled my heart with joy.

The same evening I carried away from his room a singular article which I had coveted ever since, under Gavin's direction, I had learned to manipulate it. It was an old brass compound microscope, once the possession of his sister Julia who as a girl had taken a course in natural sciences at Winton College. In type it was simple, but it had two eye pieces and two object glasses and the lens, though fixed, was actually a Smith and Beck—even in the little things Provost Blair must have the best. Accompanying the instrument were a few elementary slides and a mildewed book with yellowish pages, the first chapter headed: "What You May See in a Drop of Water"; the second: "Structure of a Fly's Wing."

I set the tube up on the table of Grandpa's room and, while he watched me covertly, began assiduously to examine the slides. Since my friendship with Gavin he had been slightly cold towards me. No one could "take the huff" more readily than Grandpa. I think in his heart he approved of my moorland roamings, but since he was not a party to them he affected an attitude of disdainful reproof. Now, however, his curiosity got the better of him.

"What newfangled nonsense have ye there, Robert?" The use of my formal given name indicated that he was not on the best of terms with me. I explained eagerly and soon he was at my elbow, one eye screwed into the mysterious tube, blundering with the adjustment, yet pretending to a consummate knowledge of the machine. I could see that it fascinated him and when I looked in after supper he was still glued to the tube, with a rapt expression on his face. "By all the powers!" he cried. "Do you see these beasties in the cheese?"

Thus began, for Grandpa and myself, an era of glorious adventure as we beat our wings into the unknown. Soon we exhausted the faded primer of Miss Julia Blair; then Grandpa, marching like a new Huxley to the public library, produced more solid works: Brooke's *Elementary Biology*, Steed's *Living Water Weeds*, and, noblest of all, Grant's *Pond Life with Thirty Coloured Plates*. During the daytime, while I was at school, he foraged amongst the neighbourhood's stagnant pools and at night, when I had finished my homework, we sat down to compare the creatures which strayed across our magic lens with the illustrations in our books. Consider our excitement when we identified a slow amoeba and were dazzled by the whirling of a rotifer. Remember, I was not yet nine, I had not fully mastered the multiplication table.

Oh, I am drunk with the wonder of new life. The nests are full of fledglings, craning their necks for food; a foal stands in the field beyond the chestnut trees; lambs bleat beside the ewes in the pastures of Snoddie's Farm. There is a word in my books I only vaguely understand: it is "reproduction"—certain of my little creatures multiply by simple division, others by a more complex process of joining together. Confusedly, I feel myself upon the threshold of a great discovery. Who will reveal to me this unknown secret? Perhaps, of all persons, Bertie Jamieson. Gavin has gone to Luss for a week, calmly removed by his omnipotent father to profit by the run of spring salmon up the Loch. I walk home every night with Jamieson and his allies but at his house, near Drumbuck Toll, they leave me, with the remark that I am "too young" to accompany them, and disappear into the washhouse, where they lock the door and shutter the window. Standing outside, disconsolate, I hear sounds and sniggering, in what must be a tenebrous interior.

When they emerge, sheepishly, Bertie tells me that, as a great favour, I may come in the following night.

I am overjoyed. I mention it to Grandpa as we sit together at our slides.

"What!" He jumps up, upsetting the precious microscope, banging the table with his fist.

"You will not go into that washhouse. Over my dead body. Never. Never."

The following evening as I emerge from the Academy he is waiting outside. He takes me by the hand and as Jamieson runs past catches the wretched boy a buffet which almost fells him to the ground. As he drags me off angrily I cannot but reflect how strange and incredible are the manifestations of spring.

CHAPTER NINE

AND still the spring continues.

Giving off Drumbuck Road to a blind ending was a short unobtrusive street of smaller cottages which bore the disappointing name of "Banks Lane" and which impaired slightly the starched gentility of its parent thoroughfare inhabited by the notables and officials of the Borough, ranging from the Provost, through the Stationmaster and the Head of the Fire Department, to Health Administrator Leckie himself. In Banks Lane dwelt several men, fitters and engineers, who cast a mild blemish on the surroundings by "working dirty" in the Boilerworks. They were not seen, fortunately, at five o'clock in the morning, when the Works hooter sounded them from their beds; but at the dinner hour, and again in the evening, their hobnail boots resounded inappropriately on the clean pavements, their soiled dungarees and grimy hands and faces seemed sadly out of place beside, for instance, the white uniform cap and shining brass buttons of Mr. Leckie.

They were a quiet lot, for their work was hard, and they succeeded, perhaps because their wages were vexatiously large, in enjoying themselves in their own inoffensive ways. Every Saturday afternoon their bright checked caps could be seen joining the stream which flowed in keen anticipation to Boghead Park, home of the local football team. Spruced and in their best clothes, they frequently took train to the city of Winton for a meat pie tea and an evening at the Palace of Varieties. On fine Sunday evenings they would stroll sedately in little bands along the country roads while one of their number improvised with great skill on a concertina or mouth harmonica —often as I lay in bed, during my early days at Lomond View, burdened with the darkness and my grandma's heavy breathing, a whiff of cigarette smoke, the waft of a gay and teasing tune, would lift me up and make me smile, unseen, reassured that all was still well with the world.

Amongst these Boilermakers, one named Jamie Nigg had begun to show me signs of his regard. He was a shortish man of about thirty, heavy about the shoulders, with big dangling hands and large, melancholy eyes. With uncanny prescience I divined that he was sad because of his legs, which were exceedingly bandy; they formed a perfect oval through which clear daylight was visible, and although, in his method of walking, he did all he could to conceal it, the deformity was enough to damp the stoutest heart. As I ran back to school at the dinner hour this bow-legged boilermaker often stopped me, viewing me with his inquiring spaniel's eyes, slowly rubbing his jaw with his calloused palm; though he shaved every day the strength of his growth kept his chin and cheeks in saturnine blue shadow.

"How are ye?"

"I'm fine, thank you, Jamie."

"All well at home?"

"Yes, thank you, Jamie."

"Mr. Leckie and the family?"

"Yes, Jamie."

"Murdoch'll be sitting his examination, soon?"

"That's right, Jamie."

"Your grandma's still away?"

"Oh, yes, Jamie."

"I saw your old grandpa on the green last Sunday."

"Did you, Jamie?"

"He looks well."

"Yes, Jamie."

"It's a bonny day."

"It is that, Jamie."

The conversation broke down at this point. A pause; then, reaching into his pocket, Jamie produced a penny and, scarcely smiling, delivered it to me with one of Levenford's oldest and funniest jokes: "Don't spend it all in the one shop." As I hopped, stepped and jumped away, clutching the coin, he called after me, standing bandy and motionless. "My best respects to all at home."

In a remote fashion, I attributed Jamie's good will to the fact that, like the Provost and Miss Julia Blair, and others in the town who had shown kindness to me, he had known my mother—this phrase, indeed, "I knew your mother," like a recurrent phrase in a piece of music, minor, yet strangely heartwarming, cropped up often during my childhood, and brought with it always a sense of reassurance, of confidence in the inherent goodness of people and of life.

But usually I was too busy darting towards the shop of Tibbie Minns, and her green glass bottles of pink-striped sweeties, to debate the causes of Jamie's interest. My experiences with Adam's half-sovereign had left me vaguely distrustful: if I did not spend my penny someone was sure to discover it, or it would fall out of my breeches as I took them off at night and roll out of the alcove, along the shiny linoleum, to Papa who would stoop and pick it up, with the righteous intention of "saving it" for me. Besides, my body, that of a young, poorly nourished animal, was crying out for sugar. Beasts of the field and forest will die amidst apparent plenty if they are deprived of certain simple and apparently unimportant substances. When I recollect the half-stilled gnawings, the after-dinner unrest of my childhood, I feel that I too might have perished but for the permeating peace afforded me by Miss Minns's sugar balls.

On the last Saturday in May, I encountered Jamie not by chance: he was actually awaiting me at the corner of Banks Lane, and "dressed," too, wearing his navy-blue suit, light brown boots, flat red-and-black-diced cap.

"Do ye want to come to the football match?"

My heart turned a quick somersault, at this sudden invasion of joy into an afternoon rendered empty and listless by the continued absence of Gavin, with his father, at Luss. The football match! The big grown-up game which I had never seen, and never hoped to see!

"Come on then," Jamie Nigg said, advancing the brown boots circuitously.

With my stomach pressed against the rope which surrounded the Boghead arena I stood beside Jamie and Jamie's gang of friends, and cheered myself hoarse as the coloured jerseys raced and mingled on the green turf. Levenford was playing its most hated rival, the neighbouring club of Ardfillan. Were there ever such tricksters, such brutes and murderers, as these men of Ardfillan, known derisively as the "Jelly Eaters" because of their contemptible custom of permitting small boys to enter their enclosure on the presentation, not of real money, but of empty jam jars which the club redeemed later, for cash, at the local rag-and-bone yard? Thank God that justice prevailed! Levenford was the victor!

After the match Jamie and I walked home in splendid comradeship; then, as we approached the deviation of our ways, our blood still surging in a rich afterglow, Jamie produced a package which had encumbered him all afternoon. His face was quite red and he had suddenly grown husky.

"Give this to your Kate," he said. "From me."

I stared at him in complete bewilderment. Kate! "Our" Kate! What had she to do with us, and our beautiful new friendship?

"That's right." He was redder than ever. "Just put it in her room."

He turned and left me standing with the package in my arms.

At Lomond View Kate was not visible—only Murdoch sat muttering and groaning at his books in the kitchen—so, obeying Jamie's instructions, I took the large wrapped oblong package to her bedroom and placed it on her chest of drawers. I had never been in Kate's room except at her express invitation, and now, with curiosity, and a sense of privilege conferred by my special mission, I dallied, studying the few bottles of lotion and the jar of face cream beside her mirror. There were a number of paper-covered booklets too. I picked them up. *Facial Beauty without Disfiguring Operations. Madame Bolsover's Method, or How to Improve the Bust in Twelve Lessons.* Another, with the mysterious, yet intriguing title: *Girls! Why Be a*

Wallflower?—I was about to probe deeper when the door opened and Kate came in.

Her chapped skin reddened with anger. Her bumps gathered instantaneously. And I only saved myself by exclaiming swiftly and adroitly:—

"Oh, Kate. I have something for you, a regular surprise."

She halted, her ears crimson, eyes still angry.

"What is it?" she asked suspiciously.

"A present, Kate!" And I indicated the package on the chest of drawers.

She gazed incredulously; then, pausing only to utter a half-hearted rebuke —"Remember, Robert, you must never, never, enter a lady's bedroom unannounced"—she approached the package, took it up, sat down with it on the bed, and, while I watched, removed the wrappings, revealing a beautiful beribboned box filled with three pounds of expensive chocolates. I was convinced Kate had never had such a lovely present in her life. I congratulated her, bending over the box with an air of complicity.

"Aren't they wonderful, Kate? They're from Jamie. He took me to the match this afternoon. You know, Jamie Nigg."

Kate's face was a study—strange mixture of pleasure, amazement, and disappointment. She said, rather haughtily: "Him, indeed! I'll have to return them."

"Oh, no, Kate. That would hurt Jamie's feelings. Besides . . ." I swallowed a bead of saliva.

Kate smiled, in spite of herself; and when she smiled, even this short dry smile, she was surprisingly agreeable. "All right, then. You may have one. But I couldn't touch them myself."

I did not delay in availing myself of this permission and at once bit into a succulent orange cream which immediately discharged its delicious flavour upon my tongue.

"Are they good?" Kate asked, swallowing, strangely, in her turn.

I made inarticulate noises.

"If only it had been anybody but Jamie Nigg!" Kate exclaimed.

"Why?" I argued loyally. "Jamie's the finest fellow you could meet. You ought to have seen him with all his friends at the match. And he knows the Levenford centre-forward."

"Oh, he's low—only a boilermaker. He works dirty. And besides, they say he takes a wee half."

Recognizing this as the idiom for a little whisky, I quoted Grandpa on the subject, staunchly: "He's none the worse of that, Kate."

"Well, then . . ." Kate reddened again, confusedly. "His legs."

"Never mind about his legs, Kate," I pressed earnestly.

"Legs are too important not to mind. Especially when you are 'walking out.'"

I paused, dismayed. "Do you like anyone else, Kate?"

"Well . . . yes . . ." Kate's gaze slipped dreamily over the pamphlet *Why*

Be a Wallflower? into the romantic distance, and I took advantage of her abstraction to select another chocolate.

"Of course I've had lots of proposals, at least several, anyhow a few, I wouldn't boast. But now I'm speaking more or less of my ideal. A man of some maturity, dark, well-bred, eloquent . . . like the Reverend Mr. Sproule, for example."

I stared at Kate with amazement: the Reverend was a middle-aged gentleman with a paunch, poetic locks, a booming voice and four children.

"Oh Kate, I'd sooner have Jamie any day. . . ." I broke off, blushing hotly, conscious that I, of all people, had no right to criticize her minister.

"Never mind," Kate said with queenly understanding. "Have another chocolate. Go on, don't mind me, I wouldn't defile my lips with them. As a matter of fact, love disgusts me. Yes, disgusts me. The woman always pays. Was that a hard or a soft centre?"

"Hard, Kate," I replied earnestly. "A kind of lovely nougat the like of which you never tasted in your life. Look, there's another exactly the same. Let me get it for you, please, please."

"No, no, I wouldn't dream of it." While Kate protested, she accepted in an absent-minded manner and as a kind of afterthought placed in her mouth the nougat I pressed upon her.

"Aren't they simply delicious, Kate?" I asked eagerly.

"No man can *buy* me, Robert. But I must say they are awfully nice."

"Have another, Kate."

"Well, I know it'll turn my stomach. Still, if you insist. Find me one of the orange kind you ate first."

Sitting on her bed, in the next half hour, we ate the entire top tray between us.

"What am I to tell Jamie, then?" I sighed at last.

Neatly tying up the box with its pink ribbon Kate suddenly began to laugh. It was the oddest experience in the world, hearing this strange, gloomy, and bad-tempered girl give way to natural laughter.

"What a pair of hypocrites we are, Robie. At least, I am. Eating the poor lad's sweeties that must have cost a fortune, and sitting in judgment on him. Just tell him the truth. Tell him we enjoyed his chocolates very much. Thank him kindly for them. And let that be the end of it."

I went down the stairs three at a time, determined that Jamie should have, at least, the first part of Kate's message.

CHAPTER TEN

JULY came, with the prospect of the summer holidays and hot winds which swayed the yellowing corn. I ran barefooted with Gavin after the watering cart in the warm, wetted dust of the Drumbuck village roads. I climbed with him to the highest point of Garshake Hill to gather the blue "bilberries" which grew there and which Mama received gratefully and made into jam much nicer than our usual rhubarb preserve. I bathed with him in the mill-dam and swam my first strokes, threshing the cool water with my arms, across a corner of the deep end, then ducked my head beneath the little waterfall while the stream cascaded into my mouth, my nose, and shoals of darting minnows, rising from the sand, tickled my legs. Transported, I heard my shrill, ecstatic laughter rise. Could water be so wonderful? It seemed to wash the last stains of sorrow from my soul. When we came out we leaped and danced, finally flung ourselves flat on the grass, staring at the bright sky with a kind of burning ecstasy. Joy! Oh, the pure, mild warm air, the light, the green of the trees, and in me those forces which awakened, the joy of breathing, the supreme joy of living!

I was too, too happy in my pagan life. The moorland wind had blown God out of my head; the postcards which Grandma sent me received scant attention; I no longer bade the Evil One emerge from dark corners of the house but fell asleep at once, barely muttering the hastiest of prayers. Ah, I had fallen from grace. The heavens were preparing fresh miseries for me.

First came the news that Gavin must again leave me. Every summer his father rented in Perthshire a lodge with a small moor offering fishing and rough shooting—another extravagance which was later to be cast, like an infamy, upon the Provost's Olympian head!—and of course Gavin would spend the school vacation there, amidst the purple of the heather and the blue of the distant hills.

There was more than a whisper originating from Miss Julia Blair that I might accompany him; but my miserable wardrobe, the cost of the railway fare, a score of chill realities, stilled that warm breath to silence. Gavin and I said good-bye at the railway station, our eyes suspiciously bright, pledging our eternal friendship in a special handclasp which we had adopted, firm as steel, with a special cabalistic interlocking of our thumbs.

Then, as I came home along the High Street, the real bolt came streaking from the sky—I found my progress barred. I glanced up and, with a start of undiluted terror, found myself before the tall dark figure of Canon Roche, who, leaning on his flapping umbrella, now transfixed me—as I might petrify a minute organism beneath my microscope—with his dark, unblinking, basilisk stare.

Though, thus far, I had tactfully avoided him, the Canon was one of the town's most striking figures. He was young, in fact the youngest canon in the diocese. He had thin features, a beaky nose, and a fine brow—his distinguished scholastic career at the Scots College in Rome gave ample evidence of a keen intelligence. On his accession to the pastorate of the Holy Angels Church he had found badly run to seed a parish always unruly because of its admixture of races: Polish, Lithuanian, Slovak and Irish emigrants had been at different times attracted to the town by reason of the work and good wages offered by the Boilerworks. Quickly, the Canon realized that one weapon above all was likely to control this rough and scarcely literate flock.

He did not hesitate to use it. With a severity foreign to his nature he thundered at them from the pulpit, flayed them with his satire on the church steps, accosted and denounced them in the public streets. In twelve months he had tamed the congregation, earned the friendship of the Marshall Brothers, owners of the Boilerworks, and won the grudging respect of the more liberal town authorities—a difficult matter in a small Scottish community where "the Catholics" were detested and despised. Strangely, too, he had gained not alone the awe but the admiration of his parish. A terror he was, yes, by God, a holy terror was the Canon, God bless and confound him!

Small wonder, though his present tone was mild, that I trembled to be singled out by such a man.

"You are Robert Shannon, are you not?"

"Yes, Father."

Ah, that "Father"—I had betrayed myself. He smiled faintly.

"And a Catholic, surely?"

"Yes, Father."

He began to furl the flapping umbrella. "I've had a letter about you from a colleague in Dublin . . . Father Shanley . . . He writes me, asking me to look you up." He shot a glance at me. "You come to Mass on Sundays, don't you?"

I hung my head. I had suffered for my allegiance to the Scarlet Woman; her mark was upon my brow; but, alone and timid, since coming to Levenford, I had not visited her Temple.

"Ah!" What a lot of trouble the umbrella was giving him. "You've made your First Communion, of course."

"No, Father."

"Your first confession, then."

The illness of my parents had got in the way of this tremendous obligation; I wished the earth would open to swallow me and my shame: "No, Father."

"Dear me. That's a sad omission for a man by the name of Shannon. We must put it right, Robert. Right, right away, if you'll forgive the pun which is, I'm sure you will agree, the lowest form of all wit and more worthy of a worthy Episcopal clergyman than of my unworthy self!"

Why did he smile? Why did he not thunder at me? My eyes, already, were smarting with tears—Gavin gone, and *this!* I knew, too, that we were the object of many curious glances from the passers-by, numerous because it was the dinner hour. Soon the shocking tale of this interview would spread far and wide, damning me once again in the eyes of my schoolfellows, upsetting everything at Lomond View.

"We have a First Communion class beginning next month at the convent. Tuesdays and Thursdays after four. Quite convenient, really. Mother Elizabeth Josephina takes it . . . I think you'll like her, if you come." He smiled at me with his compelling black eyes. "Will you come, Robert?"

"Yes, Father." I mumbled out of stiff lips.

"That's a good chap." His umbrella, though frightfully untidy, now seemed to his satisfaction. At least, he studied it amiably and began to make whirligigs with it while giving me a short talk upon my obligations. He concluded with a final injunction: "One point, Robert, not very easy, living with non-Catholic relatives as you do, but most important. It's this. Do not eat meat on Fridays. A strict rule of the Church. Remember now . . . no meat on Fridays." A parting gleam from those stern, yet kindly, eyes, and he was gone.

I tottered off in the opposite direction, still dazed by the mischance of the encounter. I was crushed, caught and convicted of my crimes. The brightness of the day was dulled. It did not for a moment occur to me that I might disregard the Canon's commands. No, no, his eye was now upon me; he loomed, in all his spiritual and temporal powers, too near and awful to be disobeyed. All Grandma's careful preparation of the vineyard of my spirit was obliterated, as by a hurricane. I felt that the mischance of my origin had finally overtaken me. It only remained for me to suffer and submit.

Then, as I approached the back door of Lomond View, a sudden recollection made the sweat break coldly on my brow. Today—this very day—was Friday. And in the air I could smell my favourite dish, beef stew. I groaned. Dear God and Canon Roche! What was I to do?

I entered the kitchen with a faltering step, took my place at the table where Kate and Murdoch were already seated. Yes, as I feared, Mama placed before me a plateful of stewed steak which seemed, indeed, a larger portion and, from its steam, more savoury than usual. I viewed it distractedly.

"Mama," I said at last, in a weak voice. "I don't think I want this stew today."

I was immediately the centre of inquiring stares. Mama considered me doubtfully. "Are you sick?"

"Well, I don't know. Perhaps a slight headache."

"Take some gravy and potatoes then."

Gravy—ah, that, too, was forbidden. I shook my head with a pale smile. "I think perhaps it would be better if I didn't eat anything."

Mama made a little clicking sound with her tongue as she did when not sure about something. Before I returned to school, where classes were going on for a few final days, she gave me a dose of Gregory's Mixture. Passing through the scullery, I had stuffed a hunk of bread furtively into my breeches pocket, and I devoured it hungrily on my way to the Academy. But all afternoon my stomach made painful empty rumbles.

That evening at the family meal Mama, with a nice air of favouring me and at the same time doing a good deed, placed before me a thin slice of the potted head on Mr. Leckie's plate—at this time he always had some "kitchen," as it was called, for his high tea. She glanced at the others self-accusingly: "Robert has not been very well today."

My soul shrank within me. I stared glassily at the tender pieces of meat, visible through the clear jelly which encased the delicacy. Why didn't I come out with the truth? Oh, no, no, a thousand no's. I could not do it. The strange and tragic history of my affiliation with the Church of Rome was too painful a subject in this family. It was veiled, buried. To resurrect it would surely bring about my ears upheaval and catastrophe, comparable only to the havoc wrought by Samson in Grandma's picture upstairs. The thought of Papa's face alone . . .

Yet it was he who, for the present, saved me.

"That boy's been at the green grosets," he suddenly declared crossly. "Get him away early to his bed." He lifted the potted head back from my plate to his own.

I had not been near his unripe gooseberries. But I welcomed the injustice, suffered myself to be sent supperless to my little curtained alcove.

On Sunday, before the family was awake, I crept through the dim lobby and scudded out to the seven o'clock Mass, sitting in the back seat of all, hiding my face as the offertory box went round. It was a fine church—built by Pugin, I afterwards discovered—in a simple Gothic style; and very "devotional," with stained-glass windows in excellent taste, the white high altar set well back, a series of high arches giving dignity to the nave. But this morning, reeling off my little incantations breathlessly, I drew no solace from it. My knees knocked together as Canon Roche mounted to the pulpit. Perhaps he would preach against me, this faithless renegade who had not the courage of his belief. What a relief . . . he did not! Yet the announcement he made was equally destructive to my peace of mind. The following week was Ember Week: Wednesday, Friday, and Saturday were days of fasting and abstinence; God would have no mercy on those weak and faithless souls who dared indulge themselves with flesh upon these days. I went home, my eyes blinking, stricken to the depths, repeating to myself, in a daze: "Wednesday, Friday *and* Saturday." To offend God was bad enough. Yet it was my terror of the terrible Canon which held me to the impossible task.

On Wednesday I was fortunate. Mama, distracted by the prospect of her "washing day," received without suspicion my whispered excuse that I must spend the dinner hour clearing up my books at the Academy, and, bending over the scullery boiler, absently bade me prepare and take along with me some slices of bread and jam. But on Friday when I tried the same device her mood was different: she sharply commanded me to return for my good hot dinner. It was mince she put before me and she left the kitchen with an air which boded ill for me if I had not cleared the plate on her return.

Oh, God, how I was suffering! No bearded Jew, confronted by a crackling loin of pork before the Inquisition, endured such tortures as were mine. I glanced desperately across at Murdoch, who, while chewing, watched me curiously. He was studying at home now, and, since Kate was delayed by the "break-up" at the Elementary School, he was the only other occupant of the table.

"Murdoch!" I gasped. "This meat gives me terrible indigestion." Swiftly, I took my plate and transferred all my mince to his.

He goggled at me. But he was a big eater, he made no protest except to remark suspiciously: "Quite a vegetarian these days." Did he guess? Impossible to tell. Trembling, with my head down, I ate up my potatoes, careful not to touch those stained with gravy.

The next day I had reached the end of my resources. Unmanned and starving, there was no invention which I could produce: I simply stayed away from Lomond View at the dinner hour, stayed away altogether, wandering round the harbour in lacklustre style, sniffing the good smells of tar and oil like a dog. As I dragged myself home in the evening I was faint with hunger. Pinched by ravening pangs, I forgot my anxiety as to how I should explain my absence to Mama. I wanted food, food.

At her front gate Mrs. Bosomley was standing with some letters in her hand. She asked me to run to the pillar box and post them. Impossible to run. Yet, weak though I was, I could not refuse a favour to this warmhearted friend. I posted her letters in the round red pillar at the corner of Banks Lane. When I returned she beckoned me to the open window. My eyes lit up. Yes, she was handing me my usual reward, a great warm double sandwich: Bovril on toast.

I stumbled round the back to the rockery, bearing the thick golden sandwich, the fragrance of which, alone, almost caused me to swoon. I sat down and bared my young fangs from which water already streamed. Then, oh, merciless Heaven, I remembered: Bovril! It was meat, pure meat; there was a poster at the railway bridge showing in bright colours the enormous ox which went into every bottle!

For a full minute, paralyzed with dismay, I stared stonily at the ox, the sublimation of all flesh meat, the occasion of sin, clasped between my small hands. Then, with a cry, I fell ravenously upon it. My teeth bit, tore and devoured. Oh, the goodness of it. I forgot the Avenging Angel and Canon Roche. I sucked in the salty, meaty juice with sinful lips. I licked my fingers in carnal joy. When it was all finished down to the last crumb, I heaved a great appeased, triumphant sigh.

Then, horrified, I realized what I had done. A sin. A mortal sin. A moment of awful silence. Then wave after wave of remorse broke over me. The Canon's dark eyes glittered before me. I could stand it no longer. I broke into tears and ran upstairs to Grandpa.

CHAPTER ELEVEN

GRANDPA was seated, with his face screwed scientifically to the microscope, when I burst upon him. And in this academic position he heard me, in silence, to the end. It did me good that he did not look at me. I dried my eyes and watched him as he rose and in his burst green slippers began to pace the floor. I felt safe in his hands. How I wished that he, and not the Canon, might ordain my religious future.

"It's very simple, boy, to straighten out your Fridays. A word from me to Mama and it is done. But," he quenched my joy with a shake of his head, "that's just the beginning of it. This thing has been brewing for some time. You're in a difficult position here, there's no denying . . . all on your own . . . It's a queer kind of legacy your poor mother left ye." He paused, stroking his beard, throwing a peculiar glance at me. "Maybe the easiest solution would be for ye just to row in with the rest of them. I mean . . . go to church at Knoxhill with the others."

Inexplicably, my tears spouted hotly again. "Oh, no, I couldn't, Grandpa. A boy's got to be what he's born to be, even if it's difficult. . . ."

He persisted, showing me all the kingdoms of the earth. "Grandma would just love you if ye went to Knoxhill. On my oath I assure ye there is nothing she would not do for you."

"No, Grandpa. I couldn't."

Strange pause. Then he smiled at me, not aloofly, but with his rare, slow, heart-warming smile. He came forward and shook me by the hand. "Well done, Robie, lad!"

Deliberately, he selected two peppermint oddfellows from the small stock in his tin, and pressed them upon me. I could not understand these supreme signs of his approval. He only called me "Robie, lad" on the rarest occasions and as the highest token of his regard.

"I might define my own position." He took an oddfellow himself, enthroned himself loftily in his chair. "I stand for religious freedom. Let a man believe what he likes, provided he doesn't interfere with what I believe. That's all over your head, boy. I'll just say, if ye'd gone to Knoxhill, I'd have disowned ye on the spot."

Philosophical silence while he lit a pipe. "I have nothing against the Catholics, except maybe their Popes. No, boy, I cannot say I approve of your Popes . . . some of these Borgias, with their poisoned rings and sichlike, were not quite the clean potato. However, say no more, you're not to blame. You believe in the same Almighty as your grandma, though she won't let you worship Him with candles and incense. Well, I will, boy. I will. I defend your right to do it. And I'll tell ye this, ye've as much chance of getting through the Pearly Gates, or whatever gates we do go through, with your Mass and vestments as she has with her psalms and Bible-banging."

I had never seen Grandpa so worked-up. He, who despised prosiness in others—who curtly dismissed every speaker he heard as "too prolix"—could, oddly enough, be magnificently long-winded himself. He moralized for half an hour in the most heated and dramatic style: burning and immortal words flowed from his tongue, like "freedom," "liberal," "tolerance," "free-thinker," "imperishable heritage" and "the dignity of man." He expressed such wonderful and high-flown sentiments I knew I must be mistaken in fancying that he several times contradicted himself—as when, for example, after extolling the virtues of universal love, he banged his fist fiercely on the table and declared that "we," meaning he and I, would "certainly *do* the old besom," meaning Grandma, "in the eye!"

Nevertheless the general effect of his oration was to bring me comfort. On subsequent Fridays, Mama, without a word, gave me discreet helpings of vegetables and, when Papa was not there, a hard-boiled egg. On the first of August—saying nothing, on Grandpa's recommendation, to anyone—I began to attend the little convent of the Holy Angels and to be prepared for my First Communion.

We were a small class under the care of Mother Elizabeth Josephina, only six or seven sniffing little girls and another little boy, Angelo Antonelli, son of the Italian ice-cream vendor in the town. He was a beautiful child, with a skin like a peach, great dark luminous imploring eyes, and soft curly brown hair. He was exactly like one of Murillo's children, though of course I did not know that then; I only knew that he delighted me and, as he was small, more than a year younger than myself, I immediately took him under my protection.

The class was held sometimes in the still twilight of the church, before the side altar, under a stained-glass window of "Our Lord Carrying His Cross"; occasionally in a prim parlour in the convent; but most frequently, since the weather was warm, on the lawn of the convent garden. Here we children would sit on the grassy bank in the shade of a blossoming syringa bush while the good nun, with the book on her knee, and placid hands in the wide sleeves of her habit, occupied a camp stool in front of us. The high walled garden was exquisitely quiet, it seemed a million miles from the busy town. Now and then one could see another of the Sisters, her face screened by her white wimple, pacing up and down one of the paths, saying her rosary. The sweep of her flowing habit was slow and gracious. Some plump pigeons strutted trustingly, quite near us. There was a low still drone of insects hovering about the white syringa flowers, which, with their delicate scent of orange blossom, seemed strangely appropriate to this enclosed place and to these pious nuns who—each with a plain gold ring on the fourth finger of her right hand—counted themselves espoused to God. Through the waving trees the stone cross of the church—its arms enclosed by a circle, the Saint Andrew's Cross—could be seen against the sky. Then our Sister would raise her forefinger to her lips for silence and, while we gazed at her with round obedient eyes, she began to speak to us of the infant Saviour. It is a moment of innocence to remember; never before, and never since, have I known such peace, such a sense of tranquil happiness.

Mother Elizabeth Josephina was quite elderly, her features lined, inclined to severity. She was a good teacher. She made those days in Palestine live for us. Listening breathlessly, we saw the poor stable and the Child who lay there. We saw the Holy Family fleeing on a donkey—think, a poor donkey!— before the wickedness of Herod. Perhaps because of my somewhat dubious past, she seemed to devote extra attention to me, and this made me proud: especially when she praised the quickness of my answers. When Canon Roche strolled in to regard us, with surprising benignity, Reverend Mother and he would put their heads together, their eyes directed towards me. Afterwards her kindness increased. She gave me scapulars, and little holy pictures, which I carried underneath my shirt. I began with all my heart to love Jesus, who I thought must have resembled little Angelo, sitting trustingly beside me. I longed for the day when, as Mother Elizabeth Josephina explained, He would come to me in the shape of the shining Host which would be placed upon my tongue.

Then she began to warn us, to speak of the horrors of a bad Communion. She cited many painful instances. There was the little boy who had "broken his fast" thoughtlessly, by nibbling some crumbs from his pocket before advancing to the altar rails; another careless little fiend who had swallowed drops of water from his toothbrush. These were bad enough; but a third story simply made us shudder. A little girl who, from wicked curiosity, had transferred the host from her tongue to her pocket handkerchief . . . Later she had found this handkerchief soaked with blood!

No one followed the progress of my instruction with more profound attention than Grandpa. He had begun by asking me if Mother Elizabeth Josephina were a good-looking woman; to which I was obliged to answer "No." When I told him of the miracle of the bloodied handkerchief, he did not move an eyelid.

"Remarkable!" he exclaimed, reflectively. "I think I will take Communion with you. A most interesting experience."

"Oh, no no, Grandpa," I cried, aghast. "It would be a sin for you, a mortal sin. And first you would have to make your confession . . . tell Canon Roche all the bad things you have done in your whole life."

"That, Robert," he said mildly, "would be a lengthy interview."

Towards the end of July, the Reverend Mother had a mild indisposition and her place on the camp stool beside the syringa bush was taken by a young, fresh-cheeked nun, Sister Cecilia. She was a sweet and gentle person who taught us even more interestingly than Reverend Mother; her blue eyes grew remote and wistful when she spoke of Our Lord; and she did not frighten us with gruesome stories. She charmed me and I ran home to tell Grandpa the news.

"We have a new teacher, Grandpa. She's a young nun. And terribly pretty."

Grandpa did not immediately answer. He twisted his moustache with that gesture I knew so well. Then: "It seems to me that I have been neglecting my duty, Robert. Tomorrow I will take you to the class. I should like to meet your Sister Cecilia."

"But, Grandpa," I said doubtfully, "I do not think gentlemen are allowed inside the convent."

He gave me his calm, confident smile, still twirling his moustaches: "We shall see."

True to his word, on the following afternoon Grandpa brushed himself thoroughly, shone his boots, set his hat sedately on his head, and taking his best bone-handled stick accompanied me to the convent, where, after some hesitation on the part of the young maidservant, who, however, was won over by my grandpa's stately demeanour, we were shown to a reception parlour. Here Grandpa seated himself with his hat at his feet, very upright, like a pillar of the church. He nodded to me once to indicate that the room had won his approval, that he was not insensitive to its atmosphere. Then he directed a chaste yet inquiring regard towards the blue-and-white statue of the Virgin, in a glass case upon the mantelpiece.

When Sister Cecilia entered he rose and gave her his most distinguished bow.

"I apologize for this intrusion, ma'am. You owe it to the fact that I am so deeply interested in the welfare," he laid his hand benevolently upon the top of my head, "of my young grandson here. My name is Alexander Gow."

"Yes, Mr. Gow," Sister Cecilia murmured a trifle uncertainly: although the order was not enclosed, but a teaching one, she was scarcely accustomed to visitors of Grandpa's calibre. "Won't you sit down?"

"Thank you, ma'am." Grandpa bowed again, waiting till Sister Cecilia had seated herself before reoccupying his chair. "I must first acknowledge, frankly and openly, that I am not of your persuasion. You are probably aware of the exceptional circumstances surrounding my little grandson here." The hand on my head again. "You may not know that it was *I* who sent him to you."

"It does you credit, Mr. Gow."

Grandpa made a deprecating gesture, rather sad. "I wish I felt worthy of your congratulations. But alas, my motives, at least in the beginning, were those of reason, the cold reason of a citizen of the world. Yet, ma'am—or perhaps I may call you Sister?" He paused, while Sister Cecilia inclined her head with slight embarrassment. "Yet, Sister, ever since my little boy began coming here—particularly since you, Sister, took over the class—I have found myself touched . . . increasingly attracted to the beautiful and simple truths that have fallen from your lips."

Sister Cecilia blushed with gratification.

"Of course," Grandpa resumed, more sadly, yet in his most winning manner, "my life has not been spotless. I have knocked about the world. My adventures . . ." Open-mouthed, I glanced at him, apprehensive that he might be on the verge of again bringing up the Zulus. But no, he did not. "My adventures, Sister Cecilia, have brought me into the face of severe temptation, all the harder to resist when a poor devil—ah, forgive me!—when a poor wretch has no one to care for him. There is no more painful deprivation in the life of any man than the lack of the love of a good woman." He sighed. "Can you wonder that now . . . one might have the impulse to come . . . in search of peace?"

I could see that Sister Cecilia was deeply moved. Her fresh cheeks were still flushed and her swimming eyes expressed a deep concern for Grandpa's soul. Pressing her hands together, she murmured: "It's very edifying. I'm sure, if you have a sincere desire for repentance, Canon Roche would be only too happy to help you."

Grandpa blew his nose; then shook his head with a regretful smile. "The Canon is a fine man, exceptionally fine . . . but perhaps a trifle unsympathetic. No, I felt that if I might come, with Robert, to the class, to sit humbly there and listen . . ."

A flutter of doubt troubled Sister Cecilia's face, like a cloud upon a limpid pool. But she seemed anxious, beyond anything, not to discourage Grandpa or to hurt his feelings.

"I'm afraid it might distract the children, Mr. Gow. However, there must be ways and means. I will certainly speak to Reverend Mother."

Grandpa gave her his most charming smile—yes, I repeat, despite his nose, it was an irresistibly charming smile. He rose and shook her hand, or rather sustained her fingers in his, as though he wished to stoop and reverently salute them. Though he restrained himself, Sister Cecilia's colour remained high long after he had gone, and during instruction, while she told us the story of the Prodigal Son, her earnest eyes were moist.

I found Grandpa waiting on me, walking up and down outside the convent, in the best of moods, swinging his stick and humming. On the way home he gave me a dissertation on the refining influences of good women, interspaced with hummings and sudden exclamations: "Delightful! Delightful!" I heard him with a certain anxiety: for in these last weeks I had come up against a fearful personal difficulty, to which I shall presently refer, on this very subject of women. Still, I was glad Sister Cecilia, and the prim, polished quiet of the convent parlour, had made such an excellent impression upon Grandpa.

He tactfully allowed a week to elapse before his next visit, choosing a sunny day on which, as he remarked, "the garden would be particularly lovely." Already, he saw himself beside me on the lawn. He spruced himself more carefully than ever and spent a long time before his mirror, trimming his beard, as he sometimes did before calling on Mrs. Bosomley. Always partial to clean linen, he wore his best white shirt, which he had starched and ironed himself. He even tucked into his buttonhole a little sprig of forget-me-not, the bright vivacious blue of which exactly matched his eyes. Then, he took my hand, threw out his chest. We set out briskly for the convent.

Alas! It was not Sister Cecilia who came to the little parlour, but Mother Elizabeth Josephina, more severe than ever, and only just recovering from jaundice. Grandpa's face fell, his opening smile was chilled, nipped in the very bud, as quickly, brusquely, Reverend Mother sent me from the room, to take my place in the class upon the lawn.

A moment later, seated on the grassy bank, I heard the sound of the front door—shut with a firm hand. Then, through the trees, I saw Grandpa descend the steps and go down the drive. Though I could scarcely distinguish at that distance, he seemed out of countenance, terribly taken-down. When, after a sharp, short instruction, Reverend Mother released us, he was not outside. Later that evening, I noticed he had removed his blue forget-me-not.

Poor Grandpa! I worried that his repentance should be cut so short, but Corpus Christi, the last Thursday of the month, was not far off and I was now in a state of exaltation alternating between misery and bliss. Before I might taste the rapture of Communion I must undergo the ordeal of my first confession. Several times Canon Roche had taken our little class upon this subject, and though his manner was restrained, I began to perceive, dimly, the horrid pitfalls which nature had prepared for unsuspecting children. A vague recognition of the difference in the sexes was borne upon me. The word "purity" was spoken gently, yet with resolution, by our pastor. Then, out of the mists, came the sudden realization of my sin. Oh, God, how I had sinned: the worst, the unforgivable sin. I could never, never tell it to the Canon.

Yet I must. The damnation attaching to a "bad" confession was worse, even, than that resulting from a "bad" Communion. With a sinking heart I saw that I must reveal my infamy. . . . Oh, the torture of knowing there was no escape!

At last the day, the fatal hour approached. From beneath the stained-glass window of "Our Lord Carrying His Cross" I staggered, in a sweat of anguished shame, into the dark confessional where Canon Roche awaited me. My bare knees sank beneath me, hitting the bare board with a hollow thud. I began to weep.

"Father, Father, forgive me. I'm so wicked, so terribly ashamed."

"What is it, my dear child?" The gentle encouragement in the hidden austere voice increased my grief. "Did you say a bad word?"

"No, Father, worse, far worse."

"What, child?"

It came with a rush. "Oh, Father, I slept with my grandmother."

Did I hear a merry laugh behind that mysterious grille? Or was it merely the echo of my sobs?

CHAPTER TWELVE

CORPUS CHRISTI has come and the morning sky is grey, grey as the body of the dead Christ when they took Him from the Cross. I have spent a fitful night on my straw mattress in the kitchen closet: only snatches of rest wherein I dream that the living Christ Child is sleeping beside me, His beautiful head on my pillow, His soft cheek against mine. I awake with a start, hoping my dream is not a sin. Lately I have been tortured by scruples: was I guilty of "immodesty" while undressing? Did I gaze "impurely" at a crucifix, at the statue of Our Lady, at anything? With sealed eyes and lips I stumble over the earth's surface, dreading the accident of sin. I am so desperately anxious to make, not just a "good," but a perfect Communion, I have even fallen to the habit of seeking heavenly signs and portents. I say to myself, gazing towards the sky: "If I see a cloud which resembles Saint Joseph's face I shall make a glorious Communion." I squint upwards, compressing my eyeballs, striving to find a paternal profile, at least a beard, amongst the celestial vapours. Or I take three pebbles from the roadway, one for each person of the Blessed Trinity, and tell myself that if I hit the corner lamp-post once in three slugs, I am sure to communicate superbly. But, no! I desist quickly in fear of sacrilege.

This morning, however, I am strangely at peace, and my thoughts are filled with love, with secret wonder that I, amongst the people who surround me in this house, clamouring for breakfast, for hot water, for shoes to be brushed, for all the humdrum things of life—that I, alone, am chosen for the sweet and joyful honour of receiving in my breast the Son of God.

Last night I washed my mouth out carefully; it is no trouble for me to forgo my breakfast. Is it possible that Mama is in Grandpa's confidence? She does not press me to eat. Barelegged, I go upstairs and find Grandpa preparing to escort me to church: he is excited and would not dream of missing what he calls "the ceremony." Though he takes the huff quickly, Grandpa does not long harbour a grudge, and he has completely got over his dismissal by Mother Elizabeth Josephina. It has been decided at the convent that I am too "big" for a white suit: a merciful judgment—the white shoes and stockings which I must wear have been hard enough to come by and it has fallen to my wonderful great-grandparent to provide them for me, how I do not know, for he has no money, and when I ask him he merely shrugs his shoulders, hinting that he has made a great sacrifice on my behalf. Later, a pawn ticket was discovered . . . for the blue vase in the parlour.

But meanwhile, I put on the new shoes and stockings with pride. I go out with Grandpa and soon we are at the church. The High Altar is adorned with white lilies: beautiful and imposing to me as I sit in the front seat of all, beside Angelo, who wears a white sailor suit, and opposite the six little girls—one of whom, I notice with disgust, is giggling from nervousness beneath her white veil fastened with a chaplet of artificial white flowers. In the seats immediately behind us are the relatives of the First Communicants. Grandpa is there—next to Mr. and Mrs. Antonelli, near Angelo's uncle and sister—interested and, I hope, not too disdainful, although he has done all the wrong things, failing to genuflect and to sign himself with holy water. Still, I am glad of him and I know he wishes to be helpful; I hear him stoop to pick up Mrs. Antonelli's glove . . . or her prayer book.

The sanctuary bell rings and the Mass begins. I follow it faithfully, reading my Preparation for Communion, but waiting, waiting only for that moment which will make this Mass different from all others, before, or after. How short the time is getting! I feel an inward tremor. Then the *Domine non sum dignus*. At last, at last! I strike my breast three times; then, with shaking knees, I rise and advance with Angelo and the others to the altar rails. I am conscious of the gaze of the congregation concentrated upon us, my poor head is whirling as I see Canon Roche advance, in his beautiful vestments, bearing the chalice, I try in vain to remember my Act of Adoration, I hope I will not make a fool of myself, I close my eyes and lift my head, opening my trembling lips as Reverend Mother has taught us, whispering in my heart a final prayer, simply the word: "Jesus."

The Host surprises me, so large and dry upon my tongue, when I had expected a moist supernatural offering. In my dry mouth it is difficult to dispose of, to swallow; I am back in my place, flushed, my throbbing temples buried in my hands, before I accomplish this. Nothing has happened to me, no sensible flow of grace, no apparent transfiguration of my soul. A wave of disappointment crashes over me. Have I made a "bad" —No, no, I check my mind from stealing down that dreadful avenue and return passionately to my prayer book, where an act of thanksgiving soothes me. I lift my head, am reassured by Angelo's tender sideways smile, by Grandpa's cough behind me. A sense of proud achievement begins to pervade me. I join with the congregation in the Prayers after Mass.

Outside the church, the sun was now shining and, after a smiling moment with the convent Sisters, I was seized upon, congratulated, shaken hands with, warmly embraced by Grandpa and the Antonellis. My remarkable relative was already bosom friends with the Italian family, which seemed delighted, nay, enchanted with him. He introduced me to Mr. and Mrs. Antonelli, their grown-up daughter Clara, and to Angelo's uncle, Vitaliano, who was about fifty, brown-faced, and with the quiet remoteness of the very deaf. Everyone smiled at me; and Mrs. Antonelli, a stoutish, dark-eyed lady with a swarthy fringe, tiny gold rings in her ears and a green velvet dress, beamed at me maternally, repeating: "Such a nice friend for our little Angelo." Then Mr. Antonelli, who was also dark but shorter than his wife and turning bald, suddenly slapped his fist into his palm and directed towards Grandpa his large soulful eyes, which were exactly like Angelo's except that they had pouches beneath them.

"Meester Gow," he exclaimed fervently yet humbly, "am goin' to ask you a favour. Da two boys are already good frien's . . . If you're nota too proud . . . come to breakfast."

Grandpa accepted on the spot. Mr. and Mrs. Antonelli were very pleased. We set off: Angelo and I walking in front, while Grandpa and the others followed behind.

The Antonellis lived above their shop, which was painted primrose and vermilion with a proud and glittering gold-lettered signboard: *Levenford Select Ice Cream Saloon, Antonio Antonelli, Sole Proprietor*. This tropical brilliance was continued upstairs. The carpets were vivid, the hangings a gorgeous shade of yellow-green. Coloured holy pictures were everywhere, for the Antonellis were very devout, but on either side of the tasseled mantelpiece two secular paintings, views of Capri and Naples, dazzled the eye with their shimmering blues. And here, good gracious, was Vesuvius, blazing in eruption. A little statue, dressed brightly in pink and white, like a doll, smiled down on me from a gilt bracket on the wall. I had never entered a house so foreign or so rich in mysterious odours. Strange cooking smells provoked my nostrils, fruity smells, acrid, tart and pungent smells, the smells of onion and perspiration, of boiling fat and damp sawdust, the sweet vanilla scent of ice cream powder rising from the cellar below.

While Mrs. Antonelli and Clara were hurrying, with many excited exclamations, to serve the breakfast, Angelo, who had taken possession of my hand, drew me shyly to the end of the first-floor corridor. Here, at the half-open door of a room which proved later to be his uncle's, he paused, with an air of promise. My heart had already bounded at the vision of a barrel organ, a real hurdy-gurdy inlaid with the name ORFEO ORGANETTO in mother-of-pearl, standing on its peg against the wall. Yet I was unprepared for the surprise which followed.

"Nicolo, Nicolo," Angelo called softly.

A monkey dressed in a red coat jumped from the bed, pattered along the floor and leaped into Angelo's arms. He was a small neat monkey with pathetic eyes and a little, wrinkled, worried face. He had, exactly, that expression which, many years after, I saw on the faces of newly born babies: a crushed, surprised, troubled, yet peevish air. Meanwhile Angelo was stroking him affectionately and offering me the same delightful privilege.

"Pet him, Robie. He won't bit you. He knows you are my dear friend. Don't you, Nicolo Nicolo? And he has no fleas, not a single one. He belongs to my Uncle Vita. Vita loves him the best in all the world. He says he is our good luck. When we first came to Levenford and were very poor my uncle used to go round the streets with his organ and Nicolo. Got a lot of pennies too. But now that we are rich, at least quite rich, though he wishes to go playing the organ Mother will not let him. She says it is not nice, that we are above such common things now. So we keep Nicolo as a pet, a great pet. He was three when my uncle brought him here. Now he is only ten, which is still young, very young for a monkey."

Here, Mrs. Antonelli called us. Enchanted, I followed Angelo, who still carried the monkey, into the front room where the others were assembled.

"Oh, not Nicolo," Mrs. Antonelli protested as we went in. "Not today, Angelo, when we have such nice company."

"Yes, Mother," Angelo insisted; "it's my First Communion."

"Oh, very well." Mrs. Antonelli gave Uncle Vita a cross look, then flashed her teeth at Grandpa. "He's just Angelo's pet!"

When Angelo had said grace, we all sat down at the table covered with an embroidered cloth and loaded with many things which did not appear at breakfast-time in Lomond View. There were large platters of meat and rice, of tomato-coloured macaroni, a chicken pie, a galantine of tongue, olives, sardines and anchovies, a dish of fruits, and, guarding a big iced cake inscribed "Bless our Angelo," several tall bottles of wine.

Grandpa, seated between Clara and Mrs. Antonelli, was tucking in with every sign of enjoyment. Beaming, at the head of the table, sat Mr. Antonelli. He looked pleased, honoured by our presence.

"A leeta wine, Mr. Gow, justa leeta. Very special. Naples imported. Frascati."

Glasses were filled, even the glass of dark, silent, smiling Uncle Vitaliano, who seemed to occupy a slightly subordinate position in the family. Rising to his feet, Grandpa proposed a toast.

"To our little ones. A happy and a holy occasion."

We all drank, even we children, for Angelo and I had each a thimbleful. The wine was sweet and warming to my inside.

"You like the Frascati, Mr. Gow?" Mr. Antonelli bent forward anxiously.

"Most refreshing," Grandpa answered cordially. He added, "Light."

"Yes, yes, verra light. Nice and light. Another glass, Mr. Gow."

"I thank you, Mr. Antonelli."

The monkey, looking rather bored on Angelo's knee, reached out casually and helped himself to a banana. I watched, spellbound, while he peeled and began to eat it—like a little man. Angelo nodded to me proudly and whispered: "He will do more tricks for us, after."

"Allow me to fill your glass again, Mrs. Antonelli," Grandpa pressed. "Yours too, my dear Miss Clara." Though they refused, laughingly covering their glasses with their hands, Grandpa was having a tremendous success with the two ladies. He replenished his own glass and after an aside which made Clara laugh again, gravely resumed the account he was giving our hostess of his recent social activities at the Provost's and other large houses in the Cemetery Road. It was plain that Mrs. Antonelli was enraptured to find herself, even remotely, in touch with such gentility.

The laughter increased; Grandpa was now teasing Clara about her young man. "Not a patch on the older generation, these youngsters," he declared grandly.

As Grandpa and Mr. Antonelli began exchanging toasts—"To Italy!" "To Scotland!"—Angelo and I received permission to leave the table. We slipped into Uncle Vitaliano's room with Nicolo and began, softly, pushing in the stop marked *Piano*, to play the hurdy-gurdy. There were four tunes: "The Bluebells of Scotland," "Onward Christian Soldiers," "God Save the King," and "Oh, Mary, We Crown Thee with Blossoms Today."

Nicolo enjoyed the music too. "The Bluebells of Scotland" was his favourite piece, and when the familiar trills and tinkles fell upon his ear he began to dance and caper for our benefit. Once he found himself the centre of attention, a stimulus which had been lacking in the other room, he increased his efforts, ran along the corridor and skipped back with a hat—it was Grandpa's. Then, using the hat, he minced up and down, like a great swell, doffing his hat and bowing, from time to time. Our laughter excited him. He began to chatter, to hold the hat up with his tail, to let it drop over his head, extinguishing himself. With a shriek of assumed rage he freed himself, kicked the hat round the room, turned a somersault over it, then curled up and pretended to go to sleep in it.

Angelo and I were rocking with laughter when the door opened and Uncle Vita came in, his grave, silent face displeased. He lifted Nicolo, soothed him and put him in his basket in the corner of the room. Then as he picked up and, with his cuff, brushed Grandpa's hat, he said something in Italian. Angelo turned to me: "He says that even for a deaf man there is too much noise in the room, and here, on such a blessed day as this . . . He wants us to sit down and sing a hymn." Angelo added of his own accord: "Uncle Vita is very holy."

"What else did he say?"

"Well . . . He said your grandpa has already drunk three bottles of wine . . . himself. And that he is squeezing our Clara's hand under the table."

Chastened, I sat down on the floor beside Angelo, while Uncle Vita, with the touch of a true virtuoso, turned the handle of the organ. We sang:—

> "Oh, Mary, we crown thee with blossoms today,
> Queen of the angels and queen of the May. . . ."

Uncle Vita smiled when we finished. Angelo translated: "He says we must never, never forget how wonderful it is to be in a state of grace. If we drop stone dead, if we are killed, cut into little pieces this very second, it does not matter. We go straight to Heaven."

Then I heard them calling me from below; it was time for me to go. Grandpa, in the hall, was saying good-bye, shaking hands repeatedly with Mr. and Mrs. Antonelli, placing his arm, in a paternal fashion, round Clara's waist; remarking: "Really, my dear, you must accord a gracious privilege to a man old enough to be your father."

"Good-bye. Good-bye." Everyone smiling, exhilarated, except Clara's young man, Thaddeus Gerrity, who had just come in and who turned very red when Grandpa kissed Clara.

Grandpa and I walked down the street. My head is reeling with the joyful events of this eventful day. Grandpa, too, seems not unmoved: his eye is bright, his cheeks are flushed; and from time to time he seems to have a little trouble, not much, with his equilibrium.

A state of grace! Uncle Vita's words returned to me, like a soaring bird, a bird which bears a message. Is it the Frascati still gurgling in my stomach which lifts me, suddenly, to a moment of blurred white ecstasy? I know. I know I have made a good Communion, yes, perhaps even a perfect Communion. I feel a long rolling platitude gathering like a ball behind Grandpa's tongue. But for once, unable to prevent myself, I forestall him. With a rush of emotion I clasp his hand.

"Oh Grandpa, I love our Blessed Saviour very much . . . but don't forget, I love you too."

CHAPTER THIRTEEN

We are marooned, in August, amidst fields of scorched stubble and dusty hedgerows, the few vagrant airs which stir the drooping trees producing only a sigh of lassitude, the protest of an earth exhausted by too much fruitfulness. Most of the good burghers of Levenford are at the seaside with their families. The empty town seems unfamiliar and as my footsteps echo across the Market Square a vista of deserted cobblestones, of roofs rising one upon another against the Castle battlements, creates the illusion of a city besieged.

Gavin is still away, his earnest postcards causing me to pine more and more for his return. Really, no drama to record in this period of stagnation; yet, beneath the surface of our household, events still move sluggishly, like fish which, although spent, are still capable of sudden and tumultuous movement.

Every evening, when I went out for a breath of air before my holiday homework—a long essay on "Mary, Queen of Scots"—I found Jamie Nigg seated on our low stone garden wall, his back directed, in studied carelessness, towards the house. He had his mouth organ with him, and was playing softly and with complete unconcern a catchy tune which, since he could not tell me either its name or origin, I simply called "Jamie's tune." What an infectious melody it was! He did not stop playing when I sat down in silence beside him, grateful for the cool beads of dew forming around us on the yellow grass, for the low line of mist creeping like a relieving army across the parched fields.

After seven o'clock Kate came out of the front door for her evening visit to her friend, Bessie Ewing, usually wearing her light grey raincoat, bareheaded, collar turned up at the back, hands in her pockets. For more than a week she had taken no notice of us, beyond a small, cool, barely perceptible nod to me. Nor had Jamie, motionless, except for his sliding mouth organ, acknowledged her passing. Only the music, growing a little stronger as she disappeared, followed her inexorably down the street. Dimly, though it lacked the lush effects of doublet, balcony, and guitar, I sensed this to be a serenade: a Scottish serenade—slow, persistent, dour.

One evening, unexpectedly, almost reluctantly, as if against her better nature, Kate stopped. She gazed at me severely: "You ought to be in at your essay."

Before I could reply Jamie took the mouth organ from his lips, shaking it free of its accumulated moisture with jerks of his wrist. "Ah, the boy's doing no harm."

Kate was forced to look at him. She did so angrily: angry about many things; angry at his persistence, at his sitting there calmly while she stood; angry most of all for being angry. But her eyes were the first to fall. Silence.

"It's a fine night," Jamie said.

"It'll probably rain." Kate spoke with bitterness.

"Maybe, maybe. We need a few good showers."

A pause. "Are you detaining me here to talk about the weather?" She made no movement to go, however. Though her plain face was cloudy, I noticed, for the first time, as she stood there in the dusk with one foot courageously advanced and her hands in her pockets visibly clenched, as in preparation for battle, what a trim sturdy figure she had, a well-turned leg, a good ankle. Perhaps Jamie noticed too. Absently, he ran off a few bars of his tune, shook the harmonica again.

"I was just thinking it was a fine night for a walk."

"Indeed! And where *to*, might I inquire?"

"Oh anywhere, just anywhere at all."

"Thank you, thank you very much indeed." Kate tossed her head, stiffly. "Quite a compliment. But as it so happens I'm going down to see my friend, Miss Ewing." She took a step preparatory to departure.

"That's my way too," Jamie remarked, getting up from the wall and dusting himself. "I'll just dauner down with you as far as her gate."

Kate, completely taken aback, could offer no protest. Her colour remained high, her manner indignant. Yet I felt, oddly enough, that she was not wholly displeased as they departed, together, walking far apart, on the pavement. The gathering darkness was merciful to Jamie's legs.

I am standing alone, enjoying my solitude and a last damp, delicious breath; then, as though pursued, I run into the house, begin, in the kitchen, to take my books from my patched satchel.

Murdoch is already bent studiously, turning few pages, but producing showers of dandruff. I often wonder if Murdoch really studies: he has never made any pretence of scholarship and once or twice I have caught sight of a seed catalogue concealed between his covers, evidence of his secret passion for all things horticultural. Through the day he keeps rising restlessly from his books, belching loudly (although he digests like an ostrich it is an article of faith that he suffers, heroically, from "the bile"), going to the mirror to squeeze blackheads from his chin, or into the garden to potter about, like a soul in limbo. Sometimes he unconsciously permits me to glimpse his thoughts.

"Do you know that in Holland they grow tulips by the square mile? Think of it. Mile after mile of tulips!"

Just now, in the corner chair behind him, silent and erect, exactly like a man driving a horse, sits his father. With the approach of the Post Office Examination next month the reins with which Papa guides the unhappy youth have become tighter; indeed, there are signs of the whip. It is necessary, not only for Murdoch's future, but for the Inspector's prestige, that Murdoch should succeed. With all the intensity of a disliked, frustrated man he wishes to announce to the Provost, to Mr. McKellar, to his chief

Dr. Laird, Medical Officer of the borough, of whom he is obsequiously jealous, to announce, in fact, all over the town: "My son, my second son . . . in the Civil Service . . ."

I put my lesson books on the table opposite Murdoch, very quietly, not to disturb him. My books, inscribed in Grandpa's hairlike copperplate, are covered with brown paper, sewn on by Mama to save them, "to keep them good"—everything must be preserved, never, never wasted, in this household. For three months I have been in a higher class. My new teacher, Mr. Singer, bald, slow, and methodical, is both gentle and encouraging towards me. Free of the tyranny of Mr. Dalgleish, I no longer blot my exercises or stand like an idiot when questioned. I display, instead, a surprising aptitude. In fact at this moment a card, a certain card which I have retained for my own secret satisfaction, falls out of my history book and flutters to the floor, causing me to blush, guiltily, under Papa's eye. He sees the blush, and the card, and is at once suspicious of both. He makes a silent gesture for me to bring him the incriminating card.

There is a long pause while Papa studies the card, my quarterly report card wherein is written, in Mr. Singer's hand:—

R. SHANNON

Arithmetic	1st.
Geography	1st.
History	1st.
English	1st.
French	1st.
Drawing	2nd.
Place in Class	1st.

Signed: GEO. SINGER, M.A.

I can see that Papa is dumbfounded. In fact, at first he glances at me sharply, convinced that it is a trick, a cheap deception. But no, the official heading, the flowing signature . . . I read his thoughts: It must be true. He is far from pleased. He hands me back the card grudgingly, with an offended air, and I return, still guilty, to my books.

Silence in the kitchen except for the ticking of the clock, the turning of a page, a restive stirring from Papa's chair . . . and, of course, I had forgotten, the click of Mama's needles, for she has come in from the scullery and is knitting a scarf for Adam. It is always for Adam, her knitting.

At nine o'clock Kate returns, does not enter the kitchen, but goes straight from the front door to her room. Good gracious! I must be mistaken. Yet I think that she is humming, humming a little run from Jamie's tune.

Half an hour later Mama looks at me significantly. I put away my books and, moving with great care, lest I knock against something and annoy Papa, I go to my little curtained closet and begin to undress. I am terribly hungry, it seems ages since my tea, and I long, with sudden ravening, for a hunk of bread and rhubarb jam. That white crust, oh, lovely white crust! Mama would give it me, no doubt, but it is preposterous, such a demand at such an hour. I kneel down, say my prayers, then I am in bed. Through the thin curtain I hear the quiet pulse of this house which harbours me: a word exchanged between Mama and Papa, the rustle of a page, the shudder of the bathroom tap, a step above my head.

Sometimes I lie awake, staring at the dim ceiling, and am only half asleep when Murdoch goes upstairs and there begins one of those long, low-voiced conferences held by Papa and Mama in the kitchen before retiring, muttered words of which reach me in the closet. The Ardfillan Hygienic Society . . . invited Papa to address them on "Refuse Disposal" . . . What did they charge for that beef today? What a price! . . . No trip to the Coast, this year . . . the money will do better in the Building Society, and when Mama pleads gently: Well, perhaps next year, if Adam "comes forward" . . . or if Papa is promoted to the Waterworks . . . meanwhile it is necessary to save . . . save . . . save.

But I no longer marvel, I am habituated to Papa's thrift, this consuming passion which seems daily to gain greater ascendancy over him, sets spinning in his brain schemes for further economizing, gives him an ascetic look of perpetual renunciation, forces Mama to endless household and culinary expedients. Mama would like to shop in the "good" stores like Donaldson's, or Bruce's, whose big plate-glass windows are a perpetual invitation to her. Given "the stuff," she is an excellent cook—her drop pancakes (on the rare occasions when there are eggs to spare) are wonderful. She would enjoy composing nice dishes for us. But instead, with a glance at her black purse, she falls back on barley-bree and sends me to Durgan's in the Vennel for a penny napbone ("And ask him to leave some meat on it, dear"), then on to Logan's, also in that poor quarter, for a half-pennyworth "between" carrot and turnip—in plain English, a farthing's worth of each. Poor Mama! . . . Last Monday when you broke the new incandescent mantle you were fitting on the hall "gasolier" (always a delicate operation) you actually gave way to tears.

Tonight I am tired, ready to sleep. As I drift into unconsciousness, I think that tomorrow I shall probably go with Grandpa to visit the Antonellis.

During the weeks that Gavin was away, I had played a good deal with little Angelo Antonelli. It was nice to have something to do in such a jaded season; and Angelo was always so touchingly glad to see me. He was like a little girl, vivacious and tender, with his lovely swimming eyes and fetching ways. He held my hand as we ran about his yard, and always cried when it was time for me to go home.

Naturally, he was a very spoiled child, there were twelve years between Clara and him. He perpetually demanded from his fat, gentle, and adoring father—and perpetually received—toys, sweets, fruits, everything. He had the complete run of the Saloon, and would rifle a tin of chocolate biscuits or break open a can of preserved pears with less compunction than I would take a glass of water at Lomond View. His childish treble troubled the air all day long: "Mama, I want a slisa melon"; "Dada, I want a limonade." Once he told me, with a little smirk, that he had made his mother get up in the middle of the night to cook him ham and eggs. Yet he never finished what was on his plate—and was always being sick.

Sometimes, when I thought of the absent Gavin's austere, cold fire, of his determined silences, his contempt for the soft and the paltry, I had an inward qualm. But despite his pampering, Angelo had a sweet side; then there was the monkey, a tremendous attraction, for we played with him continuously. Also Angelo's mother encouraged my visits.

Now that her husband, whom she ruled, had made money, Mrs. Antonelli had turned ambitious for her family, which in its poor beginnings had been scorned in Levenford. The luscious Clara was making a good match with Thaddeus Gerrity, whose father operated a successful furniture-removal company. I am sure she smiled on me—a nice little Academy boy, yet a Catholic—and fêted Grandpa with wine and cake, when he regularly visited her in the afternoon, because we represented the genteel Drumbuck Road district, and town officialdom—always important to the alien mind.

I must confess that, now and again, when I heard Grandpa "spreading himself," over the Frascati, to the eagerly attentive Clara and Mrs. Antonelli, I experienced a mild anxiety. Mrs. Antonelli, caught unawares, had a hard look; and her darkness was such I suspected, despite my innocence, that she had resort, regularly, to the razor. Yet nothing seemed to worry Grandpa; he proceeded, smooth and steady, never in difficulty, like a stately barque before a tranquil breeze.

Reassured, I would run out with Angelo to hear the band play on the Common, to take a rowboat on the pond, or to walk to Benediction at the Holy Angels with Uncle Vita: that strange, humble, simple Vita, who was barely tolerated by the family, who spent half his day in tending his beloved monkey and the other half in prayer.

The month drew to its close. One evening when, at Mama's request, I was turning down the gas in the lobby to the required "peep," Kate came in, rather late.

"Is that you, Robie?" She seemed embarrassed by even the glimmer in the hall, but her voice was warm with friendliness.

"Yes, Kate."

As I got down from the chair on which I had been standing to reach the overhead gasolier, she slipped her hand under my arm.

"Dear boy."

I flushed with pleasure: for a long time now Kate had been especially nice to me.

"Listen, Robie." Kate stopped, laughed, then suddenly went on again. "It's perfectly ridiculous . . . Jamie Nigg wants to take me to the Ardfillan Fair." She laughed again, at the preposterous notion. "Of course I can't go with him alone, it would be most unladylike. He admits that himself. So . . . he . . . that is we . . . would be glad to take you with us if you'd like to come."

Like to come! Had I not heard of, dreamed of, the Elysian delights of the Ardfillan Fair—where every kind of show, entertainment, and amusement was congregated once a year for the diversion of the countryside?

"Oh, Kate!" I whispered.

"Then it's settled." She pressed my arm again and as she began to climb the stairs she turned kindly, a sort of afterthought. "Your friend Gavin is home. I just saw him coming from the station."

Gavin home! At last. Two days before his time. So that I would see him tomorrow for certain. The thought surged within me, joined with the thought of the Ardfillan Fair. I breathed quickly. Alive with anticipation, I half-opened the front door and gazed out into the darkness. There were no stars, the sky was blotted out, but the soft cool breeze was filled with promise. Oh, life could be wonderful, simply wonderful.

CHAPTER FOURTEEN

The next morning I was out early. I had promised to return to Angelo a bundle of magazines which he had loaned me and I wished to be free, as soon as possible. But as I ran down the Cemetery Road, I met Gavin advancing in the direction of Lomond View.

"Gavin!"

He did not speak, but gave my hand the terrible clasp, still trying to master his eager smile, which he must despise as a sign of weakness. He had not grown much but was very brown and wirier than ever. The sight of him, the feel of his grey eyes searching mine, warmed me through and through. I wanted to tell him, impetuously, how much I had missed him. But this was forbidden. It was necessary to be calm and strong, sparing of all but the most essential speech.

"I was coming up to get you." Explaining his appearance at this early hour, he gazed into the distance, towards our Winton Hills. "I thought we might go up Windy Crag. There's an eagle there. The keeper told Father. We'll get on to the crags before the sun's properly up and watch for him. I have our lunch."

I saw he had his knapsack on his back. An eagle; and Gavin; all day on the hills . . . My heart jumped. "Simply grand! But first of all I must take these magazines to Angelo."

"Angelo?" he repeated, uncomprehendingly.

"Angelo Antonelli," I explained hastily. "You know, that little Italian boy. I've seen quite a bit of him while you were away. Of course he's very young . . ."

I broke off, confounded by the incredulity, the hurt look in his eyes.

"The only Italians I know of in Levenford are those ice-cream peddlers. One of them actually used to tote a barrel organ and a monkey round the town, cadging for coppers."

My ears were burning now, at this condemnation of Uncle Vita, of Nicolo and my friends. Gavin added: "You don't mean to say you've got mixed up with one of their brats?"

"Angelo has been very decent to me," I said in a queer voice.

"Angelo!" More deeply wounded, he smiled scornfully at the name. "Come on. Let's get on the crags. We can talk about all we've been doing when we're up there."

I hung my head, eyes obstinately on the pavement.

"I promised to take these back. The *Sphere*, *Graphic*, and *Illustrated London News.*" With dry lips, I defended the magazines, hoping thus to vindicate the Antonellis. "They've some wonderful photographs of the development of the death's-head moth from a chrysalis, this week. Every Saturday Mrs. Antonelli sends them to relatives in Italy. They've got to catch the mail. It's kind of Angelo to let me see them first."

Gavin had turned white. His voice was strained and jealous.

"Of course, if you prefer your tally-wally friends to me . . . that's entirely your affair. It just happens that I'm going up the Longcrags now. If you want to, you can come. If you don't I'll leave you to your Angelo."

He waited for a moment, not looking at me, with quivering lip and proud cold brow. My breast was torn asunder, I wanted to cry out how mistaken he was, to beg him to understand. But a sense of his injustice made me as palely stubborn as he. I remained silent. The next instant he was striding towards the Longcrags.

Sick with dismay, still stunned by the suddenness of the quarrel, I continued towards the town. I resolved simply to leave the magazines and come away. But when I reached the Levenford Select Saloon I found Angelo devastated by a grief perhaps greater than my own.

"Nicolo is sick. Very sick."

Between his sobs, he told me how it had occurred. Clara, wicked Clara, was to blame. Uncle Vita, who went in the evenings to pray at the Holy Angels, often for hours at a time, had the habit of putting Nicolo in the courtyard during his absence to enjoy the cool air during these stifling nights. But always he left his window open, so that if the weather turned bad, Nicolo, for whom the drainpipe was an easy ladder, could immediately regain his room. Two nights ago a heavy thunderstorm had broken and Clara, thinking only to protect the curtains, had hastily shut every window in the house. Uncle Vita was at church, the Saloon closed; poor Nicolo was caught for an hour in the drenching downpour; when Vita returned at half-past ten he found the monkey soaked to the skin, huddled in a corner of the yard.

I followed Angelo upstairs. The house was stricken, deranged. In the kitchen Mrs. Antonelli, with a distraught expression, was wringing out cloths in hot water. Clara lay flat on her face, on the front-room sofa. In Uncle Vita's bedroom Mr. Antonelli stood with a pained expression in his big eyes while Vita, in his shirt sleeves, worked over Nicolo like a man aroused.

The monkey was in bed—not his own basket, but Uncle Vita's big white bed, exactly in the centre, propped up on pillows. He wore his best woolly vest and a soft Neapolitan cap with a woollen tassel. His little worried face, isolated on the vast expanse of bed, looked more worried than ever. From time to time his teeth chattered and he shivered violently, gazing at us anxiously, in turn. Uncle Vita, with some kind of pungent oil, was rubbing his chest. While he worked on the invalid, Vita talked all the time, to himself, to the monkey, but mostly, in a voice of recrimination, to Mr. Antonelli. I glanced at Angelo, who like myself was subdued by the grandeur of the spectacle and had ceased to cry. He translated, in a whisper: "Uncle Vita says it is a judgment upon us for forgetting the good God . . . a visitation upon Father for thinking too much of business, Mother of society, and Clara of men. He says he and Nicolo have laid the foundations of our fortune, working for pennies when we were without bread. He says if Nicolo dies . . . That was when he was crying. We will all never, never have any luck again."

Mrs. Antonelli hurried in with a bowl of steaming cloths, holding them subserviently by the bedside. Clara, drifting like a wraith to the doorway, watched with red eyes while Uncle Vita applied the cloths.

They seemed to do Nicolo little good. And suddenly Vita, the saintly, the humble, threw up his hands and came out with a torrent of words. Angelo hissed in my ear. "He says Nicolo must have a doctor, the best doctor in town. That Clara, the wicked and sinful Clara, must fetch him at once."

Clara began to protest.

"She says no doctor will come to a monkey. She will try to get a veterinarian."

I saw at once from the wildness in Vita's face that a veterinarian would not do. "Yes." Angelo gave me a nod. "It is to be nothing but a doctor. We must pay anything, all the gold we have. The best doctor in town."

Clara put on her hat, weeping, but submissive, and departed with a big handful of money from Mr. Antonelli. We all sat round in chairs, watching the monkey, waiting for the doctor; all but Vita, who, beads in hand, and lips moving, was kneeling by the bed.

In half an hour Clara returned, alone. Vita jumped up and, after an interrogation which again reduced Clara to tears, he gave a terrible cry, seized his hat and rushed out.

"Clara went to four doctors and none would come. Uncle Vita has gone himself."

For nearly an hour we waited in the sickroom, then started, every one of us, as the outer door opened. It was Uncle Vita—a sigh of relief went up as we heard someone accompanying him.

The doctor entered. He was Dr. Galbraith, an elderly dried-up man with a small goatee beard, a physician recognized as skilful in the town, but rather unpopular because of his abrupt manner. What subtle persuasions the deaf, unlettered Vita had brought to bear upon this choleric practitioner remained a mystery; and the wonder of it was, he had not come for money.

For a moment he looked as if he would order us all out of the room. But he abandoned the idea, and turned his attention to the monkey. He took Nicolo's temperature and pulse; felt him all over; looked down his throat; then, for a long time, using a short wooden stethoscope, listened to his chest. The monkey's behaviour was perfect, he kept his wide frightened eyes trustingly upon the doctor, even permitted his mouth to be opened without a spoon.

Tugging at his goatee, Dr. Galbraith stared at his patient with a queer interest and approval, completely forgetful of the roomful of people who, impressed by his thoroughness, hung upon his every movement—Angelo had whispered to me: "Uncle Vita thinks he is a wonderful doctor." Then, recollecting himself, the doctor wrote out two prescriptions, a dry twist to his lips as he inscribed them: *Mr. Nick Antonelli*. He packed up his little black bag. He then said: "The medicine every four hours. Keep him warm in bed, linseed poultices night and morning, nourishing liquid diet only. He's a nice specimen of the North African rhesus, macaque. Unfortunately, as a species, they are weak in the chest. This one has double pneumonia. Good night."

He went out. Though Uncle Vita followed him all the way down the street he would not accept a single penny of a fee. I then perceived his interest to be purely scientific: that strange, beautiful, and wholly disinterested emotion which had already stirred me as I sat at my microscope and which in later years was to afford me some of the rarest joys of my life. At this instant, moved by a kinship of race and ideas, I could not repress a thrill of pride in this taciturn Scots doctor. How perfect had been his behaviour amongst these excitable Southerners!

A sense of optimism succeeded his visit; there were instructions to be carried out. I was sent running to the chemist for the medicine; Mrs. Antonelli and Clara began to mix the poultices; Vita himself set a chicken to simmer, for broth. The monkey consented to swallow some milk. He seemed sleepy after his medicine. We tiptoed from the room.

Already versed, to my sorrow, in the dangers of lung disorders, I felt sure the implications of double pneumonia were not fully understood. And, indeed, next morning Nicolo was less well. Restless and burning with fever, he uttered plaintive cries, tossing about the big bed, at which Uncle Vita knelt. All day he barely touched his chicken broth and that evening his breathing was short and rough.

All that week he grew steadily worse and a distracted hush fell upon the household, broken only by sudden hysterics from the women and by wild determined outbursts from Uncle Vita. Cast off by Gavin, and still on holiday, I threw in my lot with the Antonellis. I became a sort of page boy to the stricken monkey. Every afternoon, at three o'clock, Grandpa called, very dignified and serious, on a visit of condolence. He waited in the front room, hoping, I think, for some sympathetic conversation with Clara and, if necessary, Mrs. Antonelli, perhaps a glass of Frascati wine to restore, to cheer the spirits. But the first faint breath of the mistral was in the air. It was Mr. Antonelli who, with a long face, accepted Grandpa's sonorous commiseration. And there was no Frascati wine.

Worse, still worse. Poor Nicolo could now scarcely breathe, all the flesh had fallen from his little bones. The doctor, again approached, flatly stated that the monkey was doomed. Mr. Antonelli spoke palely of closing the Saloon, of straw spread in the street outside.

On Saturday Uncle Vita looked Mr. Antonelli fiercely in the eye. Angelo translated: "He says only God can save Nicolo. Therefore we must pray, pray terribly for a miracle. Father must go to Canon Roche to have prayers and masses said for the monkey. The convent Sisters must make a novena, and come here, to the house, to pray for Nicolo. Oh, dear, Uncle Vita is saying most awful things to my father."

Mr. Antonelli clearly did not like the commission. But Vita now dominated the household; and the monkey had, in some queer way, become a superstition, a formidable symbol whose life or death represented the collapse or survival of the Antonelli fortunes. Mr. Antonelli took his hat and slowly went out.

The following morning, Sunday, Canon Roche announced from the Holy Angels pulpit that masses would be said for the intention of Mr. Vita Antonelli. A trifle disappointed that he did not mention Nicolo by name, I was reassured that same afternoon by the arrival of Mother Elizabeth Josephina and another Sister from the convent. The Antonellis were generous contributors to the convent funds and the two nuns were graciously anxious to do all in their power to help. We all knelt down in the front room and in a low voice, so as not to disturb the dying monkey, repeated the Thirty Days' Prayer, and the *Memorare*.

Next day, a wet and dismal Monday, Nicolo was at his last gasp—he had now been ill for exactly nine days. Uncle Vita would now allow no one in the sickroom but himself, he never for a moment left the monkey's side. But at nine o'clock that morning, shortly after I arrived, he emerged; and, in the front room where we were gathered, pointed his finger, like a madman, at Clara.

"Oh, dear Saint Joseph!" Angelo wailed. "He says Clara, who alone is responsible, must make the three hundred and sixty-five steps, now, immediately. It is our only hope!"

In the midst of the ensuing commotion, while they are reasoning futilely with Uncle Vita, let me offer an explanation. This good, this simple soul, product of sunny Italy, and survival of a mediaeval age, who in the midst of the traffic of the busy High Street would suddenly stand stock still and gaze up, from beneath his flapping black hat, at the lovely heaven of Saints and Virgins, had invented for himself on this alien soil a most amazing devotion, I might even say a discipline. Upon the Castle Rock, a historic landmark which I have already mentioned, an old fortress guarding the estuary, with derelict cannon, defended in the past by Bruce and Wallace, and now a forgotten shrine, a public monument, there existed an outside winding stair, leading steeply from the portcullis below to the ruined ramparts of the Castle above and consisting, to the curiosity of succeeding generations, of precisely three hundred and sixty-five steps, one for every day of the year. Uncle Vita's penance was this: pausing to repeat an *Ave* on each step, he ascended this stairway upon his knees.

Ten minutes later Clara and I set out in the rain for the Castle Rock. Clara, the proud, the wicked, was half fainting at the ordeal, the humiliation, in prospect. But Uncle Vita must be obeyed. It was too wet for Angelo to accompany her; I was sent as an escort, to act as "watcher" for the fair penitent. Should a guide or a party of sightseers appear I was at once to warn her so that she might rise quickly and, leaning upon the ramparts, assume a position of intelligent interest in the scenery.

However, the Castle was deserted, cleared by the rain, not an onlooker in sight. We decided that I too should make the devotion. Side by side, saying our "Hail Marys," swooped upon by inquisitive gulls, we ascended, like crabs, under the dripping skies. Clara, despite her distress, had thoughtfully brought with her a soft cushion, also a small umbrella. But I, without such foresight or protection, soon found myself soaked, my bare knees completely worn out, as up, up we went, fervently, painfully, beneath the swooping gulls, the drenching clouds, the startled shades of Wallace and Bruce, the omnipotent God.

At last, it was over; we reached the top. I could barely stand . . . or see. Clara in the final throes had, accidentally but cruelly, poked her umbrella in my eye. Still we had done it, we had made the three hundred and sixty-five steps. We returned, conscious of our worth, to the Saloon.

From her martyred air I sensed that Clara was prepared for some bare acknowledgment of her efforts. But not for the scintillation of joy, of praise, which burst upon her at the threshold. The door swung open, the whole family flung themselves upon her. What gratitude! What rejoicings! During our absence the monkey had passed the crisis of his illness. Later, I was to observe and marvel at the amazing transformation which accompanies the resolution of a pneumonic infection. Abrupt and magical . . . No wonder Uncle Vita cried aloud, with shining eyes, that the good God had intervened on little Nicolo's behalf. At twenty past eleven, a moment which was calculated to coincide with the consummation of our reparation, but which, I subsequently decided, approximated more nearly to the instant when the spoke of Clara's umbrella entered my eye, Nicolo had suddenly ceased to suffocate. A mild benignant sweat had broken on him; he had

smiled feebly at his patron; then, breathing quietly, had fallen into a deep
sleep.

The monkey's recovery was rapid—there arises a memory of Uncle Vita's
face, wreathed in smiles, as he announced: "Nicolo has just eaten his first
banana." Vita had returned, already, to his usual position of humility, the
equilibrium of the household was swiftly being restored. Clara had several
new dresses of a violent hue. The good Sisters received a handsome donation,
Canon Roche a contribution to the new side-altar fund. The doctor was
presented, at dead of night, with three cases of the best preserved apricots;
his housekeeper had acknowledged to Mrs. Antonelli that he was strongly
addicted to this fruit; it was judged, too, that he would refuse a more conventional gift.

Only towards me, towards the unimportant yet worthy Robert Shannon,
was there a strange and incomprehensible coldness, at least a nullity, a
vacuum of regard. Had I not, on my bare bended knees, helped to achieve
at least half the miracle? Did I not scour the Drumbuck woods for tender
green caterpillars, to which the pampered convalescent was passionately addicted? Yet not a word, not a token of gratitude. Instead, queer looks,
conversations between Clara, Mrs. Antonelli, and Clara's young man,
significantly interrupted when I came up from the Saloon with Angelo. The
mistral was blowing colder than before. I was about to learn, early, one of
the bitter truths of life.

Several days later, as Angelo and I took the almost fully restored Nicolo
round the courtyard for an outing, I received a push which sent me spinning to the wall.

"Get away from that monkey, you." It was Thaddeus, the young man
of Clara, scowling at me vengefully. "We don't want you or your kind around
here. Get away. Go."

Paralyzed with dismay, I could not even answer him back. But my blood
rose slowly nevertheless. I refused to leave. I waited until I had Angelo to
myself in the sunny yard.

"Angelo," I said, with quiet intensity. "Something is the matter. What
have I done wrong? Tell me, Angelo?"

He would not meet my gaze. Then suddenly he raised his head. His
peachy face had turned yellow, the colour of a duck's foot. There was a
waspish look in his soulful eyes.

"We don't like you any more," he cried shrilly. "Mother says I mustn't
play with you. She says your grandpa is a drunken person who sponges for
wine, who has no money, not a lira, who lies about the grand houses he
was never inside, who is, in fact, practically the biggest liar in the world . . ."

I stared at him, dumbfounded. Was this the child whom I had stood
beside at my First Communion, the lovely babe whom I had cherished and
indulged, for whom, even, in my loyalty I had sacrificed the friendship of
Gavin, dear Gavin, the good, the true?

"Yes," he shrilled. "Thad found out everything. Your grandpa is a cheat, a pauper, a tramp. He is known all over Levenford. He chases ladies, at his age! And worst of all he puts his arm round our sweet Clara to annoy Thaddeus from bad and wicked motives . . ."

I could stand it no longer. I saw, dumbly, that all was finished between Angelo and me. I turned away. But before I did so I punched him with all my force, on his angelic little nose. A mortal sin, perhaps, to damage such an angel. But the recollection of his howl as he ran towards his mother lived joyously in my memory through many bitter weeks. I can hear it still.

CHAPTER FIFTEEN

The week of Murdoch's tests has come and that faithful student of seed catalogues stands in the lobby in his best boots and Sunday clothes being brushed all over by Mama, who plumps down on her knees to get at a spot on the back of his trouser cuff, the brush fairly flying in her work-reddened hand, an intent and proud expression on her worn face. Mama, who slaves herself to the bone for us, cooks and mends, scours, polishes and scrubs, makes every penny do the work of three, rises first and goes to bed last, and all for no apparent recompense; Mama who bears up super-humanly under Papa's increasing economies, who finds time to display the soft corner in her heart for the old man upstairs, and for a wretched boy thrown upon her hands . . . But this is Murdoch's week: no time for panegyrics. Now that the fateful days are upon him he is pleasingly confident. He has emerged unscathed from a serious talk with his father the night before. He says to us all: "I can do no more." Yes, surely these eternal fingerings have massaged enough learning beneath that dandruffed scalp. He has his lunch money in his pocket, two pairs of spectacles, in case of breakages, his pen, rubber, set squares, in fine, everything. He sets off ponderously to catch the 9:20 A.M. train for Winton, where the Civil Service tests are held. Mama and I, standing at the door, wave to him and in our hearts we wish him well. . . .

Every evening, Murdoch came back on the four o'clock local and his father, home early from the office, was already waiting in suspense.

"How did you get on?"

"Wonderful, Father, really wonderful."

As the days progressed Murdoch's confidence increased. Munching an enormous tea stolidly, while we all hung upon his words, he would throw off calm little comments on his day.

"Really, I was surprised . . . found this morning's paper so confoundedly easy. I wrote reams . . . had to ask for a second exercise book. Some of the other fellows didn't half fill theirs . . ."

"Well done . . . well done." His father voiced the rare praise grudgingly, but with a gleaming eye.

Mama, without quailing, bent forward and gave Murdoch as large a helping of potted head as his father. I knew, we all knew, that his success was assured. While this pleased me it also made me sad; I could not help contrasting how miserably I should have done in like circumstances. And I had other reasons for my dejection. The Antonelli debacle, fruit of false friendship and ingratitude, still preyed upon my mind; I had not dared mention it to Grandpa. But worst of all, I had not seen Gavin for a fortnight; once only had we met, passing each other, pale to the lips, eyes straight ahead, in the High Street. I longed for this boy whom I had betrayed, longed for him with all my heart.

One faint gleam alone illuminated the horizon. Next Wednesday was the occasion of the Ardfillan Fair, when I was to accompany Kate and Jamie to the "Shows." Grandpa had, in the past, been a regular patron of the Shows and he described their delights to me in glowing phrases. When I remarked, wistfully, that I thought I might enjoy myself, he replied, emphatically: "We shall, boy. We shall."

Jamie had promised to call for us at two o'clock, in a wagonette. He arrived punctually, but in a different vehicle. Kate and I, waiting at the parlour window, gasped our amazement as a yellow motor car chugged up.

"If your brother Adam can do it, so can I." Jamie, less saturnine than usual, under a new checked cap, gave us his explanation on the spot. He was friendly with Sam Lightbody, a mechanic at the Argyll works. Sam had borrowed a car and would drive us to Ardfillan.

We shook hands with Sam, who remained, goggled, on the driver's seat, holding, somewhat tensely, two vertical levers with handles, as though keeping the machine pulsating with his own life-blood. At his suggestion Kate ran in to get a veil to keep her hat in place. Then, as we circled admiringly, before taking our places, there strolled through the gate, brushed, trimmed, and with his best stick: Grandpa.

"Remarkable . . . remarkable," he said, eying the car; then to Jamie, sternly: "You don't imagine I'm going to let you take my granddaughter to Ardfillan . . . till all hours . . . with no one to chaperone her but a mere child."

"Oh, Grandpa," Kate said pettishly. "You're not invited."

But Jamie had broken into a rough laugh. He *knew* Grandpa; I had several times seen them emerging together from the Drumbuck Arms, wiping their mouths with the back of their hands. "Let him come," he said. "The more the merrier. Hop in."

The machine, after a few preliminary shudders, jolted into action, then began to glide in delightful style down the Drumbuck Road. Kate and Jamie sat high beside the driver in front, Kate's feather boa floating gracefully in the breeze; Grandpa and I luxuriated in the large tonneau behind. We had barely started when a hand, Jamie's, slipped backwards bearing a large cigar. Grandpa accepted, lighted it and, placing one leg on his cushion, reclined regally. "This is delightful, Robert." He spoke in his well-bred voice. "I hope he drives through the town. It'll give the bodies a chance to see us."

We were, in fact, sliding under the railway bridge on our way to the High Street. Suddenly a wild shout caused me to sit up. I saw Murdoch, standing at the station exit, waving his arms for us to stop. As we swept past he took off his bowler hat and began to pound heavily after us, still waving one arm.

"Oh, stop, Sam, stop," I cried. "There's our Murdoch!"

The machine drew up with another terrible jerk and, when stationary, began to bounce us all up and down like peas on a drum. Sam, while bouncing, turned with a pained expression: I divined that he felt this excessive stopping and starting to be no part of the duty of a normal automobile. But here was Murdoch, puffing and blowing, in his thick good clothes. He climbed in at the back and collapsing in the tonneau exclaimed: "I'm coming with you."

A pause. Was there to be no end to our self-invited guests? Grandpa, in particular, looked hurt at the intrusion, but Sam solved the difficulty by pushing in a lever and throwing us all forward in a series of short convulsions. Soon we were bowling through the town.

"How did you get on, Murdoch?" I shouted above the wind which flowed deliciously past our ears.

"Wonderful," said Murdoch. "Simply wonderful." Still blown, he crouched in his seat with his mouth partly open, his coat huddled about his ears, which stuck out more than ever. He looked pale; I thought he had run too hard. He was fanning himself, somewhat unnecessarily, with his hat. He opened his mouth wider as if to speak, then half closed it again.

Conversation was now impossible. We were out of the town and coasting down the Lea Brae. Before us, reaching out to the sea, lay the wide estuary, all sequined by the high sun; along the shore, through flat green pastures and sandy dunes, wound a white ribbon—the road we must traverse; to the west, above the blue mist, a bluer outline, watchful, ever present, the Ben. Such loveliness, such still and shimmering delight! Why could I not view it without a pang of sadness stealing round my heart? Ah, wretched boy, to whom beauty must always bring this distant, lingering pain. I sighed and surrendered myself to the sad, sweet rapture of our flight.

The car was functioning to perfection: on the down grades we approached a rapidity of twenty miles an hour. As we swept through the villages the inhabitants ran to their doors to stare after us. Men working in the fields straightened themselves, and brandished their hoes at the novelty. Only the livestock of the district seemed to regard us with resentment. It took all Sam's skill to circumvent a stubborn cow; barking dogs furiously escorted us; hens flew protestingly from beneath our wheels; once there were feathers, but the clouds of white dust rising behind mercifully left the massacre in doubt. A solitary humiliation to be recorded: the brave heart of our machine faltered on the crest of an incline; some country ruffians bound for the

Shows walked alongside; ignorant laughter—"Yah! Get out and push!" . . .

We sailed into Ardfillan at four o'clock, an hour too early for the delights of the Shows, which did not properly begin until evening. While Kate went across the street to make some purchases for Mama in a special millinery shop of this pleasant seaside resort, Sam stilled his engine, and we gazed at the galaxy of booths, tents, and roundabouts, arranged on a square of green beside the Esplanade, with the beach and plashing waves beyond.

Suddenly, crouched pale and hapless, Murdoch gave a great heave. It shook the structure of our vehicle; I thought we were starting again. But, no, the explosion came from Murdoch's soul.

"I'll commit suicide."

The threat was uttered by Murdoch in such a loud tone, almost a shout, that it instantly drew upon him our united attention. He continued, beating the cushions with his fists, his eyes bulging: "I tell you I'll commit suicide. I wanted no post in no Post Office. It's all Papa's fault. I'll kill myself. And he'll be to blame. A murderer."

"In the name of God, man!" Grandpa sat up. "What's wrong wi' ye?"

Murdoch stared at him, at all of us, with those obtuse, nearsighted eyes. Suddenly he broke down and began to blubber. "I'm plunked. Sent home by the examiners. They took me aside this morning and told me not to come back. Just told me not to come back. Not to come back. It must be a mistake. I've done wonderful, wonderful."

Failed; Murdoch failed! Silence of consternation. His bulky sobs were now shaking us all. A crowd gave evidence of forming.

"Here!" Grandpa took him by the coat collar. "Pull yourself together."

"He needs a stiff'ner." The sombre advice came from Sam.

"By God you're right. He needs something to make a man of him." Grandpa and Jamie got the helpless Murdoch out of the car while Sam held open the swing door of the Esplanade Vaults, immediately opposite. As they disappeared into the cool interior, Jamie called over his shoulder: "Hang about, boy. We'll not be long."

I stood for a while, thinking: "Poor Murdoch!" then I strolled disconsolately across the road. The fair ground was now beginning to fill up as people flocked in from the surrounding countryside. I recognized several Levenford faces. Suddenly I caught sight of a figure—small, sunburned, and resolute. It was Gavin.

He was alone, on the outskirts of a small gathering, watching, with his own particular disdain, the efforts of a cheap-jack to sell genuine gold watches to some awestruck farm hands. Then he turned and across the heads of the meaningless crowd our glances met. He reddened deeply, then went white, yet though he transferred his gaze, he did not move away. Indeed, presently he took a few steps in my direction and began, apart from everyone, to study, with concentrated immobility, a billhead advertising Willmot's Steam Bostons.

I felt the attraction of that billhead also. Though it was crudely printed and contained no information that I did not know by heart, I was soon staring at it too, standing beside Gavin, very pale, my cheek beginning to twitch—a horrible peculiarity which always affected me when I got nervous and overstrung. Impossible to say which of us spoke first. We were breathing with difficulty, our eyes remained riveted on that torn poster with its blurred representation of a swing boat standing on its head.

"It was all my fault."

"No, it was mine."

"No, mine."

"No, Robie, really it was mine. I was jealous that you had another friend. I don't want you to have a single friend in the world but me."

"You are my only friend, Gavin. And you always will be. I swear it. And I swear I was to blame. All my silly fault."

"No, mine."

"Mine."

He let me have the last word, a sublime sacrifice, since I know I am the weaker of the two. The poster had lost its attraction. We dared to look at each other. I read in his eyes that he had been as desolate as I. This moment of reunion, so poignantly desired, broke down the barriers of our restraint, evoked from us a demonstration greater even than our crushing handclasp. I took his arm in mine closely, closely, and thus linked, smiling blindly, and beyond speech, we moved off, merged with and lost ourselves in the multitude.

The brass of the roundabouts began to play, the steam whistles of the Bostons shrilly tooted. Cymbals clashed for the Animated Cakewalk; a fanfare for Cleo, the Fattest Woman upon Earth. Loud-talking gentlemen in high collars and bow ties began to swing little canes on the platforms outside the tents: "Walk up, Ladies and Gentlemen. Walk up for Leo the Leopard Man! Walk up for the Peruvian Pigmies! The one and only Talking Horse! Walk up! Walk up!" The Shows had come to life for us. We pushed our way giddily forward. Jamie had given me a florin for spending money. Gavin was equally well supplied. He had come by train from Levenford; but now he could return with me. We need not be separated. The thought gave us added joy.

We tried the coconut shies and soon had three fine milky nuts apiece; Gavin bored one with his penknife and in turn we let the clear sweet juice trickle down our throats. We visited the molly-dolly stalls, the lab-in-the-tub, the shooting gallery. We were decked with trophies, with pins, buttons, spangles and feather favours. Darkness fell and the naphtha lamps flared out. The crowd increased, the music brayed and quickened. Whoop! Whoop! Whoooop! went the Bostons. Once I caught sight of Kate and Jamie, close together, laughing, as they braved the Animated Cakewalk. And again there was a vision of Grandpa, Sam, and Murdoch, bestriding three wooden chargers, whirling giddily abreast, plunging and rearing under the lights, to the bombilation of the band. Murdoch had his bowler hat askew, a cigar braced between his teeth, a glassy jubilation in his eye. He rose in his stirrups from time to time, and yelled inhumanly.

It grows late, very late. And at last, worn out but happy, we are all gathered at the car. Kate especially seems happy, she glances frequently at Jamie and there is a bright tenderness in her eyes. Murdoch glares owlishly at Gavin, declares: "I don't care, I tell you, I simply don't care, the whole thing is a matter of complete indifference to a man of my intelligence." Then shakes him warmly by the hand. While Sam, the indispensable Sam, is beneath the bonnet, starting the car, Murdoch and Grandpa stand by with a melodious duet. "Genevieve . . . Gen . . . e . . . vieve." Halfway through, Murdoch departs hastily to the outer darkness, whence I hear sounds of prolonged and dreadful nausea.

Now we are on our way home, moving through the cool night air away from the glare, the pandemonium. In the tonneau behind, Grandpa is asleep with Murdoch lolling pallidly upon his shoulder. On the other cushion Kate and Jamie sit close together. His arm is round her waist and they are looking at the new moon.

In front I am with Gavin. Our friendship is restored, we will never again be separated. . . . At least, not until . . .

But we do not know of that, thank God. We are happy, confident. There is no sound but the steady beat of our engine, the brave hiss of our acetylene lamps. Sam, our impenetrable driver, is silent and apart. On, on, into the night. Two boys conquering the darkness, the unknown, together, under the unconquerable stars.

"*This* is what I like," Gavin whispers.

I know exactly what he means.

CHAPTER SIXTEEN

GRANDPA's philosophy, based no doubt on sad experience, was that we must pay for all our pleasures: he would warn me when I was unduly elated: "Man, ye'll suffer for this the morn." After our expedition to the Fair we suffered dreadfully upon the morn. A fateful calm hung upon the house when, later than usual, I got up. Murdoch still lay abed, Papa had gone to work, Mama was working in the scullery. Grandpa, smoking irritably, his nose redder than usual, seemed not to want me. Then, as I came downstairs, the front door opened and Grandma entered. She had returned, unknown to me, on the previous afternoon; and already, in her good bonnet and beaded cape, had been out to the Boilerworks office to draw her pension.

"Oh, Grandma," I cried. "I didn't know you were back."

She gave no answer to my pleased and excited greeting, but advanced with a strange, strained expression on her face. Opposite me, she paused, and under the dark concern of her eyes a sense of uneasiness, of anxiety descended upon me.

"Robert, Robert," she said in a quiet yet unnatural voice, "I wouldn't have believed it of you."

I shrank against the wall. I saw that she had learned, no doubt from Miss Minns, of my apostasy from all her fervent hours. Vaguely, I had been prepared for her discomfiture. But this bitter grief, that greenish look spread across her cheeks, the distracted drawing back of her lips from her teeth, startled and frightened me.

"One of these days you may be glad enough to turn to your grandma again." She said no more than that, but her tone, both pained and sad, made me tremble. Open-mouthed, I watched her continue on her way upstairs. Having knocked on his door, she firmly entered Grandpa's room.

I ran into the parlour. Why did this religion, into which I had been born, raise in Grandma such dark and savage gall? The answer defeated me. Worthy and exemplary woman, she had spoken to perhaps three members of that faith in all her life, her ignorance and misconceptions regarding it were quite ludicrous. Yet it remained her abomination. She would not lightly forgive Grandpa his connivance at my First Communion.

Indeed, at that moment, I heard voices loudly raised above me and presently, while my knees still shook, there came the sound of Grandpa's footsteps in the lobby. I peeped out—he was putting on his hat with a hasty and uneasy air.

"Come along, boy," he said to me abruptly. "It's time you and I removed ourselves."

Outside, I could see that he was troubled. No doubt she had charged him heavily with my defection, but there was stronger cause for anxiety than that. Sitting up late, at her bedroom window, Grandma had plainly observed Murdoch's "condition" on the night before, and had felt it her duty to tell Papa at breakfast.

Now Grandpa made it a practice to keep out of Papa's way, at all times, for he knew that his son-in-law detested him. Only on one occasion, in my recollection, were they together for any length of time—when Papa, in a fit of magnanimity, skilfully fostered by Mama, showed Grandpa and me over the new Levenford sewage farm—and then the event had terminated disastrously. Papa, full of pride, had talked us round the various oxidization and filtration beds, explaining with hygienic ardour that, irrespective of its beginning, the end product of the system was pure drinking water. He filled a glass and offered it to me.

"Try it and see."

I hesitated over the cloudy fluid.

"I'm afraid I'm not thirsty," I stammered.

Papa then offered the glass to Grandpa, whose well-known smile had flickered all the afternoon.

"I never was addicted to water." Grandpa spoke mildly. "And that beverage appeals to me still less."

"Don't you believe me?" Papa cried.

"I will," Grandpa smiled, "if you drink it yourself."

Papa flung down the glass and walked away.

Ordinarily, the two men rarely met; their paths did not intersect; and if Grandpa saw the Inspector in the town he would at once make a strategic detour. But now a collision was imminent. Viewed in the cold light of morning, though it had seemed fitting at the time, Murdoch's escapade took on a more sinister complexion. Papa was violently teetotal: "drink" was anathema to him—and such a wicked waste of money! Enraged by Murdoch's failure, there was no knowing to what lengths he might go to punish the reprobate who had led his son astray.

When we were well clear of the house, Grandpa slowed his rapid strides and turned to me, rather loftily. "Fortunately we have our own resources, Robie. And friends who'll give us a bite if we ask them. We'll go and call on the Antonellis."

I stopped in great embarrassment. "Oh, no, Grandpa, we can't do that."

"And why not?"

"Because . . ." I paused. Yet I had to tell him. I could not bear that he should suffer the ignominy of a door slammed in his face.

He said nothing, not a word—for all his perorations, he had, at least, the gift of suffering an injury in silence. But this was a sad blow; his face turned a queer mottled colour. I thought he might go back to Drumbuck to foregather with the Saddler and Peter Dickie. But no, he continued down the High Street and over Knoxhill, marching me into unfamiliar territory on the south side of the town.

"Where are we going, Grandpa?"

"To wash in the waters of bitterness," he answered shortly.

Whether he meant what he said, whether the salt breezes of Ardfillan had awakened in him a desire for the beaches, or whether simply he wished to put the greatest distance possible between himself and all that was distressing him, I do not know. But presently we came out through the end of the Knoxhill green and found ourselves on the shore of the estuary just below the harbour. This was no idyllic strand, but a reach of drab, ribbed silt, broken by tufts of green seaweed and flat rocks, greyly crusted with young limpets. The tide was out, such water as we saw was leaden grey; the tall chimneys of the Boilerworks, still visible, the rattle of hammers from the Shipyard, the rushing of an effluent conduit from a laundry—these raw reminders of industry increased, rather than diminished, the desolation of the scene.

Yet there was a tang in the breeze, a brackish tang. And immediately around us was that solitude which Grandpa craved. He sat down, took off his boots and socks, rolled up his trousers to the knee and, having splashed across the damp sand, began to paddle in the shallows. I watched, while the grey wavelets caressed his bony ankles; then I peeled off my own shoes and stockings, followed the wet imprints of his feet, and waded in beside him.

Presently he removed his hat: that marvellous hat which I identify, inseparably, with Grandpa—large, square, and faded, ventilated by three metal-edged holes punched on either side, hardened by age to an iron indestructibility; that hat which had contained so many rarities, from Grandpa's head to a pound of pilfered raspberries, which had served, and was still to serve, so many diverse purposes, and into which, now, stooping, he began to place cockles and mussels retrieved from this sad seashore . . .

The cockles were pure white and fluted, only a wavering spot the size of a sixpence revealed their presence beneath the flooding sand. The mussels, of a purple nacreous sheen, grew toughly in bunches in the fissures of the rocks. When we had gathered an assorted hatful, Grandpa straightened himself. "Boy," he remarked—though addressing the melancholy waters—"I may be bad . . . but not *that* bad."

On the dry part of the beach, covered with wrack and driftwood, with staved-in coops and a bunk straw mattress cast off from a ship, we made a crackling fire. While he roasted the mussels Grandpa showed me how to eat the cockles. You held the cockle over the flame until it opened, then quickly gulped the saline contents down. He judged them delicious, far better than oysters, he said, and he swallowed a great many, sadly, as though their salt astringency suited his present mood. I could not care for them, but I found the mussels exactly to my taste. The shells opened wide, wide, exposing upon pearly plates the frizzled contents, tough as meat, and nutsweet.

"No dishes to wash," Grandpa commented with a grim smile when we had done. He lit his pipe and lay on his elbow, letting his eyes roam across the scene, still indulging his reverie; he added, to himself, as though the salt fare had given him a thirst: "I could do with a dram."

Here, in the light of what ensues, I must try to establish an important aspect of Grandpa's character. He had a fondness, a weakness, for "the drink"; there were evenings when I heard his uneven footsteps on the stairs, accompanied by fumblings, and the jovial exclamations of a man undisturbed by colliding with objects in the dark; but he was not a drunkard. To dismiss him, in Adam's curt phrase, as "an old soak" was to do the man a grave injustice—he had gone on wild sprees, yet there were long sober spells between, and he never took part in Levenford's Saturday night saturnalia, which thronged the streets with reeling figures. All his life he had wanted to do brave and wonderful things—with an intensity which in his later days made him believe he had actually done them—yet in reality his career had been humdrum. His forebears had at one time been extremely well off—in partnership with two uncles, his father had once owned the well-known distillery of Glen Nevis. In a family album I had come across the yellowish photograph of a youth standing with a gun and two setter dogs on the steps of an imposing country mansion. Imagine my stupefaction when Mama told me it was Grandpa, outside his boyhood home—she had added with a faint smile and a sigh, "The Gows were gey important folks in their day, Robie." It was the malt tax which had destroyed the family fortune; and I now know that as a young man, after the "smash," Grandpa had been forced to begin, in the humble Levenford manner, as an apprentice engineer. Yet he had not "learned his trade." He was too impatient, and an enforced marriage, which he never bemoaned, with a simple girl of the people who idolized him, sent him into the hardware business. When he failed here, in high-spirited fashion, he was in turn clerk, farm hand, cabinetmaker, Scots draper, purser on a Clyde steamboat; until finally, through his Glen Nevis connections, he became, like the poet he so greatly admired, an exciseman in the Bonded Service.

Disappointment with himself and a talent for friendship, together with the fact that he "worked amongst the stuff," made him a drinker; yet he was never a graceless one; his craving was spasmodic, rather than inveterate, and sprang from the peculiarities of his temperament, that strange entanglement of opposites, which would cause him one minute to defend my innocence like a lion and the next—but we shall hear of that much later.

At present, in his dejection, there was reason to believe that his craving was coming to the surface, evoked by a bitter sense of his betrayal by Grandma.

"A *certain person*," he declared suddenly, "has been at my throat from the moment she put foot inside the house. I owe her something for all she's done to me. 'Leading Murdoch to ruin'!" He broke off to point moodily with the moist stem of his pipe. "There's the *Lord of the Isles* coming . . . on her 'Round the Kyles' trip . . . She's a braw boat."

We watched while the crowded pleasure steamer raced down the river with flashing paddles and flying bunting, her two red funnels at a jaunty angle, trailing a plume of smoke, the soft sweet music of the "German band" aboard her drifting towards us and still lingering sadly as the rush of waves came in. Poor beachcombers, downcast and penniless, how we longed to be aboard her!

"At first," Grandpa resumed, bitterly, "when I came to live at Lomond View, after the death of my wife, she pretended to be friendly with me. She mended my socks and laid out my slippers by the fire. Then she asked me to give up smoking—she objected to the smell of it. When I refused, that started it. She's worked against me ever since.

"Of course she has the best end of it. She's independent. She goes downstairs to her meals. She gets the Levenford *Herald* before me. She has the hot water on Saturday night and first use of the bathroom in the morning. I tell you, boy, it's enough to turn milk sour."

Other ships went past: some laden scows, a rusty coastal tramp, the river ferry plying on a chain cable between the harbour and Sandbank, the crack white-funnelled Inveraray steamer, the *Queen Alexandra*. Then came a liner, immeasurably huge, a "beef boat" built by Marshall Brothers for the Argentine trade. She passed slowly, impenetrably, behind a noisy tug, a pilot, Grandpa said, upon her bridge, and I followed her with watering eyes until she was only a dark smudge on the far rim of the widening estuary, behind which the sun was now setting, in purple smoke.

Grandpa meditated darkly. There was nothing like a Marshall boat, the Clyde was the noblest river in the world, Robert Burns the greatest poet . . .

one Scot could beat three Englishmen . . . even with a hand tied behind his
back . . . but it was hard for any man to get the better of a woman. A longer
silence. Suddenly Grandpa sat up and with sombre decision slapped his thigh
hard with his hand.

"By God! I'll do it."

Startled, my mind still filled with gentle meditations, with slow and
stately images of departure, I turned to Grandpa, whose thoughts I had
imagined to be similarly attuned. He was no longer brooding and dejected.
A grim determination illuminated all his features, radiated even from his
nose. He stood up.

"Come on, boy," he repeated, several times, under his breath, as with a
kind of awe at his own invention. "By God, what a bawr!"

While he hurried me back through the town, pausing to check the time
on the church steeple, I must impose another explanation. The word "bawr,"
in the local patois—which, for reasons of intelligibility, I have used sparingly
—is expressive, in essence, of a peculiar act of vengeance, a vengeance fla-
voured with devilish humour. Dismiss from your minds anything so paltry
as a practical joke. True, the bawr brings satisfaction to its perpetrator and
confusion to its victim. But there the faint resemblance ends. The bawr is
dire, traditional, the just explosion of a hatred. Where, in Corsica, in like
circumstances, they take to the maquis with a gun, in Levenford they sit
on solitary beaches, devise, then execute, a bawr.

"Where are you going, Grandpa?"

"First I am going to call on these fine Antonellis." He tempered the shock
by adding, in an indescribable tone, "By the back door."

I remained, in fear, at the corner of the alley while he went round to the
Antonelli back yard. He was absent only for a few minutes, yet I could not
repress my relief when he reappeared, apparently unscathed, even grimly
smiling. We set off into the gathering dusk and Grandpa took the unfrequented "Common way."

From time to time I threw him inquiring side glances, conscious that he
moved with a singular rigidity: the strange mobile immobility of those
porters who carry a high tower of innumerable baskets upon their heads.
Then, as by an act of levitation, I saw his hat lift, revolve, and settle back
calmly upon his brow. Still, I did not guess. It was only when a thin tail
curled from beneath the brim, and mingled with Grandpa's locks in the
manner of a queue, that I realized he had Nicolo inside his hat.

I was too surprised to speak: but Grandpa sensed that I had spotted the
monkey. He squinted at me carefully. "He aye liked my hat. No trouble in
the world to get him into it."

It was almost dark when, shortly before eight, we reached Lomond View.
Then, I realized the full finesse of Grandpa's timing: on Thursday nights at
half-past seven o'clock it was Papa's custom to attend a meeting of the
Building Society. We reached Grandpa's room unseen.

Nicolo was in rude health. He knew us perfectly—a fortunate circumstance, since strange faces always disturbed him. At the same time, the novelty of his new surroundings appeared not displeasing to him. He moved about the room, inspecting things with an air of agreeable surprise. I think he had just been fed, which accounted perhaps for his good humour. He refused the oddfellow which Grandpa offered him.

Grandpa contemplated the monkey dispassionately. He was reserved, rather on his dignity with animals; he never descended to intimacies; indeed, while he professed great affection for the Mikado in Mrs. Bosomley's presence, I had seen him take a distasteful kick at the cat when we met it, in the dark, alone.

Nine o'clock . . . A sound upon the landing indicated the passage of Grandma to the bathroom. Grandpa, waiting, darkly upon the alert, acted at once. With an agility remarkable in a man of his years he took up Nicolo and vanished through the doorway. A few seconds; then he was back—without the monkey.

I turned white. I saw at last the full import of his bawr. Yet, even as I trembled, I was conscious of an awful feeling of expectancy. I sat with Grandpa, who was biting his nails, listening tensely while Grandma heavily recrossed the landing. We heard her re-enter her room, the measured sounds of her disrobing, the groan of her bed as it received her. Silence, terrible silence. Then the air is rent: a scream . . . another . . . and another.

At this point Grandma herself must relate what happened, and in her own broad Scots—which hitherto, in the interests of lucidity, I have translated—for without this idiom, the recitation loses half its savour. Grandma told this story repeatedly in after years, mostly to her friend Miss Tibbie Minns, and always with a dreadful seriousness. No wonder I have always thought of it as "Grandma's Encounter with the Devil."

This is how it goes:—

Weel, Tibbie, on the awfu' nicht when the Thing cam' till me I was in waur nor ordinar' health and speerits. I had ta'en off my cla'es, foldit them decent-like on the rocker and put on my mutch and gownie. I had read my chapter like a Christian, ta'en oot my teeth and lichtit my dip—ye ken I aye keep a wee bit can'le by me in the nicht. Then as I put my heid down on the pillay and composed mysel' tae rest, as I aye do, in the airms o' my Saviour, I felt the Thing loup on till my cheist. I opened my e'en. And there, as I hope to be judged, gazing at me by the flickerin' dip, was the Fiend hissel'.

Na, na, it was nae dream, Tibbie, far from it. I wasna sleepin'. And forbye I'm no' a fanciful wumman. There he was, Satan, tail an' a', grinnin' and yammerin' and gnashin' his tusks at me like he wad gie a' he had tae drag me to the Pit. I'm not easy daunted, Tibbie, ye'll maybe agree, but for aince my banes turned tae watter, as weel they micht. I hadna the breath tae scream, let alane murmur the Lord's Prayer. I just lay like a corp, starin' at the Brute, while he stared back at me.

A' at yince, he ga'ed a kind o' skirl and began to jounce up and down on

my cheist like I was a pouny. I tell ye, Tibbie, if I hadna breath before I
had less then. He grippit my lugs in his twa paws and began to joggle my
heid like it was a milk kirn. He jounced and waggled and waggled and
jounced till I hadna breath in me. And a' the time the sparks was fleein' frae
his e'en like cinders. I was feared, Tibbie wumman, my skin was in a grue.
And weel the Brute kenned it for he banged and yammered and scarted his
will at me till he had a' my hair doun and, though it's no' decent to sae,
the gownie haulf off my back.

Oh, if I had juist had the presence o' mind to gi'e him the Name, but my
puir wits were fair scattered. A' I could do was to whisper, in a voice ye
couldna hear below a meal barrel: "Go, Satan, go!"

Feeble though it was, I think maybe it held the Brute. At ony rate he
stoppit his pummelin' and wi' a kind o' girn, he took a haud o' my teeth,
at the heid o' the bed, where I aye keep them, beside me. Then, as I hope
to meet my Maker, he stood up on the bed and began makin' passes wi' the
teeth, mopin' and mowin' at me, like he was puttin' them in and oot his
mouth.

I tell ye Tibbie, it was maybe that whit saved me. When I saw the Thing
abusin' my guid double set my bluid rose up in me at sic a desecration, I
stirred from my dwam, sat up and shook my fist at him. "Ye Brute, ye Brute,"
I shouted. "God send ye back below."

Nae sooner did the name o' the Almighty strike him, for it couldna' ha'
been my mere human fist what hindered him, than he gien a shriek that
wad have turned ye tae stane. He louped frae the bed, still skirlin' and
screechin'. As luck wad have it I had left my door on the keek, for the nicht
was warm and I wanted a breath o' air. Oot the room he went, like a streak o'
infernal licht while I lay shakin' in a' my limbs, thankin' Providence for my
merciful release. I couldna stir for mony a meenute. But when I did and
lichtit the gas and was praisin' Heaven that I had suffered nae ill, I saw, the
Lord save and defend me, I saw, God help me tae endure it, I saw, I tell ye,
what the Brute had done.

He hadna stole my dentures, na, na, nor smashed them neithers. But oot
o' black burning malice and revenge, he had droppit them ablow the bed
intil my nicht utensil.

CHAPTER SEVENTEEN

On the following Tuesday, the summer recess ended: Kate resumed her
teaching at the "Elementary" and I went back to the Academy. I remember
the day vividly—it marked the climax of that mood of profound dejection
which enveloped Grandpa like a cloud, one of those moods which I inherited
from him and which afflicted me when I grew older, a mood when life
seemed dark and worthless.

The weather continued enervating; Grandma remained closeted in her room; Murdoch kept out of the way—he had begun, secretly, to work for Mr. Dalrymple at the Nursery.

Grandpa evinced no desire for his friends; there was no copying to be done; nothing but to endure the heat and Papa's resentment. The old man was being nagged and persecuted. Only a small mind could have devised the expedient of stopping his tobacco. It was this, I think, which prompted Grandpa's final remark, as he fingered, mournfully, an empty pipe. "What's the use of it all, boy . . . what's the use?"

The next morning, as I dressed behind my curtain, Papa was still grumbling at breakfast, railing against the old man, when Mama came down, and in a voice which was both astonished and distraught, exclaimed: "Grandpa is not upstairs. Where can he have gone?"

A pause while Papa's surprise turned to indignation.

"This is the last straw. Have him here at the dinner hour or I'll know the reason why!"

Disturbed, but not yet alarmed, I walked with Gavin to the Academy, where we found that we were not only in the same class, but sitting next to each other. This, and the issue of new books which I brought back carefully for Mama to cover, proved a distraction during the day. But as we all sat down to the high tea that evening, I saw from Mama's red eyes and Papa's repressed manner that something was seriously amiss.

"No sign of him yet?"

Mama shook her head dolefully.

Papa began to drum his fingers on the tablecloth, crunching his toast, as though biting Grandpa's head off.

Silence. Then Murdoch, who had just come in, suggested in a subdued manner: "Maybe something has happened to him."

Papa glared at the unfortunate youth. "Shut up, you dolt. You've had your chance to be clever."

Murdoch collapsed and a more painful silence followed until irritation drove Papa to speak again.

"I must say it's hard enough, in the ordinary way, to support such an encumbrance. But when he takes to staying out, like as not going on the soak . . ."

Mama interrupted, aroused at last, a spot of indignation on her cheek. "How do you know he's doing any such thing?"

Papa gazed at her, taken aback.

"The poor old man hasn't a farthing in the world," Mama went on. "Downtrodden and miscalled by everybody. Soak, indeed. The way he's been treated lately it wouldn't surprise me a bit if he had been driven to something desperate . . ." She began to cry.

Murdoch looked justified, in a subdued way, and Kate went over to comfort Mama. "Really, Papa," she said, with a note of warning, "you ought to take some steps; with no money he can't have gone *far*."

Papa's expression was unhappy. "And set all the neighbours talking . . .

Isn't it bad enough already?" He got up from the table. "I've told my staff to keep their eyes open in the town. That's the most I can do."

Papa's staff consisted of a lanky assistant named Archibald Jupp, who always wore an air of passionate willingness because he hoped to succeed Papa, and a stout boy, who moved so slowly that he was known amongst the Boilermakers and other derisive young men as "The Fast Message." Though I was proved to be wrong, I had not much hope of this co-operation. Remembering the desolation of Grandpa's recent mood I began to feel dreadfully worried.

Next morning: no Grandpa, not a sign of him. A definite air of strain, of suspense, pervaded the household. At noon, when there was still no news, Papa struck the table, but not hard, with the flat of his hand: he said, in the tone of a man making a decisive announcement:—

"Telegraph for Adam!"

Yes, yes; send for Adam; that was the good, the logical procedure. But a telegram—Ah, this deadly missive, almost unheard-of in the household, seemed a foreboding, almost a harbinger of doom. Refusing Murdoch's aid, Mama put on her hat and went, herself, with her head on one side, to the Drumbuck sub-office, to send the telegram. In an hour there was a telegram back: WITH YOU TOMORROW THURSDAY 3 P.M. ADAM.

Insensibly our spirits rose at the promise implied in such promptitude, such businesslike decision. Mama remarked, as she put the telegram away in the private drawer where she kept all Adam's things—his letters, school reports, old pay envelopes, even a beribboned lock of his hair: "Adam's the one."

But the following day, before Adam arrived, there was a terrible development. Papa came back from the office in the middle of the forenoon, while I hung miserably about the house. He was accompanied by Archie Jupp, who stood in the lobby while Papa advanced towards Mama and, after some hesitation, with a grave, even a tender, expression, said:—

"Mama! Prepare yourself. Grandpa's hat has been found . . . floating on the Common pond."

Before our startled eyes, Jupp, who had discovered it, produced the old man's hat, pitifully battered and sodden.

"It was floating at the deep end, Mrs. Leckie. Opposite the boathouse." He spoke with ingratiating condolence. "I had an awful feeling it might be there."

I gazed with shocked anguish at the dripping relic and, as its full significance struck Mama, tears began to trickle down her cheeks.

"Come now, Mrs. Leckie," Archie Jupp said soothingly. "It may be nothing . . . nothing at all."

Papa had actually gone into the scullery to make a cup of tea for Mama. He pressed it upon her affectionately, and waited, consolingly, until she had swallowed it, before departing with Archie Jupp.

That afternoon, Adam, wearing striped trousers and a dark jacket with a pearl pin in his grey tie, took command of the situation immediately he arrived. Seated at the table, effective and calm, he heard all the evidence, even my broken tale of Grandpa's brooding melancholy and his last fateful remark. He said: "We must inform the police."

A hush fell upon us at that sinister word.

"But, Adam . . ." Papa protested. "My position . . ."

"My dear father," Adam replied coolly, "if an old man takes it into his head to drown himself you can't exactly cover *that* up. Mind you, I don't commit myself. But they'll certainly want to drag the pond."

Mama was trembling all over. "Adam! You don't mean, you don't think . . . ?"

Adam shrugged his shoulders. "I don't think he floated his hat on the pond for fun."

"Oh, Adam."

"I'm sorry I spoke so bluntly, Mama. I know how you must feel. But after all what had he to live for? I'll go down and see Chief Constable Muir. It's lucky he's a friend of mine."

He had taken to smoking Burma cheroots and now he selected one from his crocodile leather case. I gazed at him in acute distress as he pulled out the yellow straw which traversed its length and accurately lit it. With a glance which included also Papa, he turned impressively to Mama: "A good thing, Mama, a *very* good thing, I induced you to extend the policy. Let's see . . . an endowment *with* profits." With his left hand he brought out his silver pencil and began to figure on the tablecloth. "Five years at three . . . add twenty-five . . . why it makes a clear difference of one hundred and sixteen pounds."

"I don't want the money," Mama wept.

"It'll come in very handy," Papa said in a husky voice.

My grief, my growing sense of loss, was choking me as Adam put away his pencil and stood up.

"I'll look in on McKellar, too, at the Building Society Offices. He could smooth out any little difficulties in the way of immediate payment. In fact, I think I'll bring him back with me. You might whip up a really nice meat tea for us, Mama . . . something substantial like poached eggs and mince. McKellar would like that. Don't lay it in the parlour . . . not yet." He went out.

Obediently, Mama began to carry out Adam's instructions, scurrying between the kitchen and the scullery as though trying by the intensity of her activity to keep her mind off the worst. She baked several batches of scones. Papa, who could not bear the slightest extravagance, actually encouraged her to make pancakes as well, at the sacrifice of a half-dozen eggs. The unprecedented smell of rich cooking filled the air. The table was set with the best tablecloth and the parlour china.

At five o'clock Adam returned, rubbing his hands with satisfaction.

"They'll start dragging first thing, Monday. Unless he rises over the week end. And the cost will come out of the Humane Society Fund. Muir says that Common pond is getting to be an awful spot. Three drownings and a bad ice accident in the last ten years. McKellar can't come till after seven. He's a dry stick. Let's have our tea, Mama."

We sat down to the best meal I had ever eaten in Lomond View: meat, eggs, scones, pancakes, hot strong tea.

"At a time like this," Papa said, looking generously round the table, "I don't grudge a thing."

"Do you think he will rise, Adam?" Murdoch asked in a voice of morbid fascination.

"Well, now, that's a question," Adam answered with knowledgeable interest. "According to Muir they sometimes come up of their own volition within forty-eight hours. Fill up with gas." Mama shuddered and shut her eyes. "Just float up gently, and always face down—that's the curious thing. Sometimes they're stubborn though and stay down. Or they might be embedded in sand or weeds—there's a lot of weed in the pond—and can't move even though the gas is trying to rise them. In that case I'm told if you float loaves, with quicksilver in them, over the pond you often get a dip at the exact spot."

I could not bear it, this awful vision of my poor grandpa, entangled with green weed, sodden from long immersion. But suddenly, a ring at the front bell. Everyone sat up as Kate went to the door and showed in Archie Jupp.

"Sorry to disturb you—" Archie halted, discreetly, at the sight of the family meal. "But I thought you ought to know . . . there's another piece of evidence."

Archie had been hurrying, he wiped his brow; he was excited yet expressing a sense of grave commiseration.

"Mr. Parkin, who keeps the boats on the pond, remembered he heard a distinct splash late Wednesday night, opposite his boathouse, and this afternoon he went out with the boathook. He struck some clothing, a man's jacket. He took it to the police office. I've just seen it. It's Mr. Gow's."

Tears burst anew from my smarting eyes; of course Mama was crying again, gently and silently.

Papa made a noble gesture of invitation. "Sit in and take a bite with us, Archie."

Deferentially, Archie pulled up a chair. While accepting his cup from Mama he murmured, in a low voice, to Papa: "He did it once too often, Mr. Leckie."

To my surprise Papa frowned. "No, I can't allow you to say that, Jupp. It's untimely. We all have our faults. He wasn't a bad old soul. He had a certain dignity, too, when you come to think of it. That way he had of walking down the street, swinging his stick." He leaned forward and patted my shoulder, not rebuking me for my snivelling, but rather approving it as he murmured gently: "Poor boy . . . you were fond of him, too."

Another peal of the front bell—startling us, yet in a sense expected, confirming all our fears. A terrible silence; a silence of certainty as Kate rose and again went to the door. When she returned she was whiter than I had ever seen her.

"Oh, Papa," she whispered, "someone from the police station. He wants to see you."

Through the half-open doorway, I perceived in the lobby behind her the terrifying form of a policeman, red-faced and solemn, turning his helmet in his hands.

Papa immediately got up, pale but important, and made a sign to Adam, who also rose. They both went into the lobby, closing the kitchen door behind them as though, by drawing a veil upon the scene, they wished to spare us. Only the mutter of their lowered voices came to us as we sat absolutely mute, as though we ourselves were stricken by the messenger of death.

After a long time Papa came back into the room. A pause. Then Kate, the bravest of us, mustered enough strength to ask: "Have they found him?"

"Yes." Papa spoke in a low voice; he was paler than before. "They have him."

"In the mortuary?" Murdoch gasped.

"No," said Papa, "in Ardfillan jail."

He surveyed us with a glassy eye; felt his way to his chair; sat down weakly. "He's been out on the spree with the tinkers from the Skeoch wood . . . lost his coat and hat in a fight at the boathouse . . . up to God knows what these last two days . . . landed in jail at Ardfillan . . . charged with drunk and disorderly and contempt of the law. Adam has gone to bail him out."

The shades of night were falling as Adam and Grandpa came up the road. Hatless, wearing an old police tunic open and unbuttoned, in place of his lost jacket, Grandpa looked proud but subdued; there was a gleam in his eye—a chink in his armour which betrayed an inward apprehension. As I crouched at the parlour window in anxious solitude, a glimpse was enough to send me scudding upstairs to the refuge of the old man's room.

There, listening tensely, I heard the sound of the front door, followed by a dreadful chaos, filled with loud recriminations from Adam, Mama's tears and lamentations, Papa's whining abuse, but not a word, not a whisper from Grandpa.

At last he came upstairs, moving slowly, and entered his room. He was sadly tarnished; his beard needed trimming; he exhaled strange and uncomfortable odours.

He threw me a quick glance, began to potter about the room, trying unsuccessfully to hum, pretending not to care. Then he picked up his battered and still sodden hat, which, earlier that day, Mama had placed reverently upon the bed. He considered it for a moment, turned artlessly to me.

"It'll stand reblocking. It was always a grand hat."

BOOK TWO

CHAPTER ONE

THE chestnut trees, spreading more widely, were again in flourish, the setting sun was sending up a faint incense behind the Ben as, full of excitement and pride, I hurried home from the Academy one April afternoon in the year 1910. At least I must assume that it was I, though there were times when I seemed a stranger, an uncouth stranger to myself. The other morning, coming out of Baxter's after my early "round," I had caught a sudden glimpse of a strange apparition in the mirror of the baker's shop —a pale and lanky boy of fifteen who has outgrown his strength, stooping, with thin wrists and unmanageable feet, an unfamiliar profile, absorbed and melancholy, a man's nose on a boyish face—I could not repress a start of surprise, of pained unbelief.

But now I was conscious only of my splendid worth, full of my interview with Mr. Reid, held not five minutes ago, on the eve of the short Easter recess. "Jason" Reid had kept me behind the others, then crooked his forefinger for me to come to his desk. My form master was a young man, thirty-two, his stocky figure brimming over with suppressed vitality, the scar on his upper lip a diagonal white weal with tiny white beads, where the stitches had been, symmetrically alongside. This scar—which I suspected to be the result of a hare-lip operation—seemed to pull his nose down, making it flat and boneless, widening the nostrils, even making his blue eyes more prominent, almost bulging, under his fine soft blond hair. He was fair-complexioned, with a dampish skin, for he perspired easily, and was clean-shaven, disdaining to hide that slightly disfigured upper lip by a moustache, as though he welcomed and despised the cruelty of vulgar curiosity. In any case, his speech would have betrayed him, that imperfect articulation which can be reproduced exactly by placing the tongue flat against the roof of the mouth, which softens all the hard *ss* sounds to *th*'s, which in fact had given Mr. Reid his nickname on that day when we began the account of the Argonauts in the third ode of Pindar, and he spoke, with emotion, of "Jathon."

"Shannon." He drummed with his fingers, while I gazed at him adoringly. "You are not quite a plate of sour porridge"—his usual designation of the members of his form. "There's something I want to put up to you. . . ."

I was still giddy from his momentous words when I reached Lomond View.

I wanted to be alone, to hug my secret, but upstairs Grandpa was waiting at the open window with the draught board set out before him.

"What has kept you?" he asked impatiently.

"Nothing." I had become intensely secretive. Besides, Grandpa wasn't the Homeric figure he once had been to me and my announcement was much too valuable to "waste" on him.

Actually, Grandpa had altered much less than I, his movements were still charged with vigour, though I discerned less ruddy metal in his beard, a few more careless stains upon his waistcoat. He had not reached that stage in his career, to which I must later refer with pain, when his eccentricities became my bane. Lately his lifelong friend, Peter Dickie, had been overtaken by the spectre of unwanted old men and retired to the county poorhouse at Glenwoodie. This had sobered Grandpa, who always shied away from evidence of senility, and who resented, as a personal insult, the very mention of the word "death." Still, he looked quite spry, because he was enjoying his blessed annual respite: Grandma had departed on her visit to Kilmarnock. The period to be reviewed is, actually, Grandpa's Indian summer. Yet just then he was in a bad mood, for he imagined I was trying to "do him out" of his beloved game.

"What's the matter with you? Standing there like a cat on hot bricks?"

I resigned myself and sat down opposite him while he bent over the board with frowning concentration, pondering his move with a terrible deliberation, preparing a pitfall which I could easily see coming, moving his man with a pretence of innocence, enhancing this transparent cunning by tapping out his dottle, examining the stem of his pipe, and beginning to hum.

Naturally my mind was not on the game, but whizzing with that magnificent proposal of Jason's which had given me new hope for the future. Like most boys on the verge of leaving school I had worried a good deal about a career. I was ambitious, I knew what I wanted "to be," yet the circumstances of my life, although they enhanced this longing, did not offer much encouragement for its achievement.

At the Academy I had grown accustomed to finding myself at the top of my form and had passed through the hands of various masters who had prophesied in an impersonal sort of way that I should do well. There was Mr. Irwin, tall, thin, and affected, who suffered dreadfully from colds in his head and fostered in me the belief that I was good at English composition by reading approvingly to the class, in his nasal voice, my high-flown, flowery essays on such subjects as "A Battle at Sea" and "A Day in Spring." Then came Mr. Caldwell, known to the boys as "Pin" because of the short wooden peg which supported his withered leg. Meek and elderly, with gentle gestures and a small grey imperial, dressed always in clerical grey, he lived in the classics, and took me aside to tell me that, with application, I might be a Latinist. Others, equally well-meaning, had confused me with their conflicting advice.

Not until I fell into Jason's hands had I felt the warm touch of personal interest. He was the first to regard my interest in natural history as something more than a joke. How well I remember the beginning, that summer day when a pair of butterflies, common blues, flew through the open window into his classroom and we all stopped work to watch them.

"Why two?" Jason Reid asked the question idly of himself as well as the form.

A silence, then my modest voice was heard.

"Because they're mating, sir."

Jason's bulging, satiric gaze found me.

"Plate of porridge, are you suggesting that butterflies have a love life?"

"Oh, yes, sir. They can find their mate a mile away by a particular fragrance. It comes from their skin glands. It's like verbena."

"The plot thickens." Jason spoke slowly, not yet quite sure of me. "And how do they smell this delicious perfume, pray?"

"They have special knobs on the end of their antennae." I smiled, carried away by my interest. "Oh, that's nothing, sir. The Red Admiral actually tastes with its feet."

Loud shout of derision from the class. But Jason stilled them. "Quiet, clods. This dish of porridge knows something—which is more than can be said of others. Go on, Shannon. Don't our two blue friends here see each other—without the necessity for verbena?"

"Well, sir," I was blushing now, "the butterfly's eye is rather curious. It consists of about three thousand separate elements, each with a complete cornea, lens and retina. But although they have good discrimination of colours they're extremely short-sighted, a range of only about four feet . . ."

I broke off, and Reid did not press me, but at the end of the hour, as we filed out, he gave me a faint searching smile, the first time he ever smiled at me, murmuring under his breath:—

"And strange as it may seem . . . not a prig."

From then, while encouraging my biology, he began to take me far ahead of the form in physics; and a few months later set me off in the laboratory upon a line of original research on the permeability of colloids. No wonder I was devoted to him, listening open-mouthed to every word he said in class, with the doglike devotion of a lonely boy, and even, with a thoughtful frown, copying his lisp and slight stutter during my conversations with Gavin.

A year previously Gavin's father had moved him from the Academy to Larchfield College. It was a sad blow to me. Situated in the neighbouring town of Ardfillan, Larchfield was an exclusive and expensive boarding school, so select as to be almost unattainable to ordinary boys—its headmaster had been to Balliol and had actually captained a famous cricketing club at Lords! In spite of the popularity which he came quickly to enjoy in his new environment, Gavin remained loyal to me. On summer afternoons, when I borrowed Mr. Reid's bicycle and rode fifteen miles to watch him knock up a half-century for the school, he would detach himself from his flattering circle at the pavilion and come openly to the far side of the lovely playing fields where I, the lowly alien, lay hidden; fling himself in his blazer and white flannels beside me, chewing an end of grass, remarking through compressed lips: "What's been happening at home?" Nevertheless, although our friendship burned more brightly, although, when Gavin returned, we did everything together, there were long spells of separation when, rather than content myself with a second-rate companion, I fell back upon my own resources and indulged my morbid talent for solitude.

Alone, I roamed the countryside for miles around. I knew every nest, every crag, every sheeptrack on the Winton Hills. I fished the burns in spate, took dabs and pollack from the mudflats of the estuary. I made maps of the uncharted moorland which stretched, a wilderness of peat and heather, beyond the Windy Peak. All the keepers came to know me and to afford me that rare privilege, an unchallenged right of way. My collections grew. Some of my specimens were extremely rare. I had, for instance, splendid preparations of the proliferating hydra—the queer part-plant which liberates an egg—several unclassified forms of freshwater desmids, and that glorious dragonfly the *Pantala flavescens*, which, so far as I could ascertain, had never before been found in North Britain. Because of these wanderings I never missed the "holidays at the coast" which other boys looked forward to in summer—my imagination took me far beyond these tame resorts, turning the upper moorland into a wild stretch of pampas, or to the plains of Tartary over which I advanced cautiously, scanning the horizon for distant lamas . . . and sometimes, alas, for endangered missionaries.

Yes, one must admit the painful fact: I was, at this time, ardently devout. Perhaps my solitary hours had fostered this fervour. More probably it was because, like a horse pulling a load uphill, my peculiar nature strained harder in the face of difficulties. Every other day, at great inconvenience to myself, I served Canon Roche's Mass. On the friendliest terms with the Sisters, I swung the censer in the processions which wound, behind fluttering tapers, in the convent grounds. During Lent I performed prodigies of self-denial. I thanked the Almighty burningly, for having included me in the one true fold, and felt the deepest pity for all those unfortunate boys who had been born into false religions and who would, almost certainly, be lost. I shuddered to think that, but for the goodness of God, I might have come into the world as a Presbyterian or a Mohammedan, with only the thinnest chance of earning my eternal reward!

Although I shall not dwell upon them, my religious tribulations had not ceased and there were days in my calendar which I dreaded—less from physical fear than from the violence they inflicted on my spirit. Let us be honest. Levenford, like most Scottish towns, was a small Vesuvius of intolerance. The Protestants didn't like the Catholics, the Catholics were not fond of the Protestants, and both had little love for the Jews (who were mostly Poles, a small and inoffensive community congregated in the Vennel). On Saint Patrick's Day when shamrocks were sported defiantly and the Ancient Order of Hibernians paraded their banners down the High Street behind the green-sashed pipe band, the rivalry between blue and green erupted in unmentionable execrations and innumerable fights. Still more hectic was the Twelfth of July, and the massed procession of the Orange Lodges, Loyal Orders of the Great and Good King William, also with band and banners, led by a man with a tall hat and a gilt-fringed orange apron, riding a white horse and proclaiming: "Saved from popery, slavery, knavery!" while the crowd sang:—

> "Oh, dogs and dogs and a-holy dogs,
> And a-dogs and a-ho-oly wa-ter.
> King a-William slew the papish crew,
> At the Battle of-a Boyne-a Wa-ter."

The simple act of lifting my cap as I passed the Holy Angels Church usually brought upon me ridicule or contempt, but on these days of strife, the Twelfth especially, I was lucky if it did not involve me in a running fight.

But do not imagine that I mooned away my days between defending the Faith and chasing butterflies and saints in a beatific state. Papa saw to it that much of my spare time out of school was profitably occupied. Ever since I had attained employable proportions, he had hired me out in various useful directions, my present duty being to rise at six every morning to pedal Baxter's tricycle van round the empty streets, delivering fresh rolls to the half-awakened town. My small wages were received by him with the remark that they would ease the cost of my board and keep, and he would go on to tell Mama, with pale earnestness, that it was necessary to cut down further on expenses, although these had been pared to the vanishing point. Recently, indeed, Papa had taken the monthly bills into his own hands and he exasperated the tradesmen by exacting reductions or, when he set out to purchase articles for the household, by trying to knock a little off the price. When something "useful" was in question he was always anxious to buy, especially if it seemed a bargain; yet more often than not, in the end some instinct made him draw away from the purchase, bringing him back empty-handed, but, as he triumphantly declared, with the money still in his pocket. . . .

At this point an exclamation of triumph from my adversary brought back my errant thoughts. While I was dreaming Grandpa had whipped my last two men from the board.

"I knew I had you," he crowed. "You that's supposed to be the cleverest boy in the town!"

I rose quickly, so that he might not see, and so misunderstand, the look of joy springing to my eyes.

CHAPTER TWO

STILL restless and excited, I ran downstairs. I was free until eight o'clock in the evening, when I had a special and unbreakable engagement. I thought of calming myself by going to the bioscope matinee, but I had not a farthing in my pocket, or rather in Murdoch's pocket, for I had reached the size when I could wear his old suits, cast off long ago and faithfully preserved amidst camphor in the attic "kist."

I went into the scullery where Mama was damping clothes at the boiler and laying them on the ironing board, her hair and eyes more faded now, face thinner and more tiredly lined, yet still gentle, and enduring. I stood gazing at her with tremendous meaning, almost with a catch in my breath.

"You wait, Mama," I said softly. "Yes, just wait."

She gave me her queer, frowning smile.

"Wait for what?" she asked, after she had tested the hot iron near her cheek.

"Well," I said, lamely, yet with intensity. "One of these days I'll be able to do something for you . . . something big."

"Will you do something for me now? Something small. Take a note over to Kate's?"

"Oh, of course, Mama."

I often carried missives for Mama, and so saved the postage stamp, across the town to Kate, at Barloan Toll, or to Murdoch, who was now solidly established with Mr. Dalrymple at the Nursery, doing extremely well and, to his evident satisfaction, emancipated from Lomond View. These letters were a part of Mama, communications of the spirit, containing news, messages, exhortations, even requests—sent out, in patient persistence, in her unflagging effort to hold the family together.

I waited till her iron was cold. Then she entered the kitchen and brought back a sealed envelope.

"Here you are then. I wish I could send a batch of pancakes with you. But . . ." She removed the lid from the earthenware crock and peered into it in a troubled fashion. "I seem to be out of flour. Give them my love, though."

I went out and along Drumbuck Road, crossed the Common and turned left, skirting the great black shape of the Boilerworks—partly stilled by the impending holiday, yet still glowing in its depths, still alive and menacing.

Kate's house was one of the small new cottages built on a round green knoll near the old Toll-gate, on the western outskirts of the town. And as I came up the hill I suddenly discerned Kate as she came along a level side-street, pushing the perambulator before her. It was a fine navy-blue perambulator and Kate loved to push it. She walked miles with it every week, I am sure, through the town, into the shops, round the Knoxhill Park, pausing, proudly, to stoop and straighten the navy-blue cover with the white N embroidered on the corner.

I stopped to watch, smiling in sympathy, as she came along, quite unaware of me, her figure a little stouter now, bending over as she walked, smiling, clicking her tongue, her eyes intent upon the baby.

"Hello, Kate," I murmured shyly, when she had almost passed me.

"Why, *Robie*." Her tone was warm with welcome. "You poor boy. And me never looking the road you were on. It's baby. Robie, you would not believe it, he is cutting his second tooth, and with never a whimper, just as good as gold . . ." She bent again. "The pet, the precious, the mother's lamb . . ."

Ah Kate, dear Kate, you are happy with your incomparable child. And to think that, once, they prescribed for you the mandolin!

Kate's home was bright and neat, with the modern convenience of hot and cold running water, and the sharp smell of paint and polish indicating how houseproud she had become. Her marriage was a success despite the forebodings of Papa who, rent by the loss of her salary, had declared that she was throwing herself, and her career, away. When she had laid the baby in his cot she put a pan on the "main" gas stove and soon the delicious fragrance of frying steak and onions came upon the air.

"You'll wait and have a bite with us," she insisted, turning the steak expertly with a knife, and holding her head away to avoid the spark of the fat. "Jamie's upstairs in the bath. He's been on overtime lately or I'm sure he'd have wanted to take you to the football match." What sublime tact from the once churlish Kate! "He won't be a minute. You must be famished." She gave me a quick look as she said that, but looked away with equal quickness.

Jamie came down well-washed, his hair wetly plastered, and wearing, complacently, an outrageous red tartan tie.

"It's yourself, boy." That, and his little nod, had more warmth and more welcome in them, for a sensitive heart, than all the protestations in the world.

We sat down to supper at once. The steak, of which Kate gave me a very large portion, was tender and juicy, its rich substance permeated me like a transfusion. Jamie kept heaping my plate with the crisp frizzled onions. There was thick hot buttered toast and strong, scalding tea.

I think Kate and Jamie knew perfectly how poor and limited the food had become at home. Jamie, in particular, pressed me repeatedly and when I could eat no more he fixed on me a reproachful eye.

"It's there, boy," he said, simply.

All my childhood at Lomond View was dominated by a monstrous law: the necessity for saving money, even at the sacrifice of the very necessities of life. Ah, if only we could have done without money, without this Northern thrift which preferred money in the bank to a good meal in the stomach, which put gentility before generosity, this cursed penuriousness which blighted us.

When this money question bewildered and tormented me, I thought of Jamie Nigg. Jamie was never well off; yet whether he spent it upon a good steak, or on taking a forgotten boy to a football game, Jamie always got good use of his hard-won money and, what was better, he made all the money that he touched seem clean.

As we each drank one last cup of tea Jamie began to rally me, for I am sure he regarded my shy and gawky melancholy not only with compassion, but also with concern. Sensing the suppressed excitement of my mood, he remarked gravely to Kate:—

"The professor has something on his mind. These quiet clever ones . . . they're the worst."

Kate nodded, then gave me a sideways smile that advised me not to take him too seriously.

"They're deep," Jamie said. "Up to all sorts of devilments. Especially when they're good jumpers."

This delicate reference to my success in the recent Academy sports, when I had won the open high jump, gave me an inward glow and although I lowered my eyes I had again to admit to myself that it was a school record, inch and a quarter above the previous best. But that glow was nothing to the incandescence lit within me when Jamie added in a measured voice: "Of course, if you want my opinion, he's in love."

Ah, the pure white flame of pride, the deep and secret realization of this truth. With eyes still lowered I cherished the warm flush of happiness that bathed my heart.

"What's been happening at home then?" Kate asked, curbing Jamie's humour.

I hurriedly produced and gave to her Mama's letter.

"I'm sorry I forgot about this."

Kate opened the letter and read it through twice, and to my surprise her face darkened and her forehead bumps, which I had imagined gone for ever, filled up angrily. She handed the letter to Jamie, who read it in silence.

"It really is too bad. This thing of Papa's is getting to be a disease." Kate made an effort to free herself from what seemed a highly disagreeable thought. Jamie was glancing at me in a queer sort of way. There was an awkward pause.

Just then the baby woke up and Kate, seeming to welcome the interruption, gave him his bottle on her knee. For an instant, as a sign of their regard, I was allowed to take this priceless burden in my arms.

"He likes you," Kate said encouragingly. "Wait till you have one of your own, man."

I smiled, uncertainly. Terrible paradox: I was in love, but how could I reveal to her that I was morally convinced, from certain unspeakable nocturnal experiences, that I was doomed never to be able to have children?

When the baby was restored to his cot I said that it was time for me to go.

Kate saw me to the door. Now that we were alone she was again examining me intently.

"Mama didn't tell you what was in her letter?"

"No, Kate." I smiled up at her. "As a matter of fact, I'm rather taken up with some news of my own."

"Good or bad?" she inquired, with her head to one side.

"Oh, good, Kate . . . extremely good, I think . . . You see, Kate . . ." I broke off, flushing darkly, staring out at the mysterious night, spangled with misty lights, hearing the far-off whistling of a train, followed, like an echo, by the thrilling sound of a ship's foghorn from the river.

"It's all right, Robie." Now Kate was shaking her head and smiling, almost against her will. "You keep your news and I'll keep mine."

I pressed her hand and, unable to contain myself, started running at full speed down the road. Much as I liked Kate, she could not be the first to know. Again, from the unseen river, there came the slow sounding of that outward ship, making me shiver in sheer delight.

CHAPTER THREE

QUICKLY, my heart lifting at every step, I returned to Drumbuck Road; then, with a sudden quickening of my pulse, entered Sinclair Drive, a narrow street shaded by young lindens which, lightly shedding their twirling flowers, had spread a yellow carpet upon the pavement. Although there seemed nothing new in this familiar thoroughfare which in my childhood had never deeply stirred me, although its rambling old houses wore the same undisturbed air of having seen better days, now . . . ah, now its mysterious and exquisite name was engraved upon my heart. It was almost eight o'clock when my unworthy feet fell again upon the soft strewn linden flowers of that beloved drive and my blood pounded as I saw a light behind the drawn blind of the front room window of the end house. Even as I drew up, I heard the sound of Alison singing.

It was the hour of her practising: she had begun seriously to develop that talent which was widely spoken of in the town. Tonight, she had finished her scales and exercises, those clear true notes, not woven into melody, yet enchanting of their own accord, like the flutings of a bird. Now, while her mother accompanied her on the piano, she was singing "Lament for Flodden," one of those simple Scottish songs which seemed to me difficult to surpass.

> "I've heard them lilting at our ewe-milking,
> Lassies a' lilting before dawn o'day;
> But now they are moaning on ilka green loaming—
> The Flowers of the Forest are a' wede away."

A crystal bell pealed into the night, so true, so sweet, I held my breath. I shut my eyes and saw the singer, not the child whom I had often played with, but a tall, grown girl, who no longer flung her limbs about, but walked quietly, with restraint, as though conscious of a new dignity budding within her. I saw her as, on that astounding day six months ago, she came out of the cloakroom and along the school corridor with some other girls, wearing her short navy-blue drill costume, straps crossed over her white blouse, long firm legs in black stockings, speckled black gym shoes on her feet. How often had I passed her like this, with no more than a briskly casual nod. But, suddenly, as I politely stood against the wall to make way for the advancing group, Alison, still talking to her companions, raised her hand to her brown hair which clustered about her slender neck, moulding by this unconscious gesture her young breasts, and at the same time, as she brushed by, her skin warm with her recent exercise, giving me from her dark brown eyes a friendly, melting smile. Dear God, what had happened to me, all in an instant, at the hands of this heavenly creature whom I had so far practically ignored? Waves of intoxicating warmth surged through me as I leaned, bewildered yet entranced, against the wall in the empty corridor, long after she had gone. Oh, Alison, Alison of the quiet brown eyes, and the white, pure, swelling throat, I am caught up in that same rapture as I stand now, hidden by the night, and the deeper shadow of the linden tree, listening, until the last note wings, tremulous, towards the skies.

When there was silence I gathered myself and pushed through the iron gate. The garden was large, surrounded by a high wall and shaded by thick trees, with wide lawns spreading out from the drive, and rhododendron shrubberies which were straggling, somewhat overgrown. Although Alison's mother had been left comfortably off she was not wealthy, and the property was not maintained with the prim propriety of the villas in Drumbuck Road. On the front doorstep I rang the bell, and a moment later I was admitted by Janet, the elderly maid who had been with Mrs. Keith for over ten years and who always regarded me with that air of distrust peculiar to old and favoured servants, but which I then felt to be directed specially against myself. She showed me into the front room where Alison had already spread her books out on the table while Mrs. Keith, seated in a low chair by the fire, was busy with some crochet work contained in a green linen bag upon her lap.

What a bright and charming room it was, quite dazzling after the darkness—the walls light-coloured, hung with white framed water colours done by Mrs. Keith, white muslin curtains draping the drawn blinds. Two bowls of blue hyacinths perfumed the air; a fringed silk shawl hung over the open piano; the furniture was chintz-covered. In the firelight a brass Benares stand glinted beneath its load of bric-a-brac, mostly ivories, brought home from India by Captain Keith. A procession of white elephants, growing in size, marched steadily across the mantelpiece.

"You're punctual, as usual, Robert." Mrs. Keith, while I stood blinking, was endeavouring to put me at ease. "What sort of night is it?"

"Oh, very nice, Mrs. Keith," I stammered. "Misty. But you can see the stars."

She smiled as I drew up a chair beside Alison at the table. "You will always see the stars, Robert. In fact, you are a regular star-gazer."

That lenient smile lingered on her kind, sallow, slightly ironic face; I felt her watching me as I began, confusedly, to work with Alison.

Mrs. Keith was thin and rather tall, in her middle thirties, dressed simply, yet with an air of breeding and good taste. She came from a prominent county family but after the death of her husband she had gone out very little, giving herself up to her daughter's education, content with her music and the friendship of a few intimates, amongst whom were Miss Julia Blair, Mrs. Marshall—mother of Louisa, that tormentor of my childhood—and my form master, Jason Reid. Her retirement was perhaps encouraged by the fact that her health was poor—often I had the odd impression that, under her graciousness, she was suffering from headache. Yet, mainly I think for Alison's sake, she concealed her invalidism or, with a light shrug of her shoulders, gently mocked at it. Her devotion to her daughter was extreme, she was proud of Alison's talent and bent upon developing it, but since she was a clever woman with a clear sense of judgment, she seemed to realize the dangers of indulging her possessiveness. She urged Alison to have "suitable" friends of her own age, and from the beginning, after a penetrating scrutiny which ended, I must confess, in a twitch of suppressed amusement, she had encouraged me to come about the house. In my early childhood I had arrived periodically, rather overawed, burdened by the sorrows of timidity, to play staid and boring games with little Alison. On the sunny lawn, while the thin note of the piano came from the open window, or a carriage rolled up the drive bearing Mrs. Marshall to "take tea" with Alison's mother, we held a picnic for her dolls, or fed the goldfish. If it were showery we went indoors where Janet suspiciously gave us bread and butter spread with chocolate seeds and, seated at the table, the rain drumming on the panes, we engaged in a contest known as "Questions and Answers," played with small round cards which bore ridiculous queries like, "Is backgammon an old game?" and the equally preposterous response, "Yes, it was played by the Ancient Druids." Occasionally Louisa was present at these junketings, winning all the games, withering me with her scorn. Then, as we grew older, Alison and I "did our homework" together. She, a practical person, was weak in mathematics; while I, absurdly fanciful, was good at them. And Mrs. Keith, anxious that Alison should take her Intermediate Certificate, without which she could not enter the College of Music at Winton, had recently suggested that I should come in, regularly, to coach Alison in this subject.

"What are you giving my backward and wayward daughter tonight, Robert?" Mrs. Keith spoke with affectionate irony, her eyes on her work.

"Euclid, Mrs. Keith," I answered awkwardly. "The sum of the squares of the sides of a right-angled triangle . . . you know . . ."

"I don't know, Robert, but I'm sure you do." She did not smile, still trying to help me over my terrible self-consciousness. She was always helping me, without seeming to do so, giving me ideas which I could not find in the book on etiquette which I had procured from the Public Library for the special purpose of improving my behaviour.

"It does seem silly that I should have to learn this, Mother," Alison remarked tranquilly. "It's all so made-up."

"Oh, no, Alison," I said quickly. "It's really very logical. Once you admit that a straight line is the shortest distance between two points all of the thirteen books of Euclid follow automatically."

"I believe you will write a fourteenth book yourself, one day, Robert," Mrs. Keith said. "Or worse—a Life History of Beetles."

"He will, Mother," Alison exclaimed accusingly. "Do you know, in Mr. Reid's class last week he actually proved that an answer in the algebra book was wrong."

While they both smiled I lowered my head in pride and shyness, grateful to Alison for having brought this up, resuming my explanation of the theorem in a low and husky voice.

Seated close beside her, so that our knees touched under the table, I was conscious of a sweetness that made my heart faint. When our hands came in contact on the page of the book an exquisite thrill passed through me. Her rather untidy hair, which lay upon her shoulders and which, from time to time, she shook impatiently, seemed to me something wonderful and holy. I stole quick glances at her fresh cheeks, noticing the moistness of her lower lip as with a puzzled frown she sucked her pencil. I did not, could not, even contemplate the word "love." I hoped that, perhaps, she liked me. I felt that I was living, talking, smiling in a dream.

The hour passed with unbelievable rapidity. It was almost nine. Already Mrs. Keith had stifled a yawn and I had detected her looking at the clock. I did not dare to speak aloud or even whisper to Alison what was in my mind. Suddenly, with a shaking hand, I took a scrap of paper and wrote:—

"Alison, I want to see you. Will you come to the door with me tonight?"

A look of surprise came into Alison's eyes as she read the message. Taking her pencil she wrote:—

"What for?"

Trembling in all my limbs I wrote back:—

"I have something to tell you."

A pause, then Alison gave me her clear frank smile and firmly inscribed the words:—

"Very well."

A shiver of joy passed through me. Fearful that Mrs. Keith should see me, the betrayer of her trust, I took the piece of paper, folded it tight, thrust it in my mouth and swallowed it. At that moment Janet brought in a tray of milk and cracknel biscuits—positive indication that the geometry lesson was over.

Ten minutes later I stood up and said good night to Mrs. Keith. Faithful to her promise Alison accompanied me to the front porch.

"It *is* a nice night." She viewed the dewy night with a calm, untroubled gaze. "I'll come with you to the gate."

As we went down the drive I walked slowly to prolong the warm and choking rapture of being near her. Holding herself erect, Alison looked straight ahead. As we passed a dark yet familiar bush she plucked and crushed a leaf—the smell of flowering currant filled the air.

My brain was swimming, the world wavering before me. With a terrible effort I commanded my disordered breathing.

"I heard you singing tonight, Alison."

The banality of that quavering remark, which brutally parodied my pure yet destroying passion, which, in fact, horrified me the instant it was spoken, seemed lost upon her.

"Yes, I've begun to work in earnest. Miss Cramb has just started me on Schubert's songs. They are simply beautiful."

Schubert's songs: vision of the Rhine, the castles on its banks, Alison and I floating down, beneath arched bridges, on a little river steamer, disembarking at an old inn, a garden with little tables . . . Did I tell her all this? No. I croaked—in my "breaking" voice: "You are getting on terribly well, Alison."

She smiled deprecatingly, dwelling on the vagaries of her music mistress, who was, in fact, an exacting and acidulous spinster. "Miss Cramb is hard to please!"

Silence again. We had reached the gate, that point at which I must leave her. I saw her steal an inquiring glance at me. A weakness was now all over my body, a tremulous warmth was flowing about my heart. I drew a sharp quivering breath. It was the supreme moment of dedication, that moment when knighthood comes to flower.

"Alison . . . I don't suppose it matters to you . . . but today something happened to me . . . Mr. Reid told me I might sit the Marshall."

"Robie!"

In her surprise and interest she used, earnestly, my name. With hands clenched, my pale cheeks burning, I saw that she had not failed to appreciate the full significance of the secret which I had at last divulged.

The Marshall was, of course, a tremendous thing, of which the name must never, never be taken in vain. It was a scholarship to the College of Winton, founded by Sir John Marshall a century ago, open to the entire county of Winton and of tremendous monetary value—one hundred pounds per annum for five years. It stood as an expression of the passionate Scottish desire for advancement, for education, the determination to give the poor "lad of parts" his chance. Great men had first displayed their greatness by winning this prize—once, when a famous statesman died, a man from Winton whose name was echoed with respect across the seas to the corners of the world, the highest tribute paid to him was that single grave reflection by one who had been his contemporary at the Academy: "Aye . . . I mind the day he carried off the Marshall."

"I'll never win it," I said in a low voice. "But I wanted you to be the first to know I'm going to try."

"I think you have a splendid chance," Alison said generously. "It will make a tremendous difference to you if you win?"

"Yes," I answered. "All the difference in the world."

I gazed at her blindly. Lyrical words lay behind my tongue. But I could not speak them. Growing flustered, I shifted my weight from one foot to another.

"I hope it keeps up over the holiday," I said.

"Oh, I hope so," Alison answered.

"On Monday I'm going on the Loch with Gavin."

"Oh, are you?"

There was a throbbing pause.

"Good night then, Alison."

"Good night, Robie."

We parted stiffly, abruptly. As usual, I had bungled everything. Yet, as I hurried along Drumbuck Road, I felt the world still a splendid place, still rich in splendid promise.

CHAPTER FOUR

THAT sweet parting should have been the ending of my day. But alas, there remained the strange and tortuous process of getting to my bed. And tonight was my "night of the Lion's Bridge." Although unusual emotion had tired me I forced myself relentlessly past Lomond View and on to the dark country road leading to the bridge, two miles away. Have we not studied Grandma in her method of retirement? Why, therefore, should we spare this boy, this Robert Shannon, since our purpose is to reveal him truthfully, to expose him in all his dreams, strivings and follies, with as dispassionate, as merciless, a blade as that with which he dissected poor *Rana temporaria*, the frog?

The evening had turned more chill and unfriendly. When I reached the bridge, damp clouds dulled the half-moon, a gusty wind was troubling the young leaves. Tightly buttoning my jacket, Murdoch's jacket, I advanced. The bridge was an old bridge, spanning the River Leven as it poured down from the hills, bound by a narrow stone coping built out above the torrent in three semicircular bays. At each end of the coping was a masoned gargoyle, weather-worn and mutilated, yet still discernible as a grinning lion's face.

Completely alone, I climbed on to the high coping; then, with a sharp intake of breath, began to work my way across the narrow parapet of the bridge. Far below, as I edged along, I heard the unseen tumbling of the waters. The bays were the worst. There, I seemed poised on a high dark precipice while the coping, the bridge, the whole world swayed and spun about me.

I had no head for heights; the ordeal was the most frightening I could devise. But at last I had done it—across and back. Returned to the solid road, I leaned faintly, with shut eyes, against the figure of the grinning lion. No wonder the king of beasts was amused at my distress. Madness, yes, madness . . . Yet when one is poor and despised, when one trembles and blushes at a sudden laugh from passing strangers, when one has the nervous affliction of moving one's scalp and ears, it is necessary, ah, yes, it is most necessary, to prove, only to oneself, that one is not a coward.

I went home at least partially appeased. The house was in darkness—now not even a peep of gas was permitted in the lobby. I tiptoed up the stairs to the bathroom, bolted the door silently; and with great caution, since Papa would not permit the waste of a single drop of water, I ran a cold bath.

The water was frigid, even to my fingers, yet when I had removed my clothes I lay in it, motionless, with my teeth clenched, until my body was numb and senseless. This was no proof of valour but a precaution, one might say a prayer, against that wretchedness which might overtake one in the night.

I crept upstairs. I was now occupying Murdoch's old room—during the few winter weeks when Murdoch slept at home he used the larger, better, room which once was Kate's. Icy cold, almost disembodied, I lit the end of tallow candle in the enamel candlestick. Around me, shadowy as myself, were my school prizes, worthless books in pretentious bindings—there were at least three copies of Porter's *Scottish Chiefs*—also my precious microscope and natural history collections, contained in cardboard boxes, cases I had made, all of which had cost nothing. Writing materials stood on the top of the chest of drawers and another book, borrowed from the public library, entitled *The Cure of Self-Consciousness*.

Taking up this volume I opened it at Exercise Ten.

"Place yourself calmly before a looking-glass," I read. "Fold your arms and gaze at your reflection steadily. Then, narrowing your eyes, give yourself a fearless stare. You are strong, composed, cool." Without question I was cool. "Next, take a deep breath, exhale firmly and repeat three times, in a low yet potent voice, 'Julius Caesar and Napoleon! I will! I will! I will!!!'"

I obeyed the instructions implicitly—although my eyes watered and their green hue disheartened me a little. I even took a torn-out sheet of exercise book, printed in bold letters the words "I WILL" and pinned it on the wall where it would meet my fearless stare whenever I awoke. Then I knelt down by the bed.

My prayers were long and complicated, strainingly kept free from all distractions, not directed towards the vague bearded God of my early childhood, but centred ardently upon the Saviour. Occasionally I would guiltily remember the Father and the Holy Ghost and hasten to placate them. But

Jesus, in His infinite love and goodness, was the Custodian of my trusting heart. And when I thought of His Mother, whose face had lately grown suspiciously like Alison's face, tears of yearning welled from my closed eyes. Nor were the Saints forgotten. I was continually running up against new Saints I wanted to pray to; and of course once I had started I could not leave them out for fear of offending them. The newest figure in my growing calendar was Anthony, protector of youth.

The final act is at hand: opportunity for that laugh, that sudden unwanted laugh which one hears often in the theatre at a moment when the author has meant to convey something of quiet pathos, of truth, and has failed or perhaps been misunderstood. Let us laugh together, then, as, looking back, we see this lanky shivering boy, this simpleton barely purified by the ordeal of the bridge and the icy bath, take from a hiding place at the back of the drawer a strange instrument, a piece of rope to which are tied bits of old iron, two heavy door keys, a door handle, a broken piece of skate. Quickly, with the familiarity of custom, he ties this about his waist in such a manner that the disturbing metal bears upon his spine. Thus, if he lies upon his back, the position in which one dreams, he will at once awaken. At last he is beneath the patched sheet, curled stiffly upon his side. He has blown out the candle. He is girded like an anchorite and round his scraggy neck he wears a rosary, four authentic miraculous medals, one blessed by the Holy Father himself, also the brown scapulars and the blue scapulars—if there were pink or heliotrope scapulars he would certainly wear these too. He has done everything he can. Comforted by this thought, he invites the little death of sleep, with one final aspiration.

"Dear Lord . . . please let me win the Marshall."

CHAPTER FIVE

MORNING comes early and joyfully upon a holiday. On Monday, before the white sky showed its first signs of brightening, I was out of the house quietly, and waiting at the Levenford Cross for Tom Drin, who was to drop me off at Luss on his lochside delivery round.

Tom was late and in a bad humour. He should not have had to work today —even I was exempt from my obligations with the rolls—but they were very short-handed at the Blair warehouse. I climbed into the flat, open van amongst the bags of meal and we set off behind the quiet clop-clopping of the horse.

The empty cobbled streets were fresh with morning. A woman taking in milk, a man in his shirt twitching the blind of an upper window, a girl sleepily banging a bass mat at a half-open door—all this conveyed a shining sense of expedition. I was going fishing with Gavin; my last fling before I settled down to grind for the Marshall.

The sun rose but did not break through. It was one of those still silvery days, full of warmth and soft luminous light, when sounds, though muted, are heard from afar and the intervening silences are filled with the rushing of the sap in the green leaves. As the horse's back rose and fell gently, like a ship, between the shafts, the countryside slipped past—misted woods, glimpses of park land, a grey mansion with tall chimneys, terraces and glass-houses, amongst the steaming trees.

At the back doors of these big country houses I helped Tom to unload the sacks and forage. He was a shaggy, muddling sort of man and was several times hard put to propitiate an angry groom complaining that his "order" had been imperfectly executed. Once, as we lifted a heavy box, we found that the hundredweight bag of meal underneath had burst and discharged its con-tents through the floorboards of the van. Tom cursed, scratched his head, then said to me with an air of smoothing things over: "Never mind, never mind. It'll not be missed!"

When we jogged into Luss it was afternoon, and Gavin was seated, yet without impatience, on the milestone at the head of the short village street. He wore the restrained outfit of his exclusive school, grey flannel trousers and shirt, a shapeless cricketing hat of the same grey, relieved, or, rather, exalted by a thin band of blue and white, the Larchfield colours. Impossible to con-vey the distinction of this waiting figure—grown, like myself, yet still slight— the restrained unconscious pride of that face, already sunburned, beneath the careless, pulled-down hat. At least I can record the silent joy of our terrible handclasp.

"No fishing until evening, I'm afraid," Gavin murmured, as the van lumbered off. "No wind and too bright."

We walked through the quiet lochside village, passing between a score of cottages, all low, straw-thatched and whitewashed, spaced on the short white road which began at the green hill foot and ended at the silver Loch. Fuchsias and rambler roses grew up the cottages, losing themselves in the yellow thatch. The fuchsias were already in flower, dripping a crimson shower against the whitewashed walls. A brown collie dog lay stretched out, dream-ing in the white dust. There came a sweet hum of bees. Through the haze we could see the toy wooden pier with row-boats moored by bleached ropes. At such beauty, we exchanged our rare, our secret glance.

Until the hidden sun went down, Gavin and I sat on an up-turned boat, outside his father's fishing hut, sorting out tackle, practising that economy of words to which we were pledged. At seven o'clock, after Mrs. Glen, the woman of the cottage, had given us a fine tea of fresh baked scones and boiled new-laid eggs washed down with creamy milk, we righted the boat, pushed it into the water. It was still too early, but the mauve shimmer on the Loch was giving promise of the dusk. I took the oars, pulling out to the still coolness, then stopped rowing, letting the boat drift out, far out upon the calm between the high hills. As the light faded the mauve deepened to dark purple, our faces grew indistinct, then from the disappearing shore came the slow sound of the bagpipes, like the far voice of a man who has lost everything except his soul. I felt Gavin grow rigid in the boat with an anguish of feeling. Nothing was proof against this moment and that sound, not even our stoic vows. Hidden by the growing darkness, suddenly, and in a low voice, Gavin spoke.

"I understand you are sitting the Marshall, Robie?"

I started, quite taken aback. "Yes. . . . How did you know?"

"Mrs. Keith told my sister." Gavin paused, rather heavily. "I am trying for it too."

I gazed at him dumbly; even the mountains seemed to share my shocked confusion.

"But Gavin . . . you don't need the Bursary!"

His frown was palpable in the darkness.

"You'd be surprised." He spoke slowly, with deep embarrassment. "My father has been worried in the business lately. When you buy in bulk—corn and oats, for instance—sometimes you have to take a heavy loss. It isn't as easy as some people think. . . . I mean these people who envy my father and run him down for keeping up what they call too much style." He paused. "My father doesn't like display, Robie. But he has his position to keep up as Provost." A longer pause. "He's done so much for me . . . now that he's so worried I would like to do something for him."

I was silent. I had known for a long time that Gavin worshipped his father; and I had heard whispers that all was not well with the Provost's business. Yet the knowledge that we must oppose each other for the prize on which I had set my heart came as an unexpected blow. Before I could speak he went on.

"With all the cleverest boys in the county competing, one more won't make much difference. Besides, there's the honour of the town. Do you know, it's twelve years since a Levenford boy took the Bursary." He drew a fierce breath of resolution. "One of us must win it."

"You may be the one, Gavin," I said, in a strained voice, only too well aware that he was a fine scholar.

We did not now engage upon those passionate repudiations which had been a feature of our younger days. Gavin replied broodingly: "I admit I would like to win for my father's sake. But I think you have a better chance . . . it's hard for me to say that, for I'm proud . . . I suppose it's my Highland blood . . . and having so wonderful a father." He paused. "If you win, will you go on to be a doctor? . . . Or"—he lowered his voice as though he might be overheard—"do you still want to be a priest?"

Not yet recovered from the shock of his earlier communication, I nevertheless received the question with dignity. Gavin was the only person on earth before whom I would reveal myself.

"I don't think I'm good enough to be a priest," I said. "And I must admit my whole heart is set on being a medical biologist, you know, a doctor who does research. Of course when I think of Father Damien and the Curé d'Ars, especially during benediction, I want to give up everything, even falling in love with some good and beautiful girl." A wave of renunciation swept over me. "Yes, then I simply long to go away and try to be a really great saint, eating mouldy potatoes, treating money like dross—that especially would be wonderful—and living in a rough habit and a kind of trance before the altar. I wish I could make you understand what it means, Gavin, when, at benediction, we have our exposition."

"I have an idea," Gavin murmured, rather shamefaced. "Of course . . . it would be awful for you if it wasn't what you thought." He added: "I mean, if after all it was only bread."

"Yes," I agreed. "It would be awful. But by praying you can keep that thought out of your head. Prayer is really wonderful, Gavin. You can't imagine the things I've got by praying for them. And I could give you hundreds, well, dozens of other cases. You know Mrs. Rourke who keeps the dairy shop. Well, Papa was going to prosecute her for selling deficient milk. I saw her praying and praying in church. And do you know, Gavin, the milk bottle that Papa had taken the sample in burst. Yes, burst completely during the test. And it was the only time this had ever happened to Papa in all his experience." I got my breath again. "Of course one mustn't pray for unworthy intentions. Although they say that Madame de Pompadour's emerald eyes were lovely, you know I loathe the colour of mine; but one wouldn't pray to have that changed, at least, not overnight."

"Will you pray to win the Marshall?" Gavin asked rather stiffly.

"Yes . . . I'm afraid I shall, Gavin." I hung my head, then added, with a rush of generous enthusiasm: "But if I'm not to be allowed to win I'll pray that you do. You're so decent, Gavin, not like most people in the town, even some of my relatives . . . You know how they look down on Catholics. Isn't it absurd? Why, only the other day Canon Roche showed me in the almanac that all over the world there are thirty-two Catholic dukes, just think of it, thirty-two dukes . . . and all that one hears in Levenford is . . . Well, never mind. But that's why I'd like to succeed, just to show them"—a dramatic note entered my voice—"that someone who is despised could be great . . . could become a wonderful scientist . . . a kind of Saviour of humanity . . . perhaps reconcile science and religion . . . perhaps reconcile all the religions."

Overcome by my own stupendous conception, I was silent.

"Yes," Gavin said slowly. "It's pretty rotten that we've got to fight each other over the Bursary. Nothing will interfere with our friendship of course. But we must take and give no quarter." He smiled palely. "I know some prayers, too. . . ."

Out of the soft darkness the moon began to show behind the Ben, then softly it fell upon the waters, streaking the liquid blackness with a constant play of light. We had drifted inshore and there the trees stood darkly still, like plumes raised for the funeral of a god. No, they were simply trees . . . trees growing in a silent splendid land, bathed in the first twilight of creation.

Suddenly a fish jumped, unseen, in the inky shallows and, in a flash, a new mood was thrust upon us. I saw Gavin dimly, reaching for his rod, heard him whisper: "There's one at last."

I brought the boat gently along the bank, dipping my blades noiselessly. I held my breath as Gavin began to cast, sitting in the stern, motionless, except for the slow rhythmic sweep of his right forearm. Now and then I caught the gleam of the rod, the shimmer of the wet line as it cut the darkness in a silver arc and fell silently, distantly upon the water.

Suddenly there was another splash, louder than the first; and with a start of excitement, I saw Gavin's rod-tip bend like a drawn bow, felt the quivering vibration of his hands as they clasped the butt. As the reel whirred into the silence, from between his teeth Gavin said: "Keep us away, Robie. Don't let him under the boat."

The fish was now leaping, dashing madly in the liquid blackness, sending up jewels of spray when he broke the surface. Backing from the point of Gavin's throbbing rod, I did my best to keep him from beneath our keel. There was no need of silence now. My oars splashed as wildly as the splashing fish. As he started each rush I dug my blades frantically.

"Well done," Gavin panted. "He's a salmon. And a good one." A moment later, "Ship the oars."

The struggle was tearing the arms from his body, yet, though he well knew the thinness of the thread which bound him to the fish, he dared not yield an inch.

Slowly, carefully, he began to wind his reel. The moon picked out his taut figure, his resolute young face, upon which I burningly fixed my eyes, waiting for his next command.

The salmon was rushing less, Gavin was bringing him nearer.

"I see him," Gavin said in a low, husky voice. "A fresh-run fish. Get the gaff. Under this seat."

I crouched down and stretched my arm for the gaff, but as I fumblingly leaned over, my foot slipped on the wet thwarts, I fell full length across the seat, skinning my shins, almost upsetting the boat.

Not a word from Gavin, not a single reproach for my clumsiness. Only, when I had recovered myself and the rocking boat was still: "Have you got it?"

"Yes, Gavin."

A pause. Still quietly, yet with a growing urgency, Gavin whispered: "He's lightly hooked. I see the fly outside his mouth. We'll have just one chance with him. Take your gaff, and when I bring him up, don't stab at him, just slide the point under his gills."

I took the gaff with a surge of anxiety, kneeling in the well of the boat. Now I saw the salmon, deep, wide and gleaming, of a size which startled me. I had never gaffed so large a fish in my life. Gaffing was a treacherous business. Gavin, who gaffed for his father, had often told me how many salmon had been lost in this last difficult act. I began to shake, my eyes blinked. My ears, too, started their horrible twitch.

The fish was near . . . nearer . . . near enough to touch. I had a rush of panic, a frightful impulse to impale this great slippery creature with my lance. But no, pale as death, shivering with ague, I waited till Gavin turned him over, then I slipped the gaff under his jaw and brought him quietly over the gunwale. Now Gavin crouched beside me. The moon, riding serene and high in the night sky, showed two boys, near to each other, peering in silent rapture at the noble fish, curving and glimmering, in the bottom of the boat.

Yet, gazing at the defeated salmon, I felt, suddenly, a sad constriction of my heart. I thought:—

"Gavin and I . . . One of us must be defeated."

CHAPTER SIX

Next morning we slept late in our bunks at the fishing bothy, and when Mrs. Glen had given us breakfast Gavin took his father's hunting knife and in the bright sunshine outside the cottage divided the salmon cleanly in two. The firm pink flesh, with a darker core and a backbone like a pearl button, showed the fish to be in perfect condition.

"We'll toss," Gavin said. "That's the fair way. I'd say there was six pounds in each piece. But the tail-half is the best."

He spun a sixpence and I guessed right.

Gavin smiled generously. "Remember: Boil for only twenty minutes. It makes grand eating that way."

We wrapped our pieces in green rushes and placed them in the basket carrier of Gavin's bicycle. Then we said good-bye to Mrs. Glen and arranged ourselves on the bicycle—Gavin on the pedals, I perched on the "backstep" of the machine. We took turns in pedalling, dividing our labour as we had divided the fish, all the way to Levenford.

It was the dinner hour when I got to Lomond View. Papa and Mama were seated at the table as I entered the kitchen, aware that I had played truant, yet conscious of my peace offering, this precious half-salmon which would surely "do us," in Mama's phrase, for several days at least.

"Where have you been?" Sunk a little in his chair, Papa spoke in the contained, rather bloodless fashion now habitual with him and which seemed to date from that morning, months ago, when with a strange air he refused his boiled egg at breakfast, remarking steadily to Mama: "I want you to stop giving me 'kitchen.' We all eat far too much. The doctors say that heavy meals are bad for you."

"I told you, Papa," Mama now interposed. "Robie's been up the Loch. He mentioned that he mightn't be back last night."

Quickly, I put my bundle on the table. "Look what I've brought you. Gavin caught it but I gaffed it."

Mama parted the green rushes. She exclaimed, in pleased surprise, "Good for you, Robie."

I drank in her praise, eagerly, hoping also for a word from Papa. He was gazing at the fish, remotely, yet with a curious fascination. He was a man who seldom smiled; as for laughter, it was completely foreign to him; but now a kind of pale gleam lit up his face.

"It's a nice bit fish." He paused. "But what would we do with salmon? Far too rich. It would only upset our stomachs." He added, "Take it down to Donaldson's this afternoon."

"Oh, no, Papa." Mama's eyes became troubled, and her forehead furrowed. "Let us keep a few slices anyway."

"Take it all down," Papa said abstractedly. "Salmon is scarce. It's fetching three and six a pound—apparently there's fools that'll pay such a ransom. Donaldson should give us at least half a crown."

I stood aghast. Take this lovely salmon, which would enrich our meagre table, and sell it to the fishmonger! Papa could not mean it. But he had already resumed eating and Mama, with a nervous constriction of her lips, was saying to me as she spooned out the potato-bake remaining in the ashet: "Here's your lunch then, dear. Sit in."

That afternoon, I carried the fish down to Donaldson's in the High Street. Miserably, I handed my rush-covered burden to stout, red-faced Mr. Donaldson in his blue-striped apron, white jacket, and black straw hat. I was quite incapable of selling, of driving any bargain; but clearly Papa had "looked in" on his way to the office. Mr. Donaldson placed the salmon without a word on the white enamel scales. Six pounds exactly. Gavin's true eye had not lied. The big fishmonger, stroking his moustache, looking at me oddly.

"You caught it up the Loch?"

I nodded.

"Did he put up a good fight?"

"Yes." The memory of last night, the Loch, the moonlight, the comradeship, the splendid struggle, made me lower my eyes.

When Donaldson came back from his till, which was in a little glass-enclosed booth at the back, he said to me: "Six pounds at half a crown the pound makes fifteen shillings neat. Fifteen pieces of silver, boy. Give it to Mr. Leckie with my compliments." He stood watching me as I went out of the shop.

Immediately Papa came in that evening I gave him the money, which had made a heavy lump in my pocket all the afternoon. He nodded and ran it out of his cupped hand into his leather purse: he had a very expert touch with any kind of coins.

During tea he was in an agreeable mood. He told Mama that he had met Mr. Cleghorn on his way home. The Waterworks Superintendent was looking very poorly, quite failed in fact, and it was rumoured he was suffering from a stone in the kidney. There was good reason to believe that, even if this condition did not "carry him off," his retirement must be only a matter of months.

Papa's tone was unusually cheerful as he discussed Mr. Cleghorn's probable demise. As he rose he said: "Come into the parlour, Robert. I want a word with you."

We sat at the window, by the vase of dried esparto grass, behind the lace curtains in the unused room. Outside the green chestnut boughs were prancing, like mettled horses, in the breeze.

Papa studied me with reflective kindness, his pale lips pursed, the tips of his fingers pressed together.

"You're getting quite a big lad now, Robert. You've done well at school. I'm very satisfied with you."

I reddened—Papa did not praise me often. He added: "I hope you feel that we have done the right thing by you."

"Oh, I do, Papa. I'm most grateful for everything."

"Mr. Reid came into the office today with a paper he wanted signed. We had a long talk about your future." He cleared his throat. "Have you any views on the subject yourself?"

My heart was full. "Mr. Reid probably told you, Papa. I'd . . . I'd give anything to study medicine at Winton University."

Papa seemed to shrink a little, actually to diminish in size. Perhaps he was only settling deeper in his chair. He forced a smile.

"You know we are not made of money, Robert."

"But Papa . . . Didn't Mr. Reid speak to you about the Marshall?"

"He did, Robert." A spot of colour showed on Papa's transparent cheek; he looked at me earnestly, as though he were defending me, with indignation, against some deception. "And I told him it was most misguided to have raised your hopes with such a wild idea. Mr. Reid presumes beyond his position, and I don't like his radical views. Any examination is unpredictable—as Murdoch's experience showed. And the Marshall! Why, the competition for that Bursary is tremendous. Frankly—without wishing to offend you—I don't believe you are capable of winning it."

"But you'll let me try." I gulped out the words with sudden anxiety.

The "peaky" look deepened on Papa's thin face. He glanced away from me, out of the window.

"In your own interests, I can't, Robert. It would only put all sorts of wrong notions in your head. Even if you did win, I couldn't afford to let you go another five years without earning a penny piece. A great deal of outlay has been incurred in your behalf. It's high time you started to pay it back."

"But, Papa . . ." I pleaded desperately, then broke off, feeling myself turn white and sick. I wanted to explain that I would pay him back twice over if only he would give me my chance, to tell him that what I lacked in brilliance I would make up in solid work. But I sat crushed and speechless. I knew it would be useless—there was no arguing with Papa. Like most weak men he attached the utmost importance to not changing his mind. There was no rancour in his attitude—he never used me harshly; in fact it was his boast that he had not laid a finger on me in his life. Moved by the strange forces which worked within him, he had actually persuaded himself that he was "doing this for the best."

"As a matter of fact," he went on consolingly, "I saw the head timekeeper about you last week. If you go into the Works this summer you'll learn your trade before you're twenty-one. And you'll be earning good wages all the time, contributing to the upkeep of the household. Under the circumstances isn't that the most sensible thing you could do?"

I gave an inarticulate murmur. I did not want to go in for engineering, I suspected that I was unfitted for the three years' apprenticeship in the foundry. Even if he were right, all the reason in the world would not assuage the tearing bitterness in my heart.

Papa stood up. "I've no doubt it's a disappointment." He sighed and patted me on the shoulder as he left the room. "Beggars can't be choosers, my boy."

I remained seated, with bowed head. He had made all arrangements at the Works—that, no doubt, was the news Mama had written Kate the other day. As I thought of my buoyant hopes, my talks with Alison and Gavin, the whole foolish structure I had raised, water ran down the inside of my nose. I groaned.

I wanted to be like Julius Caesar and Napoleon. But I was still myself.

CHAPTER SEVEN

THE days dragged on and I was in despair. On Thursday, shortly before the close of the Easter vacation, I was mowing Mrs. Bosomley's back green— Papa had an arrangement with our neighbour whereby, for a shilling a month, I kept her grass cut and tidy. These minor earnings of mine were not paid to Papa, that would have been undignified, but, since Mrs. Bosomley owned our house as well as her own—the double property had been left her by her husband—Papa kept a careful record and deducted the exact amount every quarter from the cheque he wrote her for rent.

This afternoon, when I had finished and was putting away the machine, she came to the window, beckoned me inside and set before me a slice of cold apple dumpling and a cup of tea.

Drinking her own very strong tea, which she took without sugar, she watched me with an expression of lively disapproval. She had become stouter and more matronly, and her face, with its network of fine veins over the cheekbones, had a sort of battered look, like an old-time boxer's; but her eye was bright, and her lips had a humorous twist which showed that she was very much alive.

"Robert," she said at last, "I'm sorry to tell you that you are getting more and more like a horse."

"Am I, Mrs. Bosomley?" I stammered dismally.

She nodded. "It's your face. It grows longer every day. Why in the name of goodness are you such a melancholy boy?"

"I suppose I'm just naturally sad, Mrs. Bosomley."

"Do you enjoy being miserable?"

"No . . ." I choked dryly over the dumpling, although it was lusciously damp with fruit. "Not as a general rule, Mrs. Bosomley. But sometimes I'm sad and happy at the same time."

"Are you sad and happy now?"

"No . . . I'm afraid I'm just sad."

Mrs. Bosomley shook her head and lit a cigarette. She smoked so much her fingers were stained with nicotine—that was one of the things which made her different from the more conventional residents of Drumbuck Road. There were all sorts of stories about her but she did not seem to mind public opinion in the slightest. She was original, quick-tempered, kind. Murdoch told me she used to quarrel furiously with her husband and fling dishes at him—Murdoch could hear them through the wall—and the next minute she would be out with him in the garden, calling him pet names, with her arm round his waist.

She reached out abruptly. "Let me read your cup and see if I can't find something cheerful in it."

Revolving my empty cup between her fingers, with the cigarette in the corner of her mouth to keep the smoke out of her eyes, she examined the tea leaves at the bottom. She was an excellent cup reader, understood about dreams and the lines of the hand and could tell fortunes with the cards as well.

"Ve . . . ry interesting. Your aura is green . . . a delicate shade. You will be most successful in the neighbourhood of fields and woods. But don't linger there after dark until you are a little older. You are fierce and jealous in your attitude towards the weaker sex. Aha! What's this? Yes, indeed! You're going to meet a dark handsome woman with a beautiful figure when you're twenty-one." She raised her head. "Doesn't that buck you up?"

"I'm afraid not, Mrs. Bosomley."

"She will be of an extremely affectionate disposition . . . the Spanish type . . . and crazy about red hair."

But I merely blushed and she put down the cup and began to laugh.

"Oh, my dear boy, you make me ache all over. What *is* worrying you?"

"Oh, nothing very much, Mrs. Bosomley," I said dully.

"I can't drag it out of you." She collected the tea things and got up. "Why don't you talk things over with your grandpa?" A slightly self-conscious note came into her voice—she seemed always to have a high opinion of Grandpa. "In spite of what they say of him, Mr. Gow is a most remarkable man."

Unfortunately I did not now subscribe to this view. I was fond of Grandpa, but the days when I had run to him with my childish pains were over. Also, I had acquired the faculty of closing, like an oyster, upon a private trouble and of wrestling with it, as that mollusc might strive against its pearly irritant, in stoic solitude. I could not even bring myself to speak to Mama, who looked anxious and unhappy about me—perhaps I realized that anything I could say would only make matters worse.

However, it was apparent that Mrs. Bosomley had "had a word" with Grandpa, for on the following day he took me aside and made me tell him what was wrong.

I shall not readily forget the expression with which he heard me: the pained, bemused wrinkling of his eyes. He was a man of many sins, follies, and evasions, yet he was incapable of petty meanness—he could not understand it. There was a kind of grandeur in his face as he reached out for his hat and stick.

"Come on, boy. We'll go down and see this Mr. Reid of yours."

I did not care to be seen with Grandpa in the streets—his little peculiarities increased my own terrible self-consciousness—yet I was too dejected to offer much resistance; and presently, although I was convinced that nothing could come of his intervention, we were on our way, through streets bathed in Saturday afternoon quiet, to Reid's lodging.

Most of the Academy masters occupied respectable villas in the "good" districts, like Knoxhill and Drumbuck Road. But Jason Reid lived in a tall dingy building near the old Vennel, a far from creditable part of the town, largely inhabited by Polish and working families, by dock labourers, and other humble people. His back room overlooked a sooty court; by throwing up his front window, usually opaque from lack of cleaning, he had an excellent view of the three shining brass balls of the Levenford Mutual Aid Society and of the interesting procession which, every evening, rolled through the swing doors of the Harbour Tavern. Reid liked this dwelling for the complete freedom it afforded him; also because it outraged convention and affirmed his socialistic views.

Reid had come to the Academy two years before as a stop-gap when Mr. Douglas was appointed to the headmastership of Ardfillan High School. Reid himself made it clear that his appointment was temporary—he did not care to remain long in one place—also the Rector was obviously not impressed by Jason's careless dress, unorthodox methods and exasperating lack of deference. Yet Jason remained. He was a brilliant and original teacher; even the Rector came to admit it: and besides running the science side he could, most convenient, take the higher English class—he had both the M.A. and B.Sc. honours degrees from Trinity College. As for Reid himself, when I asked him, many years later, why he had remained so long in the dead-end of Levenford, he replied, with his peculiar flat-nosed, ox-eyed smile: "It was very handy for the pawnshop."

This flippancy was the persistence of a pose forced upon him by the circumstances of his life. He was the son of a North of Ireland clergyman and, despite his slight disfigurement, had been intended for the Church, but halfway through his studies he had fallen under the influence of Huxley and renounced the Book of Genesis. The family estrangement which resulted was something Reid never mentioned, yet I sensed it was this upheaval which had forced on him his mask of indifference, the contempt of conventional conduct which broke through, even in his teaching. On his first appearance before the English class we were following a practice introduced by Mr. Douglas, rising in turn to proclaim our views on a chosen subject— which was, that afternoon, "What I Shall Do Next Sunday." Lounging in his chair, with his feet on his desk which was the unconventional attitude in which he chose to instruct us, Reid heard us out: we were all extremely virtuous and correct. Then, in a considering voice, he declared: "Next Sunday? Why, I think I shall lie in bed and drink beer."

For all his bravado he was an unhappy and lonely soul. He kept apart from the other masters: he had nothing in common with them. Occasionally he attended a meeting of the local Fabian Society; but all the other Levenford clubs, including the famous "Philosophical," he dismissed derisively as mere "drinking dens." He had no apparent interest in women. I never at this time saw him speak, or walk, with one in the street. Yet, because of his devotion to music, he had become friendly with Mrs. Keith and her little circle. The house in Sinclair Drive was the only one he seemed to care to visit.

Perhaps Reid thought I had the makings of a scientist; more probably it was our common heritage of oddness which led him to take an interest in me. Frequently on Sunday mornings he had me to breakfast and fed me with many delicious fried sausages. He was not a great talker and was never in the smallest degree demonstrative. On the contrary he parodied the emotions. He had an austere taste in literature and did his best to knock my fine phrases out of me. He liked Addison, Locke, Hazlitt and Montaigne. He was an admirer of Schiller. Referring to his own isolation in the narrow-minded town, he would quote that philosopher: "The only relation with the public of which a man never repents, is war." Yet occasionally I surprised in his full eyes a glance which was not warlike, but affectionate.

As Grandpa and I went up the narrow staircase, dark and unhygienic, we heard the strains of music coming from Reid's rooms. Grandpa tapped with his stick on the door. And a voice from behind the panel called out: "Come in."

Jason lay exhausted in a wicker armchair by the window, jacket off, trouser ends clipped round thick socks, his feet—still incased in black lace-up bicycle shoes—resting against the table on which stood a foam-topped glass and a gramophone with a flat revolving disc and a long flower-shaped trumpet. As Grandpa began in his suavest manner to introduce himself, Jason silenced him warningly, and with a sweep of his arm motioned us to seat ourselves. When the disc came to an end he rose quickly and changed it, then flung himself back into the basket chair. From time to time he mopped his brow and drank from the glass. I saw that he had come in from one of his violent bicycle spins—spasmodically, when he felt he needed exercise, he would fling himself upon his machine and scorch furiously, up hill and down dale, head down, legs working madly, rivers of sweat running from his eyes, miles of dust floating in the air behind him. Then, safely returned, he would soothe himself with vast quantities of food and drink, and the symphonies of Beethoven recently produced on Columbia records by the Philharmonic Orchestra of London. Reid loved music, he played the piano quite beautifully, but seldom, for he despised his own talent as inadequate and amateurish.

When the symphony was finished he stopped the machine and restored the discs to an album.

"Well, sir," he addressed Grandpa politely, "what can I do for you?"

Grandpa had been slightly irked by the waiting, the lack of *éclat* in his reception. He said peevishly: "Are you quite free to attend to us?"

"Quite," said Reid.

"Well," Grandpa said, "I wanted to talk to you about this boy and the Marshall Bursary."

Jason gazed from Grandpa to me, then he went to a cupboard below the bookshelves and brought out another bottle of beer. He glanced sideways at Grandpa while he inclined the bottle. "My instructions—and of course, a contemptible usher like myself can only obey his instructions—are to keep our young friend and the Bursary as far apart as possible."

Grandpa smiled, his grim, majestic smile, and leaned forward on the handle of his stick. Waiting with pitiful eagerness, I saw that it was to be a peroration, one of his fruitiest:—

"My dear sir, it may be true that you have received these instructions. But I am here to countermand them. Not only in my own name, but in the name of decency, freedom, and justice. There are, after all, sir, even in this unenlightened age, certain essential liberties permitted to the humblest individual. Liberty of religion, liberty of speech, liberty to develop the gifts with which the Great Artificer has endowed him. Now, sir, if there is anyone low enough, and mean enough, to deny these liberties, I, for one, will not stand by and countenance it."

Grandpa's voice was rising magnificently and Jason was listening with delight, the faint smile which had appeared when Grandpa used the words "Great Artificer" still stretching the scar on his upper lip.

"Hear! Hear!" he said admiringly. "Take this, old boy, you must be dry."

He handed the glass of beer to Grandpa, and added: "Rhetoric apart, I don't in the least see how it can be done."

Grandpa sucked in the foam from his moustache, and said quickly, in a different voice:—

"Enter him on the quiet. Don't say a word to anyone."

Reid shook his head. "It couldn't be done. I have enough trouble on my hands already. Besides, the entry must be signed by his guardian."

"I'll sign it," Grandpa said.

Jason received this oddly, and began presently to pace up and down the room in his soft cycling shoes, his brows knitted, lips no longer smiling. Following him with intent eyes, I saw that he was turning over in his mind the idea presented by Grandpa; and, with an almost painful undersurge of hope, I discerned in him signs of a mounting enthusiasm.

"By Jove!" He stopped suddenly, staring straight ahead, thinking out loud. "It would be rather splendid if we could pull it off. Keep the whole thing mum. Work like fury on the quiet. And then . . . if we could do it . . . the look on all their faces, from the Rector's to that little runt Leckie's . . . at the surprise result." He spun round to me. "If you did get it, they couldn't possibly prevent you from going on to college. Good Lord! It would be something. Like a dark horse winning the Derby."

He studied me, with his full eyes, as though weighing up my points, while I flushed vividly and, turning my cap nervously in my hands, tried to sustain his stare. Whatever Mrs. Bosomley's opinion of my equine propensities, I did not feel like a Derby winner. Mama, who always cut my hair to save the barber's fee, had given me the day before a crop which made my scalp gleam through and reduced the size of my head to most unintellectual dimensions. But Jason, always, from the beginning, was my friend. And now, his Irish blood was quickening, quickening to this new and sporting flavour of the event. He struck the air with his closed fist.

"By God!" he exclaimed, his own cheeks now flushed with excitement. "We'll have a shot at it. Might as well be killed for a sheep as a lamb. You know I always wanted you to try, Shannon. And now I do, more than ever. We'll not say a word. *We'll just tear in and win!*"

That moment can never be repeated—the lifting of my insufferable disappointment—the splendour of a reopened future, of knowing that Reid believed in me—all this created in my heart a sense of singing joy. Grandpa was offering his hand to Jason; in fact we shook hands excitedly all round. Ah, it was, truly, a splendid moment. But Reid, wisely, cut it short.

"Don't let's make fools of ourselves." He drew up a chair close to us. "This thing is going to be damned difficult for you, Shannon. You're only fifteen and you'll be competing against fellows two and even three years your senior. Then you're full of faults. You know how you rush at things, jump to conclusions without proper deductions. You've got to correct all that."

I gazed at him with parted lips and shining eyes, not daring to speak, but conveying everything by my silence.

"I've a good idea of the lie of the land," Reid resumed in a tone so confidential it thrilled me through and through. "The picture for this year, as I see it, is this: A less than average entry in numbers, but high, quite high in quality. There are three boys in particular that I'm afraid of . . ." He enumerated on his fingers. "Blair of Larchfield, Allardyce of Ardfillan High, and a youngster named McEwan who's been educated privately. Blair you know—he's first-rate, a good all-rounded. Allardyce is eighteen and has been up before, which gives him a tremendous advantage. But the danger, the real danger is McEwan." Jason paused impressively—and oh, how I hated the unknown McEwan! "He's young, about your own age, the son of the classics master at Undershaws, and his father has been tutoring him specially for years. I understand he could speak Greek fluently when he was twelve years old. Knows half a dozen languages now. Quite the child prodigy, all high forehead and large spectacles. In fact, it's believed by those who know him that the Marshall is as good as in his pocket."

The slight bitterness in Reid's tone, his inflection of satire, could not disguise the fact that he was seriously afraid of this horrible boy who at breakfast probably asked his parent to pass the toast in Sanskrit. I could do no more than grit my teeth in silence.

"So you see, young Shannon," Jason concluded in a gentler tone, "we'll have to work genuinely hard. Oh, I won't kill you, not quite. You shall have an hour off every day, for exercise. You won't want to take it, once you get to the really hysterical stage, but I shall insist. You can cool your brain—God help you—walking in the country—or you can take out my bicycle—and mind you don't puncture it. I shall have quite a number of books to give you. Keep them in your bedroom. You'd better study there too. Nothing like a good blank wall for keeping you at it. I'll work out our schedule. I've got all the examination papers for the last ten years in my desk at school. We'll go over every question. We start work tomorrow . . . I think that's everything. Any comments?"

I gazed at him, my eyes lit by a white flame of ardour, my whole body quivering with the intensity of my feeling. How could I thank him? How could I tell him that I would work, fight, and die for him?

"Well, sir," I stammered, "I promise you . . ."

No use; but I am sure he understood. He rose, with alacrity, and began to select books for me from his shelves.

Grandpa helped me to carry them home. I was between heaven and earth, treading upon air.

CHAPTER EIGHT

AT THE beginning of June an event occurred, trivial in itself, yet so helpful to my purpose I felt it as an intervention of Providence upon my behalf, a direct answer to the petitions with which I was bombarding the Heavenly Throne.

Not long after our great decision in Mr. Reid's room I had come in from my morning "roll delivery" to find Adam, who seemed always to reach the house in the early hours, seated at breakfast, fresh and well-groomed, talking to Papa and Mama, having stepped out of his first-class "sleeper" on the night express from London—whenever Adam travelled on his expense sheet he did so in slap-up style. Although his Winton business connections required these periodic returns to the North, Adam was now in London: he had been appointed Southern representative of the Caledonia Insurance Com-

pany. While this change had brought him no increase in salary, Adam insisted it was a tribute to his business acumen and a step towards great things.
He was living, at this time, in a residential hotel in Hanger Hill, Ealing.

As I began my own breakfast of porridge and buttermilk, he resumed his
remarks, having broken off to give me his usual hearty greeting.

"Yes, Mama, I think it would interest you to see the house."

"What house, dear?" Mama asked.

Adam smiled. "Why, the house I've just bought . . ."

"You've bought a house?" Papa spoke with the acute, almost professional
interest of a member of the Levenford Building Society, in which, as a matter of fact, all his hard-wrung savings lay. "Where?"

"On the Bayswater Road," Adam said easily. "A first-class situation overlooking the Park. It's a first-class house, too, cream-painted stucco, seven
floors high, mahogany staircase, marble piazza, very dignified, and a freehold. But there, you don't want to hear about it."

"But we do, dear," Mama breathed. "It's the most exciting news."

Adam laughed, holding out his cup for more tea. "Well, I'd had my eye
on this property for some time, passed it every day on my way to the office.
The 'For Sale' board had been up six months when one morning I saw a
notice pasted across it: 'Auction Next Week.' Ha! I thought. Might be interesting! I'd been looking out for a suitable real estate investment ever
since I came South. So I dropped in the following Monday at the Auction
Rooms. Usual sort of place, fine panelling, lots of gents in top hats. The
auctioneer had a top hat too." Adam gave his bacon and eggs an amused
glance. "After announcing that the house had cost six thousand, which incidentally is true, he started the bidding with his eye on me, at three thousand
pounds. Up it went, up, up, all the top hats bidding against one another,
until it reached five thousand five hundred, where it hung a long, long time
before it was knocked down to the shiniest top hat of all. I sat back, never
said a word; it was funny the way they'd tried to get a rise out of me. I'd
made my inquiries, you see. I knew the bank had a mortgage of two thousand and was threatening to foreclose. The very next day I had a letter from
shiny top hat offering to sacrifice the property for four thousand. I threw
it in my wastepaper basket. Then . . ."

He took us, step by step, down the devious yet unhurried ways which had
made him, only a week before, absolute owner of this magnificent mansion
for the cash payment of nineteen hundred pounds.

"My goodness." Mama gave a little gasp, enthralled yet fearful—although
the bargain had been great the sum involved was, to her, colossal, terrifying,
and indeed it represented most of Adam's capital, saved over the last ten
years. "You certainly got the better of them . . . and London men, too.
What will you do with the house now, dear? Live in it?"

"Well, no, Mama." Adam received the naïve suggestion, enough to make
the angels laugh, with a nice consideration. "The thing's a white elephant
in its present form. My idea is to convert it. Eight self-contained flats at

rents varying from seventy to one hundred and fifty pounds. I calculate on a net six hundred after paying taxes and the caretaker's wages. Let's say a twenty per cent return. Not bad for my first real venture outside my own business."

Papa had been listening with strained attention. He moistened his lips. "Twenty per cent. And the Building Society pays me three."

Adam smiled carelessly. "Private enterprise pays higher dividends. And of course the conversion will take money. Probably another nine hundred. It's a nuisance having to find it. I'm not anxious to let all and sundry in on such a good thing."

A faint colour had crept over Papa's forehead. Always his respect for Adam had been tinged by a vague distrust, the distrust of a cautious man for the intangible operations of finance. But now, this house, solid mahogany and marble, offering a princely income—he spoke with difficulty.

"I've always believed in bricks and mortar. It's a pity I couldn't take a look at it with you, Adam."

"I don't see why you shouldn't . . . you might do worse." Adam paused thoughtfully. "Why don't you and Mama come down and spend a couple of weeks with me this summer? Take a month if necessary, combine business with pleasure. I can put you up at Ealing. You owe yourselves a holiday."

"Oh, Adam," Mama exclaimed, clasping her hands at this long-hoped-for invitation.

A great deal of discussion followed: Papa, intensely cautious, never made a decision lightly. But before Adam took his departure it was settled. And I realized, with a thrill of joy, that they would be away, leaving me free of all observation and restraint, during the final stages of my study, during the Bursary examination. Nothing could have been more blessedly opportune.

The days rushed on and soon, while I worked in my room, I heard a strange sound in the house. I had to think for several minutes before I understood that it was Mama singing—low and unmusical to be sure, but still, singing. Papa's good clothes hung all pressed and ready, the two Gladstone bags were polished till they shone. Somehow, Mama had managed to buy herself, from Miss Dobbie's, the small millinery shop which dealt in "remnants," a length of dark brown voile and, with flying needle, had "run herself up" a summer dress. But her greatest adventures were with fur—a stringy necklet which she had possessed for at least a quarter of a century, yet which she produced proudly each spring from its camphored hibernation. Mama's fur! One never knew what animal had died to give it being: although there was always, at the back of my mind, the unmentionable vision of some unfortunate cat, flattened by such a prodigious weight as had destroyed poor Samuel Leckie. Mama relined it with a strip of voile, saved from the dress length, reshaped it slightly to bring it up to date. I could see her on the back green, airing it on the clothesline, shaking it, happily, blowing into it to raise its meagre pile. . . . She had not had a holiday in five years.

Whenever she was in danger of "getting above herself," Papa brought her back to earth, with these words of warning: "Think of the fares!"

He felt that if she was not restrained there would be, in her present mood, no end to the expense, the deadly excesses, into which she might entrap him. The thought of eating in restaurants, of being forced, through some misadventure, to spend the night at a hotel, became his nightmare. He planned with redoubled care. Enough food would be taken in a cardboard hatbox to sustain them on the journey, they would sit up, third class, through the night, all the way to London. Already, Papa carried in his vest pocket a little notebook marked *Expenses of Visit to Adam*. He had, I think, the illusory hope that Adam would reimburse him. On the first line was written: "To two railway tickets . . . £-7-9-6"; and to this amount Papa returned, time and again, with the gloomy air of a man who had made a ruinous outlay. Later, I learned from Murdoch that Papa, by obsequious representations, had managed to secure "privilege tickets," which were issued to certain officials entirely free of charge.

On the eve of their departure Mama came to my room, sat down on the bed and watched me in silence.

"You're quite busy these days, dear boy." Her faint smile deepened as she added: "And no doubt you will be, while we're in London."

Did Mama know? Had Grandpa whispered a word to her? I hung my head as she continued:—

"Your boots aren't in too good a state. They'll not stand soling. If they give out before . . . well, before we come back, there's that nice strong brown pair of Kate's in the cupboard under the stairs."

"Yes, Mama." I masked my discomposure at the mention of those long narrow boots, once used by Kate for hockey, in colour a jaundiced yellow, lacing halfway up the leg, and so manifestly feminine the very thought of them gave me gooseflesh.

"They've kept their shape well," Mama murmured, persuasively. "I had a look at them the other day."

"I think I'll manage, Mama," I said.

There was a pause.

"You usually manage, don't you Robie?" Mama smiled gently. She rose, rubbed her hand over my head. Her eyes lingered a little upon me as she went out. She whispered:—

"Good luck to you . . . my own boy."

CHAPTER NINE

IMMEDIATELY Papa and Mama departed, Grandpa moved my table and all my books into the parlour, which was never used, maintained solely as a patent of gentility. How well I remember that sacred room! It had a round marble fireplace with a gilt mirror overmantel and an aspidistra in the black-leaded grate. Against one wall was a chiffonier covered by lace doilies upon which lay a Japanese fan, three cowrie shells, and a glass paperweight inscribed "A Present from Ardfillan." On the round table in the centre was a red drugget cover with a gilt-clasped copy of *Pilgrim's Progress* laid out at a tasteful angle beside a vase of esparto grass. Near by was the upright piano with a revolving stool. A green plush-framed photograph of Mama and Papa in their wedding attire stood on top. There was one picture, an oil painting entitled "The Monarch of the Glen."

The wide bay formed by the window made a splendid study for me. Here I sat, alone, and with Reid, who could now come and go with freedom. The house was very silent, intensified by the exaggerated care of Grandpa's movements. Mama had arranged that Mrs. Bosomley should come in occasionally to help us; but Grandpa, to my surprise, proved himself a resourceful housekeeper—during those periods in his life when he had been obliged to fend for himself he had picked up the knack of certain dishes, especially soups. No apparent eccentricities, not a single misdemeanour. He seemed to enjoy the freedom of the vacant house, where he was able to potter about without fear of nagging and restraint. As might be surmised, severe restrictions had been placed upon us. Most of the china and cutlery had been locked away, also the good cooking utensils, since Mama was afraid Grandpa would "singe" the pots. She had written out precise instructions for our meals, based upon a small supply of groceries delivered to us every Monday from the stores. A bare pittance had been left behind in ready cash. Nevertheless, Grandpa managed to circumvent these difficulties. He developed a habit of dropping in at the Nursery and, although Murdoch's attitude towards Grandpa could scarcely be described as amiable, we often had a fine cauliflower which did not figure on Mama's menu, or a great pot of floury potatoes which Grandpa boiled perfectly and which I particularly loved. Once or twice, as twilight fell, he departed with a dreamy air in the direction of Snoddie's Farm, and on the next day we would have for dinner a boiled chicken which could only have come from God.

Although he tried to hide it, Grandpa displayed a profound respect for my studies. He had a high regard for "book learning" and indeed for books— which was strange, for he himself possessed no more than three volumes. I must not fail, in passing, to mention these faithful friends. The first was the *Poems* of Robert Burns, most of which he knew by heart; the second, a tattered book over which Grandpa chuckled repeatedly, *The Adventures of Hajji Baba*; the third, in a broken red binding, with a frontispiece of a grimy tramp writing, "Dear Sirs, ten years ago I used your soap, since then I have used no other," was *Pears Shilling Encyclopedia*—I can still see Grandpa in our early days reaching out with an air of erudition for that wonderful compendium—"We'll see what Pears has to say about it."

Now, inevitably, the stage of his omniscience was over, but he still maintained a lofty air of piloting me through the shoals, and was delighted when I asked him to "hear" my equations or Latin verses. At the end of our first week he made me give up my early morning delivery work, which, by cutting into the best hours, when my head was clear, was proving a serious handicap. We were already deeply committed, nothing would redeem us but success; I went into the parlour and took my place at my books in the grey light of dawn, offering myself to the anguish of unremitting study. Reid had completely exempted me from the class, and all day long I laboured alone, in white and burning solitude, in that front room, bent over my small table with passionate application. Time was growing short. My rivals were working, incessantly, far harder than I. There was only one prize. How could I hope to gain it if for an instant, even, I lifted my eyes from the page?

Every evening at six o'clock Reid arrived: with a short greeting and a long look to see how I was standing it, he took a chair beside me. He tutored me until ten, when Grandpa brought in cups of cocoa, which sometimes grew cold, unnoticed, amongst the papers, at our elbows. My stability was renewed by Jason's considered sanity, by his solid figure smelling of tobacco, chalk, and perspiration, by his familiar mannerism of touching back his light blond hair that always looked newly washed, and by the human warmth of his rather "bad" breath which, mingling with the odour of his person, seemed like the exudation of an inexhaustible vitality.

When, at last, Reid has gone—having urged me to go to bed, yet knowing that I will not do so—I draw up more closely to my table, fighting my lassitude, my terrible desire for sleep. Perhaps, for a moment, I go to the bathroom to dash my head in water which, since the tank lies immediately beneath the roof, is, in summer, merely tepid. I return, flagging, yet compelled by an inner force to go on, to exact from myself the last ounce of effort. Always, I murmur a prayer before resuming, offering up all my work. To keep awake I jab my leg with a pen-nib, or knock my dull forehead with my knuckles, as if entreating it to understand. The minutes fall away, silently, into the silent night; and still my immovable figure, with coat discarded and sleeves rolled up for coolness, bare elbows on the table, hands clasping the reeling head, remains beneath the gaslight.

Two o'clock strikes. I rise and stagger to my room. Usually I sleep as though stunned the moment I fall upon my bed. But sometimes there are nightmares of my unpreparedness for the examination, of questions I cannot answer. And there are other nights when, worst of all, though dead with weariness, my brain refuses to rest, but continues to function with a hard unnatural lucidity, solving difficult quadratics, intricate problems in advanced trigonometry which normally require pages of calculation—all nothing, mere child's play to this poor brain of mine, whirling and rocketing over the fields of learning while my body lies helpless, as in a catalepsy, waiting for the first streaks of light beneath the blind that will usher me again to the tyranny of my ambition.

My sole respite came in the afternoon when towards five o'clock Grandpa forced me out for my short relaxation. On these evenings when Gavin returned home from Larchfield I employed this hour to meet him at Dalreoch stop, which was more convenient than the main Levenford station; and there, as he left the train and crossed the "goods" yard, I stood waiting at the big white gate, ready to fall into step beside him and compare despondent notes on the progress we had made.

Upon other days I went down to the Academy yard, where there was a high wall with a convenient buttress, to play a game of hand ball with Mr. Reid. Jason was good at fives and had performed, as he put it, in the Public Schools Championship at Queens Club. Our game was scarcely orthodox, for the court was not right, but it gave us lots of running about and I always felt the better for it.

Then, on my lucky afternoons, I saw Alison. Usually I met her at the end of Drumbuck Road as she returned slowly from her singing lesson, hatless, and carrying a rolled patent-leather music case under her arm. In the warm weather she wore a light dress which made her shape bud in the quiet breeze. We did not look at each other and we talked only of the most ordinary things. She would tell me what was happening at school, what Mr. Reid—for whom she had a great admiration—had said that day. Yet from time to time, despite her calmness, her eyes seemed to grow larger and softer, and her lips glowed with colour. When our ways diverged at the corner of Sinclair Drive I raced home, pausing only to pick up a stone and throw it hard. With my blood warm in my cheeks, I flung myself down at my books. Everything was going well with me. And Grandpa, who now brought to my table a cup of tea, was the best, the finest old man ever born.

No, no, I am quite wrong. It was he, the monster, who a week later plunged me to the abyss.

CHAPTER TEN

IT was a hot, still afternoon, with a threat of thunder in the air. Only four days remained before the examination and I was overwrought, my nerves painfully on edge. I had gone to dip my head in water; then, as I stood drying my face, I heard the echo of Grandpa's laugh. I came out from the bathroom to the landing and called to him; but I received no answer. Was this an hallucination? Good heavens, surely my exertions had not brought me to the point of "hearing things." I went slowly upstairs to the open door of Mama's room from which the sound, muffled though it was, had seemed to come. I entered the room, which was quite empty, and immediately heard Mrs. Bosomley's voice followed again by Grandpa's laugh.

I started, then realized that, on this still afternoon, sounds were travelling through the dividing wall; they came from the house next door. Of course! . . . I recollected seeing Grandpa trim his beard immediately after lunch.

I was on the point of turning away, when another sound brought me up short. In bewildered yet scared suspense, I gazed at the blank wall patterned with climbing roses, aware that the room through the wall was Mrs. Bosomley's bedroom. Grandpa and Mrs. Bosomley were both there, together.

Against my will, rooted by the consternation rising within me, I listened. Oh, God, surely not . . . I tried to free myself from the thought. But there was no mistake, none whatever.

Convulsively, I tore myself away, ran out of the room, straight out of the house. I was shaking all over as I hurried blindly up the road. What was the use of struggling, of fighting, the use of anything? One might make mistakes in spite of a pure and beautiful love. But then one surrendered to evil only at the last ditch, the last gasp, and with an anguished cry. To trim one's beard, before the mirror, and depart whistling, with a look of pleased anticipation —oh, God, that betrayal, by a man whom I had loved and trusted—it ground me to the dust.

Bent only on escaping the images tormenting me, I did not look where I was going. But I had taken, instinctively, the hill road, and as I passed the Nursery a shout recalled me from the tumult of my thoughts. Murdoch was pruning the hedge which flanked the entrance to the garden. I stopped, hesitated, then went over.

"What's the matter?" He had stopped pruning and was eying me as he wiped his brow with the back of his big brown hand. "Have you joined the harriers?"

I did not answer this horrible facetiousness—in fact I was quite unable to speak.

"Something gone wrong with the work?"

I shook my head abjectly, my breast still too full for words. Murdoch gazed at me speculatively, his curiosity aroused.

"I know what," he said at last. "The old boy has gone on the booze again." He read my face. "No? Well then, it's another of his tricks?"

"Tricks!" Enraged by the lightness of the word, I was shaken by a fresh spasm. "You wouldn't say 'tricks' if you knew. Oh, Murdoch!" I almost burst into tears. "If people can't at least try to live decently . . . and at his age . . ."

"Ah!" exclaimed Murdoch, enlightened, placidly pleased with his own powers of deduction. He belched, took a piece of licorice root from his pocket, bit off a piece, and began to chew it with every appearance of enjoyment.

I turned my pale face sideways, staring fixedly at a cart which was moving along the road. For some peculiar reason this solitary cart, crawling across the summer landscape, made me feel that life was endless in its monotony, that all that I now experienced was the repetition of something which had happened to me hundreds of years ago.

"You know, young fellow," Murdoch said after a pause, "it's about time you grew up. You're clever, and I was always a dunce at everything but gardening—still, at your age, I wasn't so simple. Grandpa has always been that way. A regular lady-killer all his life. Even when his wife, who I must say was very fond of him, was alive."

Silence of despair from me.

"It's just him," Murdoch went on. "And now, even though he's a good age, he can't help himself. I don't think it's anything to lose your shirt about."

"It's awful," I said faintly.

"Well, there's nothing we can do about it." Murdoch, who seemed trying not to laugh at me, clapped me upon the shoulder companionably. "The world isn't coming to an end. You'll get over all this when you're a bit older. Come along and I'll show you my new carnation. It's budding a treat."

He put the shears under his arm and opened the gate. After a moment of hesitation I went in and accompanied him, drearily, to the new greenhouse. Here he showed me half a dozen pots of milky-green shoots which were beginning to throw out buds, and explained, with pride, the method he had employed to produce the hybrid. There was something obscurely comforting in the steady movements of his large capable hands arranging the earthy pots, reaching for his clasp knife and deftly snicking off an errant shoot, binding the stems tenderly with raffia.

"If it's a success I shall call it the Murdoch Leckie! Isn't that something? More worth thinking about than . . ." He conveyed his meaning with another kindly slap upon the back.

I was calmer when I left Murdoch, but my outraged state—as ludicrous as the breaking voice that was another symptom of my age—would not let me return immediately to my books. As was to be expected, I dragged myself back, along the High Street to the church.

Here it was cool and quiet. Attending to the flowers on the side altar, the dim shape of Mother Elizabeth Josephina sent little chinking noises down the silent aisle. As she passed into the sacristy she gave me a smile of recognition and approval. I went on my knees in the still twilight, under the high window which had always solaced me, before that figure also carrying a burden, the face drawn by a spasm of pain.

Now, in this ecclesiastical atmosphere impregnated with incense and candle wax, I began to burn with a deep and just resentment against Grandpa, violator of the only virtue which really mattered. I thought of Alison, in her white dress, Alison, whom my love, this first love of puberty, had elevated to sublime and angelic heights. My face burned with shame. How would she regard a boy whose grandfather behaved like mine? Anger entered my heart, and recollected how Christ had cast the wicked men from the temple, I rose determined to have it out with Grandpa, to finish with him once and for all.

When I reached home it was he who met me in the lobby, greeting me with every appearance of welcome. From behind him there came an excellent aroma of cooking.

"I'm glad you decided to take a walk. You'll work the better for it."

I gave him a cold and scornful glance, the kind of glance with which the archangel transfixed the writhing Lucifer. "What did you do this afternoon?"

He smiled with perfect nonchalance, answered airily: "Just my usual. A game of marleys at the cemetery."

Ah! He was a liar too. Liar and lecher both! But before I could confront him he moved out of the lobby.

"Come away into the kitchen." He was rubbing his hands, full of calm, kindness, and peace of mind. "I have a vegetable soup that'll draw the teeth out your head."

I entered the kitchen and, while he was absent in the scullery, sat down at the table. In spite of my wrongs I was extremely hungry.

A moment later he entered and served me with a big bowl of steaming broth. To divert me, to add point to his culinary achievements, he had put on one of Mama's aprons, and wound a napkin, like a chef's cap, around his depraved and venerable locks. So he was a clown, a pitiful buffoon as well, this fiend who had almost, but not quite, spoiled everything.

I put my spoon in the thick soup, which was filled with peas, chopped-up carrots, and shredded pieces of chicken. I lifted it to my lips, while he watched with an expression of affectionate expectancy.

"Good?" he inquired.

It was delicious. I finished it to the last drop. Then I gazed at this absurd and abominable old man who had earned my loathing and contempt, who betrayed the sacred beliefs of youth, whom I must shun as the cause and occasion of sin. The moment of denunciation had arrived.

"Can I have another helping, Grandpa?" I asked meekly.

CHAPTER ELEVEN

THE morning of the examination was wet. On the afternoon of Thursday, the day before, Jason had taken all my books away and hidden them.

"Only the second-raters cram up to the last minute," he said. "You see them mucking over notes before they go in. They never win."

What I had learned seemed part of me. Nothing more to be assimilated. At present a mental blankness. But it is there, in the marrow of my bones. Outside my core of desperate resolution I was pale but quite calm as I dressed in the best of Murdoch's cast-offs: not a bad blue suit, though shiny at the elbows and seat. With measured strokes I shone and prepared my boots—which had caused Mama anxiety and which I must speak of later. Grandpa, hovering around, had picked me a buttonhole, to give me courage. Ah, those famous buttonholes of Grandpa's! I remember, distinctly: it was a pink moss-rosebud, with raindrops still upon it.

When he had handed it to me he produced, with a distinct "air," a small square envelope.

"Someone left this for you."

"Who?"

He shrugged his shoulders as though to say: "My dear boy, I am a gentleman, I don't spy on your affairs." But out of the corner of his eye he watched me, with a pleased expression, as though I were conforming to a pattern he approved, while with nervous fingers I opened the letter.

It was from Alison, a short note sending me her good wishes. A glow expanded round my heart . . . I reddened and put the letter in my pocket while Grandpa, whistling, smiling to himself, served my breakfast.

Jason was coming up with me to the College on this first morning. His frivolous pretext: that he did not wish me to get ensnared in the toils of a great city. Jason's kindness to me, all masked by flippancy, his unsparing generosity—for you must not imagine that three months' tutoring, given gladly and for nothing, is a natural phenomenon in a small Scots town— his support, his friendship, above all his complete understanding of my difficulties—all this, in recollection, clouds the eyes, gives one greater hope for the future of the human race than all the ideologies.

At the station we were joined by Gavin, a little pale, like myself, but calm, even smiling. He, too, had been working hard; I had not seen him for at least ten days. Now there was no sense of rivalry between us, we were partners in a tremendous enterprise. I felt a warm rush of comradeship as we exchanged our handclasp and I murmured low, so that Jason might not hear: "One of us, Gavin."

I knew now that it must be I, but if it were not . . . dear God, that was an awful thought! . . . then let it be Gavin.

The train of destiny rushed in. Our compartment was empty, smelling of cigarette and tunnel smoke, strewn with spent matches, the wooden partition scrawled with the crude wit of the apprentice engineers who travelled on this line. Reid, who did not wish us to dissipate our energies in conversation, had bought us each a *Strand Magazine* which, with a pretence of interest, we held before our faces in our corners. My copy made an excellent shield for my silently moving lips, for I was praying all the time, beseeching Heaven not to lose interest at the last ditch. Reid sat next to me, quite close, staring at the shipyards, chimney-stacks, and gasometers which sped past us in the rain, giving me courage by the communicative pressure of his thick shoulders, not withdrawing when the train threw us together, but trying, it almost seemed, to impart to me, as a final gift, his own strength, spirit, and intellectual power. Although from time to time he made desultory efforts to bring my attention back to Mr. Sherlock Holmes, a character whom he admired greatly, he was excited, yes, tensely overwrought. I could feel this, despite the check he imposed upon himself. He wanted me to win, desired it with every vital fibre of his stocky, vital frame.

The College buildings, washed by the rain as they stood ancient, spired, and grey on an eminence overlooking the Park on the west side of the city, were impressive to a boy of fifteen who had only seen them in his dreams. My old weakness, my inveterate curse, began to afflict me. I felt humble and intimidated as we left the yellow tram which had borne us from Central Station to the foot of Gilmore Hill, and, as we went up the quiet road with the professors' houses on either side, and entered a lovely quadrangle through the low cloisters, I began to question the right of a shabby and contemptible boy to penetrate such sacred precincts. Do not wholly despise me, however. Though my buttonhole and the small square note in my inside pocket should have sustained me, my left boot was already giving me concern, causing me to walk in a fashion so flat-footed that Jason asked:—

"Have you hurt your leg?"

I flushed. "Perhaps I've strained my knee."

But we were there now, on the battle ground. The other candidates were grouped round the door of the Bute Hall.

"Plates of sour porridge!" Jason, our ally, holding us apart, gave the comment as much conviction as he dared, yet I could not agree with him. They looked a fine bright crowd of boys, full of life and intelligence. I thought I discerned McEwan, a smallish, bespectacled figure leaning against a pillar, with his hands in his pockets and laughing, yes, dear God, laughing as if he did not care.

At last, a low kind of rumble, which might be from my own heart: the oak doors swung open, the boys began filing through. Suddenly, as I moved, I felt Jason grip my arm in a vice. He bent down, putting his head close to mine, so that I could feel on my cheek his warm, "bad" breath. "Take my watch, Shannon. Don't trust their old clock. And keep cool." His whisper became hoarse, his bulging eyes fastened on mine with terrible intensity. "I know you can win."

The Bute Hall is very large, with stained-glass windows like a church, organ pipes shining dully on a balcony, tattered flags round the walls, newer, brighter flags hanging from the high beams. This morning, however, at the top end, a familiar sight: varnished yellow desks, about a hundred of them, numbered and arranged before the examiner's dais. My number is nine, in the centre of the front row; several buff-covered exercise books, pen, pencil, ink and blotting sheet, all laid out for me. I add Jason's silver watch which shows three minutes to ten. Around me, the creaking and rustling has ceased. The examiner, a heavy, slow man in a faded gown, is already handing out the first paper: Trigonometry. I close my eyes, in a last desperate prayer, and when I open them the paper, printed in small clear type, lies before me. I pick it up and with a start of joy perceive that the first question is one which Jason, with unbelievable cunning, has anticipated. I know the answer almost by heart. With compressed lips and fingers that tremble slightly, I pick up my pen and draw the first virgin exercise book towards me. Then oblivion descends . . . nothing exists but that steady outflowing which comes from my bowed figure, wrapped in a pale trance.

Late that afternoon, when Gavin and I returned to Levenford, the train was so full we had little chance to compare notes, though we agreed that the Algebra and Solid Geometry papers had been horribly stiff. Now, worrying about things that perhaps I had missed, I was depressed, spent and cold. My feet especially were cold, and at this point I had better admit, not only that my boots leaked abominably, but that one of them, the left, was worn completely through in the sole, leaving a hole into which three fingers could be comfortably inserted. Still, in my vanity, I had preferred these ruins to Kate's pointed boots, which, although sound, laced halfway up the leg. With considerable ingenuity I had covered the most gaping wound by an inner sole of brown cardboard, cut from an old hatbox taken from beneath Mama's bed. However, the rain and the hard pavements soon uncovered the futility of this subterfuge. In ten minutes I had worn through the cardboard and my stocking as well, and was walking on my bare foot. No wonder I felt a little damp as I sat in the steamy compartment, crushed between workmen in dripping oilskins.

Jason met the train at Levenford station and immediately took possession of me. In his rooms, while I sat down to a hot dinner of chops and potatoes, he asked me in a queer voice, urgent yet anxious, for the papers. Seated at the desk, beneath his metal reading lamp, using logarithms and books of tables, he worked out every answer; then came over, placed them before me without a word. I compared his results with my own, then glanced up at his strained face.

"Yes," I said.

"Every one?"

"Yes," I said again, humbly, yet exalted by the long breath which broke from him.

The next day, Saturday, we had French, English, and Applied Chemistry; for the final subject, which was Physics, we must wait till Monday. I put thicker cardboard in my boot and inked the sole of my foot as a precaution against the worst. Curiously enough, my chief concern was that I should be discovered, in full view of all the candidates, with this indecent, half-naked extremity. As we came up from the tramway terminus a heavy shower caught us. Gavin shared his mackintosh with me, but, of course, he could not share his boots.

What matter! Once in the examination hall all such trivialities were forgotten, lost in the throbbing sweep of my endeavour. I thought nothing of my wet feet until I was again in the train, when, indeed, I shivered and put my hand to my brow, suddenly aware that I had a frightful headache. I was alone. Gavin had remained in Winton to meet his sister, and, during the journey, I stuck my head out of the window into the rushing air to try to cure it.

At Levenford station Jason's faithful, waiting face danced before me; I smiled, to show him that I had not completely disgraced him. He gripped my arm again, protective rather than importunate, and guided me down the steps to the cab rank.

"You're done up . . . and no wonder. Thank heaven you have all tomorrow to rest."

He took me home in the splendid luxury of a cab, and Grandpa provided us with dinner, at which, so to speak, I was the guest of honour. During the meal, contrary to my custom, I talked without reserve. Pressed by Jason, I went over the French paper and related almost word for word the English essay I had written.

"Good . . . good," Jason kept muttering, moving his hands restlessly, growing more excited every moment. "It was excellent to bring in those quotations. You did well . . . very well to say that." There was actually, on Jason's lips, a dry white spume of excitement. Grandpa was equally affected: rarely had I seen him so worked-up. He ate nothing, hung upon my words. He was not only my patron and protector, but rejuvenated, living his youth again through me; he was actually sitting the examination, and winning it, himself. He beamed at me as Reid at last declared:—

"I don't want to say things I'll regret, Shannon. But you haven't exactly made a fool of yourself. Monday's paper is your best subject. Unless God turns you into a raving lunatic over the week end—and that is quite possible —for I myself already feel like one—you cannot fail to score less than ninety-five per cent, deaf, dumb, and blindfolded. Off you go now, for heaven's sake, and sleep your head off."

As I went slowly upstairs I distinctly heard Reid add to Grandpa, as though scarcely able to trust himself:—

"He hasn't put a foot wrong. Better . . . far better than I expected."

Oh, joy, supreme and blessed transport, making me close my eyes and cling, weak with praise, to the bannister of the stairs.

Next morning, Sunday, I awakened at half-past seven and got up to attend church at eight o'clock—an act so completely automatic I was halfway along Drumbuck Road before I realized how very queer I felt. My head still ached dizzily, my throat was painfully dry, and, although the grey day gave promise of being mild, I couldn't stop shivering. Still, I knew that the strain of the examination had played havoc with my nerves. And I must go to Communion this morning, not only out of profound gratitude for favours received, but also because it was part of a solemn vow which I had made to ensure my success.

When I returned from church I found it difficult to swallow my breakfast, I was chillier than ever.

"Grandpa," I said. "I'm awfully cold. It seems silly, but I wish I could have a fire."

He had been studying me from beneath his brows, and although his face expressed some surprise he offered no objection. He remarked, slowly, "I should think you've earned a fire. And you'll have one. In the best room in the house."

He laid and lit a fire in the parlour which, recently, we had used so considerably—the only period, to my knowledge, when this useless mausoleum achieved the status of a human habitation. I felt more comfortable in the armchair by the fire, much warmer; indeed I was soon burning all over.

"What do you fancy for dinner?" Grandpa had been in and out of the room all the forenoon, attending to the fire, glancing at me.

"I don't think I'll bother with anything. I'm not in the least hungry."

"Just as you wish, boy." He hesitated, but said no more. The next time he appeared he was wearing his hat and a casual air which would have deceived no one. "I'm away out for a stroll. I won't be long."

He came back, in half an hour, with Reid. As they entered the room, I looked up from the position into which I had sunk in the chair. Jason seemed both angry and disturbed.

"Hello, hello! What's all this?" he exclaimed in a brusque voice, utterly foreign to him. "Trying to make out you're sick, eh? Well it won't work, my good fellow. If you think you're going to run out at the last hurdle, you're very much mistaken."

He blustered forward, drew a stool up to my armchair and took my hand in his, roughly, like a man who is going to stand no nonsense. "Yes, you might have some fever. But we shan't take your temperature. I haven't got a thermometer. And I don't want to put stupid notions in your head. You've simply caught a cold."

"Yes, sir," I said, with difficulty. "I'll be all right tomorrow."

"I should hope so. Don't look so damned sorry for yourself. I warned you you'd get hysterical. Pull yourself together and try and eat something." He turned to Grandpa. "Bring him in some of that milk pudding and fruit you had last night." As Grandpa went out he resumed: "After what we've been through together, I'll get you to that examination hall if I've got to fill you to the ears with brandy. Is your head clear?"

"Fairly clear, sir . . . just a little dizzy."

Grandpa had come back with a saucer of stewed apples and custard. I sat up, determined to do my best, but after I had attempted a few spoonfuls I gazed mournfully at Reid.

"It's my throat, sir."

"Your throat, eh?" There was a pause. "Well, at least we can have a look at that. Come over here."

He led me to the window and adjusted my head none too gently, so that the light fell into my mouth—which, with an effort, I held wide open. He peered for a moment; then, by the immediate change in his attitude, conveyed to me by a lessening of the pressure of his hands, I sensed the presence of disaster.

"What is it, sir?"

"Nothing. . . . I'm not sure." He turned his face away, his tone was flat, absolutely crushed. "We'll fetch the doctor."

While he went out I reeled back to my chair. I knew now that I was very sick. Worst of all was the terrible dread, growing upon me, filling my throbbing head—the dread that I might not be well enough to complete my examination next day. Grandpa was sitting erect, motionless and silent, opposite me.

Within the hour Jason was back with Dr. Galbraith. The doctor took one practised look at my throat, then nodded to Jason.

"Get him up to bed," he said.

CHAPTER TWELVE

ONCE the acute inflammation has subsided, and the membrane begins to slough from the throat, diphtheria is neither painful nor prolonged. Following the first few days of fever, a dreamy state: the pulse beats slowly and the nerves are pleasantly relaxed. Sometimes this goes too far and the larynx, or even the heart, refuses to function, causing the physician to advance, hurriedly, with a charged hypodermic. But in my case there was no such drama. It was not a severe attack and Dr. Galbraith promised that I should be up in less than two weeks. After months of agonizing effort it was restful simply to be at peace, absolutely motionless upon one's back, hands limp upon the counterpane, eyes upon the shaft of sunlight which penetrated the narrow bedroom window and swung slowly round, filled with dancing motes, as the day advanced.

Do not imagine a mind tortured by disappointment and despair—far, far from it. Consider rather a soul exquisitely sustained by hope and faith. Yes, I had the firm belief, born of my enfeeblement and the close communion which I still maintained with things celestial, the unshakable belief that God in His infinite goodness would not wilfully destroy the future of a boy who loved Him, who had propitiated Him, day and night, upon bended knees. No miracle was required, no thunderous manifestation of the divine power —simply justice, a little act of justice. The examiners need only, in fairness, allow me an average mark for the paper I had missed. Even Jason had hinted that such a thing was not impossible. When the results were announced . . . I closed my eyes, with a faint and confident smile, murmured another tranquil prayer.

Papa and Mama had not yet returned. From postcards which Mama sent to Grandpa we judged the London visit a success. Mama hinted proudly that Papa had "put money into Adam's house," and, on the strength of this investment, which seemed almost to have gone to Papa's head, they were breaking their journey on the way home to spend an extra week with Grandma's cousins at Kilmarnock. They would return, with Grandma, in about ten days. Grandpa and I calculated, looking at the calendar, that I might just be up before they got back, a stroke of good fortune which pleased us both.

Grandpa made a pretty fair nurse. During my early delirium I was aware of him, as through a veil, moving about my room in his slippers, at all hours of the night, bending to give me my medicine, to swab my throat. I heard Mrs. Bosomley's voice, too, beyond the carbolic sheet which hung outside my door, as she handed in a jelly or a blanc mange "shape" she had made. I did not now feel like a destroying angel towards her.

Although I lay in isolation I was not without visitors. Dr. Galbraith, dry, uncommunicative and a little rough, arrived every day—if he recognized me as a spectator of that strange episode at the Antonellis' he did not once refer to it. Kate came several times to the front door, but not beyond, for fear of carrying the infection to her child. Murdoch had less reason to take precautions; even so, the frequency of his visits pleased and flattered me; I began to look forward to his lumbering step, his manufactured conversation, filled with heavy pauses, his ponderous jokes (which I knew by heart), his bulletins upon the progress of the new carnation. Gavin, of course, was eager to visit me, and Grandpa nearly broke my heart by refusing to admit him. However, I was mending fast, I should see him soon.

Now there approaches a day which cannot much longer be held back—the twentieth of July, a day which is unforgettable. At times I have had nothing to relate, except lagging trivialities, the absurdities committed by a boy in the painful process of growing up. But this day—this twentieth of July . . . It lives in the memory and must again be referred to, years later —a terrible day.

It was Wednesday, and the forenoon passed, completely uneventful, except that I was out of my room, dressed, and had actually taken a few paces in the garden. After lunch, since the afternoon was so fine, Grandpa rigged up a camp chair for me on the back green, where I sat with a board under my feet and a rug on my knees, enjoying the goodness of the warm sun. In convalescence one's heart is sometimes lifted by the forgotten brightness of the outside world, lifted as by that sudden burst of bird song which comes when the sky clears after rain. Grandpa was in the house removing the evidence of my illness, which could only upset Papa and which, since Mr. Reid had made himself responsible for the doctor's fees, need not concern him.

Presently I heard a step on the pebble path: Jason's vigorous crunching step. He came round the corner of the house, smiled, and sat down on the grass.

"Feeling better?"

"Oh, I'm perfectly all right now."

"Good." He nodded, plucked a blade of grass and threw it away.

There was a silence. Then Reid meditated, his gaze moving, here and there, in a peculiar way.

"You've taken things remarkably well, Shannon. Better than I did. I must admit, that day you got sick, I could have wept tears of blood. But we must get over our disappointments, it's one of the arts of living. By the way, have you read *Candide?*"

"No, sir."

"I must lend it to you. Then you'll find out how, thanks to merciful Providence, everything happens for the best."

I stared at him, unable to penetrate his mood, yet aroused, rather flustered by this apt mention of providential intervention. Suddenly he said:—

"The results of the Marshall won't be out for another week yet." He paused, then went on steadily. "But I've just seen Professor Grant. He told me the marks."

My heart, though supported by Dr. Galbraith's strychnine medicine, took a fluttering leap, I was conscious of the clenching of my hands, the start forward, the dry choking in my throat. And, as though understanding this, Reid spoke quickly, dropping his unsuspected bitterness, fixing his large oxlike eyes, almost pathetically, on mine.

"McEwan."

The prodigy had won. These boys always win Bursaries, though occasionally it takes an attack of diphtheria to enable them to do so.

Pierced through and through, I stared at Reid as he went on, plucking more grass and throwing it away. "He only scored nine hundred and twenty marks."

I saw, dimly, that Grandpa had come through the kitchen door and joined us on the back green, saw also that he knew. Reid had told him on the way in. I lowered my head in sudden blinding pain. With pale lips I asked:—

"Who was second?"

A pause. "You . . . twenty-five marks behind . . . even without the physics paper. I tried, I nearly went down on my knees to persuade them to give you an average. I offered to show them your class marks. I told them you'd have made not twenty-five but ninety-five." His voice fell into a twisted bitterness. "No use. They couldn't, or they wouldn't, break the rule."

Again silence. Even yet I could not fully apprehend the certainty of my failure. Some further revelation was surely in store for me. As though wishing to ease the agonizing tumbling of my heart Jason added:—

"Blair is third, one mark behind you."

Two boys in a boat on the moonlit Loch: "One of us, one of us must win." Momentarily, I forgot my own misery and confusion in a sudden rush of grief for Gavin.

"Does he know?"

Reid shook his head. "Not yet."

Suddenly Grandpa spoke, in a troubled voice, not the voice of a cheap gossip, but the voice of a man who has himself known misfortune, a voice which tells, unwillingly, something sad that must sooner or later be told. Grandpa could never bring himself to offer me sympathy direct. I think he wanted, at this moment, to distract me from the crushing agony of my own defeat.

"Provost Blair has come an awful smash."

I gazed at him numbly. "What do you mean?"

"He's failed, gone bankrupt in his business at last."

I sat paralysed, wrung with an added dismay. Gavin's father a bankrupt, ruined and disgraced . . . For Gavin to lose the Marshall was nothing; nothing to this. I suddenly saw, white and proud, the face of this boy who worshipped his father, like a god upon Olympus. I knew I must go to him at once.

I had enough presence of mind not to mention my intention. No one seemed to have anything more to say. I waited until Grandpa and Jason went into the house; then, without asking permission, slipped round the side path to the road. I scarcely noticed how weak and shaky my legs were; I wanted to find Gavin.

He was not at home. There seemed nobody about the Provost's grand house; no maid, or gardener; behind the official lamp-posts an air of upheaval and confusion. After I had knocked three times Miss Julia opened the door a little way, as though afraid of what fresh disaster this might reveal. She told me in a broken voice that Gavin had been for some days with friends in Ardfillan; she had telephoned him; he was returning on the four o'clock train.

I knew he would leave the train at Dalreoch. The sky was white with heat. Men were walking in their shirt sleeves, carrying their jackets, fanning themselves with their hats. I dragged myself along, fighting the weakness in my legs, reached the gate of the station yard as the Ardfillan train came in. I waited there, in my usual place, straining my eyes across the hot dust intersected by shimmering rails.

He was there. I saw him jump from the footboard of the stationary train and begin to cross the yard. He did not see me. His face was whiter than the white sky, his eyes stared straight ahead. He knew.

The guard blew his whistle, waved his bright green flag. A goods engine was shunting waggons slowly in the yard. From a stationary waggon, very leisurely, they were rolling barrels of potatoes on to a horse van. The picture is with me still, burned into memory.

As the passenger train pulled out, Gavin, crossing the net of rail-lines, withdrawn into himself, living in his own pain, appeared unconscious of the slowly shunting train on the other track. He wasn't looking where he was going. He was walking directly in the way of the approaching engine. I started and let out a wild shout of warning. He heard me. He saw the engine. But oh God! He had stopped. His foot seemed caught between the points, he was bending, twisting and tugging with all his strength.

"Gavin! Gavin!" I shouted and ran forward.

His eyes, dark in his white face, met mine across the shimmering yard. He tried frantically to move from the rails and could not. Then the engine was upon him. Before I could cry out again his own cry came and a red haze fell upon me.

When I came to myself the yard was crowded, full of voices and confusion. The engine driver, twisting waste in his agitated hands, was explaining to a police officer that he was not to blame. People were saying in shocked voices: "What a tragedy! His father . . ." They were trying to make out that Gavin had killed himself.

I crept home, clinging to the wall, shutting my teeth upon a deathly sickness, longing for the darkness. But when night came I did not sleep. Beneath my anguish a dark resentment began to work in me. How simple, how gullible I had been. My tortured thoughts were not yet clear but, swept by a sullen revulsion of feeling, I was conscious that I had reached a crisis in my life.

Next day Papa and Mama returned with Grandma, and as I remained alone, locked in my bedroom, I heard the stir of their arrival. Grandma was calling for me. But I gave no answer.

Avoiding them, I go out, slowly down the road, past the three chestnut trees, outlined against the sky, to the house where the blinds are drawn as if against the too persistent beauty of the world.

As I walk in staring weariness, hands plunged in my pockets, my fingers encounter a little medal, a "miraculous" medal which has been given me when I sat, a trusting child who believed in fairy tales, beside the convent syringa bush. A great sob swells up in me, thrusting upwards from my breast, into my throat. I take the holy trinket and fling it tremblingly away. So much for this God who destroys children, murders them and breaks their hearts. There is no God, no justice upon earth. All hope has gone. Nothing remains but a blind defiance of the sky.

Gavin lies on his bed, in his own room, fast asleep—in a dream from which he will not awaken. He is wrapped in his dream, his eyelids closed, his face untouched, untroubled. Still proud and resolute, he is remote, far from everything.

Julia Blair, her eyes red with weeping, shows me in silence Gavin's shoe, the strong heel of which he had almost wrenched away in his effort to free his foot, trapped in the point switch of the rail. No, he did not surrender. In his dream that brave heart still lies, undefeated.

BOOK THREE

CHAPTER ONE

As I CAME through the Works gates one February evening, the ground hard under my nailed boots and the street lamps wearing frosty haloes, I caught sight of Kate's little boy, Luke, waiting on his father and wearing his new blue Academy cap with all the pride of a boy who has just gone to school. This sudden evidence of time took me by surprise: almost like a blow. Heavens, I am getting old, I am seventeen!

"Give us a penny, Robie." He ran up to me, sturdy and red-cheeked, bright-eyed with his own importance.

I felt through my soiled dungarees with insensitive fingers and found a coin. "You should say, 'Please.'"

"Please."

"Do you know who used to give me pennies when I was about your age?"

I was speaking like a patriarch and, with eyes on the penny, he was not in the least interested. Never mind. It was one of the consolations of my life, this life already heavy with years, loaded with afflictions, in fact practically over, to give him pennies, to take him on Saturday afternoons to the football match where, forgetting my sombre dignity, I cheered just as madly as he.

"Your father will be out in five minutes," I told him over my shoulder as I moved off. "He let me away early tonight."

"To go to the concert?" he called after me.

My nod was lost in the darkness. But my heart treasured the thought as I trudged less wearily across the wintry Common: the prospect of this evening banished even my overpowering and inevitable fatigue. Tonight I should not fall asleep at the table the moment I had eaten my supper. Absorbed, I passed the dark bulk of the Church of the Holy Angels without my usual gesture of defiance—a fist clenched, theatrically, in the darkness.

Soon after Gavin's death, when I was on the point of leaving the Academy, Canon Roche had summoned me to the presbytery. He received me in his room with great friendliness and, after pacing up and down with his hands in the pockets of his soutane, turned to me.

"My dear Shannon." His dark eyes burned sympathetically. "All this may be God's way of proving you, of showing you the road you must go."

I looked down.

"You are thinking of going into the Works?"

"Yes," I said. "It's about the only thing left for me to do."

"There aren't many opportunities in a small town like Levenford." He reflected. "Robert . . . have you ever thought of the priesthood?"

I flushed darkly, my eyes still fixed on the carpet.

"Yes, I have."

"It's a wonderful life, my dear boy. A great joy and privilege to serve God as one of His chosen disciples." His gaze was bent warmly upon me. "I'm not offering you empty promises. There is a diocesan fund devoted to the splendid task of educating poor boys for the priesthood. It isn't a large fund. And naturally the candidates selected are few. But, in your case—I have written about you to the Bishop—if you wish, you will be elected immediately, you can leave for the Seminary next week."

I sat silent and ashamed. I saw that Canon Roche expected me to jump at his offer. Six weeks ago I might have done so. But now everything had changed: all my gushing fervour was replaced by arid bitterness.

"Well . . ." The Canon smiled. "What have you to say?"

"I'm sorry." I choked out the words. "I'd rather not."

An expression of surprise appeared on his face. He said quickly: "But don't you want to be ordained?"

"I did once," I said. "But I don't now."

There was a silence. He seemed for the first time to realize my state of mind. But he was too wise to remonstrate. Instead he concealed his disappointment and in a thoughtful, persuasive voice began to describe the happiness of a life devoted to the service of God. He opened up broad spiritual horizons, spoke of the culture and learning freely dispensed by Holy Mother Church. He fell into a pleasant reverie, touching upon his own student days at the Scots College in Valladolid—where, of course, if I wished, I too could go. He painted a picture of the Seminary buildings, of the Spanish landscape, and wound up, with a disarming smile, by recalling a special vine under which he used to take his siesta, refreshing himself, at the same time, with the delicious sweet grapes which almost dropped into his mouth.

I felt myself carried away. I liked and admired Canon Roche. In my emotional state, his winning kindness was irresistible. But something within me refused to surrender. My lips turned pale and stiff.

"I can't," I said desperately. "I don't want to go."

A much longer silence followed, then Canon Roche spoke in a different voice.

"I have no wish to influence you. You must decide for yourself. But I might point out that such a spiritual and material favour won't come your way every day. And of course we cannot hold it open indefinitely. Pray to Almighty God for guidance, and come and see me again on Saturday."

I went out into the grey afternoon. At the end of the week I did not return to the presbytery. My boldness in defying Canon Roche amazed me. But the seeds of rebellion were growing rapidly in my breast. If God would not permit me to be a scientist I saw no reason why I should yield to Him and become a priest. Anything seemed better than that—indeed, under the circumstances, the prospect of entering the Works actually assumed a special attraction. Frustrated and full of bitterness, seething with new and terrible ideas, I wanted, recklessly, to submit to the worst that Fate could do to me. And above all, I wanted to show that I did not care.

Tonight, after eighteen months, much of these forces had expended themselves. I still dramatized my situation. Yet underneath I was growing restless and less heroic. Should I never grasp the rich and glowing future for which I yearned, and which seemed always to elude me?

Preoccupied by these thoughts, I was in no mood for interruption, yet as I turned into Drumbuck Road, a figure, a too familiar figure, detached itself from the dim shelter of the wall at the corner and, with a measured greeting, shuffled into step beside me.

My burden, which I have inherited from poor Mama: Grandpa.

"A trifle snell tonight, Robert."

I answered him under my breath, asking myself what he was up to now. The week before I had found him outside the Fitters' Bar addressing a crowd of apprentices on Woman's Suffrage.

"I was wondering, my boy, if you would care to make me a small advance. A mere nothing. Sixpence. For a postal order."

I trudged on in disapproving silence. These competitions, upon which he spends half his day, are part of what he calls his "New Era." To exact the full resources of his declining years he wants to become rich—a mere bagatelle for a man of his potentialities. In the reading room of the public library he cuts out guilelessly, under the very nose of the prim lady librarian, every advertisement which promises him wealth—and the diversity of these cuttings must be seen to be believed. In his room he initiates a voluminous correspondence, supplies missing words, rhyming phrases, the last lines of limericks, a whole vocabulary manufactured from the six letters of the alphabet thoughtfully supplied by the editor of *Home Weekly*. I cannot even pass him on the stairs without his accosting me and, with a confidential air, producing from his pocket a crumpled paper.

"Will you have the goodness to listen to this one, Robert?" He clears his throat and quotes:—

> "There was a young lady of Twickenham
> Whose boots were too tight to walk quick in 'em.
> When she came to a stile
> There she rested awhile . . ."

Triumphantly he brings out his masterstroke.

"And then took 'em off and was sick in 'em."

His envelopes fall into the red pillar-box like snowflakes into a fire. Enraged at his lack of success, he declares "Limericks" to be an utter swindle and turns, with enthusiasm, to "Bullets"—a cabinetmaker in a neighbouring town has won a thousand pounds at "Bullets." . . .

Now, as we walked through the dusk, his voice held out persuasively the incentive of reward:—

"I'll repay you out of my winnings. The post office closes at half-past six, and tomorrow is the last day."

"I won't give you a brass farthing," I answered shortly. "And what's more, you're going straight up to your room. For once I'm going out tonight, and if you upset my arrangements with any of your nonsense, I'll break your neck."

Silence; subdued silence. The worst feature of Grandpa's New Era is the new susceptibility of its initiator to a reprimand. I turned into Lomond View, annoyed with myself, but luckily I had not spoken sharply enough to upset him. I watched him slowly climb the stairs—he was now short of breath, very tremulous on any kind of ascent—and waited until reassured by the click of his door before I entered the kitchen.

Papa, seated at the table, spreading his bread thinly and methodically with margarine, gave me a nod of greeting. But it was Grandma, sustained, mellowed, and reinvigorated by her twelve months of responsibility, who, while I "took the rough off" at the scullery sink, silently yet competently brought my "kept" dinner from the oven.

* * *

Mama is gone, she who was the soul of this house—a sudden syncope on that winter night, a year ago, when Papa made the scene over Adam's letter about the money. No one suspected that she was ill, unless it was she, herself; yet looking back, in self-reproach, one remembered that gesture which became more frequent, that flight of her hand to her left breast when she was agitated, as though she were trying by the pressure of her fingers to control some pain, to support a flagging heart.

She was pressing her side like that when I found her, alone, livid and gasping for breath, in the parlour.

"Mama, you're ill. Let me get the doctor."

"No," she gasped. "It'll only upset Papa worse."

"But I must. You're really ill . . ."

There was barely time for me to run for Dr. Galbraith. When I returned with him she had already lapsed into coma.

"Worn out." Galbraith made the brief comment as the feeble thread of the artery was lost beneath his touch.

"Will you be coming tomorrow, doctor?" Papa, bewildered, yet outraged by the unusual expense, put the question feebly.

"No." Dr. Galbraith turned brutally. "She'll not be here tomorrow. And you're lucky I don't let you in for a post-mortem."

I shivered at the thought of the desecration of that defenceless body upon a mortuary slab. But Papa, even after she was gone, weeks after the funeral, while recalling with pride the number of wreaths sent in, still seemed unconvinced that she had dared to leave him.

"She always said I would outlive her," he often remarked, with an air of grievance.

To my surprise, he had not sold Mama's things, and it became a regular feature of Sunday afternoon for him to go to the bedroom, take her few dresses from the wardrobe, brush them carefully, and put them back. He was beginning to miss her.

I, too, had failed to realize how much I owed her as she scurried in timid servitude, trying always to do her best, to hold the family together, to propitiate Papa and temper his awful parsimony, to keep her head up before the town, to please everyone—this weak and colourless bondwoman, this heroic soul. Mama was not perfect, her money worries often made her sharp and cross. In my Academy days she sometimes held back the few shillings for my fee-lines until the Rector came into the class, fixed me with his eye, and announced to my unbearable shame: "One boy in this form has not paid his dues." Again, when the agent called on her for Grandpa's insurance or when she singed, and so spoiled, the porridge, fits of anguished martyrdom would seize her; and with her head on one side, a wisp of hair almost falling into the pail of soapy water, she would scrub the house from roof to cellar, her lips compressed in terrible resignation. Nevertheless she was the nearest to a saint I have ever known. Only because I had sadness enough did I compel myself, with a love acknowledged too late, to think of her as she shook her fur, before her holiday, and smiled, in the sunshine. . . .

"It is really unbelievable." Papa now took a careful mouthful of his bread and margarine, touching me with his transparent, almost friendly smile— since I had begun to bring good wages into the house he had shown open signs of regard for me and often gave me his confidence at the evening meal. "The price of butter. Elevenpence halfpenny the pound. I don't know what the world is coming to. Fortunately this new substitute is just as palatable, and even more nutritious."

Grandma was crocheting industriously behind her cup of tea, a model of contained stability. Still an active woman, she was managing the household ably, with the aid of a day girl recommended to her by a welfare organization in the town. She had the force to oppose the more grotesque of Papa's economies and had insisted upon the necessity of this daily help.

"I haven't heard a word from Adam," Papa went on palely. "It simply can't go on. I've asked Kate and Murdoch to come in about it next Sunday. I'd like you to be there also, Robert."

I gave a mutter of acquiescence and went on eating, indicating with my fork to Grandma, who at once complied, that I wished more cabbage. Although the food was poor I had enough; I even had this ready service from the old woman. There now existed, in fact, between Grandma and myself, a steady, uncommunicative alliance. Here, surely, was proof of my advancement. It afforded me as much dark satisfaction as did my calloused hands and broken fingernails, my inveterate fatigue, the cough which had begun to trouble me and which I aggravated, deliberately, by smoking.

When I had finished I went upstairs. Sophie Galt, the daily girl, having taken Grandpa his supper tray, was turning down my bed before going home for the night. Undersized and pasty-faced, with short legs concealed by a sateen dress Grandma had made her, she was about seventeen years old, one of a large family living in the Vennel. She had a slight squint, so that she seemed to be watching one all the time out of the corner of her eye. Her underprivileged manner always made me uncomfortable, a feeling intensified since that afternoon when I had surprised her posturing with terrible coquetry before the mirror in one of Mama's hats, taken from the wardrobe.

"Are you going to the Burgh Hall, tonight, Sophie?"

"Oh, no. Where would the likes of me get a ticket?" She straightened my pillow with a great display of thoroughness. "Father got one though at the Club. I expect you'll see him there."

After a pause, she glanced round the room, then over the top of my head.

"Do you think that's everything?"

"I'm sure it is, Sophie."

She lingered, gave the counterpane a final pat, coughed, sighed, at last went out.

My preparations for the concert were not elaborate. During the past two years my acute consciousness of my own person had changed to a state of studied indifference. As I pulled off my shirt there was a general effect of length, of white skin with the ribs showing through, brown blistered forearms, the ever pale face with its plume of gleaming hair. I decided perversely that I would not wear a collar; many of the workmen affected the type of scarf which I now knotted round my neck; I, myself, was a worker, a Fabian in fact, and, by heavens, I would not be ashamed of it!

When I was ready I went into Grandpa's room. He was reclining in his chair, a large new leather-bound gilt-edged book in one hand, a piece of bread and cheese from his tray in the other.

"Truly remarkable, Robert." He took a bite without raising his eyes from the page. "There are thirty-two feet of bowels inside the human form."

This expensive-looking book, the sight of which raised gooseflesh upon my spine, was one of a large stack of identical volumes, which stood against the wall, and which had arrived, express, one month before, addressed to "Alexander Gow, Esquire, Accredited Agent and Canvasser for Fireside Medical Encyclopedia Ltd." Accompanying the package was a bundle of hand-outs: "*You owe it to your loved ones . . . more than one thousand diagrams and drawings . . . remedies for forty-four poisons, ladies' ailments, blackheads . . . simple everyday language . . . sensational, daring, see for yourself . . . don't send us a penny, our accredited agent will call every week . . .*"

While Grandpa pursues a house-to-house visitation in the remote parts of the town and continues, with interest, to increase his own store of medical knowledge, I recognize forebodingly that his peculiar talents are adapted to gathering in cash receipts, rather than to accounting for them. Unluckily, although his copying days for Mr. McKellar are positively over, the old man still writes a copperplate hand, sometimes a little shaky, but deceptively fine. At this moment my eyes fall upon a letter amongst the litter of papers on his table: "*My dear good sir: In answer to your esteemed request for references I hasten to advance the name of my son-in-law, who holds the responsible position of Health Administrator to the Royal and Ancient Borough of Levenford.*" And upon another which begins simply, yet more ominously: "*Madam.*"

Grandpa's hair is now almost white—that absence of colour sentimentally referred to as "silvery"—and his once indomitable figure has shrunk considerably so that his coat and trousers sag in places which were once protuberant. His blue eye is a little brighter than it should be, he changes colour very readily, while his nose, strange symbol of his virility, is paler, less turgescent—alas, quite flaccid. I know that Grandpa has passed a sad milestone in his gay career which may be found under a section, always interesting—and profusely illustrated—in the *Medical Encyclopedia*. Mrs. Bosomley has become merely a nodding acquaintance; and his taste in feminine society has declined to those groups of schoolgirls, and attractive little "junior students," whom he stops in the Cemetery Road and sends into fits of giggles with his gallant conversation. Yet Grandpa blandly refuses to acknowledge his own decay. On the contrary, he is more open in his profession of potency, holding himself as might a stallion, a prolific sire, and frequently, with a glance of proud complacency, thumping his poor old chest with his fist. "An oak, Robert. A guid Scots oak. If I stood for the Borough Council . . ." Thank goodness his smile admits that he is being humorous. "Why, in a year's time they might even want me for Provost."

"Grandpa . . ."

"Yes, my boy."

I wait until he looks up inquiringly from the page, regretting my display of temper earlier in the evening, resolved not to bully him but to play upon his new, his absurd susceptibility to flattery, and cajole a promise from him.

"I am going out to the concert. You are too fine a man, too much the soul of honour, to take advantage of that fact. You give me your word you won't move from here till I come back."

He beams at me, well pleased, over his spectacles, still marking his place with his finger. "Of course, my boy, of course. *Noblesse oblige.*"

That must satisfy me. I nod, close his door firmly and leave him to "Disorders of the Large Intestine."

CHAPTER TWO

THE concert was not one of the ordinary performances given every Thursday during the winter by the Levenford Orchestral Society, but a gala affair arranged under "distinguished patronage" in aid of the new Cottage Hospital.

When I reached the Burgh Hall, which stood next to the Academy in the High Street, scores of people were pressing into the entrance. I joined the crowd and, inside the gaslit auditorium, already warm and humming with voices, I chose a seat deliberately, with proud exclusiveness, in a back row underneath the balcony. No matter that Reid had reserved a front seat for me, beside his own; my place was here. In any case I wished to be alone, so that none might witness the emotions which this evening must bring to me.

With the detachment of one who has failed to be a great man and now prefers, at least for the time being, to be nothing, I watched the hall fill until extra chairs had to be placed amongst the palms that lined the cream-painted, stencilled walls. In the large and quite brilliant assembly I could see Kate and Jamie, settled sedately halfway up the hall; Mr. McKellar, with a legal air of waiting to be convinced; Bertie Jamieson with sleek hair, a high collar, and two smart young ladies.

In the second row, behind Sir Thomas and Lady Marshall, and an array of town counsellors, I made out Reid with his party—Alison's mother, her music teacher, Miss Cramb, and a stranger with a narrow head and a pointed iron grey beard who must be Dr. Thomas, the noted producer of "The Messiah" and conductor of the Winton Orpheus Choir.

From time to time Jason turned round as though searching for someone —across the sea of heads I clearly observed his face. Now and then he tugged impatiently at the short blond moustache he had recently grown, and which improved his appearance considerably. A thrill passed through me at his expression—I lowered my head quickly, grateful for his friendship, but determined not to be seen, to remain an outcast, entrenched and proud.

Nevertheless, I received a nod of recognition. It was Sophie's father, squeezing in on his free "Club" ticket, looking out of place, as if this was not at all what he had expected. Galt was a pale, lacklustre man with a damp cowlick plastered on his brow and a small ingratiating eye. He was in Jamie's squad with me and, while not a good workman, he had edged himself on to the committee of the local union. In the boiler shed, I was always running into him; and because of his daughter's presence in Lomond View he seemed to find a peculiar interest in me, as though, tacitly, some kind of bond existed between us.

Fortunately there were no seats vacant in my vicinity. I turned away and almost immediately the sudden dimming of the auditorium lights made me quite safe. Amidst some scattered applause, the curtain went up; my eyes were drawn to the stage.

The opening items of the programme increased my sense of tension, they so far surpassed the ordinary level of provincial entertainment. The orchestra began with some lively selections from "Pinafore." Then came the duet from "Tosca," sung by two well-known members of the Carl Rosa Company, at present appearing in Winton. A Brahms concerto, played beautifully by the organist of the City Cathedral, next filled the hall with noble and inspiring music. Lifted up, burning with eagerness, I trembled for Alison in her ordeal, which, every moment now, was growing nearer. I began to fear that too much would be demanded of her—she was so young to make her first appearance upon a public platform and in such expert company! This audience was discriminating, its interest had been whetted by months of "talk." Now, waiting, as I was waiting, for the event of the evening, it had reached a dangerous pitch of expectancy.

At last, after perhaps an hour, a rustle passed through the hall. I felt my heart beating louder than ever, beating with fear. Except for the grand piano and the accompanist seated unobtrusively before it, the stage was empty.

Then, quietly, from the wings, Alison came on, so young and unprotected that a hush fell involuntarily. She advanced to the front of the stage, immediately behind the japanned footlights, as though wishing, from the beginning, to place herself in communication with her listeners. She had grown since those days when we knocked our knees together over the geometry book; and her long soft dress of pale blue muslin, moulding her fine strong figure, made her seem tall. She wore a ribbon of that same misty blue in her brown hair, now "put up" for the first time. As she stood there, exposed to all these eyes, I felt a deep and secret pride; yet, at the same time, I caught my breath in jealousy.

She faced the assembly, her expression serious, her hands encased in white gloves, holding a sheet of music before her in the ridiculous fashion of the period. Although she shimmered, in a haze, before my straining vision, I saw that she was composed. She waited until the audience was settled, ready to give her its attention, then she glanced at her accompanist and the first restrained chord of the piano broke the stillness. She raised her head and began to sing.

It was Schubert's "Sylvia," which often had enchanted me as I stood hidden by the darkness under the linden tree outside her window in Sinclair Drive. And now, in this hushed hall, though I must share it with so many others, the joy of listening to the song made me stop trembling. I closed my eyes, surrendering to the delight of the pure, sweet notes, assured that this voice could hold captive, not one unseen listener, but all who were privileged to hear.

A burst of hand-clapping followed the ending of the song. Alison gave no sign; she stood, as though waiting to offer up again, without pride, that gift which had been bestowed upon her. When the hall was quiet she sang, first, Schumann's "Wanderlied," followed by "Hark, Hark the Lark"; then, before the stillness could be destroyed, she began the "Mattinata" of Tosti.

This song, which Melba made so popular, full of exacting runs and high notes, soaring upwards at one dizzy moment, and the next cascading downwards, presents great difficulty; its accomplishment, with ease and perfect trueness, brought the audience, already conquered, to Alison's feet. Even the least musical could realize the quality of this youthful voice. The applause refused to die; instead it grew in volume. I could see the other artists crowding in the wings, clapping and smiling. Alison was forced to return again and again.

At last, as though about to give way to tears—and indeed, tears were making my own eyes smart—she was led back by the accompanist. Her mother had stipulated as the condition of her appearance that she should sing only one group of four songs. Also, it was the rule of these charity concerts not to permit encores. But now all that was forgotten. Alison herself seemed incapable of speech; the accompanist, smiling at her, still holding her by the hand, announced that she would give one extra song. More applause. Absolute silence as the audience, triumphant, settled back.

The piano began, repeated the opening bar, and waited; for now Alison, extremely pale, appeared to hesitate. Only for an instant, however. As though freeing herself from all distraction, she clasped her hands—no longer holding that formal sheet—and filled her breast deep. Even before the first notes broke I guessed that she would offer her vanquished listeners an old Scots song. I had not dared to hope for my favourite amongst all these native airs, "The Banks of Doon." Yet this, with beautiful simplicity, was the song she sang.

> "Ye banks and braes o' bonny Doon,
> How can ye bloom so fresh and fair?
> How can ye chant, ye little birds,
> And I sae weary fu' o' care?"

The tender words lifted me to the world of my dreams, a world which Alison and I would one day roam together, hand in hand, not far beneath the sky.

When the last note faded, the silence in the hall was profound. A rigid spell; a community entranced. Then the storm broke. The Scottish song, so exquisitely sung by this Scottish girl, had set the Scottish audience on fire. Perhaps she had won her little victory by the charm of immaturity, perhaps by a pleasant trick of voice overestimated by local sentiment. The future alone would tell. For the present everyone stood up to applaud. I was on my feet, hoarse, completely hoarse, with cheering.

When the concert ended and I made my way out of the hall, slowly, impeded by the crowd, everyone spoke of Alison. Then, in the vestibule, as I was about to escape, an arm reached out and detained me.

"Where were you?" Reid's face was flushed as my own, flushed with pleasure, yet his tone was sharply annoyed. "We've been looking out for you all evening."

"I preferred to sit by myself."

I felt him frowning at me, as I stared sideways through the arched doorway.

"I'm beginning to get angry with you, Shannon. Why can't you put on a collar and behave like a decent member of society?"

This, from a man who had prided himself on his unconventional views, brought a smile of amusement to my lips.

"Must one wear a collar to be decent?"

"Really, this pose of yours is becoming a nuisance."

"If I'm so peculiar, why bother with me?"

"Oh, don't be an ass, tonight of all nights. Thomas is delighted with Alison. Come on to the reception room. I want to introduce you to him."

Anticipating my protest, he hustled me through the vestibule, along a corridor that ran parallel to the auditorium. He was in high spirits—his love of music had brought him, long ago, into touch with Mrs. Keith, he took a great interest in Alison's talent, and it was he who had arranged for the Orpheus conductor to attend her first public performance.

He gave me a forgiving smile as we approached the end of the corridor. "Couldn't have gone better. Here we are. For heaven's sake, try to look less like Lord Chesterfield attending his own funeral."

We entered a room, opening to the stage, where a number of the performers, their friends, and the town officials stood talking while tea was served by ladies of the Hospital Committee.

Alison stood in the centre of a large group, restored to calmness, yet silent amidst the chatter, holding stiffly a small presentation bouquet of white flowers. Her gaze wandered about the room, as if searching for some recollection of ordinary events which would help her to preserve her steadiness. When our eyes met she gave me, while her lips formed into a faint smile, a glance of communicative understanding.

Awkwardly, I allowed Reid to introduce me to Dr. Thomas, who gave me his free hand and a smile while continuing his animated lecture to Miss Cramb, who for once didn't look as though she had been sucking lemons. I refused the tea which Mrs. Keith offered me—I was thirsty but I knew that my shaking fingers would never support the cup. While I stood, apart, listening to the conversation, my gaze kept straying back to Alison.

At last, an eddy of the crowd brought me beside her. Near, like this, after the remote vastness of the stage, she created in me a wistful and half-fearful excitement, a darkened joy which brought a lump to my throat and twisted my mouth so that I could scarcely speak. Yet somehow I brought out my fumbling tribute, knowing that she disliked praise and was always disinclined to discuss her singing.

She shook her head to indicate that she had not pleased herself.

"Still," she added, as though continuing that unspoken thought, "they have asked me to sing at the Orpheus Chorale."

"A solo part?"

"Yes."

"Oh, Alison . . . that's wonderful."

She shook her head again, but her round young chin was startlingly firm. "It's a beginning."

There was a silence. People were beginning to leave now, putting on their coats and wraps. Quickly, before my courage failed, I said:—

"Alison, may I see you home tonight?"

"Yes, of course," she answered quite calmly, glancing round. "Everyone seems to be going now. I'll just tell Mother."

She went over to where Mrs. Keith, looking extremely nice in a dove-grey frock and antique quaint necklace, stood talking to Reid. I watched her as she surrendered her flowers, drew on her thick tweed coat and wrapped a white shawl with a tasseled edge about her hair. I felt Mrs. Keith giving me a mildly ironic look, less kind than before, a new expression which made me redden and move towards the door. It took Alison a long time to say good night to everyone, but at last we were outside, walking from the Hall together.

"I'm cross with myself." She spoke thoughtfully, after a silence. "Just think of it. Giving way like that and almost crying. I didn't though, thank goodness."

"But, Alison. Your first concert. It would have been perfect if you had cried a little."

"No, it would have been silly. And I hate people who do silly things."

I did not press the matter to another of our arguments: I was beginning to discover that our viewpoints were quite different. Even-tempered, capable, and contained, Alison was everything that I was not. She wasn't clever perhaps, nor had she much sense of humour, but in spite of her slow way of thinking, she was full of practical common sense. Also, she was ambitious —not in my intense and highflown way, but with a logical desire to make the most of her talent. She recognized, and faced with determination, the fact that to become a singer would require study, work, and sacrifice. Her exercises, those deep breathings which enabled her to sing a "long" scale, or to maintain a phrase lasting twenty seconds, had given her a kind of physical serenity. Yet under her placidity, this smooth-brown Juno had a quiet will of her own.

"Let's go up the hill, Alison." Trembling slightly I came a little closer to her as we walked along, aware that every step was taking us nearer Sinclair Drive. "It's a lovely evening."

She smiled at my appealing tone. "It's damp and cold. I think it's going to rain. Besides, Mother'll expect me in tonight. She may be bringing a few friends home with her."

A hot lump rose in my throat; I was ready, in my intensity, to die for her, yet she calmly allowed "a few friends" to come between us.

"You don't seem to appreciate me very much," I muttered, "considering that you'll be away most of the winter."

Mrs. Keith had lately begun to speak of the old house in Sinclair Drive as being too large for her requirements. With Alison's training ahead of her she wanted to economize. She was closing her home for the cold months and spending that time with her sister-in-law in Ardfillan.

"You sound as though Ardfillan were at the other end of the earth," Alison replied with a touch of asperity. "Can't you come and see me like other people? There'll be dances, Louisa's School Reunion especially."

"You know I can't dance," I answered miserably.

"It's your own fault for not learning."

"Don't worry," I said bitterly, "you'll have plenty of beaus. All Louisa's young men. And your own."

"Thank you. I daresay I shall. And I daresay they'll be more entertaining than someone I know."

My heart was bursting; and suddenly my anger gave way to despair.

"Oh, Alison," I gasped. "Don't let's have another quarrel. I'm so terribly fond of you."

She did not answer at once. When she did her voice was troubled, sympathetic, yet struggling against the unknown.

"You know I like you too." She added, in a lower tone, "Very much."

"Then why won't you stay out with me a little longer?"

"Because I'm hungry, I've had nothing substantial since four o'clock." She laughed at herself. We were now at the entrance to her house. "Why don't you come in? The others will be here any minute. We'll have refreshments and lots of fun."

I tightened my lips in the darkness, repelled by the idea of lights, crowds of people and banal conversation in which I was too stiff and proud to join. Under such circumstances I had no capacity for gaiety, the laughter which I forced, so as not to appear unusual, sounded hollow in my ears.

"Your mother didn't invite me," I said moodily. "It's no use. I don't want to come in."

"What *do* you want?" Alison said.

She stopped and stood facing me beside the currant bush in the drive.

"I want us to be together," I mumbled. "Just you and I alone. All I would want to do would be to hold your hand . . . so long as I was near you . . ."

I broke off, incoherently. How could I tell her what I wanted when my emotions were so tangled, my desires so agonizingly confused?

She seemed touched; her smile was hesitant.

"You'd soon get tired of holding my hand."

"I swear I wouldn't."

In proof of this I reached out and caught her fingers. Then my heart began to beat madly.

"Oh, Alison," I groaned.

She did not draw back. For an instant her lips brushed against my cheek.

"There now." In the darkness she was smiling at me quietly. "Good night."

She broke away and, holding the ends of her shawl beneath her chin, ran towards the front door.

When she had gone I stood for a long time in the shadow, torn between elation and disappointment. I hoped that she would return. Surely she would come to the porch and call me in. I had been a fool to refuse and would gladly go now. But she did not come. Gradually the glow faded inside me and, turning up my coat collar, I walked slowly away, pausing several times to look over my shoulder at the lighted window of her house. The wind caught me sharply at the corner of the drive. Alison had been right. It was a damp and icy evening.

CHAPTER THREE

MY WORK at the boiler shop was not that melodramatic toil one reads of in novels, but I was not cut out for manual labour and I found it hard enough. For the most part we made marine engines which went into the vessels constructed in the shipyard; we also built feed and suction pumps, which were usually crated and shipped abroad. I had begun in the foundry, where my job for months had been to file and clean the rough castings with a steel brush. It was heavy and dirty work. Jamie kept his eye on me and was kind in many ways, but our relationship forbade his showing me favouritism, the slightest sign of which would have been resented by the whole shop. My bench was near the cupola where the cast iron was melted and poured into sand moulds. Sometimes the heat was extreme and on windy days sand blew about the shed, making me cough. Later on I moved into the machine shop. Here the shaped castings were turned and burnished by innumerable lathes. It stood next to the fitting shop, the place of assembly for all the finished parts, and resounded with the clang of hammers and the whirring of its own machines.

The apprentices were, in the main, a cheerful lot, who took life with a carefree grin, were interested in football and horse-racing, and openly ribald in their attitude towards sex. At the end of four years most of them would become seagoing engineers; while others, like myself, went on to the drawing office. A few had come for more specialized training. There was a young Siamese of noble family who appeared every morning, silent and smilingly polite, in immaculate overalls, and who would no doubt, in due course, carry the benefits of Western civilization back to his own country. At the bench next to mine a Welsh youth named Lewis gracefully idled away his time. Lewis was the son of a wealthy Cardiff shipbuilder and, since the Marshall Works enjoyed a special reputation, he had been sent there for a practical course before entering the parental business. He was a vapid, easy-going youth, with oiled hair and a receding chin, who wore vivid bow ties and equally striking shirts. But he was good-natured and generous. He kept on his bench a huge yellow tin of cigarettes, a miniature trunk in fact, and everyone was free to help himself from it. Bored to tears by his enforced sojourn in Levenford, he spent much of his spare time in Winton, where he was often seen dining at the Bodega Grill, or occupying a box at the Alhambra Music Hall. He fancied himself as a lady-killer and his remarks dealt almost exclusively with his amorous adventures in the neighbouring city.

Amongst my fellow apprentices I had tried, anxiously, to find a congenial companion. But, although I longed for friendship, my advances were clumsy, and inhibited by the fear of a rebuff. When I made the effort and went out with some of the wilder spirits, the level of the conversation, long and vociferous arguments relating to the merits of one whippet over another or to the price paid for the winner of the local pony trot, soon reduced me to a stony impotence. I wanted to find someone with whom I could discuss books and music; who would respond eagerly with his own views when I tried to articulate the new ideas towards which I was reaching out fumblingly. But whenever I brought up such subjects, I felt myself suspect of showing off, and quickly relapsed into silence. Lewis was my closest acquaintance and once or twice I had been to tea at his lodgings. But the story of his conquests could be very boring and its obvious mendacity soon ceased to amuse me. Because of my kinship with Jamie and my capacity for silence —a quality always respected in the North—I was quite well-thought-of by the others. I tried, moreover, to do my work to the best of my ability. But I was dreadfully out of my element. The thought of the years that lay ahead of me made me sick at heart.

On the Saturday following the concert, two o'clock had struck and Papa, Murdoch, Kate, Grandma, and I were seated round the cleared table while Sophie, in the scullery, washed the dishes with such complete absence of noise that one could almost hear the straining of her ear drums.

Papa wore the suppressed and anxious expression which now seldom left him. He was thinner. His face had a grey and care-worn quality, his cheeks were sunken, his lips tight over his teeth.

"It's a fortnight after quarter-day." He made the remark in a controlled voice. "And still no word from Adam."

"There's time enough, Papa." Kate spoke placatingly.

"That's what you said before. You know when the conversion fell through he promised faithfully to pay me five per cent on the nine hundred he borrowed. And there's been not a penny of interest from him for the last six months."

In my childhood I had always thought of Adam as a man who would make a fortune. He seemed earmarked for self-made success. Yet now, although our meetings remained infrequent, I had begun to perceive, underneath that genial confidence in himself, an odd limitation. Perhaps it was the tendency, so common in the Scot who thinks himself a "big man," to underestimate other people and their capacity to resist him. Adam was too sure that he could outwit others. In the private enterprise upon which he had embarked so triumphantly with Papa, he had failed to anticipate that the owners of property adjoining his Kensington house, many of whom were rich and influential, would strenuously contest his right to derange their amenities by a conversion to flats. Under the sharp scrutiny of their lawyers the freehold was not quite so watertight as it had seemed. After placing all his available capital in the venture and inveigling from Papa his entire savings, after entering into commitments with a jobbing builder, he had found himself faced with a court injunction and the threat of a devastating lawsuit. The house still remained on his hands; it was now, indeed, the "white elephant" he had once joked about, and it was only too apparent that the men in the top hats whom he so openly derided had got the better of him in the end.

"What about the school that wanted to buy it?" Kate broke the silence.

"That fell through," Papa answered gloomily. "He'll never get rid of it."

"Oh, Papa, you shouldn't worry so much. Adam has a good position, he'll pay you back eventually. And you're very comfortably off. You get a nice salary, Grandma has her compensation and Robie is bringing in a good weekly wage."

Papa, still pale, could hardly speak for indignation.

"Have you no idea of the value of money? Do you expect folks to throw their earnings away without a word . . . and be reduced to beggary in their old age?"

"Nonsense, Papa." Kate spoke soothingly but firmly. "There's your superannuation pension. Besides, you're still saving money. Why, you even have a servant in the house, a thing poor Mama never had."

"I wish your mother was alive to hear you!" Papa's eyes flashed; he dropped his voice, breathing with difficulty. "You wouldn't believe how much that girl eats over and above her wages. Not only that, she's broken two of the best plates since she came here. It's wicked, wicked."

Abandoning Kate as hopeless he turned to Murdoch. "Why don't you say something? Should I go to McKellar and start proceedings against Adam?"

Murdoch, bathed in solemn abstraction, shrugged his shoulders, which his work had made big and heavy.

"I wouldn't get myself into the lawyer's hands."

Papa winced visibly and, after a moment, a pained sigh of agreement was forced from him.

"What am I to do then, what am I to do?"

Murdoch began to speak. Always ponderous, he had, during these past months, become invested with a new profundity.

"No one ever paid much attention to me in this house, Father." With surprise I noted that he had dropped the familiar "Papa." "The fact remains, I've made my own way in spite of everything. I have my partnership with Dalrymple, I'm happy in my work in the garden, I'm doing well. At the Flower Show this spring I mean to bring out my new carnation and, if God wills it," again I started with surprise, "I'll maybe have a chance of the Alexandra Gold Medal for the best exhibit in the Show." Murdoch smiled at us all owlishly through his big glasses. "Adam always made a fool out of me, Father. His ways are not mine. Nevertheless he's my brother and I love him. That's the answer to everything. Love."

"I don't know what you're talking about," Papa burst out. "I want my money back plus the interest."

Sophie had come into the kitchen with a scuttle of coal and was replenishing the fire. Papa kept still while she was in the room, but the moment she returned to the scullery he rose with an outraged air, removed the top lump of coal, and put it back in the scuttle. He was flushed, as though the exasperation in his breast had suddenly flared beyond endurance. "No one knows what I have to contend with. One thing after another. Adam! That old fool upstairs who ought to be in Glenwoodie! Cleghorn coming through his kidney operation! What a man could do about it I don't know."

"You could love, Father," Murdoch said kindly.

"What!" Papa exclaimed.

"Yes, Father," Murdoch continued gently. "I mean exactly what I say. If only you could taste, as I have come to taste, the joy of universal love."

He stood up in a peculiar manner. I knew instinctively that he was going to make one of those pronouncements, majestic and terrible, which reared themselves, like sea serpents from a placid sea—intimations from the depths which stunned by their magnificent unexpectedness, and of which to my knowledge, he actually made three: the first at Ardfillan Fair, when he said, "I am going to kill myself"; the third, not yet born, when he declared, after the Flower Show, "I am going to be married"; and the second, now, when, as though breathing the Holy Spirit upon us, he announced:—

"I'm saved. I'm now a soldier of the Lord."

No more than that, not a single word. Wearing that same rapt smile, he took his hat and went out.

While Papa sat, stupefied, in the kitchen, Kate and I followed him, equally dazed, to the door. And there, sure enough, was the explanation, the pure fount of his conversion: Bessie Ewing, walking sedately up and down in the road outside, waiting on him. She took his arm with a proud, possessive smile. Neither of them saw us, as they walked off, communing, Murdoch's chest expanded, as if already supporting the big drum of the Salvation Army Band.

A long pause followed.

"Well, that's that," Kate said. "Religion takes this family in funny ways." There was an odd look in her eyes as she turned to me. "We're a queer lot. Why you stay on in this house beats me."

I did not answer.

Seeing my hesitancy, Kate gave a little laugh and slipped her arm about my shoulders, pressing her cheek, still dry and chapped, against mine.

"Oh, dear," she said. "Life's an awful business."

She turned and went back to the kitchen, while I slowly climbed the stairs and, still wearing my dungarees, lay down on my bed, not yet having the energy to change. Kate had persuaded Papa and Grandma to accompany her to Barloan for tea. Presently I heard the sound of the front door as they went out. Sophie had already departed for her half-day. Grandpa and I were alone in the house.

The afternoon was very quiet. With my hands behind my head I tried to conjure those visions which were my splendid avenues of escape—no wonder Reid had named me "the melancholy dreamer." But I was held to earth, bogged in the recollection of that scene which had just taken place downstairs; my mind kept turning back to it, like a dog worrying a dry bone—no hope of nutriment, a kind of nervous persistence.

It was like a conspiracy to destroy what illusions were left to me. Murdoch's conversion simply parodied my past religious fervour. Papa's obsession with money, ludicrous and degrading, had become a mania. Now he took his tea without sugar and milk, practically lived on pease brose, undressed in the dark to save the gas. His manipulations with the ends of soap and candles were unbelievable. When anything broke in the house, he mended it himself. The other day I had caught him with a strip of leather and some nails, resoling his own shoes.

Oh, God, how I hated money, the very thought of it revolted me. Yet, at the same time, I spent my days longing for enough to take me to the University to pursue the work I loved. Kate's question kept buzzing in my head. Why didn't I leave this house? Perhaps I was weak, afraid to venture into the unknown. Yet there was another reason. Less from affection than from a grinding sense of responsibility, which I inherited no doubt from some Covenanting ancestor on Grandma's side, I felt myself unable to leave Grandpa. He would be sure to meet disaster if I didn't stay to keep an eye on him. Whatever the causes, I seemed doomed to extinction in this small town.

Instinctively I thought of Alison, cut by the cruel injustice of her calmness, and, although I yearned for her, Lewis's stories of his adventures came before my mind. They were cheap enough no doubt, yet I had begun to feel it a sign of lamentable weakness that I had never enjoyed such an experience as he described. In novels which I read, young men in my position were always brought to maturity by some nice woman, separated from her husband, not a raging beauty of course, but usually a charming little creature, with humorous eyes and a wide and generous mouth. But did such a one exist in Levenford? I smiled bitterly at the utter futility of the thought. Several of the girls who worked in the dye-works were well known to the apprentices but the look of their bold red faces, the rough slang which they exchanged as they clattered past in shawls and clogs, were enough to damp even Lewis's ardour, let alone my shrinking heart. I sighed heavily, got up and started to change my working clothes.

Suddenly I heard a ring at the bell. Although the ring was polite it disturbed me: now more than ever it was a formidable business answering the front door.

I went downstairs. It was a woman who stood on the threshold, a decent middle-aged and completely strange woman, dressed in dark grey, with limp grey cotton gloves, a black hat and handbag. She looked as though she worked with her hands, perhaps a housekeeper, yet altogether a superior person and she was, strangely, more nervous than I. She conveyed the impression of having waited for the benevolent cloak of evening before venturing to approach the doorstep of Lomond View.

"Is this Mr. Gow's house?"

My heart, which had been emboldened by her timidity, dropped back into my boots. "Yes, he lives here."

A pause. Was she blushing? At least she was uncertain of how to proceed for, studying me, she went off at a tangent. "Are you his son?"

"No, not exactly . . . a relation." While I refused to commit myself I perceived the situation to be altogether too obscure, delicate, and dangerous to be handled on the doormat, in full view of the road. "Won't you come in a moment?"

"Thank you kindly, young man." She spoke with careful gentility, and followed me into the parlour where, since it was dim, I found it necessary to light the gas. Without being asked she took a chair, seated herself upon its edge and let her eyes travel round the chill sanctuary, appraising this object and that with guarded approval.

"Quite right. A nice place you have here. That's a bonny picture."

I waited in mystified silence while, not without coyness, she removed her eyes from "The Monarch of the Glen" and inspected me.

"I believe you *are* his son." She gave a little laugh. "And he told you not to say so. Never mind, I respect your discretion. Is he in?"

"If you will be so kind as to tell me your business . . ." I suggested.

"Well, I may as well tell you." Again that little laugh quickly subdued. "Mind you, I am a respectable widow woman. I think this will explain."

She opened her bag, produced and handed to me two papers. One I recognized with trepidation as a letter in Grandpa's unmistakable handwriting. The other was a marked advertisement from the *Matrimonial Post*.

> Highly respectable widow, age forty-four, dark, medium build,
> affectionate nature, artistic, moderate means, would like to hear

from gentleman of agreeable disposition, preferably churchgoer, with good home and genuine intentions. Small family no objection. References given and exchanged. Reply Box 314 M.T.

I was stunned. No need for me to read Grandpa's letter; she herself modestly referred to it.

"I had six good replies . . . but your . . . Mr. Gow's was so beautiful I just had to see him first."

I could have rocked with laughter, if I had not felt like weeping. I exclaimed, quite wildly: "See him then, madam. Go up straight away. The top floor, first door on the right."

She took back the papers, replaced them tidily in her handbag and stood up, self-conscious as a girl.

"Just tell me one thing. Is he dark or fair? My first husband was dark and I thought it would be a nice change . . ."

"Yes, yes," I broke in, waving her on. "He's fair. But go up and see for yourself. . . . Go up."

She went upstairs and I stood waiting for the short, sharp sounds of her immediate disillusionment. But there was no scene—a good half-hour passed before she descended, and then her expression, though mystified, was pleased rather than resentful.

"Your uncle is a very nice gentleman," she confided to me in a vaguely puzzled voice. "But scarcely so young as I expected."

When, with a suggestion of reluctance, she had gone, I hastened to Grandpa's room.

He was seated, pen in hand, at his table, absorbed in the composition of his favourite "Bullets."

"Robert," he declared. "I have a sure winner here. Just listen to this . . ."

"But your visitor?" I interrupted.

"Oh, her!" He dismissed the lady with disdain. "She would have wearied me to death. Besides, comparatively speaking, she hasn't a curdie to her name."

I could not help myself. I turned away in a fit of laughter that was half hysterical, while he gazed after me over his spectacles, mildly astonished, yet unperturbed, a monument of respectability.

Downstairs, I put on my cap and muffler. The dusk was deepening and it held the promise of lights and Saturday night movement in the town. My spirits, unaccountably, had risen. There would probably be music in Reid's rooms, Alison and her mother might perhaps be there. I decided that I would go and make my peace with Jason. But first there was *The Flying Highlander*.

Every Saturday night at five o'clock the Port Doran–London express made a two-minute stop at Levenford to pick up West Coast passengers. It was a superb train, painted red and gold, complete with sleepers and dining cars where white napery and gleaming silver could be seen, through the windows, beneath shaded electric candles. Simply to watch that shining train pull out slowly for the great city of the South was enough to stir the blood, to raise in my breast the wild, vain, but still undying hope that one day I, too, would take my place upon its rich upholstery, beneath its soft rose lights.

I glanced at the clock. There was just time. I hurried down the dark road.

CHAPTER FOUR

THAT winter the Levenford Philosophical Club was making an effort to recover from the run-down condition which, at an earlier date, had provoked Reid's sarcasm. It had once been a fine club, modelled upon the Edinburgh Speculative Society. Mr. McKellar was the new president, and he had arranged for the resumption of the course of public lectures for which the Philosophical had been famous.

Papa did not now belong to the Club. Overanxious to advance his promotion, he had suffered some sad rebuffs from the other members and had come to regard the annual subscription as an unjustifiable expense.

I knew nothing of the lectures until one day towards the end of November when, passing me in the street, Mr. McKellar handed me a ticket without a word. He was a silent man and this uncommunicative gesture, effected without even stopping, was typical of him. The ticket read:—

A *Lecture will be Delivered*
by
PROFESSOR MARK FLEMING
on
THE STORY OF MALARIA
at
The Philosophical Rooms
Admit one   *Nov. 30th.*

I went eagerly to the Rooms on the specified evening, yet with the feeling that wounds scarcely healed would be painfully reopened. I sat wedged incongruously amongst stout red-faced townsmen, sedate and prosperous in their fine broadcloth suits. I reddened when McKellar let his eye drift over me without the slightest recognition. But the moment Professor Fleming began to speak I fell under the fascination of the subject and the man.

Mark Fleming was Professor of Zoology at Winton University, a spare dark figure of about forty, with sharp features, a clipped moustache and bright penetrating eyes. He had done some brilliant research work on the lungfish, Lepidosiren, adventuring into unexplored country on the upper waters of the Amazon. Tonight, since he was addressing laymen, his address was semipopular. But there was enough of science in it to stir my blood.

He traced the origin of the disease, discussed its ravages and the earlier mistaken theories regarding its cause. Then he passed to the first really scientific approach to the problem, describing the attempts of Ronald Ross to isolate the parasite, that magnificent and painstaking research which was finally crowned by the discovery of "sporozoites" in the salivary glands of a special mosquito. On the white screen at the end of the room Fleming showed us lantern slides, coloured micro-photographs, demonstrating the exquisitely symmetrical stages of development of the parasite. He revealed its life history, its cycle through the blood of various hosts, of which man was one. He summarized the preventive measures which had exterminated the scourge from large tracts of country and which—he gave the classic example—had made possible the building of the Panama Canal.

When he concluded, I drew a long deep breath. I had questions to ask which would show him my burning interest in his subject. But he was surrounded by important people who, although saying stupid and unimportant things, effectually prevented my approach. And presently, looking at his watch, he departed amidst smiles and many handshakes to catch his train.

The stimulation of this lecture, which revived all my passionate love of science, lingered for a few days. It was followed by a reaction of profound depression. For a week I walked with my eyes on the ground, suffering the desolation of a lost cause. Then, quite suddenly, I had a great idea. Usually my great ideas crumbled overnight. Seemingly brilliant, they failed to withstand the remorseless logic which I myself unleashed against them. But this was different—it grew steadily, like a shaft of dawn piercing the haggard gloom. I made my plans excitedly, yet with care.

On the following Saturday, I kept back five shillings of my wages, changed quickly, made a parcel of certain articles upon my chest of drawers, and came down to the kitchen for dinner.

"Hurry, Grandma." I smiled at her. "I want to catch the one-thirty train. Big doings on hand."

The old woman was alone in the room. She brought me a plate of mutton stew, but with no answering smile, which surprised me, in view of the new friendship that had sprung up between us. Then, before sitting down with her crochet work to wait for Papa, who was always late on Saturdays, she handed me silently, with an expression of peculiar reserve, a postcard.

I took it, and read it with a gathering frown. Why couldn't people leave me alone? The interfering card bore the stamped heading, PRESBYTERY OF THE HOLY ANGELS, and it said: *Will you call and see me Sunday afternoon at four o'clock?* It was signed: J. J. ROCHE.

Still frowning, but with a passing uneasiness, I crumpled the card and threw it into the fire.

Grandma seemed very busy with her needles, but a moment later, without looking up, she said:—

"So you won't go?"

I shook my head stubbornly.

Grandma's lacework appeared to please her greatly. Yet her tone was cautious.

"Suppose he comes here. What am I to tell him?"

"Tell him I'm not in," I mumbled, red-faced.

She raised her eyes and stared at me. Gradually a smile appeared on her face, a slow smile which deepened, as she got up.

"Let me give you some more stew, my man."

Grandma's flattering approval helped me to recover my self-possession. This communication from the beyond—for so I chose to regard my fervent past—had, to be frank, given me something of a shock. I really liked Canon Roche, and felt that my behaviour towards him had been shabby; also my proud indifference towards religion hadn't saved me some rather bad moments of remorse. However, my spirits were too high to be daunted. I put the matter out of my mind and was soon racing elatedly with my bundle for the Winton train.

My purpose buoyed me during the journey. When I reached Winton at three o'clock I took the green tram to Gilmore Hill and was again confronted by the grey, immovable, inspiring edifice of my dreams. I was older now and less easily intimidated, yet as I entered the University and approached the Zoology Department I felt my heart beating rapidly. I knew my way about here fairly well. I had longingly scanned the exterior of the department when sitting the Marshall with Gavin. Now I took one swift look at the big empty lecture theatre, then knocked on the door, panelled in ground glass, and marked LABORATORY. A moment later I knocked more loudly. Then, as no one answered, I boldly pushed open the door.

It was a long high room, half-tiled and lit by many tall windows. On the low benches there were rows of microscopes, wonderful glittering Zeiss microscopes with triple swing lenses. At each place was a double-tiered rack of reagents: drop bottles of fuchsin and methylene-blue, absolute alcohol, Canada balsam, everything the heart could desire. A large electric centrifuge was whizzing under its protective wire. Some complex apparatus I had never seen before gurgled steadily beside the range of porcelain sinks. At the end of the room I made out a tall man in a buff-coloured drill-coat attending to a cage of guinea pigs.

I went slowly forward, my parcel under my arm, intoxicated by the aromatic smell of the balsam mingling with the tang of formalin and the sharp fruity scent of ether. The afternoon sunshine was pouring into this heavenly place. As I came near, the man in the drill-coat half turned and let his eyes rest on me inquiringly.

"Well?"

"Could I see Professor Fleming, please?"

He was a tall lean man of fifty, with a bilious complexion and a ragged moustache. His nose was long and his hollow cheeks had deep lines in them. He turned back to the cage, skilfully caught up a guinea pig, and with a hypodermic syringe poised between the first and second fingers of his left hand, pressed down his thumb and delicately injected the animal with a few minims of a cloudy solution. While doing this he remarked:—

"The Professor isn't here."

A sharp disappointment gripped me.

"When will he be in?"

"He seldom comes here on Saturdays. Goes down to his week-end place at Drymen." Another guinea pig received its injection and was restored to the cage. "Come back Monday."

Now thoroughly cast-down, I exclaimed: "I can only get away on Saturdays."

He had finished the injections and, having dropped the syringe into carbolic, one in twenty, he gazed at me curiously.

"Can I do anything? I'm Smith, the head attendant. What is it you want?"

There was a pause.

"I want a job." My heart took a tremendous bound as I uncovered its secret, but I continued bravely. "I want to work here, in this lab, under Professor Fleming. I saw him last week, in Levenford; that's where I come from. Any kind of job . . . even if it's only to feed these guinea pigs."

The attendant smiled dryly—at least his fixed and heavy expression lifted slightly.

"These ones don't get fed. What are you doing now?"

I told him. Then rushed on: "I hate it, though. I love science . . . zoology especially . . . I always have. I've studied it for years, at school and at home. If only I could get a start here, I'd work my way up, I'd do anything, I'd take five shillings a week and sleep on the floor." I unlimbered my package. "I brought these specimens up to show Professor Fleming. Please look at them. They'll prove to you that I'm not lying."

He was on the point of refusing, his long face had turned disagreeable again. Then, with a glance at the clock, he seemed to change his mind.

"Come on, then. I've got ten minutes before I draw the sterilizer."

He led the way over to the bench and sat down on a stool watching me while, with trembling fingers, I tore the string and brown paper from my collections. I was anxious, of course, yet eagerness and hope were surging in my breast. I felt that I could convince this dubious and saturnine man of my genuine, my unique qualities. I had brought all my specimens, everything. But I did not trouble to exhibit the commoner varieties. I went straight to my rarities, my special hydra, my unclassified Bryozoa, my incomparable Stentors.

While I nervously described them he listened attentively, scrutinizing everything from beneath his heavy lids. Once or twice he nodded and several times shook his head. When I opened my box of sections he displayed his first signs of interest. Leaning forward he took the box from me, removed the slides and held them one after another against the light. Then, pulling a microscope towards him, much as a virtuoso might tuck a violin beneath his chin, he began, while I scarcely breathed, to examine them under the high-power. His hands were stained and dirty, his wrists bony, protruding, I could see, from cheap frayed shirt cuffs. But his long fingers were incredibly sensitive, manoeuvring the oil-immersion lens with careless, impressive accuracy.

It took him a dismayingly short time to run through all my precious work. He honoured three slides with a second inspection; then, straightening himself, he faced me, tugging at his straggling moustache.

"Is that the lot?"

"Yes," I answered very nervously.

He tapped out some tobacco and rolled himself a cigarette which he lit at a Bunsen flame on the bench.

"I had a collection like that when I was your age."

I stared at him in complete surprise: it was the last thing I had expected him to say.

"Maybe not so good on sections. But I think better on Spirogyra. I'd attended Paxton's night school course at the London Polytechnic and I sweated my guts out every week end on the Surrey Ponds. I thought I'd make another Cuivier of myself. That was more than thirty years ago. Look at me now. I'm fed to the teeth with routine. I get fifty bob a week and I have an invalid wife to support." He inhaled musingly. "I tried to get in by the back door of course—the only one that was open to me. No use, my lad. If you want to be colonel of the regiment don't enlist as a private. I've been stuck as a lab attendant all my life."

I felt a sinking feeling at my heart. "But you think my work shows some promise? You said my sections were good."

He shrugged his shoulders.

"They're all right, considering you cut them with an old hollow ground Frass." He gave me a quick glance. "You see I know. I did it myself. But now we have electric microtomes. Manual dexterity is at a discount."

"At least it would get me a laboratory job?" I was trembling with anxiety. "In spite of what you say I want that. I'd even come in as a lab boy."

He gave a short laugh.

"Can you make Roux's solution? Can you smoke a hundred and fifty recording drums in half an hour? Can you separate blastomeres at the four-cell stage of cleavage? It takes five years to learn that job properly. D'you know that my lab boy is a man of sixty? I let him off today because his rheumatism's bad!" His lips were smiling but his look was bitter and sad. "If you want my advice, young fellow, you'll put the whole idea out your head. I don't deny that you have got a turn for this. But without money and a university degree the door is shut in your face. So go back to your machine, and forget it. It's not a bad life, a marine engineer. I'd give a lot myself to see the world on an old ocean-going tramp."

There was a silence. I began mechanically to put away the specimens in their boxes, to parcel them again with paper and string.

"Don't take it too hard," he said when I had finished. "I meant it for the best." He gave me his hand. "Good-bye and good luck."

I went out of the laboratory and down the deserted hill. Already the round sun was setting, streaking the dove-grey with rose. I did not take the tram, but kept on walking, across the Park. A crisp wind sent the fallen leaves scurrying along the paths, like children running out of school. I did not feel, or see, the lovely twilight. Amidst my disappointment a strange rage was burning within me. I refused to believe what Smith had told me. It was all lies. I would return to see the Professor himself next week. Nothing would stop me from achieving my ambition.

And yet, in my heart, I knew that the attendant was right. He might be soured and disagreeable but he had spoken sincerely. The longer I reflected the more surely I realized that my fine scheme for entering the department as a technician was impracticable. It was a case of the wish being father to the thought. The only way to enter was as a fee-paying student and that, of course, was impossible. What hurt most of all was the indifference with which Smith had dismissed my specimens. True, he had praised them faintly. But having, in my foolishness, expected so much, this mild approval served only to dash my high hopes to the ground. A blast of bitterness fanned the fire within me. Strangely, I was not despondent, but wounded and furious. And, as I reached the central section of the city, becoming conscious of the futile package which I still carried, I was possessed by a sudden fatalistic determination. I had failed again. I was fated never to serve my beloved science. I would finish with it for good.

Making my way down Buchanan Street, I entered the Argyll Arcade, a covered passage leading to Argyll Street and occupied by a number of odd little shops. Next to an establishment which sold model engines I found the place I wanted. In the window goldfish were swimming in a green glass tank surrounded by packets of dog biscuits and ants' eggs, amidst a confusion of mousetraps, butterfly nets, rubber articles and sheets of postage stamps. Above was the sign, NATURALISTS' BAZAAR AND EXCHANGE MART.

Inside I waited, breathing the musty odours, until a small, care-worn man in a shiny black suit dipped out from behind a curtain at the back.

"I want to sell my collection."

I undid my package again, this time with vehement fingers.

"It's good stuff," I said when I had laid out the boxes on the counter. "Just look at these dragonflies."

"We're not really buying just now." He spoke in a throaty whisper, putting on a pair of pince-nez and beginning to look carefully at everything, weighing each object with white damp fingers.

"No, there's no demand for that stuff." He said regretfully when he had finished: "I'll give you seventeen and six for the lot."

I gazed at him indignantly. "Why, that yellow *aeschna* is worth a pound itself. I've seen it priced in the London catalogues."

"This isn't London, it's the Argyll Arcade." His voice was no more than a husky murmur—either he had a dreadful cold or some affliction of the larynx. And his manner was quite indifferent. "That's the best I can do. Take it or leave it."

I felt angrier than ever. I had never before experienced the difference between buying and selling. Seventeen and six for five years' work, for these wild, difficult and dangerous climbs upon the Longcrags, these long careful hours stretching far into the night . . . It was a raging insult. Yet what could I do?

"I'll take it."

When I left the shop, no longer encumbered, my arms seemed light and my head was hot. With the coins he had given me and what remained of my original five shillings, I had more than a pound in my pocket. It was six o'clock, the city was bright with lights. I set out recklessly to enjoy myself.

At the corner of Queen Street I found a small restaurant. It looked Bohemian and in the window a tempting display of white fish and red meat was set out between two giant artichokes. I plunged through the swing door, crossed the soft carpet and sat down in a velvet-cushioned booth.

It was a cozy little place, over-upholstered in an old-fashioned way, discreetly lighted by pink-shaded candles like those I had so often admired in the diner of *The Flying Highlander*. I was nervous with the waiter who had a curly moustache and a tight white apron reaching almost to his feet. But I ordered a good dinner of kidney soup, escalope of veal with mushrooms and a Neapolitan ice cream. Then he put the wine list in my hands. Pale but determined, in a voice which shook only slightly, I ordered a flask of Chianti.

I ate slowly: I had not tasted such rich, delicious food for a long time. The wine drew my tongue and cheeks together at first, but I persevered and gradually got to like its rusty flavour, and the generous warmth which flowed all the way down with every swallow. The restaurant was not very full but one or two couples occupied the booths. Opposite me, a good-looking man was entertaining a plump dark girl in a coquettish little hat. I watched them longingly as they laughed and talked in low tones, their heads very close together.

The bill came to nine shillings. It was a colossal figure but now I simply did not care. I finished the wine, tipped the waiter a shilling, received his bow with satisfaction, and went out.

What a glorious night! Lights glittering, movement and excitement in the streets, delightful, interesting people thronging the pavements. At last I was living, I had buried my obsession, I was free. I bought an *Evening Times* from a newsboy and scanned the amusement column beneath an electric sign. There were two variety shows in town, an Edwards musical comedy, a "positively the last night" appearance of Martin Harvey in "The Only Way." None of these appealed to me. Then, at the foot of the list, I observed with delight that a repertory performance of "The Second Mrs.

Tanqueray" was being given at the old Theatre Royal. I proceeded to the Royal, took a pit stall, and went in.

Although I had read considerably, and had vague memories of being taken to "Cinderella" by my mother in Dublin, I had never been to a real play in my life. When the curtain rose I was conscious of a thrill of emotion. And soon I was quite carried away. This was the kind of world I had so often visualized, where people never spoke without being witty, where courageous souls burned away their lives in a pure white flame. With all my impressionable, thirsting senses, I drank in every word.

When I left the theatre I was wildly intoxicated. I too wanted to grasp life with both hands, to experience those joys which had so far eluded me. Glowing and voluptuous images rose sensuously before me.

The theatre had emptied early: it was only half-past ten. The streets were much less crowded now, some were quite deserted as I made my way towards James Square, a small open space in the centre of the city flanked by the General Post Office and a large department store whose plate-glass windows remained illuminated all night. Lewis, with a knowing smile, had dropped hints about James Square.

I began, nervously, to walk up and down the broad pavement of the square. Several members of the opposite sex were doing the same thing, pausing occasionally with an air of abstraction, as though waiting for a bus. One was extremely stout, bursting out in all directions. She wore a big hat covered with feathers and lace-up boots on her pianolike legs.

"Hello, dearie." She murmured to me, maternally, as we passed.

Another was tall, thin, mysteriously veiled, dressed all in black. She walked very slowly, with a slight stoop. Occasionally she coughed, but politely, into her pocket handkerchief. She gave me a weary smile which froze my blood. I halted, mystified and dismayed. I could see no one remotely approaching the lovely visions of my excited fancy. Perhaps I should do better in the centre of the square.

I crossed the street to the small ornamental garden, decorated with statues and intersected by paths. Here it was darker, more romantic. And there were more promenaders. Encouraged by the greater promise of the shadows I strolled up the central path. A girl approached, her figure young, seductive in the darkness. When she passed I drew up and turned round. She had stopped and was looking back at me. When she saw that I was interested in her, she turned, and slowly, with an inviting movement of her head, sauntered on again.

My blood was pounding dizzily in my veins. I stood for a moment. Should I follow or wait until she had again made a circuit of the little garden? It was a blind circle, she must return this way: I sat down, tremblingly, on a bench at the edge of the path. I only realized that the seat had another occupant when a man's voice addressed me.

"Got a fag, mate?"

I fumbled in my pocket and brought out a packet of cigarettes. I could see dimly that he was an oldish man, down on his luck, a regular tramp in fact.

"Thanks, pal," he said. "You wouldn't have a match?"

Hurriedly, under the leafless trees, in the dark garden, I struck a match and held it to his cigarette. The cupped flame illumined for an instant the remnants of his face. Then it went out.

I sat on the bench a long time, stiffly. I gave him the rest of my cigarettes. I walked heavily to the station. My legs were so weak I could hardly stand. I just caught the last train.

I was alone in the compartment. I sat staring at the board partition in front of me. There was nothing, after all, nothing in life that was not completely ruined. I had sold my collections, my birthright . . . for this.

Suddenly I caught sight of a little peep-hole which some mischievous passenger had cut in the wood of the dividing partition. Crushed, overwhelmed by despondency and horror, I rose nevertheless, impelled by nameless curiosity, and put my eye to the little hole.

But the next compartment was empty, quite empty too.

CHAPTER FIVE

The winter continued damp and wet. I was now in charge of a light turning-lathe and, resigned to a future at the Works, I tried to take an interest in the machine. But my mind kept wandering; I made mistakes; I saw that Jamie was becoming annoyed with me.

One day towards the middle of December he came up to my bench, frowning, with a metal connecting rod in his hand.

"Look here, Robie," he said gruffly. "You'll have to buck yourself up a bit."

I flushed to the ears; it was the first time he had ever spoken to me in such a tone.

"What have I done?"

"You've wasted eight hours' skilled time, to say nothing of the material." He held out the steel piece. "I told you to drill this with a number two x. You've used a number four and ruined the whole job."

I saw that I had been guilty of a careless blunder. But instead of feeling sorry I was conscious of a slow resentment. I kept my eyes on the ground.

"What difference does it make? Marshalls won't go bankrupt."

"That's no way to talk," Jamie replied sharply. "I tell you straight it's time you stopped crying for the moon and put your back into your job."

He lectured me heatedly for a few minutes; then, having expended his anger, he growled, before moving away: "Come up and have supper with us next Saturday."

"Thanks." I had turned white and my lips were stiff. "If it's all the same to you, I'd rather not."

He stood for a moment in silence, then walked off. I was furious at Jamie, but most of all at myself. I knew that he was justified. As I stood there, sulking, Galt came over from an adjoining bench.

"I saw his nabs putting the dog on you. He's a bit too given to that sort of thing."

Galt was only too ready to air a grudge against any exercise of authority and in his approach I sensed the sympathy of one incompetent workman for another. He had not shaved for a couple of days and his appearance was particularly slovenly. I could not contain myself.

"Oh, shut up."

He drew back with an offended air. "Don't be so high and mighty about it. Next time I'll think twice before I offer you a kindness."

I resumed my work. In the days which followed I tried to improve. But nothing went right. I handled my tools so recklessly, I gouged my thumb deeply with a cold chisel. The wound became infected and suppurated, causing an ugly abscess which Grandma poulticed for me. I felt Jamie watching me uncomfortably, looking as though he wished to speak.

"That's a sore-looking hand you have," he said at last. "It doesn't seem to heal."

"It's nothing," I answered coldly. "Just a scratch."

I almost welcomed the pain which this festering wound caused me. My mind was as dark as the wintry skies. Alison had gone to Ardfillan. She wrote regularly in answer to my frequent and passionate communications but never at great length. When the post brought a letter from her my heart swelled suffocatingly. I took the letter to my room, locked the door, and opened it with trembling fingers. Her writing was large and round, only three or four words to each line. My eager eyes soon devoured the double sheet. She was working hard at two new songs. Schubert's "Ständchen" and Schumann's "Widmung." She and her mother had gone skating with Louisa on the private pond at Ardfillan House. Dr. Thomas had been to see them once. Mr. Reid had called twice. Everyone was looking forward to the Reunion Ball. Would I not try to come to it? Again and again I read it through. What I longed for was not there. Quickly, I sat down and began my reply, ardent and reproachful, pouring out my soul.

A week before Christmas, Lewis sauntered towards me at the lunch hour.

"I say, Shannon, there's not a bad dance on in Ardfillan next Saturday. Let's go together."

I took a bite of bread and cheese, trying to maintain a stolid attitude. "I'm afraid I'm not much of a dancer."

"Never mind. You can sit them out." He smiled. "I usually do."

"I don't think I can get away."

He persisted in his good-natured effort to persuade me. "It's quite an affair. The St. Bride's Reunion. Lots of pretty girls and a top-hole buffet. I've had a couple of tickets sent me. You really must come."

In spite of my determination not to expose my feelings, an insufferable emotion mastered me. I had no dress suit; I could not dance; it was impossible for me to go. The affability of his manner, the friendliness of his insistence, above all the easy indifference with which he took the dance, like all the other good things in life, for granted, acted on me like a goad.

"Damn it all . . . Can't you leave me alone?"

He stared at me in surprise; then, with a shrug of his shoulders, left me. I was immediately ashamed of myself. All afternoon I kept my eyes fixed to my machine, cold and sick inside.

On Saturday evening I took the five o'clock workman's train to Ardfillan. For a couple of hours I wandered about the deserted promenade, now swept by a December gale. As I sheltered behind the bandstand on the vacant esplanade with my coat collar up, memories of Gavin rose from the surrounding darkness to haunt me. It was here at the Fair that we had sworn never to be separated. Such a short time ago . . . It seemed a lifetime. Now Gavin was gone, while I stood and shivered, on the very spot where, full of hope and courage, we had pledged ourselves to conquer the world.

Towards eight o'clock I made my way to the Town Hall. Mixing with the small crowd which had collected to see the local gentry arriving for the dance, I waited on the pavement outside. A fine rain began to fall. Presently the cabs and motors began to roll up.

Hidden amongst the other spectators, who were mainly domestic servants, I watched the guests enter, happy people, smiling and talking, the women in evening gowns, the men in tail coats and white ties. I saw Lewis stroll in, groomed and oiled to perfection. A moment later, with a start of surprise, I caught sight of Reid's stocky figure hurrying up the steps. At last, after an interval, Alison and her mother appeared. They came in a large party with Louisa and Mrs. Marshall. My heart stood still at the vision of Alison, in a white dress, her face quietly animated, her eyes bright as she talked to Louisa, moving over the strip of carpet. When she disappeared the first strains of the orchestra came stealing out to me from inside the Hall. My heart seemed crushed in my breast. I clenched my hands in my pockets and walked rapidly away. There was no train for three quarters of an hour. I went into a fish-and-chip shop in a poor street near the station. I had not eaten since lunch and I ordered myself a twopenny portion of chips. Hunched on a bench in the dark little shop I swilled vinegar on the greasy potatoes and ate them with my fingers. I wished I could get drunk. I wanted to degrade myself to the lowest depths.

On Monday morning at the Works I met Lewis going into the machine shop. A strange impulse made me stop and smile to him, not in apology, but with a man-of-the-world directness.

"Look here, old chap," I said. "I'm sorry I cut up so rusty last week. Did you have a good time on Saturday?"

"Yes," he answered suspiciously. "Not bad."

"The fact is"—my smile broadened—"I had a very special appointment with a lady, a young widow I met in Winton, and I got rather annoyed at you trying to drag me out of it."

His face cleared slowly. "Why didn't you say so, you ass?"

I laughed and nodded knowingly.

"Lucky devil." He looked at me enviously. "Nothing like that at Ardfillan. Very proper and correct. You were wise not to come."

This cheap lie cheered me up momentarily, although soon it brought a reaction of disgust. I retired more than ever within myself, avoiding people, making a virtue of my loneliness. When Kate asked me to her house I usually made some excuse. I saw very little of Reid. On one occasion when we met he gave me a peculiar smile.

"I'm doing my best for you, Shannon."

"In what way?" I asked, surprised.

"I'm leaving you alone."

I walked off. I could find nothing to say. I was deadeningly tired, and sick of everything. Strangely, the one person whom I turned to was Grandma—perhaps I was attracted by her rocklike stability. Where Grandpa was a mere straw in the wind, with no roots to hold him, she drew sustenance and support deep, deep from her country origins, almost it seemed from the soil from which she had sprung. I sat late at the kitchen table talking with her while she gave me glimpses of her "early days" on her father's Ayrshire farm—at the cheesemaking; bringing fresh baked bannocks to the harvesters in the fields; watching the potato pickers as they danced at night, to the fiddle, in the barn. More and more, I noticed in her little "peasant" tricks— her habit, for instance, of picking out the peas from her broth and arranging them in a neat circle round her soup plate, so that she might eat them afterwards with pepper and salt. She was full of country sayings (like "Beetroots give you lumbago" or "Ne'er cast a clout till May goes oot") and she retained her full fondness for brewing "herbals." Her memory, especially for family dates, was wonderful. With her crochet hook she could still make exquisite, intricate-patterned lace which she wore on her cap and collar and which gave to her a perennial air of freshness. Repeatedly, she assured me that her family was long-lived, that her mother remained in full possession of her faculties up to the age of ninety-six. She was quite sure that she would surpass this record, and remarked often, with a composed sigh, of Grandpa and her friend Miss Minns, "how sadly they had failed."

Christmas was almost at hand. The shops in the town were bright with holly and paper streamers. The festive season made but the slightest difference at Lomond View: Grandma would go out to the Watch Night service, Kate might send us a plum pudding; Grandpa, if unrestrained, would not stay sober. Nevertheless, as Christmas Eve approached I felt myself growing restless and uneasy. To combat this I plunged more deeply into the books which I borrowed from the public library. At night I was often so tired that when I settled to read I drowsed off at once, wakening with a start as my nostrils filled with the smoke of the expiring candlewick. But on most Sundays, during that dismal winter, I lay in bed half the day, poring over Chekhov, Dostoievski, Gorki, and the other Russian novelists. My earlier liking for romantic fiction had yielded to a more sombre and realistic taste. Also I had begun to muddle my head with philosophy: plodding through Descartes, Hume, Schopenhauer and Bergson, far out of my depth yet rewarded, now and then, by a wintry gleam which increased my sense of exclusiveness and my haughtiness towards theology. My sardonic smile crumbled the whole structure of divine revelation. Impossible for a scientist, a savant, to believe that the world had been brought to being overnight, that man was created by a process of clay modelling, and woman by the transformation of a rib. The Garden of Eden with Eve eating her apple beside the grinning serpent was a charming fairy tale. All the evidence pointed to a different conception of the origin of life: the development from primaeval scum, through millions of years, of colloidal compounds in the great seas and swamps of the cooling earth, the timeless evolution of these protoplasmic forms, through the amphibians and reptiles, to the birds and mammals, a truly remarkable cycle which—dismal thought!—made Nicolo and me brothers, practically, under our skin.

Shorn of my illusions, I sought soulful consolation in beauty. From the library I took out works upon the great painters and studied the coloured reproductions of their masterpieces. Then I came upon the Impressionists. Their new ideas of colour and form delighted me. Returning from work, I would pause to stare for a long time at the purple shadows cast by the blue chestnut trees or at the pale streaks of lemon lingering in the evening sky behind the Ben. Foolish and morbid, suffering dreadfully from the "green sickness" of youth, I invested this mountain with a portentous symbolism: it represented to me the unattainable in life. If I could not reach the summit, at least I stood, in an attitude of scornful challenge, at its base.

Although defying the lightning, and everything else, I felt miserable when Christmas Day arrived. The night before I had gone to Barloan with a present for Kate's little boy. I wanted to help fill his stocking and, in my heart, I hoped for an invitation to Christmas dinner. But they were all out when I called: I tied my parcel to the door handle and came away. Amongst the few cards which I received there was one from the convent Sisters; I smiled over it—just the correct kind of smile—but my superiority did not make me happier. When one o'clock drew near I could not face the dismal meal downstairs. I took my cap and went out.

The grey streets were deserted as I wandered through the town. There was no restaurant in Levenford where one could have a real meal. At last, in desperation, I went into the Fitters' Bar. Here I had a glass of beer and some bread and cheese. This cold fare did not make the prospect of returning to the cheerless house any more enticing. There was not even a fireplace in my room.

The public library opened between two and three o'clock, a concession to the fact that the day was not a general holiday. It was warm in the library.

I spent most of the hour there, and borrowed another book. Then I set out for home.

A raw fog had come down and darkness was not far off. As I came along Chapel Street I did not see a tall figure looming towards me, but the instant I heard the tap-tap of an umbrella on the pavement beside me I guessed who it was, and I could not repress a start.

"Why, it's you, Shannon." Canon Roche's tone was friendly. "I've been wondering if you'd gone to earth for the winter."

I kept silent, telling myself that I would not be afraid of this man who was, after all, only human and not in the least invested with mystical powers.

"I have a sick call at Drumbuck Toll. Are you going that way?"

"Yes, I'm going home."

There was a pause.

"My card to you the other week probably went astray. The post office is no respecter of postcards. I had a colleague staying with me, a South American father over here from Brazil. Knowing your interest in natural history, I thought you might have cared to meet him."

"I've lost my interest in natural history."

"Ah!" I could almost feel his eyebrows lift. "Has that gone too? Tell me, my dear fellow, has anything been saved from the wreck?"

I walked on with my head down.

"What have you got there?" He slid the book from beneath my arm. "*The Brothers Karamazov*. Not at all bad. I commend Alyosha to your notice. He's a young man with some grace in him."

He gave me back the book. For a few minutes we continued in silence.

"My dear boy, what's been the matter with you?"

His change of tone took me by surprise. I had expected a severe reprimand for "falling from grace," "missing my Easter duties" and so forth; the mildness of his voice made my eyes smart. Thank heavens it was dark—he would not catch me that way.

"Nothing's the matter."

"Then why don't you turn out as you used to? We've all missed you, the Sisters and I especially."

I gathered all my strength, determined not to remain overawed and mute. I wanted him to know what had been taking place in my mind.

"I don't believe in God any more. I've given up the whole thing."

He received this in silence. In fact he walked on so long without replying that I stole a look at his face. It was thin, tired-looking and discouraged. I realized with a shock what had never struck me before—that he too was burdened with his own sorrows, and the thought that I had probably increased them deepened my compunction. Suddenly he began to speak, gazing straight ahead, as though talking to himself.

"You don't believe in God, you've achieved a triumph of reason. . . . Well, no wonder you're rather proud of it." He paused. "But what do you know about God? For that matter, what do I know of Him? . . . I'm afraid the answer is, nothing. He is absolutely unknowable . . . incomprehensible . . . infinitely beyond the grasp of the imagination, of all the senses. We can't picture Him, or explain His treatment of us, in human terms. Believe me, Shannon, the intellectual approach to God is madness. You cannot fathom the impenetrable. The greatest mistake we can make towards God is to be always arguing when we ought simply to believe in Him blindly."

He was silent for a moment before resuming.

"Do you remember when we once discussed those creatures who live five miles down in the ocean, feeling their way, without eyes, in the blackness . . . a sort of eternal night . . . only occasionally a faint phosphorescent gleam? And if they're brought up, nearer the light of day, they simply explode. That's us, in our relation to God." Another pause. "The greatest sin of all is intellectual pride. I know pretty well what's in your mind. You've reduced everything to terms of the single cell. You can tell me exactly the chemical composition of protoplasm . . . Oh, very simple substances. But can you synthetize these substances into life? Until that happens, there's nothing for it, Shannon, but to go on in humility and faith."

Again there was a silence. We had almost reached the corner of Drum-buck Road. As he turned off towards the Toll, leaving me to continue alone, he gave me a parting glance before vanishing in the fog.

"You may not be seeking God, Robert, but He is seeking you. And He will find you, my dear boy, He will find you in the end."

I went towards Lomond View slowly, in a tangle of emotions. I should have felt proud that I had asserted myself: it was something to have the courage of one's convictions. Instead I felt shaken, afraid, and, at the bottom of my heart, horribly ashamed.

If Canon Roche had used the tricks of his trade, the usual shopworn phrases about the wiles of the Devil and so forth, I should have felt myself justified. One ill-chosen word on his part would have routed him. If he had wrung me with sentimental allusions to the Babe now lying in the Manger, I might have wept, but I should never have forgiven him.

Instead, he had met me on my own ground and quietly shown me my insignificance. Suppose, after all, that the Supreme Being existed. How absurd I should be, a tiny diatom, a feebly whirling rotifer, presuming to defy Him. And what terrors, what torments would be my punishment—worst of all the torment of knowing that I had denied Him. I had at that moment an over-powering desire to fall on my knees, to yield, in blind humility, to the solace of prayer. But I resisted, shivering and stubborn, unconsciously beginning to walk a little faster. As the outlines of Lomond View appeared, I surrendered only to unconquerable sadness. I groaned inwardly: "Oh, God . . . if there is a God . . . what kind of Christmas have you given me!"

CHAPTER SIX

In May we had a late frost followed by a thaw which turned everything to slush. Yet one evening, two weeks before the Trades Holiday, as I trudged home from the Works through the mud and melting snow, the buds were forming upon the hedgerows, I felt the coming spring stirring in my limbs. Alison was home; and on the Trades Holiday, not so far distant, we had arranged to take a trip to Ardencaple—I was looking forward to our excursion with all my heart.

At Lomond View when I entered the kitchen I immediately sensed something unusual in the air. Grandma was seated at the table with an air of resignation while Papa, his hand on her shoulder, was doing his best to propitiate her.

"Fetch your supper yourself, Robert." He straightened himself and gave me a significantly mournful glance. "Sophie has left."

The news did not strike me as especially momentous. I put down my lunch tin, washed myself in the scullery and came back. As I took my hot covered plate from the oven Grandma turned to me, amplifying Papa's explanation in a "put-out" voice.

"After all I've done for her, to walk out without a word of warning. It's past understanding."

"We'll get somebody else, sooner or later," Papa remarked softly. "After all she was very wasteful . . . and a big eater."

"I can't do it all myself," Grandma protested.

"Robie and I will make things easy for you." Papa gave a dreadful, playful kind of smirk. "I don't mind making my own bed. As a matter of fact, I'm very fond of housework."

I saw that he was secretly overjoyed to be free of the expense of the maid and that he would do his utmost to delay the engagement of another.

When I had finished my meal, to oblige the old woman I took up Grandpa's bread and cheese and cocoa, on my way up to my room. As I turned the handle of his door, and carried in the tray, he was seated by a small fire, with his coat over his shoulders.

"Thank you, Robert." He spoke in a mild and reasonable tone. "Where's Sophie?"

"Gone." I put down the tray in front of him. "Left without notice."

"Well, well!" He looked up with a surprised, slightly injured expression. "You amaze me. You never know where you are with people these days."

"It's a little awkward."

"It is indeed," he agreed. "I must say I liked the girl. Very obliging and young."

It was a relief to find Grandpa in a restrained mood, one of these blessed intermissions which filled him with his old contemplative quiet. I thought he looked frail, tonight, a trifle under the weather; and I stood a moment while he dipped his bread in his cocoa and slowly ate it.

"How's the leg?" I asked. Lately he had begun to drag his left foot as he walked.

"Fine, fine. It's only a sprain. I have a grand constitution, Robert."

Next morning, at the Works, I was conscious of Galt, Sophie's father, watching me with a peculiar air. We were working on a new generator and he kept hanging about in my vicinity, coming over now and then to borrow a wrench or a file. Selecting a moment when Jamie was at the other end of the shed he said:—

"I want to see you when we knock off."

I gazed with distaste at his colourless, unshaven face, barely lit by a lustreless eye.

"What for?"

"I'll tell you later. Meet me in the Fitters' Bar."

Before I could refuse Jamie appeared and Galt moved off. I felt puzzled and upset. What on earth did he want with me? I told myself I would not go. Yet, at five minutes past six, driven by an uneasy curiosity, I went into the Bar, immediately opposite the Works Gates, and found Galt already seated at a small table in the corner of the long sawdust-strewn saloon, which was almost empty, not yet lit up for the evening.

He greeted me with an earthy smile. "What'll you have?"

I shook my head stiffly. "I'm in a hurry. What's all this about?"

"I'll have a half first." He called for the drink and when it was brought he said: "It's about my Sophie."

I flushed indignantly.

"That has nothing to do with me."

"Maybe not." He drank his whisky in reflective fashion, his eyes wandering all round me. "But it'll be a proper scandal if it comes out."

It was as if he had dashed a bucket of water in my face. Bewildered and confused, there was no denying the thrill of intimidation which icily traversed my spine.

He gave a nod towards the other chair at the table.

"Sit down and don't be so high and mighty. You can stand me another half, too." He paused, again searching me with his small mean eye. "You've no objection?"

"Have one if you want," I muttered.

"Good health," he said when the second drink came.

Half an hour later I went along Drumbuck Road, white-faced and stiff, burning with rage and misery. The leaves were opening on the sappy chestnut trees, but now I did not see them. When I reached the house I climbed the stairs to Grandpa's room, shut the door behind me, and faced him. At my entrance he had risen with a letter in his hand.

"Look, Robie!" He sounded eager and pleased. "A consolation prize in the last competition. A coloured pencil case and a bound volume of *Good Works*."

"You and your *Good Works!*" In my bitterness I hustled him back, upsetting his books and papers.

He gazed at me, crestfallen.

"What's the matter?"

"Don't pretend you don't know." My wretchedness, rather than my rage, made my voice low and concentrated. "When I think of it, after all your promises . . . when I'm surrounded by my own troubles . . . Oh, God, it's the last straw."

"I don't understand." His head was beginning to shake.

"Then think." I bent over and shook him. "Think why Sophie left."

He repeated the words, his eyes wearing a look of blankness. Then a light seemed to break over him. He stopped shaking and confronted me with a new expression, no longer wondering but almost apostolic, raising his right hand like Moses about to bring a fountain from the rock.

"Robert, I swear to you we were always the best of friends. No more than that. Nothing."

"Indeed!" Bitterness was choking me. "You expect me to believe that . . . with your record!" He looked guilty. "You've landed yourself in a hopeless mess. And I wash my hands of you."

I turned away and went out of the room, leaving him quite frightened, on the hearthrug. While I ate my supper I struggled with the implications of this new worry—one minute it seemed trivial, the next full of limitless disaster. Moodily, I wondered if I had done wrong to conciliate Galt . . . to bribe him, in fact, by paying for his drinks. Surely that in itself was an admission of guilt. Yet, if I had taken a firmer stand, there was no knowing what he might have done. Oh, misery of miseries! While I dreamed of love as something warm and glowing, this thing came, sordid and disreputable, to mock at me.

An hour later as I went up to my room I found the old man waiting for me on the landing, a sheet of notepaper in his hand. He held this out to me, with dignity and a hint of triumph.

"I've settled everything, Robert." He placated me with a half-smile. "An open letter to the people of the town. Read it."

Wearily, I let my eyes run through the long epistle, addressed "To the Editor of the *Levenford Herald*." "Sir . . . an unwarranted aspersion has been cast against me . . . I appeal to my fellow citizens . . . nothing to conceal . . . a life without blemish . . . pure as the lily . . . respecter of true womanhood . . ."

"Goes to the point." Grandpa watched my face eagerly. "It'll just be in time for next week's issue."

"Yes." I met his gaze. "I'll take care of it for you."

"Good, good!" He patted me tremulously on the shoulder. "I didn't mean to offend you, Robie. The last thing in the world. A friend in need is a friend indeed."

I forced a smile which seemed to comfort him, at least he shook me gratefully by the hand.

As he returned to his room dragging his foot after him, suddenly, as a kind of afterthought, he put his head round the door.

"Robie," he said gravely. "My poor wife was a wonderful woman."

Oh, God, what next? I had not heard him mention her name in ten years. I went to my own room. I began to tear into small pieces his open letter to his fellow citizens.

On the following day Galt approached me as we knocked off work. I had expected this and had braced myself to meet a recriminating attitude. To my surprise his manner was quite affable.

"You're in no hurry tonight. Come on in the Bar with me. If you're not too proud."

I hesitated. Then I realized that it would relieve my mind if some sort of understanding were reached between us. We went into the Bar.

There, with his feet in the sawdust, Galt kept the conversation on his favourite topic, "the rights of man." He was a pertinacious speaker—at the Union meetings it was admitted that he had the "gift of the gab"—with a few high-sounding phrases which he brought out with a triumphant air. He believed that the workers were everywhere exploited and preyed upon, "bled white" by their employers. He wanted the men to rise and take the reins of government in their own hands. "Up with the masses, down with the classes!" was his slogan. He was beginning to use the new word "Comrade" and he spoke with unction of "the dawn of liberty."

"Well, I suppose we'll have to get down to brass tacks." He shook his head regretfully. "My worst enemy couldn't call me anything but a fair man. But I will have my rights. There's no getting over the fact that Sophie has got to be compensated."

I felt a fluttering in my inside. Long afterwards, when I discovered, in a curious way, that Grandpa had no more than put his arm around the wretched Sophie's waist—last feeble prance of the decrepit stallion—I cursed myself heartily for being such an easy victim. Now I gazed at Galt glassily.

"I'm glad you don't deny it." He approved my silence. "It shows you have the right stuff in you. Now to make no bones about it. I want five pounds. Five pounds and we wash the slate clean, everything forgiven and forgotten. These are my terms. And I can't say fairer."

I stared at him in dismay.

"I couldn't get such an amount to save my life."

"There's money in that house," Galt said accusingly. "If you don't get it, I'll go to Leckie myself. He's an old skinflint but he'll pay up sooner than have this plastered over the town."

What on earth was I to do? I saw clearly enough that he had picked me as the easiest and least resistant line of approach. Yet it seemed equally clear that if I failed to get the money he would take the matter to Papa, who had lately been grumbling horribly against Grandpa, threatening again to send him to the Institution at Glenwoodie.

"Will you give me time?" I asked at last.

Galt answered magnanimously. "I'll give you a week, Comrade. That's reasonable."

I stood up. As I went out he pressed my arm with a peculiar archness. "You're the one that somebody likes."

I walked home, shamed and outraged, my head in a whirl. In looking for a guiding principle I had turned to the shining idea of the brotherhood of man, attending meetings, studying the pamphlets, thinking feelingly in terms of "suffering humanity." We working men were allies, marching forward under the hostile sky. No one could have been more vehement than Galt in protesting the noble virtues of the downtrodden poor. Yet his own poverty was the result of indolence and shiftlessness. And now he had been given his chance to prove his nobility, he was using it to tread all over me.

During the next few days I racked my brains for ways and means of finding the money. There was only one person whom I could possibly approach. In the fitting shop, for the rest of that week, while Galt kept looking at me, I kept looking at Jamie. Recently our relations had returned to a happier footing, he seemed to feel that I was making a greater effort to "get on with the job." Several times I almost brought myself to the point of speaking to him, then my courage failed me. But on Saturday forenoon, conscious of a growing importunity in Galt's manner, I went up to the head of the assembly shed.

"Jamie." I spoke breathlessly. "Could you lend me some money?"

"I thought something was on your mind." He threw away his cigarette end and smiled at me, at the same time reaching in his pocket for a handful of cash. "How much?"

"It's more than you think." I swallowed hard. "But I promise I'll pay you back."

"How much?" he repeated, still smiling but a trifle dubious.

"Five pounds."

He stopped smiling, looked at me incredulously.

"In the name of God. Have you gone balmy? I thought you meant a couple of bob."

"I swear I'll make it up to you out of my pay."

"What do you want it for?"

"I can't say. But it's important."

He was looking at me curiously. He let the handful of change fall back into his pocket. His expression was cold, disapproving, and disappointed. He shook his head.

"I thought you were beginning to get your feet on the ground. I'm not the Bank of Scotland. I've a hard enough job to make ends meet."

I retreated, horribly humiliated by this sharp rebuff: I could wear any number of hair shirts without a murmur, but a single disparaging word would reduce me to the depths. For the rest of the shift I kept my head down, avoiding Galt's persistent stare. When the hooter blew I dodged him, bolted for the gate and ran half the way home.

During Sunday I managed to lie low, but all the next week Galt nagged me mercilessly. My first hesitation over, I had assumed, identified myself with this obligation. I had an agonizing desire to discharge it. I was a perfectionist, all my early undertakings were infused with a do-or-die intensity, and this was no exception. I wanted the final feverish satisfaction of "paying Galt off." I actually felt that I, myself, owed this money, that it was a just debt which I must at all costs repay. Galt fostered this illusion. He hinted at police court proceedings. He warned me that I was now mixed up in the affair. Remembrance of thoughts and stirrings which had troubled me when Sophie did my room added to this sense of guilt. Was I not just as bad as the old man?

When Saturday came round I was at my wit's end. I tried to elude my persecutor but Galt was waiting for me at the gates. He delivered his ultimatum. He told me in a surly voice, suggestive of the truth, that he had contracted obligations with the local bookmaker.

"If you don't bring it tonight," he said, "the fat will be in the fire with a vengeance."

As I walked away my mood turned bitter and wounded. I told myself that I was sick to death of carrying other people's burdens on my shoulders. I had done enough. I could do no more.

When I got home Grandma was coming downstairs with an air of quiet complacency, and her "Good Book" in her hands.

"He's been asking for you." She made a movement of her head back and upwards. "He had a queer turn this morning. I stopped with him a bit and read him a chapter." Lately she had adopted this worthy practice—in the face of his manifest decline a new protective attitude had replaced her old enmity towards Grandpa.

I stood, undecided, in the lobby, then against my will I went up, turned the handle of the door. He was dressed but resting on his bed, extremely subdued, and looking quite poorly. I had to say something.

"What's wrong with you?"

He smiled. "Too much spiritual reading maybe. I could do with a bit of *Hajji Baba*." He gazed at me speculatively. "You'll be going to the football match this afternoon?"

"There's no match."

He did not say anything more. He expected nothing. Yet I went down to have my dinner, resentful of his desire for my company. I had said that I would have nothing more to do with him. I meant to keep my word.

After lunch it began to rain. I hung about with my hands in my pockets staring out of the window. Then, I climbed the stairs moodily.

I made up his fire until it burned brightly. We settled ourselves and played three games of draughts, also several hands of "nap," a card game in which our stakes were matches, and to which Grandpa was much addicted. We scarcely talked at all. But afterwards, while he reclined in his chair, I read him the adventure of Hajji in the Sultan's palace, which always caused him to chuckle. At four o'clock I made tea and some hot toast and dripping. Afterwards he lit his pipe and sat back with his eyes half-closed.

"This is like old times, Robie."

I felt like breaking out and slanging him. When he was calm, relaxed, like this, the lapses which had marked his whole life seemed all the more wickedly unnecessary. I was furious with him. Yet while he sat drowsing I could not free myself from memories of his kindness to me when I was a child. Of course it was not all kindness, but in part a manifestation of his temperament. He was always something of an exhibitionist, a great character actor, and the role of benefactor was very near his heart. Still, allowing for all this, how could I resign him to his fate at this late hour? He could never endure Glenwoodie: I had seen the place when we went out to visit Peter Dickie. And to such a man as Grandpa it would be the end.

I sighed and got up. As I left the room it annoyed me horribly to see that he was fast asleep in his chair.

That night I took my microscope, which Gavin had given me—my only possession of any value, in fact a really sacred possession which I had sworn never, never to part with, not even if I were ruined and a beggar in the streets. I pawned it in the town. I got a fair price, five pounds ten shillings—slightly more than I had expected. Then I came along the Vennel and crossed the court to the chipped, chalk-scrawled, brownstone building where Galt lived. He was leaning against his doorway in his shirt sleeves.

"I've brought you the money," I said.

His fingers closed over the notes. He looked up at me. His face broke into a sheepish grin.

"That's us clear then. Come on inside a minute." He indicated an interior which was littered and untidy, the spotted wallpaper covered with his "Brotherhood" certificates, pinned cutouts of footballers and boxers.

I shook my head and began to walk away, my spirits suddenly rising by leaps and bounds. Halfway across the Common I realized that, in my nervous excitement, I had given Galt all the money I had received for the microscope, ten shillings more than he had asked. What did it matter? I was clear of him, clear and free. If I had not been so conscious of my maturity, I would have run and jumped. As it was, I went into the shop at the end of the Common and with the small change in my pocket bought myself a round puff-apple pie. I ate it slowly, going up Drumbuck Road, in the still clear evening, savouring every morsel, licking the crumbs from my fingers. How good it was! How pleasant that the evenings were drawing out! The light was limpid and tender. A thrush was singing in the chestnut branches. As I drew near I suddenly apostrophized the inoffensive bird.

"One day I'll show you! Hah! You just wait and see!"

CHAPTER SEVEN

LEVENFORD, as Mama had once said, was a smoky old town, but the woods, lochs and mountains round about were beautiful. There were all sorts of local Rambling and Photographic Clubs with nominal subscription fees of about half a crown, yet when Kate or Jamie pressed me to join, when Grandma, even, with a shrewd look, suggested that a brisk walk "would do me no harm," I merely shook my head and went up to my bed to read. I, who once lived, practically, upon the high summits of the windy crags, had not seen the real countryside for months. However, on the morning of the Trades Spring Holiday, I felt a swift resurgence of my expeditionary fever.

Unhappily, in Scotland, there is always an enemy to combat—the weather. And on this day of freedom, I saw, from my window, as I dressed, that the skies were grey and dripping. Was it to be one of these incessant downpours rendered more depressing because of the sense of a holiday spoiled? I groaned and hastened to the railway station.

Here a number of excursionists were standing, rather disconsolately, on the damp platform; and as I made my way along, my heart suddenly began to beat furiously. *She* was already there, talking to Jason Reid, wearing a sturdy mackintosh and a navy blue beret pulled over her thick hair. Immediately the entire station was illuminated by her presence. As I approached, Reid gave me a nod of greeting.

"Don't worry, Shannon. I'm not coming with you."

Alison shook the raindrops from her nose, interrogating me with a wry smile. "Isn't this the limit, Robie? Perhaps it's too wet to go?"

"Oh, no," I said hurriedly.

I longed to go, in fact I knew that we must, simply must go, even if it hailed. I was reassured when Reid said cheerily:—

"You won't melt. Only see you don't get washed overboard. My barometer registered 'Warm & Dry,' this morning. Sure sign of a typhoon."

In these last two years Reid had lost much of his moroseness. This new capacity for not getting "low" in adverse circumstances was something I envied him immensely—I so sadly lacked that quality myself. He was going to Winton on some business for Mrs. Keith, and after talking to us for a moment he left to get his train on the other side. As he did so it struck me that a look of complicity passed between Alison and him; I could not be sure, I was hurrying to the booking office, in my usual harassed fashion, to see about our tickets.

Presently Alison and I took the train to Ardfillan. After the short railway journey, making a dash from the station to the pier, dodging through stacks of barrels and coils of rope, while the fresh breeze from the sea slanted the rain against us, we boarded the North British Railway Company's paddle boat, the *Lucy Ashton*, which made the run to Ardencaple. After wandering round and viewing the engines we found a place in the lee of the deck house where we could stand in comparative shelter. Soon a bell rang below, the hawsers were cast off, the red paddles began to thrash the water, and the ship throbbed away from the quay.

Dodging the waterspouts which the wind blew round the corner into our faces, I bent forward anxiously:—

"If it's too much for you we can go below."

Alison's cheeks were beaten by the wind and the rain, the dark beret which she wore, close down on her head, seemed bejewelled with crystal drops.

"I'm enjoying it." She spoke loudly, against the breeze, smiling back at me. "Besides, I can actually see blue sky."

It was true. I followed her pointing finger and made out a break in the ragged clouds which was followed in a few minutes by another. Scarcely daring to breathe, we watched the two blue patches coalesce, expand, and gradually force back the grey. Then, to our delight, the sun burst forth, hot and brilliant. Soon the entire sky had cleared, steam began to rise from the rapidly drying decks. I saw that, by one of those amazing transformations of our northern climate, we were to have, after all, a perfect day.

"Jason's barometer was right!" I exulted.

Alison agreed warmly. "But Robie . . . please don't say Jason." She hesitated. "Mother hates us to call him that. His own name is such a fine one."

We went to the bow of the little vermilion-funnelled steamer, now gliding up the sea-loch beneath the fiery blue sky, between the high hills, stopping occasionally at a village pier to take on a consignment of early potatoes, or a crofter with a few sheep he was bringing in to market. It was wonderful to be with Alison, simply to be near her. Standing at the rail I could not escape the soft contact of her figure when she stirred. Joy and hope flooded my soul in a kind of tender ecstasy.

We reached Ardencaple, the head of the Loch, at one o'clock. The thought that I had three hours to spend with Alison in this lovely spot enchanted me. Nervously determined to do things in style, I hurried her towards the one large hotel—the West Highland Grand—which stood, with a pretentious and neglected air, amidst the few whitewashed cottages of the tiny village.

"Can we have some lunch, please?"

In the draughty hall beneath intimidating antlers, a Highland waitress, starched, elderly and formidable, opposed us. She met my request by leading us sternly into a long cold dining room, where we appeared to be the only guests. The walls were covered with stag's heads, bull's horns and improbable stuffed fish which gaped at us from varnished boards. On the sideboard a meagre buffet was laid out: sinewy-looking mutton and waxy potatoes; a blanc mange shape, pale and shivery; strong cheese and damp biscuits. A Highland major domo, with a long white beard and a tartan waistcoat, stood in the background, voicing his distrust of us in Gaelic to the waitress, who now presented her severe visage at our table.

"The season hasna' begun. She can give ye the cauld luncheon at fower an' saxpence the heid."

Filled with misgiving, I was preparing to submit to this shameless intimidation, when Alison murmured to me:—

"Do you really like this place, Robie?"

I started and reddened to the roots of my hair. I had just enough courage to shake my head.

"I don't either." Alison rose calmly and addressed the startled waitress. "We've changed our minds. We don't require luncheon after all."

Unconscious of the woman's consternation and of the agitation of the white-bearded major domo, who was now entreating us to remain, she walked composedly out of the hotel. I followed.

Across the way, Alison entered the solitary village shop and, having studied its resources carefully, persuaded the storekeeper to cut her half a dozen ham sandwiches. While this was being done she moved about, picking up a couple of apples, some ripe bananas, a bar of milk chocolate and two bottles of that splendid beverage, sustainer of my youth, Barr's Iron Brew. All this cost no more than two and six, and went into a brown paper bag, quite easy to carry.

We now set out to climb the hill, taking a path which led through a coppice of young larches, already showing feathery crimson tufts upon their branches. Following the Ardencaple stream, we pushed steadily upwards, through thick ferns and bushes of wild azalea, until at last we came out to a clearing high on the edge of the moorland. It was a forgotten little field, encroached upon by bracken and protected against the wind by stout stone dykes. Through the centre of the meadow the burn dashed and tumbled over clear rocks into an amber pool, fringed with white sand. The banks were of springy turf with clumps of primroses drooping and trailing with the current, their petals drifting down like little boats. The place held a warm air of secrecy.

We sat down on the dry grass with our backs to the wall, near the pool and amidst the soft green mitres of the new bracken. The mountains rose behind us, the Loch, with our toyish steamer anchored far below, was a mirror at our feet. Sunshine came spilling upon us. Flushed and eager, I steeped the bottles in the running stream, while Alison took off her mackintosh and spread out our picnic.

The sandwiches were made with new bread and country ham and butter; they could not have been surpassed. The Iron Brew fizzed refreshingly down my throat. Alison made me eat almost all the bananas. We scarcely spoke, but as we finished she gave me one of her odd smiles.

"Wasn't that better than the old hotel?"

I nodded inarticulately, realizing that but for her calm and decided action we might still be suffering down below.

With a contented sigh Alison removed her beret, closed her eyes and lay back against the dyke.

"This is lovely," she said. "I could go to sleep."

Her healthy, youthful body was relaxed. Her hair, that long tumbling hair with gleams in it, which always seemed a little untidy, was carelessly unloosed, framing her already sunburned face. The tender effect of her lowered eyelashes against her fair warm skin was strangely accentuated by the tiny mole high on her cheekbone. Her white blouse was open at the neck, showing the firm arch of her throat. A fine dew of perspiration was forming on her upper lip.

That joy and terror which I knew so well swept over me again.

"You aren't comfortable, Alison." I swallowed dryly and came near to her, placing my arm so that it supported her head.

She did not protest, remaining relaxed and peaceful, her eyes still closed, lips half smiling. After a moment she murmured:—

"You have a very loud heart, Robie. I can hear it bumping all over the place."

What an opening for a pretty speech! Why did I not make it? And why, oh why, did I not clasp her closely in my arms? Alas, for the tragedy of my innocent intensity! I was too simple and too gauche. Besides, my happiness was so intense, I did not dare to move. Tongue-tied, choking with emotion, I continued to support her head, my cheek close to hers, feeling the slow rise and fall of her breathing which caused her patent-leather belt to creak slightly. The sun beat upon us benevolently, warming the rough material of her skirt, so that it exhaled a perfume of tweed that mingled with the scent of thyme. The air was soft and languid and from the woods below there came the teasing echo of the cuckoo.

Rapture forced a whisper from me at last.

"This is what I meant the other night, Alison. You and I together like this. Always."

"What would happen when it rained?"

"I wouldn't mind the rain," I answered fervently. "So long as . . ."

I broke off. Alison had opened her eyes, and was looking at me sideways in a provoked fashion. There was a pause. Then with an air of resolution she sat up.

"Robie! I want to talk to you seriously. I'm worried about you. And so is Mr. Reid."

So I was right this morning at the station. Although distressed that she had drawn away from me, I felt proud to be the object of her concern.

"In the first place," she continued, frowning, "we think it's a dreadful waste that you should be stuck in the Works the way you are. You're forgetting all your biology. Do you know that they wanted to make an engineer out of Caruso? But he broke out of it."

"My dear Alison." I shrugged my shoulders with affected indifference. "I have a perfectly good job."

She was silent, her eyes fixed ahead. Had I been a little too heroic in my disavowal? I stole a glance at her profile.

"Of course I admit I get dreadfully tired . . . sometimes gouge my hand with a chisel. Then . . . there's my cough, too."

She turned to me, with an expression that perplexed me. She shook her head.

"Robie, dear . . . you're an awful boy."

What had I said? A surge of distress filled my breast. Why should she treat me with this reproving kindness? The warm air was alive with the liquid murmurs of the brook. My heart, which had been beating madly, contracted.

"Have I offended you?"

"No, of course not." She bit her lip, struggling with her feelings. "You just make me feel how different we are. I'm so practical, a little too solid perhaps, while you are, and always will be, in the clouds. Goodness knows what you'll do when Mr. Reid goes away from Levenford."

I gazed at her in confused surprise. "Reid? Going away?"

Her eyes were lowered, she was twisting the stem of a primrose in her fingers.

"He has applied for a post in England. A school near Horsham, in Sussex. He's been at the Academy too long. This place is small but it goes in for modern methods and will give him more opportunity."

I exclaimed: "Do you mean that Reid has got the post?"

"Well, yes . . . I think it is practically settled. He had made up his mind to let you know this evening."

I felt chilled. Although, from time to time, Reid had thrown out hints, this was a sudden and unexpected blow. And why had it been arranged and settled without a word to me? Perhaps he had not wished to hurt me. Yet an unhappy sense of exclusion took hold of me. Before I could express any of these thoughts, Alison continued in a low voice, avoiding my eyes, her colour coming and going:—

"I know you're upset that Mr. Reid is leaving. It's horrid to lose one's friends. Although of course people can keep in touch with each other even when they do leave."

There was a queer silence.

"The fact is, Robie . . ." Suddenly Alison raised her head. "Mother and I are going away too."

I must have turned pale, my lips could scarcely form the word.

"Where?"

Leaning towards me she went on rapidly, earnestly.

"It's my training, for one thing. You know how important Mother thinks it, how specialized it must be. Miss Cramb can't teach me any more. In Winton there is no one much better. It's been decided I shall go to the Royal Conservatory of Music in London."

"London!" It was the other end of the earth; and it was near, extremely near to Sussex.

Alison's colour was now out of control, she was deeply, almost painfully embarrassed.

"For a boy who is so clever you are terribly blind to what's going on. Everyone has known it but you. Mother and Mr. Reid are going to be married."

Stunned, I could find nothing to say. Of course I had to admit that Mrs. Keith was still an attractive woman, that she and Reid shared the same tastes and interests. But, instead of rejoicing, I was appalled.

There was a long silence.

At last, I said, wretchedly: "If you go, I have nobody."

"I'm not going for ever." Her voice was soft, full of kindness and affection. "You know I must think of my singing. But it isn't the end of the world, Robie. And don't jump to conclusions—remember, there's always another day."

As I stared ahead, mournful and desolate, the sun began to slip behind the mountains and there came three sharp blasts from the steamer at the pier, warning that her departure was not far off.

"We must hurry!" Alison exclaimed. "They'll be casting off quite soon."

She gave me, unexpectedly, a hesitant, almost pleading smile and, rising, extended her hand to help me to my feet. As we hastened down towards the boat, I had the strange impression that, for all her firmness, she was swayed by uncertainty equal to my own. The steamer whistled again—a prolonged note, like the siren at the Works. My holiday was over. Suddenly, with a sinking heart, I saw myself alone and lost. The future rose before me like a wall.

CHAPTER EIGHT

The last Saturday in July . . . Preoccupied by my own woes, I had forgotten that this was the date of the Flower Show, and only recollected the fact at noon, on my way home from the Works. When I reached Lomond View, I was in no mood for the afternoon's event. But I had promised Murdoch to attend the Show, and at two o'clock I went to my room to get ready. The sound of heavy, if uncertain, footsteps above my head caused me, once or twice, to pause; and in the end I was driven to go up.

The old man, washed and trimmed, was posed before his mirror, attempting, with trembling fingers, and very red in the face, to knot his tie. His clothes had been brushed, his boots polished in the best style of his palmy days. He wore a starched white shirt which was tight around his throat.

"That you, Robert?" In spite of his shakiness, his tone was equable, he did not remove his eyes from the glass.

I remained silent for a moment, chilled, despite the heat, by the signs of his activity.

"Where are you going?"

"Where am I going?" He made the knot, successfully, his neck stretched out. "What a question. I am going to the Flower Show, of course."

"No . . . no . . . You're not well enough to go."

"I was never better in my life."

"It's terribly hot. Sure to upset you. You ought to rest."

"I've been resting all week. You've no idea how tiresome it is to rest."

"But your leg—" I tried a final argument. "You're much too lame to walk."

He turned from the mirror and, although his head was shaking a little, gave me one of his quiet smiles.

"My dear boy, the difference between you and me is that you give up too easily. How often have I told you not to be so easy beat? You wouldn't expect me, the head of the family, to stay away on Murdoch's big day. Besides, I've always liked flowers. Flowers and pretty women."

I had reddened at his analysis of my character, which I felt to be only too true, and now, dismayed, I watched him get into his jacket and, with an air, shoot out his stiff cuffs. He had been ailing these past weeks; yet, with tremulous indifference, he was preparing to disport himself. It was enough to paralyse all my powers of diplomacy. Impossible to turn him from his purpose . . .

"Well!" he said, satisfied at last with his appearance, and taking up his stick. "Am I to have the pleasure of your company? Or do you wish me to go alone?"

Of course I must go with him. How could I let him loose in such a crowd, on such a day as this? I followed him as, holding the bannisters rather too tightly, and not very sure of his footing, he descended the stairs.

Outside, numbers of the townspeople, men in straw hats, women in light dresses, were moving along the road to the gardens of Overton House where the Show was being held. As we joined the leisurely stream I reflected that at least we should not meet any of Grandpa's less reputable friends in this gathering. Vaguely relieved, yet afraid of his slight unsteadiness, I offered to take his arm.

It was a horrible blunder. Grandpa repudiated my assistance irritably.

"What do you think I am? A fossil . . . a mummy?" Doing his best to disguise his dragging foot, he drew himself up, and tried to inflate his chest in the old manner. "In five years' time perhaps I'll ask you to order my Bath chair. I'm not done yet by any means."

Even the remotest allusion to his waning powers was a dreadful mistake. He hated to think that he was failing, and shut his eyes firmly to the fact that he could not go on for ever. Actually, he was succeeding in carrying himself erect: in spite of my anxiety I was compelled to own it. Turned out better than usual, he was, even admitting his erratic feet, and that slight agitation of his head, a presentable figure. Indeed, his white hair, bushy beneath his hat, made him rather striking—eyes were turned towards him, he felt himself a centre of attraction, preened himself, as we strolled along.

"You observe, Robert," he murmured to me, with restored complacency, "these two ladies on the left. Very elegant. Beautiful sunshine too. I wouldn't have missed this for the world."

As we approached the lodge entrance gates, where temporary wooden turnstiles had been installed, Grandpa produced, with a flourish, two free passes, which he had obtained in advance from Murdoch. He was incorrigible.

It was pleasant within the enclosure, one of the finest and largest gardens in the county, now made festive by half a dozen red-striped marquees for the exhibits, by several tents given over to displays of seeds and garden implements, and an open-air tea-court where, deployed round the fountain, the town band was playing a soft waltz. The trim lawns and shady trees, the bright movement of the ladies' dresses, the scarlet and gold of the bandsmen's uniform, the tinkle of the music and the fountain, the sound of well-bred conversation, all this caused Grandpa to blossom out more. He let his feet sink into the velvet turf. His nostrils expanded.

"I aye had a taste for the genteel, Robert. It's my proper element."

He bowed to several persons who did not seem to recognize him, then, in no way discomposed, he began to hum, limping along in a survey of the scene.

"Handsome, very handsome." The excitement was going to his head a little. He remained polite and restrained. Yet he had begun to accept everything as being in his honour. "Look! Is that not Mrs. Bosomley over there?"

"No, it isn't." He was always mistaking people, the "long sight" of which he had been so proud was gone for ever.

"Well, never mind. A fine woman, too. We'll speak to her later. Take me to Murdoch's carnations now. I always liked carnations. And I want to see if he's won the prize."

I moved him on with relief. I had made out Alison and her mother in the distance and it was my earnest desire to avoid them. We entered the marquees, which were filled with flowers, hothouse fruits and choice vegetables. It must not be forgotten that the Scots are famous gardeners. In one tent was an array of roses of marvellous scent and colour; in another masses of sweet peas exhaling a fragrance delicate as their own petals. We admired baskets of downy peaches; splendid asparagus tied with blue ribbon; bunches of luscious muscat grapes; a giant pumpkin bursting with its own juice. Grandpa viewed them all with mounting pleasure, barely tempered by his air of a connoisseur, his face redder than ever from the sultry heat beneath the blistering canvas. Seeing him so happy, I felt ashamed of my misgivings and glad that he had not been deprived of this hour.

We reached the display of carnations. Here, amongst the considerable gathering which had assembled to regard, with curiosity and respect, a large bunch of blossoms on the front of the stand, we found Kate and Jamie with little Luke. A moment later Murdoch came over from the booth reserved for exhibitors, accompanied by Miss Ewing. The old man was deeply gratified by this family encounter. He shook hands all round, even with Kate's child, whom he addressed affectionately as "Robie." Then, glancing at the surrounding spectators as though favouring them with his confidence, he whispered to Murdoch loudly, so that all could hear:—

"What's the verdict, my boy? Have we won the medal?"

Murdoch gave a self-conscious nod towards the stand. "See for yourself."

Hung on the central bunch of carnations—lovely unusual blossoms of a delicate shade of yellow with tinges of mauve upon the petal edges—was a gilt-edged card with ink barely dry: *Bowers Silver Medal for Best Floral Exhibit. Mr. Murdoch Leckie of Dalrymple and Leckie, Nurserymen, Drumbuck.*

"It's just as good as the Alexandra," Miss Ewing explained quickly. "We're very pleased."

Although he had done well, Murdoch had not quite achieved his ambition. It made no difference to Grandpa however. To him a medal was a medal. His face was crimson.

"Murdoch, I'm proud of you. You do me honour. If you will permit me the privilege of being the first to wear your bonny flower . . ."

He stretched out his hand, took a carnation from the bunch, snapped the stem and slipped it in his buttonhole.

It was a typical gesture and although Murdoch did not look especially well-pleased the buttonhole undoubtedly made Grandpa complete. His smile went round us all before it wavered.

"Take me to where they'll give out the prizes. I'm not tired, mind you. But I'll sit down there, and wait till they give us the medal."

When he was settled in a garden chair on the lawn in the shade of a tall acacia tree, pleasantly near the band, and beside Kate and Jamie, I felt a temporary lifting of my responsibility and took the opportunity to slip away. He would not miss me for the next half hour—already he had taken Kate's son upon his knee and was asking, with a dim indulgent smile:—

"Robie, do you mind that day we went skating on the pond?"

As I crossed the lawn I could hear the little boy's shrill answer:—

"Never mind the skating, Grandpa. Tell me about the Zulus."

I wandered through several marquees, aimlessly, yet with the corner of my eye sensitively alert for *them*. Reid was leaving for the South the following week, while Alison and Mrs. Keith would join him a few days later—the wedding would be held quietly in London at the end of the month. Strangely, my distress was increased by the fact that, since I had last seen her, Alison had sung beautifully at the St. Andrew's Hall. Wounded and already alone, I shrank from meeting my friends, yet I felt it necessary to say good-bye to them.

"Please don't look so tragic, Robie. You ought to be proud of Murdoch's success."

Mrs. Keith, standing with Reid near the band, wearing a wide hat of soft straw with a white trimming, was glancing at me sideways, giving me her faint smile, less critical than it had been of late.

"Do I look tragic?" I started, and stammered. "Murdoch didn't win the gold medal."

"How could he," Jason said, "when I've been secretly growing vegetable marrows in my window boxes for months?"

"My dear boy." Mrs. Keith's dark eyes were gay. "You're perfectly all right. Still, it would be nice if you cheered up just for a bit."

Under my breath I made a stiff attempt to defend myself.

"Naturally one can't expect to be grinning all over one's face when certain people one is fond of happen to be going away."

Reid shook his head. "Life's a desperate business, Robert; suppose you come and have strawberries and cream with us. We're meeting Alison in the tea-garden in half an hour."

"Yes, do come," said Mrs. Keith. "We'll be there at four."

"Very well."

When they strolled off I turned and went into another marquee where, for a long time, I stared fixedly at a prime bunch of parsnips. I hated parsnips, and I wasn't really thinking of them. The mild satire which had pervaded the genuine friendship in Jason's tone made me suddenly see myself as I must appear to others. Oh, God! What a fool I was! I knew nothing about life, I didn't understand the first thing about it. I existed in a world of dreams, the pale victim of my own fancies. Pray Heaven for just one thing—that I would not break down and make an idiot of myself before them.

At five minutes to four I set out for the tea-garden.

And then, as I came through the crowd, I became aware of Kate, waving to me from the place where Grandpa had been sitting. Something imperative in her signals broke into my utter desolation, caused me to start and hurry forward.

"Grandpa's taken ill." She spoke breathlessly. "I sent Jamie for the doctor but he's taken worse now. Run down to the lodge and telephone for a cab."

Surrounded by a few good Samaritans, the old man lay on the grass which, an hour ago, he had proudly trodden. He was curled on his side, one arm twisted in, as though contorted. His eyes were fixed and open, one side of his mouth breathed noisily, the other half was still. His white hair was disheveled. He had the wild, sad look of the dethroned Lear after that night of storm. Though I did not know much about it, I saw that it was a stroke. As I started running for the lodge they were preparing to make the awards. The band, having completed its programme, struck up, with a finality that sounded dreadful in my ears: "God Save the King."

CHAPTER NINE

SUNDAY; and nearly midnight. This time there is no mistake; the old man is dying. The consciousness of this pervades his room where I sit watching him, pervades the sleeping house, even the night beyond. All day there has been an air of expectancy, of correct behaviour—Murdoch and Jamie talking with Papa in subdued voices downstairs; Kate hushing the eager cries of her little boy as he plays ball in the back garden; Grandma on tiptoe baking a big batch of scones. This is called "waiting for the end," and the family retires with a sense of respectful disappointment that the old man should be "lingering," despite the three shattering electric strokes he has sustained in quick succession, and Dr. Galbraith's prediction that he cannot last. There are no protests when I claim the privilege of sitting up with him: the rights of my affection are recognized, and they are convenient when one has no desire to miss a good night's sleep.

The stillness is frightening; although I have drawn up the blind and opened the window the invasion of the warm and starless night brings no relief. Grandpa lies on his back, no longer snoring, barely breathing through a mouth drawn open by the recession of all his features. Before retiring Grandma has sponged the sharpened, half-conscious face, brushed the white hair, reviving a shadowy impression of that last magnificent appearance at the Flower Show. Age has reduced this body to ruins but has somehow failed to degrade it.

As I gaze at him, melancholy, yet relieved that he is solving a bad problem in the easiest way, I fall into an involuntary meditation: this, surely, is the moment to assay the value of a life, this awful moment of departure which we all must take. What follies, what sins he has committed! No one knows better than I the weaknesses and obstinacies of the old man's character; for already, with a tinge of horror, I recognize, in that sad and foolish boy, myself, these same traits which have descended to me from him. Yet I defend them, these troubled depths of personality: for already, like Grandpa, I have my doubts of the accepted code. These faint ennobling virtues: never to be mean, to be kind, to inspire affection—perhaps they outweigh a hundred besetting sins.

I must have dozed by the bedside. I am aroused by the old man trying to speak. I bend close and manage to catch the word: "Spirit."

It is no deathbed repentance, no reference to the Holy Ghost. He means that drink to which he has long been addicted, of which he now sorely feels the need. It is not good for him, but neither were his other predilections, and since the doctor has not troubled to impose a ban, I feel my way down to the parlour cupboard, where I find the bottle already purchased, not without disapproval, for those visitors that the bereavement will bring to the house and who, like Mr. McKellar, "partake." I pour a little into a cup, neat—he could never bear water with it—thinking it the final irony that the old man should sip the goblet of his own funeral feast.

He is grateful for the whisky, which he swallows with great difficulty. He mutters: "Meat and drink."

These are his last words. I find in that accidental phrase a strange meaning, a terse evaluation of his philosophy of life.

The clock strikes three, shaking me from my drooping fatigue. I see that the old man is now sinking fast, his instant of greatness is at hand. Suddenly the door opens and Grandma, carrying a candle, wearing her mutch and long white "gownie," comes into the room, drawn by instinct, the peasant's instinct which senses unerringly, and with awe, the approach of death. She does not, on this occasion, read aloud a chapter from her "Book." She glances from the dying man to me, silently accepts my chair, while I move over to the window.

The imminence of dawn can be felt: unseen stirrings, the incautious movement of a bird, vague looming of the three chestnut trees. Grandma's behaviour is superb. She is afraid of the dark presence now standing in the room with us, this reminder of her own mortality. But she is purged of hatred. The bitterness, the animosity which once dominated that little world wherein we three people lived, now seems childish and remote. During these last months, as he sank, so she has risen; not in pity, but rather in mournful realization of her own worth, she has grown quite fond of her old enemy.

Yes, at last. Something has slipped away. The death of a man in the full height of his vigour is a dreadful business, a wrenching, unwilling orgasm. But this old man is tired. A skiff slips away from the shore easily, without splashing. Grandma looks at me, gives a faint nod of affirmation, and rises.

I watch while she binds up the sagging chin, places pennies—another peasant trick—on the closed eyes. I gaze, with great sadness, at the face fixed in this final rigidity. He has reached a place, whether of light or darkness I do not know, where no more follies can be committed; he has escaped from all his persecutors and pursuers—most of all, from himself.

At Grandma's whispered instruction I turn to pull down the blind. The dawn is coming: the chestnuts taking shape, the fields less huddled, a stain of saffron in the east. I blow out the candle. Suddenly from the farm on the hill, as if in mockery of the extinguished flame, there uprises the loud derisive challenge of a cock.

CHAPTER TEN

ON TUESDAY we all sat down in the parlour to a ham-and-egg tea after the funeral, which though not lavish was, at Papa's command, done handsomely, by the second-best undertaker in the town. Papa, rubbing his hands and full of courtesies, had brought back Mr. McKellar from the cemetery.

Grandma sat on the lawyer's right and Kate on his left; Murdoch and Jamie were at the bottom end on either side of me; Adam occupied the head of the table, next to Papa.

"Everything passed off very nicely, I think." Papa, eager for approval, interrogated Mr. McKellar with his eyes. "Oh, take two eggs, man. Yes, I didn't want to make a splurge. On the other hand I always like to do the right thing. And besides, in a sense, if you understand me, it was due to him."

Some reply was expected from the lawyer. As he accepted his cup of tea from Kate he said dryly:—

"I think the funeral was appropriate to the circumstances."

Papa looked slightly irked: it was one of his annoyances never to have been able to make McKellar like him. He looked grateful as Adam remarked:—

"No one could have wished for better."

McKellar shrugged his solid shoulders. "When you get to that stage you don't wish for anything at all."

Papa and Adam exchanged a glance of understanding, of alliance against this surly intruder. Although he had arrived only that morning Adam had already assuaged Papa, reassured him on the question of the house, which, after all, was probably going to be sold to the kindergarten school, had calmly offered and, when Papa vacillated, as calmly torn up a cheque, had, in fact, won him so completely, that in the cab home they had fallen to discussing, in low tones, possible "openings" for Papa's new capital, the insurance money which had come to him at last.

"Try some of my scones, Mr. McKellar," Grandma said.

"I will, indeed." The lawyer was making a good tea and, though taciturn to Papa and Adam, he talked amiably, in his heavy style, to Kate and the old lady. He was an ardent advocate of Home Rule for Scotland and here he met Grandma on common ground. He seemed to crouch over his plate, and his eye went darting about the table, in a disconcerting manner.

I must confess that I avoided this steely glance. At the graveside, raw gash in the greensward, where the dignity of "a cord" was conferred on me, I had in a weak and ridiculous manner made a ghastly fool of myself. As we lowered the coffin my body began to shake, I burst into blubbering tears . . . at my age! The recollection of it made me hang my head in shame.

"Have you the exact amount of the policy?" Adam inquired casually.

"Yes, I have." McKellar spoke with formality. There was no love between these two: the city insurance man, dabbler in odd affairs, and the small town solicitor-actuary. An interesting character, this McKellar, who had always given me a nod across the street over a period of years—slow, stolid, firm as a rock, he would die sooner than change one halfpenny in his balance sheet. To say that he was honest is a preposterous understatement. He was a watchdog of probity; for all affairs beyond the solid three per cents he had a shake of his head and this peculiar phrase: "A bad business. Aye, aye, a bad business." Clearly he distrusted Adam as an opportunist, a young man who left his office at rather short notice and who had always shoved himself up at the expense of others.

"What might the accrued sum be?" Adam was still pressing ahead.

"Seven hundred and eighty-nine pounds, seven shillings and threepence . . . precisely."

Adam inclined his head while Papa paled at the magnitude, the luscious magnitude of the sum. I could not help thinking of Grandpa, who had hated this policy so much that he had forbidden me ever to mention it in his presence. Thank heaven he was spared Papa's joyful whisper:—

"When can you pay it?"

"At once." McKellar placed his knife and fork methodically together and pushed away his plate.

"More tea, Mr. McKellar."

"Thank you no, I've done brawly."

"A drop of spirits then." Papa, the prim abstainer, actually made the hospitable offering.

"Well, if you insist."

When the full tumbler had been placed before McKellar, I slipped from my chair with the intention of escaping unobserved. But that steady and penetrating orb fell upon me like a searchlight.

"Where are you going?"

Papa came to my rescue. "He's still a bit upset . . . Maybe you noticed at the funeral. That's all right, we'll excuse you, Robert."

"Sit down, boy." McKellar took a firm dram of spirits. "It's hardly respectful to the old man's memory to slink out in the middle of the proceedings. If you have any regard for him at all—and you're the only one that pretends to have—you might have the decency to bide till I have finished."

I sank into my chair in confusion. McKellar had never used that tone to me before. It stung and humiliated me.

"Let's get ahead with it then," Adam said sharply.

"As you wish." McKellar took some papers from his inside pocket. "Here is the policy, No. 57430, an endowment assurance in the name of Alexander Gow. And here is the will. I'll read it through."

"What for?" Adam was losing his temper at the lawyer's pedantic slowness. "Why all this rigmarole? I was in your office when you drew it, I witnessed it, and I know it by heart."

McKellar gave the impression of being taken aback. "It'll be more regular if I read it. It won't take me a moment."

"Of course." Papa smoothed things over.

McKellar put on his glasses and in a slow broad voice read out the will. It was a short and simple document. Grandpa left everything to Mama, and, in the event of her decease, to her executor, Papa.

"Well." Papa exhaled a satisfied breath. "That's just as it should be. Now there's nothing to detain us."

"Wait!" McKellar almost shouted the word and at the same time thumped the table with his large fist. In the silence which succeeded he glanced round, crouching over the parchment, that slow grim smile, carefully hidden until now, contracting his bushy brows, tightening his firm mouth. He was like a man free at last to unleash and to enjoy some exquisite secret.

His eye found me again, dwelt upon me with open kindness, as he said: "There is a codicil to this will, a holograph codicil dated July 20th, 1910."

An exclamation from Papa, which I scarcely heard. How clearly I remembered that day: that day of mortal sadness, when I lost the Marshall and Gavin was killed.

McKellar went on, letting every word sink in—yes, as though it afforded him excruciating pleasure to stab Papa with each individual word:—

"On that day, the twentieth of July, Dandie Gow came into my office. I called him Dandie because, in spite of all his failings and misfortunes, I'm proud to say he was my friend. He asked me outright if he could divert the proceeds of his policy. We had a long talk, he and I, that afternoon. As a result, every penny of the money, I say every penny, and my God, I mean every penny, is left to the boy here, Robert Shannon, under my trusteeship, to enable him to take his medical degrees at Winton College."

Deathly silence. I had turned white; my throat, my heart constricted; I could not believe it, I was too used to misfortune, too beaten-down—it was just another device of the blind sky to pretend to raise me up so that I could be dashed down again, more cruelly.

"You are trying to impose on me," Papa whimpered. "He couldn't do such a thing. He had no right."

The grim smile deepened. "Every right, under this policy, which could not be mortgaged or compounded during his lifetime, but was his to devise and bequeath, voluntarily."

Papa threw a piteous glance at Adam. "Is that so?"

"It's the only way Mama would have it." Adam glared at McKellar. "He was out of his mind."

"Not when he drew the codicil two years ago. He was as sane as you are."

"I'll contest the will," Papa said in a high strange voice. "I'll take it to law."

"Do so." McKellar ceased to smile. He glanced from Adam to Papa in a very threatening manner. "Yes, do so. And I promise you I'll fight you of my own accord, fight you if need be to the County Court, and the High Court. Fight you to the floor of the Parliament itself. It would be a bad business for you, Leckie. There would be no Waterworks for you then, my man." He paused, relishing to the full this little bit of melodrama which, after years of staid practice, had come his way. "Your wife didn't wish to take out this policy, though she paid most of the premiums herself. As for the old man—he had no chance to get a farthing from it. But he wanted it to serve a good and useful purpose. It will serve that purpose, or my name is not Duncan McKellar."

Oh, God, was it really true then . . . this wonderful gift from Grandpa, who had never breathed a word of it to me? I kept my eyes lowered, scarcely breathing, the muscles of my face twitching beneath their fixed rigidity. Suddenly I heard Kate's voice, felt her arm go round my shoulders.

"I don't know what the others think . . . in my opinion it's the best use that could be made of this money . . . yes, the very best use."

"Hear! Hear!" Jamie added in a loud whisper.

Blessed Kate of the bad tempers and the bumps on her forehead, and Jamie, who makes money seem clean and decent . . . I humbly trust their little boy will have less difficulty in growing up than did I. McKellar, folding up the papers, addressed me as he stood up.

"Ten o'clock tomorrow at my office. But meantime you can walk down the road with me. A breath of air will do you no harm."

I left the room with him blindly. There comes a point when nature, strung to the breaking-point, can endure no more.

CHAPTER ELEVEN

LATE that evening there returns from Lawyer McKellar's house an excited small-town mammal of the genus *Homo sapiens*, in brief, that woeful yet warm-blooded vertebrate, Robert Shannon. Although this peculiar biped is actually eighteen and has not so long ago felt upon his stooping shoulders the awful burden of the years, of an almost unrequited love and of countless other miseries as well, he is still unhardened and immature. Now, while conscious of the calm still beauty of the night, a vast pellucid night singing with stars, beneath which his heart also is singing, he gazes straight ahead, flushed, and intent.

The future is wide and open to him. The dry Scots lawyer, who has talked with him so long, will act as his trustee and counsellor, as his friend. He will never go back to the Works. At the beginning of the new session, next month, he will go to the University, living in the students' hostel there, entering with joy upon his medical studies. Biology . . . practical zoology . . . these magic names have brought that high colour to his cheeks. Already he sniffs the intoxicating odours of formalin and Canada balsam, views that long line of Zeiss microscopes, each with its wonderful oil-immersion lenses, and one of which will be his—in spite of poor Mr. Smith, whom he will be pleased to see again. To think of it! Why, they will probably let him dissect the dogfish, *mustelus canis*, if he is lucky, in his first term!

There is enough money to see him through: the few loose ends left by Grandpa can be cleared up by McKellar for less than twenty pounds. If unpleasant things are said to him when he goes home—and his expression hardens here—he has been told to take no notice. He will soon leave Lomond View for good.

Ah, yes, the future is open and shining. Reid and Alison may be going, but he is going also. . . . He will show them that he is not fated to be a failure. His feelings towards Alison have subtly changed, his passion is more sternly contained. Perhaps there is no place for women in the life of a great zoologist? Or perhaps one day in Vienna, when a famous prima donna is singing the title role in *Carmen*, a grave distinguished doctor with a decoration in his buttonhole and a small trim beard will come quietly into the stage box. . . .

No, no, these fancies belong to the phase of adolescence which the boy has put behind him. Ahead there is work to be done . . . serious, oh, glorious laboratory work.

But wait . . . one last moment, one final inconsistency before we let him go. As he passes along Chapel Street there rises before him on his right the dark despised structure of the Holy Angels Church. He needs nothing, this bright spirit, from that place, which no longer deludes him. Bravely, he has resisted all the wiles of Canon Roche to bring him back to it. Sadness has not brought him to his knees. . . . Oh, he's past being hoodwinked; practically, in fact, on the verge of being a freethinker.

And yet at this moment he is caught unawares, seized and strangled, by an overmastering force. Remember—he has read everything, from the *Origin of Species* to Renan's *Life of Jesus*, he has smiled at the fable of Adam's rib, and agreed with the witty French Cardinal, whose name he has forgotten, that Christianity rests upon a charming myth. Yet this is something which surges up, which is in his blood, his bones, his very marrow, something he will never be rid of, which will haunt him till the instant of his death.

We are faced with an anticlimax of the first magnitude. But we have sworn, beyond everything, to be truthful. How many times in the future this Robert Shannon will shuttle between apathy and ardour, rise and be smitten down again, we are not at liberty to predict—or how often he will make, and break, his peace with the Being towards whom all human impulses ascend. The fact remains that now, uncontrollably, he feels the need of communicating the exaltation of his spirit, in the listening stillness. He feels suddenly that his prayer of gratitude will not fall into the void. And with a shamefaced air, he darts into the dark church.

The least we can say is that he is not absent long. Perhaps he has only stayed to light a penny candle, or murmur some incoherent words before the sombre altar. Yet perhaps it is more than that. When he emerges, dazzled a little by the lucid stars and the Northern Lights now searching the polar sky, he sets off more briskly, his footsteps ringing clear in the empty street.

THE END

SHANNON'S
WAY

BOOK ONE

CHAPTER ONE

ON A DAMP evening in December, the fifth of that month, in the year
1919—a date which marked the beginning of a great change in my life—
six o'clock had struck from the University tower and the soft mist from the
Eldon River was creeping round the Experimental Pathology buildings at the
foot of Fenner Hill, invading our long work-room that smelled faintly of
formalin, and was lit only by low, green-shaded lamps.

Professor Usher was still in his study—from behind the closed door on
my right, with eardrums unnaturally attuned, I could hear his precise tones
as he spoke, at length, upon the telephone. Surreptitiously, I glanced at
the two other assistants who, with myself, made up the Professor's team.

Directly opposite, Spence stood at his bench, racking culture tubes,
awaiting the arrival of his wife. She called for him regularly, every Friday
night, and they went out together to dinner and the theatre. A slanting
beam drew a cruel caricature of his broken profile upon the wall.

In the far corner of the laboratory Lomax had knocked off work and was
idly tapping a cigarette upon his thumbnail—signal for a departure which he
generally contrived to make easy and negligent. Presently, in a bored
manner, surrounded by a languid cloud of smoke, he stood up, adjusting
the wave in his hair at the mirror he kept over his sink.

"Let's go somewhere tonight, Shannon. Have dinner with me and we'll
take in a cinema."

The invitation was flattering, but of course, this evening I declined it.

"How about you, Spence?" Lomax turned towards the other bench.

"I'm afraid Muriel and I are going out."

"This is a beastly unsociable town," Lomax complained.

Neil Spence hesitated, almost apologetic, covering his chin with his left
hand, an instinctive gesture, which seemed to give him confidence and which
always touched me, increasing the sympathy and deep affection which I
felt for him.

"Why don't you come along with us?"

The suggestion halted Lomax.

"I shouldn't want to butt in and spoil your evening."

"You wouldn't."

Just then there came the sound of a motor horn, and almost at once
Smith, the attendant, entered and announced that Mrs. Spence had arrived
and was outside.

"Don't let's keep Muriel." Spence, having put on his overcoat, waited
companionably for Lomax at the door. "I think you'll enjoy the show . . .
it's *The Maid of the Mountains*. Good night, Robert."

"Good night."

When they had gone I breathed a little faster and my eyes, wandering round this world I loved, this inner, secret, mysterious world of the laboratory, came to rest, with apprehensive expectation, upon the Professor's door.

At the same instant it opened and Hugo Usher came out. His exits and entrances, indeed all his movements, had a slightly theatrical quality, which so completely fitted his severe figure, iron-grey hair, and cropped imperial that he gave me always the uncomfortable impression of being less a distinguished scientist than an actor playing too perfectly that part. He drew up by the Hoffman centrifuge, near my bench. Despite his well-controlled expression it was not difficult for me to read, in the faint constriction of his frontal muscles, a disapproval of my peculiarities, from the shabby naval uniform I persisted in wearing, to my failure, during the past six weeks, to evince enthusiasm for the research he had compelled me to take up.

There was a pause. Then, with that infusion of geniality which he assumed to temper his severity, he said, briefly:

"No, Shannon . . . I'm afraid not."

My heart ceased its bounding and sank slowly, while my face coloured with disappointment and mortification.

"But, surely, sir, if you've read my memorandum . . ."

"I have read it," he interrupted me and, by way of evidence, laid upon my bench the typewritten sheet which, earlier that day, I had presented to him and which now, to my burning eyes, presented the soiled and deplorable appearance of a rejected manuscript. "I regret that I cannot accept your suggestion. The work upon which you are engaged is of very considerable importance. Impossible . . . to allow you to discontinue it."

I lowered my eyes, debarred by my hurt pride from pressing my request, knowing also that his decisions were always irrevocable. Although my head was bent, I could feel his gaze resting upon the batch of slides stacked on the acid-charred wood of my bench.

"You've finished our latest counts?"

"Not yet," I told him without looking up.

"You know I particularly want our paper ready for the Spring Congress. As I shall be away for several weeks it is imperative you press forward with all possible speed."

When I did not answer his half-frown deepened. He cleared his throat. I thought I was about to receive a dissertation on the nobility of pathological investigation, particularly as it related to his favourite subject, the theory of opsonins. However, after playing for a moment with his wide-brimmed soft black hat he flung it on the back of his head.

"Good evening, Shannon."

With that formal withdrawing bow he had picked up abroad, he went out.

I sat for a long moment, completely still.

"I'm ready to close up, sir."

Lean and cadaverous as ever, out of the corner of his eye Smith, the attendant, was watching me, the same Herbert Smith who, when I first entered the Zoology laboratory six years before, had damped my youthful enthusiasm with his pessimism. Now he was head attendant in the Pathological Department, but the attainment of this better position had not changed him, and he displayed towards me a morose suspicion which my few successes, including an honours M.D. and the winning of the Lister Gold Medal, had increased rather than dispelled.

Without a word I shrouded my microscope, put away the slides, took my cap and went out. My thoughts were bitter as I walked down the dark, dripping avenue of Fenner Hill, crossed the crowded thoroughfare of Pardyke Road—where, beneath misty arc lights, the trams clanged and bounded over greasy cobblestones—then entered the drab district of Kirkhead. Here, terraces of old-fashioned houses, clinging desperately to respectability against an invasion of public-houses, ice-cream saloons and tenements for the workers at the near-by docks, raised their tall grimy fronts, with broken stucco cornices, slipped porticos and fallen gutters, weeping, it seemed, for their former glory, beneath the eternally smoky sky.

At Number 52, which bore on the fanlight the polite name ROTHESAY, and below, in discreet letters of peeling gilt, GUESTS, I mounted the steps and went in.

CHAPTER TWO

MY ROOM, at the top of the boarding-house, was small, almost an attic, furnished sparsely with an iron cot, a white wooden washstand and a black-framed woolwork text. But it had the advantage of communicating with a little green-painted glass conservatory still equipped with stands and benches, a relic of the palmy days of the mansion. Although cold in winter and sweltering in summer, this served me adequately as a study.

For this accommodation, with two meals a day, I paid the Misses Dearie, co-owners of the establishment, the moderate sum of thirty-four shillings a week—which, I must at once acknowledge, was quite as much as I could afford. The money I had inherited from my grandfather, "to put me through college," had no more than fulfilled its purpose, while the honorarium for my assistantship, and for the extra work of demonstrating in Bacteriology to the third-year students, amounted to one hundred guineas a year, a delusive suggestion of gold pieces which concealed the fact that in Scotland they are cautious about spoiling their budding genius. Thus, on Saturday, when I had paid my board and lodgings, I had barely five shillings in my pocket to provide myself with midday luncheons at the Union, with clothing, shoes, books, tobacco—in brief, I was outrageously poor, compelled to wear my obsolete uniform, which so offended Professor Usher's sense of propriety, not from choice, but because it was the only suit that I possessed.

However, these pinched circumstances scarcely troubled me. My upbringing in Levenford had inured me to such vicissitudes of the Spartan life as lumpy porridge, watery milk of singular and unforgettable blueness, made-down clothing, and thick-soled boots studded with "tackets" to make them last. Besides, I regarded my present state as purely transitory, precursor of a splendid future, and my mind was too desperately engaged by the enterprise which would carry me to a great and immediate success to worry about trifles.

When I reached my lofty garret, from which I had a view of a blank brick wall topped by the smoke-stack of the city incinerator, I stood for a moment in determined thought, studying the paper which Usher had restored to me.

"You'll be late for tea."

With a start, I turned to the intruder who stood diffidently upon my threshold. It was, of course, Miss Jean Law, my next-door neighbour in the corridor. This young woman, one of the five medical students who lodged at Rothesay, was taking my Bacteriology class, and all through the present session had made me the object of her neighbourly attentions.

"The gong went five minutes ago," she murmured, in her Northern accent; and, observing my irritation, she had the grace to blush—a warm, modest flush which suffused her fair skin yet did not cause her to lower her brown eyes. "I knocked, but you didn't hear me."

I crumpled up the paper.

"I've asked you, Miss Law, not to disturb me when I'm busy."

"Yes . . . but your *tea*," she protested, more than ever rolling her r's in her confusion.

I could not help it—at the sight of her, in her blue serge skirt, her plain white blouse, black stockings, and sturdy shoes, entreating me with such earnest solicitude, as though the loss of my tea were a mortal calamity, I was obliged to smile.

"All right," I consented, imitating her tone. "I'll come this very minute."

We went down together to the dining-room, an appalling chamber, furnished in worn red plush, the very linoleum inpregnated with the smell of boiled cabbage. Upon the mantelpiece, which had a tasseled velvet fringe, stood the pride of the Misses Dearie, token of their departed sire's prestige and of their own "ladylike" upbringing: a hideous green marble clock, stopped, but supported by two gilt-helmeted figures carrying axes and inscribed *Presented to Captain Hamish Dearie on his retirement from command of the Winton Fire Brigade.*

The meal, pale and meagre shadow of the traditional substantial Scots "high" tea, had already begun, and Miss Beth Dearie was presiding at the mahogany table covered with a mended but clean white cloth, bearing a few plates of bread, scones and seedcake, an ashet of kippers, one for each person, and a Britannia metal tea-pot, encased in a blue knitted "cozy."

As she poured our tea Miss Beth, a tall, correct, angular spinster of forty-five, with faded good looks, whose hairnet and a high bone-necked lace dress seemed to emphasize her air of reduced gentility, gave us—although she had due respect for my medical degree, and Miss Law was certainly her favourite—her pale, "suffering" smile, which vanished only when I dropped a penny in the little wooden box placed beside the empty biscuit barrel in the centre of the table, and marked "For the Blind." Punctuality, like politeness, was one of the elder Miss Dearie's many principles, and all who came after she had "asked the blessing" were supposed to make atonement, although one must be forgiven for doubting, in unguarded moments, if this tribute ever reached its proper destination.

I began in silence to eat my kipper, which was salt, greasy, and more than usually undergrown. These two worthy gentlewomen had a hard struggle to make ends meet, and Miss Beth—who "managed" the establishment out in front, while Miss Ailie cooked and cleaned in the background—saw to it that the sin of gluttony was never committed in her presence. In spite of this, the scrupulous reputation of her house was recognized by those connected with the University, and she seldom had a vacancy. Tonight, I saw that out of her complement of six, Galbraith and Harrington, both fourth-year undergraduates, were absent, having gone home for the week end, but opposite me sat the two other medical students, Harold Muss and Babu Lal Chatterjee.

Muss was an undersized youth of eighteen, perpetually spotted with acne pimples, and endowed with a most striking set of protuberant buck teeth. He was only in his first year, and for the most part maintained deferential silence, but occasionally, when he thought someone had made a joke, he would burst suddenly into a wild and hoarse guffaw.

Lal Chatterjee, a Parsee from Calcutta, was older than Muss, actually about thirty-three, extremely plump and podgy, with a smooth saffron complexion set off by a voluminous pink turban and a beaming, ineffably stupid face. For at least fifteen years he had been waddling in and out of the Winton classrooms, wearing baggy trousers which hung down at the seat like an empty potato sack, and carrying a large green umbrella, trying without success to obtain his medical degree. Good-natured and garrulous, with an incessant flow of amiable small talk, he was nicknamed "the Babu" and had become, at the University, a comic institution. Immediately we entered, in a high "singsong" voice which seemed always, like the cry of the muezzin proclaiming the hours of prayer, to be pitched in the minor key, he began:

"Ah, good evening Dr. Robert Shannon and Miss Jean Law. I am afraid we have almost eaten all the food. For your lateness you may perhaps perish of malnutrition. Oh, yes, perhaps, ha, ha. Mr. Harold Muss, please to pass me the mustard, thank you. I appeal to my fellow doctor, I ask you Dr. Robert Shannon, does not mustard stimulate the salivary glands, of which there are two, the sublingual and another whose name I have safely in my note-book? Sir, excuse me, how does that other gland call itself?"

"The pancreas," I suggested.

"Ah, yes, sir, the pancreas," agreed the Babu, beaming. "That is exactly my own view."

Muss, who was drinking tea, suddenly choked violently.

"The pancreas!" he gasped. "I don't know much, but that's in the stummick!"

Lal Chatterjee gazed reproachfully upon his convulsed fellow student. "Oh, poor Mr. Harold Muss! Do not exhibit your ignorance. Please to remember that I am many more years an undergraduate than you. I had the honour to fail B.A., Calcutta University, probably before you were born."

Miss Law was attempting to catch my eye and to draw me into her conversation with Miss Beth. They were discussing, with the grave yet eager interest of those banded by evangelical sympathies, the coming performance of "The Messiah" at St. Andrew's Hall—always a notable winter event in Winton—but since I had, for reasons of my own, a particular reticence towards religious matters, I fixed my gaze upon my plate.

"I do so like choral music, don't you, Mr. Shannon?"

"No," I said. "I'm afraid I don't."

At this point, Miss Ailie Dearie entered from the kitchen, silently, in her broken-down felt slippers, bearing the "crystal," the glass dish of stewed but stony prunes which, on "kipper-nights," with the inevitability of death, terminated our grim repast.

Unlike her sister, Miss Ailie was a soft and tender creature, rather untidy in her appearance, with a thickset, slow-moving figure and hands knotted and disfigured by housework. It was rumoured—probably a piece of student nonsense, encouraged by the fact that her one relaxation, in the evenings, was the reading of romantic novels from the public library—that as a young girl she had suffered a tragic love affair. Her kind face, flushed from the stove, patient under her sister's acid tongue, was sad and wistful, with a thin strand of hair falling so constantly over her forehead that she had the curious habit of pursing her lips and, with a gentle upward breath, puffing it away. Perhaps her own difficulties made her sympathetic towards my problems. Now, with kindly interest, she bent over and murmured in my ear:

"How did things go today, Robert?"

To reassure her I forced a smile, at which she nodded with a pleased expression, puffed away her hair and went out.

Miss Ailie's heart was softer than her prunes! For the next five minutes, no sounds were audible but those of troubled mastication, the clash of Muss's errant canines upon the flinty fruit.

When nothing edible remained on the table, the meal ended with Beth Dearie rising like the chatelaine of a castle who has dispensed a banquet. We then dispersed to our rooms, Harold Muss absently extracting fish-bones with his forefinger, Lal Chatterjee belching musically, with a kind of Oriental majesty, en route.

"Mr. Shannon." Hastening after me, Miss Law breathed my name—I had at last broken her of the habit of addressing me as "Doctor," a title which, with its implications of professional mediocrity, I at this stage thoroughly resented. "I'm not sure of the paper I've written on *Trypanosoma gambiense* . . . you know the question you set us today. It's so specially interesting to me . . . Would you . . . could you be so terribly good as to look it over?"

Although harassed and preoccupied, I had not the strength of will to refuse—somehow that unguarded freshness in her face turned back my rudest answers.

"Bring it along," I growled.

Five minutes later, sustained by the broken springs of the one chair in the conservatory, I read her paper, while she sat very erect on the edge of a stool covered with cracked wax-cloth, her hands clasping her serge skirt across her ankles, watching me with an earnest and anxious air.

"Will it do?" she asked, when I had finished.

The essay was remarkably well done, with several quite original observations, and a series of sketches of the flagellated parasite's development, extremely accurate. As I considered her, I had to admit that she was not like most of the young women who came in droves to the University, presuming to "go in" for medicine. Some of these came for a lark, others were pushed forward by aspiring middle-class parents, a few were merely seeking to get married to an eligible young man who would one day, in some suburban community, become a stodgily respectable practitioner, more or less incompetent but financially secure. None had any real talent or capacity for the profession.

"You see," she murmured, as though to encourage my opinion, "there's work waiting for me. I am so anxious to get my degree."

"This is well above pass standard," I said. "In fact, it's extremely good."

A warmth crept into her soft cheeks.

"Oh, thank you, Dr. . . . Mr. Shannon. That means everything, coming from you. I can't tell you how much we students respect your opinion . . . and your . . . Yes, please let me say it, your brilliance. . . . And of course I know what a hard time you had in the war."

I took off my slipper and examined the crack beginning in the toe. I have tried to explain why I could not wound this strange neighbour of mine; nevertheless I had to have some outlet for my vexed sensibilities. My nature was reserved and secretive, I was not constitutionally a liar, yet under that starry, trustful gaze, some devil, which perhaps I had inherited from my incorrigible grandfather, had begun, in these past weeks, screened by my thoughtful, even melancholy visage, to play outrageous pranks.

During our frequent conversations I had confided in her that I came of a wealthy and aristocratic Levenford family, but that, being left an orphan and preferring medical research to the career mapped out for me, I had been cut off and forbidden my ancestral home.

Her innocent credulity goaded me to further efforts.

For the four years of the war I had led an uneventful, dreary existence as the surgeon of a light cruiser detailed for duty with submarines in the

North Sea. Our weekly missions through the enemy mine fields were probably dangerous enough, but they were unutterably dull. In harbour we drank gin, played van-john, and fished for eels. Once our senior officer was surprised in undress uniform in his cabin with a pretty woman to whom, he subsequently told us, he was teaching the abstruse arts of navigation. Beyond this, nothing broke the monotony until we got into the Battle of Jutland, then everything happened so quickly that there remained only a confused impression of noise and light flashes, of myself sweating between decks in the sick-bay, doing everything badly, with shaking fingers, my inside so turned to water that for a whole week afterwards I suffered abominably from colic.

Naturally this would not do for Miss Jean Law, so while she hung upon my words I invented a new and more picturesque adventure. We had been torpedoed, marooned for days in mid-Pacific on a raft, there were dramatic scenes of thirst and hunger, we fought off sharks, and so on, through the most horrific hazards, until I woke up, pale but triumphant, a hero in fact, in a South American hospital.

During my present silence she had apparently been nerving herself, and now her eyelashes began to flicker, always a sign of her inner stress.

"I've been thinking . . . I mean . . . it seems scarcely fair, Mr. Shannon, that I should have learned so much about you . . . while you know nothing about me." She faltered slightly, then continued valiantly, her colour high. "I was wondering if, some Saturday, you would care to come out to my home at Blairhill."

"Well," I said, rather taken aback. "I'm going to be pretty busy all winter."

"I realize that. But you have been so kind to me I'd like you to meet my people. Of course," she added hurriedly, "we're very simple folk, not like you. My father"—and again she flushed, yet, with the air of one who after long self-communion has taken a difficult resolution, went on bravely—"is not a very important person. He is . . . a baker."

There was a longish pause. Not knowing what to say, or do, I sat rather too still. I was beginning to feel uncomfortable, when suddenly she smiled, showing that some spark of humour enlivened her seraphic fervour.

"Yes, he bakes bread. Works in the bakehouse with my young brother and another man. And sends the batches round the countryside by a horse-drawn van. Quite a small business, but old-established, as you might gather. So although you are so well-connected, please don't look down on us."

"Good Lord, what do you take me for?" Stung, I threw her a quick glance, but she was quite innocent of any double meaning.

"Then you'll come." With a pleased expression she rose, took up her paper from the arm of my chair and stood looking at it. "I'm most grateful for your help with these trypanosomes. Tropical medicine interests me so much." My inquiring glance provoked a final confidence. "You see . . . we belong to the Brethren in Blairhill . . . and . . . immediately I get my degree . . . I am going out as a doctor to our settlement . . . at Kumasi, in West Africa."

My jaw must have dropped at least an inch. Was there no end to her preposterous capacity to startle me? My first impulse was to laugh, but the look in her eyes, which shone as though she glimpsed the Holy Grail, restrained me. And as I considered her, I had to admit that at least she had the virtue of sincerity.

"How long have you had this wild idea?"

"Ever since I started Medicine. That's why I went in for it."

So she hadn't come to the University for a lark, or to get married, like the others. Even so, I still was unconvinced.

"It all sounds very noble," I said slowly. "Romantic and self-sacrificing . . . on paper. But if you did go . . . I wonder if you really know what you'll be up against."

"I ought to." She smiled calmly. "My sister has been out there as a nurse for the last five years."

That silenced me. She paused at the door and with a smile slipped from the room. After an interval during which I sat motionless, staring somewhat foolishly at nothing, and listening unconsciously, rather uncomfortably, to her quiet movements next door, I shrugged my shoulders and, with compressed lips, turned to the consideration of my own situation.

Must I submit to Professor Usher's direction or should I in my own way, seen as unclear and hazardous, take issue with authority and fate?

CHAPTER THREE

THE next day, Saturday, was my weekly holiday, and at six o'clock in the morning, I set out from the sleeping house to walk to the village of Dreem, some twenty-six miles away. The Winton streets were still dark, damp with dew, and except for the footfalls of an early workman, silent and deserted. When the sun broke through I had passed the city outskirts, leaving behind, with relief, the last of the bungalows scattered among market gardens, and was in open country, with the broad estuary of the Clyde reaching away to the sea before me, a luminous, familiar vision which always lifted up my heart.

Towards noon I ate an apple which Miss Ailie, daring her sister's displeasure, had slipped in my pocket the night before. Then, crossing the river at Erskine Ferry, five miles above the town of Levenford, I entered the stretch of splendid farm land which fringed the waters of the Firth, a terrain richly pastoral, with sheep and cattle grazing on the rolling meadows, enclosed by grey stone walls.

As I approached my destination, the purpose of this journey, naïve though it might be, dominated my mind. All that year, since the University Senate, following my demobilization in 1918, had awarded me the Eldon Fellowship,

I had been employed by Professor Usher upon a routine investigation of certain opsonins, a subject interesting to him, but regarded by me as of slight importance—indeed, the entire opsonic theory was already being discredited by advanced scientific workers.

Perhaps I was prejudiced by my deep regard for the previous head of the Department, Professor Challis, who, at the University, had taught and inspired me: a fine old man, now retired, at the age of seventy, to the obscurity of private life. Yet I neither liked nor trusted his successor. Frigid, at times ingratiating, spurred by a rich and socially ambitious wife, Hugo Usher seemed lacking in inspiration or creative force, unprepared to make the sacrifice of blood and tears demanded by research, an opportunist who had achieved his position through a facility for tabulating statistics, but more especially through push, well-timed publicity, and a remarkable capacity for picking other people's brains. By attaching promising young men to his department, he had acquired a reputation for original investigation—my previous monograph, for example, on Pituitary Function, a small drudgery perhaps, yet painfully achieved, had been published as the joint work of Professor Hugo Usher and Dr. Robert Shannon.

While under this bondage, I had been seeking, with pathetic eagerness, a really significant subject for research, a broad, original thesis, a thesis so unmistakably momentous that it would influence, or even alter, the course of general medicine.

A tall order, naturally. But I was young, only twenty-four, passionately bound up in my work, burning with the painful ambition of a silent and retiring nature, longing, in my poverty and obscurity, to astound the world.

For months I had sought in vain until suddenly, out of the blue, an opportunity presented itself. During that autumn a number of rural areas all over the country had been stricken by a curious epidemic which, perhaps for lack of a better term, had been loosely classified as influenza. The death rate of the infection was high and its incidence wide—in the popular press there had been sporadic headlines of a sensational nature and indeed, in the medical journals I had traced several reports from America, Holland, Belgium, and other foreign sources recording outbreaks of a comparable condition. The symptoms of acute chill, fever, intense headache, and body pains were of considerable severity, often leading to a fatal pneumonia or, in cases which recovered, to prolonged aftereffects of debility. And as I studied them I began to feel that here was a new and different disease, a suspicion which increased as time went on, and sent a current of excitement through my veins.

My interest in this matter was further heightened by the fact that one of the main local centres of the epidemic was the neighbourhood of Dreem. And now, at three o'clock in the afternoon, as I trudged into that little village of low grey houses, straggling along the bank of a placid stream, always a quiet place but at present, because of the recent sickness, even more silent and deserted, my eagerness, conquering fatigue, made me go faster. Without pausing for my usual bread and cheese at the one small village tavern, I went immediately to Alex Duthie.

He was in his cottage, seated, pipe in mouth, in his cozy kitchen, while Simon, his little boy, played on the rug at his feet and Alice, his wife, a sedate, matronly woman, rolled out a pastry at the table.

Alex was a short, steady-looking man of thirty-five, dressed in clean moleskin trousers, thick socks, and a striped flannel shirt. He greeted me with an impenetrable motion of his head, a flicker rather, of his features, so faint as to be almost invisible, yet which somehow had more welcome than the longest speech. At the same time he took in, not without irony, my tired and dusty appearance.

"Did you miss the bus?"

"No, Alex. I wanted the walk." Unable to restrain myself, I went on: "I hope I'm not late. Did you . . . make the arrangements?"

He appeared not to have heard; then, guardedly, he smiled, and removed the pipe from his lips.

"Ye're a fine chap to choose Saturday afternoon. Most folks like a rest then . . . especially after what we've been through." He paused long enough to make me anxious. "But I managed the most of them for ye. We'll drop down to the Institute now."

As I gave an exclamation of gratitude, he got up, went over to the fender and began to lace on his boots.

"Do you fancy a cup of tea, Doctor?" Mrs. Duthie asked. "A body needs something hot, a time like this."

"No, thank you, Alice. I'd rather get to work."

"You're having supper and spending the night with us," Alex announced, in the tone of one who will take no refusal. "Sim here wants to show you the new fishing rod I cut down for him."

He took his peaked cap and we went out. Sim, five years old, a self-contained and silent soul like his father, followed us to the door.

"I'm a confounded nuisance to you, Alex," I said as we walked down the road. "I wouldn't have asked you to do this if I didn't think it was important."

"Ay," he agreed wryly. "Ye're a bit of a bother, Rob. But as we happen to be fond of ye, we maun put up wi' it."

My association with Alex Duthie, and indeed, with Dreem, went back six years, to before the war, when as a lonely student at the University I had forsaken my books to indulge my passion for fishing in those tidal waters where, each spring, the silvery sea trout make a wonderful run. On the river-bank, one evening, Alex had helped me to land a tremendous fish; and in that hectic encounter, in the exquisite triumph which succeeded it, the seeds of enduring friendship had been sown. Although a working man, being employed as head herdsman by the Dreem Farms Company, Duthie was locally a highly respected figure and for several years past had been elected to the office of "provost" of the little community. His manner could be difficult at times and his tongue, when he used it, was often rough, but never once had I known him do a mean or shabby thing. Since the village was too remote to possess a resident doctor, it was to him that I made my present unorthodox request, a request which could have come only from an ingenuous and enthusiastic young man, which in fact had in it a touch of the absurd.

The Institute was a small brick building, recently erected by the Farms Combine, and containing various club-rooms and a library. Alex led the way into one of the rooms off the main corridor where about thirty persons were gathered, reading and talking, but with an air of expectancy. A silence fell as we went in.

"Well!" Alex exclaimed. "Here's Dr. Shannon. Most of ye know him as a pretty fair fisherman. But forbye, he's a sort of professor at the University, and he wants to find out about this damn 'flu that's laid us out here. He's come to ask a favour of you."

This struck the right note and several of the people smiled, though many of them still looked pale and ill. When I thanked them for coming I explained what was wanted and promised not to keep them long. Then I removed my haversack, took out a series of numbered capillary tubes and systematically set to work.

They were, of course, all village folk, most of them men who worked in the fields, and they had all had the recent infection. Some I knew personally, big Sam Louden, who often tied flies for me, keen-eyed Harry Vence, and others whom I had met, at twilight, knee-deep in the water, casting their long greenheart rods. It was a simple operation to obtain from each a small blood specimen and their friendly, good-natured patience made things easier. Even so, I took longer than I had expected for, as I went on, a fine tremor crept into my fingers as I realized what this might mean to me.

At last it was over, my final subject had rolled down his sleeve, shaken hands with me and gone out. Then, as I looked up from my note-book, I saw Alex, seated on a near-by bench, watching me in alert summation of my character—a queer penetrating look, mingled, too, with intelligent interest which, as our eyes met, he took pains to conceal.

There was a pause. I had already told him what was in my mind. I said steadily:

"I have to do it this way, Alex. I can't help myself . . . I simply must find out."

A silence followed; then, slowly, Duthie came over and gripped me by the hand.

"Ye're a clever chap, Rob, and I'm sure I wish you luck. If I can help again, in any way, just let me know." A dry smile wrinkled the corners of his eyes. "Meantime, come on back to supper. Alice has a grand steak-and-kidney puddin' for us."

I smiled back at him.

"You go ahead, Alex. I'll join you when I finish off my notes."

"All right, lad. Don't be long."

When he had gone I worked for half an hour, checking and tabulating the specimens, then with my rucksack across my shoulder I left the Institute and walked up the narrow wynd towards Duthie's cottage. A clear darkness was falling and a thin moon with its attendant star had risen in the frosty sky. The lightly textured air was cold and still, and suddenly my mind lifted in a surge of exhilaration at the prospect which lay before me, this voyage of discovery, beset with difficulty and danger, into uncharted seas.

Outside Alex's door I paused. The lights of the village twinkled around me and beyond flowed the waters of the estuary, shadowy and mysteriously spangled. While I stood there, quite motionless, watching the moon drift higher in the heavens, listening, as the last whisperings of the earth died in the boreal stillness, I felt the mantle of an eternal solitude enwrap my spirit. I knew then what I was, and must always be—alone, one against the world.

I shivered, recollected that I was hungry; and aware that I should find food, fire, and friendship there, and the quiet laughter of little Sim, I went in to Alex's house.

CHAPTER FOUR

On the following Friday, there took place the event I had anticipated, and upon which my plan of action was based.

All that week, at the University, as I automatically performed the task to which I was handcuffed, I observed that Professor Usher was unusually pleasant to us, moving about incisive as ever, yet wearing a smile so artificially agreeable it caused the hairs on the back of my neck to bristle.

On Friday afternoon this bland assumption of the co-operative spirit reached its height as he made a little tour of the laboratory and finally, having cleared his throat, faced us with a confidential smile.

"Gentlemen, as you are no doubt aware, I have been honoured with an invitation to act as chairman of the advisory committee for the coming Pathological Congress, a distinction which obliges me to make a tour of the various universities with my distinguished colleague, Professor Harrington, in order that we may draw up a suitable and comprehensive agenda."

After an impressive pause he went on.

"Mrs. Usher and I leave for London tonight at six. We shall be away for eight weeks. I know, of course, that in my absence the work of the Department will proceed smoothly and expeditiously, in accordance with the best traditions of research. Are there any questions?"

No one answered. He nodded, as though establishing the fact that an understanding had been reached between us; then, looking at his watch, he bowed to each of us in turn and left the Department. Smith went with him to see to the luggage.

I could scarcely contain my emotions as the door swung shut, for although I had expected a brief respite from the attentions of my taskmaster, the news that he had gone, actually, for eight weeks was so wonderful it bowled me over. What could I not accomplish in that time!

Lomax had already risen and, lighting a cigarette, was glancing across at me with his fatigued smile.

"Didn't you sense we were being put in the frame of mind to work continuously while he was away? I'm so fond of him, I can't bear to see him go."

Pale, with discontented eyes and blond wavy hair, and wearing usually a faintly cynical expression, Adrian Lomax was about four years older than I, one of those fortunate persons who attract instinctively by their charm and good looks. He was an only son, with a rich mother, a widow who lived in London, and he had been educated at Winchester and Oxford, impressed at these colleges with a stamp of manners and good breeding. After his graduation he had meant to continue his studies abroad but the war had intervened and now, because of some remote connection between Professor Usher and his family, he had come to Winton to "put in" twelve months' post-graduate research. In his tastes, he affected the exotic, despised most things, aloofly, and cast down all that could not be explained in terms of natural science. His languid scepticism suggested deep reserves of knowledge; and with his half-shrug, his supercilious smile, his metaphysical expositions, he attempted frequently to put nails in the coffin of my belief. Self-centred and affected, his too conscious absence of condescension towards Spence and myself concealed a spoiled vanity. Yet he had a most engaging way with him. Preparing for a distinguished career, but disdaining the vulgarity of too obvious effort, he worked spasmodically; and, while bewailing his exile, carelessly contrived, in his comfortable rooms furnished expensively by himself, to exceed his generous allowance and have the best of everything.

Meanwhile he had been rummaging in his locker, from which he now produced, with an amused air, a bottle of Benedictine.

"This happens to be on hand. Let's mark the occasion. Immediately." He drew the cork and poured generous measures of the golden liquid into three clean beakers.

Neil Spence, the third member of Usher's team, apart from those regular weekly outings with his wife was not inclined to gaiety—like the hermit crab, he ventured out of his shell only on the rarest occasions—but now he came over sociably and joined Lomax.

So too did I. The thought of my tremendous decision to use the University laboratory for my own experiments gave to me a sense of freedom and excitement, which rose almost to exaltation, and sent a desire to celebrate surging recklessly within me.

"Absent friends." Lomax drank. "Coupled with the name of Herr Professor

Hugo. I hope you like this stuff. Nothing too good for my distinguished colleagues."

"It's extremely nice," Spence said in his quiet, matter-of-fact voice.

"Made by the monks." Lomax turned his ironic gaze towards me. "That should please you, Shannon. You are a Catholic, aren't you?"

"Yes . . . of course." I gave my answer a disarming assurance.

Lomax refilled the beakers with a faintly quizzical smile.

"But Robert, I thought you were a scientist. You can't reconcile Genesis and the mutation of species."

"I don't try to." I took a sip of the warm and mellow liqueur. "The one is a sordid fact . . . the other a romantic mystery."

"Hmm," said Lomax. "What about the Pope?"

"He's all right with me."

"You're fond of him?"

"Absolutely." I stopped smiling—Lomax's wit on this topic usually ended by annoying me. "I admit I'm not a shining example . . . quite the reverse, in fact. All the same, there's something that I can't ever get away from . . . against reason if you like. . . . I hope you don't wish me to say that I regret it."

"Far from it, my dear fellow," Lomax said easily.

Neil Spence was glancing at his watch.

"Nearly six o'clock. Muriel ought to be here any minute."

He took his handkerchief and began, surreptitiously, to remove the moisture that escaped from the corners of his lips.

One night, in a trench near the Marne, in the muddy darkness, as he rose unguardedly to ease his cramped position, Spence's lower jaw had been shattered by a burst of German shrapnel; and although the plastic surgeons had patched him wonderfully with one of his own ribs, the result was a sad distortion of the human face: the chin supplanted by an angry scar, with drawn lips emerging from the cicatrix, a cruel contrast to his fine broad brow, beneath which his dark, rather haunted eyes retreated instinctively. What made the disfigurement worse was the fact that Spence had been a handsome youth, much sought after at the local dances, picnics and tennis tournaments in the staid but comfortable society of Winton.

"Your wife is charming," Lomax remarked politely. "I enjoyed the theatre last week immensely. Shall I pour another libation to Herr Hugo?"

"No, don't," Spence said, sensibly. "We've had enough."

"But he asked us to drink in the best traditions of the Department," I said.

We all laughed, even Spence. It was a thing he rarely did, it contorted his face so badly. At that moment we were interrupted by a sound behind us.

Mrs. Spence had come in to the laboratory, unannounced, with the daring air of one who has broken rules and knows it. She smiled at us vivaciously from behind the dotted veil which fringed her hat and gave piquancy to the slightly hollow contours of her face.

"Smith wasn't to be found, and I waited . . . and waited . . . like a lost soul."

Muriel Spence was about twenty-seven, of medium height, rather thin, yet graceful, with delicate wrists and ankles, light brown hair and a narrow, somewhat colourless face in which however, at times, her grey eyes were wide and girlish. Without exaggeration, she could be regarded as the alleviation of Spence's misfortune. Before the war he had been engaged to her and when he returned, quite broken up, she had stood by him, resisting the pressure of her family and his own efforts to give her back her freedom. Their wedding, largely attended, had created widespread interest. Now, although she had lost much of her youthful prettiness and was somewhat artificial in her manner, she still was attractive, and in her dark costume and necklet of brown fur she brightened our dull work-room. Because of Spence, who was my closest friend, I had tried to like Muriel; yet my nature, awkward and difficult no doubt, found always in her a quality which threw me back, as though unwanted, upon myself.

She raised her veil and kissed her husband lightly on the cheek, remarking, with a tinge of reproof:

"We shall be late for our dinner engagement, dear. Why aren't you ready?"

"Of course, Mrs. Spence," said Lomax, elevating one eyebrow in his best manner, "now you're in, you may never get out of this chamber of horrors."

She tilted her head to one side, touching me with her bright, provoking glance.

"I feel quite safe with Mr. Shannon here."

At this, for some reason, Lomax and Mrs. Spence smiled. Spence, whose dark eyes rested with almost doglike devotion upon his wife's face, had put on his overcoat, and now she tucked her gloved hand under his arm.

"Neil and I are going your way, Mr. Lomax." She spoke invitingly. "Can we drop you?"

There was a slight pause.

"Thank you," he said, at length. "You're very kind."

I left with them and at Muriel's runabout, parked outside the entrance to the building, we parted. While they set off in the car towards the city, I walked down Fenner Hill, bent on retrieving the Dreem specimens from my lodgings and returning with them, immediately, to the laboratory.

In Eldon Park, to my right, the ornamental lake was "bearing," crowded with skaters. I could hear in the still air the keen, gay ring of the steel blades upon the ice. Elevated by the Benedictine, and the delicious thought of Usher's departure, I felt like singing. There was a pleasant giddiness in my head, the world seemed an altogether delightful place.

As I approached the familiar boarding-house, the door of Rothesay opened and there appeared Harold Muss, accompanied by Miss Law, both bearing skates which swung from straps upon their wrists. At this, the liqueur, belying its monastic origin, proved more potent than I had imagined. I couldn't explain why, but the sudden apparition in such company of Miss Law, wearing a neat white sweater and a woollen cap, with a red tassel, upon her hair, bent, not on succour and salvation, but upon healthful exercise, sent me into a silent fit of laughter.

"What's the matter, Mr. Shannon?" At the sight of me she drew up. "Are you ill?"

"Not at all," I answered, leaving hold of the railings. "I am in perfect mental and physical condition . . . ready for an effort which may shake the world. Do I make myself clear?"

Muss suppressed a snigger, he guessed the nature of my symptoms, but Miss Law's modest countenance expressed only sympathy and a deeper concern.

"Won't you come with us to the lake? The breeze might do you good."

"No," I said, "I won't come to the lake." I added logically: "I have no skates."

"I could lend you skates," Muss suggested slyly, "but the ice is slippery."

"Shut up, Muss," I said sternly. "Don't I work my fingers to the bone for you . . . and for all humanity?"

"You've been keeping at it much too hard, Mr. Shannon." In her perplexity Miss Jean had taken my words quite literally. "You know you promised to come out to Blairhill. I go home tonight. Do take the day off and visit us tomorrow."

Gazing into her soft brown eyes, my powers of invention seemed suddenly to fail me. Finding no excuse, after a moment, lamely, I muttered:

"All right, I'll come."

CHAPTER FIVE

THE one-thirty train for Blairhill was painfully slow, its ancient compartments so foul that with every jolt of the engine a puff of dust exhaled from the mouldy seat covers. As it dragged across the smoky industrial Lowlands, past belching factory chimneys, with never a blade of grass in sight, stopping at every little station, I blamed myself for fulfilling a promise I had never meant to make and took little comfort in arguing that a day off would send me back refreshed to my research.

At last, about an hour after leaving Winton Low Level, having escaped the worst of the "black country," we bumped into Blairhill. So that the unhappy traveller should not miss his fate, the name was worked in white pebbles, between two fierce-looking Scots firs, upon the station embankment. And there, waiting on the platform, rising a little on her toes, scanning eagerly with bright eyes the curved flank of the stationary train, was Miss Jean Law.

As I opened the door and came towards her, I perceived that, in honour of my visit, or merely, perhaps, because of her week-end vacation, she was wearing, beneath a loose coat, her knitted white sweater and, upon her brown curls, which seemed more noticeable than usual, that little tasselled woollen cap known in Scotland as a "cool." Discerning me amongst the milling passengers, her face lit up in welcome. We shook hands.

"Oh, Mr. Shannon," she exclaimed, happily. "It's so nice you could come. I was almost afraid . . ."

She broke off, but I finished the sentence for her.

"That I would let you down."

"Well . . ." She coloured, as she did so easily. "I know you're a busy man. But you're here anyway, and it's a lovely afternoon, and I've so much to show you, and although I shouldn't say it, I think you'll enjoy it."

As she spoke we were walking together up the narrow main street. The town was less spoiled than I had expected, it lay within the wide domain of the ducal family of Blairhill and had the air of an old-fashioned country borough, with hand-hewn setts upon the pavements, unexpected winding alleys, and an old market-place. Full of pride in her native place, my companion explained that "the present Duke," in conjunction with the Blairhill Historical Society, had done much to preserve the local antiquities and she assured me, seriously, enthusiastically, that, when the formalities of introduction were completed, she would take me upon a comprehensive tour of inspection.

At the head of the incline she paused suddenly, opposite a little low-browed building, and, with a nervously conscious air betrayed by her fluttering lashes, she remarked:

"This is our bakehouse, Mr. Shannon. You must come in and meet my father."

I followed her, beneath a low archway into a little cobbled yard, past a varnished van, its shafts directed towards the sky, then down, through a narrow doorway, between piled sacks of flour, into a dim, sweet-smelling, earth-floored basement lit by the dull red radiation of two charcoal ovens. Gradually, as my eyes became accustomed to the dark interior, I made out two shirt-sleeved figures, each armed with a long wooden paddle, working energetically at the open ovens, their white aprons made ruddy by the glow as they drew the batches of bread on to long wooden trays.

For several minutes we watched in silence this operation, which appeared to demand energy, adroitness, and speed. Then, as the new batch slid into the ovens and the iron doors clanged shut, the foremost of the two turned immediately and came towards us, wiping his hand upon his apron and holding it out, the nails still slightly encrusted with dried dough.

Daniel Law was about fifty-five, of medium height, pallid from his occupation, yet vigorous-looking, with thick shoulders, and a sturdy frame. Despite his steel spectacles and the close black beard which somewhat masked his features, he had a frank, earnest expression and an open brow, at present beaded with sweat. Obviously he did not smile easily; yet as his warm fingers grasped mine his lips parted slightly, in greeting, exposing strong teeth, somewhat spoiled, however, by the flour, which was everywhere.

"I am glad to make your acquaintance, sir. My daughter has told me of your great kindness to her at the coll-edge. Any friend of my daughter is welcome here."

His deep voice had a patriarchal quality, enhanced by his pronunciation of the word "college," and his bespectacled eyes, as he made reference to Miss Jean Law, glinted fondly. He went on to apologize.

"I'm sorry we're so rushed the now. My son and I manage by ourselves, Saturday afternoons." He called over his shoulder. "Luke! Step up here a minute."

The young lad of seventeen, who advanced, smiling and pulling on his jacket, bore a close resemblance to his sister, having similar colouring of complexion and eyes. He had a warm, cheerful, human air which made me take to him at once. He could not stay, having to harness the horse and drive the van upon its country round. Indeed, I perceived that Law himself, despite his courtesy, was pressed; so, with a side glance at my companion, I indicated that we must not trespass upon his time.

Law nodded.

"Our customers maun have bread, sir. And tomorrow's the Sabbath day. But we'll see you later at the house. Around five o'clock. Meantime, my daughter will take ye in hand."

Outside, and continuing our way to the outer fringes of the town, past newer houses standing in little garden plots, my companion kept stealing glances at me, half anxious, half eager, as though trying to gauge my opinion of her relatives. Presently, at a turn of the quiet avenue, overhung by the bare but drooping branches of some chestnut trees, we approached a small stone villa, neat and unpretentious, with a trim privet hedge in front and immaculate lace curtains shrouding the windows. Here, unable to contain herself, with her hand upon the iron gate bearing, on a brass plate, the name SILOAM, Miss Law exclaimed:

"They both liked you—my father and Luke. I could see that. Now you'll meet my mother."

While she spoke, the front door opened and a slight woman, silver-haired and comely, with a delicate transparent skin, her figure shielded by a black alpaca wrapper, appeared to greet us. After a quick glance at her daughter, making no effort to conceal the feather duster in her hand, she turned upon me for a long moment the scrutiny of her confidently tranquil eyes. Then, as though reassured, she fell into the vein of small talk.

"You caught me before I got changed, Mr. Shannon. I was just finishing my parlour when I happened to see you walking up the avenue. Come in and sit down."

"No, Mother," Miss Jean protested quickly. "We're going out to make the best of the afternoon."

Mrs. Law bent upon my companion her calm experienced gaze, which, though fond and tolerant of such youthful impatience, preserved a certain element of maternal condescension.

"You've plenty time, child."

"Not for what I've planned."

"Are you taking Malcolm with you?"

"Of course not, Mother." Her daughter answered a trifle fretfully. "You know he's away this afternoon."

Who was Malcolm? I wondered absently, perhaps some juvenile relation, possibly a dog.

"Well, well . . . Off you go then," agreed Mrs. Law with her air of quiet reasoning. "But be sure you're back for supper. We'll all be here and I'll be ready to dish at six o'clock sharp. Good-bye for just now, Mr. Shannon."

While she smiled and retired, competently, to her parlour, Miss Jean Law, with the slightly relieved air of one who has successfully gone through the preliminaries, took me exclusively in hand.

"Now," she exclaimed, with energy, "I can show you round."

Leading the way, she took me out, into the back garden of about half an acre, and toured me painstakingly along its gravel paths, between the tidy beds, the rhubarb patch, the washing green. When I approved its order, she flashed me a grateful smile.

"Of course, it's very tiny . . . suburban you might even say. I'm sure, Mr. Shannon, it's nothing like your home."

Affecting not to hear the mildly searching lift in her tone, I pointed, hastily, to the toolshed, where a red motor-cycle was propped upon its stand.

"Luke's." She answered my unspoken inquiry indulgently. "He's mad on motor engines and knows a lot about them, too—although Father doesn't approve. But poor fellow, he has to go so slow in the van, he likes to make up for it on his Indian."

My opinion of Luke, already high, rose considerably. For a long time, as one yearns for the moon, I had coveted such a machine, which was capable of bearing its rider exquisitely through the air at a speed of at least seventy miles an hour. I should have liked to halt to inspect its perfections, but Miss Jean was hastening me back, past the house, and into the public roadway. Tucking her "cool" more firmly upon her curls, she glanced methodically at her watch and remarked crisply:

"We have a good three hours. We'll try to get in everything."

"Shouldn't we rest for a bit, first?" I suggested, casting a glance towards two chairs which stood in a sheltered corner of the verandah. I had been up half the night trying to plan out a culture technique for my specimens.

She laughed quite gaily and remarked, archly, as though I had said something funny:

"Really, Mr. Shannon, you are a *cure*. Why, we've only just begun."

We set out, at a good round pace.

Never was there a more scrupulous sightseer, a more devoted cicerone

—that I am prepared to swear—than this pretty daughter of the baker of Blairhill.

Earnestly, indefatigably, she paraded me round the royal and ancient borough. She showed me the Town Hall, the public library, the Masonic Temple, the ducal mausoleum, the old weavers' houses on Cottar's Row, the remains of the Roman wall (three decayed boulders), and, with a reverent air, in Lamb Lane, the Meeting Hall of the Brethren. She even exhibited to me the exact spot at the Cross where Claverhouse, dispersing a Conventicle, had been providentially thrown from his charger.

Then, while I rejoiced that our pilgrimage was over, she gave me, scarcely pausing for breath and with a bright nod, the mysterious glance of one who has saved the best treat for the end.

"We can't miss the White Cattle," she declared, adding, primly, as though quoting from a guide-book: "They are quite unique."

To view these fabulous animals, which, she advised me, were part of the famous herd of Château-le-roi, imported from France by "the late Duke's father," we were obliged to retrace our steps for about two miles and to enter, through pillared gates, an extensive demesne known as "the High Parks," which "the late Duke" had graciously detached from his own policies and donated to the town.

It was undoubtedly a lovely stretch of woods and meadows, still maintaining—since not a soul was in sight—its previous air of privacy.

But Miss Law could not find the cattle. Although she sought them vigorously, ardently, as though her honour were at stake, drawing me with her, up hill and down dale, over wooden stiles and under bushy glades, her seeking eyes meanwhile exhibiting an increased concern, her expression lengthening with dismay, she was forced, eventually, to pull up upon the summit of the last grassy hill and, facing me, with shame, to admit defeat.

"I'm afraid . . . Mr. Shannon . . ." Then, with a final explosion of pique: "Really, it's beyond understanding."

"They're probably hiding from us, up the trees."

She shook her head, refusing to see humour in the subject.

"Such lovely animals. Milky-white and with beautiful curving horns. They must be 'in' for the winter. I'll show you them another time."

"Do," I said. "Meanwhile let's sit down."

The afternoon was extremely calm, warm for the season, with the sun, partly veiled, diffusing an amber light, which seemed to steep the landscape in the stillness of an undiscovered world. The contours of the muted woods fell away beneath our feet, hiding a little stream which, hushed by the prevailing mood, crept from pool to pool, holding its breath, imposing an equal silence upon us.

Beside me, chewing a blade of the brown tussocky grass and gazing straight ahead, Miss Jean Law sat erect, still nursing her discomfiture and, as I rested on my elbow, I began, unconsciously, to study her, trying, in a random fashion, to dissect her personality. I could not of course revise my opinion

of her naïvety yet I was compelled to admit that of the few young women
I had met, she was the most supremely natural. She had, especially in this
setting, a striking, youthful freshness. Her brown eyes, hair, and skin
matched the woodlands, as did her firm little throat and chin. Her teeth,
as she munched the wiry grass, were white and wholesome. Observing from
underneath, one could almost see the flow of warm blood through the soft
curve of her upper lip. But, more than anything, she looked, and smelled,
so extraordinarily clean. I decided, idly, that, since this virtue came next
to godliness, she must wash thoroughly, all over, night and morning, with
Windsor soap. Everything visible about her and, I felt sure, the invisible
also, was neat and spotless.

Suddenly, while I critically took stock of her, she turned her head and
met, unexpectedly, my examining gaze. For a moment she sustained it with
her usual fearless honesty, then her modest eyes fell and a slow, sweet flush
spread all over her cheeks. There was a strained pause, a silence that was
part, somehow, of the greater surrounding stillness of Nature and which,
as though inviting a word, an action upon my part that did not come, was
filled with an almost painful expectation. Then, almost angrily, as though
refusing to surrender to confusion, she glanced at her round silver watch,
jumped quickly to her feet.

"It's time we got back." She added in a low voice, which she tried to make
practical, "You must be starving for your tea."

When we reached Siloam the entire family awaited us in the immaculate
back parlour, Mrs. Law wearing her "company" dove-grey silk, Mr. Law and
Luke spruced-up in linen collars and decent broadcloth suits. There was
also present, rather to my surprise, another guest, introduced to me as Mr.
Hodden, who answered, with an agreeable smile, to the name Malcolm,
who at once attached himself to Jean, and who was, indeed, on terms of
devoted intimacy with all the members of the Law family.

He was a correct, dependable-looking young man of about twenty-five, with
a well-set-up figure, an open, faintly serious expression, firm lips, and a
square, compact head, dressed with methodical neatness in a brown tweed
suit and a high stiff collar. Prone always to envy in others those qualities
opposite to my own, I felt myself dim slightly in his presence, for he had
about him a calm solidity, the air of one who exercises every day at the
Y.M.C.A., a look of manly frankness as though, conscious of his own up-
rightness, he was resolved to find in his fellow man an equal attribute. His
top right vest-pocket carried a tuning fork and a row of sharpened pencils,
which served doubtless to facilitate his occupation, which I soon learned was
that of a teacher in the Blairhill elementary school.

When he had offered me a friendly hand, Mrs. Law set the seal upon
our meeting.

"You two young men ought to have much in common. Malcolm is quite
one of ourselves, Mr. Shannon. He takes our Sunday school every week.
A real worker, I can tell you."

Since supper was ready we took our places at the table, Daniel gravely repeated a lengthy grace in which, with a veiled glance towards her photograph, in nurse's uniform upon the mantelpiece, he made a rather touching reference to his absent daughter Agnes "now working in foreign fields." Then Mrs. Law began generously to portion out the large cut of boiled salmon that stood before her.

Sharp set, I fell to with the appetite to be expected from one of Miss Dearie's boarders. There was in addition to the generous fish a plenitude of everything, potatoes boiled in their jackets, winter greens, cold ham and tongue, pickles, pots of home-made preserve; indeed, the simple goodness of the meal would have delighted a palate far more expert than mine. In honour of my visit the baker had made a special sponge cake, iced with marzipan and adorned with frosted cherries. But what pleased me most was the bread. Light and well risen, with a crisp, crackling crust, it exhaled a delicious fragrance and melted upon one's tongue. When I ventured to compliment him upon his product Law looked gravely pleased. He picked up a slice from the plate, tested its consistency, sniffed it delicately, then broke it, with a sacramental air, between his fingers. Glancing across the table, professionally, at his son, he remarked:

"A shade underfired today, Luke . . . but not at all bad." Then, turning to me, he went on, with great simplicity, "We take our trade seriously, sir. The staff of life, that's what our bread is to many of the poor country folks. They don't get much else—colliers, ploughmen, farm labourers, with large families, working maybe for thirty-five shillings a week. That's why we make it wi' nowt but the best flour, and the sweetest barm, all mixed by hand."

"The finest bread in the country," Malcolm interposed, with a nod towards me. He was sitting next to Jean and passing plates in an undercurrent of quiet merriment.

Daniel smiled.

"Ay, they walk five miles, some of these bodies, to meet our van to buy it." He paused, drawing himself erect, with dignity. "You are probably aware, Mr. Shannon, of the scriptural significance of the article we produce. You will mind how the Saviour multiplied the loaves to feed the multitude, how He broke bread wi' his disciples at the Last Supper."

I gave a confused murmur of assent and, as Luke relieved my embarrassment by passing me the strawberry jam, with the faintest droop of his left eyelid, I attempted, in an undertone, to engage him in conversation on the merits of his motor-cycle. Daniel, however, was not to be denied. Head of this household, preacher at the Meetings, he was accustomed to hold forth, and now, beaming his grave and well-disposed regard across the table, he seemed determined to sound me out.

"Of course, Doctor, you follow a noble profession yourself. To heal the sick, restore the maimed, cause the lame to walk, what could be more meritorious? It was a proud and happy moment for me, sir, when my daughter decided to dedicate herself to that great and splendid work."

I kept silent, since I could not well advise him that it was my intention never to practice, but to devote myself exclusively to the pursuit of pure science.

Undeterred by my reticence, and with that strange interplay of dignity and humility which characterized him, Daniel returned to the subject, touched upon the brotherhood of man, upon the Christian virtue of helping one another; then, having worked himself into position, he faced me directly.

"May I ask, sir, what is your persuasion?"

I took a prolonged draught of tea. Except for Hodden, whose gaze betrayed a mild alertness, they were all viewing me with kindly attention, waiting in warm interest for my reply as though, in fact, it were the crux, the necessary keystone which would complete the firm edifice of their united approval. Miss Jean in particular, a trifle flushed from the strong hot beverage, was viewing me with parted lips and starry eyes.

What on earth was I to say? I knew enough of these small town interdenomination feuds to realize what a commotion I would cause if I spoke the naked truth—that I was a Catholic, who had strayed occasionally into the less dark corridors of scepticism, but who still, at heart, clung to his first belief. The thought caused me to fall back for support upon the structure I had already created for Miss Law. After all, what did it matter? I should never see this worthy family again, I preferred not to disrupt the harmony of the occasion, and if I were skilful I need not lie.

"Well, sir," I said, with a fluency which shocked me, as though this congregation of goodness evoked the worst subtleties of my character, "I must confess that my biological work has somewhat restricted my opportunities for churchgoing. But I was brought up, in Levenford, in an exceedingly strict Nonconformist atmosphere. In fact"—still drawing upon the facts of my chequered upbringing, I improved modestly upon one of my grandmother's less credible boasts—"a great-uncle on my mother's side was one of the Covenanters who gave testimony, with his blood, on Marston Moor."

There was a pause. Then as my answer slowly sank in, I perceived that its effect was not only satisfactory, but highly impressive.

"Do you tell me!" Daniel inclined his head with excusable interest. "Marston Moor! Ay, that was a martyrdom of the saints. You should be proud of such a forebear, Mr. Shannon. And," he added with gentle cunning, "I hope in future you'll mind his good example."

This obstacle surmounted, the evening continued on a note of amiable concord. When Malcolm, with profuse expressions of regret, was obliged to take his departure to conduct some night classes at the Blairhill Institute —extra work, Mrs. Law confided to me, which he was undertaking to support his widowed mother—we adjoined to the parlour where Miss Jean was induced to perform upon the piano, a piece by Grieg. Then there was talk of the distant Agnes. Her latest letter, extremely cheerful, was proudly read aloud. Snapshots were passed, tenderly, one by one, all yellowish and slightly fogged—native children in groups, spindly and large-eyed, wearing white pinafores, strangely pathetic, sustained by a staunch and smiling nurse's figure; clusters of wooden huts, a glimpse of a barren compound, and always the lush background of forest beyond, strange fernlike trees, the whole shot with shafts of sunlight and sullen, blinding shadow.

When eight o'clock struck, I rose to leave amidst protests and cordial handclasps.

"We were honoured, sir," said Daniel—and, with an unexpected warmth in his eye: "Maybe next time ye visit us, ye'll bide overnight."

"Yes, come again soon." Mrs. Law pressed a package into my hand, murmuring confidentially, "That's a nice bit Scots shortbread to help out things at Miss Dearie's."

Darkness had fallen as Luke and his sister escorted me to the station. On the way down Luke generously offered to lend me the motor bike whenever I could use it. As the train gathered steam, Miss Jean Law walked along beside my window.

"I hope you enjoyed your visit, Mr. Shannon. I know we all did, very much."

Alone, in the compartment, I subsided in a corner, exhausted by this excess of sociability, trying to assess my own reactions to it. To be truthful, contact with this simple, zealous family had filled me with a distaste for myself stronger even than usual—I felt cheap and shabby, yes, for some reason I felt a regular sneak.

And suddenly I had a vision of Jean Law's face as, innocently, she blushed with downcast eyes, beside me, in the High Parks. I had slight experience of women, and in this respect was entirely without conceit. But now a thought went through me like an arrow. I started, sat up, shocked, in the empty carriage.

"Oh, no!" I exclaimed aloud. "She couldn't . . . she can't . . . It would be too absurd."

CHAPTER SIX

FEBRUARY came in with sharper frost, with cold clear sparkling days which stirred the blood. For over a month now I had flung myself, with complete abandon, into my own work. It felt good to be alive.

Naturally, Lomax and Spence noticed my activity, but Smith, although I occasionally caught him staring at me and biting the ends of his ragged moustache, could not guess what I was up to. Now that Professor Usher was away, he spent most of the day in the bar of the University Arms.

It was not an easy process I had set myself. Do not imagine that original research is accomplished in a fine poetic rapture; before the dawn appears one must drudge along the labyrinthine ways, or roll the stone like Sisyphus, endlessly uphill.

Yet, after experimenting with many media, and finding them useless for my purpose, I had at last succeeded in growing, in peptone broth, from the Dreem specimens, a culture which I believed to contain the causal organism of the epidemic disease. As I gazed at the delicate yellow strands forming in saffron threads within the topaz clear liquid, enlarging and coalescing, like a glowing crocus, yet more beautiful to me than the rarest flower, my heart kept pounding with a deep excitement. This was a growth I did not recognize, which gave promise of something strange and new, which reinforced the trembling structure of my hopes.

As the time at my disposal lessened, I increased my efforts, by a method of selective culture, to produce a strong pure strain of this precious organism. I had a key for the side door of the Pathology building that gave me access to the laboratory when everyone had gone. After tea at Miss Dearie's, I returned to the Department, remaining there, submerged like a diver, connected to the world by only the thinnest cord of consciousness, in the cool, green-shaded solitude, until midnight boomed across the silent University. These were the most productive hours of all.

I was confident that I could finish this essential phase by the following Saturday, February 1st, and remove all traces of my experiments that same night. It fitted beautifully, like a well-designed mosaic—Professor Usher had written that he would return on Monday, the 3rd, and I should be at my bench, busy with his tests, when he came back.

On the Wednesday evening of that last week, shortly after nine o'clock, I felt that, at last, the culture was ripe for examination and with a platinum loop I smeared and stained a microscope slide. It was a crucial moment. Holding my breath, I placed the slide under the oil immersion lens; then, as the dark forms leaped up against the shining background, I gave a sharp involuntary gasp.

The field was loaded with a small, comma-shaped bacillus which I had never seen before.

For a long time I sat immobile, gazing at my discovery, suffused by an exaltation which turned me giddy. At last, collecting myself, I opened my note-book and began, with scientific accuracy, to write a specific description of the organism, which from its shape, I named, provisionally, Bacillus C. For perhaps fifteen minutes I continued, but suddenly my concentration was broken by a flood of light through the work-room fanlight. A few seconds later I heard steps in the passage, the door opened, and, while I turned cold with consternation, Professor Usher walked into the laboratory. He wore a grey suit with a dark cloth cape thrown across his shoulders, and his pale, stiff face was stained with the grime of travel. At first I could not believe that he was real. Then I saw he had just come off the train.

"Good evening, Shannon." He advanced slowly, in a measured fashion. "Still here?"

I blinked at him across the culture flasks. He was looking at them.

"You show remarkable industry. What's this?"

Utterly unnerved at being caught, I was silent. Why, oh, why had he come back before his time?

Suddenly, behind Professor Usher, I saw that bird of ill omen, standing, without his white coat, in an ill-fitting street suit, his long neck drooping, his orbits hollow—Smith. I realized, then, that I would have to tell him.

As I began haltingly, yet with jealous reserve, to speak, Usher's manner grew more distant and severe. When I finished his face was wintry.

"Do you mean that you have deliberately shelved my work in favour of your own?"

"I'll resume the counts next week."

"Since I've been away how many have you done?"

I hesitated.

"None."

His narrow, ingrained features turned grey with anger.

"I especially told you I wished our paper finished by the end of this month . . . for Professor Harrington . . . whose hospitality I have been enjoying . . . my old friend and colleague. Yet the minute my back was turned . . ." He stuttered slightly. "Why? Why?"

I kept looking at the lining of his cape. It was made of dark green silk. I muttered:

"I have to find out about this . . ."

"Indeed." Even his nostrils turned white. "Well, sir, let us not beat about the bush. You will abandon it at once."

I felt myself wince, but steadied my unruly nerves.

"Surely my fellowship gives me some say in the matter?"

"As Professor of Experimental Pathology, I have the last word."

I was not easily aroused, in fact my nature was retiring and inoffensive, I believed profoundly in universal tolerance, in that blessed motto, "Live and let live," yet now a reddish haze swam up before me.

"I can't give up this investigation. I consider it of far greater importance than the opsonin tests."

In the background Smith swallowed suddenly, his bony Adam's apple shuttling up and down his throat, as though relishing a savoury morsel. Usher drew himself to his full height, his lips wire-thin.

"You are a singularly graceless fellow, Shannon. I observe it in your manners, which are deplorable, in your dress, totally unsuited to your professional standing, and in your outrageous disrespect towards myself. I am accustomed to co-operating with gentlemen. If I have been lenient towards you it was because of my belief that with proper guidance you might go far. But if you choose to behave like a boor, we know how to deal with you. Unless by Monday you hand me a written apology for this almost unpardonable lapse I must ask you to leave my Department."

A dead stillness followed.

After a fitting interval, Usher took out his handkerchief and wiped his lips. He saw that he had silenced me and, as usual, his sense of self-interest came to the surface.

"Seriously, Shannon, for your own good, I advise you to take yourself in hand. In spite of everything, I am reluctant to break up our collaboration. Now, if you will excuse me, I have not been home yet."

With a matador-like sweep of his cape, he spun round and went out. At his departure, Smith stood a moment, then began to whistle softly under his ragged moustache, and, not looking at me, to make pretence of cleaning out Spence's sink.

He was waiting for me to speak, of course, and I was a fool to fall into the trap.

"Well," I said, bitterly. "I suppose you think you've queered my pitch."

"You heard the Chief, sir. I must carry out his orders. I have my responsibilities."

I knew this to be sheer hypocrisy. The truth was that, for the most incredible of reasons, Smith nursed against me, in his heart, an almost morbid jealousy. A poor youngster, like myself, he had once aspired towards the highest scientific goal. Now, beaten, frustrated, and consumed with envy, he could not endure that I might succeed where he had failed.

"It's no fault of mine, sir." He swabbed at the sink with a defiant smirk. "I only done my duty."

"I congratulate you."

I put away my cultures, set the regulator of the incubator to the requisite temperature, while he stared at me, sideways, in an odd manner. Then I took my cap and went out.

Sick with resentment, I walked down Fenner Hill, in the darkness.

At the intersection of Pardyke Road and Kirkhead Terrace, to clear my head, I stepped into the cabman's shelter upon the corner, and ordered a mug of coffee. Seated on a high stool, with my elbows on the counter, I sipped the dark gritty fluid, blind to the surrounding swirl of the night life of this poor quarter—the familiar crowds gathered round the pubs and fried-fish shops, the hucksters shouting at their barrows under naphtha flares, the slowly promenading women, the newsboys darting between the traffic, shouting the latest sensation.

A moment later, as I sat brooding, I felt the tap of an umbrella upon my shoulder and, turning, I saw the Babu at my elbow, beaming, full of friendship and affection for his fellow men.

"Good evening, sir."

I scowled at him but he slid forward a stool and pantingly elevated his flabby bulk to the level of the counter.

"Most fortunate meeting. I have been to Alhambra Varieties, second house naturally, so extremely jolly." He rapped for attention with his umbrella. "Coffee, please, with plenty sugar. And one large portion fruit cake. Give nice piece, please."

I turned my back. But Chatterjee, between noisy draughts, and with many giggles, persisted in describing his evening's entertainment, in which the famous Scots comedian, Sir Harry Lauder, had played a prominent part.

"Tee, hee, hee. At the frolics of that hilarious nobleman, I laugh so heartily I nearly fall from my front position in the balcony. I tell you, sir, I am so fearfully enamoured of the Scottish music, I am sincerely wishful of learning to play bagpipes. Can you suggest instructor, sir?"

"For God's sake leave me alone."

"But how nice, sir, for my Calcutta friends if, when returning with my degree, I also dispense Scottish airs while attired in kilt." Waving a pudgy forefinger he lilted in a high falsetto, "Ay, *ay, ay . . . la, la, la . . . lassee by the side . . . on banks of bonnee Clyde . . . When sun go down to rest . . . that is hour that I love best . . . roaming in the . . . roaming in the gloaming.* Excuse me, Dr. Robert Shannon, what is precise meaning of Scottish 'gloaming'? A wood, forest, nullah or concealed place, probably, suitable for love? Hee, hee, hee. Am I right, sir?"

I felt in my pocket for a coin, placed it on the counter to pay for my coffee and got abruptly to my feet.

"Wait, wait, wait, Dr. Robert Shannon." He tried to detain me, with the crook of his umbrella. "Guess, sir. In the audience tonight, who do I see from my high front place in the balcony? It is two of your friends, in front stalls, Dr. Adrian Lomax and the lady of Dr. Spence, both together, enjoying performance. Don't go, sir, I wish to accompany you."

But I was already outside the shelter. A new fear had entered my mind, driving me to retrace my steps hastily towards the Department.

" 'I must carry out his orders.' "

As I raced back, I kept thinking with increased foreboding of that last gleam in the attendant's eye.

The place was in total darkness when I got there. Hurriedly, I opened the side door, went into the laboratory. Even as I entered I missed the faint reassuring hum of the heater. With a sinking heart I switched on the light above my bench and opened the incubator. Then I saw with certainty. Smith had thrown out my cultures, the flasks stood empty on the bench, and four weeks of my hardest work had gone to waste.

CHAPTER SEVEN

UPON the following morning I did not go to the University but made my way, after breakfast, to Parkside Crescent where, in a quiet and unobtrusive terrace overlooking Kelvingrove Gardens, Professor Challis lived in retirement. I felt sure I should get advice and help from this good old man who had so often encouraged me in the past. When I rang the bell it was Beatrice, his married daughter, who opened the door—a pleasant young woman, wearing an art print overall, with her children, two bright-eyed little girls, peeping at me from behind her skirts.

"I'm sorry to trouble you so early, Beatrice. Could I see the Professor?"

"But, Robert," she exclaimed in her warm voice, smiling in spite of herself at my anxious face, "didn't you know . . . ? He's away."

My disappointment must have shown only too plainly, for, with a change of manner, she went on quickly to explain that her father, who suffered severely from arthritis, had been taken by some friends upon a trip to Egypt for his health. He would be away all winter.

"Won't you come in a moment?" she added kindly. "The children and I are having biscuits and hot cocoa."

"No, thank you, Beatrice." I tried to smile as I turned away.

Most of the day, which was grey and overcast, I walked aimlessly about the city, along Sinclair and Manfield Streets, staring unseeingly into the windows of the large shops; then, in the afternoon, I wandered to the docks where, wrapped in a chilly mist, the black and white river steamers lay paddle to paddle, laid up for the winter. I came back to the boarding-house and, more from habit than anything else, drifted into tea.

Out of the corner of my eye I noticed that Miss Jean Law, who had been away—where, I did not know—for the past three days, was again in her usual place. I thought she looked queer, quite ill, in fact—she was pale and her nose and eyes were swollen, slightly inflamed, as though she had been suffering from a severe head cold—but I was too moodily preoccupied to give her more than a single glance. She left the table early.

However, when I went upstairs, ten minutes later, I found her standing, erect, in the corridor, with her back to my door. She addressed me in a stiff, unnatural tone.

"Mr. Shannon, I should like a word with you."

"Not just now." I answered. "I'm tired. I'm busy. And my room's in a mess."

"Then come into mine." Her lips became resolute.

She opened her own door and, before I could protest I was in her small room which was, in contrast to my littered and untidy den, a model of cool propriety. As, for the first time, I viewed the narrow, neatly "made" white bed, the hand-hooked rug, the shining, silver-framed photograph of her parents placed on the little table precisely set out with her comb and brush, I vaguely recollected her having told me that, to help Miss Ailie, she "did" her room herself.

"Sit down, Mr. Shannon." As I was about to rest on the window ledge she interposed with a sudden quiver of irony: "No, not there . . . take the chair, please . . . it's much more suitable for a gentleman like you."

I glanced at her sharply. She was breathing quickly and was paler than ever—a pallor that darkened her swollen brown eyes and made deeper the shadows which lay beneath them. I also saw, with surprise, that she was trembling. But, keeping her gaze unwaveringly upon me, she began, steadily, and with a curl of her lip:

"Mr. Shannon, I owe a great deal to you. It's really remarkable, in fact, that one in your exalted position should have condescended to be good to a poor creature like myself, a petty tradesman's daughter."

In spite of myself, I was now listening to her with moody attentiveness.

"You may have observed that I've been absent for a few days. Perhaps you'd care to guess where I've been?"

"No," I said. "I wouldn't."

"Then I'll tell you, Mr. Shannon." Her dark eyes sparked. "I've been visiting in your part of the country. Every year my father goes to speak at the Tent Meeting and, though it may amuse you, I go with him. This year the Tent was pitched at Levenford."

I began vaguely to see the shape of things to come and an added bitterness corroded me.

"I hope it didn't blow down on you."

"No, it didn't," she answered hotly, "though I'm sure you wish it had."

"Far from it, I rather like a circus. What did you do? Jump through paper hoops?"

"No, Mr. Shannon." Her voice quivered. "We had a splendid, fruitful mission. There are some good people in Levenford, you see. I met one of them, after our first meeting. A fine old lady . . . Mrs. Leckie."

In spite of having steeled myself, I flinched. Although I had not seen her for more than twelve months, I had every reason to remember this indomitable woman, the support yet flail of my childhood, this paragon who wore six petticoats and elastic-sided boots, whose bed I had occupied at the tender age of seven, the patron of open-air Conventicles, of Gregory powder and peppermint imperials; now—I computed rapidly—eighty-four years old. She was my great-grandmother.

Standing there, her eyes flashing fire, Miss Law saw that she had touched me on the raw. She began to tremble all over.

"Naturally, in your native place, we spoke to her of you. My father inquired, in fact, if some of your wealthy relatives might not be induced to support our cause. She stared at us, then she laughed. Yes, Mr. Shannon, she laughed *out loud*."

I felt myself redden at the vision of that wrinkled, ochreous grin, but my tormentor, relentlessly, cuttingly, went on.

"Yes, she told us all about you. At first we couldn't believe it. 'There's some mistake' my father said. 'This young man is most highly connected.' Then she took us across the Common."

"Shut up," I exclaimed, in a rage. "I'm not interested in what she did."

"She took us and showed us your country estate." Pale and quivering, almost gasping for breath, Miss Jean Law choked out the words. "A dreary, poky little semi-detached, with weeds all round and washing on the line. One by one, she exposed all your beastly lies. She told us you were never wrecked on a raft in the war. 'You'll not drown that one,' she said, 'he's like his wicked old grandfather.' Yes, she even told us"—her voice broke upon the culminating odium—"what church you go to."

I jumped furiously to my feet. On top of all my troubles, this was the last straw.

"What right have you to preach at me? I only did it for a joke."

"A joke! That makes it more shameful."

"Oh, be quiet," I shouted. "I wouldn't have done it at all if you hadn't run after me, imposed yourself on me at every turn with your blasted medical papers and your . . . your inane white cows."

"So that's the way of it." She bit her lip fiercely, but could not keep back the tears. "Now we're getting the truth. Oh, you fine gentleman, you hero, you aristocrat . . . you miserable Ananias, it would serve you right if you were struck down too." Her colour came and went, she made the motion of swallowing, then suddenly, passionately, unrestrainedly she gave way to her sobs. "I never want to see you again, never, never, as long as I live."

"That suits me. I never wanted to see you in the first place. And for all I care you can go to Blairhill, or West Africa, or Timbuktu. In fact you can go to hell. Good-bye."

I walked out of the room and slammed the door.

CHAPTER EIGHT

Most of that night I lay awake, thinking of my own uncertain future. It was cold in my room. Through the window, which I always kept open, I heard the night trams banging along Pardyke Road. The noise went through my head. Occasionally from the docks came the low wail of a ship, slipping down river on the tide. There were no sounds from next door, none. I lay on my back, with my hands behind my head, gnawing the bitter bone of reflection.

What Usher did not understand was the inner compulsion, call it if you choose the inspiration, which motivated my research. How could I abandon it without betraying my scientific conscience, without, in fact, selling myself? The desire to find out the truth concerning this epidemic, this strange bacillus, was irresistible. I could not let it go.

When morning came I rose stiffly. While dressing I burst the knitted sweater that I wore underneath my jacket, an old garment I had kept all through the war and to which I had become attached. Annoyed, I cut myself while shaving. After a cup of tea I smoked a cigarette; then set out for the University.

It was a fine crisp morning, everyone seemed in the best of spirits. I passed a group of girls with shawls round their heads, laughing and chattering, on their way to work at the Gilmore Laundry. The corner tobacconist was polishing his shop window.

My mood was still hard and bitter, yet the nearer I drew to the Pathology buildings the more my nervousness increased; for alas, to display myself to advantage in a crisis was a feat beyond my powers. When I entered the laboratory and saw that the entire staff was present, I felt that I was pale.

Everyone was watching me. I went to my bench, opened all the drawers and began to empty them of my books and papers. At this, Professor Usher approached me.

"Clearing the decks for action, Shannon?" His manner was brisk, as though my submission were understood. "When you're ready, I'd like to discuss our scheme of work."

I took a quick breath, striving to keep my voice even.

"I can't undertake that work. I'm leaving the Department this morning."

Complete silence. I had certainly achieved a sensation, yet it brought me no satisfaction. I felt a dry smarting behind my eyes. Usher was frowning in a provoked fashion. I saw he had not expected this.

"Don't you realize what it means, if you give up your fellowship at a moment's notice?"

"I've considered all that."

"The Senate will undoubtedly put a black mark against your name. You'll never get another opportunity."

"I'll have to take my chance."

Why was I mumbling? I wanted to be calm and cold, especially since the perplexed annoyance had now left his face and he was considering me with an expression of open dislike.

"Very well, Shannon," he said severely. "You are acting with extreme stupidity. But if you persist I can't stop you. I simply wash my hands of the whole affair. Your blood is on your own head."

He shrugged his shoulders and, turning towards his office, left me to gather up the remainder of my notes. When the pile was complete, I lifted it in both arms, at the same time darting a glance round the laboratory. Lomax, with his usual half-smile, sat examining his finger nails, while Smith, his back to me, was attending to the cages with apparent indifference. Only Spence showed evidence of concern, and, as I passed his bench, he said, under his breath:

"Anything I can do, let me know."

This, at least, was some slight tribute to my passing. I nodded to Spence then raised my head but, as I went through the swing doors, my edifice of books became unbalanced, and despite my efforts, shot from my arms all over the outer corridor. I had to go down upon my knees in the dark passage and grope about for my belongings.

Outside, with the cool air striking upon my heated face, I felt oddly lost to be going home in the middle of the forenoon, an emotion intensified when I almost stumbled over a pail of soapy water in the dark hall of

Rothesay. The house had a strange feel about it and an even fustier smell.

I went upstairs, washed my hands from habit, sat down at my table and stared at the dingy wallpaper. What was I to do? Before I could answer that question the door opened and Miss Ailie, carrying a broom and dust pan, wearing an old wrapper and her list slippers, came into my room. She started slightly at the unexpected sight of me.

"Why, Rob, what's the matter? You're not sick?"

I shook my head, while she considered me with anxious kindness.

"Then why aren't you at the University?"

I hesitated for a moment, then blurted out the truth.

"I've chucked my job, Miss Ailie."

She did not press for more information but looked at me quietly, for a long time, with a beautiful expression, which was almost tender. Blowing the wisp of hair out of her faded blue eyes she said:

"Well, never mind, Rob. You'll get another."

There was a pause; then, as though wishing to distract me from my own misfortune, she added:

"It never rains but it pours. Miss Law left us this morning. Quite unexpected. Such a nice lass too. She's going back to work for her examination at home."

I received this information in silence; yet, under Miss Ailie's guileless gaze, my face, already downcast, reddened guiltily.

"Tut, tut," she declared. "This'll never do."

Without further comment she left the room, returning presently with a glass of buttermilk and a slice of sponge cake. How she had spirited these precious things out of the kitchen, under the sharp eyes of her sister, I could not imagine. She sat down and with open satisfaction watched me as, unwilling to offend her, I consumed them. Food was Miss Ailie's remedy for most ills, a belief easy to understand in that household.

"*There!*" she exclaimed, when I had finished. No more than that single word. But what a wealth of feeling she put into it! And what heart her kindness put into me!

Now the outlook looked less bad. Slowly, like a sun swimming out of grey mist, a resolution grew within my troubled breast. I would continue my work independently—yes, somehow, somewhere, alone, I would bring it, successfully, to completion. Why not? Others had worked under almost insuperable difficulties. I clenched my fist and banged the table hard. . . . By heavens, I would do it. I'd get a job somewhere, now . . . at once . . . and go on.

CHAPTER NINE

WITH my belief in myself restored, I went out confidently enough, setting my course towards the Northern Infirmary, which lay quite near, on the left bank of the Eldon, within sight of the University Tower. Clearly, my best course—although it might be construed as a "step down"—was to take an appointment as house physician in one of the large city hospitals where I should have at least definite, if restricted, facilities for continuing my research. And I selected the Northern not only because of its convenience and high reputation, but because I knew the registrar, George Cox.

The entrance to a metropolitan hospital is apt to be a confusing place, but with the indifference of familiarity I went past the intimidating army of white-clad porters, attendants, and nurses, through a series of tiled corridors, and into the registrar's office, where I sat down beside Cox's desk and watched him for a few minutes as, amongst the papers which encumbered him, he rapidly signed a batch of diet sheets.

"Cox," I said, when he had finished. "I'd like to join the staff."

Returning my gaze he grinned heartily, then lit a cigarette. He was a stocky, solidly muscled figure, about thirty-two, with a flat, ugly, good-natured face, a cropped blond moustache, and a coarse, ruddy, greasy skin, full of enlarged pores. He was enormously strong, in fact he seemed to exude a careless vitality, and the many liberties which he took with himself, from chain smoking to, in his own phrase, "stopping out on the tiles," made not the slightest inroads upon his constitution. Devoted to athletics, he had as a medical student, represented the University at every known game and, loth to sever a connection in which he had happily broken practically all the bones in his body, he had dropped breezily into this administrative position in the College teaching hospital.

He answered me at last, with heavy humour. "The Superintendent isn't quite ready to retire yet. When he is I'll let you know."

"I'm not joking," I said quickly. "I really want to come in as a house physician."

He was so surprised he found it difficult to dispose of his smile.

"What's happened to the fellowship?"

"That passed away suddenly . . . this morning."

Cox shifted in his chair, carefully flicked his cigarette ash to the floor.

"It's unfortunate, Shannon. We haven't a single vacancy. You see, we just made our appointments for the next six months, and all the interns look depressingly healthy."

There was a pause, filled by the rattle of a typewriter through the glass partition. I could see that this good fellow was uncomfortable, almost uneasy, that a person of my attainments should be chasing round, at short notice, for a junior's job. Yet I knew his answer to be absolutely honest.

"That's all right, Cox. I'll try the Alexandra."

"Yes, do," he said eagerly. "Shall I ring them for you?"

"Thanks all the same," I said, getting up. "But I'll go over myself."

I did go over to the Alexandra Infirmary. I went to the Great Eastern, the King George, the Royal Free; I made in fact, with increasing chagrin, an exhaustive and fruitless tour of all the city hospitals. The possibility of failing in my quest had never entered my head. I had forgotten that during the war years, to meet the national emergency, the medical curriculum had been so shortened and speeded up that hundreds of young men and women were roughly machined into shape, then disgorged, diploma in hand, off the assembly line, as it were, into the open market. As a result, the profession had become thoroughly overcrowded, and I was now merely one of the crowd.

This fact was borne in upon me even more sharply during the next few days, when, like a candidate for the dole, I presented myself, in line, at the Winton medical agency. There were no available hospital appointments. I might purchase a general practice for a mere three thousand pounds. I might also, if I wished, secure a fortnight's "locum" in the remote island of Skye, but while I debated the desirability of such a stop-gap, the opportunity was snatched from under my nose by the pale, bespectacled youngster behind me. At the end of the week I was constrained, shamefully, to seek out the elder Miss Dearie in her little cubby-hole office under the stairs.

"I'm sorry, Miss Beth. I can't pay you this week. I'm flat broke."

She reared herself, in the shadows, like a pallid boa-constrictor, and fixing upon me a suffering and reproachful eye, with her most prayerful, most ladylike expression, replied:

"I had guessed as much, Doctor . . . not being without a certain experience . . . to my sorrow. Naturally our rules in such contingencies are strict. But you are an old client of this establishment. You may remain."

As I left her sanctum I felt, with gratitude, that Miss Beth had shown much forbearance towards me. But, alas, it was not her nature to display this virtue long, and as my days passed in unsuccessful seeking, she turned up increasingly at table the whites of her eyes, with many mournful and martyred sighs, viewing me from time to time with a saintly resignation as though I were piling faggots round her at the stake, and turning the conversation pointedly to such disconcerting topics as the cost of electric light and the rising price of meat. I noticed also that my portions tended, progressively, with almost mathematical precision, to diminish. Finally, rather than be made to feel a cadger, I began to absent myself altogether from the evening meal, relying upon the hunk of bread and cheese, which Miss Ailie smuggled to my room, to blunt the edge of my hunger.

At the end of the month, although I had dodged Miss Beth as much as possible, I felt in my bones that the crisis was not distant, that presently, in fact, I should find myself upon the pavement, outside Rothesay, with no other lodging than the sky. Then, one Saturday, from the sanctuary of my room, I was called to the telephone by Miss Ailie. Spence's voice came to me over the line.

"Have fixed up yet, Shannon?" While I hesitated, ashamed to confess my defeat, he went on. "If you haven't, I've just heard of a vacancy at the Dalnair Cottage Hospital. It's a small place, for infectious fevers, and Haines, the doctor there, is leaving rather unexpectedly. Do you remember

Haines? Always seemed half asleep. He says there isn't a lot of work. You'd
have plenty of spare time. I thought it might interest you . . . especially
as it's down Levenford way . . . in your part of the country."

While I began to thank him he rang off, and I hung up the receiver,
thinking what a good friend Spence was, in his quiet and unobtrusive way.
I had not heard a word from Lomax. I must get this job at all costs, and
as Dalnair was near Levenford, I knew instinctively how I must do it. It
was time for me to pocket the last vestiges of my pride.

Back in my room, with much heart-burning, I composed a letter to the
one man upon whom I knew I could depend. I borrowed a stamp from
Miss Ailie and posted this letter in the hall mail-box. Then, as twilight
began to fall, I shrouded my microscope in its green baize cover and
carried it across the Park to Hillier's, the pawnshop behind the University, which catered especially for impecunious and bankrupt students.
Here, I pledged my instrument for eight pounds, fifteen shillings. It was
a Leitz and probably worth twenty guineas, but I was no good at haggling,
and took the money without protest.

Ignoring the long-haired young clerk behind the counter whose pencil,
protruding from an ear, intensified his general air of sharpness, and who,
having driven a hard bargain by deprecating, one by one, the qualities of
my microscope, was now disposed to discourse, agreeably, upon the weather,
I placed seven pounds, four weeks' rent, in an envelope to give to Miss
Beth. Five shillings, the price of a return railway ticket to Levenford, I
stowed securely in my top waistcoat pocket. This left a balance of thirty
shillings which, as a wave of recollection of my month's privations, my
stinted meals, my crusts of bread and rinds of cheese, swept over me, I
resolved recklessly to spend, immediately, on a dinner, at the neighbouring Rob Roy Tavern, a noted restaurant, patronized by the University faculty,
which offered a native cuisine of the highest excellence.

Then, as I came out of Hillier's, and, already licking my lips, began the
ascent of the back avenue—little more than a flagged pathway—which wound
up between the sycamore trees towards that summit upon which the
University stood, I suddenly discerned a solitary female figure approaching,
weighted slightly to one side by her textbooks, descending the path towards
the tramway terminus slowly, with a peculiar air of reverie and sadness
which, since I immediately recognized the young woman as Miss Jean Law,
caused me a sharp stab of discomfort. Since her head was drooping, her
gaze downcast, she did not see me for some seconds; but when about twenty
paces distant, as though forewarned by all her instincts of a disturbing
presence, an uncongenial protoplasm, she lifted her clouded eyes—which
instantly encountered mine.

She started, quite distinctly faltered, then resumed her way, while her
face, which seemed apathetic, smudged in places by her day's work, also
smaller and more strained than I had ever known it, turned white as her
father's flour. She wanted to look away, but she could not, and her dark

eyes, compelled against their will, remained upon me, haunted and frightened, almost as though guilty of a sin, while she approached. Now we were level with each other, and so close that the scent of Windsor soap struck upon my nostrils. What was happening to me? At that instant of near contact a sudden palpitating surge gathered and broke within my breast. Then she had passed me stiffly, head rigid in the air, and was immediately beyond my field of vision.

I did not glance behind me, yet the sight of that wan and solitary figure had stirred and upset me beyond belief. Why had I not spoken to her? It would have been so easy, at this moment, with money in my pocket, to make a graceful atonement and ask her to share my meal. Disconsolate, stung by my stupidity, I at last swung round. But she was gone, vanished in the soft dusk swiftly gathering beneath the budding sycamores. I let out a very bad word.

And then . . . I cannot explain my next action, which I regretted immediately I had performed it, nor can I attempt to defend what is so clearly indefensible, yet, since I am sworn to truth, I must shamefully record the facts.

As I went uphill, through the narrow old streets behind the University, continuing to heap abuse upon myself, I came upon the Church of the Nativity, which in my early student days I had visited every day and where, still, despite the irregularity of my life and the damaging conflicts of my mind, I attended Mass; where, indeed, borne by the irrevocable instinct in my bones, I came occasionally, on a wave of tenderness, to make, in the dimness, an act of reparation, a promise of amendment—an outpouring of the heart from which I arose, comforted.

Now, caught by an irresistible impulse, rather as one is seized by a garrotter from behind, I drew up, blinked, then hurried automatically into the little church filled with the sweet smell of incense, candle-wax, and damp. There, at the door, hastily, as though committing a crime, I stuffed my three crisp ten-shilling notes into the padlocked iron box marked in grey letters St. Vincent de Paul, and without even looking at the altar, stalked out.

"There!" I prayed without satisfaction to whatever saints observed me. "Do without your dinner, you blasted fool."

CHAPTER TEN

Next afternoon, at two o'clock, I arrived in Levenford. Often I had promised myself a sentimental pilgrimage to this Clydeside borough where I had grown up, where the grey façade of the Academy, the grassy stretch of Common with its little iron bandstand, the elephantine outline of the "Castle Rock" seen through the tall stacks of the Shipyards, with the distant view of Ben Lomond beyond, seemed impregnated with memories of these tender years. Yet, somehow, I had not found the occasion for this indulgence—time had severed so many of the ties which bound me to the town. And now, as I walked up the High Street towards the office of Duncan McKellar, my thoughts fixed on the approaching interview which I had sought, I was conscious of a prosaic drabness, rather than of any romantic quality, in my surroundings. The town seemed small and dirty, its inhabitants depressingly ordinary in appearance, and the once imposing solicitor's office, crouching opposite a sadly diminished Borough Hall, badly in need of a coat of paint.

However, McKellar himself was little changed, perhaps a trifle more veined around the nose, but still clean-shaven and close-cropped, eyes dry and penetrating beneath his sandy brows, manner contained, deliberate, judicial. He did not keep me waiting, and when I was seated before his broad mahogany desk, he began gravely to stroke his full underlip and, against the background of japanned deed-boxes, to contemplate me.

"Well, Robert." His survey completed, he spoke, at last, in a moderate tone. "What is it, this time?"

The question was ordinary enough but the note of quiet disapproval running through it made me gaze at him defensively. Ever since those early days when, without a word, he had, while passing me in the street, pressed into my hand tickets for the Mechanics Concerts, I had been conscious of a current of sympathy, of interest, flowing towards me from this man. He had taken my part when I was a boy, had administered the money left me for my education, a very watchdog of probity, and, as a sort of unofficial guardian, had advised and encouraged me during my student days. But now he was shaking his head in sombre disappointment.

"Come on. Let's have it, lad. What do you want?"

"Nothing," I answered. "If this is how you feel about it."

"Tut, tut. Don't be a young fool. Out with it."

Suppressing my sense of injury, I told him, as best I could.

"You see how important it is. If I'm to go on with this research I must get a hospital job. Perhaps Dalnair isn't a big place, but that would give me all the more spare time to do my own work."

"Do you think I carry appointments, like marbles, in my pocket?"

"No. But you're treasurer to the County Health Board. You have influence. You could get me in."

McKellar studied me again, his brows contracted; then, no longer able to restrain his irritation, he burst out:

"Just look at you, man. Shabby and down-at-heel. You've a button off your coat, your collar's cracked, you need a hair-cut. There's a burst in your boot, too. I tell you, sir, you're a disgrace to me, to yourself, and the whole medical profession. Damn it all, you don't look like a doctor. After all that's been done for ye! Ye look like a tramp."

Under this withering attack, I bit my lip in silence.

"And the worst o't is," he went on, lapsing more and more into broad Scots as his anger grew, "it's a' your own perverse and ediotic fault. When

I think on the career ye've had, on the way ye've taken medals and honours and fellowships, and then, after folks have built on ye . . . to come to *this* . . . Oh, man alive, it's fair deplorable."

"All right." I stood up. "I'll say good-bye. And thanks."

"Sit down," he shouted.

There was a pause. I sat down. With an effort he mastered his feelings and, in a constrained voice, remarked:

"I just cannot carry the sole responsibility any longer, Robert. I've asked here for a conference a certain person who is interested in you also, and whose sound common sense I value."

He pressed the bell upon the desk and a moment later Miss Glennie, his faithful servitor, respectfully ushered into the room a figure, unchangeable as destiny, fateful as doom, wearing her historic black-beaded cape, elastic-sided boots, and crape-bedizened, white-frilled mutch.

Of all my relatives, the others having wandered far afield, Great-grandmother Leckie was now the sole representative in Levenford. Since her son had died of a stroke shortly after his retirement from the Borough Health Department, she had continued to inhabit his house, Lomond View, now aged eighty-four, yet physically active and in alert possession of all her faculties, unconquerable and indestructible, the last prop supporting the structure of a disintegrating family.

The old woman seated herself, very erect, with a prim bow to McKellar, who had half risen in his chair, then turned towards me observantly, but without visible recognition upon her long, firm, yellowish, deeply wrinkled face. Her purse was still treasured in her mittened hand. Her hair, still parted in the middle, seemed a trifle thinner than of old but was still untouched by grey, as also were the crinkling whiskers which sprouted from the brown mole upon her upper lip. She still made the same clicking noises with her teeth.

"Well, ma'am," said McKellar, formally opening the inquest, "here we are."

Again the old woman inclined her head and, as though in church and about to enjoy a sermon of excellent severity, she took from her bag a peppermint imperial and placed it austerely between her lips.

"The position simply is," the lawyer continued, "that Robert here, with everything in his favour and the best prospects in the world, is sitting before us *without a curdie in his pocket.*"

At this accusation, which was quite true, for, beyond my return ticket to Winton, I had in the way of available currency precisely nothing, my grandmother once more bent forward her head rigidly, to indicate her comprehension of my lamentable situation.

"He ought," McKellar reasoned, getting warm again, "he ought to be in his own practice. There's those would help him to that if he only said the word. He has brains. He's personable. When he chooses, he has a way with him. Here, in Levenford, he could earn his thousand a year in good

hard siller without the slightest trouble. He could settle down, get married
to a decent lass and become a solid and respectable member of the community, like his friends have aye wished him to. But instead, what does
he do? Starts out on a wild goose chase that will never put a farthing in
the bank for him. And now, here he is, begging me to get him a job in a
poky, outlandish fever hospital, an old cottage hospital where he'll be lost,
buried in the wilds, with no more nor a hundred and twenty pound a
year!"

"You're forgetting something," I said. "In this hospital I'll be able to do
the work I want to do, work that may take me out of the wilds, and by
your own material standards, bring me far more recognition than I could
ever earn as a general practitioner in Levenford."

"*Tch!*" McKellar dismissed my argument with an angry shrug. "That's
all up in the air. That's the trouble with you. You're too impractical for
words."

"I'm not so sure!" For the first time the old woman spoke, gazing at the
lawyer inscrutably. "Robert is still young. He's trying for big things. If we
make him a general practitioner he'll never forgive us."

I could scarcely believe it. McKellar, who had clearly banked on her strong
support, gazed towards her with a fallen expression.

"We must remember that Robert was subject to very mixed influences
when he was a boy. He must be given time to shake these off. I don't think
it would be a bad thing if he were to have this chance. If he brings it off,
well and good. If not . . ." She paused, and I saw what was coming. "He
will have to accept our conditions."

The lawyer was now looking queerly at Grandma, darting peculiar, com-
prehending glances at her, while he pursed his lips and played with the
heavy ruler on his desk.

I took advantage of the silence. "Help me get this job at Dalnair. If I
don't succeed in what I'm after and have to come back to you for help, I
give you my word I'll do what you ask."

"Hmm!" McKellar hummed and hawed, still consulting with the old
woman from beneath his brows with a mixed expression, through which,
however, there predominated a reluctant respect.

"That seems to me a sound proposal," she remarked mildly, but with a
faint, meaningful relaxation of her features towards him.

"Hmm!" said McKellar again. "I daresay . . . I daresay . . . Well—" He
made up his mind. "So be it. Mind ye, Robert, I can't promise you the post,
but I'll do my best, I know Masters pretty well, the chairman of the committee. And if I get it for you I'll expect you, without fail, to keep your
side of the bargain."

We shook hands upon this and, after some further conversation, I went
out of the office.

I wanted to leave before the old woman could get hold of me. But as
I swung into the street I heard her following close behind me.

"Robert."

I had to turn round.

"Don't be in such a hurry."

"I have a train to catch."

She took no notice of the excuse.

"Give me your arm. I'm not so young as I was, Robert."

I gritted my teeth. I was twenty-four, a bacteriologist who handled with contempt the deadliest germs, who, after the war, had gained a sharp experience of life. But in her presence the years fell away from me and I was again a child. She reduced me. She humiliated me. And I knew, from her possessive touch, that I should have to put up with her for the rest of the afternoon, that she would extract from me, using her tongue like a scourge, the full story of my doings.

As, arm in arm, we rounded, in stately fashion, the bend of Church Street, she leaned towards me, sweeping aside the last of my resistance.

"First thing we do is get that old uniform off your back. We'll go up the town to the Co-operative Stores and get ye into a decent homespun suit. Then, instead of these broken-down bauchles, we'll put a new pair of shoes on your misguided feet. Ay, ay, my man, I'll have ye half-human again, before ye're an hour older."

I shuddered at the prospect of being "fitted," under her eagle eye, by the female assistants of the Boot and Drapery departments.

Leaning closer, exhaling a powerful odour of peppermint, she breathed warmly into my ear:

"Now tell me everything, Robert, about this young woman Law."

BOOK TWO

CHAPTER ONE

I was met at Dalnair village station by the hospital chauffeur and handyman, with an old brass-bound Argyll ambulance, the paintwork washed away, but the glass glittering, rather like a hearse. When he had introduced himself as Peter Pim, he placed my bag aboard in sluggish fashion and, after many crankings, started up the machine. We lumbered off, past a jumble of ramshackle houses, a dingy little store, some clay pits, and a disused brickworks; then across a stream, striving valiantly to purify its muddy course, and into a bedraggled semi-urban countryside, upon which, however, the early spring had imposed a fresh green mantle.

From time to time, as I bounced upon the hard front seat, I stole inquiring glances at my companion's expressionless profile, which, beneath his peaked cap, conveyed such an impression of lethargy I hesitated to break into speech. However, at last I ventured to compliment him upon the sound condition of his antique vehicle, which, from his handling of the controls, was clearly a source of pride to him.

He did not immediately reply, then with his gaze fixed on the road ahead he made a sort of considered pronouncement.

"I am interested in mechanics, sir."

If this was so, I felt he could be of service to me, and I expressed the democratic hope that we might be friends.

Again he communed with himself.

"I think we'll get along, sir. I always do my best. I was on excellent terms with Dr. Haines. A nice easy gentleman, was Dr. Haines, sir. I was sorry to see him go."

Chilled somewhat by this laudation of my predecessor and by the melancholy intonation with which it was delivered, I lapsed into silence that persisted until we laboured to the summit of a narrow lane and swept into a circular gravel driveway giving access to a little group of trim brick buildings. Opposite the largest of these we drew up and, descending from the ambulance, I became conscious of a short, swart-complexioned woman in uniform, whom I guessed to be the matron, standing upon the steps, protecting her winged white cap from the breeze and radiantly smiling her welcome.

"Dr. Shannon, I presume. Delighted to make your acquaintance. I'm Miss Trudgeon."

While Pim made himself scarce with an astringent expression, she greeted me jovially and, almost before I knew where I was, had shown me to my quarters: sitting-room, bedroom, and bathroom all on the east side of the central building. Then, bustling me along, full of energy and enthusiasm, she took me proudly round the entire institution.

It was quite small, consisting of four little detached pavilions, spaced at the corners of a square, behind the administrative block, devoted respectively to the treatment of scarlet fever, diphtheria, measles, and "mixed infections." The arrangements were primitive, nevertheless the old-fashioned wards, with their well-waxed floors and spotless little cots, shone with cleanliness. Most of the few patients were children and as they sat up in their red bed-jackets, smiling as we went past, while the afternoon sun streamed through the long windows, they made me feel that my duties would be agreeable. The Ward Sisters, too—one presiding over each pavilion—had a reassuringly quiet and sensible air. In short, the general effect of this unpretentious little hospital, which, from its high and wind-swept hill-top, commanded a view of the valley townships it served, was one of efficiency and usefulness.

At the foot of the grounds, some distance from the four pavilions, there stood a peculiar maroon-coloured edifice of corrugated iron, somewhat dilapidated, and almost entirely surrounded by shrubbery.

"That was our smallpox ward," Miss Trudgeon explained, her small shrewd eyes interpreting my thought. "As you can see, it isn't used . . . so we won't go in. Luckily, the laurel bushes hide it." She added complacently: "We haven't had a case in the last five years."

From here, always with that air of justifiable pride, she conducted me to the nurses' recreation room, the kitchen, and the receiving-office—all of which exhibited the same immaculate gloss—and finally, to a room with a long wooden counter into which were set gas and electricity fittings and two porcelain sinks. Some varnished desks and a couple of benches were piled against the wall.

"This is our test room," Matron remarked. "Don't you think it's nice?"

"Very."

I said nothing more, of course. Yet I knew at once that I had found the ideal place for my laboratory. As we retraced our steps along the driveway I was already, in my mind's eye, allocating the available space and making my arrangements.

Back in the main building, Miss Trudgeon insisted on giving me afternoon tea in her own parlour, an airy, charming room facing to the front, with a bow window, chintz-covered chairs and sofa, and a china bowl of flowering hyacinths on the piano, an apartment which, I could not but observe, was even nicer than any we had previously entered. When she had pressed the bell a red-cheeked country girl in a starched cap and apron, whom she introduced to me as Katie, our "joint" maid, brought in a tea service and a tiered cake stand. Talking all the time, Miss Trudgeon presided officiously behind this equipage, offering me a choice of India or China tea with an excellent cut of plum cake just out of the hospital oven.

She was about fifty, I judged, and before "settling down" at Dalnair, had, she informed me, spent ten years in Bengal as an army nurse, an experience which had no doubt imparted to her large and prominent features their distinct coppery tinge, and which also, perhaps, had given to her voice and manner characteristics closely resembling those of the sergeant-major. I had noticed particularly her projecting bust, her chesty swagger, and the lateral oscillation of her short but far from inconsiderable haunches, as she preceded me through the wards. And now, her bluff heartiness, the loudness of her laugh, her downright and decisive gestures, seemed to complete the picture of a personality better suited to the barrack square than the sick-room.

Yet what impressed me most was her determined pride in the hospital, a sense almost of ownership. Again, half jocularly, she reverted to that dominant theme.

"I'm glad you approve of our little place, Doctor. It's a bit out of date, of course, but I've tried to get over that with a few army dodges. I've worked hard to bring things to their present state. Yes, I've really put my back into it."

A brief, odd silence followed, but presently, to my relief, there came a discreet tap upon the door, and in answer to Miss Trudgeon's "Come in," the handle turned noiselessly and a tall, thin, red-haired Sister appeared upon the threshold. Upon seeing me, she started, and her pale green eyes, fringed by straw-coloured lashes, sought out Miss Trudgeon's with a deprecating humility which brought to the matron's bronzed face an indulgent smile.

"Come, come, my dear, don't run away. Doctor, this is Night Sister Effie Peek. She usually has tea with me when she gets up in the afternoon. Sit down, my dear."

Modestly, Sister Peek entered the room and, seating herself on a low chair, accepted the cup which was offered her.

"I'm very pleased that you should meet Sister Peek," continued Miss Trudgeon. "She is quite the most helpful member of my staff."

"Oh, no." The pale, red-haired Sister repudiated the compliment with a quiver of her unworthy flesh; then turning towards me, she murmured: "Matron is much too kind. But of course a word from her means so much. You see, everyone looks up to her. And she has been here so long, we simply couldn't get on without her. After all, our doctors come and go. But Matron goes on for ever."

Having thus paraphrased Tennyson's "Brook" for my benefit, this blanched creature—even her red hair was pale, and her skin was milky-white—subsided to a respectful silence. In a few minutes, as though not daring to trespass further upon our time, she rose and with a fawnlike glance towards the matron glided from the room to begin her night's duty. I did not long outstay her. I stood up and, having expressed to Miss Trudgeon my appreciation of the warmth of her welcome, excused myself on the grounds that I must unpack.

"That's all right, Doctor. We ought to rub along together. As Sister Peek says, I'm an old-timer here." Bouncing to her feet, her large face wreathed in smiles, she gave me, for an instant, a penetrating glance, adding, with jovial emphasis, "I think you'll find that my ways are the best."

With curiously mixed feelings I found my way to my own quarters, satisfied by my reception, telling myself, as I pottered round the room, examining its severe yet adequate furnishings with the eye of one who must live and become intimate with these unknown articles, that, although perhaps rather blunt, Miss Trudgeon was a cheery, hearty soul, but at the same time vaguely disturbed by the *brio* of her manner and by impressions and reactions which I could not quite define.

CHAPTER TWO

YET nothing, nothing could depress my spirits, nor damp my satisfaction at the prospect of resuming my research after those weeks of maddening delay.

As I had surmised, my official duties were pleasant and inexacting. The actual capacity of the hospital was small, not more than fifty patients when absolutely full, and now, since no epidemics were prevalent, at this particular season we had only about a dozen children, all convalescent, mostly from simple measles and, no matter how conscientiously I prolonged my round of the wards, I was finished, and free, by noon.

The test room was better than I had imagined. In the cupboards and drawers I found a variety of equipment which I could convert and use. Material accumulates easily in hospitals—ordered in a burst of enthusiasm, it is put away and forgotten. My own pieces of apparatus were soon installed and by mortgaging my first month's salary, I redeemed my microscope from Hillier's. Already, on the hospital note-paper, I had initiated a lively correspondence with several doctors in other rural areas affected by the epidemic, and from the specimens which they kindly sent me, together with those which still remained from Dreem, I began again to try to cultivate Bacillus C.

All this, of course, was achieved discreetly. I took care to perform my official duties scrupulously, and I was pleasantly assiduous in my attentions to the matron who, during these early days, beneath her smiling heartiness, was studying me, rather as an experienced pugilist might study an opponent for the first round in the ring.

She was a strange mixture. When she came to Dalnair, in the "good old days" lamented by Pim—whom I soon found to be a professional grumbler —the hospital had been slackly run. Step by step she had changed the system, worked herself into the good graces of the Hospital Committee, won into her own hands complete authority. Now she managed the place, from attic to cellar, with firmness, economy, and tireless efficiency.

"I'm at her beck and call all day long," Pim confided in me with woeful dignity as, seated on an upturned pail, he was taking all morning to polish the ancient ambulance. "All my little perks have gone. Why, would you be-lieve it, sir, she even checks the soap for my outdoor wash-room!"

Although I took breakfast and supper alone, it was the Dalnair custom for doctor and matron to lunch together. Thus at one o'clock each day she came to my room for "tiffin," as she called it, seated herself at table, and tucked her napkin into her bosom. She was fond of her food, especially of spicy dishes and curries, which appeared frequently upon the menu, served with mango chutney and shredded coconut. Heaping her plate she would mix the ingredients thoroughly, then delve into the savoury mess, using a spoon—the only way to eat curry, she told me—and washing her mouthfuls down with lime-juice and soda. She was proud of her Bengali recipes, and had a fund of anecdotes bearing upon her army experiences, which went with them, her favourite being a spirited account of how she and Colonel Sutler of the Bengal Medical Service had fought the cholera in Bogra in 1902.

Despite these repetitious stories, she had a sense of humour which, although too boisterous for my taste, had saved me thus far from disliking her. She might be a little martinet, yet her deep chuckle was disarming, and on occasions she could be kind. To those of her nurses who worked well and did not cross her she was, on the whole, good-hearted and fair. Over a period of years she had done her best with the committee—no easy task—to improve the working conditions and inadequate pay of her staff. In a hospital such as Dalnair there was always the serious risk of contracting an infectious fever, and when a nurse was laid up in this fashion Miss Trudgeon, who might very well have slanged her head off the week before, looked after her like a mother.

One of her predilections was a decided fondness for the game of draughts; and occasionally, early in the evening, she honoured me with an invitation to her room to play. Now my great-grandfather, past master of the art, had taught me, when I was a boy, all the deep and diabolical subtleties of "the dambrod" and during our innumerable encounters across the chequered board I had acquired from him that particular brand of low cunning which lures an opponent to his doom. At my first meeting with the matron it took me only thirty seconds to discover that she was far from being a match for me—indeed I was hard put to it to lose. Yet lose I did, with sound diplo-macy, upon every occasion, to her extreme delight. When she had beaten me she would lie back in her chair, crowing with satisfaction, taunting me with my inability to get the better of her, and winding up, invariably, with an account of the historic game she had played against Colonel Sutler, during the cholera epidemic, at Bogra, in 1902.

The provocation was severe, yet keeping in mind my main objective, I suffered it with commendable patience. One evening, however, she went over the score, and her taunts got under my skin.

"Poor fellow," she jeered. "Where are your brains? How on earth did you get your medical degree? I'll have to give you lessons. Did I ever tell you the story of my game with . . ."

"I'm beginning to know it off by heart," I snapped. "Set up your men again."

She did so, shaking with laughter at having finally provoked me. The game began and in five moves I got through her defense and wiped the board with her.

"Eh, what a fluke!" she exclaimed, hardly able to believe her eyes. "Let's have another."

"By all means."

This time she played more cautiously but she had not the ghost of a chance. Twice I got three men for one, and in four minutes she was beaten.

There was a strained silence. Her face had turned a dusky red. But still she couldn't think that her second defeat was anything but the wildest chance.

"I shan't let you get away with that. One more game."

I ought, at this stage, to have used better judgement, but I was still smarting from her sharp tongue. Besides, these repeated sessions were encroaching upon the time available for my work; I wanted to put an end to them. Using the double shift opening that old Dandy Gow had perfected I sacrificed four men in rapid succession; then, with two sweeping moves, cleared every one of her pieces off the board.

The triumphant smile which had begun to dawn upon her face stiffened to an angry grimace while the veins of her neck and forehead swelled. She shut the board and rattled the pieces into their box.

"That will be all for this evening, thank you, Doctor."

Already regretting what I had done, I gave a deprecating laugh.

"Extraordinary how these games turned out."

"Most extraordinary," she agreed stiffly. "There seems to be a little more in you than meets the eye."

"I can't always be so absurdly lucky. I'm sure you'll win next time."

Her exasperation got the better of her. She stood up.

"What do you take me for? A complete fool?"

"Oh, no, indeed, Matron."

With an effort she controlled herself.

"Close the door then, on your way out."

Back in my room, I began to see how stupid I had been in offending her, and with hands thrust moodily in my pockets I stood staring out of my window, more annoyed with myself than with her.

At that moment, a burst of rapid reports struck my ear and a red motorcycle swung round the drive and came to rest outside my room. As the bareheaded rider heaved the heavy machine on to its stand and removed his goggles I recognized him, with a start of surprise. It was Luke Law.

I opened the window.

"Hello, Luke."

"Hello, yourself."

His cheerful smile dispelled my misgivings and, when he had come into the room, by the simple expedient of sliding over the sill, he took off his long leather gauntlets and shook me by the hand.

"I've brought you the bike," he announced and, observing my mystified expression, added: "You remember? I said I would lend it you for a spell."

"Don't you want it yourself?"

"No." He shook his head. "Not for the next few weeks anyway. I'm going to the Tyne Home Bakery in Newcastle. To learn how they fire stone-milled flour. Father knows the manager."

I had not expected this kindness and felt some embarrassment in accepting it, but Luke brushed aside my protests with the most natural air in the world and, stretching himself out in a chair, lit up one of my cigarettes.

"Yours truly isn't allowed to smoke." He grinned. "But I do like a fag— and I have one too, when I think they won't smell it on me. You've no idea what a sell it is, being held in at every turn. I want to be like the other fellows." He blew smoke rebelliously, yet humorously down his nose. "And I wish I could do the work I'm set on. Who wants to be a hand baker? Stone-milled flour! Huh! Twenty years behind the times. I want to work with machinery, with bicycles and motor cars, have my own little factory. I'm good at that. . . . I can make things go. If only I could modernize our plant . . . put in mechanical mixers . . . an electric oven . . ."

"You'll do it . . . later."

"Well," he sighed. "Maybe."

I could see that, despite his youth and good nature, he was beginning to chafe at parental restrictions, and to demand the right to his own existence.

After a pause he threw me a glance which, while holding nothing of reproach, while deprecating, in fact, half-humorously, the folly and weakness of the whole female sex, nevertheless conveyed a certain sense of troubled compunction.

"We're a little under the weather at home, Robert. It's Jean . . ."

To hide my feelings I bent forward and took a cigarette from the box. The very mention of that name had sent a wave of feeling over me. Luke was so absurdly like her, with his open expression, his brown eyes, curly hair, and fresh, brown colouring, that at this moment I scarcely dared look at him.

"Hasn't she been well?" I asked, cautiously.

"She's been awful!" he exclaimed. "At first she went about raging at the terrible scoundrels and blackguards in the world." He chuckled. "That was you of course. Then gradually she fell into the dumps. And for the last few weeks she's done nothing but cry. She tries to hide it, but I can tell."

"Perhaps she's worried about her exam," I suggested. "Doesn't she sit the final this summer?"

"No exam ever upset Jean like that." He paused and added in a confidential, man-of-the-world tone: "You know what it's all about as well as I do. Here! She asked me to give you this note."

After some fumbling in the inside pocket of his Norfolk jacket he produced a folded slip of paper, which I accepted with a curious acceleration of my pulse.

> Dear Mr. Shannon,
>
> Having discovered, by the merest chance, that my brother proposes visiting you on some business of his own, I take the opportunity of sending you these few lines.
>
> The fact is that I have something to say to you, something quite impersonal and unimportant, and if you should, by any chance, be in Winton next Wednesday, I am wondering if you would care to have tea with me at Grant's in Botanic Road, about five o'clock. Probably you have something better to do. Possibly you have forgotten all about me. In which case, it does not matter. Please excuse my presumption.
>
> I am,
Yours as always,
JEAN LAW
>
> P.S. I was walking alone in the High Parks last Saturday and found out why we did not see the White Cattle. There has been an outbreak in the herd and a number of them have died. Isn't it a shame?
>
> P.P.S. I know I have many faults but at least I speak the truth.

I put down the note and gazed across at young Law's inquiring and ingenuous face, wondering if Jean had not arranged the whole affair—Luke's visit, the offer of the motor-cycle, the invitation to tea upon the following week—with quiet yet definite intention. My earlier moodiness had vanished, currents of elation were tingling all over my skin.

"You'll go?" asked Luke.

"I suppose so," I answered, in a voice which, despite the beating of my heart, I tried to make prosaic and mature.

"Women are a nuisance, aren't they?" Luke said, with sudden sympathy.

I laughed and, in a rush of spirits, pressed him to remain for supper. We had a good meal together, followed by coffee and cigarettes, during which, as superior beings, we loosened our collars and discussed fast motorcycles, aeroplane design, the brotherhood of man, electric dough-mixers, and the incomprehensible perverseness of the opposite sex.

CHAPTER THREE

WINTON was a drab enough city, grey, beneath a pall of smoke, ringed by belching chimneys, much rained on, oppressed by monumental architecture and some fearful statuary; but its glory, if it could lay claim to glory, was in its tea-rooms. They animated the dreary streets, scores of them, little oases of rest and refreshment where, having traversed the outer premises devoted to the sale of cakes and cookies, the Winton citizens—clerks, typists, shop girls, students, even staid merchants and men of business—gathered at all hours of the day around white-capped tables loaded with scones and short-bread and innumerable pastries, to seek solace in a cup of tea or coffee.

Of these establishments the one most patronized by members of the University was Grant's, where, in addition to a celebrated make of cream buns, one could enjoy the select sense of "tone" conveyed by an interior of dark oak, with real oil paintings, by members of the Scottish Academy, inter-spersed with crossed dirks and claymores, upon the panelled walls.

Upon the following Wednesday then, with a strange mingling of eagerness and apprehension, I arrived at Grant's. I had decided to take all the after-noon off work, for I had a special errand which I wished to do in connection with my research. I was early for my appointment, but even so, Miss Law was earlier. As I entered the crowded café, filled with the buzz of conversa-tion and the tinkle of teaspoons, a small figure half rose at the back, beneath the most formidable of the claymores, and, with a nervous gesture, beckoned me to the table which, in the face of considerable opposition, she was bravely reserving for us. Otherwise she did not greet me, and as I crushed my way forward and sat down silently beside her I observed that, in contrast to those easy days of "cool" and sweater, she was dressed with some severity in a dark grey costume and a prim black hat. Also she was pale, extremely pale, definitely thinner, and, though she exerted herself to conceal it, quite painfully agitated.

There was a constrained pause while, by the process of crooking her fore-finger and holding it aloft, she at last overcame the difficulty of securing service.

"Lemon or cream?"

These were her first words, and she made the inquiry in subdued tones without daring to look at me, while the waitress stood over us, impatiently fingering her pencil.

I ordered lemon tea.

"And would you care for cream buns?"

I agreed to the buns, adding:

"Of course this is my treat."

"No," she answered with quivering lips, but a firming of her chin. "I asked *you*."

We sat in silence till the waitress returned, then, in silence, began our repast.

"Very full here, isn't it?" I ventured at length. "Popular sort of place."

"Yes, it is." A pause. "Extremely popular. And deservedly so."

"Oh, yes. Wonderful buns these are."

"Are they? I'm very glad."

"Won't you have one?"

"No, thank you. I'm not particularly hungry."

"I was sorry to hear about your White Cattle."

"Yes, poor things . . . it's been quite bad."

Another pause.

"Rather a wet summer it's been so far, don't you think?"

"Very wet. I don't know what the weather's coming to."

A still longer pause. Then, nerving herself with a sip of tea—and I noticed that her hand shook as she lowered her cup—she turned to me with a look of serious intentness.

"Mr. Shannon," she exclaimed with a gulp, and all in one breath. "I've been wondering if, after all, it would be possible for us to be friends."

While I stared at her, nonplussed, she went on, her colour coming and going, her voice breaking occasionally, as she strove to be calm and reasonable.

"When I say friends, I mean friends . . . nothing less, nothing more. Friendship is such a wonderful thing. And one meets it so seldom. True friendship that is to say. Of course you may feel that you don't wish to be friends with me. I'm just nothing. And I admit it was stupid of me to take things so much to heart and quarrel with you. But now I see that you were only joking, and that I was very childish about it. After all, we are practical, adult people, aren't we? We do belong to different religions, but although that's a serious thing, it isn't a crime, at least it's no bar to our having an occasional cup of tea together. It would be a great pity if we stopped being friends, simply for nothing . . . and drifted apart . . . like ships that pass in the night . . . I mean, if we never saw each other again . . . when, if we were sensible we could be meeting often, that's to say, once in a while, as friends . . ."

She broke off, playing with her teaspoon, a bright flush upon her cheeks, her brown eyes bright also, rather frightened, yet resolutely meeting mine.

"Well," I said, doubtfully. "It's a little difficult, isn't it? I have my work. And you're studying hard for your exam."

"Yes, I know you're busy. And I suppose I have to keep at it, too." There was a strange lack of enthusiasm in the voice of this once-eager student of Pathology, and she added quickly, as though pleading for a rational approach to the whole question of the acquirement of knowledge: "We have to take a spell off once in a while. I mean, it's impossible to work *all* the time."

There was a silence. As though conscious of her high colour, she at last lowered her gaze and drew back in her chair, to hide herself from the curiosity of the tea-room. Glancing at her covertly, I was amazed that I should ever have treated her with disdain. Her flush, her lowered lashes, throwing a soft shadow upon the soft bloom of her cheek, gave her a sensitive, yes, a quite angelic air. Nothing, not her prim black kid gloves, nor the old-fashioned round gold watch she wore upon one wrist, not even her absurd hard little hat, could spoil the stinging charm of her beauty.

And suddenly, to my own surprise, I felt a warm tide welling up within me. I found myself answering, with an air of logical decision:

"There's no law against it I suppose. I daresay we could see each other once in a while."

Her face lighted up. She bent forward with a tremulous and happy smile and in a tone which paid high tribute to my superior wisdom, she exclaimed:

"I'm so glad. I was afraid . . . I mean, it's such a sensible way to look at things."

"Good." I acknowledged her flattery with a generous nod and, spurred by some incomprehensible impulse, gazed into her shining eyes. "What are you doing this evening?"

An imperceptible stiffening of her figure attended this unexpected remark.

"Well . . . I am going to see the Miss Dearies . . . they were so kind to me, you know. Then, I'm taking the six-thirty train home to Blairhill."

The spurt of recklessness expanded in me further. I remarked coolly:

"Come to the theatre with me, instead?"

She started, perceptibly, and the faint look of fright came back into her eyes, increasing as I went on.

"I have some business that will take about an hour. Let's meet at the Theatre Royal at seven. Martin Harvey is on there, in *The Only Way*. You ought to enjoy that."

Still she gazed at me in stricken silence as though my invitation had exposed to her all the secret terrors and dangers of the world. Then she gulped.

"Mr. Shannon, I'm afraid you don't understand. I've never been to the theatre in my life."

"Good heavens!" Although I ought to have been prepared for this, I could scarcely believe my ears. "Why on earth not?"

"Well, you know how strict we are at home."

Lowering her gaze, she drew patterns on the cloth with her finger. "In the Brethren, we don't hold with cards, or dances, or going to the theatre. Of course Father doesn't exactly forbid us . . . but we just never seemed to think of it."

I studied her in wonder.

"Then it's high time you thought of it now. Why," I spoke largely, "the theatre is one of the greatest cultural influences in the world. Mind you, I don't think too much of *The Only Way*. But it'll do for a start."

She was silent, continuing to make designs in painful, downcast indecision. Then slowly, as her Puritan grain refused to yield, she raised her head and faltered.

"I'm afraid, Mr. Shannon, I couldn't go."

"But why?"

She made no answer, but her melting gaze was sorely troubled. Weighing down the scale against her natural inclination, so vivid and ardent, were all the sad and sombre teachings of her childhood, these austere warnings against the world, those apocalyptic prophesies of doom.

"Well!" I exclaimed in annoyance. "If that isn't the limit. You waste half the afternoon trying to convince me that we ought to spend some time together. And, when I offer to take you out, to a perfectly innocent entertainment, in fact, a classical performance, based on a famous novel by Charles Dickens, you flatly refuse to come."

"Oh, Dickens . . ." she murmured faintly, as though partly reassured. "Charles Dickens. He was a very worthy writer."

But in my resentment I had buttoned my jacket and was looking round for the waitress to obtain the bill.

Scorched by my displeasure, she observed, with renewed agitation, these signs of imminent departure; then with a little gasp, her breast rising and falling, she tremblingly surrendered.

"Very well," she whispered helplessly. "I'll come."

Despite the entreaty of her gaze, I did not immediately forgive her, not until I had paid the check—an action which now she did not dare dispute—and escorted her to the street. There I turned and, as we said good-bye, I addressed her in a friendly yet warning tone.

"Seven o'clock at the theatre. Don't be late."

"Yes, Mr. Shannon," she murmured submissively and, with a last quivering glance, she swung round and went off.

After standing a moment, I departed for the Pathology Department, where, since I had written him beforehand, I expected that Spence would be awaiting me.

It was quarter past six when I reached the building and, since the last thing I wished was to run into Usher or Smith, I reconnoitred the corridors carefully before entering the laboratory. There, as I had hoped, Spence was alone, bent in close study at his bench.

Since my approach was quiet I was at his elbow before he became aware of my presence. Then I saw, with some surprise, that he was not working, but examining, meditatively, a photograph.

"It's you, Robert." He looked me over, rather heavily. "I've missed you. How goes it at Dalnair?"

"Pretty well," I answered cheerfully. "I'm scrapping with the matron. But I've cultured my bacillus again—a pure strain."

"Good work. Have you identified it?"

"No, but I shall. I'm working on that now."

He nodded his head.

"I wish I could get out of here too, Robert. If only I could land a professorship at one of the smaller schools . . . Aberdeen or St. Andrews."

"You will," I said encouragingly.

"Yes." His tone was curiously reflective. "I've plodded along pretty hard these last four years . . . for Muriel's sake. She would like it at St. Andrews."

"How is Lomax?" I asked.

Spence gave me his expressionless glance. There was a perceptible pause.

"Handsome and dashing as ever. Quite pleased with life . . . and himself."

"I haven't seen him for ages."

"He appears to have been rather busy lately. Well, it's good to know you're getting ahead. I had your letter. I can give you all the glycerine medium you want."

"Thanks, Spence. I knew I could count on you."

He made a deprecating gesture. There was an odd silence. Awkwardly I shifted my gaze, which came to rest on the photograph before him. His eyes followed mine.

"Take a better look," he said, and handed me the photograph. It was the pleasing likeness of a youngster with well-cut features and a clean, vigorous air.

"Very nice," I commented. "Who is it?"

He began to laugh, a strange sound, for although he often smiled, in his twisted fashion, I had seldom heard him laugh.

"Could you believe it?" he said. "That's me."

I gave an inarticulate murmur. I didn't know what to say. And I glanced at him uncomfortably. He was so unlike his usual mild and quiet self.

"Yes, I was like that at eighteen. Extraordinary how important a face is . . . I don't mean a good-looking face . . . just an ordinary, even an ugly face. You know what you read in novels. 'His face had a kind of charming ugliness.' But you can't romanticize half a face. Impossible. The Colosseum is quite a spectacle. But only by moonlight, and for half an hour. Who wants to look at a blasted ruin all the time? In fact, if you were to ask me, Shannon, I'd say in the end it would get most hellishly upon your nerves."

No, I had never before seen Spence in this overwrought, this morbid frame of mind. His quiet reserve made one forget that he must always exercise upon himself a rigid discipline against self-pity. Touched, vaguely uneasy, I wondered if I should speak. But at that moment, when he seemed almost on the point of breaking down, he suddenly took himself in hand, jumped up and went over to the storage shelves.

"Come along," he said briskly. "Let's pack up your stuff."

I followed, slowly.

Together we selected a dozen half-litre flasks of the medium, which we packed with straw in a portable hamper, made of stout wicker. Then I left, warmly thanking Spence once more. I was relieved to see that he seemed almost himself again. That odd spell of his had given me quite a shock.

CHAPTER FOUR

AT THE foot of the hill I took the red tram to Central Station and at the Left Luggage Office checked in my hamper. Then I went into the Railway Buffet and fortified myself hurriedly with a cold sausage roll and a glass of beer. I was beginning to have qualms about the evening and to wonder if Miss

Jean's tender conscience might not prove an insurmountable barrier to our enjoyment.

However, when I met her at the theatre she had thrown off her scruples, her expression was eager and responsive, her dark irises held a sparkle of excitement.

"I've been looking at the posters," she said, as we entered the foyer. "I can see nothing wrong in them whatever."

Our seats, although inexpensive, were reasonably good, two pit stalls in the third row, and as we occupied them, the orchestra began tuning up. My companion gave me a glance of communicative ardour and burrowed into the programme which I handed her. Then, as though wishing to be free of all encumbrance, she took off and entrusted to me her wristlet watch.

"Please keep this safe for me. It's loose. And has worried me all afternoon."

Presently the lights went down; then, after a short overture, the curtain rose upon a scene of eighteenth-century Paris, and the crashing melodrama of the French Revolution began slowly to unfold its interwoven themes of hopeless love and heroic self-sacrifice.

This was the evergreen play from A Tale of Two Cities, with which that superb trouper, Martin Harvey, yielding himself nobly to the scaffold night after night and at Wednesday matinées, had enthralled provincial audiences for at least a score of years.

At first my companion seemed, circumspectly, to reserve her judgement; then gradually she sat up straight, her clear eyes kindling with interest and delight. Without removing her gaze from the stage she murmured to me in a human undertone:

"What a lovely scene!"

Then she yielded herself to the pale, dark glamour of Sydney Carton, to the frail and sylphlike charm of Lucie Manette.

At the first interval she relaxed slowly, with a sigh, and, fanning her flushed cheeks with her programme, bent a grateful glance upon me.

"It's splendid, Mr. Shannon. So different from what I expected. I can't tell you what a treat it is for me."

"Would you like an ice?"

"Oh, no, I couldn't dream of it. After what we've seen it would be like sacrilege."

"Of course it's not a really first-rate play."

"Oh, it is, it is," she insisted. "It's lovely. I feel so sorry for poor Sydney Carton. He's so much in love with Lucie and she . . . Oh, it must be a frightful thing, Mr. Shannon, to be terribly in love with someone and not to be loved in return."

"Quite," I agreed gravely. "Of course, they're extremely good friends. And friendship is a wonderful thing."

She consulted her programme to conceal her blush.

"I like them all," she said. "The girl who does Lucie is very sweet, she has such lovely long blond hair. Miss N. de Silva is her name."

"She," I answered, "in real life, is Martin Harvey's wife."

"No!" she exclaimed, looking up, with animation. "How interesting."

"She is probably forty-five years of age and that blond hair is a wig."

"Please, don't, Mr. Shannon," she cried, in a shocked voice. "How can you joke about such things? I'm loving every minute of it. Hush! The curtain's going up."

The second act began with green lights and soft, sad music. And more and more, the sensitive features of my companion reflected the emotions awakened in her breast. At the intermission, deeply affected, she barely spoke at all. But, as the last act got under way and she became once more a rapt being, a strange phenomenon occurred, how I could not guess, yet in some manner her hand, small and rather damp, became entangled with my own. So stimulating was the warm current of her blood I did not break the contact. And thus we sat, with fingers interlocked, linked together as though to sustain each other while the drama of Carton's self-sacrifice worked to its heart-rending end. As the noble fellow made the supreme sacrifice, mounting to the guillotine firmly, with pallid countenance and carefully ruffled raven locks, his speaking eye soulfully sweeping the gallery and pit, I felt a convulsive tremor pass through my companion's body, which was very close to mine; then, one by one, like pattering raindrops in springtime, her warm, tender tears fell upon the back of my hand.

At last, the end, with a clamorous house and many, many curtain-calls for Miss de Silva and Martin Harvey—now looking, in fact, happy and handsome in his silk shirt and varnished top-boots, marvellously resurrected from the tomb. Miss Jean Law, however, was too overcome to join in such banal applause. Silently, as though crushed by feelings too deep for words, she rose and accompanied me from the theatre. Only when we reached the street did she turn to me.

"Oh, Robert, Robert," she whispered, with brimming eyes. "You can't believe how much I've enjoyed myself."

It was the first time she had used my Christian name.

We walked to Central Station in silence and, since her train, the last of the day, did not leave for fifteen minutes, we stood somewhat self-consciously together under the bookstall clock.

Suddenly, as though awakening from a dream, Miss Jean gave a little start of recollection.

"My watch!" she exclaimed. "I was almost forgetting it."

"Oh, of course." I smiled. "I had quite forgotten too." And I felt in my jacket pocket for the trinket she had entrusted to me.

But I could not find it. I searched unsuccessfully through all the pockets of my jacket, inside and out. Then, with growing consternation I began to fumble in my waistcoat pockets.

"Good heavens," I muttered. "I don't seem to have it."

"But you must have it." Her voice sounded stiff and queer. "I gave it to you."

"I know you did. But I'm such an absent-minded beggar. I mislay everything."

I was now searching, vainly, and somewhat desperately, in my trousers when, chancing to glance up, I caught sight of the look upon Miss Jean's face, the look of a pure young woman, who finds, after all, that she is indeed dealing with a blackguard and has been deceived, duped, and deluded by him, such a look of pain, doubt and consternation I stopped my futile fumblings in dismay.

"What's the matter?"

"It isn't my watch." Her lips had turned deathly white, her voice was smaller than ever. "It's my mother's watch, given her by my father. I borrowed it, out of vanity, to impress you. Oh dear, oh dear." The inexhaustible fountains of her eyes overflowed again. "After this lovely evening . . . when I was trusting you and . . . liking you . . ."

"Good Lord," I shouted. "Do you think I've stolen the blasted thing?"

By way of answer she broke down completely. Then, as she opened her handbag to find her sodden handkerchief, a sudden gleam of gold illumined the dimness of the station arches. Even as she started, I remembered that, while she sat entranced—fearing, indeed, that I might lose the thing—I had slipped it for safety in her bag.

"Oh!" she gasped, petrified. "Oh, dear, goodness . . ." She stared at me in horrified contrition and stammered: "How can I . . . ever apologize . . . for doubting you?"

Stony silence on my part.

From behind us came the shrill blast of a guard's whistle, followed by the warning shriek of an engine.

"Robert!" she cried wildly. "What can I say . . . oh, my dear, what can I do?"

I gazed upon her coldly. Again the engine shrieked.

"Unless you wish to spend the night on the Winton pavements, I advise you to catch your train."

Frantically, she gazed from me to the platform where, with slow, reverberating chuffs, her train was beginning to move. For an instant she hesitated, then, with a little moan, she turned and ran.

When I saw that she was safely aboard I turned, collected my hamper, and, a few minutes later, took the last train for Dalnair, not altogether displeased with myself. That I was a bit of a fraud, I fully realized; but somehow, like Sydney Carton, I had acquired a halo, at least for the time being, and I rather liked the cozy feel of it.

CHAPTER FIVE

I GOT back to the hospital shortly before midnight and, to my surprise, observed that a light was still showing in Miss Trudgeon's window. As the slate in the hall indicated that there were no new admissions, I locked up, meaning to turn in at once. But I had no sooner entered my own quarters than I heard, from the corridor, those ingratiating tones which belonged only to Sister Peek.

"Doctor . . . Dr. Shannon."

I opened my door.

"Doctor." She gave me her meek, downcast smile. "The matron wishes to see you."

"What!"

"Yes, at once, Doctor, in her office."

This peremptory summons, delivered secondhand, at such an hour, struck me as an impertinence. For an instant, anxious to preserve the peace, I thought of complying. Then I felt it was too much to swallow.

"Give the matron my compliments. If she wants to speak to me, she knows where to find me."

Sister Peek turned up the whites of her eyes in dismay, yet from the manner in which she scurried off, I could see that she was not sorry to act as the virtuous intermediary in promoting the differenec between the matron and myself. She must, indeed, have delivered my message with considerable *empressement* for, a minute later, Miss Trudgeon bore in upon me, wearing her dark uniform but without her cap, cuffs, and collar. Shorn of these embellishments of white linen, her face looked yellower than ever.

"Dr. Shannon. On my monthly inspection today I went into the test room. I found it in the most atrocious disorder, littered with all sorts of rubbish —untidy, messed up and muddled."

"Well, what about it?"

"Is it your doing?"

"Yes."

"You had no right to do such a thing, no right whatsoever. You should have asked me first."

"Why?"

"Because you should. It's my department."

"Isn't the whole hospital your department?" I was beginning to lose my calm. "You want to run the entire show. You're not content unless you have everyone bowing and scraping to you. In fact, you treat this place as though it were your own private property. Well, it isn't. I have my rights, as well as you. I happen to be doing some important scientific work at present. That's why I took the test room."

"Then you'll kindly give it back."

"Are you suggesting that I stop my work?"

"It's a matter of indifference to me what you do, so long as you carry out your job. But I want my test room back, clean and tidy again."

"Why? The room's never used."

She gave a short laugh.

"That's where you're wrong. It's used at this time every year. For my nurses' lectures. Didn't you notice the desks? The session begins on Saturday."

"You can use some other room," I protested, feeling as though my feet had been swept from under me.

She shook her head deliberately.

"There are no other rooms with proper accommodation. Only the isolation ward. And that's much too damp and miserable. Apart from the nurses, I wouldn't wish you to be uncomfortable, Doctor. You see," with acrid humour she launched her final shaft, "*you* are the one who gives the lectures."

Outmanœuvred, in fact, completely cornered, I could only glare at her in helpless silence. The flicker of derisive amusement in her eyes, as she moved to the door, showed her satisfaction at having evened the score between us and put me in my place.

I went to bed threshing out this new difficulty in my mind. Seasoned by a life of brawls and bluster, toughened by interminable rows with servants, tradesmen, nurses and Sisters, waddling forward, victoriously, with a gory trail of doctors in her wake, she was a hard nut to crack. Much as it galled me, there was nothing for it, at present, but a strategic retreat.

At lunch next day, after a period of silence, I told her formally that I would clear out of the test room.

In reward for my capitulation she gave me a grim smile.

"I thought you'd see reason, Doctor. May I have the chutney, please. Now I recollect when I was in Bogra . . ."

I felt like breaking the bottle on her head. Instead, I passed it to her with a smile of equal grimness.

An hour later, at half-past two, I walked down casually to the old smallpox isolation pavilion, then quickly dodged into the protection of the shrubbery which concealed it. Miss Trudgeon was busy in the linen room; nevertheless, I wanted to be careful.

The isolation pavilion was a ruin—no other word is possible—I effected an entry only by breaking in a decayed corrugated iron panel. Darkly shuttered, chilly as a sepulchre, and empty of everything but dust and cobwebs, it obviously hadn't been opened for years. Striking matches, which burned my fingers, I surveyed the abandoned ruin. There was a hole in the boards where the stove had been ripped out. A chipped enamel basin, yellow and corroded, lay on the floor. Even the water was cut off, and the tap had almost rusted away.

Disconsolately, I came out, found Pim at the garage, and explained my situation to him.

"I'm going to move into the old smallpox pavilion."

He laughed incredulously.

"That place. It's no use for anything."

"We could recondition it."

"Never."

He continued to insist that it was impossible; but, when I pressed ten shillings into his palm, he finally consented, although with a bad grace, to my plan.

That same evening, when it was dusk, we moved all my gear from the test room to the derelict pavilion. Then Pim, grumbling all the time, began to restore the place to a primitive sort of order, fitting a new faucet for me, connecting up the cut-off electric wires, restoring the worst of the rotted woodwork. Dirty and tired, we stopped at ten o'clock, when he had to fetch some of the Sisters from the station.

It took two more nights to complete the job, and the result was poor enough. Still, it was my own place, draughty and unheated, but with a stout bench, water, electricity, four walls, and a roof. Sister Cameron, who was in charge of the scarlatina ward, had made for me, from old bed-jackets, three curtains of red flannel which, rigged up behind the shutters, permitted not a blink of light to escape. A new lock, fitted to the door, gave to me the sole right of entry and of egress. And by running an invisible wire from the bell-push on the door of my living quarters, Pim had arranged an indicator which would give me warning when I was wanted. I had, in short, a secret laboratory, a fort, an arsenal of research, from which no one could dislodge me. Every evening, after my final round of the wards, I made a detour to the shrubbery and, in the falling darkness, I slipped into the thick laurel bushes and gained the sanctuary of the pavilion. I was hard at work by nine o'clock.

Keeping myself going with black coffee, which I brewed myself, I worked usually until one in the morning; and sometimes, in the absorption of my quest, I kept on until dawn and did not go to bed at all, relying on a cold shower and hard rub-down to freshen me for breakfast, and the duties of the coming day.

I progressed rapidly, but this constant application was taking toll of my nerves, and in the afternoons I began to make use of Luke's motor-cycle. Nothing was more soothing than a swift rush along the empty country roads, this whizzing anæsthesia of speed. And the bike, as though imbued with a homing instinct, brought me always to the vicinity of Blairhill, bearing me, with a roar and a crackle, past the gate of the villa Siloam.

One afternoon, instead of flashing past, I slowed down, ran the machine up the little back lane, and stopped behind the garden wall. It was not a high stone wall and I scaled it easily. And there, in the latticed summer-house, almost at my feet, was the daughter of the baker of Blairhill.

Still unconscious of my presence, she was seated at a rustic table, bareheaded and wearing a short jacket, with her chin in her cupped hand, a medical textbook and a paper bag of plums before her. She was studying, of course. Yet so pensive was her air, so absent her manner, so remote her gaze, and so frequently did her fingers dip into the paper bag, I began to fear that her application to Osler's *Practice of Medicine* was not all that it might be. She had indeed, since my arrival, without once turning a page, consumed, in a melancholy fashion, three ripe plums; and now, sadly selecting her fourth, had, with a faint sigh, plunged her white teeth into its succulent flesh, so that little drops of ruddy juice ran down her chin when, glancing up suddenly, she caught sight of me upon the wall. She started, and almost swallowed the plum-stone.

"It's all right," I said. "I haven't come to steal anything."

She still choked on the stone.

"Oh, Mr. Shannon . . . I'm so glad to see you . . . I was just thinking . . . about our awful misunderstanding . . . and wondering how on earth I could put it right."

"I thought you were working."

"Yes, I was," she admitted, but with a faint blush. "In a sort of a way. My exam's in four weeks' time." She sighed. "I don't seem to be getting on."

"Perhaps you need some fresh air," I suggested. "I have Luke's bike here. Will you come for a spin?"

Her eyes sparkled.

"I should love it."

She got to her feet and, reaching down, I helped her, quite unnecessarily, for she was light and agile, to the top of the wall. We dropped down on the other side. The next minute she was seated on the pillion, I had kicked at the starter, and we were off.

It was a brilliant August day and, as we escaped from the winding streets of Blairhill, encouraged by the sunshine and the delightful rapidity of our motion, guided, also, by some strange nostalgic compulsion, I set our course for the village of Markinch upon the southern shore of Loch Lomond. The countryside was superb, the Darroch foothills agleam with wheatfields in full ear and starred with patches of scarlet poppies. On the fertile slopes of Gowrie the orchards of pear, apple, and plum lay heavy with ripe fruit, and the pickers, filling, with seeming indolence, the pannier baskets strapped about their waists, waved to us as we sped past. Defying the rush of air, I shouted over my shoulder to my companion:

"Fine, isn't it?" We survived a series of exhilarating bounces and dodged, by inches, a stationary farm-cart. "You hang on well. I suppose you often go out with Luke?"

With her lips close to my ear she shouted back:

"Oh, yes, quite often." But in her tone there was that which disparaged all previous excursions, which put Luke severely in his place as a mere brother, which exalted this present moment to an incomparable plane. More and more I became conscious of the circlet of her arms about my waist, the light contact of her form behind me, the pressure of her cheek against my ribs, as she burrowed for protection against the wind.

About five o'clock we swept over the crest of Markinch Brae; and there, before us, was the Loch, cool and unruffled, bearing the deep blue of the unclouded sky, with richly wooded slopes rising from its edges to the sharp, ridged mountains of a paler blue, beyond. Breaking the surface of the still expanse, a chain of small green islands lay mirrored, like a jade necklace, and, upon the nearer shore, there was clustered a little clachan of white-washed cottages, embowered in honeysuckle and wild dog-roses.

This was Markinch, the most favoured of all my boyhood haunts, whither I had so often come, alone, or with my friend Gavin Blair, to find solace for my wounded soul. And now, as we descended the steep winding hill, I experienced again, and more intensely, that inner glow always awakened in my breast by this sleepy, forgotten little spot, steeped in summer quiet, drenched in the scent of honeysuckle, with no sounds but the drone of bees, the splash of a fish in the shallows, and no sign of life but a single collie dog, a drowsy sentinel, stretched in the white dust by the little pier at which the toy red-funnelled steamer of the Loch called once a week.

At the end of the short village street I drew up and we detached ourselves stiffly and somewhat self-consciously from the machine, which, although fuming and smelling of hot oil, had nobly withstood the heat and burden of the day.

"Well . . ." I said, finding it strangely difficult to meet her eye after the close communion of our journey. "That was a glorious run. I expect it's given you an appetite for tea."

She glanced around appreciatively, but, having failed to discover even a single village store, she turned to me smiling, and with an air of intimate comradeship.

"It's beautiful. But we'll never get anything to eat."

"I can't let you starve." I led the way to the last little white cottage of the row, where, above the porch, almost concealed by climbing scarlet fuchsias, there was a weathered sign bearing the cryptic word: *Minerals*—which in that Northern district is to be interpreted as meaning "soft drinks."

I knocked at the door and presently there appeared a small bent woman in a dark tartan dress.

"Good afternoon. Can you give us some tea?"

She gazed up at us with a discouraging shake of her head.

"Na, na. I dinna sell ought but the aërated watters . . . Reid's Lemonade and Barr's Iron Brew."

My companion shot me a justified glance but I continued:

"You surprise me, Janet. Many a time you've given me a lovely tea. Don't you remember when we used to come fishing . . . Gavin and I . . . and the salmon we caught for you . . . ? I'm Robert Shannon."

At my use of her Christian name she had started and now, peering closely at me like a little old witch, she uttered an exclamation of affectionate recognition, that cry which springs instinctively from the Highland heart, so slow always to recognize strangers but warm, ever warm to a friend.

"Guid sakes alive. If I'd had my specs I would have kenned you. It's you, yourself, Robert."

"Indeed it is, Janet. And this is Miss Law. And if you turn us from your door we'll just fade away and never come back."

"I'll no do that, though," cried Janet vigorously. "Na, na. Heaven forbid. Ye'll have the finest tea in Markinch inside ten minutes."

"Can we have it in the garden, Janet?"

"Ye can that! Well, well! It beats a'. Robert Shannon, grown up now, and a doctor . . . Ay, ay, ye canna deny it. I read a' about ye in the *Lennox Herald* . . ."

With these, and many other ejaculations, Janet ushered us through to her back garden, then scurried off to the dark little kitchen where through the fixed window we caught glimpses of her bent figure bustling about with a big iron griddle.

As a result of her willing labours we were soon seated, under the wooden trellis, before that plain but delicious fare I had savoured, here, in the past—new baked scones and home churned butter, boiled fresh eggs, heather honey in the comb, and strong black tea. Jean said grace gravely, with closed eyes, then, naturally, and with good appetite, she began the wholesome country meal.

At first, old Janet hung about, eager for all my news, and glancing at us with native shrewdness, embarrassing us considerably by her questions. After a while, however, when she had replenished the tea-pot, she left us. And, with a sigh of contentment, Miss Jean turned towards me.

"This is so lovely," she exclaimed, happily, guilelessly. "And to think that we nearly missed it all. If I hadn't asked you to be friends, that day in Grant's . . . You've no idea what a lot of nerve it took . . . I was shaking all over."

"Do you regret it?"

"No." She blushed faintly. "Do you?"

I shook my head silently, still looking at her, causing her gaze to fall, a gesture of timidity, which, as on that occasion when I had passed her, sad and solitary, outside Hillier's on Fenner Hill, sent over me a throbbing wave of tenderness. How pretty she was, in this country setting, wind-swept and glowing, virginal and sweet. A gipsy, perhaps. Her clustered hair was brown, held by a brown ribbon, brown also were her eyes, and her face, which had tiny freckles of a deeper brown dusted upon it.

Playing nervously with her teaspoon, she remarked, as though attempting to return the conversation to an ordinary level:

"Can you smell the honeysuckle? I'm sure it's somewhere in the garden."

I did not answer, though the scent of the flower, or of something sweeter, was mounting in my blood. Beset by an emotion that was strange and new, I tried to direct my thoughts into the plane of reason, to my research experiments, towards the innumerable dissections which I had coldly performed in the Department mortuary. How, in the light of these, could I ever find beauty in the human form? But, alas, I could. I thought then, in desperation, of those amœbae, lowest form of all cellular life, which, when placed together beneath the microscope upon a slide, are instinctively attracted. Had I not a mind, an understanding, and a will to save me from that blind reaction? I heard myself saying, independent of my own volition:

"Shall we take a stroll? It's not late yet. We'll not go far."

She hesitated. Yet she also was reluctant to break the spell that lay upon us.

"Do come," I urged. "It's still early."

"For a little way then," she consented, in a low voice.

I left a generous present upon the table and we took our leave of Janet. Then we set out slowly over the narrow pathway to the winding shore of the Loch. Twilight was beginning to fall, a crescent moon swung high in the eastern sky and was bosomed in the mysterious depths of the dark water beneath. The air was soft, gentle as a caress. Away in the distance a grey heron cried and was answered remotely by its mate. Then the low lapping of the lake became part of the stillness of the night.

In silence we followed the muted water's edge until, reaching a little sandy cove, sheltered by banks of meadowsweet and mint, we stopped, suddenly, and turned towards each other. An instant of expectation. Her lips were warm and dry, parted as though in sacrifice, offering themselves in the pure and perfect knowledge that never before had they been kissed by any man.

Not a word was spoken. I held my breath, my heart was beating in my breast, as though fearful of a kind of death. But no, the enchantment was prolonged, there was nothing but that sweet, that single kiss. Her innocence had conquered.

As we walked back slowly, a pure white mist crept over the water like breath upon a mirror. Veils of vapour loomed over the land, filling the valleys with a rimed and ghostly air. And although for me the moon shone with a brighter radiance, strangely, my dear companion shivered.

CHAPTER SIX

On the afternoon of September 29, in my laboratory day-book, which I used as a diary and a record of my work, I made this elated entry:

This morning at 2 A.M. I finally identified Bacillus C.

It is none other than *Brucella melitensis*, an obscure coccobacillus which David Bruce isolated in 1886 during an outbreak of fever in Malta caused by the milk of infected goats.

This bacillus, confined, apparently, to the Mediterranean littoral, and, according to the text-books, transmitted only by goats, had always been regarded as of mere historical interest or at least of minor importance in the field of general medicine. This belief is wholly incorrect.

On the contrary *Brucella melitensis* is the causal organism of the recent severe epidemic here, and almost certainly, of other clinically similar epidemics currently reported in Europe and the United States. From careful checking of the data at my command

> I am convinced that, in the present instance, transmission by goats'
> milk may be ruled out as an impossibility. I suspect, in fact, as the
> infective agent, the milk of cows. Should this be so, the importance
> of this discovery cannot be overestimated.

I threw down the pen and, with a glance at the clock, snatched up my
cap and hurried from the hospital to Dalnair station to catch my train. I
was meeting Jean in Winton at three o'clock and, glowing with excitement,
I could scarcely wait to give her my wonderful news.

All that lingering summer, which, by the dreamlike beauty of its days,
conspired to defeat the force of reason, we had drawn more closely to each
other. I, perhaps, was a willing victim, but my companion, by her temperament and denomination, by every intimate beat of her family life, was better
able to appreciate the barrier to our attachment which, on that evening at
Markinch, had been blindingly revealed to her. Bound by the web of parental
ties, enclosed by the inexorable limits of her creed, no nightmare was more
fearful to her than the grim phantom of my religion. More than once she
had, with tears, protested that our relationship was impossible. But when,
after a sad good-bye, I returned to Dalnair, the telephone in my room would
ring and her voice would tremble across the wire:

"Oh, no, Robert, no . . . we can't give each other up."

Rent by the wonder of this new emotion, swept away as by a cataract, we
were hopelessly in love.

In Winton, half an hour later, an autumn rain was falling as I left the train
and hastened to the quiet café which we had discovered near the Central
Station. She was already there, a lonely figure, at the far end of the almost
deserted lounge.

"Jean," I exclaimed, going forward and taking both her hands, "I've got
it at last."

Seating myself beside her on the wall settee, I poured out the account of
my success.

"Don't you see the tremendous significance of it? Not just goats' milk . . .
on the island of Malta. But cows' milk, everywhere. Cows' milk, cheese,
butter, all dairy produce . . . the most generally used foods in the world
. . . that's how this germ is transmitted. And there's more. I telephoned Alex
Duthie this morning. He told me they had a lot of trouble with their dairy
herd just before the epidemic. Several of the animals died. That's no coinci-
dence . . . must be some relationship. In fact he said there's been severe
outbreaks among cattle herds all over the country . . . 35 per cent affected.
If they get another sick animal at Dreem, Alex's going to let me have milk
samples. Don't you see the possibility, Jean . . . heavens, if there should be
a connection between the two . . ."

I broke off, in a ferment of feeling, while she gazed at me with quiet
sympathy.

"I'm so glad, Robert." She hesitated, and her smile became subdued. "I wouldn't mind if they gave me that question at my exam tomorrow."

There was a pause, during which my effervescence slowly ebbed. I had actually forgotten that it was the eve of that important event, her degree examination, and her anxiety for the ordeal which would begin upon the following morning and endure for five days was now so apparent it awakened in me a sudden stab of contrition. I had pushed ahead with my research, every night, pressing on, full of inexhaustible energy, avoiding pitfalls by a kind of magic. But what of her? When she spoke palely of hours filled with anxiety for the future I had remonstrated that she also had her work, and I had, it is true, from time to time, at Dalnair, taken her over certain subjects which I thought likely to crop up in her papers. Yet could I not have coached her more thoroughly, more patiently, instead of proving a perpetual distraction?

"You'll be all right," I said encouragingly. "You've studied pretty hard."

"I suppose so," she answered, wanly. "I don't seem to have much confidence. Professor Kennerly's the examiner . . . and he's very strict."

Again my heart and conscience smote me. Was this the same bright and bustling neophyte who, fervent for her mission, with enthusiasm to heal, had come to my room to probe the exciting mysteries of trypanosomes?

"Jean," I said in a low voice. "I've been a selfish brute."

She shook her head listlessly, with drooping lip.

"I'm as much to blame as you."

In silence I bent forward and pressed her fingers tight. She whispered: "At least we have each other."

When we left the café I was still accusing myself and, on our way to the station, in an effort to cheer her, also, perhaps, to appease my sense of guilt, I stopped at a little antique shop at the corner of Woolmarket. In my journeyings through this back street I had observed in the window a green necklace, extremely simple, for the beads were only of glass, but pretty, in good taste, and genuinely old. Before my companion knew what I was about I asked her to wait, went in and purchased it. A moment later, as we entered the station and stood at our usual place of leave-taking, under the bookstall clock, I gave the beads to her.

"That's for good luck," I said. "Green is my lucky colour."

She flushed with surprise and her face, losing its despondency, slowly lit up with pleasure. I had never given her anything before.

"They're beautiful," she said.

"No, no. They're nothing. But let me put them on."

I took the beads and fastened them around her neck. Then, carried away by this new tenderness, careless of the passing crowds, the public place, I held her in my arms and kissed her.

She had to leave immediately for her train. As I turned away, I suddenly caught sight of a tall and ladylike figure, standing as though petrified, her eyes fixed upon me in a shocked and unbelieving stare. With a sinking of my heart, I recognized her, knew instantly that she had witnessed the gift of the necklace, the close embrace. I took a step towards her, but with the glassiest of glances, and a frigid, an imperceptible inclination of her head, she had begun already to move away. It was Miss Beth Dearie.

For the rest of that week, according to our arrangement, I made no attempt to communicate with Jean. But while I worked hard at Dalnair, I thought of her, and on the following Monday morning, I rose early and hurried down to the lodge to get the *Herald* before it was sent into Miss Trudgeon's parlour. The medical passes appeared always at the top of the last page and, standing in the drive in my pyjamas and overcoat, I ran my eye hastily over the printed list. Then again, more carefully, but with a growing sense of misgiving, I scanned it.

Jean's name was not there. I could not believe it. She had failed.

Although she had warned me not to do so, swept by a deep commiseration, I felt I must telephone her at once. I went to the switchboard in the hall and, while Sister Peek scurried around with her ears alertly cocked, I called the number in Blairhill.

"Hello. I want to speak to Miss Law."

It was a woman's voice that answered, not Jean's, alas, but almost certainly her mother's.

"Who is speaking?"

I hesitated.

"A friend."

There was a pause, then the voice came back.

"I am sorry. Miss Law is not here."

"But please listen," I said. Then I broke off, for the sharp crackle against my ear-drum told me that the other party had hung up.

All that day, scarcely knowing what to do, I laboured under a dismal oppression. After supper, when seven o'clock struck, I was preparing to restore myself by my nightly session in the laboratory when Katie, the maid, who had already cleared away the dishes, tapped upon my door.

"There's a gentleman to see you, sir."

"Is it a patient?"

"Oh, no, sir."

"Relative?"

"I don't think so, sir."

I gazed at her in perplexity: I wasn't used to visitors at this hour.

"Well . . . you'd better show him in."

There must, that evening, have been a blind spot upon my intelligence. I got the shock of my life when, with a firm tread, Daniel Law came into the room.

As the door closed behind him, he bestowed upon me his grave and steady gaze.

"I hope I am not intruding at an awkward time, Doctor? If convenient, I should greatly like to have a word with you."

"Why . . . certainly," I stammered.

At this he bowed and removed his heavy black coat, which he folded methodically and placed, with his hat, upon the couch. Then, pulling a hard chair near to me, he sat down, very formal in his best dark suit, white dickey, and string tie, laid his hands upon his knees, and again transfixed me with unhesitating eyes.

"Doctor," he quietly began. "It was not an easy step for me to come to you like this. Before doing so I wrestled long in prayer." He paused. "You have been seeing much of my daughter lately?"

I turned extremely red.

"I'm afraid I have."

"Might one ask why?"

"Well . . . as a matter of fact . . . I'm very fond of her."

"Ah!" There was neither irony nor condemnation in the simple exclamation, merely a sombre, somewhat cold concern. "We are fond of her too, Doctor. Indeed, ever since she became a child of light, she has been to us as the lamb to the shepherd. You will appreciate, therefore, how great was our disappointment when we learned today that she had failed to obtain her medical degree. And I fear the main reason was that, instead of working, she was wasting her time in frivolous pursuits."

I was silent.

"Of course," he went on, with a visionary air, "I have every confidence in my daughter. We must bear the hand of the Lord when it presses upon us, and she will be sanctified by this affliction. My sainted wife and I have taken counsel with her and she will try again, after some months of uninterrupted study. What concerns us is a much more serious issue. I do not know how far your acquaintance has gone, Doctor—I can get no word of this from my daughter and am indebted to Miss Dearie for the little information I possess—nevertheless, I fear you must agree that, under the circumstances, it has gone far enough."

"I don't understand," I said quickly. "Why do you object to my knowing your daughter?"

He made no immediate answer. Pressing his finger tips together, he meditated intently.

"Doctor," he said suddenly and with greater firmness, "I hope my daughter will marry. One day I hope she will be a happy wife. But she will never find that happiness except with one of her own religious persuasion."

We were in deep water now but, uncaring, I plunged forward.

"I don't agree with you," I said. "Religion is a private affair. We can't help what creed we're born into. It's quite possible for two people to be tolerant of each other's belief."

He shook his head, darkly, with a cold and strangely baffling smile which seemed, if anything, to indicate his exclusive familiarity with the ways and ordinances of an Omniscient God.

"I make allowance for your youth and inexperience. There can be only one true testimony to the Blood, one true congregation of the saints. In that true congregation of the Lord's anointed my daughter has been reared. She can never commingle with the waters of Babylon."

As he spoke, by some strange antithesis, my thoughts flew suddenly, and heavily, to the lovely waters of Markinch, beside which Jean and I had wandered, to exchange, under the soft, indulgent dome of heaven, our first sweet kiss.

"Young man." Observing my bitterness, and the signs of rebellion in my face, his tone grew harsh. "I wish you well, and hope that light will one day break upon you. But it is only just that you should understand, finally, that my daughter is not for you. There is, in our communion, a ministering brother to whom she is virtually affianced. I refer to Malcolm Hodden. You have met him under my roof. At present he is a teacher, but he aspires one day to be a minister of the Gospel and to bear the torch into the wilderness. By every affinity of mind and spirit he has shown himself worthy to lead and guide her along the pathways of this earthly life."

There was a silence. He seemed to wait for me to speak but as, sunk in my chair, I said nothing, he rose, quiet as ever, and methodically put on his coat. When the last button was in place he gazed at me between sad forbearance and frigid admonition.

"I am glad that our conversation has been salutary, Doctor. We must all learn to submit to the Lord . . . to come to a true knowledge of His will. . . . In parting, I commit you to His care."

Taking up his hat, with firm footsteps, and that air of serene and steady discipline, he passed from the room.

I did not move for a long time. Despite his rigid and narrow views, I was constrained, in honesty, to admit that he was acting according to his lights. This did not help me. The tone of his discourse, as though every word were sacred and prophetic, drawn from Revelation, had cut me to the quick. And Hodden . . . ah, that was a bitter pill to swallow.

Full of hurt and angry love, I thought of Jean. I set my jaw firmly. At least I had not promised not to see her.

CHAPTER SEVEN

IN THIS restless and uneasy mood I made my night round of the wards. When I had given Sister Peek her instructions, I went, as usual, to the isolation pavilion, but I could not concentrate. The pursuit of pure science, to which I was dedicated, demanded complete detachment from all the entanglements of life. Yet now I cared nothing for that solemn covenant. The vision of Jean was before me, slim and fresh, her brown eyes misted with the bloom of youth. I loved her. I must see her.

On the following afternoon, the moment I was free, I hurried to the garage. Twice already I had telephoned to the villa Siloam, but on each occasion the voice of Mrs. Law had answered, and without a word, as though it were a hot iron, I had dropped the receiver back upon its hook. Now, despite the drizzle, I set off upon the motor-cycle for Blairhill.

At the rear of Siloam, with beating heart, I made my way to the summer-house. I found it empty, the chair untenanted, the rustic table bare of Osler's *Practice of Medicine*. Uncertainly, I sat on the wall watching the rain drip from the green painted lattice-work; then, dropping down on the near side, I skirted the garden and gained the front of the house. For almost half an hour, I hung about in the bushes, straining my eyes towards the mysterious lace-curtained windows. But although I several times caught sight of her mother, moving about in the dim interior of the "front room," I was not once rewarded by a glimpse of Jean.

Suddenly I heard the sound of approaching footsteps in the avenue. At first I thought that it was Daniel Law, but a moment later Luke's figure swung into view. I came forward.

"Luke!" I exclaimed. "I didn't know you were back."

"Yes, I'm back," he admitted.

"Why didn't you let me know? You're the very one who can help me."

"Am I?"

"Yes, Luke. Now listen." I spoke with painful urgency. "I must see Jean, at once."

"You'll not do that," he answered, hesitantly, glancing from me to the silent front of the house. Then, taking apparently a decision in my favour, he added: "We can't talk here. Come on down the street with me."

He led the way back to the town, gazing occasionally over his shoulder, then at a rather disreputable corner near the Market Square, dived into a gaudily painted saloon which bore the sign: BLAIRHILL SPORTS BAR. Seated in a booth at the back of this depressing emporium, which from its convenient array of pin-ball and fruit machines, I saw to be the resort of Blairhill's gilded youth, Luke ordered two glasses of beer. Then he gave me a long, equivocal stare.

"You've done it this time," he said at last. "If you ask me . . . it's all *up*."

I leaned forward quickly.

"What happened?"

"The worst I remember. When Mother heard from Miss Dearie, about you I mean, she took Jean aside, very quiet and sad, and had her crying all over the place. When Father came in at tea-time there was a long consultation. Then, while Mother went and fetched Malcolm, Father went up and prayed with Jean, for about an hour, in her room. Even in the kitchen, I could hear her sobbing, as if her heart would break. When they came down she had stopped. She was white-looking, but quiet. You see, it was all over then."

"Luke! What do you mean?"

"I think they made her promise she would never see you again."

It took me a minute to fully grasp his meaning, but presently there fell

upon me an iron conviction that he spoke the truth. Although in this age
of progress one could barely credit the fact, there existed in this family an
authority which went back to those days of the Old Testament, when the
tribes of Gilead and Gad followed their destiny across the plains of Moab,
tending their flocks and herds, submitting to the elders, trusting blindly in
the Lord.

Daniel Law was such a patriarch. He still lived in and by the books of
Kings, Numbers, and Deuteronomy. And amidst the roar of the machine
age, the distracting blare of jazz, and the enticing flicker of the cinema, he
had raised his children in that tradition, not by fear, for he was no tyrant, but
by a rule of tempered firmness, above all by the inflexible display of his
conviction, the unwavering light of his example. The popular, slightly comic
conception of the street-corner evangelist was as remote from Daniel Law
as a sickly weed from a stalwart oak. He was no weak-kneed tract passer, no
whining intoner of the Psalms. He was, indeed, a veritable Paul, righteous
and valiant, with a gleam in his eye which cowed the evil serpent before he
crushed it beneath his heel. He had, of course, the defect of his qualities.
His gaze was steady, yet he could see only straight ahead. Compromise was
beyond him—a thing, to him, was either black or white. Outside the shining
orbit of his own interior light, there existed only darkness, beset with tempta-
tions for the elect and, like twisted roots in a dark forest, the snares of
Satan. Tolerance was a forbidden weakness, indeed, a word he did not understand. If one were not "saved" then, alas, one was eternally damned. This
it was which for years had kept his daughter upon the stony path, saved her
from the iniquities of dances, card playing, and the theatre, reduced her
reading to *Good Words* and *Pilgrim's Progress*, and now, by the exercise of
prayer and pressure, had wrung from her that tearful promise to renounce her
unworthy lover.

All this flashed across my mind as I sat opposite Luke in the cheap and
chilly beer parlour, and although my reflections gave me the dizzy sensation
of having run into a stone wall, although also I felt a smouldering resentment
against Jean for having surrendered me, nevertheless, I could not, simply
could not, give her up.

"Luke," I said, tensely. "You've got to help me."

"Yes?" he queried, without much conviction.

"I simply must see your sister." I made the statement with a certain desperation.

He did not answer. Wiping his lips with his floury cuff, he gazed at me
with a sorrowing smile.

"You can do it, you know," I went on. "I'll wait here while you go back
to the house and tell Jean to step out and meet me."

Still quiet and pitying, he shook his head.

"Jean's not at the house. She's away."

I stared at him, motionless, while slowly he nodded his head.

"It's well seen you don't know Father. She was sent off last night to our

Aunt Elizabeth in Bethnal Green. She's to stay there, studying, for the next
four months, until she sits her exam again." He paused. "And Mrs. Russell,
that's our aunt, has instructions to open all her letters."

Bethnal Green, a suburb of London, more than three hundred miles
away—destination impossible of achievement by the villain Shannon. And
no letters, by request! Oh, wise, resourceful Daniel. In fact, a Daniel come
to judgement. I sat there, quite still, but my eyes fell wretchedly.

There was a protracted silence from which I was roused by the voice
of Luke as, in a sympathetic manner, he inquired:

"Would you like another beer?"

I lifted my bowed head.

"No, thanks, Luke." At least he meant well. "And that reminds me. You
want your bike back."

"Ah, there's no hurry."

"Yes, you must." I saw he was protesting only for politeness' sake. "It's
in the lane at the back of your house. I took good care of it. Here's the key."

He accepted the ignition key without further demur; then we got up and
went out. In the street, after a glance up and down, he shook my hand with
a kind of melancholy comradeship. I set out to walk to the station.

The rain was falling more heavily now, running in the gutters, plastering
the narrow thoroughfare with mud, making everything grey and miserable.

Oh, God, I thought to myself, in a sudden access of heartache, what am
I doing in this dreary and forsaken little town? I want to be in the sunshine,
away from this mess, uncertainty, and endless striving. I'd like to be on a
dubbeh, floating down the Nile, or on the bright hills of Sorrento, basking
above the blue Tyrrhenian Sea. No, damn it, I'd rather be in the fog and
grime of Bethnal Green.

But I knew I could not be there.

CHAPTER EIGHT

AFTER that, everything fell on me at once . . . but I will try, calmly, to keep
the sequence. I don't intend to harp on my state of mind. It was like the
weather, which continued with incessant rain and blustering equinoctial gales
that tore from our trees leaves and twigs not yet dead, strewing a sodden
litter upon the drive.

We were now extremely busy in the wards, mostly with diphtheria cases—
an epidemic of this disease had developed in the western district of Winton-
shire. I'd had this infection myself, a circumstance which, I daresay, gave me
a fellow feeling for the children who came in with it. So far, we could boast
of a clean sheet, not a single death, and Miss Trudgeon proudly paraded
about the place as though she, personally, were responsible. And perhaps she
was—her efficiency impressed me more and more, and in my heart I had
begun, unwillingly, to admire this conscientious, capable, indomitable little

war horse, whose hidden qualities far outweighed her obvious, and less attractive, attributes. But I took care not to tell her so. In my present mood I was sullen and rude to everyone.

Then, on the night of the third of November—this exact and fatal date is inscribed indelibly upon my recollection—I came back with bent head and flagging steps from the pavilion to my quarters and flung myself into a chair.

I hadn't been there ten minutes before a persistent buzzing struck my ear. It was the telephone on my bedside table, the bell sounding faintly because I had forgotten to throw back the switch before leaving the pavilion. I went into the bedroom and wearily picked up the receiver.

"Hello."

"Hello. Is that you, Doctor? I'm right glad to have reached you." Despite the bad connection, the relief in the voice was evident. "This is Duthie, Alex Duthie, at Dreem. Doctor . . . Robert . . . you must do something for me."

Before I could answer he went on:

"It's our Sim. He's been sick for a week with diphtheria. And he's not getting on. I want to bring him over to you at the hospital."

I did not hesitate an instant. We were already full and Alex, living across the border of the county, had no call upon our resources. Yet I couldn't dream of refusing him.

"All right. Get your doctor to sign a certificate and I'll send the ambulance over, first thing in the morning."

"No, no." His voice came back quickly. "The boy's right bad, Robert. We have a car at the door and he's all wrapped in blankets. I want to fetch him to you now."

I wasn't sure that it was correct to make this irregular admission, on short notice. However, because of my deep regard for Alex, I had to take the risk.

"Go ahead then. I'll expect you in about an hour. See you keep him warm on the way."

"I will. And thanks, lad . . . thanks."

I replaced the receiver and went along the corridor to the matron's room. Here, however, the lights were out and I was obliged to press the night bell, which summoned Sister Peek. When she arrived I gave her curt instructions to prepare a cot in the side room of Ward B, a comfortable little annex usually reserved for private patients and now the only space remaining unoccupied. Then I sat down to wait.

It was not a long vigil. Shortly before midnight a closed hired car drove up to the front entrance and as I pushed open the door against the wind and heavy, driving rain, Alex appeared carrying his son, all bundled up in blankets, in his arms. I showed him into the reception room. His face was white and drawn.

When he had deposited the boy upon the couch, where Sister Peek began to prepare him for examination, Alex wiped his forehead with the back of his hand and stood aside in silence, fixing upon me a look of haggard inquiry.

"Don't look so worried. When did Sim take ill?"

"The beginning of the week."

"And he's had his antitoxin injections?"

"Two lots. But it hasn't helped him much." Duthie spoke faster. "It's deep down in the throat. When we saw that every minute he was getting worse, I just had to bring him over. We have faith in you, Rob. Take a look at him, for pity's sake."

"All right. Don't get excited."

I turned towards the couch and immediately the reassuring expression which I had assumed for Duthie's benefit left my face. In fact, as my gaze fell upon the livid child who, with closed eyes and clutching hands, was fighting for every breath, I received a painful shock. Silently, I went on to examine him. The temperature was 103, the pulse so thin as to be almost imperceptible. I did not try to count the respirations. A tough yellow membrane covered the back of the throat and extended viciously into the larynx. The child was clearly *in extremis,* already almost moribund.

I glanced at Duthie, who, standing mutely by, was trying, with even greater anxiety, to read my face; and although moved by pity, I felt a sharp anger against him for the predicament in which he had placed me.

"You should never have brought him out. He's desperately ill."

He swallowed dryly.

"What like's the matter?"

"Laryngeal diphtheria. The membrane is blocking the windpipe . . . keeping him from breathing."

"Can't anything be done?"

"Tracheotomy . . . and at once. But we can't do it here. We've no theatre, no facilities. He should have been moved to one of the big city fever hospitals long ago." I moved across to the telephone. "I'll ring up the Alexandra now and make arrangements to get him in at once."

I had begun to dial the emergency number when suddenly the child began to crow, a thin, desperate stridor which rasped and echoed in the room.

Alex pulled at my arm.

"We'll never get him to another hospital. God knows it was bad enough coming here. You do what's necessary yourself."

"I can't. It's a job for an expert."

"Go on, do it, do it."

Arrested, I stood staring at him, in a startled and helpless manner, like a fool. As I have explained elsewhere, I had the most limited experience in the practice of medicine, and had never attempted a serious operation in my life. From the clear heights of pure science I had always affected to despise the bustling practitioner who, in a pinch, would tackle anything. Yet there was no denying the dreadful urgency of this case. It was, indeed, a question of minutes—for I now perceived that if I evaded the issue, on the pretext of transferring the case to the Alexandra, the child would never reach that hospital alive. Aware of my own hopeless inadequacy, I groaned inwardly.

"Get Matron up." I turned to Sister Peek. "And move the patient over to the side room at once."

Six minutes later we were in the side room, Miss Trudgeon, Sister Peek, and myself, gathered round the plain deal table upon which, in a clean hospital nightdress, lay the gasping form of the unconscious child. Apart from that convulsive breathing there was dead silence in the cramped little room. I had rolled up my sleeves, washed my hands hurriedly in carbolic solution, and now I was in such a mortal funk, I glanced instinctively, incredibly almost, towards the matron for support.

She was admirably calm, impersonal, efficient, and, although she had just awakened from sleep and thrown on her uniform at short order, correctly dressed. Even her starched headdress was adjusted so that not a hair seemed out of place. Despite the feud between us, I couldn't suppress a surge of admiration, and of envy too. She knew her job inside out, and her courage was superb.

"You won't want an anæsthetic?" she asked me in an undertone.

I shook my head. The state of the breathing simply wouldn't permit it. In any case the child was too far gone.

"Very good, then," said Miss Trudgeon, cheerfully. "I'll take the head and arms. You steady the legs, Sister Peek."

As she spoke she handed me a lancet from the square of white gauze in the enamel basin and, staunchly setting herself at the head of the table, took a firm grip of Sim's arms. The night Sister, in a wobbly fashion, grasped the boy's ankles.

Although doubtless it was only for an instant, it seemed to me that I stood there, with the knife in my inept and nerveless hand, for a timeless eternity.

"We're all ready then, Doctor," the matron reminded me and, believe it or not, there was again a firm encouragement in her tone.

I took a deep breath, clenched my teeth, and, holding the skin tense, made an incision in the child's throat. The blood oozed thick and dark, obscuring the wound. I swabbed, again and again, and cut deeper. Sim was unconscious, and felt nothing, I am sure; yet at every touch he writhed and squirmed on the table in a kind of feeble agony. At the same time there came, intermittently, that frightful heave for breath, which convulsed all his body, as though he were a fish, gasping upon a slab. These sudden uncontrollable movements increased my difficulties. I tried to get a retractor into the opening. It went in, but immediately fell out and went clattering to the floor. Then the blood welled thicker, not a bright, spurting stream which I could have controlled, but a slow treacly flow which choked up everything. I couldn't use the lancet any more. I was too near the great vessels of the neck. One false snick and I would sever the jugular vein. I tried with my forefinger to part the tissues, muddling about in the mess, seeking desperately for the trachea. If I didn't find it quickly it was all up with Sim. He was almost black in the face now. His efforts to get air, which sucked in all his ribs, and breastbone, till his small white chest was hollow, had a more frantic quality, but were less frequent and more feeble. There were long intervals when he didn't breathe at all. Already his body had a cold and clammy feel.

The perspiration burst in great beads upon my forehead. I felt so sick I thought I was going to faint. I couldn't find the windpipe, I simply couldn't, and the child was almost gone. Oh, God . . . for Christ's sake . . . help me find that trachea.

"No pulse, now, Doctor." It was a soft, reproachful bleat from Sister Peek who, from time to time, had laid her fingers on the boy's wrist. But still, at the head of the table, the matron never said a word.

I don't know what came over me—with the courage of despair I took the lancet and cut deep. Suddenly, as by a kind of magic, there sprang up in the wound, thin, white, and shining, like a silver reed, the object of my blundering, frantic search. My own breast gave a great convulsive heave and, dashing the perspiration from my eyes, I slit the exposed trachea. Instantly, there was a whistling inrush of free air, a blessed draught which filled those choked and suffocating lungs. Once, twice, the starved chest heaved deeply, to its full extent. Again and again, in a kind of ecstasy of relief. Then, slowly, at first, but with increasing force, the moribund child began regularly to breathe. The dusky tinge faded from his skin, the bluish lips slowly turned to red, he ceased to struggle.

Quickly, with trembling fingers, I slipped in the double tracheotomy tube, sutured a few small bleeding points, stitched up the wound and bandaged it so that the narrow metal orifice of the tube protruded. My knees were knocking under me, my heart bumping against my ribs, and the worst of my agitation was that I had to hide it. I stood limply by, damp and dishevelled, with bloodied fingers, while Matron expertly tucked Sim into the side-room cot, with hot bottles round him and his head well-pillowed.

"There now," Miss Trudgeon remarked at last. "He ought to do very nicely. You'll take over this case, Sister, and special on it all night."

As she swung round to go out, she gave me a quick half glance, neither of approval nor disapproval, as though to say: It was touch and go, but you came out of it better than you deserved. For the first time we understood each other.

Even when Matron had gone I could scarcely bring myself to leave. Sister Peek had drawn up a chair to the cot, with a tray of swabs handy to clear the mucus which occasionally bubbled in the mouth of the tube, and behind her, I remained watching the boy, now resting, a good colour in his cheeks. From sheer exhaustion he had begun to drowse, but suddenly, briefly, his eyes opened and, by a strange chance, encountered mine. For an instant he smiled, at least the shadowy suspicion of a smile faintly moved his lips. Then his lids drooped and he was asleep.

Nothing could have so deeply moved me as that tremulous and childish smile. I could have wished no greater reward.

"I'm going now, Sister," I said in a matter-of-fact tone. "You know what to do?"

"Oh, yes, Doctor."

Only as I went out did I remember Alex Duthie, still waiting in the reception room, and at the prospect of ending his suspense I increased my pace, under the bright and singing stars. Yes, he was there, seated stiffly in a hard chair, facing the door, holding his cold and empty pipe, as though he had not stirred since we had left him. When I entered, his attitude became more rigid, then he rose, confronting me in silence, his eyes burning with the question he could not bring himself to utter.

"He's all right now."

So set was his expression, he could not immediately relax it. I could see the sinews of his jaw muscles drawn tautly under the skin. Then, all at once, his mouth began to twitch. He said, at last, in a low voice:

"You did it?"

I nodded.

"Now he can breathe. In fact he's asleep. When he's got over his diphtheria, in ten days or so, we'll take out the tube and the wound will heal up. There'll hardly even be a scar."

Duthie took a step forward and seized my hand, wrung it so gratefully, with such fervour and feeling, he made me flinch.

"I'll never forget what ye've done for us this night. Never, never. I told you we had faith in ye, the wife and me." Mercifully, he relinquished my crushed fingers. "Can I ring her up? She's waiting at the farm manager's house."

A moment later he was in the hall, relating the good news, inarticulately. When he had finished I rejoined him, went out with him to the hired landaulet, beside which the forgotten driver, his cap pulled over his ears, patiently paced up and down.

"All's well, Joe!" cried Duthie in an uplifted tone. "The young-un's ower the worst."

In his gratitude the good fellow leaned through the window, his voice tense with feeling.

"I'll be over tomorrow, lad, and bring the missus. And again . . . from the bottom of my heart . . . *I thank ye.*"

When the car had gone I lingered in the cool, windy darkness. Then, as I heard the clock in the vestibule strike one, I made my way rather dizzily to my bedroom. I was so confused I didn't want to think about anything. I only knew that amidst my disappointment and perplexities there was a queer peace in my heart. I fell asleep almost at once, thinking, of all things, of Sim's smile.

CHAPTER NINE

I MUST have slept for about four hours when I was again aroused, and forcibly, by someone tugging at my arm. I opened my eyes to find the light full on and Sister Peek at my bedside, with a stricken face, exclaiming hysterically in my ear:

"Come at once . . . at once."

She almost pulled me from the sheets and, as I struggled into my coat and slippers, I realized, though half awake, that only a catastrophe could have caused this shrinking creature to burst into my room in such a fashion and at such an hour. Indeed, she seemed almost at her wits' end and as I set out beside her, half running, towards Ward B, she kept on repeating, like a lesson she had learned, while she scurried along:

"I didn't do it. I didn't do it."

In the dim, warm side room Sim was lying back upon his pillows, propped up as I had left him, very peaceful and quiet. Yet he seemed unnaturally still, and as I knocked the shade off the night-light and peered closer I saw, with a start, that the shining orifice was missing from his bandages, the tube was no longer in his throat. Hastily, I snatched up a pair of forceps and cleared the plug of mucus from the wound then, taking hold of his slack arms, I began to apply artificial respiration.

I worked on Sim, like one demented, for over an hour. But even before I arrived, he had been dead, quite dead. I stopped, buttoned up the crumpled nightdress, composed that inconsiderable frame which had struggled so hard and endured so much, laid back the head upon the pillow.

Suddenly, as I straightened out the bed, I uncovered, in a fold of the wrinkled sheets, the tracheotomy tube, all choked and foul with membrane. I stared at it stupidly, then I turned towards Sister Peek, who all this time had remained pressed against the door.

"It's blocked," I said in a tone of wonder. "He must have coughed it out."

Then I saw everything, and even before I could accuse her, the expression upon her face told me that my suspicion was correct. Another thought struck me. I walked slowly past her into the ward kitchen. Yes, on the table —that same deal table on which had been fought out the battle for Sim's life—there stood a tea-pot, a plate of sardine sandwiches, and a cold, half-finished cup of tea. Tempting little repast.

"Oh, Doctor." She had followed me, wringing her hands. "I never thought . . . he was sleeping so comfortable . . . I only left him for a minute."

I couldn't bear it. I thought my heart would burst. I went out of the kitchen, through the ward and into the open. Outside the few stars were fading and the first faint fingers of dawn had erased the darkness from the eastern sky. Beating my forehead with my clenched fists, I reached my sitting-room, where I fell into a chair by the table. It was not that my own slight achievement had been torn from me. What burned and rankled in my breast, and poisoned all my being, was the senseless turning of victory to defeat, the selfish, criminal waste of life. Sunk in a blind stupor, I surrendered to despair.

I must have sat without moving for a long time, for I was still there, in my overcoat and my pyjamas, when Katie appeared at nine o'clock to lay the breakfast table. Unable to bear her solicitous glances, I went through my bedroom to the bathroom, shaved automatically, and dressed. When I came back an extra good breakfast was awaiting me, toast, coffee, bacon and eggs under the metal cover. But although I needed food I could eat nothing, my stomach revolted even at a few sips of coffee. I went to the window and looked out. It was a cold and foggy morning, forerunner of the overcast damp of winter.

A knock on the door. As I turned, slowly Miss Trudgeon came into the room, composed, as usual, but showing in her eyes some signs of strain. Her manner was friendly. She crossed over to the fireplace where a few green sticks were spluttering and throwing out eddies of damp smoke.

"Sister Peek has been to see me." Her voice, when she did speak, was serious and restrained. "She is very much upset."

"I'm not surprised," I said bitterly.

"I know how you must feel, Doctor. Especially after all your efforts. The whole thing is highly regrettable." She paused. "For my own part, I regret it exceedingly, for no one could take the interests of this hospital more to heart than I. But these accidents do occur, Doctor, even in the best-regulated institutions. And, in a long experience, I have found that there is only one thing to do about them."

"And what's that?" I couldn't help asking.

"Overlook them."

I caught my breath sharply.

"You can't overlook this. It wasn't an accident. It was a case of gross negligence, which must be punished."

"Suppose we do as you suggest. What happens? Sister Peek is dismissed, there is a deal of talk and scandal, the hospital gets a bad name, and nobody is a bit the better for it."

"She'll have to go," I answered doggedly. "She's a bad nurse and she cost that child his life."

Miss Trudgeon made a soothing gesture.

"I understand your point of view, Doctor. And I sympathize with it. But . . . in this hospital . . . there are other considerations of a practical nature to be borne in mind."

"She can't be allowed to stay here to do the same thing over again."

"She won't," Matron said quickly. "This will be a lesson she'll never forget. I'll guarantee that. I can assure you, Doctor, that Sister Peek has many good points, and it would be altogether unwise, I won't say unjust, to ruin her career, for that's what it would amount to, because of this single incident."

I gazed at her heavily, recollecting how she went out of her way to make a favourite of the night sister. I wondered if a vague sense of privilege did not attach to Effie Peek. I was about to speak when there came a subdued knock upon the door and Katie again presented herself upon the threshold.

"Mr. and Mrs. Duthie waiting to see you, in the reception room, sir."

I felt myself turn cold, indeed an involuntary shiver passed through all my limbs. My reply to the matron was frozen upon my lips. I looked dully at the floor for a moment; then, by an effort, forced myself to move towards the door.

As I went out Miss Trudgeon came close to me and urged, in a voice of unmistakable sincerity:

"Be careful, Doctor. In your own interests . . . and mine."

My vision was so blurred and uncertain, the corridor seemed full of fog; but as I stumbled into the reception room I could see clearly enough that Duthie and his wife were smiling as though unable to contain a deep and intimate happiness. In fact when I entered Alex got up, with a beaming face, and gripped me by the hand.

"I hope we're not too early for you, lad. But there's no holding the missus and me this morning. We felt like singing on the way down here."

"That's right, Doctor." Alice Duthie had risen and was standing beside her husband, her simple careworn face quite radiant. "And we owe it all to your skill and cleverness."

I steadied myself against the table. My legs were failing me, my head seemed stuffed with cotton wool and, worst of all, I felt every second that I was going to break down and cry.

"Eh, lad!" Alex exclaimed. "Ye're quite done up. And no wonder either, after losing your sleep on our behalf. We'll not be bothering you a minute longer. We'll just gang over and take a look at Sim."

"Stop . . ." In a weak and broken manner I brought out the word.

They looked at me, at first amazed, then with concern, finally in sharp anxiety.

"What's like the matter?" Alex said in an altered voice. Then, after a pause, as though it were dragged from him: "Is our boy bad again?"

I nodded my head, blindly.

"Much worse? Good God, man, don't stand like that, tell us how he is."

I couldn't look at Alice; the sight of Alex's face, emptied of its light, turned grey and pitiful, was as much as I could bear.

"God in Heaven," he said in a low extinguished tone. "It's not *that*."

There was a long silence, how long I don't know. Time ceased to have any meaning, everything was blurred and blank. But I could see that Alice was weeping and that Duthie had his arm round her. When at last he did speak, his voice was cold and hard.

"Can we go over and see him?"

"Yes," I muttered. "Shall I come with you?"

"If you don't mind, we'll go alone."

On his way to the door he turned to me as to a stranger.

"This would have come easier if last night ye hadna let me think ye'd saved our boy. I never want to set eyes on ye again."

I went back to my room, where I wandered about, without purpose, picking up things and laying them down again.

And then, as I gazed through the window, I saw Alex and Mrs. Duthie come round the corner of the building and proceed slowly down the drive. His figure looked bowed and crushed, his arm was still about his wife's shoulders, holding her closely and supporting her as she moved forward, blind and helpless with weeping.

Then everything boiled over inside me. I swung round and went down the corridor to the Sisters' sitting-room. As I had guessed, Sister Peek was there, alone. She was seated in a comfortable chair before a good fire, her eyes red, but her expression vaguely relieved, as though, having had "a good cry," she now felt that the worst was over. She had just finished her lunch, that early meal which she took before retiring, and on her plate I made out two chop-bones, picked clean.

A spasm of rage, of wild and senseless fury, choked me.

"You cheap, useless, callous slut! How dare you sit there, swilling and guzzling and warming yourself, after what you've done? Don't you understand that your selfish carelessness cost that poor kid his life? It's your fault, your cursed rotten fault that he's lying there, dead, at this minute."

The look on my face must have frightened her. She slid from the chair and retreated to the corner of the room. I followed her, caught her by the shoulders, and shook her till her teeth rattled.

"Call yourself a nurse. Hell and damnation, it's enough to make a cat laugh. If you stay on here, I'll see you get it in the neck. You ought to be hanged for what you've done. Think that over the next time you want to slink away from your patient for a cup of tea."

She did not attempt to answer. As she cringed there, limp and shaken, her green eyes glinted up at me.

I turned and went out. Although I didn't regret it, I was painfully aware that my outburst had been mistaken and stupid. But I didn't realize how stupid until later.

CHAPTER TEN

THREE weeks later, while we sat drinking our coffee after lunch, Miss Trudgeon, with a companionable air, produced a letter. That night of the tracheotomy had marked the end of our strife. She no longer put my back up, I was prepared to swear by her honesty and dependability. Indeed, I had almost begun to feel that she was, reluctantly, taking a liking to me.

"We'll be having our annual visit from the management committee this afternoon."

I studied the typewritten notice which she handed me.

"I'd better put on a clean collar in honour of the event."

"It might be advisable." Her small eyes twinkled. "There are only three members . . . Masters, Hone, and Gloag. But they're quite particular. They're earlier than usual this year."

"What's the procedure?"

"We feed them—that's half the battle—then take them round." She glanced at me wryly. "You don't have to worry. I'm the one who gets rapped on the knuckles."

I did not give much heed to the impending visitation. I was still oppressed and suffering from reaction, and only recently had begun to pick up the thread of my research. No word at all had come from Jean and two letters which I wrote her had been sent back, redirected in a strange hand. Vaguely, throughout the afternoon, I was conscious of an air of preparation, of sweepings and scurryings in the corridors, of a final polish being laid upon floors and walls already spotless. Also, in my room, a tantalus of spirits arrived upon the sideboard, while extra leaves were put in the table which was then ornamented with a centrepiece of flowers and set for a massive repast.

At half-past four, a closed car drove up to the front door and, after a few minutes of conversation and laughter in the hall, Matron appeared, all smiles, in her best uniform, bringing into the room the members of the committee.

"Dr. Shannon . . . this is Mr. Ben Masters . . . Mr. Hone . . . and Mr. Gloag."

She introduced me with a genial sparkle in her eye, almost coyly, as though we had never been anything but the best of friends and had always lived together in perfect harmony, then immediately proceeded to pour out for the newcomers large tumblers of whisky which, with an air of dignity and responsibility, they accepted as their due.

The leader of the party, Mr. Masters, was a tall, spare, rough-looking man of about fifty, with hard, weather-beaten features, deepset eyes, and the loud, harsh voice of one accustomed to shouting orders in the open air. He looked to me like a gang foreman and was, I afterwards discovered, a jobbing builder and contractor in the near-by town of Prenton. As he drank his whisky, listening without comment to the matron's stream of small talk, I felt him gazing at me speculatively over the rim of his glass.

Meanwhile, I had been buttonholed by the second member of the committee, Mr. Hone, a plump, natty figure with a waxed moustache, a tight blue suit, and spats. He seemed fussy and loquacious, yet his manner, though commercial, was agreeable.

"You know, Doctor," he confided in me, "nothing fits a man better than to serve his fellow creatures on a hospital committee. It takes time mind

you, and time's money these days, especially when you have your own business—I'm in the drapery and upholstery line myself—but look at the good
you accomplish. . . . Thank you, Matron, I don't mind if I do. The
labourer is worthy of his hire. Very fair whisky this, I wonder what it costs
us. . . . And the interest, Doctor, you've no idea the things I've learned
about medicine. Only the other day the wife showed me a rash on our
youngest—a bonny baby, though I say it as shouldn't—and when I told her
not to worry—it was only from the blood you understand—why Albert, she
says, I have to compliment you, even though you are my husband, you know
all the fevers, you're as good as a doctor any day! I'll leave this card with
you!" Producing a trade card from his top waistcoat pocket he pressed it
confidentially into my hand. "As you observe, I do a little undertaking
on the side. In case any bereaved relatives of your better-off patients should
require my assistance it's nice to be prepared. We do everything very dignified, Doctor. And reasonable."

So far, Mr. Gloag, the last member of the party, a small, sharp-eyed man
of middle age, had remained dumb; nevertheless, he had a way of cocking
his head towards the conversation as though determined to let nothing go
past him, and from time to time, as a sign of his agreement with his colleagues, he emitted a half-grudging exclamation of assent.

"Well, gentlemen," Miss Trudgeon remarked, in her most dulcet tones, "I
hope you've brought good appetites. Shall we sit in?"

Our guests showed little hesitation in accepting the invitation. They had
undoubtedly come prepared to do justice to this annual, free repast, and
although occasionally Mr. Masters, at the head of the table, threw out a
rough witticism, for most of the meal nothing was heard but the clink of
knives and forks, the steady grinding of jaws.

Yet, at last, despite Miss Trudgeon's hospitable pressings, the efforts of the
committee flagged and failed. After a pause, Mr. Masters pushed back his
chair and rose to his feet, dusting the crumbs from his waistcoat, with a
businesslike air.

"Now, Matron, if convenient we'd like to go round with you. And the
doctor."

His official manner set the general tone as they began their tour of
inspection, and I soon perceived, from the matron's air of tension and slightly
heightened colour, that this was rather more of a trial than she had been
prepared to admit to me.

In the administrative building the visiting members systematically viewed
the office, the laundry, and the kitchen, where Mr. Gloag, in particular,
showed a remarkable talent for prying into cupboards, sniffing in dark
corners, and lifting the lids of pots and pans, to sample the flavour of the
staff's supper.

Next our party passed to the wards, where, facing their main task, the
committee-men began a slow and almost royal progress. Determined to miss
nothing, Gloag went everywhere, even peering under the beds in his efforts

to find illicit dust. Once we lost him in the lavatory of Ward B, but he reappeared with an expression of defeat, having found everything in working order. Masters was equally thorough, interrogating the patients, inquiring of each in hoarse whispers, which could be heard all over the place, if there were any cause for complaints. Hone, meantime, made it his duty to sound out the members of the staff, especially the younger nurses, inquiring with unctuous familiarity into their health and habits. Once he paused and, pointing to a well-marked case of measles, remarked to me over his shoulder, in a stage whisper, with the air of a connoisseur:

"Beautiful rash, Doctor. Chicken pox, eh? I could tell it a mile away."

I did not contradict him. In fact I effaced myself as much as possible. This was obviously the matron's responsibility and, while I couldn't but sympathize with her, I had no wish to draw the enemy's fire upon myself.

Perhaps I was prejudiced, and the committee was carrying out its task from the highest motives, yet I couldn't suppress the thought that these three were uninformed and ill-mannered busybodies, each in his own way a small-town politician of the type which pushes forward in public affairs to secure some personal advantage and, invested with a petty authority, takes good care to exercise it to the full.

At last it was over; we emerged from the end ward into the crisp November air and, with a sense of relief, I was preparing to see our unwelcome guests depart, when suddenly, in a tone of purpose, Masters exclaimed:

"Now we'll take a look at Pavilion E."

For an instant I was puzzled and, indeed, a general air of surprise fell upon the party; then, with a start, I observed the direction of his gaze.

"You mean the old smallpox ward?" Matron asked in a doubtful tone.

"What else?" Masters replied testily. "It's part of the hospital buildings. I want to see it like the rest." He hesitated for a moment. "I'm thinking we might reconstruct it."

"Of course"—Matron spoke without moving—"it hasn't been used for some time."

"Yes, indeed," I broke in hastily. "It's quite derelict."

"We'll be the judge of that. Let's get a move on."

I allowed myself to be swept forward with the others, at a loss as to how this had been sprung upon me. From her ill-concealed surprise and annoyance, I was perfectly convinced that Matron had no hand in it. Masters was at the door now, turning the handle, thrusting with his shoulder against the panel. As this held fast, I took a completely wrong decision.

"It's probably nailed up. We'll never get in."

There was an odd sort of silence. Then Hone remarked softly:

"Don't you want us to get in, Doctor?"

Meanwhile Masters had struck a wax vesta and, bent down, was fiddling at the keyhole. In a tone of discovery he exclaimed:

"This is a new lock . . . a brand-new lock." He straightened himself. "What's going on here? Gloag, go and tell Pim to bring a crowbar."

I saw then that I had to face it. I did not wish Pim to be involved, and Matron was looking worried, so I fumbled in my inside pocket, and brought out the key.

"I can let you in." Making the best of a bad job, I unlocked the door and switched on the light.

With their instincts of detection fully aroused, all three of them pushed forward and stared in an outraged fashion at my equipment. After their hitherto fruitless excursion it was meat and drink to them to discover this iniquity.

"God damn it!" Masters exclaimed. "What's all this?"

I smiled at them propitiatingly.

"It's very simple, gentlemen. I am doing some research work, and as this pavilion was completely unoccupied I ventured to make use of it as my laboratory."

"Who gave you permission?"

In spite of my resolution to be meek, I reddened at Masters's tone.

"Was it necessary to have permission?"

Masters's brows drew down. He glared at me.

"Don't you realize that you are responsible to the committee for everything? You had no right whatsoever to take such a liberty."

"I don't understand your point of view. Am I taking a liberty in applying myself to scientific research?"

"Certainly you are. You're the doctor of this fever hospital, not a bloody experimenter."

Hone coughed gently behind his hand.

"May we inquire whose time you utilized for this so-called research of yours? I presoom you were doing it when you should have been in the wards, caring for our patients."

"I worked in my own time, at night, when my official duties were over."

"Your official duties are never over," Masters cut in rudely. "This is a whole-time job. We pay you to be on your toes twenty-four hours of the day, not to sneak off and shut yourself up with a lot of germs. What the hell have you been doing with them?"

Forgetting the wise example of the matron—that the only way to deal with a self-important official is to flatter and cajole him—I lost my temper.

"What the hell d'you think I've been doing? Keeping them as pets?"

Genuinely shocked, Hone interposed.

"Insolence won't help you, Doctor. Most improper. It's a nasty business this, a very nasty business. Who do you think pays for the electricity you burn, and the gas to light these burners? We represent the ratepayers of the district. You can't run a private business on public time and public money."

"We'll have to report the whole thing to the main committee," Masters declared. "I'll bring it up myself."

"Uh-huh," added Gloag.

I bit my lip impotently. The grain of truth in Hone's remarks made them even more unpalatable. Although I had never dreamed that it was necessary, I saw now that it would have been wiser for me, in the first instance, to have secured permission. I could only grind my teeth in silent rage, my misery enhanced by the odd glance of commiseration which Miss Trudgeon gave me, as I shut the door of that fatal pavilion and followed the others to the main building where, after a quick nip of spirits to fortify themselves against the cold, my three oppressors bundled into their coats and scarves and prepared to take their departure.

Their leave-taking of the matron was cordial, but they barely said good-bye to me, and that with the chilliest of glances.

Glumly, I wandered back to my room. My ill-luck was colossal; still, I couldn't believe that they would come down upon me severely. It wasn't a crime I had committed, and when, in calmer mood, they considered the matter, they must surely see the honesty of my motives. Resolved to leave nothing to chance, I went there and then to my desk and wrote them a full account of all that I was attempting in my research. I felt more confident when I had posted it.

That night, when I returned from my last round, I met Sister Peek in the corridor. She hadn't gone on duty—the night report book was clutched under her arm. Apparently she had been waiting for me. Whenever I appeared she took a quick breath.

"Good evening, Dr. Shannon. I hope you enjoyed yourself this afternoon."

"What do you say?" I asked her.

"I hope you liked the visit this afternoon."

Her voice was strangely shrill, indeed, the very fact that she should address me directly was, in itself, odd enough to arrest my attention. Lately she had kept out of my way, and when we did meet had passed me without raising her eyes. Peering at her in the dim corridor, I saw that she was crouching, almost, against the wall. Yet, for all her shrinking, she went on, with a gasp and a rush:

"It must have been nice for you when they walked into the isolation pavilion. And found out about your fine laboratory. I'm sure you enjoyed it thoroughly."

I kept watching her face. It surprised me how much she hated me.

"Oh, yes, indeed, my fine Dr. Shannon, I'm not the one that's going to be kicked out. So there! Perhaps that will teach you not to insult a lady. For in case you may not know it," she gulped with fearful triumph, "*the chairman of the committee, Mr. Masters, is my brother-in-law.*"

Before I could speak, as though afraid I might strike her, she swung round and scuttled off.

I stood quite still . . . long after she had gone.

Now everything was clear, the last thing in the world I had ever dreamed would happen. At one time I had feared that Matron might report me, but never, of all people, never Effie Peek. On her night duty she had seen me leave the pavilion and, after further spying, had informed on me to her worthy relative. It was a sweet revenge. When my first wild fury died, I felt sick and hopeless. How could one fight a thing like this? I had outraged her shrinking sensibilities beyond forgiveness. It wasn't ordinary vindictiveness or spite, but something more. She probably was the victim of a neurotic compulsion, she could not help herself. Yet I had no redress. And after this, I hadn't a spark of hope.

On the last day of the month I received an official communication from the committee of management, signed by Ben Masters, requesting my resignation from my position as medical officer at Dalnair Hospital. I read the letter with a stony face.

The staff were very sympathetic about it. Headed by the matron, they got up a subscription and at a little ceremony, after several agreeable speeches, presented me with a nice umbrella. Then, with an air of melancholy justification, Pim took me to the station in the aged ambulance. I was loose again in the world, faced with the prospect of conducting my experiments in the street. And for a start, as I walked blindly from the platform at Winton station, I left my new umbrella in the train and lost it.

BOOK THREE

CHAPTER ONE

AT THE Globe Commercial Hotel, in a mean street off the Trongate in the noisy heart of the city, I found a room, uncarpeted, fusty from unopened windows, the wallpaper discoloured, the wooden washstand charred by cigarette ends. I did not like the room, which seemed alien, defiled by the innumerable travellers who had occupied it. But it was cheap.

After a cup of tea in the greasy coffee-room downstairs, I set out for Parkside Crescent, on the far side of Winton. When I reached that quiet residential quarter I found, to my relief, that Professor Challis was at home and would see me.

He came almost at once into the dim, maroon-curtained, book-lined study, moving a little uncertainly, his thin, blue-veined hand shakily outstretched, and a grave welcome in his ash-grey eyes, which, though clear, were deep with age.

"This is an unexpected pleasure, Robert. You called some months ago. I was sorry to miss you."

Wilfred Challis was now over seventy, a frail little bowed figure, dressed in an out-of-fashion frock coat, tight black trousers, and button boots which gave to him an Old World appearance that was both touching and absurd. Because of failing health, he had retired from the University, being superseded by Professor Usher, and, outside of a limited circle of experts in France and Switzerland, where much of his best work had been done, his name was almost unknown. Yet he was a true scientist who, through the purity of his motives and the nobility of his mind, had without any material reward brought light to the darkness of the world. During my student days he had become my ideal and he had given me in many ways evidence of his regard. His aged face, with its high brow, its look of tranquil distinction, of warm humanity, was mild and serene.

He took an arm-chair beside me, followed by his old brown spaniel dog, Gulliver, which immediately lay down at his feet; then, giving me his close attention, he listened with deepening sympathy while I told him my story. After a brief pause he asked a few technical questions, then passed his long, sensitive fingers meditatively through his thin white hair.

"Interesting," he said. "Most interesting. Robert, I always felt that you would not disappoint me."

Unexpectedly, I felt my eyes fill up with tears.

"If only I could get a grant, sir," I pressed, earnestly. "Surely I'm entitled to it? I don't want to tie myself up with another job. You see how I've been hampered by lack of money."

"My dear boy . . ." He smiled gently. "A lifelong experience has taught

me that the hardest thing about scientific research is to get the money for
it."

"But surely, sir, that's what the Research Council is for . . . I'd only
need a lab and about a hundred pounds. If you approach them, you have
such influence."

He shook his head, with a faint, regretful smile.

"I am a back number now, an old fogey laid away upon the shelf. And
what you ask is difficult. But I assure you I will try. Not only to get the
grant but to help you in every way I can." He paused. "One day, Robert,
I should really like to find you a Continental appointment. Here, we are
still tied down by insular prejudice. In Paris or Stockholm you would have
a freer hand."

He would not let me thank him, but led me back with warm interest
to the subject of my research. While I talked, the dog, Gulliver, licked
his hand, the fire burned clear, from upstairs I could hear the cheerful
chatter of his grandchildren. I felt my heart expand towards this kindly
old man who, through his hatred of the pompous, still seemed young, and
from whom there emanated a sense of gentle humour. Half an hour later,
as I took my leave, he made a careful note of my address, and promised
he would get in touch with me soon.

Cheered and encouraged, I made my way back across the city. It was a
clear afternoon, with high luminous clouds, and the pavements of Manfield
Street, the main shopping thoroughfare, were thick with people taking advantage of the mildness of the weather to examine the bargains offered in
the spring sales. Near the General Post Office I crossed to the south side
of the street.

· Then, all at once, I started, my abstraction gone, my body suddenly
alive. Directly ahead of me, standing with her mother, holding a number
of parcels, and gazing into the window of one of the large department stores,
was Jean.

Although I had known she must return for her examination, now only
two weeks away, this unexpected sight of her caught me by the throat and
left me breathless. My heart began to beat like mad. I started towards her,
then held myself in check. Sheltered by the crowd, my pulse still thudding
in my ears, I watched her with straining eyes. She looked older, more mature,
and although no apparent sadness was discernible in her expression, her
interest in her mother's conversation, which related, no doubt, to a dark
coat displayed behind the plate glass, was no more than passive and obedient.
From time to time, indeed, her attention wandered, and she looked about
her with an air of pensive inquiry which sent a fresh pang through me. Why,
oh why, was she not alone?

Presently, with a wise shake of her head, Mrs. Law took Jean's arm and
the two women moved away from the window. I saw that they had finished
their shopping and were proceeding in the direction of Central Station to
go home. I followed them, like a thief, my heart burning with desire, long-

SHANNON'S WAY

ing to approach, yet debarred by a vision of the consternation which my appearance must produce.

Outside a little creamery Mrs. Law paused and looked at her watch. After a moment's consultation, they went inside and sat down at a small marble-topped table. From outside, torn by love and indecision, I watched them order and drink hot milk. When they stepped out I tracked them into the busy station. There, amongst the crowd, under the bookstall, which had so often been our meeting place, I was almost close enough to touch Jean. Why did she not turn and see me? I willed, desperately, with all my force, that she might do so. But no, arm in arm with her mother, she slowly passed the barrier, entered the waiting train, and was lost to view.

Immediately she was gone I blamed myself for my stupidity in bungling this opportunity, and hastening back to my shabby room, after restively pacing its narrow confines, I took a sheet of paper and my pen, sat down on the creaky bed. I wanted to release my long suppressed feelings in a flood of words, but the thought that the letter might be intercepted held me back. Finally, under cover of an envelope addressed to Luke, I sent this message:

> Dear Jean,
> I saw you today in Winton without having a chance to speak to you. I realize that you will soon be taking your examination again and have no wish to disturb you before or during that event. But when it is over I ask you to meet me without fail. I have missed you terribly and have so very much to say to you. Please reply to this address. Best of luck in the exam.
>
> Yours,
> ROBERT

For the next few days I watched the hotel mail-rack feverishly, waiting for an answer to this letter, my love for her reawakened and renewed. Surely she must reply? My longing to be with her was irresistible.

At the same time, since my funds were running so perilously low that I must soon reach a decision about the future, I was anxious to have word from Professor Challis. I did not wish to commit myself to another job for fear the grant from the Research Council materialized. But as I began to economize on food, to eat a single sausage roll for lunch, and, a little later, to miss my dinner altogether, I began to wish I had more strongly impressed the critical nature of circumstances upon my old Professor. Could it be that he had forgotten, that the main purpose of my visit had slipped from his failing memory? As a precaution I went to the Medical Employment Agency and left my name there, but in the process I had a disagreement with the clerk in charge, an exchange of words which did little to improve my prospects. My failure to hear from Challis, Jean's continued silence, the miserable conditions under which I was living, and, above all, the mounting sense of delay in the progress of my work began to prey upon me intolerably.

In desperation, I rummaged out a flask from the equipment which encumbered the floor space at the foot of my bed and began to try upon myself a series of skin reactions with heat-killed suspensions of the bacilli, scratching the surface of my arm and inoculating the abrasion with dilutions of attenuated cultures. To my joy, a series of typical ulcers developed, thus enabling me to study the important processes of dermal reaction. I watched these carefully and, since I could do no more, made notes and drawings as the condition spread.

In the intervals, I walked the streets endlessly and took to haunting the approaches to Winton Central, in an effort to catch sight of Jean, coming from the Blairhill train. Several times in the crowds I would glimpse some girl who so resembled her that my heart stopped beating. But as I hastened forward, eager and anxious, it was only to find myself gazing into the eyes of a total stranger.

One wet night while I vainly hung about the station, after a particularly wretched day, I felt a hand upon my shoulder.

"How are you, Robert?"

I swung round, a light of expectation leaping to my face. But it was Spence, buttoned up in a raincoat, the evening paper which he had just purchased tucked beneath his arm. I lowered my head quickly, glad, of course, to see him, yet confused that he should find me here, like this.

There was a pause. Neil never could make conversation but after an awkward moment he said, in his halting style:

"What are you doing in Winton? Taking a day off?"

I kept my eyes averted, afraid of his pity.

"Yes," I said. "I just got in from Dalnair."

He looked me over, in his sidelong apologetic way.

"Come on home and have dinner with us tonight."

I hesitated. I had nothing to look forward to but another wasted, dismal evening at the Globe, where, if I did not wish to listen to the noisy conversation of commercial travellers in the draughty lounge, I must shut myself in my room. I was damp, cold, and hungry. My head was ringing from a day in the streets, my arm kept throbbing painfully. I had not had a decent meal for a week, in fact for twenty-four hours I had eaten practically nothing. I felt faint and ill. It was a severe temptation.

"That's settled," he said, before I could refuse.

We took the bus, which ran to Mount Pleasant, the outlying district where, ever since their marriage, Spence and his wife had rented a small half-timbered house, one of many standing in a row in a modest suburban drive. During the journey we did not talk. Pretending to read his paper, Spence left me alone, but once or twice I felt his eye upon me and, as we got off and approached his home, he said, as though to put me at my ease:

"Muriel will be so glad you've come."

The house, although not spacious, was brightly lit and warm. When we entered, the change from the outer chill gave me an absurd giddy spell, so that I had to steady myself against the wall. Before he removed his things, Spence took me through the lobby to his study and, having seated me before the fire, insisted on giving me a glass of sherry and a biscuit. There was a look of concern upon his honest face which made me feel most uncomfortable.

"You're sure you're all right?"

I forced a laugh.

"Why shouldn't I be?"

For a moment or two he pottered about, pretending not to watch me, then he left, with the remark:

"Make yourself at home . . . Muriel will be down presently."

I lay back and closed my eyes, still feeling weak, and fighting an inane desire to break down because of the kindness Spence had shown me. Presently, I relaxed a little; the sherry had revived me and the comfortable chair almost made me doze off. Ten minutes later I roused myself with a start to find Mrs. Spence standing in the doorway.

"Don't get up." She made a gesture of restraint as she came in.

In spite of Neil's assurance and her own polite smile, she did not seem particularly pleased to see me. She was as attractive as ever, even more so, I thought, wearing a pink, young-looking dress, cut low round the neck, with a tight-fitting bodice covered with sequins. Her hair had been freshly set and there were reddish lights in it which I had not noticed before. She had on a good deal of make-up, and the heavy lipstick gave her thin lips an artificial warmth.

"I hope I'm not putting you about," I said, awkwardly.

"Oh, no." She shook her head, lighting a cigarette with little affected movements. "Mr. Lomax was coming, anyway. It will be quite like old times for you three to get together."

A silence fell between us which was growing difficult when Spence appeared, washed and changed. He had put on a black tie and a dinner jacket.

"I apologize for these glad rags, Shannon." He smiled placatingly towards his wife. "Muriel insists."

"We don't entertain much," Mrs. Spence said sharply. "At least let us do it like gentlepeople."

Spence flushed slightly, but he busied himself filling up the decanters, and did not say anything. Muriel, with one eye upon the clock, was occupying herself in rearranging, with a slight frown of dissatisfaction, the row of miniature ivory elephants which stood upon the mantelpiece.

"Shall I help you, dear?" said Spence. "These things never stand up." She shook her head. "I wish we had some decent ornaments."

Somehow it hurt me to see Spence so solicitous, so overanxious to please his wife—I also observed that he had poured himself a second whisky, and much more of it than usual.

Towards eight o'clock, when dinner had been ready for half an hour, there was the sound of a taxi and Lomax arrived, full of apologies for his lateness. He was charming, easy and composed, delighted, he said, to see me again, his clothes and his manners both quite perfect.

In the dining-room the table was covered by a lace-edged cloth and lit by green wax candles with frilled paper shades. Previously, when I had visited Spence, there was usually a plain and simple meal, but now the dinner was pretentious with lots of courses and nothing much to eat. I did not mind, for although, an hour before, I was ravenously hungry, now my stomach had turned against food and I had no appetite at all. The parlourmaid who waited, drilled by her mistress as to the usages of "the best people," stood at attention by the door, in the intervals of serving, breathing through her mouth and staring at us while we ate. Spence spoke very little, but Muriel chattered all the time, mostly to Lomax, in a gay and vivacious style, knowingly discussing items of society news, picked up, no doubt, from the fashion journals she so eagerly perused, and covering up the delays in the service with an exaggeration of her best social manner which set my teeth on edge.

At last it ended, the rattle of crockery in the kitchen ceased, the waitress disappeared, and Mrs. Spence addressed us prettily.

"You three may go and smoke your pipes in the study. Join me in the drawing-room in half an hour." At the door she detained Lomax with her little laugh. "First you must help me blow out the candles."

Spence and I moved into the study where, silently, he stirred up the fire, poured out some whisky, and passed me a cigarette. He looked on the mantelpiece, then felt in his pockets.

"Have you a match, Robert?"

"I'll get some," I said.

I returned to the hall and there, through the open door of the dining-room, I saw Lomax and Mrs. Spence. Encircled by his arms, she was standing close to him, her hands resting intimately on his shoulders, looking up adoringly into his eyes. It was not her attitude alone but the expression of complete infatuation upon her face which stunned me. I stood for an instant, then, as their lips met, I turned away, found a box of matches in my coat pocket, and went back to the study.

Spence was crouched forward in his chair, staring into the fire. He lit his pipe slowly.

"These evenings cheer Muriel up," he said without looking at me. "I think Lomax does her good."

"Of course," I agreed.

"I sometimes wish I weren't such a dull sort of chap, Robert. I try to be bright, but I can't. I've no small talk at all."

"Thank God for that, Neil."

He threw me a grateful glance.

A moment later Lomax joined us. A brief silence followed his appearance but it did not disconcert him; nothing seemed ever to leave Adrian Lomax at a loss. Taking a cigarette from his case, he occupied the hearthrug, began to describe his conversation with the taxi-driver who had brought him out. He was graceful and amusing, and before long Spence, who had at first gazed at him with brooding eyes, was listening with a smile. But I could not smile. I was not squeamish, and I had half suspected Lomax all along, yet even so, I felt within me a sort of burning nausea. If it had been anyone but Spence . . . I kept thinking.

I could not restrain myself. While Lomax went on talking I got up, left the study with a muttered excuse, and crossed the hall to the drawing-room.

Mrs. Spence was standing by the fireplace, one foot upon the brass fender, her elbow upon the mantelpiece, gazing with an absent smile at her reflection in the mirror. She seemed restless, pleased with herself, yet filled with a flickering disquiet. As I came in and closed the door behind me she spun round quickly.

"Oh, it's you. Where are the others?"

"In the study."

She must have guessed from my tone that something was wrong. With a sudden lift of her eyelashes she sped a swift glance at me.

"Mrs. Spence," I said at last in a stony voice, "I saw you and Lomax a few minutes ago."

She paled slightly, then coloured deeply and angrily.

"So you spied on us."

"No. I saw you quite by accident."

Speechless, she struggled for words, her cheeks aflame with vexation. I went on:

"Your husband is my best friend. And the best fellow in the world. I can't compel you in any way. But I beg of you to think of him."

"Think of him!" she exclaimed. "Why doesn't someone think of me for a change?" She choked, overcome by a sudden uprush of passionate resentment. "Have you any idea what I've gone through in these last five years?"

"You were happy enough till Lomax came along."

"That's all you know. I was miserable."

"Why did you marry Neil?"

"Because I was a perfect fool, carried away by sentiment, pity, and popular approval. . . . Such a nice girl, doing a fine thing, so wonderfully noble." Her lip drew back. "I didn't realize what I was letting myself in for. Oh, it was all right at first, during the war. There was lots of excitement then. The bands were playing and the flags flying. They even stood up and applauded him when we went to the theatre. But that's all over and forgotten now. He isn't a hero any more. He's a freak. People stare at him in the street. The boys shout after him. Can you imagine my feelings? Only the other day we were in a restaurant and a group at the next table started laughing at him behind his back, till I could have sunk through the floor."

I gazed at her stiffly, frozen by the cheapness of her mind, but I did not give up.

"People can be horribly unkind. You don't have to go out. You have a nice home."

"A poky little house in the suburbs," she flung back scornfully. "That's not what I was brought up to. I'm bored, yes, bored to death. Sitting here night after night, I could scream. When I was engaged to him we planned he would be a consultant. Can you see him in a fashionable practice now, with that bedside appearance? Once he was called in to a little girl down the street and when he bent over the cot the child nearly had a fit. He'll never be anything but a laboratory hack."

"That should make you very gentle with him."

"Oh, shut up!" She threw the words at me. "You half-baked idealists are all the same. I've given him enough. I'm tired of making jellies and soups for him. I can't go on wasting the best years of my life."

"He loves you," I said. "That's worth something to both of you. Don't throw it away."

Her eyes met mine, fiercely, like a blow. I expected an outburst. Instead, she turned away and gazed into the fireplace. The slow ticking of the clock sounded in the room like the heartbeats of a mechanical doll. When she faced me again her expression was calm, her gaze open and beguiling.

"Now listen, Robert. You're making a great fuss about nothing. It's only a flirtation really, between Adrian and me. I swear to you there's no harm in it."

She came forward and laid her hand lightly on my sleeve.

"Life is rather dull in this hateful suburb. One does deserve a little cheering-up sometimes. Every woman likes to be flattered and made up to . . . to feel she has some fascination. That's all there is to it. You won't tell Neil?"

I shook my head, looking at her fixedly, wondering if she spoke anything like the truth.

"I do make it up to him. I am nice to him really." She smiled, persuasively, still stroking my sleeve. "Promise you won't say a word?"

"No," I said. "I won't tell him. I'm going now. Good night, Mrs. Spence."

In the study, on the pretext that I must take the ten o'clock train for Dalnair, I announced that I must leave, and said good night to Lomax. Spence came with me to the door, rather put out at my abrupt departure. In the porch he slipped an arm round my shoulders.

"I wish you wouldn't rush off, Robert." His dark eyes rested on mine. "In fact . . . I was going to ask you to stay here for a few days . . . if things were difficult for you."

"Difficult?" I echoed.

He glanced away.

"I rang Dalnair last week. They told me you had gone." He groped for words which seemed to come from deep down in his unselfish heart. "You

see, I'd love to help . . . I'm so well off here . . . I don't like to think of
you knocking around, on the loose."

"Thanks, Spence, thanks. I'm quite all right." My feelings overpowered me,
I could not go on. I wrung his hand and ran down the steps into the wet
darkness of the night.

I walked all the way back to the city in an effort to pull myself together.
My arm felt hot and swollen but that ache was less than the pain that
burned in my breast. A sense of the cruelty of life overwhelmed me.

It was eleven o'clock when I reached the Globe and as I entered the chilly
lobby I saw a letter for me in the rack. I took it hurriedly.

> My dear Shannon,
>   I am sorry to report that despite my strongest representations,
> the Research Council has refused to make a grant towards your work.
> This I am afraid is final. I shall, however, continue to bear your
> needs in mind. If in the meantime you should require a room for
> your equipment I have arranged that you may have this at the
> old Apothecaries Hall in St. Andrew's Lane. Do not be discouraged.
>   Very sincerely yours,
>   WILFRED CHALLIS

I could not read any more, I simply could not see the words. I had to
clench my teeth, to keep the tears from rolling from my eyes.

CHAPTER TWO

NEXT morning, like an unskilled boxer who, although knocked down, must
struggle to his feet, I went, but without much hope, to the Apothecaries
Hall. This was a rambling old building, situated near the Wellgate, a branch
of the Pharmaceutical College, where students for the Licenciate of the
Society of Apothecaries took their classes. It was in every sense inferior to
the University.

The janitor had been notified of my coming, and when I gave him my
name he conducted me to a room on the ground floor, a long low room,
rather dark, with a table, a leather couch, an agate balance in a glass case,
a rack of test tubes and two small shelves of simple chemical reagents. It
was, in fact, the sort of room I had feared that I might find, a room suited
to a student in pharmacy, and as I surveyed its limitations I asked myself if
I should ever, under high heaven, secure the proper background for my
work. Here, by constant improvising, by straining every nerve, one might push
ahead. But alone, without money or adequate assistance, that progress would
be slow.

Outside, I gave the janitor a shilling and asked him to call at the Globe
with a hand-barrow and bring over my apparatus. At least I should have
free storage for my things. This, since I did not know how long I should

be able to remain at the hotel, would be some advantage. Whether I should make the effort to carry on here I could not at this moment decide. In my heart, as I came through the ivy-covered archway of the Hall, I was conscious of a slight rankling towards Professor Challis. Yet I could not believe that he would willingly fail me.

On the way back to the hotel, struggling with these thoughts, I went by the Trongate Cross. This was a noisy, congested triangle in the poor section of the city, formed by the intersection of three narrow, busy streets, and hemmed in by cheap shops and tall tenements. All the traffic from the docks flowed through it, a steady stream of drays and lorries, mingling and intermingling with the trams and buses from Old High Street.

I was about to turn the corner into Trongate proper when, suddenly, through my preoccupation, there flashed that strange premonition occasioned by disaster. Amongst the crowd on the opposite pavement a schoolgirl of about fourteen, her satchel under her arm, had been standing with a companion, waiting for an opportunity to cross the street. Now, thinking the intersection clear, with a laughing good-bye to her friend, she stepped off the kerb. At that instant a motor waggon swung out of Old High Street at unexpected speed. The child saw it and ran forward. It seemed that she would escape. But in the same second a heavy lorry lumbered up from the other direction. The space between the two vehicles drew in. She halted dizzily, saw that she was trapped, made an awkward effort to turn back, then slipped full length on the wet asphalt. Her satchel shot across the street, spilling her school-books at my feet. There was a screech of brakes, a shrill scream of terror, and with a grinding noise the wheel of the lorry, weighted with pig-iron from the docks, passed over her body.

A cry of horror arose, there was a general rush forward, and immediately a crowd surrounded the victim. I could not help myself. Although my whole instinct was to shun the public exhibition of my profession, I thrust through the milling throng and knelt beside the injured girl. Beneath the mud which soiled her face she was deathly pale, inert, and moaning feebly. A policeman was supporting her head in the crook of his arm, hampered by well-meaning persons, pressing close and offering advice.

"Get her in somewhere," I said. "I'm a doctor."

His red, resentful face cleared at once. Willing hands passed down a plank from the stationary truck. Amidst more shouting and confusion she was placed on this impromptu stretcher, carried to the back premises of a small surgery, set amongst the shops across the way, and laid upon a couch. A score of curious individuals poured in after us. Immediately the policeman telephoned for an ambulance. But as he joined me at the couch, he said:

"It'll take a good ten minutes in this traffic."

"Please move these people out of here," I told him.

While he cleared the shabby consulting-room I bent down and opened the child's stained and torn blouse. Her rent undervest fell away, exposing her

flat little chest. It was the left shoulder, I saw, an impacted compound
fracture of the humerus. Her broken left arm hung deformed and limp,
but worse than that was the large bluish swelling, growing steadily larger, in
the left axilla. With my fingers on her wrist I threw a quick glance of
anxiety at her face, completely blanched now, the eyes fixed and slightly
upturned.

The police officer was beside me again. We were joined by the surgery
dispenser, an elderly man in a short white jacket.

"Whose place is this?" I asked him.

"Dr. Mathers's. It's unlucky he's not here."

"She don't look too well," the officer said in a low voice.

With my gaze upon that pulsing swelling I was thinking rapidly. The
brachial artery was undoubtedly ruptured, too high up to apply a tourni-
quet, and the bleeding was so profuse it might easily prove fatal before
the ambulance arrived.

I could not hesitate. Without a word to the others I dragged the couch to
the window, went to the small enamel instrument cabinet in the corner,
took out a scalpel, Spencer forceps, and a glass container of catgut sutures.
The ether bottle was on the bottom shelf. I poured some on a pad of
gauze, placed this upon the child's nostrils. She whimpered faintly, then
lay still.

No time for routine antisepsis. I dashed some iodine over my hands,
swabbed the swollen armpit with the same pungent fluid. The other two
were watching me with staring eyes. Framed in the doorway was a group
of silent spectators. Ignoring them, I took the knife and cut into the puffy
arm.

Immediately a great clot of blood welled out. Through it I saw the ragged spurting gap in the torn artery. Instantly I clamped the forceps on it.
Then, deliberately, almost at my leisure, I ligatured the vessel. It was very
easy, all over in five minutes. Removing the ether mask, I unclipped the
forceps, lightly packed the wound, and applied a bandage, reverse spica, to
make it extra neat. Already the pulse was stronger, the breathing deeper and
more regular. I took the coarse grey blanket from the foot of the couch and
wrapped it tight about her skinny form. They might give her a transfusion
at the hospital, perhaps an intravenous saline, but the real emergency was
over.

"She'll do now," I said briefly.

The policeman gave a gratified sigh and from the doorway there came
a murmur of approval. But, as I turned, I became aware of a short, stocky,
vigorous man, with a fiery complexion and a shock of frizzy hair, staring at
me with unfriendly eyes.

This jarring personality annoyed me.

"I thought I said to clear the room."

"All right, then," he said brusquely. "Push off."

"You push off," I answered with some heat.

"Why should I? It's my surgery."

I realized that I was in the presence of Dr. Mathers.

At this point the ambulance arrived, a diversion which caused considerable commotion. When at last the little patient had been made completely comfortable and carefully removed, the police officer closed his note-book, shook my hand solemnly, and took his leave. The dispenser went into the front premises, the remnants of the crowd dissolved, the traffic resumed its roar. Dr. Mathers and I were alone.

"You have a nerve," he resumed. "Walking into my office. Messing it up with blood. And I don't even get a fee for it."

I rolled down my sleeves and put on my jacket.

"When I'm in funds I'll send you a cheque for ten guineas."

He bit his thumbnail for a moment, as though chewing upon my remark. All his nails were bitten close.

"What's your name?"

"Shannon."

"I suppose you're some sort of doctor."

I glanced at his framed diploma, hung on the wall behind him. It was the certificate of the Conjoint Board, the lowest possible qualification with which a man was entitled to practice.

"Yes," I said. "Are you?"

He reddened slightly and, with an air of uncovering a fraud, turned abruptly to his desk and picked up the *Medical Directory*. Slashing through the pages with the energy which characterized all his movements, he quickly found my name.

"Shannon," he said. "Robert Shannon. We'll soon see." But as he read the list of my qualifications and the prizes which I had taken, his face fell. He closed the book, sat down on the Rexine-covered revolving chair, tilted back on his head the bowler hat which he still wore, and fell to studying me in a new manner.

"You've heard of me," he said, at length.

"Never."

"You must have. James Mathers. I've the biggest practice in the city. Three thousand on the panel. The maximum. All the other doctors hate me. I cut the feet from under them. I'm very popular with the people."

Still watching me, he rolled a cigarette, expertly, with his left hand, and stuck it, drooping, in his mouth. His cockiness was amazing. He was dressed in a loud professional style, with broad striped trousers, short black jacket, winged collar, and a stock with a diamond pin in it. But his chin was blue; he needed a shave.

"So you're out of a job?" he asked, suddenly. "What is it . . . booze or women?"

"Both," I said. "I'm also a morphine addict."

He did not answer—then with a brisk movement sat up.

"How would you like to work for me? Three nights a week. Surgery and late calls. I need time off. The practice is killing me."

Surprised, I reflected for a minute.

"What would you pay?"

"Three guineas a week."

I considered again. It was quite a generous offer which would keep me at the Globe, and save me the humiliation of lining up at the Medical Agency. I'd have time for my research too, if only I could get things going at Apothecaries Hall.

"All right."

"It's a deal then. Be here tonight, six o'clock sharp. I warn you I've had assistants before. None of them were any damn good. They went out on their ear."

"Thank you for the hint."

I was on my way to the door when, with a grim smile, he called me back.

"Here. You look as though you needed something in advance."

From his hip pocket he took an overstuffed leather purse and, carefully selecting the money, pushed across to me three shillings and three pound notes.

I had learned a little sense. Without a word, I picked up the money as carefully as he had put it down.

CHAPTER THREE

THAT same evening, at six, and thereafter on three nights of the week, I attended at the surgery in Trongate Cross. When I arrived the waiting-room was always packed to the door with patients—women in shawls, ragged children, workmen from the docks—and the hectic session which followed often ran on until eleven o'clock at night, after which there were usually one or two urgent calls which Thompson, the dispenser, gave me as he finally closed up. It was hard work. Dr. Mathers had been guilty of no exaggeration when he spoke of his enormous practice. I soon found that he had an extraordinary reputation amongst the poor people who inhabited this slum district.

His fiery personality alone gave him great prestige and his methods were abrupt, forceful, and dramatic. He had an instinct for diagnosis and did not hesitate to give his opinion, usually in the broad vernacular. He never spared himself, worked like a galley slave, and bullied his people a good deal. They liked him for it. His prescriptions were drastic. He used the maximum dose of every drug and a patient who had been severely purged or violently sweated would remark with a knowing shake of his head: "Ay, there's something *in* the wee doctor's medicine."

Mathers was sensitive about his diminutive stature, yet he had all the vanity of the small man, and thoroughly enjoyed his success. He loved to feel that he could triumph where the neighbouring doctors failed and would chuckle over a case where he had "wiped the eye" of one of his colleagues. But most of all he delighted in the fact that from this drab little surgery, in a poor-class district, with no more than a Conjoint diploma, he was able to reside in style in a large villa in the suburbs, to run a Sunbeam car, educate his only daughter handsomely, present his wife with a fine fur coat, in short, to live, as he put it, like a lord. His money sense was extremely strong. Although he charged only small fees, from a shilling to half a crown, he was insistent upon payment in cash.

"Once they know they can get you for nothing, Doctor," he warned me, "you're done."

In a drawer of his desk he kept a long chamois bag which had once contained midwifery forceps and into which all the fees were poured. Towards the end of the surgery hours it was bulging with cash. Upon my first night, as the surgery concluded, Dr. Mathers walked in unexpectedly, took up the bag and weighed it expertly. He glanced at me but said nothing. Although he tried not to show it, I could see that he was satisfied.

At the beginning of the second week, when I arrived on Monday evening to begin my consultations, I put my hand in my pocket and brought out a pound note.

"This is yours." As he looked at me sharply, I went on, "The child that was run over is getting on famously. Her father came in last Friday and insisted on paying this fee. He's a decent fellow and very grateful."

Mathers's expression was extremely queer. He rolled a cigarette and bit away the loose threads, which he spat on the floor.

"Keep it," he said at last.

I refused irritably.

"You pay me a salary. Everything I earn is yours."

There was a pause. He walked to the window and came back, having forgotten to light his cigarette.

"Shall I tell you something, Shannon?" he said slowly. "You're the first straight assistant I've ever had. Let's take the quid and send the kid a bunch of black grapes and some flowers."

That was the strange thing about this little man—he loved money, but he was not mean, and could spend freely upon himself and others.

After this incident Dr. Mathers's attitude was much more cordial. Indeed he became quite intimate, proudly showing me snapshots of his wife and of his seventeen-year-old daughter Ada, now finishing her schooling at the exclusive, and expensive, Convent of the Sacred Heart in Grantley. He also exhibited a photograph of his grandiose villa with the big car standing at the door and threw out hints that he would soon invite me there. From time to time he gave me advice as to how to run a practice, and one day, in an expansive mood, confessed that he was actually making three thousand pounds a year. Intensely curious as to how I spent the rest of my time, he often tried to exact some information from me, but I maintained always a

discreet reserve. Although I disliked the work my spirits were high, for I had
an odd premonition that my luck had turned at last. And so, indeed, it
seemed.

On Thursday of that week, as I returned late in the afternoon to the Globe,
I made out in the gathering dusk, across the street, a man's figure which
seemed familiar. As I appeared, he stirred from his attitude of patient waiting, and slowly approached me. Remembering the circumstances under
which we had parted, my heart came into my mouth as I recognized Alex
Duthie.

A long silence succeeded our meeting and, to my surprise, I perceived that
his hesitation and emotion were greater than my own. At last, in a low voice,
he said:

"I'd like a word with you, Robert. Can we go inside?"

I took him through the swing doors and up to my room where, having
deposited upon the floor the box which he carried beneath his arm, he sat
down on the edge of a chair. Twisting his round stiff cap in his capable
hands, he fixed his troubled, candid gaze upon me.

"Rob . . . I've come here to beg your pardon."

It cost him an effort to get out these words, but when he had done so
he drew an easier breath.

"Last week we were out to Dalnair. We had gathered all of Sim's toys
out of the attic and the wife took the notion to leave them at the hospital
for the children. When we were there we had a long talk with the matron.
In confidence, she told us everything. I'm sorry I blamed you, Robert. I
could cut my tongue out now."

I scarcely knew what to say. Gratitude of any sort embarrassed me beyond
belief. At the same time, the break in my friendship with Duthie had
worried me, and it was a relief to find myself no longer misunderstood.
Without speaking, I held out my hand. He gripped it like a vice, and a slow
grave smile spread over his ruddy face.

"We're all right again then, lad."

"Of course, Alex."

"You'll come fishing with me in the autumn?"

"If you feel like it."

"I'll feel like it," he answered slowly. "One gets over things in time, you
know, Rob."

There was a short pause. He rubbed his hands together and with an air
of inquiry glanced round the room.

"You're still on with your research?"

"Yes."

"That's good. You remember the milk samples you wanted? I've fetched
them along to you today."

I sat up, electrified.

"You've had another cattle outbreak?"

He nodded.

"Severe?"

"Quite bad, Rob. Five of our heifers dropped their calves and died in spite of all we could do for them."

"And you saved me milk samples?" I was tense with excitement.

"From all of them. In sterile containers." He inclined his head towards the package he had put down. "In that zinc-lined box."

I gazed at him with overflowing gratitude. So much had gone against me I could scarcely believe this splendid stroke of fortune.

"Alex," I exulted, "you've no idea how much this means to me. Exactly what I wanted . . ."

"It's not so one-sided," he answered, seriously. "I tell you straight, Rob, this business has got us badly worried at the Farms. All the best herds seem to have it. The manager says if you can help us in any way he'll surely appreciate it."

"I'll try, Alex, I promise you I'll try." For a moment I could not continue. "If there was anything needed to make up . . . you couldn't have chosen a better way . . ."

"If you're pleased, then I'm pleased too." He inspected his big silver watch. "Now it's time I was moving."

"Stay a bit longer," I pressed him. "Let me get you a drink."

I would gladly have given him all I possessed.

"No, lad . . . I have to catch that old six-fifteen bus." He gave me his slow, quiet smile. "I waited outside here for over an hour before you showed up."

I went downstairs with him and sent him on his way with my warmest thanks. Having watched his solid figure disappear in the darkness, I came back into the hotel filled with an eager happiness.

I was about to bound upstairs towards the Dreem Farms box when, in the hall rack, I saw a letter for me. The handwriting was unmistakable, it was from Jean. Breathless, clutching the letter, I made my way upstairs, shut the door and, with trembling fingers, tore open the envelope.

Dear Robert,

Luke has been away at Tynecastle for the past three weeks. Because of this I did not receive your letter until this afternoon and now I scarcely know how to reply. If I am to be truthful I cannot deny that it made me happy to hear from you and that I have missed you greatly. Perhaps I am wrong to tell you this. Perhaps I ought not to write this letter at all. But I have some news, and shall make that my excuse.

For these last few days I have been taking the examination again and, although I made some mistakes, I am so glad to tell you that I did not too badly. Professor Kennerly, for a wonder, was quite nice. And yesterday when I had my final oral he took me aside and

informed me that I had passed with distinction, in all subjects.
A fluke, of course, but what a relief!

The graduation won't be till the end of term, July 31, until then
I intend taking a course in Tropical Medicine, which starts next
week at the Sanderson Institute. The lecture is at 9 o'clock every
morning and lasts one hour.

Yours,
JEAN LAW

Passed . . . passed with distinction . . . and missing me . . . missing me
greatly. My eyes glistened towards the words, which after those weary months
of sadness and frustration came like a divine balm to my lonely heart. My
wretched bedroom was transformed. I wanted to leap, to laugh, to sing.
Again and again I read those lines which, because she had written them,
seemed invested with a unique and tender beauty. There was a hidden note
of longing in the letter which raised me to a kind of ecstasy which gave me,
suddenly, an idea, a plan of future action that sent the blood rushing to
my head, in a shiver of delight. I took the sheet of note-paper which, so
recently, she had touched, and pressed it to my lips.

CHAPTER FOUR

THE Sanderson Institute stood on the far side of the river, in an almost forgotten part of the city, between the Pensioners' Hospice and the ancient
St. Enoch's Church. It was a quiet district and the gardens in St. Enoch's
Square gave to it a country look. Rain had fallen the night before, a soft
spring rain, and as I made my way along the flagged pavement of Old George
Street there was a smell of sap and young grass in the air. A warm breeze
came from the river and swung the buds of the tall elm trees where the
sparrows were chirping. All at once the cold grip of winter seemed to have
relaxed and the moist earth, opening to the sunshine, gave forth a heady
sweetness that filled me with longing, with an ineffable yearning, that was
like a pain.

Outside the Hospice an old flower woman had her stand. On an impulse
I stopped and bought a sixpenny bunch of the snowdrops which hung over
the edge of her basket. Too shy to carry them openly, I wrapped the fragile
blossoms in my handkerchief and placed them in my pocket. As I hurried
into the courtyard of the Institute and took up my position outside the
lecture-room, the old clock of St. Enoch's, as though intoxicated by the balmy
air, struck ten merry strokes.

A few minutes later the Institute lecture-room began to empty itself.
There were not more than half a dozen students. Last of all, emerging with
an absent air, alone, came Jean. She was in grey, which always suited her so
well, the lines of her slight thin figure outlined as the fresh wind moulded

the stuff of her dress about her. Her lips were slightly parted. Her hands, in their worn gloves, clasped a note-book. Her soft brown eyes were downcast.

Suddenly she looked up, our glances met, and going forward, I took both her hands in mine.

"Jean . . . at last."

"Robert."

She had spoken my name haltingly, as though struggling, with confusion, against a pang of conscience. But now her face was filled with light, a bright warmth flooded her cheeks. I wanted to hold her tightly in my arms. But no, I dared not. Words came huskily.

"It's so wonderful to see you again."

For a moment, gazing into each other's eyes in a kind of rapt intoxication, neither of us could speak. Behind us in the elms the sparrows twittered and, down the river, a dog was barking, far away. At last, still breathless, I exclaimed:

"And you're through . . . with distinction . . . I congratulate you."

"It's nothing." She smiled.

"It's splendid. You'd have done it before, but for my pernicious influence."

She laughed shyly. We both laughed. I was still holding her hands as though I would never let them go.

"You've left Dalnair?" she asked.

"Yes," I answered gaily. "I got kicked out. You see what a rotter I am. Now I'm part-time assistant to a slum doctor in the Trongate."

"But your research?" She spoke quickly.

"Ah," I said. "It's about that I want to talk to you."

I led her across the road to the Square Gardens. We sat down on a green bench which encircled the trunk of a gnarled tree. Pigeons fluttered and strutted before us, giddy as the other birds with the delicious surge of spring. No one was in sight but an old pensioner, hobbling down a path, in his black peaked cap and bright scarlet coat. I took from my pocket the bunch of snowdrops and gave them to her.

"Oh!" she cried, with delight, then paused, afraid that her words or look might say too much.

"Wear them, Jean," I said, in a low voice. "It isn't a crime. Tell me, did they make you promise not to see me?"

There was a sudden pause.

"No," she said slowly. "If I had I couldn't very well be here."

I watched while, with a slightly saddened expression, she deeply inhaled the delicate perfume, then pinned to her bodice, below the soft little necklet of camphory fur around her neck, these white and fragile flowers which so miraculously suited her. Seated close beside her, I felt a glow run through my limbs, my cheeks and forehead were hot. I knew that if I did not quickly broach the subject on my mind, this terrible emotion would conquer me.

"Jean," I said, striving to take a grip upon myself. "Apart from your lecture, your days are free now . . . I mean, after ten o'clock you have nothing much to occupy you?"

"Yes." There was a note of inquiry in her eyes and, as I did not speak, she added: "Why?"

"I need your help," I answered firmly and sincerely, aware that I spoke the truth. Gazing at her steadily I went on. "I'm half-way through my investigation, ready to begin the next step and I'm quite wildly excited about it. You know the difficulty I've had, going on by myself . . . Oh, I'm not complaining, but now for this new phase I must have some assistance. There are tests which I can't possibly manage single-handed. Professor Challis has given me a room." I paused. "Would you . . . will you work with me?"

She had flushed slightly and now, for a moment, she looked at me eagerly, then slowly she lowered her eyes. There was a silence.

"Oh, Robert, I wish I could. But I can't. Surely you know how it is with me now. My parents . . . I owe so much to them . . . they've built everything on me . . . I love them . . . Mother especially . . . she's the best in the whole world. And they . . . while they haven't exactly forced me"—she seemed to seek for words to temper the blow—"they don't want me to see you. Even at this moment . . . I'm disobeying them."

I bit my lip. For all her softness there was something irreconcilable about her, a strong fidelity, loyalties that were not mine, a sense of duty which gave her a horror of dissimulation.

"They must hate me pretty thoroughly."

"No, Robert. They simply understand that our ways must be apart."

"It isn't as if this were a personal matter," I burst out. "You're a doctor now and it's for science."

"I'd love to do it. I'm so interested. But it isn't possible."

"It's entirely possible," I insisted. "No one need know. Your people would merely think you were doing some practical work in tropical medicine . . ."

She silenced me with a strained glance.

"It isn't that I'm afraid of, Robert."

"What then?"

"We'd be together."

"Is that so terrible?"

She raised her dark lashes, and gazed at me mournfully.

"I know I'm to blame . . . I didn't realize at first that our feeling for each other was . . . so deep. And if we go on it will get deeper. That will only make it worse for us in the end."

This simple declaration brought back warmth to my heart. I took a quick breath, resolved, at all costs, to persuade her.

"Listen, Jean. If I promise, swear to you that I'll never once make love to you, never even mention the word, will you assist me? I need help so badly. If I don't get it, I'm done."

A long, still pause. She gazed at me doubtfully, her colour coming and going, lost in a trance of uncertainty. And quickly I pressed home my advantage.

"It's such a wonderful chance. I'm on the verge of something tremendous. Come and see for yourself."

Carried away, I jumped up and held out my hand. After a moment she got slowly to her feet.

It was not a long walk to Apothecaries Hall. We were there in ten minutes. I led her directly to my work-room and there, taking from my small incubator one of the culture tubes which I had inoculated with the recent specimens from Duthie, I held it eagerly before her.

"There," I said. "I have it. And it's growing pretty fast. You don't recognize it?"

She shook her head, her interest awakened, a quick look of interrogation in her wide dark pupils.

I returned the tube to the water bath, glanced at the regulator and closed the zinc door. Then, quite simply, I explained what was in my mind.

A flush of enthusiasm crept into her cheeks. Her eyes, bright yet deeply troubled, wandered round the room, back to the culture, then again to me. My heart was beating fast. To hide my emotion I went to the window and threw it up, letting in a flood of sunlight. Outside, fleecy clouds were racing in the bright blue sky. I turned towards her.

"Robert," she said slowly. "If I work with you . . . because I believe your work to be important . . . will you promise, faithfully, to keep your word?"

"Yes," I said.

I saw her breast heave in a sudden sigh. While I kept my gaze upon her, she put down her book, removed her hat, and began to take off her gloves.

"Very well," she said. "Let's begin."

CHAPTER FIVE

EVERY morning regularly, shortly after ten o'clock, when her lecture was over, Jean came into the room where I was already at work and, taking her smock from the hook behind the door, slipped it on and began to busy herself, methodically, at the other end of the long table. We did not exchange more than a few words, perhaps only a smile of greeting. Sometimes, when I was occupied with a calculation, I pretended not to notice her arrival—an impersonal attitude which I felt might reassure her. Yet she was there, and later when I guardedly looked up I would see her, measuring and titrating, behind the clamped burettes, entering each reading in the battered black record-book, her expression serious and intent.

As I had foreseen, her neatness and careful accuracy were of the utmost help to me, especially in preparing the hundreds of slides which it was necessary to examine. It was a difficult staining technique, and a dangerous one, for these mass bouillon cultures were highly virulent. But working quietly, with steady fingers, her features deeply absorbed, her eyes unwavering, she never once made a mistake. When she felt my gaze upon her she would give me, interrupting her work, a silent yet speaking glance, binding us more closely in this community of effort to which we were pledged. The light spring airs streamed through the wide open window into our dim little room, bringing faintly the sounds of another world—a hum of traffic, the whistle of a steamboat, a strain of tinkling music from a distant barrel-organ. Her presence, with its control and quietude, stimulated me to a pitch I had never known before.

At one o'clock we stopped for lunch. Although there were one or two good cafés in this neighbourhood, it was easier, more agreeable, and cheaper to take our meal in the laboratory. To this end we clubbed our money and from the market, which she passed through, on her way from the train, Jean would bring, each day, an assortment of provisions. Having steeped our hands for three minutes in corrosive sublimate solution, a precaution which I insisted upon with inflexible firmness, we sat on the window-sill and, balancing a plate upon our knees, enjoyed an alfresco repast. When the day was grey and chilly we had soup, heated over the Bunsen burner. But usually our fare consisted of fresh scones, slices of cold sausage, and Dunlop cheese, with an apple, or a bag of cherries, for dessert. In the courtyard outside there was a blackbird which came faithfully every day, to share our good things. When he saw that we had cherries, he would perch upon Jean's wrist, whistling his heart out with greedy delight.

Upon the seventh afternoon, as we worked in silence, I heard a step and turned round. Professor Challis stood on the threshold, bent and buttoned-up in his faded frock coat, plucking at his silver moustache, his eyes screwed up towards us.

"I thought I'd look in on you, Robert," he said, "to see how you were getting on." ·

I rose at once and introduced him to Jean, to whom he bowed with his Old World air. He was surprised, I could see, and although too courteous to show it, both curious and doubtful. But soon it was evident that she pleased him and, reassured, he gave me his twinkling smile.

"Half the battle in research, Robert, is a suitable assistant."

He chuckled at that, as though he had made an excellent joke, then wandered about the room, gently activating the cultures, examining the slides, peering through the pages of our notes, in silence, but with a quiet approval more exciting to us than words.

When the survey was complete he turned and gazed at us.

"I shall get you more samples, more specimens from other areas . . . from the Continent . . . where they still have some regard for me." He broke off and threw out his hands. "Go on, go on. Pay no attention to an old fossil like me. Simply go on."

The words were nothing, but in his eyes I saw a lively gleam which had not been there before.

After that he came regularly to visit us, often at the lunch hour, bringing not only the promised specimens but, more than once, a contribution to our meal. Seated in a chair, his stick between his knees, leaning forward rather shakily on the bone handle, he watched us from beneath his bushy brows, with bright eyes, while we divided a meat pie or a jar of Strasbourg *pâté*. His attachment to Jean had steadily increased, and his manner to her was charming, gently chivalrous, yet with a kind of mischievous benevolence, like a schoolboy. He never ate anything, but when she made coffee he would accept a cup and, having asked her permission with that special gallantry he now displayed towards her, would snip delicately and light one of the small cigars he occasionally permitted himself. While the blue spirals drifted upwards and dispersed, he would recount to us his early experiences as a young research student in Paris, at the Sorbonne, where he worked under the great Duclaux.

"I had no money then." He chuckled, after describing to us a Sunday spent at Barbizon. "And I've none now. But I've always been happy, doing the work that's not like anything else in the world."

When he had gone Jean drew a deep breath. Her eyes were glowing.

"He's sweet, Robert. A great man. And I love him."

"If I'm any judge the old chap loves you too." I smiled a trifle wryly. "But would your family approve of him?"

She lowered her gaze.

"Let's get back to work."

We had by this time isolated in a pure state, from the numerous milk samples, a Gram-negative organism which I identified as Bang's bacillus, originally discovered by the Danish scientist Bang, and shown by him to be the cause of acute disease in cattle widely prevalent all over the world. This, therefore, was the cause of the trouble in the dairy herds. Indeed, from figures which I worked out, we estimated that probably 35 per cent of all cattle in the country, to say nothing of sheep, goats, and other farm stock, were harbourers of this germ which we now had cultivated in massive quantity, in a special broth medium.

We also possessed, in a pure state, the Bruce bacillus of Malta fever, which, of course, during my sojourn at Dalnair, I had recovered from human beings stricken during the epidemic of so-called influenza, and which also we had in many instances isolated from the recent human specimens procured by Challis. Thus we were in a position to compare these two organisms —the one from cattle, the other from man—to analyze their varying reactions, and to discover the possible relationship between them.

The tests which we employed were exceedingly complex and at first it was difficult to assess their value. But gradually, as one positive result succeeded another, there emerged a supposition, built in the beginning upon conjecture, but later upon solid proof, which truly staggered us. When it dawned upon us, we gazed at each other incredulously.

"It can't be," I said slowly. "It's impossible."

"It could be," she answered, logically. "And it is just possible."

I pressed both hands to my head, irritated for once by her quiet simplicity. Dr. Mathers had kept me late at the surgery the night before, he was increasing his demands upon me, and the strain of this double duty was beginning to tell.

"For God's sake," I said, "don't let's cross bridges before we come to them. We've weeks of work yet before we make the final antigen test."

But still the evidence piled up and, at the end of three months, as we drew nearer to this crucial test, a deep and increasing excitement imposed itself upon us. In the hours when we were obliged to wait for the process of agglutination to take place, we found this nervous strain almost unbearable—and since there was no need to remain in the laboratory we sought relief by escaping for an hour or so to the country immediately surrounding Winton.

Now there was no question of the motor-cycle, for even Luke was unaware that we were together; but the tramway was convenient and took us in twenty minutes to our favourite resort, the Longcrag Hill, a wooded height, not yet built upon, which overlooked the river. Here, on a mossy rock, we would sit and watch the ferry boats and tiny paddle steamers plying up and down the broad stream, with the city, lost in a golden haze, revealed only by a glittering dome or tenuous spire, lying far below at our feet. We spoke mainly of the problems confronting us in our work, and discussed, with agitated hope, the prospects of success. Sometimes, tired out, yet overcome by the magic of the moment, I would lie back, shut my eyes and, with all the longing of my provincial soul, dream aloud, dream of the Sorbonne, pictured so vividly to us by Challis, dream of a life of pure, unhampered research.

Faithful to my promise, although it was not easy, I did not once speak to her of love. Aware of her scruples, of the niceties of conscience she had overcome to help me, I was resolved to prove to her how false was her suspicion that she could not really trust me. Only thus could I justify myself in her eyes and my own.

When the day of decision arrived we set the final batch of agglutinin tubes and went out. It was Thursday, the last day of June, a more than usually lovely afternoon; and, afraid almost of what we might find on our return, we were disinclined to leave the Hill. As we sat there, a little steamer, away beneath us, was setting out upon an evening cruise to the islands of the lower estuary, and upon its after-deck we could see the tiny figures of a German band. They were playing a Strauss waltz. The little ship with flags flying, and paddles churning, swept gaily down the river, and disappeared from sight. But behind there lingered a whisper of the melody, ascending to us faintly yet sweetly, tender as a caress. It was a precious moment. I dared not look at my companion, but in a dazzling flash I felt the exaltation of these days of joint endeavour which, almost without my knowledge, had deepened and strengthened our intimacy. I knew now that, in every way, she had become indispensable to me.

We rose to go. I had no surgery that evening and Jean, because of the importance of the occasion, had arranged to remain in Winton until eight o'clock.

Five o'clock was striking when we got to our little laboratory. It was now or never. I went to the incubator and opening the door, made an abrupt gesture to my companion to remove the racked tray of tubes. There were, in that tray, twenty-four tubes, each containing a liquid, perfectly clear some hours ago, but which, if the test were successful, would now show a cloudy deposit. Holding my breath, I watched her nervously take out the tray. Then I gave a short gasp.

Every tube in the rack showed a flocculent white precipitate. I could not speak. Caught by a sudden weakness I sat down on the leather settee while Jean, still holding the tray of tubes, continued to gaze at me with a transfigured face.

It was true then: these two organisms, regarded for twenty-one years as separate and unrelated species, were the same. Yes, I had proved it. Morphologically, culturally, and by agglutination tests, they were identical. This widespread disease of cattle was intensely communicable to humans, not only by direct contact, but through milk, butter, cheese, and every variety of dairy produce. The Bang's disease of animals was the Malta fever of Bruce and the "influenza" epidemic, all in one, all due to the same bacillus, which we had cultivated here in the lab. I shut my eyes dizzily. We had actually established the existence, and the cause, of a new infection in man, not a minor condition of local interest, but a serious disease capable of producing major epidemics as well as continued ill-health in its milder and more chronic forms, a disease which must number its victims in hundreds of thousands in every country all over the world. As I considered these ramifications I swallowed dryly. Like Cortez, upon his mountain peak, I saw, with startling clarity, the vast extent of our discovery.

At last Jean broke the silence.

"It's wonderful," she said in a low voice. "Oh, Robert, you can publish everything now."

I shook my head. Before me, in a shining glow, I saw a still more splendid vision. Holding down my swelling excitement, trying to behave with modesty and dignity, like a real scientist, I answered:

"We have discovered the disease. And the germ which causes that disease. Now we must produce the vaccine which will cure it. When we have that, we have everything, perfect and complete."

It was a glorious, a dazzling thought. Her eyes kindled.

"We should telephone Professor Challis."

"Tomorrow," I said. I felt, jealously, that for the present our triumph must belong to us alone.

She seemed to understand, and as she smiled, a further surge of elation swept over me, toppling my dignity, undermining my pretence of calm.

"My dear Dr. Law," I smiled back at her, "this is an occasion which will go down in history. We really ought to celebrate. Will you have dinner with me tonight?"

She hesitated, her cheeks still warm with ardour, and glanced at her watch. "They'll be expecting me at home."

"Oh, do come," I said eagerly. "It's early. You'll get your train all right."

As she looked at me with bright eyes in which there lay also a faint entreaty, I jumped to my feet, full of confidence and joy. I laughed as I helped her into her coat.

"We've worked pretty hard. We deserve a little treat."

I took her arm gaily as we went out.

CHAPTER SIX

IN OLD George Street, not far away, there stood a small French restaurant, the Continental, which I had occasionally patronized in company with Spence and which I now decided was exactly right for our present entertainment. Kept by a widow, an Alsatian named Madame Brossard, whose husband had taught languages at the neighbouring public school, it was a humble establishment, but it was clean, the cuisine was good, and even in this northern atmosphere it had maintained something of a native character. The floor was sanded, the coarse checked napkins were folded like fans and tucked into tinted wine glasses, each little table bore a red-shaded rush-light which cast a romantic glow upon the bone-handled cutlery.

As we entered, Madame bowed to us from her desk behind the *caisse* and the youthful waiter, clad in a seedy dress suit too large for him, showed us to a table in the corner. We were early and, apart from some regular customers dining at a long table in the centre of the room, the place was pleasantly empty. In high spirits we discussed the menu, written with violet copying ink in an angular hand, and ordered *soupe aux oignons, escalope de veau, soufflé à l'orange,* and coffee.

"It's awfully nice here," Jean said, looking about her with an animated expression. "We might be in Paris." She saved herself with a little grimace. "For all I know about it."

"Let's pretend we are," I answered gaily. "We've come in from the Sorbonne . . . as described by our friend Challis. We're immensely famous scientists . . . can't you see my beard! . . . And we've just made a world-shaking discovery which will cover us with unbounded glory."

"So we have," she exclaimed, practically.

I gave a little shout of laughter. Thrilled by a sense of triumph, escaped from the heavy harness of routine, my usual reticence was gone, a joyous intoxication pervaded me. When the waiter brought our soup and a long thin crusty roll I addressed him in French. As he shook his head, looked apologetic, and answered me in broad Scots, Jean burst out laughing too.

"What were you saying to that poor boy?" she asked when he had gone.

"Something he was too young to understand." I leaned across the table. "I shall tell you later."

We began our soup, which was delicious, filled with thin slices of crisp onion and heaped with grated cheese. In the elation which possessed us we were lifted high above ourselves, buoyant on the crest of our success. The waiter, now our friend, brought, with an air, the carafe of red wine which was included with the *table d'hôte*. Tremulous with excitement, my heart singing with happiness, I poured out two glasses of this simple vintage which was still foaming from the cask.

"Let's drink to our success."

Her gaze wavered slightly, but only for an instant for, as though carried away by a consciousness of the occasion, she took first a sip, then finished the glass.

"Not bad." I nodded approvingly. "When in Paris do as the Parisians. Besides . . . remember that you are now a stout, though still attractive, middle-aged woman who has had a hard day chasing agglutinins at the Sorbonne. As Saint Paul suggested, you need a little wine for your stomach's sake."

She gazed at me reprovingly then, unexpectedly, her composure gave way, she smiled, and a moment later was again dissolved in laughter, a gay and playful laughter which sprang from nothing but the sweet exhilaration of her mood.

"Oh, Robert, you shouldn't . . ." she cried, wiping her eyes. "We're behaving like children."

From behind the cash register Madame Brossard, a stately figure, was regarding us with a benign and sympathetic eye.

When the *escalope* arrived I refilled our glasses and, irresistibly drawn, we began to discuss our adventures during the past three months, smiling now at the difficulties we had encountered, savouring again in every detail the splendour of achievement.

"Do you remember that day you lost your temper, Robert?"

"I deny, emphatically, that I ever lost my temper."

"Oh yes, you did. When I broke the centrifuge. You nearly boxed my ears!"

"Well, now I wish I had."

It was enough to set us off again.

As I bent towards my companion, now so bright and animated, with flushed cheeks and mischievous, laughing eyes, I saw more clearly than ever before the dual nature of her personality. The grave, devoted little Calvinist was gone, and from beneath that imprint of her upbringing, there emerged a warm and vivid creature who, having taken off her hat, leaned her elbows intimately on the table and surrendered unconsciously to her instincts as a woman.

A ground-swell of emotion caught me. As a vision of our relationship flashed before me I felt suddenly that I could not continue to endure the alternate blows of suffering and joy which had composed it. I had kept my word in this strange comradeship; yet, without my knowing it, the deep and painful charm of her presence in the laboratory had worn me down. Freed from the obsession of my work, I could no longer suppress the natural instinct of my heart. I swallowed the last of my coffee to get rid of the sudden choking in my throat.

"Jean," I said. "You've helped me so much in these last three months. Why?"

"Sense of duty." She smiled.

"Then you haven't minded working with me?"

"I've loved it!" she exclaimed and added absently, "The experience will be so useful to me when I get to the settlement at Kumasi."

The remark, uttered without thinking, sent a knife into my heart.

"Don't," I said. "For God's sake . . . not tonight."

"No, Robert." She gave me a swift and swimming glance.

An immediate silence followed. As though fearful of having betrayed herself, she let her eyes fall.

This evening there was about her a warmth, a quick and vivid pulse of life which made me catch my breath. Overcome with love, I fought to preserve my sanity against this mounting enchantment. It was useless, everything yielded to the wild sweetness of this hour. In my side, fostered by our nearness, there came an actual pain, an inexpressible longing which found a momentary ease when, involuntarily, I took her hand and pressed it tight in mine.

She made no effort to withdraw her imprisoned fingers but, as though she too were striving to be calm, at last she sighed:

"I suppose we ought to go."

During these silent moments which brought us closer than ever before, which seemed formed of the longing that swirled between us, I had quite lost count of time. Now, as I summoned the waiter for the bill while Jean, with a subdued air, slowly put on her hat, I caught sight of the clock above the cash desk. It showed five minutes past eight.

"It's later than I thought," I said, in a low voice. "I'm afraid you've missed your train."

She turned to glance at the clock, then looked back at me. The warmth in her cheeks had deepened, her eyes were bright as stars, so bright that once again, she lowered her lashes in defense.

"I don't suppose it matters."

"When is the next?"

"Not until quarter to ten."

There was a pause. She had begun, almost agitatedly, to crumble a fragment of roll. The nervous movement of her fingers, her downcast gaze, the quick pulse in her throat, made my heart miss a beat.

"Let's go then."

I paid the bill and we went outside. The street was quiet, the sky overcast, the night air warm and still.

"What shall we do?" I only spoke for the sake of something to say. "Take a stroll in the Gardens?"

"Don't they close the gates at eight?"

"I forgot," I muttered. "I think they do."

We were standing under a street lamp in the deserted thoroughfare. A wave of recklessness passed over me. She was near to me, so near that all my resolutions were swept away in a wild torrent of desire. My heart was beating like mad. I could scarcely speak.

"Let's go back to the laboratory for a bit."

As we started to walk along the pavement I took her arm. We did not say a word. When we reached the Hall I opened the door of our work-room with my key. It was dark, but from the old gas-lamp in the courtyard there stole in a faint glimmer, which cast a lustre that was like a spell, both fatal and predestined, upon her upturned face. Her eyes were closed, the lids translucent, expectant and foredoomed. I felt her sweet breath upon my cheek. As though to still the trembling of her limbs, she clung to me, then we were in each other's arms, upon the little couch.

In the timeless and enchanted twilight, a warm numbness drugged my limbs, a stupor of happiness. The past was forgotten, the future extinguished, this moment now was everything. Her head lay back, exposing the thin arch of her throat, the tender hollow of her neck. Her eyes still were shuttered against the unearthly light, and her pale brow, gathered in a strange deep furrow, was drawn as though by pain. Then, through her quick and troubled breathing, and the rapid pulsing of her heart, which fluttered against her thin opened blouse, like a frightened bird, I felt the upward rushing of all her being, uniting, soaring into oblivion with mine. Nothing, no tie of heaven or earth, restrained that ecstasy of flight.

CHAPTER SEVEN

ON MONDAY afternoon, four days later, Professor Challis came to see me. He had been away for the week-end at a hydropathic in Bute which he frequented occasionally to have treatment for the arthritis which was slowly crippling him. Finding my message upon his return, he had taken a cab from his house to the laboratory.

When he had shaken hands he laid down his hat and, flicking the raindrops from his umbrella, gazed round the room with an air of mild inquiry.

"Where is our young friend?"

Although I had been prepared for the question, to my annoyance, I coloured slightly.

"She isn't here today."

Standing warming his finger tips at the little charcoal stove, he gave me an oddly searching glance, as though surprised to find me here, alone, with a silent air.

"So everything has turned out well."

"Yes."

He shook his head.

"You are suffering from reaction, Robert. You are tired. Sit still and let me look for myself."

A few minutes later he turned to the bench and for the next half-hour occupied himself intently with the report I had prepared, making calculations in pencil upon the margin. Then, with great deliberation, he examined all my cultures. He stooped for a long time over the microscope, and finally, slewed round stiffly upon the stool. He looked old, worn, and a little wistful, his cheeks more hollow than before. I saw that he was considerably affected.

"Robert . . ." He said, at last, with his mild eyes fixed on mine: "You must not become proud. Never. Science has no place for vanity or self-seeking. And after all you are only at the beginning of your career. You have been lucky. Also you have much to learn, everything in fact. But what you have done warms my old heart."

After a moment of complete silence he went on.

"Of course you could announce your discovery immediately. It is without doubt of immense importance. But I agree that it would be better, more perfect and scientific, to take a further three months and finish the work completely by producing a vaccine therapeutically effective in controlling this new disease. Is that what you wish to do?"

"Yes."

"Then you shall do it. But"—his eyes swept the room—"you cannot do it here."

He acknowledged my look of surprise with a slow nod of his head.

"It would be quite impossible to effect the final highly technical stages of your research under these makeshift conditions. I make no apologies, Robert, this was the best I could do for you at the time. But now I must do better. You require, absolutely, a modern, well-equipped laboratory. And there are three possible ways in which you can secure it."

Despite my suffering I was listening to him with attention.

"In the first place, you can go to one of the large manufacturing drug houses, such as Wilson's or Harlett's. In the face of your present findings either would be delighted, unquestionably, to offer you all their resources, a highly trained staff, and a large salary to produce your vaccine for sale, commercially, in bulk." He added: "That would be very profitable for every one concerned."

He waited. Then, as I continued to gaze at him in silence, without attempting to answer, a faint smile irradiated his lined features.

"So far so good," he said. "The second possibility: To go to Professor Usher."

This time I started involuntarily, but before I could speak he made a gesture of restraint with his thin brown hand.

"The good Professor is beginning to regret that he let you go." He gave a short chuckle, amused, rather than malicious. "From time to time I have caused him some curiosity . . . not to say chagrin . . . by speaking about your work."

"No," I said, in a low tone, and all the secret unrest now within me found expression in that single word.

"Why not? I assure you he would welcome you back to the Department."

"He put me out of the Department," I answered, from between my teeth. "I must go through with this on my own."

"Very well," Challis said. "There remains . . . Eastershaws."

Forgetting momentarily the turmoil seething in my breast, I stared at him in utter amazement. Was he joking? Or had he suddenly gone out of his wits?

"You know that place?" he inquired.

"Of course."

Again he gave me his faint, grave smile.

"I am quite serious, Robert. They have a vacancy there for a resident medical officer. I have made representations to the superintendent, Dr. Goodall, and he is agreeable that you have the position for the next few months. It is an old institution, you understand, but they have made a recent addition, a complete modern laboratory, in which you would have full and unrestricted opportunity to finish, absolutely, your work."

There was a pause. I looked round the improvised test room which I had at first despised but to which I had now, in every way, become attached. Another change, I thought; why can't I for once be left alone?

"I'd rather not leave," I said slowly. "I'm used to it here."

He shook his head.

"It is a necessity, my boy, which was bound to arise. Not even Pasteur could produce a vaccine with this equipage. That is why I have all along been seeking another opening for you." As I still hesitated he asked mildly: "Perhaps you object to living in such a place as Eastershaws?"

"No," I answered, after a moment. "I suppose I could stick it."

"Then think it over, and let me know tonight. Without question, it is a laboratory of which one dreams." He stood up, patted me on the shoulder and pulled on his light-coloured gloves. "Now I must go. Again my congratulations." He took his umbrella, glanced at me over his shoulder. "And do not forget to give my regards to Dr. Law."

I made an indistinct answer as he went out.

I could not bring myself to tell him that I had not seen Jean for the past four days, that in my pocket there burned a letter from her, a pitiful, tear-stained note, filled with self-reproaches, with the deepest, the most desperate anguish of remorse.

Oh, God, what a fool I had been. In the warm delirium of those irretrievable moments I had not paused to consider how deeply the sense of wrongdoing would wound her artless and unaffected soul. I could still see her, as she left me, late that night, her face white and piteous, her lips quivering, and in her eyes the look of a wounded bird, a look so hurt, so mournful and despairing, it almost rent my heart.

Goodness was something one never thought of, at which perhaps one laughed. Yet it was the very substance of her being.

Once, when a child, I had broken a fragile vase of crystal. The same cruel sense of unconsolable bereavement occasioned by those scattered fragments was striking at me now. There were others, I knew, who went through "an affair" with apparent carelessness. Yet we, alas, unlike in every way, had this in common: we could not lay upon our wounds the salve of indifference. A phrase from her letter kept grinding through my brain.

The mistake we made was in thinking we could be together. We must never make that mistake again. I cannot, must not see you again.

A deep sigh broke from me. I felt, desolately, as though I had cast away, and lost for ever, a pearl of great price. Weary and unsettled, filled with a sort of burning sickness, I blamed myself bitterly. Yet we had crossed this invisible brink less because we were together than because of those forces which would have drawn us apart. And now? The end of enchantment . . . death of the heart? No. I longed for her more than ever, desired her with all my soul.

Abruptly, I stood up. Although since I had received her letter I had thought of nothing else, I made a great effort now to shake off my despondency and to fix my mind on this offer which had come from Challis. My mood was not attuned to the idea, yet I had to admit the justice of his arguments. And after, in restless brooding fashion, I had paced the floor for perhaps an hour, I decided to accept. As it was nearly half-past five, I locked up and set out for the surgery in the Trongate.

The waiting-room, as usual, was hot and overcrowded, filled with a prevailing odour, with hushed murmurs, coughs, heavy breathing and the shuffling of feet on the bare floor. Condensed moisture was running down the chocolate-coloured walls. As I took my place at the desk Dr. Mathers came bustling in with a slip of paper in his hand.

"Full house tonight, Shannon. Business is good. I wonder if you'd mind doing these calls for me when you get through."

There were five visits written on the slip he handed me. Gradually, in an off-hand, genial manner, he had been increasing my work until now I was doing far more than that originally agreed between us.

"All right," I said, in a flat voice. "But I'd like to talk to you."

"Go ahead."

"I'm afraid I'm leaving."

According to his custom, he had begun to transfer handfuls of cash, the fees taken during his afternoon round, from his trouser pockets into the chamois bag, but now he stopped abruptly and looked at me sharply. After a moment he began to laugh.

"I wondered how long it would be before you tried to hold me up for a raise. How much do you want?"

"Nothing."

"Come off it, Shannon. You're not a bad chap. I'll give you another guinea a week."

"No," I said, with averted eyes.

"Two guineas then, damn it."

When I shook my head his expression altered and became serious. With his foot he closed the door in the face of the waiting patients, sat down on the edge of the desk and considered me.

"This is a fine thing to land on a man when he's going off for the evening. I'm taking the missus and Ada to Hengler's Circus. You've no idea how much they liked you when they met you the other day. Now tell me. How much do you really want?"

I had to hold myself in check. In my present state of mind it revolted me, the manner in which he reduced everything to the common denominator of cash.

"Money has nothing to do with it."

He did not believe me—impossible that I should not care for the precious stuff. He bit his thumb-nail, eyeing me calculatingly, all the time.

"Look here, Shannon." It came with a rush. "I've taken to you. We've all taken to you. I don't say you're much of a doctor yet, but I could teach you. The thing is, you're dependable. You're honest. You don't let the half-crowns stick to your fingers. I've been meaning to put this proposition up to you for a long time. Now listen. Come in with me here, as a full-time assistant, at two fifty, no, say even three hundred a year. If you do well, in twelve months, I'll take you into partnership, and let you pay out of receipts. Can you beat that? This practice is a regular gold mine. We'll work it together. Why, if Ada and you was to hit it off, we might make it a family business and in the fulness of time you would succeed me."

"Oh, go to hell." My nerves suddenly gave way. "I don't want to succeed you. I don't want your money. Or anything else."

"Oh, come now," he muttered, quite taken aback. "I gave you a job, didn't I, when you were down and out?"

"Yes," I almost shouted. "And I'm grateful for it. That's why I've let you sweat me to death these past three months. But now I've had enough. I'm sick of picking half-crowns out of one-room tenements to shove in your shammy bag. Keep your gold mine to yourself. I want no part of it."

"It's not possible," he said, staring at me. "I make you a gilt-edged offer. And you throw it in my teeth. You're crazy."

"All right," I said. "We'll leave it that way. Now let me get on with the work."

I banged the admission bell on the desk and straight away the first patient, an old man, came shambling in. As I began to examine him Dr. Mathers continued to stare at me with his hat pushed back on his head, in complete bewilderment. Finally he took up the bag of money, locked it securely in the safe and, without another word, went out. I regretted my outburst immediately he had gone. He was not a bad-hearted fellow, and he gave good service to the district, but his relentless quest of a full money-bag was more than I could bear.

It was past eleven o'clock when I finished the last call. I made my way towards the Globe, tired out, yet knowing that I would not sleep. Now that I was no longer occupied, the pain returned and, like a sharp-toothed animal, started gnawing at my breast. Yet, as I tramped through the damp streets, I sneered at my suffering. What a model I would make for the gay, successful Lothario! Young Romeo . . . Casanova . . . these were the names I threw at myself with bitter self-derision.

When I reached my hotel room I tore off my clothing and flung myself into bed. I lay there in the darkness, stiffly, with tight-shut eyes. But as I tried to get to sleep these words branded themselves upon my brain: *I must never see you again . . . never . . . never.*

BOOK FOUR

CHAPTER ONE

A WEEK later, towards nine o'clock in the evening, I was carrying my bag along a deserted road, straining my eyes in the misty darkness for the first sight of Eastershaws Place, still quite invisible in the illusory emptiness of the night. I had missed my train at Winton and, arriving an hour late at Shaws Junction, which lies in the lonely wooded pastures of Lothian, some forty miles from the city, I found no conveyance awaiting me. At the village station they had given me directions, yet in that deserted countryside I would almost certainly have lost my way but for striking a high and solid wall, topped by a row of iron spikes. I had followed this for the past ten minutes and now, with a sudden sweep, it brought me to the entrance gates, sentinelled by a turreted stone lodge with a lantern in the window.

Setting down my bag, I knocked upon the heavy nail-studded door which gave access to the lodge. After a short interval someone plucked the lantern from the window and came out of the lodge, an unseen figure peering from behind the gate.

"Who is it?"

I gave him my name, adding:

"You're expecting me, I think."

"I know nothing about you. Where's your pass?"

"I haven't a pass. But surely they told you I was coming?"

"They did not."

The gateman appeared on the point of returning to the lodge and of leaving me in the outer darkness. But at that moment, another lantern swung into being, and a feminine voice, high, rather pretentiously cultured, and with an Irish accent, came from behind the porter.

"Is that Dr. Shannon? All right, Gunn, open up and let him in."

Not without some grumbling from the lodge-keeper, the wrought-iron gates swung open. I picked up my bag and stepped forward.

"You've got your gear with you. Good. Come along."

My conductress, so far as could be made out by the sickly lantern light, was a woman of about forty, bare-headed, wearing blue glasses and a loose ulster of rough tweed. As the gates clanged shut, while we set off up a long, dark drive, she introduced herself.

"I'm Dr. Maitland, in charge of the Women's Side." I brushed against a clump of shrubs, and almost missed my footing. "Dr. Palfrey would have met you . . . he looks after Men's East and West, but it's his half-day and he has gone to Winton." After a due pause, she added: "That's our main building straight ahead."

I raised my eyes. Some distance in front, upon a slight eminence, a castellated shape was dimly visible, a honeycomb of lights which swam hazily in the moist blackness. The mist subdued these lights, gave to them a quality luminous and elusive. As I watched, striding on, some lights went out and others came to being, which made the constellation dance and flutter.

The end of the avenue brought us at last under the high façade, and Maitland advanced to a stone portico illuminated by an overhead lamp in a metal grille. Pausing, key in hand, at the top of the wide and shallow granite steps, she explained:

"This is Gentlemen's South. Your quarters are here."

Within, the hall was large and lofty, tessellated in black and white marble, with an alabaster statue at the end and three dark enormous landscapes, in oils and heavy gilt, upon the walls. Two buhl cabinets flanked by green-and-gold state chairs completed a picture which stupefied the senses by its rococo splendour.

"I hope you approve." Maitland seemed to be hiding a smile. "Entrance to Valhalla, eh?"

Without waiting for an answer, she continued up the broad carpeted staircase, to the third floor. Here, using, with remarkable dexterity, the same key, which I now saw to be attached to her waist by a thin steel cable, she threw open the door of a self-contained suite.

"Here we are. And you know the worst. Bedroom, sitting-room and bath. Complete Victorian—Gothic."

Despite her cool amusement, the rooms, although somewhat archaic in their style of furnishing, were unusually comfortable. In the sitting-room, where the chenille curtains were already drawn, a coal fire threw a warm glow upon the brass fender and red pile carpet. There were two easy chairs and a sofa, a reading lamp beside a secretaire which held shelves of leather-bound books. The bedroom beyond showed a snug mahogany bed, the tub in the bathroom was of thick rounded porcelain. I was tempted, with a stab of bitterness, to tell my superior companion that, by contrast with the inadequacies I had experienced at the Globe, this was luxury.

"Want to unpack?" she asked, standing discreetly near the doorway. "Or perhaps you'd like some supper sent up?"

"Yes, I would. If it isn't too much trouble."

I dropped my bag behind the sofa and while she rang the bell beside the mantelpiece and ordered something for me, I had a better look at her. She was extremely plain, with a mottled, shiny pink complexion and drab-coloured hair untidily gathered into a knot at the back of her head. Her eyes were obviously weak, for even behind her violet lenses, the lids were visibly red and everted. As though deliberately to accentuate her lack of beauty, she was dowdily dressed, beneath her ulster, in a pink-striped flannel blouse and a baggy tweed skirt.

In five minutes a maidservant wearing a bulgy black uniform and starched white apron came in silently with the tray. She was short and stocky, almost a dwarf, with muscular black-stockinged calves and a grey expressionless face.

"Thank you, Sarah," Maitland said pleasantly. "That seems nice. By-the-by, this is Dr. Shannon. I know you'll look after him well."

The maid kept her eyes upon the carpet, with no relaxation of her drawn blankness. But suddenly she bobbed, an automatic little curtsey. Without speaking she went out.

I followed her with my eyes, then turned to my companion in meaning interrogation.

"Yes." Maitland nodded carelessly. She watched me with her challenging, half-mocking smile as I poured a cup of coffee and began to eat a sandwich.

"They do one rather well here. Miss Indre, who looks after the house-keeping, is most efficient. Incidentally, I'm not going to drag you round the staff for introductions. Palfrey is the man you'll see most of, you breakfast with him at Men's East every morning. Then there's Dr. Goodall . . . our Chief . . . that was his house, with the red blinds, on the left of your entrance."

"Oughtn't I to report to him tonight?" I looked up.

"I'll let him know you're here," Maitland answered.

"What are my duties?"

"Morning and evening rounds. Deputize for Palfrey on his day off and for me on mine. Official duty in the refectory. Occasional dispensary. Otherwise make yourself generally useful and agreeable to the good people of our little world. It's quite simple. I understand you're doing some research. You'll have ample chance for that between times. Here's your pass key."

From her coat pocket she produced a key, similar to her own, with a length of fine steel chain attached.

"You'll soon get the knack of it. I warn you that you'll get nowhere without it in Eastershaws. Don't lose it."

There was no mockery in Maitland's manner as she handed over the large, old-fashioned key, incredibly smooth and polished like silver from constant use.

"Well, I fancy that's about everything. I'm off now to see the Dutchess. She's been quite obstreperous and needs a good lecture and a spot of heroin."

When she had gone I finished my supper, which was very different from the usual hospital food, and altogether in keeping with this sumptuous establishment. I wondered if I should make a short tour of inspection with my new, indispensable key. As I came up the staircase with Maitland I had observed, on each landing, a mahogany door with faded lettering above, and thick glass panels through which there was a vista of a long gallery, faintly illumined, reaching out mysteriously to another door, a further gallery.

Despite Professor Challis's recommendation, already borne out, that this place was one of the best of its kind, a vague disquiet troubled me. In the profession one always tends to look askance at asylum work as being just a little off the normal track. There are some splendid people in that service, of course, but on the other hand some who are distinctly queer—and who get queerer, as time goes on. It is an easy life and much medical flotsam drifts into it. Besides, once you're in, somehow it is less easy to get out. Not to put too fine a point on it, some of these peculiar mental states are as "catching" as the infectious fevers.

However, I would have to take these chances. I got up abruptly. My bed had been neatly turned down, disclosing linen whiter and finer than any I had known. Retrieving my bag from behind the sofa, I unpacked, distributing my textbooks, papers, and few poor belongings to the best advantage. The previous incumbent, name unknown, had not troubled to remove all his possessions, leaving a half-tin of cigarettes, an old red-striped bath robe, several novels, and a score of knickknacks scattered in careless profusion.

I had only one small photograph, cheaply framed in passe-partout, a snapshot taken, one sunny day, on the moors behind Gowrie: a simple, open little face, in sepia, with wind-blown curls and a pointed, courageous chin . . . with dark eyes smiling . . . could one believe it . . . actually, smiling with a strange awakened happiness. Were they smiling now? At least, as I placed it on the mantelpiece, beside the clock, I had no answering smile. Instead, I went over to the calendar on the secretaire and, with a queer, fixed expression, I put a mark opposite the date July 31.

At that moment, a quick knock upon the door caused me instinctively to start and, as I saw the tall and craggy figure upon the threshold, I realized that my visitor was the Superintendent.

"Good evening, Dr. Shannon." His voice was mild and halting. "Welcome to Eastershaws."

Long and loosely built, Dr. Goodall had a gaunt and sagging air, with iron-grey hair that needed cutting hanging untidily over his collar. His face was long and saturnine, with a biggish nose, undershot chin, and heavy-lidded jaundiced eyes which, although aloof, were deeply human, warm with understanding, and holding strange hypnotic depths.

"I have heard much of you from Professor Challis." He smiled meditatively. "It struck me you must be anxious to see our laboratory."

With a gesture he indicated that I should accompany him. We went downstairs and, by a tiled subway, lit by electric frosted domes, he led me a considerable distance under the main building, then up an incline to a small central courtyard, open to the stars, but surrounded by high walls. Silently unlocking another door he switched on the light.

"Here we are then, Dr. Shannon. I trust you will find it satisfactory."

I was speechless. I could only gaze in dumb wonder, completely overcome. Naturally I had hoped for a reasonably good work-room, although in the light of my past experience I had not dared to build upon it. But this exceeded even my wildest expectation. It was the finest small unit I had ever seen, better even than the Department laboratory, with rack upon rack of stoppered reagents, an Exton scopometer, conditioned hoods, electric grinder, and sterilizing vault—all fitted up, from the tiled walls to the last pipette, regardless of expense.

"I'm afraid," Goodall commented with mild apology, "it hasn't been used much. Some of the apparatus may need adjusting."

"But it's perfect." My voice failed me.

He smiled faintly.

"It is a recent addition. And we had the best technical advice when we installed it. I am happy to think that it is to see some service."

In that remote yet sympathetic manner he concluded:

"We shall expect great things of you. I am a lonely bachelor, Dr. Shannon. Eastershaws is my child. If you can bring credit to it, you will make me happy."

We retraced our steps. In the hallway, beneath the staircase which led to my rooms, he paused, that heavy-lidded gaze once again barely touching mine.

"I trust you are satisfied with what Eastershaws can do for you. Your quarters are quite comfortable?"

"More than comfortable."

Another pause.

"Good night then, Dr. Shannon."

"Good night."

When he had gone, I entered my room, my head whirling from the impact of his strange, compelling personality.

I undressed slowly, took a hot bath, and got into bed. As I settled myself to sleep I heard, through the overhanging silence, a sudden wailing cry. It came like the wild and desolate hooting of an owl. I knew that it was not an owl, yet I did not care, I had no place now for dismay.

The cry was repeated, fading slowly into the outer darkness.

CHAPTER TWO

NEXT morning, from the small iron balcony which spanned the coping of my window, I was able to view the impressive prospect of Eastershaws.

The mansion, built of grey granite, shimmering in the morning air, was in the baronial style, with castellated gables, and four massive turrets. In front lay a broad balustraded terrace with a central fountain surrounded by ornamental designs in boxwood. A lawn, edged by rose beds, stretched beyond, merging to a stretch of playing sward, served by a little Tyrolean chalet. Avenues cut across the green acres, and the high stone wall which circled the wide estate gave to it an air of privacy, as though it were some privileged domain.

I shaved and dressed; then, as it struck eight o'clock, I set out to breakfast with Dr. Palfrey. In the sitting-room above Men's East I discovered a short plump pink baldish man of fifty seated at table eating vigorously behind the morning paper. Our eyes met.

"My dear fellow, come along in." Still eating, he raised his hand in welcome, then completed the gesture by filling his mouth with buttered toast. "You're Shannon, of course. I'm Palfrey—Edinburgh man, took my degree in '99. Kedgeree, bacon and eggs over there . . . and here . . . the coffee. A lovely morning . . . blue sky and clear air . . . what we call a 'real Easter- shaws day.'"

Palfrey had a warm, inoffensive, and slightly foolish air, his cheeks were smooth and chubby—with every movement they wobbled like jellies. He looked thoroughly washed and manicured, his cuffs were starched, gold pince- nez hung primly round his neck by an invisible cord. Across his pink scalp a few strands of pale hair, faintly speckled with ginger, were carefully arranged from the fringe behind his ears. He kept dabbing his rosy lips and white moustache with his napkin.

"I should have made your acquaintance last night. But I was out. Out in the outland, as we say. At the opera. *Carmen*. Ah! Wonderful, unhappy Bizet. To think that he died, brokenhearted, after the failure of the opening production at the Opéra Comique, without an inkling of the glorious suc- cess it would afterwards attain. I have been to that opera precisely thirty- seven times. I have heard Bressler-Gianoli, Lehmann, Mary Garden, Destinn . . . de Reszke as Don José, Amato as Escamillo. We are most fortunate to have a Carl Rosa season in Winton." He hummed a few bars from the "Toreador Song," strumming with his fingers on the *Herald* before him. "In the critique here it says Scotti was in good voice. I should think so! Ah, that moment when Micaela, emblem of sweetness, enters the wild and rocky defile of the smugglers' camp! '*I try not to own that I tremble*.' Exquisite . . . melodious . . . superb! Are you interested in music?"

I gave an inarticulate murmur.

"Ah! You must come down to the piano in the auditorium with me. I go there most evenings, to run through a few things. I might as well confess, music is my delight. I count the three great moments in my life . . . when I heard Patti sing 'Sicilian Vespers,' Galli-Curci 'Pretty Bird' from *The Pearl of Brazil*, and Melba, Massenet's 'Sevillana.'"

He ran on like this until I had finished breakfast; then, with a ladylike gesture, examined his wrist watch.

"The Chief has asked me to take you round. Come along."

He led off fussily, his short plump legs twinkling with unexpected speed along the subway—then, taking a concrete incline to the left, as by an astral materialization, he brought us unexpectedly to daylight in the corridor be- neath my own quarters.

Here an obese, stupid-looking man of fifty in an untidy grease-stained grey uniform and rubber-soled shoes was padding up and down officiously. At Palfrey's appearance he threw out his stomach and saluted with a mixture of obsequiousness and pomp.

"Morning, Scammon. Dr. Shannon—this is Samuel Scammon—our Head Attendant . . . and also, may I add, our valued conductor of the Easter- shaws Brass Band."

Joined by Scammon's assistant, Attendant Brogan, a young good-looking fellow with a bold blue eye, we advanced towards the first gallery, over which I now saw, in faded gold, the name BALACLAVA. Like a conjuror, Scammon manipulated his key. We were inside.

The gallery was long, lofty and restful, well lit by a row of high windows upon one side and with a score of doors, leading to the individual bedrooms, upon the other. The furniture, like that in the entrance below, was of buhl, the carpets and hangings, though faded, were rich. There were easy chairs in plenty, racks of books and periodicals, in one corner a revolving globe of the world. The atmosphere was that of a comfortable but old-fashioned club, smelling of age, soap, leather and furniture polish, just faintly tinged with the scent of the commode.

About twenty gentlemen sat quietly enjoying the gallery's amenities. In the foreground two were occupied by a game of chess. Another, in the corner, with a meditative finger, was revolving the geographic sphere. Several had their morning newspaper. Others had nothing, but kept still, very erect, on chairs.

Palfrey, having scanned the report which Scammon handed to him, swept forward blithely.

"Morning, gentlemen. Having a good game?" Beaming, he placed a companionable hand on the shoulder of each chess player. "It's the most glorious day, outside. You'll enjoy your little walk, I promise you. I shan't be a moment running through . . . then you may be off."

He moved down the gallery, pausing at intervals, full of good humour and affable advice. His flow of small talk, though somewhat to a pattern, never failed. He heard complaints with an indulgent and soothing ear. He hummed between times. Yet he wasted not a minute in his expeditious passage.

ALMA was the next gallery, then came INKERMAN; altogether there were six and when, at last, we emerged to the ground-floor vestibule, having completed the entire circuit, it was almost one o'clock. Palfrey, without delay, escorted me into the fresh air and along the terrace towards the West Wing for luncheon.

"By-the-by, Shannon, perhaps I ought to warn you . . . Maitland and our housekeeper, Miss Indre, are a very close little mutual admiration society. They're not particularly enamoured of me." He passed this off airily. "I don't mind a bit. But it's all the more reason for us to support each other."

In a small parlour off the vestibule of Ladies' West, tastefully arranged as a dining-room, the square table set with fine linen and shining silver for four, Miss Indre and Maitland were already waiting. The housekeeper greeted me with a small quiet inclination of her head, a slender, faded, aristocratic woman of over fifty, immaculate and fragile in a blue voile uniform with narrow soft white wrist-bands and collar.

As we sat down veiled glances of understanding and quiet, intimate remarks passed between the two women. It was a strained and uncomfortable meal. After the soup a joint of meat was brought in and placed before

Palfrey, who carved in an embarrassed manner, humming strenuously as he sliced the undercut on to the various plates. Occasionally, with masculine directness, Maitland addressed a breezy remark in my direction—she asked me if I would make up the stock solutions after lunch for her Sister in charge. Once or twice when Palfrey spoke she shot an amused glance at Miss Indre.

Oppressed by my morning experiences, and by the unexpected difficulty of adjusting myself to this strange environment, I kept silent. When Palfrey rose, after the dessert, with a muttered excuse, I followed him towards the terrace.

"These women!" he exclaimed. "Didn't I tell you? I can't stand these two, Shannon. In fact I detest all women. I thank Heaven I have never had anything to do with one of them in my life."

He flounced off to take duty in the refectory, leaving me to proceed, with mixed emotions, towards the dispensary.

Here, Sister Shadd and a nurse were awaiting me, with an official air. Shadd was a coarse, middle-aged, strongly bosomed woman with a good-natured eye. She was examining her watch, pinned on the front of her uniform, as I came in.

"Good afternoon, Doctor. This is Nurse Stanway. May we have our supplies?"

As Shadd placed her empty basket on the counter, the nurse glanced at me, sideways, and across her pale, composed, flattened face there passed a faint smile. She was about twenty-five years of age, dark-haired, carrying herself with an air of indifference, and wearing a wedding ring on her right hand.

"Let me show you where things are," Shadd said. "A friend in need is a friend indeed."

I was to discover that Sister Shadd had a collection of proverbs such as, 'Six and half a dozen,' 'It never rains but it pours,' 'A stitch in time saves nine,' which she constantly produced with an air of wisdom. Now, very cheerfully, she aided me to fill her basket with the standard drugs, mostly hypnotics; then, with another glance at her pinned-on watch, she took her departure, remarking over her shoulder, as she went through the door, in that friendly, well-disposed tone she adopted towards Stanway:

"Get the East dressings from Dr. Shannon, Nurse. Then come back and help me in the linen-room."

There was a pause when Nurse Stanway and I were left alone, an alteration of the atmosphere, an imperceptible drop from the official plane. As she slid forward her basket she gave me a casual glance.

"You don't mind if I sit down?"

I made no objection. I guessed she wanted to get into talk with me, but although I had a rule of never looking twice at any nurse, this place, frankly, was getting on my nerves and I felt that a little human conversation might help.

Perching herself upon the counter, she gazed at me, expressionless, yet with slightly mocking air. She was not exactly good-looking, she was too pale, with pale, full lips, flat high cheek-bones, and a pushed-in nose. Yet she had an attractive quality. Under her eyes there were faint blue shadows and the skin there was stretched tight. Her black hair, cut square across her forehead, had a bluish sheen.

"Well," she said, coolly. "What brought you to Eastershaws?"

In the same manner, I answered:

"I just came in for a rest."

"You'll get it. This place is practically a morgue."

"Some of it seems pretty old-fashioned."

"It was built over a century ago. I shouldn't think it's changed much since then."

"Don't they use any modern methods?"

"Oh, yes. Not Palfrey, poor dear. He only eats, sleeps, and hums. But Maitland sweats away at hydrotherapy, shock-treatment, and psychoanalysis. She's very earnest, means well, quite decent, in fact. Goodall's idea is the best. He lets well alone. But he sees that the patients are taken care of, and he sort of helps them along by pretending that they're normal."

"I like Goodall. I met him last night."

"He's all right. Only he's a little cracked himself." She glanced at me satirically. "We're all slightly off the beam."

I filled the East list for her, gauze, lint, and g.p. tissue, solutions of valerian, bromide, and chloral hydrate. I had never met paraldehyde before and as I took the stopper from the bottle the ether smell of it almost knocked me over.

"That's powerful stuff."

"Yes. It has a kick in it. Not bad for a hangover."

She laughed briefly at my surprised expression and crooked her arm in the handle of the basket. As she moved to the door, she gave me, from her oblique eyes, that peculiar, direct half-smile.

"It's not so bad here, when you know your way around. Some of us manage to have a fairly decent time. Drop into our sitting-room when you're bored."

As she went out I found myself frowning slightly. Not that I was puzzled. Although she was quite young, her air of experience, the stretched blue skin beneath her eyes, that pushed-in, expressionless face which gave nothing away, suggested an eventful history.

When I had finished in the dispensary it was only three o'clock and now I was free to begin my own work. With a sigh of relief I went outside. But there I drew up suddenly, arrested by the scene before me.

On the lawn beneath the terrace a group of gentlemen had been marshalled by Chief Attendant Scammon for a game of bowls which, from their frequent exclamations, was proving highly exciting. The tennis courts on the other side of the Tyrolean pavilion were in full blast, with Palfrey umpiring one match. From the pavilion itself came the strains of brass music: pleasant little broken snatches, runs and rallentandos from one of Sousa's marches: indicating that the Eastershaws band was engaged in practice. Colour was added by a party of ladies, headed by Sister Shadd, trailing in elegant fashion—some were even sporting parasols—round the orchard. Nor was the picture entirely given over to diversion. In the kitchen gardens a large body of men from the East Wing were working industriously, spaced at regular intervals, hoeing the newly planted furrows with well-directed strokes.

I looked at the scene for a long time, then gradually a strange and startled feeling came upon me, a recurrence, an intensification of the sensation which had troubled me ever since I set foot in the Place. This was pleasant, this was pretty but, my God, it was almost more than I could stand. My nerves were not in a good state, perhaps, but I'd had about enough of Eastershaws for the present, with these Crimean galleries, and the gentlemen inside them, and Palfrey, and the pass key with chain attached, the doors with no handles, the smell of Sanitas, and all the rest of it. In fact I was getting a queer confused dizziness at the back of my head. I spun round sharply, went straight to the laboratory and locked the door. As I shut my window against the distant cries of the bowlers, a terrible weight of desolation, of loneliness, struck at me and crushed me down. Suddenly, despairingly, with all my heart I longed for Jean. What was I doing in this accursed spot? I should be with her. We should be together, I couldn't stand it here . . . alone.

But at last I conquered myself and, at the bench, set myself to begin the last phase of my research.

CHAPTER THREE

On the thirty-first of July, that date I had so determinedly anticipated, I obtained Dr. Goodall's consent and started, early, for the graduation ceremony at the University. Although Palfrey had occasionally tried to enveigle me to one of his favourite operas and Maitland several times had suggested that I ought to "go out," because of my activities in the laboratory, since my arrival I had not once been beyond the confines of the Place. I was beginning to settle down. In fact, it felt unreal to be in a tram again, and to see cars and people moving at will about the streets.

When, towards eleven o'clock, I reached the summit of Fenner Hill, the Moray Hall was already crowded with students and their relatives, buzzing with the usual anticipation, its musty dignity rent, from time to time, by the demonstrations of the younger and more exuberant undergraduates who were singing student songs, chasing up the aisles, whooping and catcalling, unrolling paper streamers. It all looked childish and stupid to me. I did not go in but hung about in the crowd standing by the door, hoping to meet in with Spence or Lomax and, in the meantime, searching the auditorium and balconies with a strained and nervous gaze.

Jean was not visible. But suddenly, amongst that sea of faces, I caught sight of her family, her father, mother, and Luke, seated in the second row of the left side balcony, with Malcolm Hodden beside them. All were in their best clothes, bending forward eagerly, with such animation, so pleased, proud and expectant, I had to repress an instinctive reaction of hostility. I took cover behind the nearest pillar.

At that moment, by the dexterous use of his umbrella, a corpulent spectator poked and manœuvred into position beside me—then, with a gasp of triumph, accosted me.

"Hello, my dear Dr. Robert Shannon."

I found myself confronted by that fount of gossip and good nature, the ever-beaming Babu Chatterjee.

"How extremely agreeable to meet you, sir. We miss you continually at Rothesay, but of course follow your career with interest. Is it not a splendid assembly here today?"

"Splendid," I agreed, without enthusiasm.

"Oh, come, sir! Tee hee! No disparagement to our dear Alma Mater." His remarks were punctuated by little grunts as, periodically, from the thrusting crowd, he received an elbow in his abdomen. "Although I am not myself graduating, hoping to do so shortly, the splendid ceremonial pleases me greatly. I have not once missed it the past ten years. Come, sir. Shall we press forward and secure two front adjacent seats?"

"I think I'll wait here. I'm looking out for Spence and Lomax."

At that instant the great organ above us pealed out, drowning all other sounds; and, realizing that the proceedings had begun, a fresh wave of people pressed into the hall, swirling us apart, sweeping the Babu up the central aisle.

I held my ground for a few minutes, while the Principal made a short speech and, aided by Professor Usher, who stood beside him with the parchments, started the usual business of "capping" the long procession of graduates. But the crowd was too dense for me to view the spectacle, in any case I had no wish to see all of it, and, since my frustrated gaze kept stealing upwards to the balcony, the sight of Hodden and the Law family, smiling and applauding, became more than I could endure. In the face of protests and opposition, I fought my way out of the hall. A public telephone booth stood in a corner of the cloisters, and, on an impulse, I entered and rang up the Pathology Department. But Spence was not there. Nor could I find him at his house. The phone simply rang, no one answered.

Defeated, I came out of the cabinet and went slowly up the worn, shallow stone stairway, along the corridor, to the robing-room. It was here that, for a fee of half a guinea or so, the students hired their gowns and hoods, and I knew that after the ceremony Jean would come back, to return her borrowed robes. This was the only place where I could be sure of finding her alone and I sat down in a corner by the long wooden counter, to wait.

Under the depressing sound of forced applause, which rattled out every thirty seconds beneath me, my mood sank to depths of bitter sadness. A rush of returning graduates caused me to raise my head abruptly and presently, amongst the others, I saw Jean, hurrying along the corridor, wearing her gown over a new brown costume, new brown stockings and shoes. She was flushed, talking to the girl beside her, with an air of excitement, of momentary animation which, after these weeks of separation, cut me to the heart. Because I loved her I wished to find her bathed in tears.

She had not noticed me. Slowly and carefully, I got up and stood by the counter, close beside her. I was at her elbow but she did not dream that I was there and I did not say a word.

For several seconds nothing happened; then, all at once, she paused, arrested in the act of handing in her gown. She could not have seen me, yet the warm blood ebbed, slowly, from her face and neck, leaving her very white. For a long, long moment she remained inanimate—then, as by the exercise of an immense, an almost superhuman, effort she forced herself to turn her head.

I looked straight into her eyes. She seemed turned to stone.

"I wasn't invited, but all the same, I came."

A long pause. Her pale lips may have shaped an answer. But she could not speak it. I went on:

"I don't suppose you have a few minutes to waste? I'd like to speak to you alone."

"I am alone now."

"Yes, but we're sure to be interrupted here. Can't we go off somewhere for a bit? I seem to recollect that we've done it before."

"My people are waiting for me downstairs. I have to go back to them at once."

Although all my bones were melting towards her, I answered bitterly:

"I've kept out of your way for four weeks, I haven't contaminated you with my presence. I think I'm due a short conversation with you."

She moistened those pale dry lips.

"What good would it do?"

I looked at her cruelly. I had longed to see her and now that we were, at last, together, my one desire was to wound her as deeply as I could. I searched for the hardest and most cutting words.

"At least it would give us a chance to say good-bye. Now you've got your degree I've no doubt you'll be only too glad to be rid of me. You probably know I'm at Eastershaws. Yes. The asylum. I've come down even more in the world."

As I went on like this, causing the dark look of pain to deepen in her eyes, I suddenly saw a solid form advancing towards us. Quickly, I bent forward and, in a different tone, said:

"Jean. Come out and see me at Eastershaws . . . some afternoon . . . just once . . . for old time's sake."

I could see the struggle going on behind her pale, tormented brow then, even as I realized what it must mean to her, she barely whispered:

"Next Thursday, then . . . I may come."

No sooner had she spoken than Malcolm Hodden was upon us, breathing a little rapidly from having bounded upstairs, curving his arm around Jean's shoulders, as though to protect her from the jostling crowd, and at the same time giving me, with his steady blue eyes, a glance of quiet recognition.

"Come, Jean, dear," he reasoned, but without reproach. "We've all been wondering what was delaying you."

"Am I late?" she asked nervously.

"Oh, no." He smiled with reassuring calm, escorting her towards the steps. "I engaged the table for one o'clock—we have plenty of time. But Professor Kennerly is with your father and asking for you."

At the foot of the staircase, while Jean slipped away, without even a glance, to join her parents, who stood in a group near the quadrangle, Malcolm turned upon me his serious yet unhostile gaze.

"Don't look at me like that, Shannon. We are not enemies. Since we have a few minutes together, let us talk things over sensibly."

He led the way through the stone archway to the front terrace, where, at the University flagstaff, there stood, in an open space upon the summit of the hill, a circular iron bench. Seating himself, he made a sign for me to do likewise. His calm was admirable. He was, in fact, all that I was not. Strong, practical, dependable, with a clear eye and a fine physique, conscious of his own inner equilibrium, he showed no sensitive flinchings. There were no secret doubts or dark places in his soul. I envied him with all my imperfect, anguished heart.

"At least we have one thing in common," he began, as though reading my mind. "We both want Jean to be happy."

"Yes," I said, my lips compressed.

"Then think, Shannon," he argued, logically. "Don't you see it is impossible? You and she are unsuited in every way."

"I love her," I said doggedly.

"But love isn't marriage," he answered quickly. "That is a serious undertaking. One simply cannot rush into it. You would be wretched, married."

"How can you tell? We would take our chance. Marriage is something inevitable . . . a calamity, perhaps, from which there is no escape . . . but not a blueprint for a new mission hall."

"No, no, Shannon." He countered my jibe with greater earnestness. "Marriage should confirm, and not disrupt two lives. Before you met Jean everything was arranged . . . her work . . . her life. She was settled, contented in her mind. And now you are asking her to give up all this, to estrange her family, cut herself off from the very sources of her being."

"None of these things need happen."

"Ah, that's what you think. Let me ask you a simple question. Would you like to attend service at Jean's chapel?"

"No."

"Exactly. Then how can you expect her to go to yours?"

"That's just the point. I don't. I have no wish to force her into anything. We should each have complete freedom of thought and action."

He shook his head, unconvinced.

"It's a pretty theory, Shannon. In practice it won't work. There are scores of opportunities for friction. And what about the children? Ask your own priest. He will tell you that I'm right. Your church has always frowned on mixed marriages."

"Some have succeeded," I maintained, with heavy stubbornness. "We would be happy together."

"For a little while perhaps," he said, almost with pity. "But in five years' time, just consider . . . a hymn tune overheard, a revival meeting in the street, some recollection of her childhood, the realization of what she has given up . . . she will look at you and hate you."

The words fell upon my ears like a knell. In the silence which followed I could hear the heavy drumming of the flag, transmitted through the pole, as though the vibrant wood were striving to be alive.

"Believe me, Shannon, I am trying to think only of Jean. Today she had almost regained happiness when you reappeared. Do you wish to hurt her always? Ah, I know you better than that! As man to man, Shannon, I am sure your better nature will prevail."

He brought out his watch, encased in a horn guard, studied it, and, in a lighter key, declared:

"We are giving a little celebration for Jean. Lunch at the Windsor Hotel." He paused. "If circumstances were different, I would wish you to be with us. Is there anything more that I can say?"

"No," I said.

He stood up and, after a firm forbearing pressure upon my arm, moved steadily away. And there I sat, hearing the drumming and singing of the flag, isolated by my own acts, trying not to hate Malcolm, feeling myself more and more an outlaw. A party of well-dressed visitors glanced at me curiously, in passing, then turned away polite eyes.

CHAPTER FOUR

BREAKING the long spell of fine weather, Thursday dawned damp and misty. I watched anxiously for it to clear, but even at noon the sun was blanketed and, although it was not raining heavily, the lawns were drenched, and in the avenues a steady dripping came from the trees.

Immediately after lunch I walked to the lodge, keyed, nervously, with longing. I was in good time, yet she had already arrived, and was sitting, neglected and distraught, in the waiting-room, which, since this was visiting day, was noisy and steamy, crowded with the relatives of East Wing patients.

Concerned, I went forward and would have taken her hand had she not risen to her feet.

"Why didn't you ask the porter to telephone me?"

"It's my own fault." She gave me a distant, wavering smile. "I took an earlier train. It was a little difficult at home . . . and as I had nothing else to do, I just came out here."

"If I'd only known."

"It's nothing. I didn't want to disturb you. But they might have let me walk about the gardens."

"Well," I explained, "they have to take a few precautions here. It's like crossing from one country to another. We're an exclusive lot. But if you'd told Gunn you were a doctor he'd have let you in right away."

Although I was trying to win her from her depression, she remained silent and withdrawn, looking small and forlorn in her raincoat and a soft hat with a grey wing all beaded with raindrops. My longing for her hurt me, yet I tried to force my stiff features to a semblance of composure.

"Well, never mind," I said, making a fresh start. "You're here . . . and we are together."

"Yes," she answered in a subdued voice. "It's a shame it's turned so damp."

In silence we walked up South Avenue, past the wet-roofed chalet, under the dripping trees, which stood silent, bent over the wet path as though cowed by the rain.

The misery of the weather hung over us, blurring all outlines in this lost and silent city. Would she never speak?

Suddenly as we approached the main building she raised her gaze slowly —then, at something visible behind me, gave a startled cry.

A body of men from the East Wing had loomed out of the mist, led by Scammon and his assistant Brogan, approaching in mass formation at the double. They were only exercising, but as the dark figures swung down on us, closely packed, their feet thudding rhythmically on the soft gravel, Jean closed her eyes, holding herself rigid until they had passed and the sound of their pounding footsteps was lost in the grey fog.

"I'm sorry," she said, at last, miserably. "I know it's absurd of me: I'm all on edge."

Everything was going wrong. Under my breath I cursed myself. The rain came on, quite heavy.

"Let's go in," I said. "I want to show you the laboratory."

After the raw outer air, it was comfortable in the laboratory, but although she removed her gloves she did not unbutton the collar of her raincoat. We stood side by side at the bench and, when her eyes had swept the place, she took up all the cultures, one by one, in a reminiscent way, as of something past, clouded by memory, never to be renewed.

"Careful," I murmured, as she touched the stopper of the strongest culture.

She turned towards me, and her dark dilated pupils softened slightly. Yet she said nothing. No one was there, we were together, but we were not alone.

"I've made a vaccine," I told her in a low voice. "But now I have a better idea. To extract and concentrate the nucleo-protein. Challis agrees it should be far more efficacious."

"Have you seen him lately?"

"No. I'm sorry to say he's laid up again, at Bute."

There was a pause. Her apparent calmness, this pretence of normality, made everything unreal. We stood and looked at each other as though hypnotized. It was suddenly chilly.

"You're cold," I said.

We went to my sitting-room, where Sarah had already lit a good fire. I rang the bell and almost at once she brought up the well-laden tray I had asked her to prepare.

Sunk in a wide chair and warming her hands at the blaze, Jean drank a cup of tea gratefully, and ate one of the *petits fours* which I had brought in specially from Grant's. Her mood seemed flagging, as though the prospect of life were a load from which she shrank. I simply could not break this cold constraint which lay upon us. Yet, watching the colour flow back slowly to her pinched cheeks, I hoped that she was thawing out. She looked pathetically small and slight. As her fresh and tender bloom returned, a white heat burned in my breast. But my pride would not let me show it. In a stiff voice I said:

"I hope you feel better."

"Yes, thank you."

"This Place takes some getting used to."

"I'm sorry I was so silly outside. But here . . . It's as though someone never stops watching you."

Again there fell a silence in which the slow tick of the clock sounded like fate. The room was beginning to darken. Except for a flicker from the hearth there was barely enough light for me to see her face, so still, as if asleep. A quiver went over my nerves.

"You have barely spoken all afternoon. You cannot forgive me . . . for what happened . . ."

She did not raise her head.

"I am ashamed," I said. "But I could not have been different."

"It is terrible to fall in love against one's will," she said at last. "When I am with you I no longer belong to myself."

This admission gave to me a feeling of hope, that grew, gradually, into a strange sense of power. I gazed at her across the shadows.

"I want to ask you something."

"Do you?" she said. Her face had a tense look, the look of someone expecting a blow.

"Let us get married. At once. At the registry office."

She seemed to feel, rather than to hear me, sitting silent and stricken, her head averted, as though trying to turn away.

Seeing her so helpless, a sudden exultation flamed over me.

"Why shouldn't we?" I insisted softly, rapidly. "Say you'll marry me. This afternoon."

Breathless, I waited for her to answer. Her eyelids were lowered, her face half dazed, as though the world rocked about her and she were lost.

"Say yes."

"Oh, I can't," she murmured, inarticulately, tormented, in the tone of one about to die.

"You can."

"No," she cried, facing round to me hysterically. "It is impossible."

A long, a heavy pause. That sudden cry had made of me an enemy, her enemy, the enemy of her people. I tried to collect myself.

"For God's sake, don't be so unloving, Jean."

"I must be. We have suffered enough. And others too. My mother goes about the house, looking at me, simply saying nothing. And she is ill. I have to tell you, Robert. I am going away for good."

The finality in her voice stunned me.

"It's all arranged. There's a party of us going out to West Africa on the maiden voyage of the new Clan liner, the *Algoa*. We sail in three months' time."

"Three months." I echoed her words—at least it was not tomorrow. But sadly, with enforced calmness, she shook her head.

"No, Robert . . . I shall be busy all that time . . . doing temporary work."

"Where?"

She flushed slightly, but her gaze did not waver.

"At Dalnair."

"The cottage hospital?" Surprise broke through my despair.

"Yes."

I sat dumb and overcome. She went on:

"There is a vacancy there again. They want to try a woman doctor for a change . . . a short experimental appointment. The matron recommended me to the committee."

Crushed by the news of her departure, I nevertheless kept trying, in a stupid sort of way, to picture her against the familiar background of the hospital, traversing the wards and corridors, occupying the very quarters that I had used. At last, I muttered brokenly:

"You did get on with Matron. You get on with everyone but me."

Her breast heaved. She gave me a strange, unnatural smile.

"If we had never met . . . it would have been better. With us, there is a penalty for everything."

I guessed her meaning. But although my eyes were smarting and my heart almost bursting, I struck back with a last, despairing bitterness.

"I won't give you up."

She was still calm but tears were flowing down her cheeks.

"Robert . . . I'm going to marry Malcolm Hodden."

I stared at her, frozen. I barely whispered:

"Oh, no . . . no . . . you don't care for him."

"Yes, I do." Pale and tremulous, she defended herself with quivering distress. "He is a worthy, honourable man. We grew up together, went to school, yes, to Sunday school together. We worship in the same chapel. We have the same aims and objectives, he will be good for me in every way. In fact, when we are married we shall go out together on the *Algoa*, I as a doctor, Malcolm as head teacher in the settlement school."

I swallowed the enormous lump which had risen in my throat.

"It can't be true," I muttered, inaudibly. "It's all a dream."

"You and I are the dream, Robert. We must go back to reality."

I clenched my fists against my forehead and while, helplessly, I did so, she began in real earnest to cry.

It was more than I could stand. I got to my feet. At the same instant she rose, blindly, as though driven by the instinct to escape. We met. Then, for a moment, she was in my arms, weeping as though her heart would break, while my own heart was choked by a wild intoxication and delight. But as I held her more closely, she seemed suddenly to summon all her strength. Abruptly and passionately, she broke away.

"No . . . Robert . . . no."

The anguish in her face, in every line of her fragile, flinching form, held me rooted to the spot.

"Jean."

"No, no . . . never again . . . never."

She could not stop the sobs which choked her, sobs which wrung my heart, and made me long to soothe her upon my breast. But that look in her glistening eyes, broken and tortured, yet fiercely unwavering, welling up from the depths of her soul, drained me slowly of all hope. The burning words of love I meant to speak died upon my lips. The arms I had raised towards her fell to my side. There was a dull and heavy beating in my head.

At last, stiffly, she brushed away her tears with the back of her hand, then wiped her lips. With a face hard as iron I helped her to put on her raincoat.

"I'll come with you to the gate."

We walked to the entrance lodge without a single word. The rivulets which channeled the avenue had a sound almost living, but our steps were dead upon the sodden ground. We drew up at the gateway. I took her fingers, wet with rain and tears, but quickly she disengaged them.

"Good-bye, Robert."

I looked at her as for the last time. A car rushed past in the road outside.

"Good-bye."

She faltered at that, but recovered herself with a shiver and hurried off, her eyes wrinkled up against fresh tears, not looking back. The next minute the heavy gate clanged shut; she was gone.

I came up the drive, sullen and wretched. Twilight was falling and the rain at last had ceased. Above the western horizon the sky was livid, as though the sunset had committed bloody murder amongst the clouds. Suddenly, over the still Place, the evening bugle sounded and from the tall flagpole on the hill the flag descended, slowly, slowly, while outlined upon the ridge there stood, rigidly, in the tense attitude of salute, the erect and solitary figure of the inmate deputed to this task.

Long live Eastershaws, I thought bitterly.

Back in my room I found the fire almost dead. I gazed at the dull grey ashes.

CHAPTER FIVE

It was Sunday, and the bells of the ivy-clad church broke upon the Eastershaws air. As though to aggravate the darkness of my mind, the morning once again shone bright and warm. Fruit hung heavily on the orchard trees, and in the formal beds of the balustraded terrace geraniums and begonias traced out vivid arabesques.

From my window, as I finished dressing, heavy, and only half awake, I could see the inmates of the Place converging upon the holy building, a goodly sized Gothic structure of mellow brick, appropriately shaded by a cluster of tall elms.

The men of the East Wing came first, flanked by Brogan and three of Scammon's staff, a large and solid body, dressed in workmanlike grey, with strong boots and serviceable caps, most of whom worked in the fields or craft shops. Some were cheerful and smiling, others silent, a few gloomy —for there were "bad" morons amongst the "good" who were often at odds with the authorities. One group had a superior, though less hardy air, with darker suits and white starched collars—these were men who had risen and were entrusted with special tasks such as checking cartloads of coal or wood at the weighbridge, or marking off the laundry, on paper sheets, with pen and ink. Palfrey, already in the porch, shepherded them in with a benign smile and pink nods of welcome.

The women of the North Wing approached a minute later, wearing their Sunday black, some of them recognizable as the waitresses and chambermaids of the Place. They fell into the same category as the men.

Next upon the scene were the gentlemen of the Place, accompanied by Scammon who, in the full finery of his best uniform, set the tone of sartorial perfection. At least a dozen of the party sported morning coats and top hats. Here, if you like, was the "upper crust" of Eastershaws.

A moment's pause when the gentlemen had crossed the sacred acre. . . . Inside the church an organ voluntary had begun; then, as though aware that they brought the final touch, the ladies of West Wing made their appearance, not in a solid troop like those of lesser consequence, but singly and in pairs, chaperoned by Sister Shadd. They came leisurely, in all their finery, careful that their skirts did not touch the dust. In the very centre of the group, surrounded by her own adulatory coterie, a lady advanced with great dignity towards the porch. Small, grey-haired and slight, with a drawn little beak and bright darting eyes in a parchment face, she was attired in lavender silk, with lace at her bosom and a large hat with an ostrich plume upon her head.

They were all in now, the bells had ceased and, stepping briskly up the path, in a plain everyday suit, came Goodall, to conduct the service. When he had vanished into the church I turned from the window with a bitter frown, clipped on my key and went downstairs.

This was the third Sunday of the month, I was on official duty all day, at least until six; but I went first to the laboratory, which I had left only six hours before, to check upon the collodion sac I was using as a dialyzing membrane. Yes, it was functioning perfectly. That was the way of it now. In my work everything went well. I took the rack of twenty sterile paraffined tubes, and ran into each 1 c.c. of the dialyzed fluid, corked the test-tubes carefully, numbered them, and put them in the incubator.

I stood a moment, heavy and brooding, feeling at the back of my head that hard pain which comes from overwork. I wanted my coffee, but could scarcely gather myself to go for it. Yes, this time there was no mistake. I was not far from isolating the nucleo-protein which should prove far more effective than the primary vaccine. Then I should have finished. Everything. My nerves bunched together at the thought. But I felt no real excitement. Only a kind of sullen, bitter satisfaction.

In the breakfast-room at Men's North I ate a slice of toast and drank three cups of black coffee. It was good to be alone—not that I minded Palfrey much, he was an amiable, inoffensive creature. The rhyme Nurse Stanway had made suited him.

> I like little Palfrey, his coat is so warm,
> And if you don't hurt him, he'll do you no harm.

I lit a cigarette and inhaled deeply, as though to dull down that perpetual ache in my side. It was over, yet there came always an unguarded moment when Jean was close to me, when, with a wincing spasm, I must thrust her savagely away. At first, in sadness, I had pitied myself. Now a slow burning resentment had mingled with the pain, and tempered it like steel. There raged in me a deep, corroding anger against life.

I rose and went down to the dispensary where I began to make up the stock bromide and chloral solutions for the galleries. The dispensary was quiet and dim, panelled in dark mahogany, with an aromatic smell of drugs, old wood, and sealing wax which vaguely soothed my warring senses. Lately, the Place had grown upon me. My earlier uneasiness was gone, I accepted, without a second thought, the key, the warm rococo galleries, the social structure of this cut-off little world.

Footsteps sounded in the passage and, an instant later, the hatch went up, framing Nurse Stanway's head and shoulders.

"Ready?" she asked.

I answered briefly:

"In a minute."

She stood watching while I filled the last of the West Side list.

"You didn't go to church?"

"No," I said. "Did you?"

"It's much too nice a day. Besides it isn't in my line."

I looked at her. She met my gaze without any discernible change in her expressionless face. Her bang of glossy hair had a bluish glint and showed square on her white forehead under her uniform cap. I knew now that during the war she had married a flying officer who had later divorced her. She did not appear to care. One never knew what she was feeling, it seemed that nothing could break her casual air, her complete indifference, as though life were something worthless, to be spent carelessly, or simply thrown away.

"You haven't come to our sitting-room yet." She spoke deliberately, almost with the slowness of mockery. "Sister Shadd's very cut up about it."

"I haven't had time."

I made the excuse abruptly.

"Why don't you look in tonight? You might find it amusing. One never knows."

There was a faintly malicious challenge in her tone which sent a stark impulse along my worn nerves. I gazed at her with moody attention. Her rather full eyes still were mocking, yet they held a glint of meaning.

"All right," I said, suddenly. "I'll come."

She smiled slightly and, still looking at me, gathered up the medicines I had placed on the ledge of the hatch. Then, without a word, she turned away. Her slow movements had a physical casualness, a sensual grace.

For the rest of the day I was unsettled, ill at ease. After lunch I wrote up the case-book for Men's East, and at three o'clock went to deliver it at Dr. Goodall's house, set in the façade of the main building.

An elderly maidservant answered the bell and, having gone within to inquire, returned a moment later to say that the Superintendent was resting but would see me. I followed her to the study, a large untidy room, panelled in nondescript brown wood and sparsely lit by a yellowish leaded Gothic window with a stained-glass coat of arms inset. Stretched upon a sofa by the wide fireplace, covered by a plaid rug, was Goodall.

"You must excuse me, Dr. Shannon. The fact is, after church I did not feel well, and took a stiff dose of morphine." He proclaimed the fact simply, his eyes heavy in the griped and sallow face. "Wasn't it Montaigne who compared biliary colic to the tortures of the damned? I am a sufferer too."

He laid down the book I handed him and fixed his lined and heavy-lidded gaze upon me.

"You seem to be settling down very nicely. I am glad. I don't like changes in my staff. We have a great opportunity here, Dr. Shannon . . . in this little planet of ours." He paused, with a musing, strangely distant air. "Has it never struck you that we are a race apart, with our own laws and customs, virtues and vices, our social and intellectual strata, our reactions to the stress of living? People of the other world do not understand us, laugh at us, perhaps fear us. But we are citizens of the universe, nevertheless, a symbol of Man's indestructibility under the forces of Nature and of Fate."

My heart missed a beat as, leaning towards me, he went on with that remote gleam in his dark, pin-point irises.

"My task, Dr. Shannon, my life's endeavour is to create a new society, out of an order that is diseased and decadent. Difficult . . . ah, yes, but not impossible. And what a chance, Doctor! . . . When you have finished your present research I can open up for you a scientific field of unimaginable scope. We are only upon the threshold of understanding those maladies which affect our people. The brain, Dr. Shannon, the human brain, in all its mystery and majesty, pink and translucent, shining like a lovely fruit within its delicate membranes, its cranial sheath . . . What a subject for investiga-tion . . . what a fascinating enigma to be solved!"

There was exaltation in his voice. For a moment I thought he was about to soar to dizzier heights but, as with an effort, he recollected himself. He threw me a quick glance and after a moment of silence, dismissed me with his dark yet winning smile.

"Don't work too hard, Doctor. One must occasionally pay tribute to the senses."

I came away from his house in an even greater tumult of my feelings, attracted, yet excited and confused. He always had that effect upon me. But this evening it was worse than ever.

I simply could not rest. A surging ferment overcharged my veins, ready to burst forth. One must occasionally pay tribute to the senses, he had said.

Although, several times, I had told myself I would not go, towards eight o'clock I knocked on the door of the Sisters' sitting-room and opened it. I must find a way of escape from these fevered and tormenting thoughts.

Seated at the end of the long table, which gave evidence that most of the staff had already supped and left the room, were Shadd, in uniform, Miss Paton, the dietician, and Nurse Stanway, dressed for "off duty" in a blue skirt and white silk blouse. The three were talking in intimate voices and it was Shadd, perking up like a pouter pigeon, who saw me first.

"Why, Mahomet has come to the mountain." She brought out the "saying" in a pleased voice. "We're highly honoured, I'm sure."

As I entered Miss Paton, a middle-aged woman with a ruddy face, gave me a nod of greeting. Nurse Stanway's expression was calm and indifferent. It was the first time I had seen her out of uniform. Her bang of glossy hair fell more conspicuously over her forehead, and the soft, shiny stuff of her blouse was loose over her flat chest and breasts.

"Haven't you finished?" I asked.

"As a matter of fact, we haven't begun." Shadd met my inquiring gaze with a robust laugh. "We may as well tell you . . . since you're one of us now. Sometimes we get tired of our menu. It wouldn't be good discipline, for the others, to complain. So we just wait and go down for supper, we three, to the kitchens."

"Ah, I see!"

At my tone, a faint blush penetrated Shadd's dermal toughness. She rose. "If you breathe a word of it I'll never speak to you again."

The kitchens, reached by the subway, were entirely underground, but lofty, cool and softly lit by clusters of frosted ceiling globes. Against one white tiled wall stood an array of old-fashioned ranges, on another hung a copper *batterie de cuisine,* while along a third ran a series of insulated white doors leading to the cold-rooms. Three mixing troughs, a bread cutter and a ham-slicing machine with a heavy steel wheel stood at the far end beside a scrubbed deal table on which a great pan of oatmeal was already soaking for the next morning's porridge. A gentle whirring from the ventilation system filled the air of the immaculate vault.

Miss Paton had acquired a new briskness in her own domain. She advanced to the refrigerator marked Ladies' West, and with a turn of her wrist on the nickel handle threw open the heavy door, disclosing an assortment of cold meats, tongue, ham, sardines in a glass container, blanc mange, jellies, and preserved fruits.

Sister Shadd smacked her lips.

"I'm hungry," she said.

When plates and forks had been passed round we began to eat in picnic fashion. Out of the corner of my eye, I saw Stanway perch herself on the wooden table with a detachment and assurance which swelled the dark forces of exasperation within me. Her legs were crossed, so that one swung loose, stressing the silken slimness of the limb. Her posture, slightly inclined backwards, emphasized the line of her thigh, waist, and breasts.

A harsh tightness rose in my throat. The desire to subdue her, to break through the barriers which restrained me, to destroy and desecrate, dominated me like a fever. I took no notice of her, remaining beside Sister Shadd, replenishing her plate from time to time, bearing with her stupid conversation. Yet while I pretended to listen, I could still see Stanway, balancing a plate of salad, her eyes charged with a sly and secret irony.

At last, having finished her dessert, Shadd heaved a regretful sigh.

"Well! All good things come to an end. I must go now and check my wretched linen-room. Be a sport, Paton, and come with me. It'll only take me half an hour if you help me."

On our way back through the underground the two older women took the

West incline. I continued with Nurse Stanway towards the North Wing
vestibule. We stood there.

"What next?"

"I think I'll take a walk," Stanway said, carelessly.

"I'll come with you."

She indicated her indifference with a slight shrug, an instinct of cruelty,
yet flattered, in a feline way, by my attention.

Outside, the night was dark, a few stars showing, but moonless. Once she
was free of the buildings Stanway halted to light a cigarette. The cupped
flame haloed for an instant her pale unconcerned face, with its high cheekbones and flattened nose. Why, I asked myself, am I doing this? I knew
practically nothing about her and cared less. An accommodating stranger
who would help me to roll in the gutter, to escape. A greater hardness took
hold of me. In a controlled voice I said:

"Which way?"

"Down to the farm . . ." She seemed to smile. "And back."

"Just as you like."

Setting off along the West drive, suiting my step to hers, I kept a distance
between us, looking straight in front. But, in the darkness, her own sense
of space was less exact and from time to time she brushed against me. The
soft collision of her hip-bone as it made contact with mine increased the
tortured hardness of my thoughts.

"Why don't you talk?" she asked with a light laugh. She was like a cat,
in that the night seemed to excite and strengthen her.

"What about?"

"Anything. I don't care. What star is that ahead of us?"

"The Pole star. Look for it when you get lost in the woods."

Again she laughed, less scornfully than usual.

"Are we likely to get lost? You don't see Venus, by any chance?"

"Not just yet."

"Well . . ." She was still laughing. "There's still hope."

I did not say anything. I felt myself harder and more uncaring now,
despising myself and her. That laugh, keyed too high, shorn of assurance,
had given her away, revealed her pretence of indifference as a sham, a secret
invitation, from the beginning.

At the turn of the road under the farm elms there was a five-barred gate,
held by two high turf walls. I stopped.

"This is as far as you want to go?"

She stubbed out her cigarette against the gate. I took her by the shoulders.
I said:

"I'd like to break your neck."

"Why don't you try?"

Pressed back against the turf wall her face was dead-white, the stretched
skin under her eyes bluer than ever. Her nostrils were slightly dilated. Her

smile was fixed, almost a grimace. A wave of repugnance went over me, but the desire for oblivion had gone too far to be dispelled.

Her lips were dry and slightly bitter from the cigarette. They opened in an experienced manner. I could feel a shred of tobacco on her tongue. Her breath came quicker than mine.

There was an instant while Jean's face floated up before me, then the moon went behind a cloud and it was dark beneath the elms where nothing remained but disillusion and despair.

CHAPTER SIX

AUGUST passed in a wave of stifling heat. Although the watering cart went round each morning, clouds of dust rose from the driveways of the Place, and the leaves hung limply on the trees. The sun, streaming through the window-panes, upon which a fly buzzed quietly, gave to the dim galleries a mellow and nostalgic charm.

On the last evening of that torrid month it was so close I left the door of the laboratory half open. As I bent over the Duboscq colorimeter, with my shirt-sleeves rolled up and sweat rolling down under my unloosened collar, I heard a step behind me.

"Good evening, Shannon." To my surprise, it was Maitland's voice. "No, don't let me disturb you."

She had never visited me here before. Judging by the wool-stuffed workbag upon her arm, she was returning from one of her long, close sessions with Miss Indre, wherein the two women, knitting together, confidentially reviewed the current problems of the Place. Now, pulling forward a stool, she seated herself near me.

"How is it going?"

I laid down my pen, and rubbed my strained and slightly bloodshot eyes. I could feel the twitching of my left supraorbital nerve. I said shortly:

"In a few hours I'll have finished."

"I'm so glad. I guessed you were near the end."

She had taken no offence at my abruptness. I did not dislike Maitland, but it was annoying to have her in the way at this particular moment. I could see her better now, her mottled face had a serious expression, as she gazed at me steadily through her violet lenses, studying me, and at the same time nerving herself to speak.

"I'm not an interfering person, Shannon . . . under my shell of bravado, I am rather a weak and pitiful creature. And I am wondering if I dare offer you some advice."

I stared at her in complete surprise. With a formal gravity which increased my irritation, she resumed:

"It's terribly important to find one's proper place in life, Shannon. Take my own case, for instance—dull though it is. I'm Irish, as you know, but

actually my family is English, settled in Wexford on a demesne granted them
by Cromwell. For over three hundred years we Maitlands have lived there,
isolated, alien, separated from the people by blood and tears, burned out
twice in five generations, suffering an insidious decay, a blight, soft and relentless as a sea fog, which rots the soul."

There was a pause. I looked at her coldly.

"You seem to have escaped that unhappy fate."

"Yes, Shannon. I escaped. But only by running away."

Her gaze was charged with such significance I moved impatiently.

"Frankly, I don't know what you mean."

"Don't you recall Freud's definition of a psychosis? A flight away from
life into the realm of disease."

"What's that got to do with me?"

"Can't you guess?"

"No, I can't." My temper unexpectedly got out of hand, my voice was
disturbingly shrill. "What are you driving at?"

She took off her glasses and slowly polished them. Then, forgetfully, she
let them fall into her lap, gazed at me with those weak and browless eyes.

"Shannon . . . you should leave Eastershaws."

I was absolutely staggered.

"What! Leave?"

"Yes," she repeated. "Whenever you complete your research."

I felt myself flush, deeply. I stared at her with angry, incredulous eyes.

"That's an excellent joke. I thought for a moment you were serious."

"I am entirely serious . . . and so is my advice."

"Then wait until I ask for it. I happen to like this Place as well as you.
And I have friends here too."

"Nurse Stanway?" Her lip curled faintly. "She's had a few followers in
her time. Attendant Brogan, for instance . . . and your predecessor . . ."

"That's none of your business. I've been treated pretty badly outside. I'm
not going to throw up a good job and a first-class laboratory because you
get some wild idea in your head."

That, I could see, had silenced her.

She sat still for a few moments, then stood up.

"All right, Shannon. Let's forget about it. Good night."

She smiled and quickly went out.

I turned angrily to my bench. At the back of my mind I was dully aware
of how I had spent myself in this final effort. I had lost weight and there
were hollows in my cheeks; when I caught a glimpse of myself in the mirror
I seemed to be confronted by a stranger. In the past, I had been able to do
with three or four hours' sleep. But now I couldn't sleep at all. Complete
insomnia. To calm my nerves during these night long seances I smoked so
constantly my tongue and throat were raw. And there were these strange
tricks and fancies, fetishes in fact, which I had developed under this growing
strain. Every time I left my bench, I had to go back, three times, to reassure

myself that I had actually turned off the tap of my burette. I had developed the habit of shutting my left eye when I made my readings, and of writing my figures backwards. Each day, before I began work, I counted all the tiles in the section of wall above the incubator. There was a word, too, which somehow had got into my head, "abracadabra," and I found myself muttering it to myself, as a kind of invocation, as a spur to goad myself on, and as a low exclamation of triumph, whenever I completed another step in my experiments. And still I went on, like an automaton, testing and titrating, bearing forward, forward . . . I had to go on. I'd gone too far to draw back, it was all or nothing now . . . yes, all or nothing.

At eight o'clock I set the vaccine extract to filter, and as this process would take about an hour, I rose, switched off the lights, and left the laboratory, bent upon a short respite in my room.

Outside, I could hear preliminary tunings from the auditorium where, at the end of each month, an entertainment was held, half-dance, half-concert, sponsored by Palfrey, ostensibly for the benefit of the patients, but mainly to permit the little *maestro* to sing, with his hand upon his heart, Gounod's "Even bravest heart may swell . . ."

I rarely went to these junketings and tonight I assuredly would not go.

Anxious to stretch out on my sofa, I entered my room, but as I did so I found that I was not alone. Seated by the open window, with a droop to his shoulders, and a peculiar fixity in his gaze, was Neil Spence.

"Why, Spence!" I exclaimed. "It's good to see you again."

He acknowledged my welcome with a faint smile in his wide, immobile eyes, and after we had shaken hands, sank back in his chair, his face shadowed by the curtain.

"I can't stay long, Robert. But I took a notion to look you up. You don't mind?"

"Of course not." I had often pressed him to visit me—yet, strangely, I wondered why he had come. "You'll have a drink?"

He looked at me broodingly, that shadowy smile still flickering in his dark pupils.

"Please."

I saw then that he had already had several, but that made no difference, besides I wanted one myself. It was easy to come by good spirits from the stimulant cupboard and lately I had drawn pretty heavily upon that store. I scarcely ate anything now, but kept myself going on black coffee, whisky, and cigarettes. I poured out two stiff drinks.

"Here's luck then, Robert."

"Good health."

He nursed his tumbler between his hands, his eyes wandering about the room. There was in his calmness something which made me uneasy.

"How is Muriel?" I asked.

"Quite well, I believe."

"You should have brought her along."

He sat stock-still; his immobility was strangely terrifying.

"Muriel left me last week. She's with Lomax—in London."

He made the statement in a tone so matter-of-fact it took my breath away. There was a pause. I had not guessed it was as bad as this.

"What a rotten trick!" I muttered at last.

"Oh, I don't know," he answered logically, with that same inhuman self-control. "Lomax is a good-looking fellow and Muriel is still a most attractive girl. And after all, I'm not much fun to live with."

I looked at him quickly. He went on, musingly, in that same flat tone:

"I suppose she went on as long as she could, before she fell for Lomax."

I had to say something.

"What a swine he must be!"

Spence shook his head. In spite of the whisky he was completely sober.

"He's probably not any worse than the rest of us." A long, low breath escaped him. "I ought never to have married her in the first place. But I was so damned fond of her. And God knows I did my best. Took her out every Friday night." He repeated this, as though it comforted him. "Every Friday night in life."

"She'll come back to you," I said. "You can make a fresh start."

He looked full at me and the smile in his dark eyes was tragic.

"Don't be a fool, Robert. It's all over." He paused, reflectively. "She has asked for a divorce. Wants to be free. Well, I'll attend to that for her. Isn't it extraordinary . . . I see now that she is shallow and worthless . . . but I can't hate her."

I poured him another drink, and one for myself. I scarcely knew what to say. In a vain effort to divert his mind I asked:

"Have you been going to the Department?"

"Yes. You see, no one knows about this yet. Lomax is on vacation . . . Muriel supposed to be visiting her sister. But what's the use, I've lost interest. I'm not like you, Robert. I never was cut out for research." He added, in a flat voice: "It wouldn't have been so bad, except that when I saw how things were going and spoke to her she said, 'Leave me alone. I hate the sight of you.'"

There was a prolonged silence. Then, softly, the sound of a two-step came through the open window, stealing across the night air into the room. Spence looked at me, his impassive features showing a vague inquiry.

"It's a dance they have once a month," I told him. "The staff and some of the patients."

He considered for a moment.

"Muriel would have enjoyed that . . . we occasionally used to dance on Friday nights. I daresay Lomax will take her out."

He listened till the two-step was over, then put down his empty glass.

"I have to go now, Robert."

"Oh, nonsense. It's quite early."

"I must. I have an appointment. There's a good train at nine."

"Have another spot then?"

"No thanks. I want to be right for my appointment."

I guessed he had to see his lawyer about the divorce. I wasn't happy about him, but there seemed nothing I could say. It was twenty minutes to nine.

I went down to the lodge with him and opened the gates—Gunn had gone up to the dance.

"I'll walk to the station with you."

He shook his head.

"If I know anything you want to be back in that laboratory."

There was a slight flush on his thin cheeks and the expression in his fine sombre eyes startled me.

"Are you all right, Spence?"

"Perfectly." His voice held a hint of ghostly laughter.

A pause.

We shook hands. As I gazed at him doubtfully, he did actually smile, his old distorted smile.

"Good luck, Robert. . . . Bless you."

I made my way back up the drive slowly. What he said was quite true. I had to finish, absolutely, or it would finish me. In the darkness, as I went towards the laboratory, I could still hear the soft beat of the music. That night fog we so often got was coming down.

As I entered, the white cool room was silent, save for the low and muffled throbbing of the music. I freed my mind of everything, except my work. Despite the barred double windows of frosted glass, the stealthy fog had penetrated, and floated in a soft swathe, like a disembodied spirit, under the domed roof. Beneath, in the centre of the tiled floor, upon my bench, stood the filtration apparatus. I saw that the flask was nearly filled by a clear, translucent fluid. It took me but a moment to remove my jacket, roll up my shirt-sleeves, and pull on my soiled smock. Advancing to the bench, I took up the flask, gazed at it with a strange and thrilling emotion. Then, intently, I set to work.

It was only a short process to standardize and encapsulate the final product. At quarter to ten I had done it. At last, in spite of everything, I had reached the summit of the endless hill and looked down upon the kingdoms spread before me.

I felt so dizzy I had to hang on to the edge of the bench. The buzzing elation in my ears transformed the distant music. Faintly, then more clearly, I conceived the strains as a celestial symphony, with high angelic voices, clarion-sweet, mingling with bells and a sonorous counterpoint of drums. As these ecstatic harmonies swelled I kept muttering to myself tensely:

"I've done it . . . oh, God Almighty . . . I've finished it at last."

With an effort I broke off, put away the ampules carefully in the ice box, locked up the laboratory, and went out.

I directed my exhausted footsteps towards my room. As I reached the vestibule I heard someone call my name, and turning, I saw Brogan, the attendant, running after me.

I stopped and waited till he came up. He was white and breathing fast.

"Dr. Shannon, I've been looking for you all over." He caught his breath. "There's been a little accident, sir."

I stood quite still, staring at him.

"Look, sir." Despite his experience the man shuddered. "It's your friend . . . we just had word from the station."

Spence! I suddenly felt sick. A cold sweat broke on my brow. I swallowed with an effort.

"He slipped and fell, sir. Just as the nine o'clock train came in. It was instantaneous."

CHAPTER SEVEN

THE next few days were raw and foggy, a chill and early breath of autumn, melancholy presage of the coming winter and, as I went about my duties, I felt an equal foreboding bearing coldly down upon me. Spence's funeral had been held in his native town of Ullapool in the distant county of Ross, and I had been unable to attend it. But in a letter to his parents I had tried to temper the blow by attributing the occurrence solely to tragic chance. I had heard nothing of Lomax and Muriel.

The laboratory was locked, the key in my pocket, and it seemed strange that I should not be going there. Professor Challis would return to Winton at the end of the week, I would leave all arrangements concerning the announcement in his hands. Inevitably, news of my achievement pervaded Eastershaws and I was obliged to endure the embarrassment of congratulations—restrained from Maitland and Miss Indre, effusive from Palfrey, warm and dignified from Dr. Goodall. There came also an extraordinary trunk call from Wilson's, the great pharmaceutical house in London, which, until Challis should advise me, I refused to answer.

But on Thursday I received a visitor whom I had expected least of all. After supper, as I paced up and down my room, smoking endless cigarettes, trying to concentrate my scattered thoughts and to control my still unruly nerves, Professor Usher was shown in.

I gazed blankly at his tall, distinguished figure as he came forward and shook my hand with a cordial smile.

"My dear Shannon, how are you? I hope I haven't come at an inconvenient moment?"

"No . . ." I said stiffly. "Not at all."

"May I sit down?" He took a chair and crossed one leg over the other. "I daresay I should have let you know I was coming, but I enjoy acting upon impulse. And I did wish to be amongst the first to felicitate you."

"Thank you."

"I was in my office when Professor Challis telephoned me from Bute, working out a little idea." He smiled and caressed his neat imperial. "Despite my heavy administrative burdens, I try to get down occasionally to some real research. Well, I did not hesitate a moment."

I could not think of a suitable response, so I said nothing at all.

"Of course, I knew this was coming. I flatter myself I keep my ear pretty close to the ground. After all, the main purpose of my Department is to foster all that is worth while in modern scientific advancement and, despite our little disagreement, I realized that one day you would justify my belief in you."

I bit my lip at this airy insincerity.

"It would have saved me considerable trouble if you had acted upon that assumption."

"Yes," he agreed in his most winning manner. "I'm prepared to admit frankly that I was hasty. And now I've said it, I hope you'll meet me half-way and forget what's past."

My head was aching more than ever. I could not fathom his purpose. His tone grew more confidential.

"Now, listen, Shannon. I'll be perfectly open with you. Lately, we've had a run of shocking bad luck at the Department. We have not been getting satisfactory results. To cut a long story short, I want you back."

I made an instinctive gesture of refusal, but he held me with an impressive eye.

"Don't misunderstand me. I mean something considerably more important than merely handing you back your old position. Significant changes have been shaping up at the University. At last I have been won over to the idea of incorporating a bio-chemical laboratory in the Pathology building, and the Board of Trustees has decided to found a chair for experimental research in that particular field. The salary has been fixed at seven hundred pounds per annum, and the duties of the new director, subject, of course, to my most cordial co-operation, will be to organize and promote the work of the laboratory. He will have the status of a junior professor, with the privilege of delivering a course of lectures each session. Now, Shannon—" He drew a long, important breath. "I want you to consider the results a young and brilliant man might achieve in this position, aided by trained technicians and eager young students." He leaned forward and tapped me on the knee. "What would you say if the chance were given to you?"

I tried to keep steady in my chair. The offer took my breath away, an opportunity the like of which I had never dared, even, to contemplate. I saw that Usher's motives were completely selfish, he wanted me for the sake of the Department, and for his own sake too. The scientific and popular interest created by the publication of my discovery, the newspaper acclaim, the new health legislation which would be introduced in Parliament, all this was too infinitely valuable for him to miss. Even so, was he less human on that account? In my perplexity and distress I pressed my hand across my forehead, not knowing how to answer him.

"There, there," Usher said, easily. "I've a fair idea of how hard you've been at it. I won't bother you any more at present. What I suggest is this. You'll come to dinner at my house, Monday night. The Chancellor will be there, together with a few of my colleagues, members of the Senate who are keenly interested, to meet and congratulate you. There may also be present, though whisper it not in Gath"—his incisive expression became arch—"an editor or two, distinguished representatives of the press. I think I can promise you a stimulating evening."

I tried to express my thanks, but he stopped me with a smile.

"Not a word, my dear fellow. You must accept this as my *amende honorable*. Eight o'clock sharp then, at my house on Monday. Splendid. Again my congratulations coupled with the hope that in the future we may further the noble cause of science together."

He stood up, clasped my hand, flashed upon me his histrionic smile and left the room.

I sank back in my chair. This brilliant turn of events was too much for my tired brain, I still could scarcely grasp it. The first start of excitement was over, I felt no elation, only a strange inner tensity. This was the copybook reward of industry, perseverance, and high endeavour. I was the prize student now, at the head of the list. They all professed their friendship, were eager to shake my hand, even the Dalnair committee would want to claim acquaintance with me now. But they had been against me, every one of them, when I was really struggling, bogged in the morass of adversity.

Yet I knew I would not be so heroic as to disown success. I had suffered too long the cruel pangs, the back-breaking effort of independent effort. Usher wouldn't interfere too much. And the money . . . seven hundred pounds a year . . . I had never once thought of that, but now, despite myself, I would be rich, I might even dress like a well-off practitioner, quite the gentleman . . . it was all going to end up well, after all.

It was not good for me, this bitterness, but I could not check it, my future had never seemed brighter, yet a shroud seemed cast over my joy. Only one person would truly care, honestly rejoice in my success. I could see her face at this moment. For weeks I had buried that picture in the secret recesses of my mind, now I could not free myself of it. And suddenly, through the hardness which pervaded me, there came a soft and tender yearning. She had broken with me. Her prolonged silence indicated that. And I had betrayed her. But I wanted to speak with her, only for a moment, to tell her that my research was over; only for a moment, to hear her voice.

And so, against common sense, against my pride, against everything, I got up, went slowly to the telephone and, after a final moment of hesitation, called up the cottage hospital at Dalnair.

It was a toll call and I had to wait some time, but at last I succeeded in getting through. My voice sounded harsh and forced.

"I'd like to speak to Dr. Law, please."

"Oh, I'm sorry, sir, you can't."

The abrupt refusal surprised and disconcerted me.

"Isn't she in?" I asked.

"Oh, yes, sir, she's in."

"You mean she's on duty?"

"Oh, no, sir, not on duty."

"Then what do you mean? Please go to her room and tell her I'm here."

"She's not in her room, sir. She's in the wards."

Who was at the other end? I tried to recognize the voice, but could not. In addition, the country exchange was acting in its usual fashion and the wire began to sing and crackle loudly. Restraining my impatience, I changed the receiver to my other ear.

"Hello, hello . . . Who is that talking?"

"It's the maid, sir."

"Katie?"

"No, sir, the under-maid. I'm new, sir."

My nerves were now so taut I had to shut my eyes.

"Please fetch the matron. Tell her Dr. Shannon wishes to speak to her."

"Very good, sir. Will you hold on, please."

I hung on, with increasing vexation and anxiety, for what seemed an interminable period. But finally, with relief, I heard a sharp step, followed by Miss Trudgeon's unmistakable tones.

"Yes, Dr. Shannon?"

"Matron," I exclaimed. "I'm sorry to trouble you, but I did want to have a word with Dr. Law. Could you reach her for me?"

"I'm afraid you can't speak with her, Doctor. You haven't heard our news?"

"No."

There was an appreciable pause. Then:

"Dr. Law has been ill, quite ill, for the past three weeks."

As my heart turned over in my breast, there came a crackle in the instrument which cut off further speech. But I had already heard enough to turn my swift suspicion into certainty. I hung up the receiver. It was always my failing to leap impetuously to a premature conclusion and that, precisely, was what I did just now.

CHAPTER EIGHT

NEXT morning I went early to the laboratory, then across to Dr. Goodall's house. He had not risen, but when I sent in word that I was obliged to take the day off, he gave me his permission.

The sky was still grey as I walked down the drive and through the big gates. After my long and unbroken sojourn within the high walls it was painful to make this journey to Dalnair. I reached Winton at ten o'clock. The city lay damp and warm beneath a low smoke pall. The noise and bustle of the streets, the crowds pushing with luggage towards the barrier at the Central Station, were strangely jarring after the order and tranquillity of Easter-shaws. But I had to see Jean, yes, at whatever cost, I must see her.

Yet, as I sat brooding in the swaying train, while the sooty fields and sidings drifted past, my feeling was less pity than a slow and smouldering anger. More and more I was obsessed by the vision of her fingers—touching the cultures . . . crumbling the biscuit to her lips.

At Dalnair station I couldn't get a cab, so, under the grey and humid sky, I walked to the hospital by the steep path which I used to race up at top speed. But now I climbed slowly, wishing I had stopped at the Railway Tavern for a drink. I was out of breath as I reached the crest of the hill, entered the drive, and rang the front door bell.

There was no delay. It was Katie who answered my ring. I had not told them I was coming and she gave me a queer look. But she had always liked me and, with a restrained air of welcome, she admitted me to the reception room. A moment later Miss Trudgeon appeared.

"Well," she exclaimed, bustling in with her brisk and energetic smile. "This is a surprise. I'm very glad to see you again."

Gazing at her heavily, I saw that she had spoken quite sincerely; yet, while I felt grateful for her friendly reception, I was not deceived by the specious brightness of her manner, which I recognized at once as a mere professional disguise, a cloak that I had often seen her adopt when interviewing anxious relatives.

"But I must say," she went on with a sideways glance, "you don't flatter your new job. You're thin as a rake. What have they been doing to you? You look as though they'd put you through a mangle."

"Oh, I'm all right."

"Don't they feed you out there?"

"Yes . . . the food's excellent."

She shook her head slightly, as though doubting the truth of my words.

"You need a course of my good nourishing curries."

There was an awkward pause during which, as she hadn't asked me to sit down, we both remained standing. The cheerful, rather encouraging smile, which from long practice her tough facial muscles seemed capable of sus-taining endlessly, had lost a little of its glitter.

I moistened my lips.

"How is she?"

"As well as can be expected. She's been ill three weeks now." The matron hesitated; then, observing that I was waiting for further information, she proceeded on that same note of optimism, choosing her words so as not to commit herself. "At first she seemed to be holding her own. But these last few days there's been a slight loss of ground."

I felt my heart contract. I knew that phrase so well.

"Who's looking after her?"

"Dr. Fraser, the Medical Officer of Health."

I had a vision of this middle-aged man, with thinning sandy hair, thick fair eyebrows, and a plain, square, lined face made coarsely ruddy by a reticulation of red veins upon the cheeks.

"He's a good man."

"Excellent."

"Tell me the truth. What does he say?"

The matron was silent. She shrugged her shoulders slightly.

"She's quite ill. If only she'd gone down with it at once, she'd have had a better chance. She went on for a week with persistent headache and temperature, before she collapsed. But that often happens with scarlet fever."

"Scarlet fever!" I exclaimed, in an indescribable tone.

"Yes, of course," Matron said, surprised. "I told you on the phone last night."

A rending silence. I drew a quick sharp breath, which seemed to burn to my finger-tips. So rooted was my idea I could not bring myself to surrender it.

"I'd like to see her," I said.

Miss Trudgeon's gaze slid over my head.

"She's not altogether conscious."

"All the same, I would like to."

"What good can it possibly do?"

"All the same . . ." I said.

The matron now looked thoroughly embarrassed. She spoke directly.

"Her parents and her brother are here . . . in the sitting-room. And her fiancé. Unless they were willing, Doctor, I couldn't take the responsibility."

I felt a sinking of dismay. This was something unthought-of, a difficulty to be overcome, a penance to be endured. Yet for nothing, nothing must I abandon the purpose which had brought me here. I sighed.

"I'll go in and see them."

Once again she shrugged.

"Very well. You know your own business best. If you want me I'll be in the ward."

Without further comment Miss Trudgeon briefly nodded, spun round and moved off, leaving me to make my way, as best I could, along the corridor to my old sitting-room. Outside the door I stood for a full minute, hearing the sound of a deep voice within, then summoning all my courage I turned the handle and went in.

Daniel Law was at the table, reading aloud from a Bible, with Luke, in the next chair, close beside him. Seated in the window embrasure and facing in my direction were Mrs. Law and Malcolm Hodden. I stood there in hang-dog fashion, holding my breath until the recital finished.

There was a momentous silence. Daniel removed his glasses and, with his handkerchief, dried them openly, then half-turned in his chair. Although his attitude was fixed, his grave, anxious countenance gave no sign of anger or accusation. He simply gazed at me with silent dignity.

Malcolm, however, had risen. He came towards me. His undertone was audible in the silent room.

"How can you intrude at a time like this?" His full eyes, near to me, were veined. "Can't you respect our privacy . . . forcing yourself . . ."

"No, Malcolm," Jean's mother interposed in a low tone.

I kept my gaze on the floor, all that I had meant to say congealed upon my lips.

"He has no right to be here!" Hodden cried, suddenly, in a racked voice.

"Oh, be quiet," Luke muttered.

"Hush, son," whispered Mrs. Law. With a steady glance towards me she stood up. "I am going to see our daughter now. Will you come with me to the ward?"

Speechless, not having spoken a word, I accompanied her from the room, across the driveway, to the side room of the little pavilion. Waves of light rippled across the clean gravel yard, a young nurse crossed before us, under a verandah a group of children, convalescent, in red coats, were throwing a rubber ball.

My heart was hammering unbearably in my side as Matron opened the door and we joined her in the white-painted room. Only one of the three beds was occupied, half-surrounded by a screen, with a white enamel chair at one side. Upon this chair, leaning forward in an attitude of watching, was Sister Peek. As I followed Matron slowly round the edge of the screen and stood at the foot of the bed, I dared not raise my eyes. Only by the greatest exercise of will did I succeed in lifting my head, inch by inch, until my gaze, travelling along the white counterpane, came to rest on Jean.

She lay upon her back, her eyes wide open, constantly muttering, with tremulous movements of her dry lips and tongue, her thin hands all the while plucking at the bedclothes. Against the low white pillow, beneath her tied-back hair, her facial bones were sharp and fine. Her cheeks showed, not the usual bright patches of fever, but a dull and heavy flush, while a crop of reddish points, some of which had already faded, leaving brownish stains, disfigured her drawn brow . . . the typical rash of toxic scarlatina.

Already, amidst the rushing in my ears, I felt myself slipping down the slope.

Above the bed, beyond reach of those plucking fingers and twitching wrists, there hung the chart upon which was traced the sharp ridges, the depths and hilly contours, of the fever. My eyes went straining towards it. Yes, I thought, after a long moment, there is no doubt at all. What a fool I had been, what a fool I always was. . . . It was, with certainty, scarlet fever.

In muted voices Mrs. Law and Matron began to talk together. I was not there. Useless as a piece of unwanted furniture, I was ignored. I did not exist. My eyes fell, in anguished confusion, wandering amongst the paraphernalia of sickness which neatly covered the bedside table, medicine bottles, feeding cup, a hypodermic, ether, and camphor in oil. If it had reached that stage it was bad enough.

The scene hung, suspended, from a remorseless thread of time which swung slightly from side to side, and slowly attenuated, became more fragile as seconds were stripped away and cast one by one into an unknown void. You could not bear this indefinitely. I went out, crossed the narrow passage to the opposite side room, which was quite empty, and there sat down upon the edge of a bed, staring at the blank yellow distempered wall with direct and haggard eyes. I had hoped to do so much, and now I could do nothing . . . no dramatic and impassioned act to prove myself, to establish a reason for existing . . . nothing. Filled, more and more, with self-contempt, denying myself all value, I took from my pocket the large ampule I had wrapped in cotton wool that morning and, under the unconscious pressure of my fingers, the brittle snap of the glass was magnified to a high resonance, ringing in my ears like bells. Shreds of damp wool stuck to my fingers. Impossible to describe the white heat burning in my mind, my sense of distressed ineptitude, the burden, without feeling, which bore upon me, the string of mocking echoes in the silence which encircled me.

Still, time kept swinging, the seconds falling, feather-soft. How had this come upon her? Ah, if one were tired, or wrapped, despite oneself, in some melancholy dream, might it not then be easy to forget those simple precautions which make the difference between health and sickness? Voices fell upon my ear through the frozen emptiness of thought. I heard Mrs. Law and Matron come out of the sick-room and move along the passage. Miss Trudgeon was trying to soothe the troubled mother.

"Rest assured, everything is being done. We should know in twenty-four hours. Dr. Fraser is giving every attention. As for Sister Peek, nothing could surpass her devotion to this case. She's been specialling on it for over three weeks, and has often taken double duty. I've never known such self-sacrifice."

So I had been wrong there also. It was like me to think the worst of everyone. I'd misjudged the matron, too, fought with her, distrusted her. That was my special quality, getting on the wrong side of people, acting against convention and the grain of decency, standing against the universe, belonging to no place, and to no one, but myself.

A gong vibrated in the far main building, sounding for the nurses' luncheon, a sign of normal life which deepened the hollow present. The two women had passed through the outer door now, their voices, faint and sad, dwindled away to nothing. I stood up, automatically, and, like a figure moved by strings, went out of the pavilion. No one was in sight. As though wearing shackles, I started down the hill towards the station. Huddled in an empty compartment of the returning train I was still in the ward, up there, on the darkening hill.

WHEN I got back to Eastershaws I found a note saying that Professor Usher had telephoned me twice, leaving word that I should call him when I came in. I hesitated, then told myself I would put it off till later. I had a splitting headache, I wanted to be let alone, to cut myself off, to nurse my sadness, and my fears, in secret.

At five o'clock I drank a cup of tea. I was glad of it. All my faculties seemed numbed. On the tray was another slip.

> Mr. Smith of the Pathology Department telephoned you at 3 P.M. Urgent.

Vaguely, through the weight that was myself, I felt annoyed by this persistence, and puzzled, until I remembered that Usher had hinted at sending a reporter from the *Herald*. Smith must have been deputed to arrange that interview. I could not bear that just now. Time enough at the dinner on Monday. I rolled up the slip and dropped it in the fire.

Goodall had given me the whole day off. There was no need for me to leave my room. I sat, in a heavy daze, counting the hours, until nine o'clock; then, rousing myself, I telephoned the hospital at Dalnair. There was no change in Jean's condition. They could tell me nothing more.

Dead-tired, throbbing with anxiety, I supposed I had better turn in, but my neuralgia was so bad I knew I would not sleep. The aspirin bottle in my bathroom cabinet was empty. I went downstairs and, as I was in the dispensary, took some pyramidon. Then, on my way back, in the central subway, I saw one of the nurses approaching. It was Stanway.

She was alone, walking slowly towards the hostel. When she noticed me she stopped, leaned back casually against the wall of the passage until I came near.

"Where have you been?"

"Nowhere in particular."

"You're quite a stranger."

Although she spoke with an assumption of indifference she was studying me closely. She added:

"I hope you don't think I missed you."

"No," I said.

"There are lots of others I can go out with."

"Yes."

There was a pause. I looked at her, and looked away, overcome by a revulsion of feeling which turned me sick and cold. There is a penalty for everything, I thought, bitterly regretting those many dreary nights when, skirting the walls like a thief, I had gone to her room. Promiscuous and cheap . . . all without meaning . . . or a single tender thought. The frosted lights crackled overhead, artificial and unreal. She cared nothing for me and I, oh, God, how tired I was of her.

"What's the matter?" She spoke sharply, still watching the changes in my face.

Still I didn't answer. And, mistaking my hesitation, a slow provocative smile touched her lips.

"I'm going off duty now." She glanced at me indolently. "If you want to come along."

"No," I said heavily, gazing straight ahead.

Quite taken aback, she stiffened, from wounded vanity, and, for once, her pale skin reddened, an angry and unexpected stain. There was a pause.

"All right." She shrugged. "Don't think I care. But don't come round, disturbing me, when you happen to change your mind."

She stared at me, with open contempt, her small head silhouetted like a skull against the light, then she spun round and went off, along the subway, her heels clicking on the concrete, clicking away to silence.

Well, that was the end, thank God. I turned and went back to my room and flung myself upon my bed. After a while the pyramidon took effect. I slept heavily.

But next morning, when I awoke, I felt worse than ever. My sleep had merely prepared me for the day to come.

During the forenoon, I got through my work somehow, and without meeting Maitland or Palfrey—lately, I had become adept at avoiding the other members of the staff.

After one o'clock, with a deep foreboding, having forced delay upon myself until I could no longer bear it, I telephoned Dalnair again. Sister Cameron spoke to me. Her voice sounded cheerful, but she was always cheerful. And the answer which she gave me was the same. No change. Holding her own. No change at all.

In a burst of good intention she tried to help me.

"At any rate, the worst hasn't happened yet. While there's life there's hope."

Outside it was raining, a heavy shower which darkened the sky and cast a stormy shadow over all the grounds. I mounted the staircase slowly to my room. Then, as I entered, I perceived in the indistinct light that someone was seated on the sofa, at the far side of the fire. I switched on the shaded lamp above the bookcase and, with dull surprise, I saw that my visitor was Adrian Lomax.

Without altering his position he met my long, heavy stare in a manner which at least simulated his habitual and superior calm, but which, at the same time, betrayed, underneath, uncertainty as to how I might receive him.

"Lomax," I said, finally, as from a distance. "You're the last person I expected here."

"You don't seem very glad to see me."

I made no answer. There was a pause. He had not changed much, indeed, scarcely at all. I had imagined that, after what he had come through, he must be broken up by a sense of responsibility and guilt. On the contrary, he was still as well turned out as ever, paler perhaps, with a more listless droop to his lips, but perfectly composed, and prepared to defend himself.

"You didn't know I was back?"

"No."

Although actually there had been little scandal, I saw that his pride had driven him to return. He lit a cigarette, with an attempt at his former ease. Yes, he was embarrassed and was trying, with this air of bravura, to hide it.

"I suppose you have your knife in me. But I wasn't altogether to blame."

"Weren't you?"

"Far from it. From the very beginning it was Muriel who ran after me. Wouldn't leave me alone. Oh, I daresay it was foolish of me but I just couldn't disentangle myself."

"Where is she now?"

"I offered to marry her. I wanted to do the right thing. But we had a filthy row. She's gone back to her people. I'm not sorry. She would have been a damned nuisance."

"You've got out of it very well. Better than Spence."

"You know it was an accident. It was a foggy night. He missed his footing on the platform. It all came out at the inquest."

"For God's sake don't excuse yourself. You sound as though you felt you'd pushed him over."

The colour went out of his face.

"Don't you think that was a little uncalled-for? At any rate I mean to show that I'm not the rotter they say I am. I'm going to work, really work at the Department, do something this time that'll make them all sit up."

He gave the impression that he had been the victim of uncontrollable circumstances and that the future would completely justify him. I knew that he would never achieve anything, that he was, under his air of brilliant superiority, weak, vapid, and self-indulgent. It made me uneasy to have him in the room. I stood up and poked the fire, hoping that he would take the hint and go.

But he did not go. He kept looking at me in a curious manner.

"You've been doing good work lately."

Standing away from him, I made a gesture of dissent.

"They were very excited about it at the Department."

I raised my eyes slowly. Through the mists which encircled me his use of the past tense struck me as strange. A moment's silence followed.

He sat up and leaned towards me, that odd, thin smile of condolence more apparent upon his lips.

"Usher has asked me to come and see you, Shannon . . . to break the news. You've been forestalled. Someone has published your work before you."

I stared at him, wondering, dully, what he was driving at; then suddenly I started.

"What do you mean?" I could scarcely bring out the words. "I checked all the literature before I began. There was nothing."

"No, Shannon, there wasn't. But now there is. A research worker in America, a woman doctor named Evans, has just come out in this month's *Medical Review* with a full report of her experiments. Two years' work. Her conclusions are practically the same as yours. She has isolated the bacillus, shown the world-wide incidence of the disease—the figures are amazingly large—identified the infection in dairy herds, in fact, everything."

A long silence. The room was spinning round me.

Lomax was speaking again, with too obvious tact.

"It was Smith who told us first. He's been following Dr. Evans's work for months. He actually had an advance proof of the report in his possession. He brought it into the Department yesterday."

"I see."

My lips were stiff and cold, I felt as though I had been turned to stone. Eighteen months of unsparing effort, of feverish application by day and night, in the face of every difficulty, all wasted, and of no avail. If the results were already before the scientific world, proved and published, I should get no credit now for what I had done, the problems I had solved at such cost to myself. It had happened before, of course; as though by some strange telepathy, a current passed between two workers, continents apart, starting them off, unknown to each other, upon the same quest. And doubtless it would happen again. Yet this did not ease the frightful pang of finding another at the goal before me, nor dull the deathly bitterness of defeat.

"It's a damned shame." Lomax spoke without looking at me. "I needn't say how sorry I am."

His pretence of pity was more crushing than indifference. He got up from his chair.

"By-the-by, in case you wanted to read it, I brought along the article." He took some printed sheets from his coat pocket and laid them upon the table. "Now I'll push off. Good night, Shannon."

"Good night."

When he had gone I sat staring at nothing, in a hollow, hopeless calm. Then, with a deep sigh, which seemed to spring from the bottom of my heart, I rose, went over to the table, and taking up the report, steeled myself to read it.

As Lomax had said, it was a masterly investigation of the disease, later to be named brucellosis, and one that came to be regarded as a monumental work. When I had twice gone over it carefully I had to acknowledge, with a swift surge of jealousy, that Dr. Evans was a brilliant and resourceful scientist, whose work was perhaps better than mine.

I folded the sheets with intense calm, and stood up. This new calm, false though it might be, was like a sudden intoxication filling my head with a

sense of power and light. It was now three o'clock and time for me to ring
Dalnair again. Without a tremor, I went towards the telephone. But before
I could take up the instrument there came a knock upon the door, the
maid entered and handed me a telegram. I opened it with steady fingers.

ACCEPT MY SINCERE SYMPATHY PUBLICATION IN REVIEW WHICH
IN NO WAY DETRACTS INTRINSIC MERIT YOUR EFFORT. AM STILL UN-
ABLE TO TRAVEL BUT HOPE SEE YOU SOON TO ARRANGE FUTURE WORK.
REGARDS. WILFRED CHALLIS.

If reaction had been delayed, now it fell upon me with an added force.
I had leaned on Challis, forgetful of his years and gathering enfeeblement.
This message of condolence struck away the last support, and as I gazed at
the blurred words I felt, suddenly, a queer snap behind my brow, as though
an elastic band, stretched too tight, had finally yielded to the strain. At
the same instant my nerves escaped me, the world spun round, and the
splendid humour of the whole thing came before me in a flash. I smiled,
at first vaguely, yet after a moment with growing conviction, until, presently,
I began to laugh . . . at myself, my present situation—then, like a quick-
change artist, upon whom is forced the necessity of another part, I suddenly
became sedate, serious and resourceful.

With an air of purpose, I looked at my watch, forgetful that I had done
so a few minutes before. It was only a quarter after three, which reassured
me, for I suddenly was filled by a pressing desire to be busy. All sense of
disappointment was gone and, through the general insensibility which affected me, I was conscious of a vague pervading comfort, a recognition that
what occurred outside, at the Department or Dalnair, was of slight importance in the general movement of my life. Was I not safe here, well-
housed and fed, insulated from the shocks and sadness of the outer world,
in this splendid, this sheltered, retreat? For that matter, if it pleased me,
I need never leave it.

Reinforced by this thought, I set out briskly to the West Wing where, on
Maitland's day off, it was my duty to make the afternoon round. Lately I
had been remiss in this obligation, perhaps I had not been pulling my full
weight in the Place. That would not do at all, it was not fair to Dr. Goodall,
not up to Eastershaws standards. Reproachfully, I told myself I must make
fitting reparation. There were many things I could attend to before the day
was over.

In the West vestibule I joined Sister Shadd and made a thorough round
of the six galleries. I did not rush or scamp the work but was painstaking and
solicitous. The quiet of the galleries was strangely soothing and I talked
at length with several of the inmates, even drank a cup of tea with the
Duchess in her own room, a lofty apartment with faded green curtains, a
bearskin hearthrug and an ormolu chandelier. She wore a mauve velvet dress
with a great deal of ornate jewellery and several necklaces of freshly strung
melon seeds. At first she kept her beady eyes appraisingly upon me, but as

I exerted myself to please she gradually unbent and, when I rose to go, extended to me, coquettishly, her parchment-yellow hand.

Mildly amused by my success, I turned to Shadd as we stood together at the outer door.

"Remarkable, Sister, isn't it . . . how the Duchess, despite her extravagances, epitomizes certain phenomena observable amongst your ladies here."

"Most remarkable." All through my visit she had been constrained and silent. Now, she gave me a peculiar, sharply disapproving look.

"I mean," I smiled, "they're all interested in dress. Even the oldest of them keeps trying to come out with something new, adding a ribbon here, altering a flounce there, in an effort to outvie the rest. Often their creations are grotesque, yet if they're sufficiently different they immediately become the vogue. Of course, the Duchess's large wardrobe enables her to reign supreme."

Sister Shadd, still staring at me, opened her lips, then compressed them tightly in acute displeasure.

"Their attitude towards the opposite sex is interesting also . . ." I went on. "Take, for example, the passive virgins who blench at the very sight of man . . . and those others, of a mild romantic strain, who give coy glances while walking in the grounds, towards the male of their fancy . . . And those desperate creatures who alternately beseech and complain of ravishment by lightning, thunderbolt, electric waves, solar and lunar rays, or even through the supernatural visitation of Goodall himself!"

"Excuse me, Doctor," Shadd cut in abruptly. "Miss Indre wants me. I have to go now." As she went off, her brow like thunder, she added, "Really, you surprise me. Why don't you go and lie down for a bit?"

So she thought I had been drinking, confound her. Philosophy was wasted on her anyhow. I resented her departure yet refused, positively, to permit it to upset me. I turned with renewed briskness, and made my way to the dispensary.

The stock solutions had got very low. It took a full hour's work to replenish them. As I measured the crystals of chloral hydrate and shook them into the blue glass bottles I found myself humming—Palfrey's favourite phrase from *Carmen* . . . by poor, unhappy Bizet. Very pleasant and agreeable. If my head had not felt so numb, as though beaten by hammers, I should have been thoroughly at ease.

Suddenly the house phone rang. The sharp, shrill note gave me an agonizing start. Yet I was calm as I picked up the receiver.

"Dr. Shannon?" It was the porter at the lodge.

"Yes."

"I've been trying to find you all over the building. There's a young fellow here who wants to speak with you."

"With me?" I stared blankly at the wall in front of me. "What's his name?"

"Law . . . he says, Luke Law."

Oh, of course, I remembered Luke, my young friend with the motor-cycle. What did he want at this time of day?

I'd barely time to begin humming again when Luke's voice came through, eager and excited, the words tumbling over one another.

"Is that you, Robert . . . come down at once . . . I want to see you."

"What's the matter?"

"Nothing . . . everything . . . it's good news . . . Jean's much better."

"I beg your pardon?"

"She's out of danger. At two o'clock this afternoon she had her crisis. She's conscious now. She's talked to us. Isn't it wonderful?"

"Quite so. I'm delighted."

"I just had to get on the bike and come flying over to tell you. Come down to the lodge. I want to see you."

"Sorry, dear boy." My tone conveyed the polite regret of one preoccupied by many affairs. "I couldn't possibly manage it at the moment."

"What!" A pause. "After me coming all that way . . . ? Robert . . . Hello . . . hello . . ."

Although, remotely, it hurt me to do so, I cut him off, hooking up the receiver with a quiet smile. Much as I liked Luke, I had no time to waste on futile errands! Naturally, it was quite a relief that Miss Law should be better, no doubt very gratifying to her relatives. A quiet sort of girl, she was, with brown eyes and hair. I recollected the song . . . *Jeannie with the light brown hair* . . . Charming melody, I must mention it to Palfrey. I remembered her, vaguely, as a student in my class, clever, but something of a nuisance. Of course, I bore her no ill-feeling, not the slightest ill-will in the world.

Bizet, again . . . poor, unhappy Bizet . . . *I try not to own that I tremble* . . . I finished my stock solutions, tidied up the dispensary, and again, briskly, with unclear gaze, deciphered the time on my watch.

Seven o'clock. I had always disliked duty in the refectory, but now, despite the pain in my head, it seemed a pleasing, a logical necessity.

Supper had begun when I entered the dining-hall and the waitresses were bringing tray after tray of food to the long tables where, amidst a great clatter of dishes, scraping of chairs, and chatter of voices, everyone had begun to eat.

I stood for a moment; then, not mounting the dais, strolled up and down, watching with benign, possessive interest. The rising clouds of steam and the spicy smell of food made me feel my lack of sleep, and as my thoughts drifted, the scene grew rich and warm, feudal, almost, in its trenchered assembly of hind and gentle, its constant flow of servitors, like a canvas by Breughel in its life and colour, its bizarre diversity of human physiognomy, its abundance, movement, and high hubbub. . . .

Ah, I was back in the subway again, returning, with measured paces to my room. Outside the pantry of Balaclava the night attendant had come on duty and was mixing the evening cocoa.

"I brought up the mail, Doctor. There's a letter for you."

"Thank you, my good fellow."

In passing, I took the stiff envelope, stamped with the University crest. My smile was fixed now, as though printed upon my face, a mask for all the whirling chaos that went on behind. The heavy sledges struck harder on my skull, a sudden sweat broke over me, and in a transient, haggard gleam I knew that I was ill. But swiftly, the light went out, and eager to go on, aware of work waiting to be done, smiling more fixedly, I entered the vestibule and opened the letter.

Department of Pathology, University of Winton. From Usher, Professor Usher, head of that most excellent foundation. A nice letter, yes, indeed, a charming letter. The good Professor regretted, in fact, he deeply regretted that, under the circumstances, it was impossible to hold out any hope of the new appointment. If only the results had been published sooner. The delay was tragic, the disappointment intense, and his feelings quite understandable. There was a postscript over the page. Ah, yes, the dinner party was off too. Most unfortunate, when the invitation for Monday was extended, a previous engagement had been overlooked. Profuse excuses. Some other time. Why, yes, of course, it was all perfectly agreeable and correct. Come back to your bench in the laboratory. Work under me in a less intractable spirit with proper co-operation and supervision. A generous offer. But thank you, no.

Under the high light in the vestibule, beside the statue of Demeter and the tall buhl cabinets, I tore the letter carefully into four pieces. I wanted suddenly to shout out loud. But my lips were too stiff, as though glued together, and the pain in my head had risen, swelled in a crescendo of sound and shivering vibrations, as though someone were smashing wood with blunt axes on the back of my neck. In spite of this, I saw at last, with my wavering and dream-like gaze, what I wanted to do. Essential and important. On, on . . . don't stop . . . not an instant to be lost.

I went outside and hastened towards the laboratory. It was quite dark now and a wind had risen, swaying the trees and bushes, sending strange whisperings across the night. A leaf, brushing my cheek like ghostly fingers, made me spur my flagging footsteps to a stumbling run.

Now I was in the laboratory. Surveying the scene of my labours with an expressionless yet tortured eye, I advanced, independent of my own volition, and opened up the storage cabinet. The round, cotton-wool-stoppered flasks stood there in a row, opalescent and glittering, like luminous suns. Dazzled, I faltered and hung back. But that weakness was momentary. Collecting myself, I took up the precious flasks and smashed them quietly and carefully in the porcelain sink. I turned on both taps. When the last drop of fluid had run through the drain I bunched together the sheaf of papers on the bench, those pages filled with my calculations and conclusions, the toil of many midnight hours. Again, quietly, carefully, I struck a match to set a light to them, to hold them, burning, over the sink until the last charred fragment should be destroyed. But before I could do so the sound of quick footsteps made me turn round, slowly, balancing the insufferable burden of my head. Maitland stood in the doorway.

"Don't, Shannon," she cried, and hurried forward.

The match scorched my fingers and went out. The hammer strokes rang harder in my brain. I put both hands to my brow. Then everything gave way.

CHAPTER TEN

THE October afternoon was still and golden, filled with tranquil space. In my old room at Lomond View the slanting daylight made a bright patch upon the wallpaper, brought to life from beneath the yellow varnish its faded roses, glinted, also, upon the brass end knobs of my bed, dented years ago, when I had tried to straighten a crooked skate. Through the window I could see the early tinge of autumn upon the crimson curled leaves of the beech across the road, and in the distance, above the violet haze, the blue humped shoulders of Ben Lomond. As a boy, in this same room, I had often gazed with ardour upon that far-off prospect of the mountain. I gazed upon it now.

Lying comfortably on my side, I felt relaxed, conscious that my indolence was sanctioned, since Dr. Galbraith, supported by Grandma Leckie, was always insisting that I must rest. Yet the splendour of the afternoon was irresistible—I decided I must be up. Was I not practically well again and able to be about, after lunch, for a few hours each day? I threw off the bed-clothes and began to dress, carefully however, for I was still unsteady on my feet and had proved how slowly one may gather strength after a complete breakdown. Well, I had deserved it. All my own misguided fault.

I went downstairs, demonstrating my progress towards recovery by not even holding to the bannister. I had not got used to the queer sensation of living again in this house which, during my childhood in Levenford, had been my home. Now the property of my grandmother, it was quite unchanged, and although peopled only by the shades of most of its former inhabitants, still maintained its familiar air of pinched but aspiring respectability. They had brought me here after my smash-up, and with a grim devotion which made me heartily ashamed of all the hard things I had said of her, the old woman had nursed me back to health.

In the parlour the paper fan had been removed, a good fire burned in the black-leaded grate. Grandma had lit it for me before departing upon one of those shopping pilgrimages to the town, from which she returned, slowly, encumbered by packages of good things for me to eat. She had nourished me nobly, and according to her own peculiar precepts, on such proved restoratives as were sanctioned by her country traditions. Ten minutes ago, before leaving, she had whispered in my ear, with an air of significant promise:

"A nice boiled fowl for tonight, Robert." She was a staunch believer in a boiled fowl, served with the broth, which she named "the goodness" of the dish.

Alone in the house, this silent house filled with memories of the past, I had always to struggle against reverie, and the intolerable nostalgia which it evoked in me. Here was the couch on which Dandie Gow had bade me rest when I came in from my schoolboy combat with Gavin Blair. There, on the mantelpiece, lay the old wooden pen he had used for his legal copying. On that window-seat I had studied hard and fruitlessly to win the Marshall Bursary. At this very table they had told me I could not go to the University to study medicine. But I had gone. Ah, yes, I had always followed stubbornly my own solitary path, that tortuously winding path which had brought me back to where I had begun.

Quickly, I took myself in hand and, with a glance at the weather, decided on a short walk. In the hall, conscious of my cropped head, I pulled my cap well down, slid the key under the doormat in case the old woman should return before me, and set out.

Although the air was crisp and cool, my paces were not lively, and once or twice I had to pause as I strolled up the road to the hamlet of Drumbuck. It was the same quiet little village, set beneath a slow rise of moors, traversed by a brook which ran beneath two stone bridges. Some children were bowling their hoops towards the smithy and their thin, high cries broke cheerfully upon the scene. On the village green I rested upon the seat under the great Scots fir which had stood there for a hundred years. From fissures in the blue-grey trunk little streams of sap had run and hardened. I scraped one with my finger nail and, rubbing the grey dust between my palms, inhaled the clean resinous tang. It made me feel that strength was coming back to me, that my life, after all, was not without a future.

Yet by the time I had made the round of Barloan Toll, I had more than had enough. I was glad to get back to the arm-chair, to put on my slippers and warm my feet at the fire. The morning paper lay folded on the table beside me, the *Herald*, which I always enjoyed, the main diversion in my convalescent day. I lifted it and laid it upon my knees, at the same time hearing the front door open and shut. There were steps in the hall, sounds of bustling movements in the back of the house. Presently the old woman came into the parlour. We looked at each other. I smiled.

"Did you get your fowl?"

"I got two," she answered. "I've asked McKellar for supper."

"That sounds like a party."

"Aye." She nodded calmly. "Dr. Galbraith will be here as well."

"I see."

Before I could engage her in controversy, she changed the subject.

"It's time you had your hot milk. Don't scorch your shoes like that. They'll go through in the soles."

She turned and went out, leaving me thoughtful and subdued.

I had sensed for some time what was coming, and now I knew that it was here. Dr. Galbraith was getting on in years. His large practice, which extended widely from Levenford town into the Winton countryside, had become too much for him. He wanted a partner and, to my sorrow, the suggestion had been made that he might want me.

Yes, the trap had been long and patiently prepared, the hands that had set the trap were kind and friendly hands. Yet, alas, despite the promise I had given, I shrank away from it. It touched me that the hard-headed McKellar should be willing to advance the purchase price—a thousand pounds was a deal of money to a Scots lawyer. I liked the old doctor well enough, with his weather-beaten face, his grey goatee beard, and that dry twist to his lips, his manner, once abrupt and choleric, now mellowed by age. As I drowsed by the fire I tried to see myself driving a Ford along the country roads, bumping over dry ruts in summer, ploughing through winter snow, calling at outlying farms, bearing my black bag into snug steadings and white-washed cottages standing lonely on the moor. But my heart was not in it. I understood myself too well to feel anything but unwillingness towards such a prospect. I was not suited to general practice, and from my past experience I knew that I should grind along, without interest, blunting the edges of my ambition, mediocre, indifferent, and defeated.

Suppressing a sigh, I took up the paper and in an effort to distract my mind began to scan the sheets. I read here and there, all the pieces that looked interesting. There was not much news. I was turning to the editorial columns when, on the back page, an item caught my eye. It was a small item, a bare three lines, but it caused me to start painfully; then, for a long time, held me motionless.

Under the heading, *Departure of Ships*, was the simple announcement:

> The Clan Liner, S.S. *Algoa*, sailed today from Winton for Lagos and the Gold Coast. She carries a group of workers bound for the settlement at Kumasi.

I read the notice several times, like a child learning a lesson, as though uncertain of its meaning, and as I did so, the warm room chilled, and that faint quickening, sanguine and instinctive, which I had felt in the afternoon beneath the pine tree, diminished within me. So that was over, too . . . finished for ever. Since I had known that Jean would sail upon this ship I had dreaded the moment of its departure. Now it had gone. And, in that act, that separation of the vessel from these shores, that slow recession towards the horizon, there was a sense of final, irrevocable cleavage . . . a lonely lighthouse searching the empty sea, the flickering beam extinguished. And she had not come, had not even written her good-bye. That failure was the real martyrdom of love, it hurt me most of all.

For a long time, perhaps an hour, yet how long I did not know, I remained staring into the fire. Distantly, through my sad and painful thoughts, I heard the sound of an arrival, of footsteps and voices in the hall. I did not stir. Whether it was McKellar or the doctor, I could not bring myself to face the hearty handclasp, the tactful sympathy, which either would surely offer me.

Then, as I sat mute and motionless, the door opened almost without sound, behind me. Awaiting the impact of a robust voice, I did not trouble to move, but gradually the consciousness of someone standing there, standing with perfect stillness, at my back, caused me to turn my head. And then, slowly, I raised my apathetic eyes.

At first I thought I was ill again. This must be some fresh hallucination, another of these fevered visions which had not so long ago afflicted me. Then, in a flash of understanding, I saw that it was she, saw also the explanation of her presence.

I had forgotten that out-going vessels often lay overnight at the tail of the Bank to pick up passengers, and await a favourable tide. She had come, after all, to say good-bye.

The heavy thudding of my poor heart sounded in my ears, and a mist rose up before me, through which I gazed at her in utter silence. In equal silence she gazed at me. Although she still was thin, with a slight pallor persisting in her cheeks, little trace of her recent illness could be seen in those brown eyes, that clear complexion and lustrous hair. I could not but contrast my own condition with this serenity. Here I crouched, spent and broken, while she set out, steady and intent, almost fully restored to health. Her dress, too, of dark grey material edged with a lighter braid of silk, was quite new, bought, no doubt, in preparation for her journey. I saw, with a further stab of pain, that around her neck were clasped the green beads I had given her.

Slowly, I straightened in my chair. I could see her lips shaping to speak to me. I wanted to be ready to meet the blow.

"How are you, Robert?"

"Never better. Won't you sit down?"

"Thank you." Her voice was low yet controlled.

She seated herself, opposite me, very erect, her gloved hands clasped together, her eyes still bent upon me. Like a little plaster saint, I told myself, embittered by a composure that I could not match. I gritted my teeth to keep back the weak exhibition of my emotion.

"You have quite recovered," I said.

"I was very lucky."

"The sea voyage should set you up."

She took no notice of this thrust. Her silence caused me a fresh paroxysm of heartache. I tapped the news-sheet on my knee.

"I just happened to read that you were sailing. Nice of you to look me up. How is Malcolm? Has he gone on board?"

"Yes, Robert, he has gone on board."

The barb, turned back, gently, without rancour, sank deep in my breast. I tried not to flinch. Because of her glove, I could not see the ring, but if Malcolm were going with her they must certainly be married.

"Well—" I tried, casually, to smile, but my pale lips were drawn back in an anguished spasm. "I ought to congratulate you. He's a good fellow. I hope you have a nice trip."

She did not immediately answer; then, seriously, she said:

"And what about you, Robert?"

"I'm quite all right. I have a chance to get into a good practice here in Levenford."

"No."

The single word, uttered with a burst of feeling, drew me up short.

"What do you mean? It's virtually settled."

"No," she repeated. "You must not do it."

A short, strained pause. She was less calm now, and her eyes had taken on a sudden depth.

"Robert," she said, earnestly. "You cannot, you must not throw yourself away in a country practice. Oh, I'm not decrying country doctors. But they are not you. You've had a bitter disappointment, a terrible reverse, but that isn't the end. You'll try again, you'll do finer, greater work. You can't bury your talents. You must, you must go on."

"Where?" I asked, bitterly. "In another back room . . . another asylum?"

With greater earnestness she leaned a little forward.

"You feel badly towards Professor Challis, don't you? It was a mistake to send you to Eastershaws. But he's an old man, and he never really had an opportunity to put you in the right place." Her throat swelled. "Well, now he has. Robert, how would you like to lecture in Bacteriology at the University of Lausanne?"

I gazed at her, immobile, in fact scarcely breathing, as she went on, more rapidly:

"They wrote to Professor Challis, asking him to recommend the best man he knew, a young man who could organize the laboratory. He sent them a full report of your research. Yesterday he showed me their reply. If you wish it, the appointment is yours."

I brushed my hand across my eyes as though shading them from too bright a light. A fresh start, away from the restrictions of this narrow land, in Lausanne, that lovely Swiss city on the sparkling waters of Lake Leman. But no, no . . . my confidence was gone . . . I dared not undertake it.

"I couldn't," I muttered. "I'm not fit."

Her lips came together. Under her cloak of stiff formality I saw a sudden trembling of resolution. She took a quick grave breath.

"You must, Robert. All your future is at stake. You cannot admit that you are beaten."

I was silent, my eyes, unseeing, fixed upon the floor.

"I am beaten," I said, in a leaden voice. "I've given them my word. They are coming here tonight. It's easy to fight one's enemies. But against friends . . . and kindness . . . and my own promise . . . I can't argue . . . I can't fight any more."

"I will help you."

In slow surprise, I raised my gaze.

"You? . . . You'll be away."

She was very pale and for a moment her lips quivered so convulsively that she was unable to answer. She sat looking at her clasped hands.

"I am not going."

"But Malcolm?" I cried.

"The *Algoa* sailed at six this morning. Malcolm was on board."

There was a mortal silence. Bewildered, incapable of believing, I felt myself grow rigid. Before I could speak she went on again in a voice that seemed strangled by the immensity of her effort.

"When I was ill, Robert . . . and afterwards, I seemed to see things which were not apparent to me before." She almost broke down, but forced herself to go on. "I had always recognized my obligations to my parents, to the people with whom I meant to work. I didn't realize my obligation to you . . . and because I love you most in all the world, it is a greater obligation than to any of the others. If you had succeeded, if you hadn't had your breakdown, I might never have understood this . . . but now . . . I do."

She paused, striving for breath, gazing at me with strained intensity, as though burdened by the burning necessity of conveying to me difficult and unformed thoughts which recently had come to her. In the stress of her emotion tears began to roll down her cheeks. Her words came quickly.

"All the time, as I was lying there, in a kind of dream, I kept wondering why I had refused to marry you . . . I loved you . . . really I had got ill through loving you, and not caring what I did in the wards . . . but behind that love there was pride and fear and prejudice against your religion, of which I really knew nothing. God had caused you to be born a Catholic and me a member of the Brethren. Did that mean he hated one of us and loved the other . . . wished that one should live in the darkness of lies, and the other in the light of truth? If so, Christianity was meaningless. Oh, Robert, you were kinder towards my belief than I was to yours. And I felt so terribly ashamed I told myself, if I got better, I would come and beg you to forgive me."

Now she was weeping uncontrollably and, while I sat white and rigid, unable to move my stiff lips, she whispered:

"Robert, dear Robert, you must think me the most difficult . . . the most inconsistent person in the world. But there is a pressure in events we cannot withstand. Oh, my dear, I've left Blairhill, left my parents, left everything, for good. And if you still want me, I will marry you, when and where you wish . . . We will go to Lausanne . . . work together . . . be kind and considerate of each other . . ."

The next instant she was in my arms, her heart against mine, her voice stifled by sobs. My lips moved without making a sound. My breast, dilated with an immense joy, seemed about to burst.

As from a distant world I heard the front door open again, heard the stamping arrival of McKellar and Dr. Galbraith, the cautious undertones of the old woman as she met them in the hall.

It did not matter now. I was no longer alone, darkness had turned to the light of day, life was for ever remade. We should make our way into the unknown together. Yes, in the mystical warmth of that moment everything became possible, there was no thought of failure, and happiness seemed eternal.

THE END